First Printing: 2019 Amazon Publishing
Bristol, UK

www.KimWedlock.com

@KimWedlock

The Devoted
Book Two

The Sah'niir

Kim Wedlock

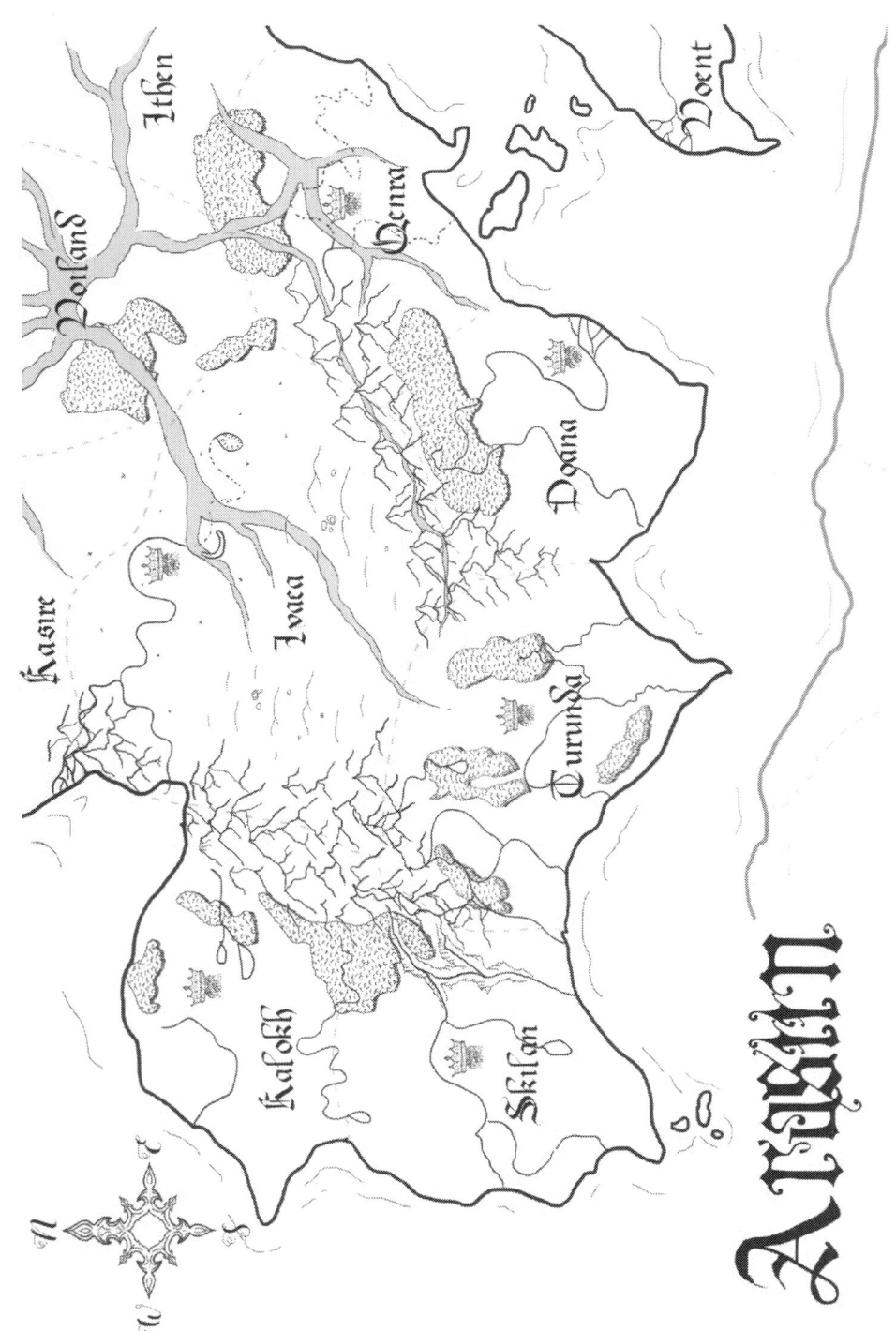

Norland

Ithen

Denra

Doent

Kasire

Doana

Ivaca

Turunda

Kafokk

Skifon

Arasun

N

E

S

W

4

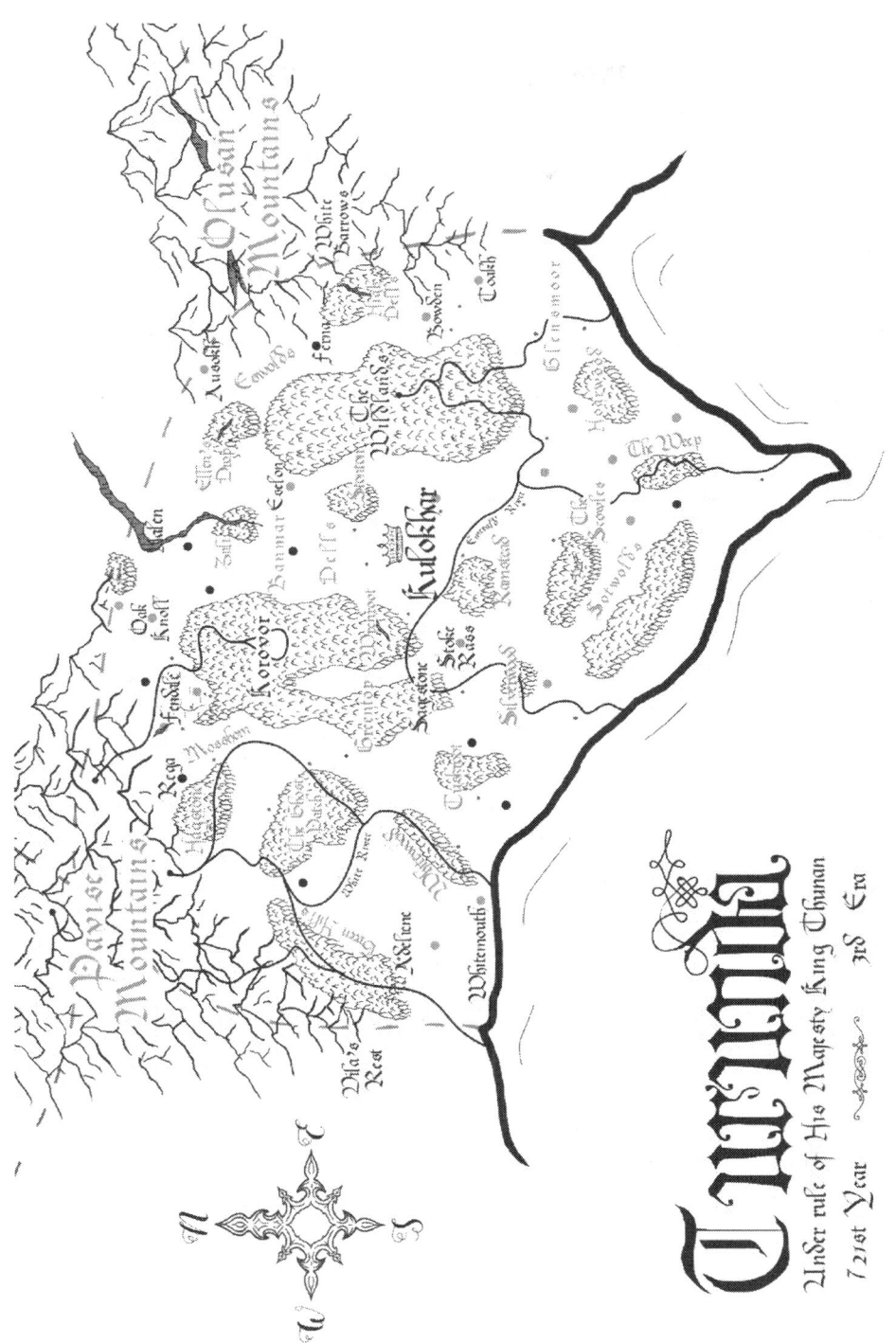

Prologue

The air shuddered beneath the clamour of crashing porcelain.

Priceless amphora toppled from ornate pedestals to shatter across the decaying ground, sending fragments of antiquity scattering over marble, vanishing amongst the creeping greenery.

Paintings the size of a man dropped heavily from the walls; gilded filigree frames bent and dulled as they struck the rubble, while sharp edges tore canvas and severed haughty silver faces.

A statue of onyx; carved with such impossible perfection, the seductive, dancing figure could have completed her pirouette at any moment, but dropped lifelessly instead at the jerk of the rug beneath its dais, helpless to its obliteration.

Another substantial portrait plummeted at the splintering impact of a body thrown into the wall, but the surrounding destruction continued unobserved, the cacophony overshadowed by grunts, bellows and roughly cut curses. The frame landed just a hand's breadth away.

With a bitter and oblivious wince, Rathen snatched together his bearings and moved to shove himself free of his entrapment, only to be pinned right back into the crumbling wall before he could even shift his weight. Anthis set upon him in a flash.

He was undeterred by Rathen's hands as they pushed, slapped and scrunched his face, nor his knuckles as they pummelled his jaw and ribs. His once-astute green eyes were clouded by a desperate frenzy, fuelled by something Rathen could easily guess at but didn't dare try to understand.

His fist cracked into Anthis's cheekbone, jerking his head to the side. But Anthis didn't falter. He roared, his fevered assault undying while the sleek, sharp, unadorned dagger cut through the air. It moved as though sentient, dragging his hand along with it in its hunger for blood. Somehow, the steel failed to find him.

Rathen fought to shove him away, but his every effort only pushed him deeper into the plaster.

The blade neared for another attempt. Rathen grasped his forearm. They grappled, and he struck with his knee. He hit. But it wasn't his target, for again Anthis didn't react. He tore his arm free.

Rathen's palm slammed immediately into his forehead and his foot hooked around behind his heel. The daze lasted for half a second, but it was enough. He jerked his foot and Anthis collapsed, clawing for Rathen on his way down.

He seized the opportunity to escape.

Within a moment he was back under rabid pursuit, the historian trampling parchments, books, relics and blankets in his hysteria. Neither noticed another of the walls begin to melt and slump.

*

Several scrolls lay open side by side across the fractured ground, their every face graced by tidy, slender lettering accentuated with long and flourishing streaks, yet shaped with angles just jagged enough to betray the harshness of their pronunciation. A handful of illustrations were nestled among them to enlighten the subjects, wonderfully elegant images of unrecognisable objects and places, beautiful in their own right. But whatever their significance, their intention was lost.

Rathen stared at the cryptic markings through the jittery firelight, the dead sun's shine still cold and weak in the midnight sky. His eyes tumbled from one parchment to the next, picking out what few shapes and runes he could recognise in an attempt to draw as much meaning from the jumble as he could. His tired vision strained, but he continued scanning the scripts, over and over and over again. He closed his mind against the hopelessness that twirled in circles through his gut.

Giggling rose nearby. It was a wonderfully alluring sound. But he ignored it. He also ignored the deeper and just as vacant chuckle that followed.

He read for the thirty seventh time. The thirty eighth. Upon the forty first, he stalled, his warily thoughtful frown deepening. He then took up two of the scrolls, rose to his feet, and approached the makeshift wall of fallen portraits, panels and side-turned tables that divided the decrepit room, from behind which the giggles continued to roll. He rounded it, and ignored the three naked, faceless women surrounding the shirtless young man.

"Anthis." He crouched beside him, paying no attention to the illusion that turned her fascinations onto him, nor the void-black holes of nothingness that severed her body and half of her head. He pointed to one particular line on the parchment, "what does this say, right here?"

Anthis snickered stupidly as one of the women ran her silver fingertips lightly along his collarbone.

Rathen shoved the parchment into his face. "Anthis."

He gave it a cursory glance before returning his full attention to the women. "'Hang'."

Rathen pushed the second scroll in front of his nose. "And this?"

He looked again, but his attention slipped before it landed, stolen by another of the horrific yet benign figures as she began kissing the scar tissue over his abdomen, despite having no lips with which to kiss.

Rathen slapped his head. Anthis looked back with the expected absence. "'Grain'."

"You're sure?"

"Mmm..." Again, his attention fluttered away.

Rathen rose, his eyes returning to their scouring of the scrolls, and retreated to his side of the slowly flooding room.

Rathen thundered around the divide. "Where is it?"

Anthis scowled back at him. "Where's what?"

"My blanket. Where is it?"

"Why would I know?"

Rathen's poisonous expression darkened. He stormed across the iced floor and violently shoved him aside, away from his crude bed of broken panels and torn tapestries, and snatched the third blanket that had been hidden hastily behind an upturned chair.

"No, that's *mine!*" Anthis lunged forwards, but Rathen easily shoved him back.

"Four blankets," he snapped, holding it out of his reach, "two bodies. It isn't hard."

"You don't need it!"

"*I'll freeze!*"

"*Use your damned magic!*" He lunged for a second time, and again Rathen pushed him away. Anthis's footing slipped. He steadied a heartbeat later and shot Rathen a murderous look, the undying madness that had been overridden by arcane pleasures elbowing its way back to the forefront. "Cocky bastard. Half-elf. Half-breed! You *freak!*"

"You'll live." Rathen turned away.

Anthis spat and dove forwards.

Evading was impossible.

They dragged one another down, punching, clawing, cursing and kicking. The glistening ice that was scarred first by the black marble floor that lay half-hidden beneath was soon spattered with flecks of crimson.

Anthis wept. He hugged his knees, shrinking deeper into the concealed nook among the debris of the dividing wall, sobbing silently in terror. He could hear the crashing, the shattering, the ripping, and soon the crackle of fire, close one moment, distant the next; right upon him and then from the furthest edge of the derelict hall.

Sepulchral cries rent the air, streaked for a moment with desperation, then nothing more than savagery.

Fierce claws skittered over marble with impossible speed, approaching him, passing him, and veering off to the furthest side before another scream pierced his ears and another piece of history shattered into dust.

Anthis did his best to choke back his cries. He was hidden, but he would be found.

Another shriek, and, somehow, Anthis summoned the courage to move. But the blanket of oppressive, primordial dread reclaimed him at once, and he crumbled beneath the desire it evoked to freeze as the monstrous claws returned. He drew himself in further, deeper into his hiding place, and squeezed his eyes shut tight against the image of the abhorrent visage. A desperate prayer fell silently from his lips, to any god that would listen, as he rocked himself against the ferocious and plaintive, booming, inhuman cries.

Neither paid heed to the overgrown tree roots that snaked their way in through a widening crack in the wall.

Chapter 1

At first glance, the city of Rega appeared quite untroubled - perhaps even at ease. People nodded and smiled politely at one another as they passed in the narrow streets, and greeted eagerly familiar faces with whom they shuffled beneath projecting roofs to exchange gossip out of the rain. Others toughed out the drizzle to browse the goods on the cramped market stalls, haggling wherever possible, though the selections of meats, vegetables and cautiously covered spices weren't as varied as they could have been, while everyone in between kept to themselves, heads bowed beneath weather cloaks as they made their way to their destinations without troubling anyone, lost in their own thoughts.

It was only after lingering in the marketplace for half an hour, with eyes and ears wide open, that one eventually noticed the shadow of tension blanketing the city. A shadow that, once revealed, was quite impossible to ignore. It tainted everything; it followed everyone around like a spectre, lingering behind smiles and pleasant greetings. People cast looks that lasted a fraction of a second too long, shoulders stiffened as they neared strangers, conspicuously brief sideways glances accompanied whispered gossip, the merchants' hawking had less heart.

It crept into Petra's muscles. She forced herself to release the breath she'd been unconsciously holding and tugged her hood down a little lower over her face, her blood red hair tucked back out of sight. She peered as coolly as she could at the array of flowers that lined the front of the shop, local blooms, unlike food and game, unaffected by the demands of war, and tried to keep her hands from seeking the hilt of the single dagger concealed within the back of her cinch. So unarmed, she felt positively naked, and painfully vulnerable. But Garon had insisted.

She couldn't help another impatient glance across the square towards the bootblack's bench. It was obscured by a twist in the road, but she could see the polish-stained boy kneeling at its foot well enough. He didn't rise or turn despite the weight of her eyes on him.

Tightening again, she dragged her gaze back to the gerberas. She glanced over six more times before the boy finally stood and accepted with far too much animation a large, shiny coin for his trouble, and his customer at last stepped down and into sight. She abandoned the shop and the hopeful stares of its merchant immediately.

"Well?" She demanded once she'd wended through the isolated crowds, but Garon's rigid expression offered little promise. Her shoulders sagged, and she fell into step beside him as he headed back across the market, adjusting the bag of recently procured food on his aching shoulder. She wondered why she'd expected anything more from his encounter than polished boots.

They remained silent until they neared the city gates, where the only ears in such dreary weather belonged to soggy guards and urgent citizens who sought to complete their business and return as quickly as possible to the comfort of their homes.

"People are uneasy," Garon finally murmured when the road ahead was clear of all but two crestfallen sentries. "But it's not just Doana or mages. The tribes are moving closer. Local hunters have tripped some of their traps in the woods, and two have died."

Petra nodded stiffly. "So I overheard. But what can be done? Their issues aren't our business. At best, the soldiers can patrol the borders, but if they want to move closer, any effort we make to push them back will just drag us in."

"I'm inclined to agree, but it can't go on." He cast her an askance look, swift and severe. "Don't tell Eyila."

"She already knows what's going on out there."

"But she doesn't need to hear of *this*."

"If she wants to get involved, let her. The right is hers."

"And you would charge in after her. Your presence alone would get all of Turunda involved."

"Is that concern?" She asked flatly.

"For everyone else."

She rolled her eyes and folded her arms, growling 'of course it is' beneath her breath. "Fine," she spoke up. "I won't say anything. But don't think she's stupid."

"I don't think she's stupid. I think she's reckless. You *both* are. And there are far bigger things at stake at the moment than tribal conflicts."

They left the city gates, making a show of pulling their cloaks tighter about themselves against the rain while watched far too closely by the guards, and followed the rough, wet roads at a justifiably hurried pace until they were back in the cover of the outlying forest. Once hidden among its shadows, they veered right and tracked through the trees, dropping their hoods at a safe distance beneath the canopy's shelter. The patter of raindrops against broad leaves undertoned the warm air, muffling the sounds of life undiscouraged by the downpour. But though it surrounded them and seemed increasingly deafening the longer Petra focused on it, preferring that to the thick silence that encapsulated the two, neither missed the deep, flat, mournful sound of a horn blown in the distance.

Garon stopped immediately and halted Petra with a swift, barring arm. They both held their breath, straining their ears through the incessant drizzle for any answering calls, but there came no further blasts, nor shouts, nor wails. It was a long moment before they dared to continue, stepping far more lightly along their winding route as they scoured the surroundings for the traps they'd heard mention of in the city. They breathed the slightest sigh of relief when the trees finally parted for the thick, knotted trunk of an old oak up ahead.

They slipped carefully down into the long-dead stream bed that bowed around its roots, and found as they followed it a cloaked figure standing upon the opposite bank. Petra slowed and frowned. "Eyila?"

The figure turned and fixed them both with eyes of shocking ice-blue. They were sharp, though a wisp of arcane distraction remained at their edges, and Petra found herself feeling a sudden and immense guilt beneath the gaze, though she wasn't sure why.

"This," Eyila declared bitterly, "is you cityfolks' fault."

Petra sighed in defeat. The horn. Of course she'd recognised the horn.

Even in her anger the tribal girl swept gracefully down the stream bank, returning to the substantial recess within the old, gnarled roots, her bronze face still troubled as she muttered something about trees and dropped heavily upon her blanket. "Find anything?" She asked just as shortly as the others followed, and Garon shook his head. "I'm not surprised. Your White Hammer has nothing to do with the Arana, as I understand it. Why would they know anything of their plans?"

"I never said they were associated with the Hall," he reminded her dispassionately, dropping the bag of food behind the bedrolls before searching out his waterskin. "They're contacts, not colleagues. People who see and hear things; people in a position to collect, compare and corroborate information."

Eyila frowned.

"People no one notice and talk around without thinking they'll repeat it to anyone else," Petra clarified. "Like bootblacks, apparently."

"What's a bootblack?"

Garon sighed tiresomely and returned his waterskin to the pile, then, without a word, turned and walked off into the trees. The others watched him go.

Eyila's eyes shifted onto Petra, whose unreadable gaze lingered after him. "He's still--"

"Mhm." She sighed and shook her head in self-reproach, leaning over for her own flask. She shrugged disparagingly as she unstoppered it. "It's just the way he is. I don't know why I expected anything else."

"But he kissed *you*."

"He did. And since then I've been little more than a density in the air." She took a draught and shrugged again. "But I get it. This is serious. It's been three weeks and we've seen and heard nothing of Salus since we escaped that accursed place, and while he's certainly up to *something*, all we've managed to uncover in that time is that he's been giving his orders by proxy and it's making some of his subordinates nervous. How Garon's contacts learned even that much still eludes me, but the fountain cleaner he spoke to in White Heath also knew an awful lot about the workings of the palace's wine cellar. Regardless, it took Kienza two days to find us after we got out, and if the Arana actually has translocators - which they *must* for him to have gotten to Dolunokh so suddenly - then he probably returned to Turunda far sooner than we did. He said he didn't need the Zi'veyn anymore, so he's most likely turned his focus onto his new plans instead, and for the sake of *everyone*, we need to uncover what they are." She shook her head as hopelessness began creeping over her. "But without Rathen, the Zi'veyn, or Anthis and his damned educated guesses, we're... Ugh, and we're almost certainly being followed..."

Eyila nodded slowly. "Have you talked to him?"

"Oh Vastal *save* me. *Leave it alone*, Eyila! I don't know why he kissed me - something in his head must have broken on that island. Just *forget* about it! I have!"

She studied the duelist for another long moment, then nodded slowly again. "All right." She turned her attention onto the bag they'd brought back and began rummaging through its contents.

"Do you think they're okay?"

She looked back up at Petra's suddenly softened tone and found her staring off for miles into the forest behind her, her hazel eyes steeped in even deeper fret. She set the bag aside. "I'm sure they're fine. Neither of them are fools."

"But the place was tearing itself apart when we left..."

A sadness flickered across Eyila's brow, at which she lowered her hood, shook free her asymmetrical white hair, and turned her face into the subtlest breeze that seemed to rise from nowhere. Her expression eased as its cool ribbons caressed her cheek, but she didn't manage to smile. So when she looked back, she forced one. "They're fine. I'm sure of it. Though I admit that I'm surprised by your concern for Anthis."

Petra stiffened for a moment and failed to conceal the curl of her lip at the mention of the cultist's name. "Well, I'm not...*unfeeling*..."

"But his faith disturbs you."

"Of *course* it disturbs me! I can't fathom why it doesn't disturb *you!*"

"Because," Eyila smiled softly, "I can see his heart. He *is* Craitic, like you - immensely so. He believes so very strongly and fully in your goddess, he makes no lie of that. And I believe it's that devotion to Vastal, and for all the good She represents, that has driven him to take upon himself the duty of protecting us all from the fate your Craitic scrolls dictate."

"By *killing* people? Taking them as sacrifice to a supposed demigod and 'saviour' because their souls are considered 'valuable'?!"

"In a sense," she continued to smile, "yes. Because he could take the life of *anyone* with a free spirit, but he chooses instead those who bring only pain and misery. People whose actions, if allowed to continue, would perhaps throw into question for some the love your goddess has for them."

"But he thinks his 'god' uses them to...build a...a *dead-soul-shield*, or something!"

"Life doesn't cease to be, only our bodies die. Our energy continues - in your culture, without purpose. But he believes that his demigod, Vokaad, can put that energy to use to protect your people from any future wrath of the gods, be that Zikhon's victory over Vastal, or something...more complex."

"His demigod does not *exist*."

Eyila's expression twisted softly into something Petra couldn't read, and she remembered far too late that she was speaking to someone with a faith very different to her own. Her cheeks turned a deep crimson, but whatever Eyila may have said - in defence of her own wind goddess, or a similar observation towards Vastal - was replaced instead by a pitying smile.

"If that is true, then he is still doing your people a service by destroying the wretched among you. But need I remind you that you recently uncovered information that could upturn your *own* entire belief system? That the elves, from whom Craitism grew, originally held *five* gods in regard, not merely two, and that both Vastal and Zikhon were not the icons of good and evil your people today believe Them to be?"

Petra gritted her teeth behind her lips, trapping any heated retort or argument born of the blinding insult that burned away her shame. "It's *not* true."

Eyila smiled softly. "Well, I can't attest to either side. I mean only that faith is also perception. The elves regarded five *faces* of gods equally, for Their good and

Their bad. You have regarded only two, one for good and the other for bad. My people and those of the other tribes hold love and devotion to other gods still, gods that have no place in your culture, while yours have no place in mine. And what bad has befallen any of us for it?"

"Yes but, apparently, those five gods *destroyed* the elves!"

"If what Anthis has learned is correct, the elves were destroyed for challenging their gods' power and being in a position to act upon it. They had already turned their faith away from the gods by then, and nothing bad had befallen them before."

Petra growled and snapped her head away, her hand absently clutching at the chain about her neck.

"I mean simply," the girl continued with only a flicker more tact, "that the *truth* bears little consequence. Day will always flow into night, which will always flow into day; the moon will always fade and be reborn and the sun will always tan the sands. The wind will always blow. As long as we stay true to who we are, are grateful for all we have, and take time to consider what is beyond us, to trust in what we cannot always see, to have *faith*, what does it matter who we choose to worship? As long as their teachings are noble and harmonic, and their followers uphold the true essence of good, what need is there in knowing whose god is real, or whose beliefs are right? If they are good, they are *all* 'right'."

"You speak of other faiths and truths so easily," Petra sighed tediously, but looked around in surprise as Eyila's musical voice rose in a lilting chuckle.

"Because I *know* that *my* goddess is real."

She stared at her in confusion for a moment, but found she could only breathe a bewildered laugh.

Eyila's eyes dropped to the chain she continued to run absently through her fingers, at the circular talisman of Vastal and at the solid oval locket strung beside it. She watched as she traced them both with equal care, and a frown of understanding slowly crossed her brow. "It's...about your father, isn't it?"

Petra's hazel eyes widened in another wash of surprise.

"It's not the idea that Anthis believes something different to you, nor even really that he kills for it. You've known him far longer than I - you know who he is, you know his convictions, and you understand that he chooses his sacrifices carefully. What troubles you is that he kills *at all*."

Petra stared at the tribal girl. A warm breeze picked up, shifting the leaves and dislodging settled raindrops, shaking them down upon their boots as they poked out from the root-woven cave. She scoffed and turned away. Eyila didn't try to regain her attention.

"They will be back," she said instead, returning to her rummaging. "Both of them, with the Zi'veyn."

"We should still consider an alternative."

Both spun in fright as Garon returned from his patrol, but Eyila quickly straightened, her eyes flaring with even greater conviction. "Rathen is a great mage--"

"And the destruction of that place was far greater."

"Kienza will get them out if Rathen can't."

His hard, grey eyes flicked only briefly onto Petra before turning to the trees beyond them. "Don't you remember how alarmed she was by the fact that he was still in there? There may well be nothing even *she* can do. It's been three weeks. They would be out by now, and we'd have heard something."

"Rathen is smarter than to go around shouting about his return," Petra snapped. "They'd lie low. Kienza told us to go to Fendale--"

"And in the mean time? She never told us *why* we had to go there, it could have nothing at all to do with them. No, we can't afford to waste time waiting, we need to *do* something. We need...information..."

Petra's eyes narrowed as she watched him fold his arms in thought. "And?"

His eyes flicked back to her, briefly once again. "With or without the Zi'veyn, whatever happens, we *will* need a mage."

Her eyes flashed incredulously and she leapt suddenly to her feet. "Do *not* tell me you're thinking about the Order. Not after what we saw in Stonbridge."

"What about Kienza?" Eyila offered.

"And just how are we supposed to find her?"

Petra stepped up to him, her jaw tight in frustration despite her steadying breath, and ignored the fact that he still barely looked at her. "You're right, Garon: we need *information*. But we are *not* giving up on Rathen. If, like he says, Salus has elven magic, then how could anyone with anything *less* than that stand up to him? And as *you* pointed out, we could never find Kienza ourselves. I get the feeling that even *Rathen* wouldn't be able to find her." She watched the inquisitor's jaw clench, and his eyes finally rested upon her for more than a heartbeat.

"Your suggestion?" He asked coolly.

"We go to Fendale, like Kienza told us to, and we see what happens. We're only five or six days away."

"And then--"

"And then, if there's nothing there to suggest they're out, or safe, or at the very least *alive*...we consider an alternative. Because, as you *keep* reminding us, there are far bigger things at stake than anything Eyila and I might worry our little heads about."

"I never said that."

"You don't need to." She turned away, ignoring the pinprick of injury in his eyes which he was very quick to hide, and began strapping her weapons back about her torso. "Let's be off. I want to find somewhere dry before nightfall."

Chapter 2

"I am warning you," Riken rumbled, his deep voice harsh as he leaned over the organised desk and fixed the patient old man with even plainer threat, "if you don't get your people under control, the Crown will place *all* of you under house arrest and pin *you*, Arator, under investigation. All licences, orders and privileges will be revoked - and I dare say the unrest in the cities would be quelled. A solution to *all* problems."

"Mm." Arator leaned calmly back in his chair and clasped his hands neatly upon his lap, staring past the liaison in consideration. "I dare say you would be correct. Of course such a solution would present *new* problems - such as our part in Turunda's defence - which could, unfortunately, only be overcome by a reversal, which would revive the *original* problems. It's a tricky circle. Of course," his eyes fell onto him, "there is another option: you could trust my word that every step *is* being taken to put an end to the matter."

"And just what results are there to be seen for it?"

"Unfortunately nothing yet so absolute, but progress is certainly being made."

Riken held him in the grips of a venomously mistrustful stare and suppressed a snarl at the easy calm the grand magister met it with. He pushed himself back from the desk and turned away to spare his patience. Arator continued to watch him. "Doana," he said after a long moment, his voice tight. "Has anything been detected?"

"Nothing."

"You're sure your mages aren't withholding anything? Plotting something?"

Arator managed to keep the flash of rage from his old eyes. "Quite sure."

"But you cannot guarantee there won't be a repeat of Rosh."

With a deep breath, he eased his hidden yet fraying temper and straightened. "Rosh's actions were his alone. They do not represent the intentions of the Order. What he has done has shamed himself and his family; his commission of sivaan has been revoked posthumously and his family have lost the adjoining privileges. None more will follow his lead."

"For fear of what happens after they're *dead?* What use is that? What of those who have no family to bear their punishment? What's to stop *them?*" Riken slammed his hands upon the desk and revived his penetrating stare, but again the mage was not moved. His eyes narrowed suspiciously. "And what of Koraaz? He was one of yours, once. A sahrot - a colonel. Another high rank. What about him? He returned from the dead, attacked Carenna and then vanished again like a wisp of smoke."

Arator was already shaking his head. "That was not Rathen Koraaz."

"So you've claimed. But then just who *was* it?"

"I assure you, my lord, it was no mage. It was nothing more than a malformed opiac addict in the contemptible district of a contemptible city who lost control of what faculties he retained from his drug-dictated existence. Most of the witnesses themselves were quite likely intoxicated. No one died - no one was even injured. Someone had a fit, thrashed around, frightened everyone and was chased away in a frenzy."

"There were guards as witnesses."

A small, regretful smile passed over Arator's face. "Guards in a contemptible district of a contemptible city. They are not beyond temptation, nor corruption, my lord." He maintained an assuring softness in his eyes while Riken continued to stare at him in silence, and the middle aged liaison's nostrils soon flared with the release of a long and tightly controlled breath. He pushed himself back from the table and straightened his regal, stately robes.

"Repair this matter, Grand Magister, and fast. Doana are hidden all around us, and they surely have many more underhand tricks to throw our way. Turunda is in no position to withstand an insurrection, *especially* not by mages. The Crown has given you the space to deal with your subordinates, but if it goes on for much longer, we will have no choice but to revoke that right and your jurisdiction and turn the matter over to another body."

"I understand, of course."

"I know you do. And I hope it doesn't come to that." He inclined his head, a gesture returned by the old mage as he rose from his desk. "Good afternoon, Grand Magister."

"Good afternoon, Lord Riken."

The liaison left, the door closed, and Arator dropped heavily back into his seat. Ten seconds later, as expected, another knock came, and he wearily called his permission to enter. The two high magisters did so swiftly.

"I understand the need for it," the elder of the pair began brusquely as the door closed behind them, "but it blisters every time we have to dishonour Sivaan Rosh. Whatever truly happened to him *wasn't* his own doing!"

Arator sighed and ran his hand over his neatly combed and tied grey hair. "You don't need to remind me, Delas, but dishonouring him is the only way to maintain the Crown's trust. We don't truly know what happened, after all."

"Yes, well, the king and his council are fools."

He gave her a flat, disapproving look as she settled serenely into the chair before his desk, while the second mage, mid-thirties and far younger than either, remained standing in respect. "How many times have I told you not to eavesdrop?"

"I've lost count, but if you raised auditory barriers it wouldn't be an issue. Now," she leaned forwards, the flame of intent in her dark eyes made more vivid by the breaking of the clouds outside, "what are we to do?"

"For now, nothing."

"*Nothing?*"

"Delas, there's nothing we can, not right now. Not with the Arana watching us so closely. You can deflect their eyes from this room for a while but we can't keep them from the entire Order House, and *especially* not for good. They're everywhere. Like spiders. They get into every little hole, make themselves comfortable and watch the world with eight attentive eyes. We can misdirect them, at best, but they *will* notice if we move."

Delas, the head of the spell-preservation department, curled her lip in distaste. "Why has the Crown allowed this?" Her eyes narrowed as he hesitated. "You don't think they did."

"I don't, but I also have no proof. You heard Riken, if we can't do something about these rebels, someone else is going to step in to do it. It's not impossible that the Arana has already been posed with the task and are presently moving into position for the swiftest of results when they're finally given the nod."

"It's not just the rebels, though, is it?"

Both pairs of eyes turned up onto the third. The younger man, rigid in bearing, looked back at them with the same cautious pause of someone far inferior, and yet with a spark of innate confidence. That well-earned self-assurance was one of the factors that had brought him up to the level of high magister and stand-in for the head of the Order's military, but it would take time before he became comfortable with his new equals - and far, far longer still before he displayed the same casual familiarity with the grand magister, the head of the Order, that Delas did.

He straightened beneath their gazes, but the conviction in his eyes remained steady. "As Lady Delas pointed out, Sivaan Rosh wasn't responsible for the calamity among the soldiers, and neither were any of the other mages who died with him. Nor, from identical reports, has been *any* mage to have...taken his life. We all know this."

"Lord Roane is correct, of course," Delas agreed. "It's the fault of all these strange arcane goings on out in the wilds - but *how?* Arator, we *need* more information!"

"We can't get close to any such site, especially with--"

"With the Arana watching us, yes yes yes, but if the Crown wants the matter resolved, is this not also relevant?"

"It is. But we're thought to be to blame. Every mage within the Order is being watched, dogged as soon as they leave the gates. There's no hiding from them. The only mages capable of spells of concealment are the diz'al in the military wing, and despite the Crown's mistrust of us, they're all on standby for war. And they're not trained to decipher such issues."

"Then we teach the spell to those who *are!*"

"So you've said many times, Lord Roane, but if it were to get out that such a hard-nailed regulation had been breached, we would be under even greater suspicion. Now, more than ever, we must play by the rules."

"We've always played by the rules, Arator, and look where it's gotten us." Delas shook her elaborately coiffured head and hammered her sharp fingernails into the chair's arm rest. "Every mage in the Order..." She pursed her lips, and her eyes slighted again in thought. "Rathen--"

"We've had neither sight nor sound of him since Carenna."

"But young Owan says--"

"That he is out there in an inquisitor's custody studying these places with a historian. Yes, I am aware, I was present when he delivered me the report. But Rathen Koraaz does not answer to us any longer."

"No, apparently he answers to the Hall of the White Hammer instead."

"I doubt he answers even to them. But I have been in contact with the Hall regarding the matter and they will not confirm a thing."

"They like their secrets almost as much as the Arana. But at least they're open about their existence." Delas sighed wearily. "And yet, he is our only option."

"Absolutely not."

"Oh, Roane, *do* be quiet," she grumbled. "Rathen Koraaz is *not* a monster. Don't succumb to the rumours your classmates fell to so easily. You're too young to have served beneath him but surely you know of his deeds in service."

"Yes, Lady Delas, I do - just as I know that we have no explanation at all for the actions that brought that service to an *end*." Roane's burning eyes crashed onto his superior, who watched him with calculation. "We *cannot* turn to him."

"Then you will be glad to hear, Lord Roane, that I fear this is a pointless conversation anyway. As I have said: we don't know where he is, nor what he's doing. We couldn't reach out to him if we wanted to. And...as much as it pains me to admit this, for I knew him well, we *don't* have an explanation for his turns. We have no way of knowing what could come of them, for those around him or for the Order itself. And our position is precarious enough." He looked to Delas, who sat with tight lips and confliction clear in her eyes. He knew she agreed, and that she did so with the same reluctance as he. But Sahrakh Roane Forlin, having graduated from the Order's schooling two years before the sahrot's disgrace, knew nothing of the man's nature to soothe his frets, as neither did his classmates nor those of the years that followed. And, above all else, his position in the military wing meant that he prioritised the safety of the people above all else. And quite rightly, for it was his job.

The light in the office dimmed behind the gathering clouds. Arator sighed heavily and ran his hand over his tidy head. "We must find those responsible for the rebellion. The leaders. Whomever is inciting dissent. We need to regain order in our ranks."

"And then? That won't stop whatever it is driving a handful to destruction. They're causing greater calamity than the rebellion."

He nodded slowly, his eyes suddenly lost in distant thought. "When we come to it."

Delas's lined brow creased deeper in apprehension. Roane, too, displayed his unease. But neither put it to voice. They inclined their heads and vacated the office at the grand magister's bidding, leaving him to rise, wander, and find himself standing grimly at the window.

The capital city of Kulokhar spilled out all around the trio of towers, and from his position mid way up the tallest, he had a grand view. But today, he didn't see it. His eyes travelled further, past the city walls, around the scattered military encampments, across the forests and villages severed by the slow-moving cataclysm; he stared well beyond the realms of sight and off into space and thought, where the same weighty matters circled his mind like vultures, plaguing his waking moments.

The Order was under his command, and it was falling. What had he done to allow it? Where had he gone wrong? When had he taken the first step down the path to this, the beginnings of a collapse of an entire authority? For it had to be his fault, or surely it would have happened sooner.

And this magic...the pandemonium of magic that couldn't be, and yet was, and was now tearing the land apart. Voiland, Hin'ua and Ithen to the north had each been rent into pieces; Dolunokh was barely standing. The continent of Arasiin was riven, scarred by chasms and canyons that were reaching further and further south. They'd appeared in the north of Turunda already; Halen was the first to fall. And the Order, *his* Order, the body whose jurisdiction this precise predicament fell under, knew barely the first thing about it.

There was too much else going on, things the Crown deemed more immediate threats. He had spread his people thin trying to bend to the Crown's demands, and he'd neglected the magic because of it. He could spare too few. And that had left them blind. They were *still* blind, and as they groped about in the dark, the ground was collapsing beneath them.

He should have tried harder, but war could never be taken lightly. They'd kept out of it all for so long; even as surrounding countries fell into a blood frenzy, Turunda had remained untouched. It was inevitable that they would succumb sooner or later, and it was far from a surprise that Skilan had been involved when they finally did, even if they were merely high on their winnings. But Doana... Doana. They hadn't seen them coming. Even now the details, the motives, eluded him. But it was not his task to think on them.

And yet, perhaps it should have been. Perhaps, if...

No. No, second-guessing himself would never do. Once he started, he'd never make a confident decision again, and a leader couldn't be so crippled. It had been Sivaan Rosh's place to decipher the arcanised heralds of war, and if Doana had slipped past him, and slipped past General Moore - and slipped even past the Arana - then how could *he* ever have hoped to spot it?

No. He couldn't second-guess himself. He could only reflect and admit his mistakes and try to avoid making them again. He was at fault for ignoring the magic when it was still beyond their borders, for presuming it to be the result of foreign mages' hands in war. But that hadn't been an unreasonable conclusion - it had certainly been far more likely than what had been discovered since it had barrelled through into their domain. Spell chains, loose magic, broken elven spells that were collecting at magnetic sites rather than dispersing into nothingness... Such should not have been possible.

But, possible or not, it was there, and it had to be tackled.

But how could they tackle it if they were being *blamed* for it, and being set upon by the Arana's ghosts before they could reach such places to investigate? How many of his mages had been imprisoned on such work? Twenty? Twenty five? He'd been quick to assert his position and rescue them into his custody, but such interruptions made it impossible to learn anything.

And yet Rathen Koraaz...that most unfortunate child prodigy...he *was* out there. And if Owan, a long-ago friend and the scholar who had encountered him on a similar task - one of the lucky ones who had avoided capture - was to be believed, he also had the chance to work it out.

But...Rathen Koraaz had never been a scholar. His aptitude for learning was weak; he'd always been more of a...*physical* man, one interested in action and results, not theory and speculation. He was impatient. That was why he'd been drawn to the military wing, why he'd made Sahrot at the impressively young age of twenty seven and could have risen so much further, had fate been kinder. He wanted to *do* things, and to see the results of his actions immediately. Picking scrolls apart, constructing spells, analysing technicalities - such had never been his strengths.

How could a man like that ever hope to unravel this impossible dilemma? To present an end to its impossible results, the tearing of the land, the crippling of mages' minds, the strengthening of the underpowered?

Arator sighed and squeezed his arms about his chest. His head was pounding, and his guilt at the matter being so far out of his hands - like so many others whose shadows weighed like lead upon his shoulders - chased away the beginnings of hunger from the appetite that had been eluding him.

But he couldn't indulge nausea. Stress was no reason to starve himself. The Order would only suffer more for it.

He pushed himself away from the window and left his tidy office to fill the silent pit in his stomach.

Chapter 3

The sour taint of the forges was inescapable all across Emberton; day and night it thickened the air while the ring of hammer against steel drummed an incessant rhythm into the lives of residents, dictating all from their breath to synchronous footsteps. It wasn't quite as bad when a favourable breeze picked up, and though work in Turunda's smithing capital never ceased, its hardened residents made a point of pausing to savour the cleaner, clearer air the moment the smog relented.

One such breeze purified the town that afternoon, and the streets were more cheerful for it. The riverside docks were busy with children diving from the quays, the small fountain square was filled with the bouncing, spirited music of passing minstrels, and the dancing, clapping and foot-tapping it incited spread into the equally lively if equally small market, where even the unvaried produce on display seemed curiously delectable.

It was, in short, a pleasant place to be, and like all others around him, the returning smith wore a smile of enjoyment as he passed leisurely among the crowds. A stall cleared up ahead of him, the departing customers revealing a wealth of fruits made more vivid by the atmosphere. He stopped, fished around in his pockets, and purchased an apple patched in red and green, which he bit into immediately to silence the impending rumble of his stomach. He hadn't stopped to eat since breakfast, and that itself had been meagre.

He slowed his trek through the market, looking around as he wandered at the various displays of joy from the children to the elderly. But as infectious as their pleasure was, he had to fight to keep the smile on his face. Such celebration had become a rare sight lately, and for reasons everyone was aware of yet no one would speak of.

His heart weakened, and he moved on.

Nearing the edge of the market and the reach of the minstrels' pipes and drums, a small but sharp movement caught his eye. A casually dressed figure turned down a quiet street, a man who wore no distinguishing marks and yet one he recognised immediately. Tanner Erson - a mage, without his cloak. And he, too, was heading towards the forging district.

He slowed down, noting the path the mage was taking, and adjusted his own against it. A mage without his cloak could only herald trouble.

He discarded the core of his apple, having bitten it to the bone, and lightened his steps. He knew Emberton's streets well enough to guess at the route such a suspicious figure would take, as well as chart another for himself that wouldn't overlap it, and he was soon passing through streets and lanes in parallel, half a beat behind so that he wouldn't catch the mage's eye. He took to wider streets rather than follow small mazes of alleys when a lane would later intercept them, or the main road when there was a fork up ahead that would take him the same way. At one moment he dropped to his knee and appeared to remove a stone from his boot when the mage's pace had slowed, just to hang back. He peered carefully around each corner before proceeding, but the mage continued to take the expected turns.

He didn't ease, however, and his predictions inevitably failed.

Following an unavoidable, twisting route between towering buildings where the noise of life had grown distant, he heard footsteps approaching. He leapt back on silent feet, slipping behind a corner, and peered around through the shade only once the footsteps had taken the lead once again. The mage had deviated.

He adjusted his route, but soon crossed him again. The mage seemed none the wiser, but on the third occurrence, in the middle of a straight lane devoid of shafts or corridors, he was forced to drop to the foot of a bottle-laden doorway, muss up his hair and pretend to be in a drunken stupor against the wall. The footsteps didn't pause. He rose again only once they'd faded around the distant corner.

And this time, he followed him.

He turned the bend and saw the mage take a left. He followed, silently. When the mage took a right, he continued straight on. When the mage appeared, crossing his lane on an intersecting path, he took the same direction at the nearest turning, tracking parallel once more.

A tavern was close; the air was tinged with ale and pipeweed. He slowed as he neared. He passed its back door, turned a corner and knelt to dislodge another stone. And listened.

He glanced behind him, back towards the tavern. He counted to three, then rose. And jumped.

The mage had no chance even to shout out in surprise. His head struck the ground, his mouth was gagged, and his fingers broken one by one before being dragged away towards the rear entrance of the building.

"Mm." The old man grunted in satisfaction, having correctly guessed the identity behind the impatient knock, and moved away from the door and its fine insect net draping to let his visitor in. "Can I get you a cup of tea?"

Salus's nose wrinkled against the odour of musk and fruit as he stepped into the dark, cramped room, but a smile still flickered as usual at Tom's tightrope of respect and familiarity. He shook his head, closing the door tightly behind himself. "No, thank you, Tom." His eyes drew through the torchlight, first across the various mesh cages lining the walls and the fist-sized moths that occupied them, before settling upon the cluttered table at the far end. "I just wondered--"

"I always pass on everything as it comes in, Keliceran, you know that. If it's not on your desk, it hasn't arrived." The master lepidopterist glanced up from chopping fruit at the silence that followed, and noted the keenness around his eyes. As well, belatedly, as his soot-dusted clothing. "Just get in, did you? Get him?"

Salus nodded as he peered into the nearest cage.

"Good - you stopped the attack before it happened, then?"

"This one, yes. But there are so many directions we're trying to look in that it's impossible to prevent them all..."

"Yes, well, little victories."

"Mm..." Salus straightened and nodded towards the old man. "Thank you, Tom."

"Of course, Keliceran."

He wasted no time in leaving the dank old cellar, and at the escape of the offending smell, he was able to breathe a little easier. Unfortunately his remaining tensions and their deep, steel roots proved far more stubborn, but he had grown accustomed to them.

His fingers flexed restlessly as he covered the short, torchlit passage, pausing only to emerge from the hatch secreted beneath the grand staircase of Arana House's foyer. His veins tingled as he darted around and climbed them, shaping intentions in his mind - light, heat, ball or flame - with every step, and his fingers twitched along with them, instinctively trying to relay those thoughts into signs. But he stilled them, restrained them and interlaced them, and focused his energy into intent alone.

For the past three weeks he'd been training his magic urgently and barely keeping at bay the regret that had seeded itself within him. He had killed Denek. He'd had no choice at the time, the mage - the *elf* - had become a rabid beast and lunged at him with his own intent to kill. Salus had simply protected himself. But now...what could *Erran* possibly teach him? An Aranan mage and powerful in his own right, certainly, but neither he nor anyone else could ever hold a candle to an elf. Nor even part-elf, like himself.

He had conjured that blue fire, the fire that had consumed and obliterated his teacher in seconds, summoning it from nowhere, on impulse, without any signs. Just like an elf. Just as Denek had taught him. He was capable of more than any ordinary mage, so what could any ordinary mage teach him?

A growl shook free from his throat when he reached the second floor, and his silent, motionless spells continued to go unanswered.

Whether he was capable of more or not, he had no choice but to stick with Erran's instruction - grudgingly, impatiently - because he was in no position to reject his help. Elven magic he may have had, but he had no idea how to wield it.

It had been three and a half weeks since he'd cast that cold blue fire, and his training had grown beyond feverish trying to recreate it. He was racked with fatigue, sleeping only when Taliel commanded it, and his judgement should surely have been impaired. But it wasn't. In fact, he was curiously alert; acutely aware of the blood in his veins, the beat of his heart, and capable even of calculating stolen time from the office to take on a handful of missions himself, securing their success with his never-forgotten portian training.

But, between the trifling matters of upholding the Arana's reputation, eluding Lord Malson and working around the Crown's ineptitude with every decision that needed making, it was yet more magic, and that of another, that harassed his sleepless nights.

Koraaz. He had gotten to the Zi'veyn first, and while he had no idea what they truly intended to do with it, it was a priority to keep it out of the Order's hands. Because while Denek had assured him that it would take elven magic to use, *Salus* had elven magic himself. And he just couldn't ignore the odds that, in a body of one and a half thousand mages, there could well be another in the Order.

Or that elves themselves were hiding amongst them.

Rathen Koraaz had elven magic, at the very least. Of that he was sure. Mages could cast illusionary spells - the Arana had begun work on altering appearances, and a handful within the rear- and advance-guard of the Order's military could conceal, but that was all. But Denek had *transformed*. By sight, strength and speed - tangible and impossible for anyone less. And his transformation matched perfectly the reports of Koraaz's attacks in Kulokhar eleven years ago, and again in Carenna just recently. He'd teleported, too, taking himself and his comrades to Dolunokh, just as Denek had done for him.

Yes. Koraaz, at least, had elven magic...and quite probably elven training for him to have been able to use it so easily.

And the Order had used that very same magic to move him out of sight; they'd orchestrated a catastrophe, drawing full attention to him and the resulting banishment, and soon reported him dead. All to conceal an asset. So that no one would notice him move into position when the time was right.

All of that meant that the Order certainly had the means of using the Zi'veyn.

So why *hadn't* they?

He all but sprinted up the final flight of stairs and along the corridor to his office. He was doing his best to make the most of the opportunity the Order's hesitance had presented. He *had* to get it away from them. But all he'd managed under Erran's instruction of magic were Aranan basics - moving things, conjuring fire, extinguishing light, and intensifying it to deepen shadows and divert attention. He was working on freezing people, certainly a valuable skill, but his expectations of his newly discovered elven blood were slowing him down. He tried relentlessly to cast his spells without signs, and failed every time.

At present, he had neither the plan *nor* the skill to steal the Zi'veyn away.

Salus barely slowed as he reached the loathsome office door. He burst inside and provoked a vaguely startled jerk from the man sat behind his desk.

Teagan rose from the chair immediately and stared past the keliceran to the wall behind him.

Salus ignored the formality. Slamming the door, he marched across the room he loathed from the very bottom of his heart and took his place at the seat of torment behind the desk, which Teagan promptly vacated. But he didn't sit down. He leaned over and raked through the reports that his favoured subordinate had so neatly stacked, scanning over their varied concerns: the watch over Doana's scattered camps, the deterrent against tribes and non-humans, the weeding out of foreigners from Turunda's towns and cities, the continued observations of suspicious Order activity, and the quashing of anticipated attacks after the confirmation of such suspicions - to which he would add his own report, for the records.

Only once he'd soaked up every necessary detail with a practised if fervid eye did he drop heavily into the accursed chair, and he felt its shackles ensnare him. He puffed a sigh of resignation and looked up towards Teagan. The dark haired man stood now on the opposite side of the desk, impassive, gaze still fixed over his superior's head. Salus didn't bother to try to set him at ease. He looked back down at the reports, and the office remained silent for a long time. "Until we know which camps are being genuinely fortified," he said finally, barely a fraction above a hiss, "we can do *nothing* against Doana."

"They know we're watching them."

"And they're feeding us nonsense." He shoved the reports away, scattering them across and off of the polished walnut desk. Teagan didn't react to the collapse of his organisation. "Without that intel, the military is frozen. Doana may even be waiting for *us* to make the first move, to act rashly in impatience so they can strike from somewhere else while our back is turned! Skilan may have been a swift victory, but our military has been in action for three months, they *have* taken losses, *especially* with Rosh's *damned internal strike!* They *cannot* stand against a fresh force *without intel!*" He leapt hotly from his seat, but Teagan remained unaffected. "We've been hindered from the first step - they're being too careful, we can't seem to glean *any* of their plans - or perhaps we *have*, but there's so much disinformation floating around that it's *impossible* to tell just which it is! It's like a game of thimblerig! Infiltrating and replacing any of them isn't an option, and even a controlled provocation, a nudge, a poke with a *stick* could turn out to be anticipated!"

"It is an unconventional situation," Teagan agreed calmly.

"And Doana is in full sodding control." He snapped away as a torrent of helplessness surged up inside him, seizing his muscles, spinning circles in his gut like a whirlpool. Sweat beaded on his skin, his heart thundered. The chair disintegrated beneath the power of his foot. "*Why is there nothing I can do?!*"

He scowled down at his hands as the air grew dense, tightening his fingers, staring at what moved in the veins beneath his flesh. He hissed and curled them into fists. "With this magic...I could *obliterate* them...but I have no idea *how!*"

"They don't seem to be doing anything--"

"Except waiting for us to attack! But we can't risk going first, so we're trapped in a deadlock!" He spun back towards his subordinate, whom he noticed flinch beneath his gaze. He brushed it aside. Then his voice dropped suspiciously. "The mages report nothing, either. But how can we trust *them?* They've thrown the country into turmoil themselves, and they're attacking openly now, in *groups*... The only ease we have over that matter is the apparent trend of suicidal mages moving alone. Groups are destructive, but they have yet to kill anyone...though that doesn't make them any less suspicious..."

He turned away again, leaving Teagan to release a very slow and uneven breath, and wandered towards the window. He peered out over the nearby estates and towards the city beyond, and the spiralling ebon towers at its centre, gilded in gold and silver, observing them so attentively it was as if he could see through the walls to their occupants' activities. "We're watching them, and yet seeing nothing. Whether they're hiding it all behind spells too advanced for us to detect, or they're just being that careful... But there are so few mages in the Arana's ranks...and so many have been sent out to protect the city from the mages that the Order House itself is thinly guarded... It feels counter-productive. Treating symptoms, not the cause..." He flexed his fingers again.

Rain clouds emptied in the distance, their edges blurred in the downpour. The sun shone intermittently over the city. The local clouds parted for one such stint of brightness, then quickly knitted themselves back together.

His thoughts cascaded. The room was silent.

"What of the tribes?" He asked casually, without turning. "They're moving closer, getting in the way - are we actually affecting their numbers? At this rate, we'll have more evacuations on our hands."

"They're not killing one another anymore," Teagan confirmed with a sturdy voice, no trace remaining of his previous disturbance. "Their numbers are dropping by the Arana's actions alone. They're wisening up to each other's tactics and traps remain untripped by their intended victims."

"No, instead by innocent people, honest hunters."

"They're paying no attention to boundaries; their arguments are spreading out of their terrain. There's no telling just how far out their traps have been set, nor what the traps themselves may be."

"Mm. One was impaled on a hinged barricade of sharpened sticks, the other crushed beneath a rigged boulder." Salus looked around from the window, his visage calmer, his eyes human. "Malson wants them lured away."

"I know. So I have issued the order to cease framing the opposing sides. It will only encourage them to remain beyond their borders with the intent of finding the responsible individuals. They will be removed instead, and we will set up our own blockades."

He looked back out of the window, watching a spider on the glass wrap a fly in its web as he chewed over his proxy's decision. Finally, he nodded his agreement. "But it will take time. The tribes are mobile - by the time we've raised defences in one area, they'll have moved off into another. They're strange like that, they don't hold advantageous ground, they just keep moving and lay traps behind them..." He cocked his head in thought, his tone growing even more distant. "Yes, they are strange creatures...neither human nor anything less...living in a culture of barbarism. Are they even aware of what's happening outside their little world?"

He grunted to himself. Yes, they were. Because there was one such barbarian travelling with Koraaz. For reasons as far from his understanding as the stars were from the soil, he had recruited into his band of misfits an untamed, savage spell caster from the Ivaean deserts. What was it that *she* could do that he could not himself? What could *she* bring him that Karth, an inquisitor, a duelist and a *child* could not?!

Just *what* was the Order planning?!

His knuckles thumped into the window frame, and he gritted his teeth against the blunt pain that spread through his hand. His eyes flicked hatefully towards the distant towers before he spun back to the dark and confining office. "The Order hasn't used the Zi'veyn, and we've had no hint of their intentions. We need to find Koraaz, *now*. Find him, find where he's taken it and imprison him so they *can't*."

"No one has seen him - operatives or civilians."

"Then follow the tracks in Dolunokh!"

"There were only three, sir - you have been informed of this. One limping, the other stumbling and heavily supported by the third. They rested an hour away, then moved off to the south towards the nearest settlement. Then we lost the tracks. Vague reports have since come in from eastern Turunda of an inquisitor with the correct build, and of rumours of the duelist, Petra Dalton, appearing in cities, but no one has been able to confirm either and any attempts to track them have been hampered by various factors of war."

Salus's burning, raging stare drilled into his core, but this time, Teagan didn't flinch. His brow didn't flicker even as Salus spoke, even though he had expected rancour and received instead a tone startlingly calm, even though his inferno was stilled only by the slow dawn of understanding. "They were injured... I saw *five* go in, but only three came out...and they *lingered*. There was no urgency, they...they were *waiting*..."

Salus wavered as if physically struck, his face empty of anything but shock as he steadied himself against the window frame. "That's why the Order haven't... Koraaz hasn't returned. They *don't* have the Zi'veyn." His wide eyes flicked towards Teagan for an explanation, but the portian was already shaking his head.

"We don't know what this means. He could be dead and the Zi'veyn itself destroyed, or he could simply be trapped."

"But the site--"

"Dolunokh is under surveillance across a fifteen mile square radius encompassing the point where they entered, where the tracks were discovered, and where they ended. If Koraaz returns, we will know."

"Who else is missing?"

"Karth. Two sets of footprints were booted, one bare; one of the booted was female, and the other matched those of the White Hammer uniform."

"Karth..." Salus nodded vigorously. "Good. That's good. Without those two, the rest are stuck...but we still need to find them." He straightened, professionalism abruptly reasserting itself and cooling his fever. "They teleported to Dolunokh, just like we did. They couldn't have gotten there so fast from Ivaea, not even by boat. So they probably teleported away afterwards, too. You didn't lose the tracks, they *stopped*. There is still a mage among the three who returned..."

"You believe a *tribal* mage could be capable of teleporting?"

"Don't be foolish, Teagan, of course not. She didn't do it alone. The elves created vessels for their spells, that's what the Zi'veyn itself is - perhaps Koraaz gave her something, a quick get-away to familiar ground... Why weren't those sightings followed up?!"

"They--"

"This isn't *good enough!*" His eyes flashed, and Teagan's immediately flicked away. "I can't train magic *and* juggle this place! I left you in charge because I thought you were capable of making decisions! Of handling whatever came up in my absence! And now I find that you've *let them* slip past us?!"

"S-Sir, the reports were--"

"*Don't interrupt me!*"

The walls shook, but Salus didn't notice. He thundered across the room in an instant, coming to a sudden stop a hair's breadth from the portian who wouldn't meet his eyes. Their quick, almost nervous shifting irritated him. His lip curled further, revealing even more sharp teeth through the monstrous snarl. "I would expect this level of ineptitude from a phaeacian," he growled fiercely, "and quite possibly a phidipan. But *never* from a portian, and *certainly* not from you. You had *better* fix this, Teagan, and fix it *fast*, because if you don't the whole country will fall and I will hold *you* responsible, and if I can't rely on you, I can't rely on *anyone*. So *get after them* - with people who *won't* allow themselves to be interrupted by 'factors of war', because this is *much* bigger than traps and sodding barricades. If he gets out, Koraaz *will* join them - find them, and we will find *him*.

28

They're still sticking together for a reason - but don't get too close. Send a portian. Watch them. Listen. Follow. I want constant updates." His black eyes narrowed. "Why are you shaking? Actually, no, I don't care. You have your orders. See to them. Now."

Teagan turned and left without a moment to lose, sparing no promises, no formalities, not even a nod of understanding. As though he was desperate to be away. But it didn't matter. At that point, all that mattered to Salus were results, and the ceasing of the pain in his head.

Once the door had swung shut, he dashed forwards to lock it and began to pace the office, forcing deep breaths into his lungs and shaking out the tension in his arms and legs. It took a while for his blood to cool, but as soon as his body began to feel familiar, he sat himself down on the floor, in the centre of the rug.

Closing his eyes, he straightened, raised his head, dropped his shoulder blades down his back, relaxed his face, and let his feet fall into the floor and the crown of his head float. His breathing came easier, and his thoughts began settling into some kind of order.

Koraaz hadn't gotten out; the Order didn't have the Zi'veyn. That was why they hadn't used it. But they were still up to no good, and the remnants of Koraaz's merry band could still prove themselves to be a problem, even without him or Karth. And if Koraaz *did* get out...

The man was too great a nuisance. He would get out, of course he would. And then Salus would confront him himself. It was pointless to send any Aranan mage after him; they could do nothing against his elven magic except get themselves killed, and that would certainly alert him to any tails. Then he would take hasty action - he may even teleport away again. Only Salus could oppose him.

'What are you striving for?' He heard Taliel's softly spoken question repeat in his mind. *'Absolute protection,'* he had replied. *'But what does that mean?'*

What *did* it mean? Did he even know? He wanted to protect Turunda, but its threats came from everywhere. How could he protect, absolutely, from things he couldn't foresee?

What was that old idiom? 'The roots of foresight are knowledge'.

Prediction. Preparation. Threats against a country did not occur on a whim. They were planned. And if they were planned, they could be prevented. He needed only to know what such plans were. And he had planted agents for that, observing towns and cities from the most advantageous positions, gathering valuable intel merely by listening.

But they couldn't have eyes and ears everywhere. Things would always slip past. Whispers and looks, the slightest of hand-offs. And how much would they catch but brush off as being insignificant? Was such a judgement not the *keliceran's* to make? Or Teagan's? For even he was not usually so incompetent - though, evidently there was a first time for everything.

To protect the country, he needed to know when and where things were happening and exactly who was involved - every subtle glance, every polite marketplace collision, every hushed meeting in a corner of a tavern. How could he prevent calamities before they happened with anything less?

He wondered, abstractly, if he could trust all the eyes he had out there. Why could they not be his *own?* If *he* could see things unfold as and when they happened, observe the birth of every conspiracy, catch every step of a growing scheme...

Then a thought appeared, and he forced his racing heart back into check and seized control of his breath.

There had been tell in children's stories of elves spying on one another with seeing mirrors and scrying pools. Surely, if the elves could create a place made of nothing but magic, such spells would have been trivial...

His eyes flickered open as his thoughts tumbled away, but he swiftly caught himself and forced them shut again. He hadn't noticed his body grow rigid, nor his breath shorten.

There had to be signs that could form a foundation; in a body of spies, his mages had to know *something* of arcane surveillance techniques...

There were records, details of what his mages could do, a reference for assignments if magic was the only way, for matters out of the ordinary - records expanded upon whenever new spells were developed. Though trained by the Order once upon a time, his mages had long since been independent; Order mages were capable of so very much more than his, and without collaboration they had kept the Arana's abilities distinctly stunted - but the Arana had created many of the spells in those records themselves. Necessity had forced their abilities and knowledge to grow, and they had thrived beyond the condemning eyes of high magisters, both their power and creativity proving valuable assets to the country.

If those records noted no such spell of distant observation, his mages could certainly create it.

His eyes flooded over the spines of the hundreds of ledgers lining the broadest wall, following the bookshelves from one end of the room to the other, sparing not a moment to wonder at when he had abandoned his efforts for calm.

The shelves were fit to burst with accounts and reports reaching back for three and a half centuries, linens increasingly tattered and bindings more weathered the further in time they stretched. But though he knew the file he sought should have been nestled among the most recent of the extensive archive, it was quickly apparent that it was not there. And after almost twenty minutes of racing up and down the room, neither was it anywhere else.

The usual roar of frustration at the world stacking itself against him ensnared him, as did the subsequent victimisation of nearby inanimate objects. A second chair shattered, side tables collapsed, the teapot was actively sought out. It was only through the most fortunate of chances that the ledgers themselves were left untouched.

How was it possible to have such power, power *no one* but he could wield, and wield for the good of the entire *country*, and yet be so restrained by its technicalities that it rendered him no better a protector than a common guard?! All he wished for was the safety of his people, the people he had given his entire being to, his past, his present and his future, since he'd been little more than twelve years old! But it seemed the world would not allow it!

To have eyes and ears everywhere, to locate every threat - to be in two, three, five, *seven* places at once! To have the power and the reach to eradicate *every* threat, *every* enemy with a sweep of his arm so they might fall as easily as pieces on a chessboard!

To be rid of them, by blood or by chain, or even just raise the borders so they couldn't get in at all! Or--

He whirled as a rap on the door interrupted his mental ravings. He bellowed admittance, hoping instead to frighten them off, and his frustration pricked deeper when the handle turned anyway.

But the door didn't open. It took him a moment to recall he'd locked it, and an even longer back and forth to decide upon leaving it that way.

Until a soft voice, half a whisper, spoke his name from behind it.

What rage that gripped him evaporated as suddenly as it had formed. His feet moved long before he gave them the order, and his fingers fumbled with the lock - but at least the hammering of his heart, though still unwelcome, was fuelled now by something altogether more pleasant.

Finally the latch clicked out of place, and he opened the door to the brown haired woman, both plain and incredibly beautiful, standing to attention outside. Her fine lips were pursed in her resting thoughtfulness and her eyes stared past him to whatever lay beyond. But though she didn't smile, he saw a sparkle in her formality that he knew was meant only for him.

His expression remained equally neutral. He straightened and widened the door, stepping to one side to let her in, which she did promptly and without a word. Only once the footsteps they'd both heard approaching from further along the hallway had passed did a change flicker across either, and only once the door had closed was it allowed to take any hold.

Taliel turned suddenly and threw her arms about his neck, and as his stomach fluttered, he embraced her in return, and the moment her soft lips sought his, he felt his every tension diminish.

Chapter 4

Twilight enshrouded the butchered landscape, though the golden sun hung only just past its zenith. The darkness smothered every rise, flooded every crevice, and what meagre slivers of light persisted cast deeper shadows beyond the colossal shards of stone that pierced the upturned fields, tangled further the knots and gnarls of tree roots that rose from the dirt like the claws of the dead. Forests were swallowed, hills had collapsed, and jagged, miniature peaks had been thrust up from the depths of the earth. Amethyst lightning shattered the sky, flashing in and out of existence but for a few violet streaks, inexplicably frozen in time.

And yet the air was near silent, stirred only by the intermittent rustle of dry leaves disturbed by a whispering breeze, and the constant hum pulsating in long, droning rifts, but weak, like the rumble of a most distant torrent of water.

Nothing moved. Nothing breathed. There was not even the buzz of the smallest insect's wings.

Dolunokh was as still as death, watched only by the eyes of ghosts.

Until the air shuddered and a disembodied cry obliterated the silence.

"*--nds off me!*"

In that same instant a flash of endless black tore itself into being, shifting and jerking its shapeless form, expelling pops of light, threads of heat, a tinkling melody, and two figures in a flurry of leaves before imploding on a whim and leaving the ravaged land to its sorrows and the rages of these sudden arrivals.

They struck the ground. One of the two staggered immediately back to his feet and lunged forwards in desperation, sparing not a moment for the portal nor his sudden and decrepit surroundings. The impossible twilight would have made little difference had he tried to observe it - their world had been much darker and much less possible a moment before - but the urgency firing his blood seized him to his core and continued to overpower any thought for anything other than escape.

The second figure moved close behind him, and unwillingly. Even as he limped, the first dragged him along by the collar of his soiled shirt, which was only half as tattered and blood-stained as his own. Their bodies were in little better state, but despite cuts and burns, atrophied muscles and devouring hunger, the second maintained a bestial fury, clawing at his captor, trying one moment to free himself and the next to pull himself closer so that he might rip out his throat. The first managed easily to stay ahead of it.

"*Let go of me!*" The captive roared, groping up his arm in an attempt to grasp and violently wrench his long, black hair. "*I'll kill you!*"

"I'd like to see you try." But the retort was weary, forlorn and without heart even as he continued to evade the attacks.

Finally, Rathen's haunted eyes began to rake the surroundings.

His heart faltered immediately. Doubt seeped in, but this, he remembered painfully, was Dolunokh. Dolunokh, after a torrent of agitated magic had surged from Khry's Glory with Garon, Petra and Eyila's escape, and ravaged the real world. It had been a site of cataclysm before that moment, but now it was only a floating river and faceless harlot away from mirroring that cursed arcane realm.

And if the turbulent magic had devastated this immediate land so immensely, what had it done to the rest?

What had become of Turunda?

He swallowed hard and forced the cascading images from his mind in favour of movement. He had no idea where they were going, but he knew they couldn't stay. They had to find the others.

Anthis raged and bellowed about half breeds and arrogance. Rathen ignored him.

How long had they been trapped? The false sun had never once moved, hanging eternally in a midnight sky; it had felt like an age... Then the others would not be nearby. Salus had been there when they'd first leapt through the doorway, and he would surely have waited for their return. He may even have captured them the moment they'd gotten out.

Perhaps the pair's entrapment had been a blessing, keeping the Zi'veyn from his clutches.

He tightened his grip on the strap of the near-empty bag slung over his shoulder, and gave Anthis an encouraging jerk as his efforts turned once more away from attack and onto freeing himself from his grasp. Their first priority was to get as far from the riven fields as possible.

Anthis suddenly ceased his struggle, and Rathen looked back in sickening understanding. The young man's eyes were desperate, flicking around in a fever until his head snapped around to the right and behind. Someone was following them. And Rathen didn't need long to work out who.

He slowed and looked around, but, as he'd expected, there was no sign at all of any movement. He looked back to Anthis; the direction of his focus hadn't changed.

He released the bag and quickly flexed his fingers, shaping and releasing a single spell. He swallowed hard. Twenty, twenty five feet behind them and to the right, where the cracked ground was several feet higher and jagged, a lone man was following them. On perfectly silent feet.

Rathen's bearded jaw tightened. He grasped the bag and continued onwards, urgency renewed, and pulled Anthis along in his impassioned distraction. "Eyes front," he whispered, though he knew it was hopeless, and focused instead upon keeping the figure in the centre of his mind's eye.

He continued to track them, remaining out of sight, hidden beneath the peak of the ledge, footsteps light and soundless.

Rathen glanced further along to the right. Ahead, the high ground dropped and a series of tusk-like rocks rose from its lowest point, while on the left the ground dropped sheer into a chasm. The path became constricted. It was an ideal location for a small and precise ambush - and what else would an Aranan hunter deliver?

But he didn't deviate. There was nowhere else to go but along that narrowing path. And it seemed that Anthis had heard him, and more impressively yet had understood. Or perhaps Rathen had simply returned to being the focus of his rage, for his frenzied clawing, snarling and nonsensical cursing had been revived.

But, again, Rathen ignored it. He kept his eyes locked forwards and his focus to the right. The assassin was drawing nearer. With every step they took, the tracker took two. Soon they were level, and the ground began its descent. The stone tusks were ten paces away. Eight. Five.

He released Anthis's collar.

In an instant the young man spun and launched himself like a manticore completing its ground stalk. The face of the ghostly assassin as he left his cover had barely a moment to flicker in shock. The meagre sunlight was caught in a flash of steel. The air was pierced by a manic cackling. Anthis leapt upon him.

Rathen turned away while the man gasped and gargled as his throat was cut, and chose not to hear the archaic elven words that fell so easily from the insane historian's lips, nor the carnal gasp that rose with the other's last breath. He didn't look back for some time.

"We need to keep moving," he said at last, and heard Anthis rise. A strike to his shoulder shoved him forwards.

"You," Anthis snarled as Rathen caught himself, his voice still elated but tainted with a lingering venom, "you don't tell me what to do. I'm so *sick* of you."

Rathen turned slowly and levelled his gaze, in part to keep his eyes from wandering down to the cut along Anthis's forearm as it knitted itself back together. Instead, he saw the lust over his kill and the high from the power he could almost physically feel emanating from him ringing the young man's green eyes. But comprehension had also returned; for the first time in Vastal only knew how long, Anthis appeared almost like a man again. And so Rathen had no qualms with planting his fist in his gut.

"And I," he said coolly as Anthis wheezed, "am sick of you."

He turned away to survey the area, broadening his magic to detect anyone else nearby, and so he noticed immediately when Anthis's false magic shifted. It was little trouble to deflect the phantom burst of energy thrown towards him.

Anthis grunted when it returned to hit him in full force, throwing him backwards several feet, and Rathen's stoic facade collapsed as he rallied his withering energy to storm the distance. "*Don't ever* use that filth against me."

"It *would* be filth to you, wouldn't it?" He puffed. "Anything *beneath* you is filth!"

Rathen's lip curled, but he snatched back his composure, straightening and ignoring the daggers shot by Anthis's bitter eyes as he fought to reclaim his breath. "I'm not going to keep arguing with you."

"Why? Because I'm beneath you too?!" He watched the black haired mage turn in silence, lift the slackened bag from the ground and begin to limp away. The heat of rage flashed through his chest like a bolt of amethyst lightning, encouraging his weary body to pick itself back up. "What a surprise," he jeered. "Walking away all tall and rigid, so very high and mighty. You were always insufferable, treating your magic like a curse, like you were too good for it, too good for everything and everyone around you, *lowering* yourself to our level just to make us more comfortable in your magnificently formidable presence!"

"What are you prattling on about?"

"Acknowledgement! How *generous* of you! When all I was doing was 'prattling' - but that's all I ever do, isn't it? Like the rest of the riff raff." Anthis chased after him, falling in step just behind and burning his sight through the back of his head. "We have nothing of value to say; if it didn't come from your lips it's not worth being heard. We're not worth talking to - your company is the best there is, why bother with the rest of us? But I suppose that's what comes from hiding all alone in a corner of the world, crying over your fate, wallowing in your own self pity and enjoying every moment of it." Again he said nothing, and Anthis's fury doubled.

Rathen grunted, shoved again, but he didn't slow or turn. "I'm not fighting with you."

"No, why would you? What would be the point? You could tear my throat open in a heartbeat. Why would you even feel threatened with what you're capable of--"

Now he whirled. "*What I'm capable of?!*"

"Oh," Anthis's green eyes flashed in satisfaction, "have I trodden on a golden nerve?"

Rathen shook his head, searching the historian's eyes in disbelief. "You actually think I *enjoy* it, don't you? You *really* believe that I hold some value--"

"Why wouldn't you?! You're half-elf! You're superior to all of us! Stronger than any mage!"

"And you're...what, you're *jealous?!*" His incredulity swelled as Anthis scoffed.

"Why would I be *jealous?!* I've studied the elves my whole life! I've single-handedly unravelled a number of their mysteries and I'm acknowledged as a nuisance for it among my peers! I even possess a 'filthy' form of magic! *Why would I be jealous?!*"

The air seemed to fall notably silent at the sound of knuckles crunching into a jawbone.

Anthis spat blood and scowled, but before he could begin to struggle back to his feet with another acrid remark, a great weight pressed against his chest, and another clasped about his long-unshaven throat. He panicked and stared up into eyes that boiled with barely suppressed rage.

"*Believe me,*" Rathen growled, pressing his knee harder into his sternum, "I am cursed. What you would apparently consider a blessing has *ruined* my life, and I would *never* wish my misfortunes upon even *you.*" Anthis clawed at his arm, but Rathen's grip was not tight enough to damage him. Somehow, he had restrained himself that much. "You like history - let me share some: all through the Order I was dogged by unreachable expectations, and when the underlying power my superiors were so *convinced* I carried finally reared its sickening head, *I killed sixteen people*, and was *banished* for it - an insult disguised as leniency, a 'mercy' for my service to the country, when really they just didn't have the *courage* to do the responsible thing and *kill me.*" He fought to keep his blood from boiling, but this time he couldn't prevent the force of his knee nor his grip from closing. "They took my whole life, sure enough - my career, my family, my *future* - and held it all out of my reach, forcing me either to die slowly and painfully from my wounds or continue to exist without them. I left my home in the middle of the night rather than see through the week of grace, all so my wife wouldn't follow me and share my sentence or watch me die. But through no fault of my own, I *survived.* Kienza found me, and she saved me, but she couldn't keep the ugly grudge from consuming what small world I found myself living in, one directed towards any figure of authority, and one, to this day, I am still disinclined to change.

"Then the Crown had the *audacity* to reach out and ask for my help, and I *loathe* them for it. I am here *only* because I want to keep Aria safe. And you may spit on that fact, call me a liar, tell me that I'm seeking glory, or even - and I *dare* you to say it - that as long as Aria is with me, she is *always* in danger. And that is true. *Everyone* is. But believe me when I say she has *no one* else. She shouldn't even have *me*. So don't tell me that I don't feel *threatened* because of what I'm *capable of*, because it's what I'm capable of that *does* threaten me, *constantly*, I have no control over it--"

"Oh," Anthis rasped as he dug his fingernails deeper into Rathen's bloodied arm, "no control? Not even with such direct attention from the elves? But, then, what could they teach you that--*mmph!* That you don't already know?!"

Rathen's eyes flashed again, but somehow he forced himself back in check. Choking him would achieve nothing. He withdrew his hand. With effort. "You have looked at me with disdain from the moment my secret came out," he said heavily after a moment of collection. "Perhaps it was irresponsible of me to conceal it, but what good would it have done to tell you? Probably as much as had you told us *your* secret. Because," his eyes softened, causing more than a flicker of mistrust through Anthis's, "you're as much a victim of your...*faith*, as I am my own blood."

He shifted his weight and rose from Anthis's chest, leaving him lying in another wheezing battle for breath, lifted the bag and began to stagger away. "Come on. There will be others." He glanced back as Anthis stared after him, choking, but pensive, his eyes an open mixture of surprise and confusion, equally intense. "Hurry up!"

Anthis closed his mouth. He stifled his sudden questions, pushed himself up in spite of the dead and heavy weight of his limbs, and followed him along the narrow path through the ruined landscape at a wary, silent distance.

The twilight had neither faded nor deepened, but the sun had dropped beyond the horizon - it made a nice change to finally have some indication of the passage of time beyond beard growth, which Rathen still couldn't shave through his weakness to conjure a blade. He needed to conserve what little strength he had in case the need for defence arose, for he still had no idea where they were, and if Anthis knew, he wasn't telling. He hadn't said a word in hours. But at least he wasn't attacking him now.

Concealed within one short and shallow crevasse among the riddle of arcane destruction, Rathen turned the small onyx-gold relic over in his hands. He'd long stopped marvelling at its lightness, its perfect lines, its central lotus and geometric hooks and thorns. Instead his attention was focused deep inside at the spells that filled it, the complex chains and irregular connections that linked each together at least four times over, creating an impossibly intricate web of information. A few weeks ago it would have overwhelmed him, but he'd since had far too much time to analyse it. Even under his present fatigue and the hallucinations that would surely return before too much longer, he observed the labyrinth of magic with logic and direction, following the path through the apparent chaos like a child's puzzle completed so many times.

His task was still daunting, and now that he was in a position to safely use his magic again, he felt the pressure despite his weakness to repair the relic as soon as possible. But with every moment he took to penetrate the magic of the Zi'veyn, the clearer the frays and breakages became, and after an age of nothing but staring at the thing, he was sure he'd found a way to achieve it. And with little idea of what had become of the world after the surge that had followed the others out, there was no time like the present.

"Have you..."

Rathen jumped and looked up, further along the crevasse. The camp was black but for a sliver of moonlight slipping through the gathering clouds; they hadn't risked a fire, certain they were still being stalked though neither could detect a thing, but there hadn't been any kindling nearby anyway. And so all there was to reveal Anthis sitting against the opposite earthen wall some ten paces away was a trace of light glinting back from his eyes.

Rathen looked back down to the elven relic. "I'm there, I think. But patching it won't work, like I thought. The spell is too complicated. I might cover more than I should. I'll have to..." he shrugged, deciding that such detail was needlessly elaborate. Perhaps even arrogant. "I can fix it."

Anthis nodded slowly and said no more, leaving Rathen to further ponder the artefact and finally dare the first of his highly tentative reparations, until the deathly rumble of the young man's stomach forced him at last to his feet. "I'll see if I can find some food."

Rathen watched him stagger off. He didn't bother telling him not to go far, nor to be careful, nor that he was most likely wasting his time. Because he was just as starved and didn't want to put him off. His eyes dropped back to the relic and his attention returned to the spell, and after ten minutes of intense concentration interspersed with a few careful injections of magic, exhaustion finally beat him to sleep.

He awoke the following twilight morning to a handful of berries left in a hollow in the ground beside him, which he ate without question in a single, voracious mouthful, but almost half an hour passed before he finally saw Anthis. He appeared at the end of the chasm, lurching forwards and tightly hugging his chest. Rathen leapt to his feet in a panic, certainly using what little energy he'd gained from the berries in that single, urgent movement, but as Anthis moved closer, Rathen noticed that his clumsy movements were listless but devoid of severity, and it was not his chest he hugged, but the husks of some kind of fruit.

The five scaled shells, he discovered when he hurried to help, were filled with water from a nearby stream. Anthis had already drank his fill; these were for Rathen, who had just enough energy to express surprise. But that was all. Once drained, they set back out on painful limbs, eyes peeled in the hope of finding more berries or the ripened fruit the husks had once encased, their guard ever raised against pursuers.

The day passed in a blur of tedious motion; the uneven ground rolled along incessantly beneath their feet, tripping and staggering them when they couldn't keep up with it. Their vision hazed and legs buckled, but when one collapsed the other picked them up, and they continued to struggle over the rotating land, too debilitated to even mutter complaint.

But the haggard landscape did begin to subdue; the rifts and fissures became smaller and fewer, as did their detours around them, while the outcrops of stone grew more weathered and natural, and the few trees began standing upright. But the changes came too slowly for them to notice. It was only when Anthis fell for the seventh time and Rathen followed while trying to help him back up that awareness struck, and they finally noticed the most drastic change of all. Lying on their backs, staring towards the midday sun in exhaustion, they found that the sky was blue. Not indigo, not streaked in violet, but blue, partially clouded, and delightfully ordinary.

Neither could help a laugh of joy. They pushed themselves back to their feet and continued onwards through genuine daylight, their spirits finally buoyed.

Luck, too, suddenly smiled upon them: within a copse of trees that stood strangely but welcomely untouched in the desolation, they found an abundance of blueberries. After gorging themselves ravenously, they filled the bag with as many as they could find, then followed the sound of trickling water as it gurgled delightfully in their ears. A stream cut through the miniature forest, most likely the very same Anthis had found that morning, where Rathen spared the energy to conjure two waterskins. They drank their fill and stored what they could, and as they stopped to rest, he dared and achieved further progress over the ancient relic.

Their fatigue subsided, at least for the moment, and as they followed the stream which, they decided with much effort, must have been uninterrupted all the way back to its source for it to still be flowing, their spirits were as high as the clouds.

It led them along to another curious copse, which they reached just as the stars began to twinkle, and after a sleep far less fitful than those they'd become accustomed to, they ate their fill of berries, adding to their hoard what few they could scrounge from these sparser bushes, and set back out in the correct morning light to face the same trials yet again. But where the world became familiar with elements of the ordinary, they found it easier to put one foot in front of the other, and they had both gathered bearings enough to note their direction from the sun. Finally, they were heading south, towards Voiland and on to Ivaea.

But with those bearings came clarity, and their morale dampened as their minds wandered again towards the others. Where were they? *Had* they been captured? Or had they taken this very same trek south? Were they in Ivaea? Or even back in Turunda?

Or had they fallen victim to the rigours of the world, caught in the tides of war and fallen to Ivaean or Kasiri blade? Or simply starved? In their haste to escape the collapse of Khry's Glory, their supplies had been forgotten - a silver lining, at least, for the pair trapped inside - and Dolunokh, as they had seen, was almost empty of any sustenance. Would they soon come across three corpses? Or would they find only scattered bones after the feasting of opportunistic scavengers?

Rathen gritted his teeth against the thought as they crossed the widening stream through its shallows, neglecting in their wealth to pause and take a drink, and waded through the reeds to the far bank where an apple tree grew in another verdant grove.

They'd found no trace of pursuers since that lone assassin days ago, and as neither were sure how much distance they'd covered, they weren't inclined to relax their guard. The Arana would certainly have the area under watch - the simple fact that Salus, the obsessively-driven head of those spies, wanted the Zi'veyn that was currently half-repaired inside Rathen's bag was enough to justify that assumption, and the fact that there had been no sign of pursuers equally meant nothing. They were professionals, after all.

A light splash behind them forced hearts into throats and the quickest movements either had made in weeks. But while Anthis had drawn in a flash the plainest of his two concealed daggers and Rathen had raised one empty hand and tightened his grasp on the bag with the other, neither, it seemed, were quite so prepared to utilise their weapons.

Their tracker was upon Rathen in a moment, gripping him tightly and pinning his arms to his sides. He attempted to free himself, but his body was still too weak to put up any kind of fight, and as Anthis had not yet come to his rescue, he could only assume that he was similarly incapacitated.

But at the very moment he felt a desperate helplessness begin to overshadow his being, he caught the warming scent of forest and the fever in the muffled words spoken into his shoulder. It took him a long while to comprehend them, and even as the figure pulled away and he stared into a perfectly beautiful face accented by piercing emerald eyes and framed by a tangle of brown waves, curls and ringlets, it wasn't until she embraced him again that he finally recognised her.

"Kienza?" He felt her nod against his shoulder, and when she pulled away again, he was almost knocked down by the intensity of emotion in her watery eyes.

She raised her hand and stroked his gaunt, hairy, salt-and-peppered cheek, smiling in amusement through her tears, though sorrow lingered at its centre. He caught her hand as the sorrow began to dominate and smiled himself, with nothing but relief. He leaned down and kissed her. She returned it vigorously.

"You have no idea how relieved I am to see you," she told him before they'd even parted, and grasped him firmly by the arms, though her grip quickly loosened. "You're so thin..."

"There wasn't much to eat." He stared into her eyes, his sudden severity not in the least compromised by his starvation. "Aria? Is she all right? Tell me."

Kienza nodded earnestly. "She's fine. Just fine. She's been working very hard."

"Working hard?" His frown passed as he recalled the task he'd set her, then returned in shame. He shrugged the bag from his back, rummaged through the berries and withdrew the gilded onyx pyramid which sat snugly in the palm of his hand. "I'm afraid I won't need it..."

Her eyes brimmed with an intense and sudden intrigue, and her hand rose instinctively to reach out for it. Catching herself, she promptly forced it back into her other and diverted her gaze onto him with abruptly veiled thoughts. His own, troubled eyes were already lost in the tangle of black and gold.

She turned away, leaving him to his guilt-riddled ponderings, and pulled Anthis up from the floor where he'd dropped in exhaustion and into an embrace of his own. He looked on in shock, though not devoid of appreciation, then received from her the same look of concern. She stepped back and regarded them both, then ordered them to remove their shirts and sit before thrusting a plate summoned from nowhere into their hands, each bearing a generous chunk of bread, meat, cheese, grapes, and a tall glass of chilled milk. "Summoned, not conjured," she declared before Rathen could protest to the false nutrition of equally false food, and set about looking over their multitude of severe cuts, bruises, burns and fractured bones.

Rathen eased a deep breath, certain at last in the safety of her presence, and as he felt the movement of her magic weave first into Anthis's skin, he recalled, not for the first time, the words she'd given them before they'd departed Ivaea for the Roquna sea. "'Where we need to go'."

Anthis glanced at him in confusion while he crammed bread into his mouth, but Kienza merely smiled from behind them.

"You knew everything, didn't you?"

"Of course I did," she replied easily.

"About my mother?"

"Mhm."

"And that there was an island full of elves out there?"

"Well your mother had to come from *somewhere*."

"And--"

"And that you would be ensnared in the enchanted mists and twisting current and reach said island rather than the Ronar Coast of Kasire?" She shrugged easily again. "Yep."

Anthis's shoulders sagged. Whether it was for the ease of pain or in shame for having been so easily tricked, Rathen wasn't sure, but he knew for which of those reasons a defeated smile graced his own lips. He nodded and asked nothing more about it. "And Aria is safe? She's being looked after?"

"You've already asked. Don't worry - your father's care would surprise you."

Anthis looked again in curiosity, but his mouth was full now with cheese.

"And the others? Are they--"

"Fine, all fine. Relax, my love. The world has not crumbled in your absence."

Reluctantly, Rathen eased in acceptance. At a pleading gurgle from his stomach, he finally made a start on the food, having neglected it in his nausea. It didn't take him long to pick the plate spotless, and after a brief wave of dizziness, he felt energy overflowing. Mind racing, heart pumping, determination aflame, he seized the Zi'veyn from the blueberry bag.

Anthis and Kienza both stared on in silent fascination, each wishing to snatch the thing and marvel at it in their own hands but unwilling to interrupt Rathen's immense concentration. His focus was suddenly and absolutely consumed. A thing so small, so insignificant - not even truly a beauty by the standards of most recovered elven pieces. But as they stared, they soon began to squirm beneath its presence. This tiny little thing, the tiny little thing they had searched two months for, could block the magic of elves. It could render the original spell casters defenceless. Made as a weapon, a show of power, to end elven conflicts in the favour of its wielder - who could then obliterate them with his own magic without resistance. For what did elves know of swinging a sword? Or of using their hands at all?

Truly, it was a terrible thing.

But it had the potential to be a saviour. Nothing else could remove elven magic, in the veins of its caster nor the spells they left behind. But while the latter could, at least, be countered once understood, the shattered chains that had seeped like a plague from the elven-made realm were too clueless and chaotic to truly be deciphered. A counter-spell could not be created, not against every individual and half-degraded chain that gathered in uncountable pools all across Turunda and well beyond. In such an unnatural state, it would take nothing less than an unnatural, barbarically conceived spell to oppose it.

Kienza dragged her attention back to her own work, and soon gave Anthis a gentle pat on the shoulder. "All finished, Mister Karth."

He was already sitting taller, and now rolled his shoulders and flexed his back, discovering right away the absence of every single twinge and crack that had hounded him for the past two days - or at least since he'd regained his faculties. His muscles, too, felt lighter and stronger. He was very nearly seized by the urge to leap up and climb the apple tree. "Thank you," he said with evident surprise, "and Anthis, please."

She nodded graciously and her hands then fell upon Rathen's bare skin, but he didn't react, and nor did he notice her immediate recoil.

She glanced towards Anthis, who noticed her shock, and only then did *he* truly see the extent of Rathen's wounds - most of which seemed more like rips than cuts, as if his body had grown without his skin.

Or his bones had broadened and reshaped themselves beneath it.

He looked back towards Kienza, whose perfect lips were puckered in thought as her hands returned to his skin, her forest green eyes just as pensive, and recalled through the haze of creeping wilds, floating paths and melting walls two incidents in which a monster had set upon him - one with a startling likeness to Rathen.

He turned away, his eyes grazing his shirt and the two blades he'd hidden from the sylvan sorceress within it, and suppressed the shame that came with the return of the equally hazy memories of his own bestial attacks.

Silently, he slunk away to redress.

"You transformed, didn't you?" She asked Rathen quietly as she pretended not to notice Anthis disappear around the other side of the tree. But he didn't answer. She inhaled to ask him again, thinking him too absorbed to have heard, but was cut off before she could begin.

"Yes."

The single word was hollowed out by so much contempt she could almost hear its echo. Only then did she notice the stiffness of his muscles. "And you're ashamed."

"What sort of thing is that to say?" He spoke emptily.

"A silly thing, I suppose," she conceded, "but I do think it might be necessary to remind you that, when it happened, I was not there."

"And why would you need to remind me of that?"

Her eyes narrowed, and a smile twitched over her lips. She knew that tone, and knew he was being deliberately obtuse. But she would play along and spell out for him what he was already well aware of. "Because there was no one there to heal you."

She smiled again as he failed to retort and watched the scabbed-over tears across the back of his ribs vanish into smooth skin. "So that means - and correct me if I'm wrong - that you have some kind of control over it now."

He jolted with what at first seemed like a bark. "Control." He shook his head and scoffed again. "I couldn't stop it from happening at all."

"Stop it from *happening*, no, but stop it from *continuing*, yes." She moved around to his front and set to work on the additional rips and what seemed like knife wounds across his front. She paused to stroke his cheek which was suddenly not so gaunt anymore, though it did appear more aged. "Usually," she continued just as lightly as he stared down into the reflective onyx, "you're damn near dead. It takes my magic, or Eyila's, for you to recover - or standard medics and two to three weeks of bed rest just to be able to sit up. And yet here you are, moving around, *fighting*, it would seem, and healed but for cuts and bruises without the help of magic nor medics. And after what your body goes through, that can only happen internally."

He growled tiresomely. "What are you talking about?"

"That whatever the elves tried to teach you, something of it got through. And now you have to grasp it and use it, sharpen it and perfect it. And then it *will* stop happening, unless you will it."

"Why would I ever *will* it?"

"Because its foundation, as the elves themselves have told you, is defence. A deterrent against violence, to strike such fear into the hearts of enemies with the dreadful visage of the God of *Eternal Peace* that they would not want to even *try* raising a hand against you ever again, and so saving *both* sides from harm." She abandoned her magic and lifted his bearded chin, running her fingers through the tangled black and white hairs. She smiled at them, then at him, and her green eyes softened, revealing her heart. Her gaze gripped him, and his anger similarly melted. "You are not fully elven. That is why it shreds you. It isn't meant for you. But with the understanding you're cultivating, in your mind and in your magic, your body can better steel itself against it. You will learn to control it, and learning to force it into submission once it has taken hold is the first - and biggest - step."

He stared back at her doubtfully, his eyes flicking between hers, but she was hiding nothing. He nodded. "But to reach that point, it will have to happen again."

She moved around to his side and lifted his emaciated arm to erase the streaks of burns from around his waist. She glanced only briefly at the steel cuff about his bicep, shrunken to keep itself in place. "Perhaps. But at the same time, every occurrence is also an opportunity to fight it into submission from the moment of onset - is it not?"

He sighed and looked back to the Zi'veyn. She smiled. He agreed.

But then he looked up again, a new spark in his eye as he regarded her with a burning thought.

"Uh-oh," she jested, but he ignored it.

"Tell me something: the elves cast spells without seals or signs, they can teleport, they--"

She chuckled softly and smiled. "No, Rathen, my love, my dearest, I am not an elf. Strikingly beautiful and disgustingly knowledgable about all things magic, but *not* an elf."

The spark died and his eyes turned away again, brimming now with confusion and defeated assumptions.

She saw quickly to the wounds beneath his shredded trousers before Anthis reappeared from around the tree, then rose to her feet, pulled him up, kissed him and declared that she had 'things to do'.

"Wait!" Rathen abruptly thrust the artefact forwards, inches from her face. "Can you...?"

She blinked in confusion while Anthis looked on, itching to take it and finally look it over himself. "Can I...? What? Juggle it?"

"No," he smiled despite himself, "can you check it?"

"Check it?" She frowned and took it - tentatively. It was remarkably light. "You mean you've repaired it already? Then again, I suppose you've had a month to work it out..."

The two blanched, but neither could find their tongues.

She frowned and concentrated into its depths just as he had, though with noticeably more composure, but soon shook her head and handed it back to him. "I can't detect anything broken," she said carefully, "but it's such an intricate spell that I might have missed something..." She watched him curiously as he reclaimed it, turned it over and dropped it back into the bag of berries. She didn't voice her suspicions even as her eyes flicked again to the glinting of the cuff through his torn sleeve.

Her lips pursed at another passing thought as he slung the sack over his shoulder, and their clothes suddenly refreshed; frays sealed, rips stitched, filth evaporated. Then she dragged them together, embraced them both fondly, and their stomachs lurched with the abrupt shift of the world.

Chapter 5

The world brightened. At first it seemed to be the curious displacement of light that always accompanied the casting of such invasive and unnatural spells, but when it didn't diminish, there followed the belated recollection that while such a phenomenon was always expected, it was also absolutely always imagined.

The thought was lost an instant later when a chill joined the blinding air, crisp, fresh and welcome, if fleeting, and the suddenly notable absence of running water was marked by the green chirp of a grasshopper and the gradual arrival of distant braying and bleating. As senses grounded, the subtle aroma of damp soil and summer blossoms trailed in the wake of the breeze, and a hint of earthy bark, with the slightest, smoothest note of sweet almond.

Aryll trees.

Turunda.

A roughly snapped curse renewed the abating nausea in a panic, and the ring of steel over scabbard lockets silenced the insects. Efforts were enforced to subdue the somersaulting of their stomachs, and their bearings urgently tumbled back into place.

Rathen was seized immediately, but even as the breath was once again squeezed out of him, a flash of red infused with spices and rosehip assured him there was no need for alarm, and he observed a black-clad officer of fine bearing sheath his sword from beyond the woman's embrace.

As suddenly and as roughly as he was grasped, he was released, but as a smile of relief began to twitch into place, it was promptly slapped away. Rubbing his cheek, which Kienza had not seen fit to shave while making him otherwise presentable, he stared instead into a visage of fury.

"*Where were you?!*" Petra struck him hard in the shoulder.

He looked defensively from her to Garon, who seemed *almost* to smile in amusement despite his usual bleak rigidity, then on to Eyila who grinned quite openly beside him. She incited another flicker of surprise with the lack of white, grey and black paint smeared across her bronze skin.

Anthis, too, appeared just as startled, for he stared at her, mouth slightly but certainly agape. His cheeks flushed as she stepped towards him, and his eyes flicked away for something else - *anything* else - to look at. The rosiness deepened when she embraced him just as fondly as Petra had Rathen.

Who still stared at him in expectation. "Well?"

He grappled for an explanation, but after a moment of stuttering and stammering, quite unsure where to start, Petra shoved him by the shoulder again and sighed, her fury abating to leave behind nothing but fierce relief. "Well...it's good to have you back."

"Thank you. I'm sorry if we made you worry..."

"Do you have it?"

Rathen's eyes flicked back towards Garon while Eyila moved over to hug him. He'd lost all trace of his amusement and looked distinctly dull and official again. He chose not to take his lack of concern as offence - though there was a certain shortness to the way he shrugged the bag from his shoulder and withdrew the Zi'veyn.

All eyes dropped with the weight of lead upon the small up-turned pyramid, each coloured by the shared mixture of unease and fascination the relic seemed to have a habit of invoking.

Garon was the first to pull his eyes away from it, looking instead towards Anthis. "And this is it? You're *sure?*"

"Positive."

He looked then to Rathen. "And--"

"They are weary." Eyila stepped in front of the inquisitor of the Hall of the White Hammer, silencing his impending flurry of questions with her stern but musical voice. Her pale eyes were no less piercing for the lack of a streak of black clay. "Perhaps we should let them rest and gather themselves. After all, they have just appeared out of nowhere, presumably by the hands of our own rescuer - which suggests they've only recently returned."

The pair spared a moment to look about themselves and notice, belatedly, that Kienza was not with them.

Petra nodded, but didn't turn towards the inquisitor despite addressing him. "Eyila's right. And I think there are a few things they should know..."

Apprehension brushed the two of them with the breeze, and Garon straightened, his air of duty rising. But instead of explaining, he strode past them, leading the way down a worn road lined on one side by trees while the other rolled into farmland. The rest followed, one at a time - Petra first, then Rathen, then Anthis and Eyila, who stared at him closely with an unreadable thoughtfulness. Anthis felt his cheeks redden and suppressed the heat as best he could until she soon nodded to herself in decision and looked away, though she kept her mysterious conclusion to herself.

They soon branched off from the road where the trees thickened and disappeared into the shadows. Rathen frowned uneasily at their haste as the perfectly good road continued to wind away through the hills, but he kept his tongue still until Garon brought them to a narrow, steep-sided river and down into a groove made flat by thirsty animals.

Food was handed out, and despite the simple but nourishing meal Kienza had provided them, neither Rathen nor Anthis declined what they were offered. Garon told them as they ate of what had transpired over the past month, starting orderly at the very beginning.

As expected, Salus had still been there when they'd escaped, searching for them in a frenzy. It was unclear whether he'd noticed the portal open and spit them out, or if he'd simply been groping in the darkness, but they had fled the area as quickly as they were able - with Garon's injured leg, a detail Petra had offered quite to his irritation. They'd stopped at a reasonable distance to wait for the two of them, but the land was buckling violently, and after an hour had passed and the world seemed to begin falling around them, they had little choice but to move on.

They'd headed south towards the nearest settlement, assuming that it was still standing, but Kienza had appeared out of thin air long before they were able to find out.

In the blink of an eye, she had teleported them all the way to Turunda and out from beneath the watchful eyes of the Arana's hunters, where she had then healed the worst of their injuries. She hadn't seemed surprised by the news of where they'd been, but she'd been clearly distracted, lost in thought, and said little but to ask where the two of them were. When they'd explained, she said she'd guessed as much, but when they asked if there was anything she could do, she'd fallen silent again. When she'd finished with her healing spells, she'd told them to head towards Fendale, gave them some food, and left. Her quiet alarm had exacerbated their own.

Their sudden return to Turunda had allowed them to evade the Arana's notice, granting them some degree of freedom, so they headed north from somewhere south of White Rapids towards Fendale, stopping to gather information on Salus's actions wherever they could along their way. But such was, of course, hard to come by. And though Eyila had remained hidden outside of settlements, and the others had replaced or covered their garments, they couldn't avoid the eyes of everyone and were soon pursued. Garon had managed to lose them with abrupt course changes, but they could never know when they'd picked up a new tail.

"Otherwise," Garon finished, with a whisper of defeat, "we've uncovered next to nothing about what Salus is up to. Not that that's a surprise. But we'll find something, one way or another - and with your return, we have the Zi'veyn, at least. We can return our focus to the magic in the mean time."

"It's gotten worse, hasn't it?" Anthis asked, turning away from the water as he washed the last of the cut hairs from his skin, but the quick looks exchanged among the three answered his question long before Garon could nod.

Petra looked hesitantly between the two of them. "What...happened in there? Why didn't you follow us?"

"The, uh...place was collapsing." Rathen turned his eyes away. "The magic gave way."

"But why?"

He became suddenly engrossed in the surface of the passing water. "When I...cancelled out the spell protecting the Zi'veyn...I...upset the local balance. I didn't trigger any of the traps, I just...destabilised the surrounding magic. And with the whole place rearranging itself on a whim, the door had moved - we would have followed, but I couldn't risk using my magic to find it so quickly, so I had to..." He paused, feeling Anthis's eyes on him. He cleared his throat, watched a passing piece of driftwood, then looked up at last with glassy eyes. "Well, it took a while, but I located it eventually and here we are."

"You were in there for--"

"A month. We know."

"What did you *do* for all that time?"

The pair looked away from each other. "We worked through Eizariin's scrolls."

"Eizariin's scrolls? *You* did?"

Rathen's expression flattened. "I did what I could. That's also why it took a while."

"I don't understand."

He leaned over and fished about in the bag for a moment, then withdrew a scroll nowhere near as aged as they'd expected, unrolled it and presented it to them. It was covered in illegible writing, slender lettering with angles just a little too harsh, and multiple inkblots. It had been written in a hurry. And recently. "It seems," he said as Anthis took it with a frown, "that Eizariin had set us a task that went *beyond* retrieving the Zi'veyn."

All eyes lingered expectantly, and the young historian soon shook his head, his frown growing in awe. "Destroying Khryu'vahz..." He looked towards the mage with even more astonishment. "You *did* this?"

"You don't remember?" Petra frowned, but his eyes flicked quickly away from her in shame.

"There won't be any more magic leaking out of that place," Rathen declared, sparing him her scrutiny. "I can assure you of that. Khry's Glory imploded behind us." He glanced towards Anthis who regarded him again in shock, no doubt for having been able to read the elf's hand at all, hurried scribblings or not, let alone for casting the spell it described. It was, no doubt, only the threat of incriminating himself again that prevented him from voicing his surprise.

"What about the Zi'veyn?" Garon asked. "Have you made any progress?"

"I couldn't risk casting any more spells in there, but I had plenty of time to analyse it."

"And? Can you repair it?"

Rathen took it again from the bag and held it out before them all. He didn't notice himself sit taller in pride. "It's already done."

"What?"

"Well we've been out for two days--"

"No, I mean are you *sure* it's done?"

Rathen's posture deflated. "I...well I've not tried to *use* it, if that's what you mean, but Kienza couldn't detect anything wrong with it."

"So, in short, no. You're not sure."

His lip curled. "How I've missed you, Garon. No. I'm *not* sure. But I've spent a *month* analysing it, thoroughly probing it, and through no small effort, all the links *have* been repaired. I can see how it works, *perfectly.*"

Petra's hand reached slowly out towards it, lured by fascination. Rathen handed it over with surprising ease and heard Anthis stifle some kind of noise, unintelligible even had it been released. "How *does* it work?"

"The elves perceived their magic as its own being," he explained just as easily, "something alive, not owned, just like the tribes do. The elves may have been arrogant, but that perception wouldn't have changed, it's too fundamental a thing in their culture, a physical truth. And after Eyila explained to me how she perceives *her* magic and helped me make the water in Ut'hala turn blue, I started to grasp the concept. It's almost like symbiosis; magic forms and resides within them - within *us* - and we are able to use it. It moves on its own, willingly; we have no control over it. We can't force it to multiply any more than we can stop it from forming.

"The Zi'veyn, however, *can*, but only because it is external, separate from the magic and the caster, and its spell is *immensely* complicated, uncastable by any individual in any single moment. Magic is formed in the heart, but the Zi'veyn doesn't affect the organ. For it to be viable as a weapon, it would need to be immediately effective, so there's no use halting the production of the magic by affecting the heart and leaving whatever is already in the blood. So it halts the magic itself." He withdrew another scroll and pointed to two neat and anciently scripted words. "'Suspend' and 'particle', or 'fragment'," he read. He didn't glance towards Anthis, who hadn't translated them quite so precisely, but had at least given him what he'd needed to muddle through. "It picks out the motes of magic in the bloodstream and suspends them while the blood continues to flow past it. This renders the magic - and *only* the magic - unusable, and highly vulnerable."

"It sounds very..." Petra pulled a sceptical face, "precise."

"Yes, but it's not about picking out minuscule details one by one. Magic is very nearly its own element, its construction is that unique, and the Zi'veyn itself uses elemental magic, almost. The spell has been designed to touch things *only* like itself: magic, in any form. In any setting."

"Even outside of blood..."

"Exactly."

"...And it works?"

He glanced towards Eyila. "I presume so, but only against elven magic. Elven magic is formed in an elven heart, perfectly suited to one another, whereas human magic is formed in a human heart with elven adaptations - the third ventricle - without the...physical *essence* of the elf to influence its formation. Human magic is..." his lip curled in personal offence, "impure. It won't react the same way."

"It will not work on me," she concluded without insult. "You are half elven - would it work on you?"

"To a degree; not completely..."

"Then it will not work on Salus."

Rathen straightened "No." He looked at Garon critically, who himself had straightened at the impending question. "What did he mean when he said he doesn't need the Zi'veyn?"

"We don't know, but we presume he has plans."

"And he's not been giving out orders himself?"

"It seems not, but my contacts are not among the Arana's ranks, so anything we uncover is second- or third-hand, or completely untrue."

"And you base your work on their word?" Petra scoffed, drawing a flicker of interest from Rathen and Anthis. But Garon didn't seem troubled by her subtle yet directed venom.

"I've learned to identify a lead worth pursuing. And I believe them. Salus's orders are being given by proxy."

"So he can work on his plans, no doubt, *whatever* they are. Or train his magic...he's likely growing more adept every day..." Rathen sighed dubiously. "And you have no idea what he's up to?"

"Nothing beyond assumptions; nothing at all we can act upon."

A rustle on the opposite bank reined the tense conversation to a halt. A water vole scurried out along a projection beneath the overhang and vanished among the reeds.

Rathen's dark eyes dragged back onto the inquisitor. "You say you've been pursued. By the Arana?"

"Presumably."

"*Only* them?"

"...I hope so."

"The elves would know where we are," Petra reminded them, just as quietly. "It would be no trouble for them to locate us, reach us and abduct us, or destroy us. And they haven't."

"Perhaps they were waiting for *us*. Without the Zi'veyn, you three are no threat."

"Why would they think *any* of us were a threat?"

"Our recovery of the Zi'veyn could be enough to undo every effort their ancestors have made to conceal their past from their descendants," Anthis suggested, his eyes still scouring the far bank. "While I don't think Eizariin shares in the sentiment, he's made it clear that Tekhest and her followers would take any means to preserve ignorance in order to prevent their history from repeating itself."

"Tekhest has a darkness inside her," Rathen agreed. "I wouldn't want to find out what 'means' were within her reach."

"Of course, it's also possible that they were uninformed at the time Eizariin sent us on our way. If they know now that we have the Zi'veyn - as you say, it would be no trouble for them to find us, nor to spy on us from a distance - then surely they also know what we intend to do with it. And we've destroyed Khryu'vahz. They could conclude that we're handling their ancestors' mistake for them, slowly but surely, without the need for them to step in and reveal themselves to the world nor their past to their younger. If they leave us alone, they can continue to disown their responsibility."

"Unfortunately," Rathen sighed, "not even Garon's contacts can enlighten us. Whatever the case, we should keep our eyes open. We have the Zi'veyn; we're safe from them."

"Assuming you can use it. Understanding how it works and *making* it work are two different things."

"We will find out soon enough." Petra rose tightly at another rustle from the bank and snatched up the bags as the water vole hurried again about its business. "Fendale's been ruined by magic. If we continue as we were, we'll arrive tomorrow morning and you can try it then."

Rathen and Anthis looked about them as the others followed her lead, searching for any distinguishing landmarks in the compact, unremarkable forest. "Where exactly *are* we?"

"Mosshorn."

They moved quickly and quietly, suddenly uneasy, throwing glances over their shoulders for movement in the shadows. Only Garon didn't seem to succumb, his sights set calmly on their path through the trees.

Rathen moved up beside him, rubbing his raw but hairless cheek. "How is Eyila?" He asked quietly, though she was too distracted to overhear. "There's a shadow of something in her eyes that I don't like."

Garon nodded slightly. "She's improved since we left Dolunokh; she's cogent, but she's not perfect. And she's still haunted by what happened to her people. She withdraws into herself often, and from time to time it looks as though she can see or hear something the rest of us can't. It's hard to tell when she's lost in thought or when she's affected by magic. Kienza did nothing for her, but there may not have been anything she could."

"If there was, she'd have done it. The elf did warn us that she'd be affected if she went in there, but it was so much more concentrated than I'd expected. I doubt there's any way of knowing if it was just the potency, or if she's just as vulnerable as those few in the Order." He glanced towards him, then looked nonchalantly off to the side. "The magic has gotten worse, you say. Has the Order?"

"In regards to mages losing control of themselves, I don't believe the rate has changed."

Now he frowned, and looked openly towards him. "'In regards' - Garon, what else has happened?" He watched the inquisitor's face remain conspicuously unchanged, and quickly drew his own conclusion. He paled. "No..."

Unfortunately, Garon nodded. "The Order has now truly rebelled. Four weeks ago the populace finally broke, began rioting, and groups of mages began actively standing against them. The first attack was in Orton - one mage struck out, obliterated the tavern, the high street and the western gate. No one was killed, but since then groups have followed his lead, and they're organised." He rolled his left shoulder, an absent habit. "We witnessed an attack in Stonbridge a couple of weeks ago. A group of mages - about four or five - stole casks from the tavern and spread their contents around the square, then set them alight. The flames grew quickly, but they enhanced them with their magic and started to control them. The watermill burned down, as did their grain stores. The tavern, I think, was an accident, but none of them tried to correct it." His lip curled, his shoulder rolled again, and there was, for a moment, a clear presence of shame and disgust, for himself and for the mages, in his grey eyes. "The flames were... People were hurt. And we could do nothing. Even had we not been concerned with being hunted, we couldn't have stood against five mages. We couldn't even risk bringing Eyila in to heal anyone."

They walked in silence, consumed by thought, until Garon spoke up again, his voice suddenly unaffected. "Why didn't Anthis follow us out?"

"All four of you were entranced," Rathen explained, grateful for the change of subject. "The magic's hold over you and Petra, at the very least, was broken when the rest of it started collapsing, but not him. I went back to drag him out and when I turned around, the door was gone. He remained under its influence throughout."

"For a month." He regarded him gravely. "And his condition?"

He wasn't speaking of the magic. Rathen stiffened and looked away. "Sated."

They trekked through the afternoon and soon descended into a valley, thickly wooded, steeply sloped and carpeted where the sun broke through with bluebells. The air was fragrant and fresh, and the breeze, when it flowed to cool the warm, summer air, was channelled down into the ravine and billowed up along the sides. They stopped only when the light had grown too weak to cover the ground safely, making camp in a large, open hollow long unused by beasts if the aged bones of prey and lack of faeces were any indication.

The landscape was treacherous but their tracks were thin, and for both those facts, they were safe. That night the atmosphere was almost jovial; Rathen and Anthis were grateful for the company of more than just each other, and the rest for answers to worries and a distraction from constantly glancing over their shoulders. Questions were abound as they ate, directed mostly towards the pair and their time in Khry's Glory, which they - meaning mostly Rathen - answered as best they could, many of which with successful evasion. In time they tired and dispersed for their own matters - Eyila meditated near the bottom of the ravine where the funnelled breeze was at its strongest, Petra tended her blades, and Garon patrolled just beyond the reach of the small campfire. Rathen had noticed a strange charge between the latter two, but he spared it little thought.

Instead, he approached the fire where Anthis was sat, peering into scrolls through the flickering light, staring with the most profound concentration and drinking their cryptic contents with the steadiest focus he'd had for weeks. He sat down next to him and dropped something into his lap.

Anthis flinched in his engrossment, but after flashing him a look of irritation for the fright, his eyes dropped down to what had assaulted him.

The scrolls were forgotten in a heartbeat.

He watched him lift the Zi'veyn with a grasp so delicate it bordered on reverence and turn it in the light. He stared closely, ran his fingers gently along its lines, tapped the ends of several of its sharp thorns, watched the firelight glitter across the lotus petals. He was silent for a long while, and it absorbed his attention in the same way that a good piece of wood gripped Aria.

Rathen's heart jumped, and he forced the thought urgently from his mind. "Well?" He said in an attempt to wall it out. "Is it all you hoped?"

Anthis guffawed, sputtering a response that at the very least suggested that his expectations had been inadequate. "How elaborate were the traps around it?" He managed after another long minute or two of marvelling.

"Elaborate. And vicious."

"Vicious how?" He couldn't have torn his eyes away from it if he'd tried.

"Without falling victim to them myself, I can't truly tell you, but on paper, *villainous*. Mental torment, like summoning phantoms - conjuring things at the edge of your vision, gone the moment you turn, and raising your very greatest fear from something deeper than memory, whether you're consciously aware of what that is or not. Or rotating your perception of left and right, up and down. Implanting the certainty that the world is an illusion, that life is just a dream - even imposing the nature of infinity..."

Anthis didn't seem to have caught a word. "Anything physical?" He asked eventually.

"The worst of it was a bio-chemical response that turned the would-be thief's own magic into a weapon against him."

"Sounds grisly."

"Mm..."

His gaze was still devouring the relic. "How complex is the spell? Do you think casting it was a collaborative effort?"

"It was suggested that it *was* cast by a single individual, but piece by piece."

"Oh? Did Kienza suggest that?"

"Aria."

The light in Anthis's eyes suddenly dimmed, and they moved at last, if sluggishly, onto the fire in front of him. When he glanced towards Rathen, he found his gaze had shifted in the same direction and had dulled with an unmissable heartache that stalled him. He lowered the artefact, and after a long hesitation, inhaled to speak. But he remained silent for another uncertain moment. "W...What do you intend to do? Will you go get her now we're out? We never did make it to Kasire..."

"I...want to," he admitted guiltily, equally as indecisive about speaking, "but you heard everything Garon said. She's safer where she is."

"With your father. But you don't think highly of him."

"I don't, but Kienza has been checking in...and, perhaps he's changed. It's been nearly forty years since he released me to the Order, and I don't think I've spent more than an hour in his presence since then. And they say with age comes wisdom..."

"I don't see it."

Rathen smiled, fleetingly, but his gaze remained among the hypnotic flames.

"What - forgive me - what did you mean when you said she 'shouldn't even have you'?" He watched Rathen remain perfectly still. "Sorry, it's none of--"

"Aria isn't my daughter."

The crackling of the fire became immense. Neither said a word. When Rathen eventually spoke, his voice was soft and reflective.

"I found her one morning in my garden. She was sitting in a tuft of arenaria, eating my strawberries. She was alone, she was wet and thin - *tiny*. I have no idea how she got there, and...well, my home is far from people, so she must have been extremely lost to have found her way into my garden. I took pity, made her something to eat," he smiled to himself, "scrambled eggs, it was. She devoured it in a moment... I put her in some dry clothes and went out to see if I could find her parents. I searched for a few hours, dared to set foot into villages and listened for anyone looking for a lost child. But no one was, so I headed back to make sure she was okay. I was going to go back out and look again, search the other villages, but..." He stared into the fire for another silent moment. "It transpired that a nearby village had been razed about a week before, by bandits. Kienza had told me about it. The girl had come from there, and her parents had been killed. Somehow she escaped and hid, and was found by guards sent to investigate a few days later once news of the attack had spread. One of them was tasked with taking her somewhere safe until extended family could be found, but he was killed before he could reach the next village. She must have found her way into the forest on her own, found my garden and eaten the first thing she saw."

Anthis nodded. "Strawberries..." A smile flickered across his face, though his expression was quick to sober. "Arenaria."

"Arenaria." Rathen straightened in an attempt to shrug the melancholy atmosphere from his shoulders. "None of her family made any appeal, if they even knew she'd survived - or if she even had any. So she just sort of stayed with me, and I..." he smiled. "I was thoroughly unprepared for the power she had over me. She wriggled into my heart and made herself much too comfortable. But she...she's dogged by tragedy. Truly, I'm sure of it. She lost her parents, her escort, and she wound up living in isolation with a...with me..." He picked up a stick and poked heavily at the flames. It took some time for Anthis to finally speak.

"Or is she graced with luck?"

Rathen flashed him a frown.

"Think about it," the young man said thoughtfully, "she *escaped* a bandit attack, she *escaped* whatever or whoever killed the guard, and she *found* the home of an isolated, banished man who came to love her as if she was his own. And she's...escaped every..." He brushed that aside. "She has the most lively and inspiring fascination, it's not stifled by tragedy or even the minutiae of the world. *Everything* around her is a marvel."

"Because she's been shut away from it all her life."

"And she's turned out wonderfully for it."

"She would have been better off with her true parents."

Anthis regarded him carefully. "Do you really believe that?"

He didn't respond. He drew in his knees and rested his chin upon them. He looked older through the shifting light of the flames.

Anthis straightened, uneasy thoughts slipping into his mind, and he also looked back into the fire. But though he was reluctant to speak them, he was convinced that they had to be said. Rathen needed to hear them; Anthis needed to share them. "I was born into it."

"Born into what?" The mage asked distantly.

"The Sulyax Dizan."

Rathen lifted his chin, but didn't look towards him. Anthis took up the crucial task of poking the flames.

"My parents introduced me to it. It wasn't voluntary on my part, but I knew no different. They didn't make sacrifices in front of me - they didn't talk about it or even show me the knives. But it was always there, and when I was ten, they sat me down and told me of their ways, and it...all sounded so...*reasonable*. They spoke of it so easily, so coolly, that it seemed there was nothing at all sinister in taking the life of one person to protect the whole *world* from Zikhon. And I think, in a way, that's why they encouraged my passion for the elves - because their deaths at Zikhon's hands justified the Sulyax Dizan's actions. We've all been taught by the Temple that Zikhon destroyed them - though we five may now know that that's not the case - and the ruins I hungered over were evidence of that dead society. And my parents were *adamant*, so very convinced that what they were doing was for the purest ends. They made it seem as though they had been *chosen* for the duty - the *honour* - of serving Vokaad's work, of protecting our entire civilisation, and I felt that I had been, too. I felt so privileged, and I kept it a secret from my friends, as my parents told me to, to 'avoid envy' or hindrance from those who didn't understand. And I did my duty with the greatest pride..."

Embers fluttered as the harshly probing stick dislodged several larger alder branches. Rathen's eyes travelled towards him as he continued to prod. "After everything you've said before, you don't sound entirely convinced right now..."

He tossed the stick into the fire. "A few years after I was inducted, the mother and both sisters of one of my friends were raped and murdered. I began to wonder then if the hurt caused by the loss of a life was really worth it when there were others out there who, through the...through certain means of detection, bore souls far more useful to Vokaad than those of harmless wanderers or merchants, and who wouldn't be at all missed. Why use the souls of those we were trying to protect when we could use the--...you understand my point. Well, when I found my mother moments after she'd taken a life, intoxicated by the magic even while still kneeling in the blood of her kill - an enthusiastic baker, very well-loved in the community - I was disgusted. I took my own convictions to heart that day, and, since then, I have *never* taken a life that didn't...deserve it." He turned his gaze, hard and level, onto the black haired man beside him, who stared into the flames with an expression torn between shock and pity. "Now tell me again that true parents are always the best choice."

He didn't. He didn't move at all beyond a flickering tension in his jaw. But the thoughts that consumed him were clearer than the moon.

Anthis turned away and lifted the Zi'veyn from the ground, rotating it once more in the light. But the intricate lines and subtle, flourishing metal brushwork that covered its ebon faces did not absorb his attention as it had ten minutes ago. "About...in Khry's Glory--"

"It's forgotten."

He nodded slowly, though the relief was a fair stretch more than he'd expected. "Same."

Rathen, too, nodded, then shifted awkwardly. "And, uh..." Mercifully, Anthis waved it away. He nodded again, even more uncomfortable, then rose at last to his feet. "Well, good night, Anthis."

"Good night, Rathen."

He all but fled the campfire.

Turning quickly into the darkness, weariness barrelled over him. It felt different from that which had tormented him for weeks. It was an energised fatigue, if such a thing was possible; he knew that he was heading to a bed roll to rest and dream rather than curling up on the ground or a bed made of torn tapestries, too haggard to notice the sharp rocks or puddles beneath him, and descending uncontrollably into a dead sleep. And he knew that he would awake the following morning as a living being rather than a walking corpse to stagger through the wilderness without recallable aim, only to fall into another dead sleep when the need next hit.

It felt good. He couldn't wait to sleep.

He made for the end of the hollow where the blankets had been left, sheltered by rock shelves and overhanging bushes, and passed by Petra along his way. She was sat upon another projection a little further down the slope, expertly tending the hilt wrapping even while her eyes were looking off further along the valley. Curious, Rathen followed her gaze, and found himself unsurprised when he spotted Garon on patrol, making his way down to the ravine. And less surprised, still, when he glanced back and saw that her eyes were filled with force, willing the inquisitor to look towards her, but also with a quickness that suggested she would only look away and ignore him if he did.

Her eyes flicked suddenly onto him and Rathen smiled abashedly for having been caught as good as eavesdropping on a private moment. She smiled back just as shamefully, nodded good night, then looked down at her blade with far too much concentration, as though she hadn't been looking towards Garon at all.

He shook his head to himself as he passed, at which point her gaze surely returned, and left the matter and the rest of the world behind as he clambered beneath the blankets with little thought to even removing his boots.

He sighed in the utmost contentment as he made himself comfortable and observed the night sky through the trees on the far bank. It was a true night sky; there was no cold, ashen sun, only the light from the moon hanging somewhere to the east, out of sight through the leaves. The air was crisp and cool, as it was on Turundan summer nights, and it was silent but for the crackle of fire and Petra's quiet work. There was no empyrean music, no creeping roots, no rising tides, melting walls or flaming tapestries. It was so very ordinary. And the animosity in the air was minimal.

It was nice to have things back to normal.

But his smile didn't stick.

How could it ever be normal if Aria wasn't there?

Chapter 6

To have food is to have power. Physically, and politically. If one doesn't eat, one weakens. If farmhands don't harvest, business weakens. With no grain to sell and no grain to eat, villages, towns and cities weaken. Thus the country weakens. The same is true for war. A hungry force is a disadvantaged force, and the larger its ranks, the more food is needed to stave off that disadvantage. But only so much can be carried and ferried, and so it has always been standard practise to reap what your enemies sow; pillage the fields and stores of your intended prize, where the food is fresh and plentiful, and the peasantry slow-witted and defenceless.

Fenard Milson had known this well. Born to a milling family and enlisted in his youth to fight in what became a long and exhausting war, he learned the true value of food, and developed a great respect for the labours of his family which, upon finally returning home, he took up with dutiful enthusiasm.

It was some three decades later, when the mill had expanded and the village around it, that the Red Nest War began. The dictatorship that had swallowed Angra, Sarunokh, Antide and Dweron had set its sights on the northern lands of Arasiin, and Turunda's 'tail' was the closest and swiftest place for the consolidated armies to make landfall. His Supreme Majesty, Emperor Rasjh swept across the Boral Channel and split those forces, laying waste both to Turunda and Skilan while they were embroiled in one of their own countless spats. Foaming at the mouth, both sides had their armies at the ready and sights locked exclusively on one another. The invading force found little resistance. They swarmed over the land like locusts and set about their plans for the fortified bordering countries, who had not missed the results of their neighbours' foolishness.

Unfortunately, His Supreme Majesty Emperor Rasjh had overlooked the peasantry, and it was not so slow-witted.

Fenard, the war-wisened miller, had ordered his farmhands and convinced the owners of neighbouring crop lands to take their harvest early, to gather it before the light of dawn in water-tight hide sacks, donated by a few trusting leather workers, and bury them in the earth by the lake before burning their fields. He then convinced the rest of his expanding village and a few others beyond to gather as much whitetip as they could find, the tiny seeds of a small but common fern cultivated for its healing properties once shelled and boiled. But, as with many remedies, while a small dose can be beneficial to immunity, work against infections or even counter a greater dose, too much becomes a lethal poison.

Toxic whitetip oils had rendered Fenard's mill unusable by the time his plan came to fruition, but that had not been the full cost he was to pay for the swathes of dictatorial forces eradicated by his poisonous 'grain'. How the emperor's forces discovered that he had been responsible was unknown. No one ever admitted to having been the one to hand him over. But it didn't matter. Fenard Milson's very slow and very public execution had martyred him, and farmland across the country followed his rebellious strategy in outrage. The torched fields would hinder locals for a few years, but it was overcome, especially with the help of the grateful and relieved neighbouring allied forces.

But the invaders could not wait. With their numbers starved, weakened, and a great deal diminished, Turunda's army quashed them, and even the slow-witted, defenceless peasantry rallied, using anything at hand to defend their homes, be that house, farm or country.

And ninety three years on, the town of Fendale, represented by a fern and renamed in the miller's honour, had been rent and riven by an invading force entirely unaffected by the needs of food.

The fissures on the outskirts were short and narrow at first, but they grew beside every step until they gaped ominously and swallowed whole stretches of the road, coaxing travellers into the black world deep beneath the surface. And if one managed to avoid the abyssal lure and continued along the route, for whatever their purpose, to the top of the hill where the town's walls finally fell into sight, magic suddenly tumbled over them. But what lay beneath the arcane blanket was not beautiful. It was not peaceful. Whatever spells of fictitious sentiments that had been intended to ease elven hearts in Khryu'vahz had not gathered in Fendale. In Fendale, there was only foreboding. A distressing mixture of solitude, once perhaps comfortable, and anticipation, a sense of being on the brink of something wonderful never to come that raised an immediate itch of impatience.

And that sickening, sublime melody that had stitched itself into every desperately forgotten and clearly recalled moment of entrapment, but only six bars, replaying on an endless loop, prickling the skin beneath beads of sweat while the heart was sent hammering into a frenzy.

Rathen swallowed hard. He was sure he would succumb to madness here.

His eyes flicked towards Anthis. The young man, a little more than half his own age, carried himself identically: tight and hunched, his footsteps spiritless.

He looked then to Eyila. She'd walked all morning in silence, displaying open distaste towards the cluttered trees, roots and mud, but now there was something new in her eyes, something that had been trapped in the background and was now uncaged, released to prowl at the surface. Her arm was looped through Petra's, who was surreptitiously restraining her from racing on ahead in her strange state. And as they neared the looming gates, open and unmanned, the intangible had seized her like the grasp of a rusted gauntlet.

His eyes turned forwards again and he continued, internally braced, along Garon's lead.

The town appeared unharmed from the road, but the moment they stepped through the gates, the tense mood plummeted even further.

The guardhouse just inside the walls had been raised and split by a thrust of the land so abrupt it was as though the meagre town walls had contained the worst of the magic themselves. Its front and furthest faces had crumbled with the force, their stones laying scattered over the road which itself had been tilted at a sudden and dramatic angle like a scuffed carpet runner, while the rest of the abandoned building remained upright and exposed along with everything that remained inside - the desks, the cells, the reports, the teacups.

On the other side of the road, the houses appeared unaffected, but the windows were too illuminated; a single glance through revealed that only the facades still stood. Everything behind them had fallen into crevasses which had also claimed a portion of the town wall, a detail obscured on their approach by the outlying stables.

They tread slowly, carefully, staring at the desolation and speaking not a word. Fendale had been evacuated to Morton as soon as the crisis had struck, but not everyone had made it out alive. And so every pile of rubble and every snaking crack in the road drew the eye, conjuring the dreadful wonder at whether that particular calamity had claimed a life. The crevasses summoned the worst of their thoughts; bodies couldn't be retrieved so easily, if, from some, at all.

Rathen chose to turn his mind away. He, at least, had other things to think about, and he leapt into them eagerly, walling out the world around him and stifling the beginnings of an anxious sweat. He wasted no time in withdrawing the Zi'veyn, and in doing so immediately grasped the desperate attention of the others.

"What will happen when you use it?" Petra asked as she moved closer to him, dragging the transient Eyila along with her. Her voice was low, wary of being overheard, though there was none but the dead to disturb. "Will all this be returned to normal?"

Rathen's head twitched. "I couldn't say. But I guess we'll find out..." Reluctant necessity seized his stride, carrying him ahead to survey the area with more than sight alone. The others watched him uneasily as his eyes discovered and chased something beyond the realms of vision, and hesitated to follow as he set off purposefully after it. But whatever had grasped him had missed Eyila; she continued to stare up towards the top windows. No one could decide just how discomforting that was.

They wound through the shattered streets, following his steadfast trail, climbing over the fallen walls and carts that blocked their way, jumping over fissures, avoiding the touch of pools of golden sunset, vibrant enough to rival the true sun, and breathed none too deep of the apple-scented breeze. They had all been in Khryu'vahz, they had all witnessed the disturbingly sanguine nature of the magic, but that it could also cause such havoc, such destruction, such death...

More than a few of them felt themselves itch under its contact. No one wished to linger. But their pace faltered in spite of themselves when they spotted the edge of a sail rising from the muddy ground.

No...from a monstrous chasm. One filled with brown, red and golden autumnal leaves, each perfectly shaped, perfectly coloured, like a funerary bouquet, gently enshrouding the remains of Fendale's iconic mill. A mill that had stood as a memorial for nearly a century, as a testament to the value of every skill, the strength that lies in ordinary folk, a bravery not limited to soldiers.

A mill that had been sundered by a force unconcerned by the skills, strength or bravery of either.

Absorbed in grim matters, they were slow to notice the huge and ancient oak tree that loomed at the head of the road. Still and silent with an imposing beauty, it was curiously untouched by the chaos as equally as the road veered around it. But despite its apparently unnatural protection, the tree was not born of the displaced magic; its full, vibrant boughs had always shaded the clearing, a village square that had grown into a town garden as the settlement had flourished, and its knotted roots pushed apart the flagstones laid once out of their reach. The Grandmother Tree; it was once believed to house an oak wife, a relict woodland spirit, as a means of explaining how it could grow to such a great age and size without succumbing to disease or a woodman's axe. A child's fairytale - but a fairytale that, perhaps, had some kind of credence after all.

For Rathen had finally come to a stop, just at the edge of its shadow.

The others slowed behind him and stared up into its reaches.

"This is the point of magnetic focus," Rathen told them with a touch of effort, his attention still somewhere between the tree and the air. "Seems the most likely place to start."

"It doesn't *look* like the centre," Anthis murmured as he glanced from the untouched garden and back to the ruined mill that stood like a ghost at the edge of all their sights. "Are you sure it's not--"

"Of *course* he's sure."

"I'm sure," Rathen replied over Petra's sudden and malicious retort, but it surprised neither after the sharp and mistrustful looks she'd sent the historian once her relief at their return had subsided. Anthis barely acknowledged it, and Rathen's eyes dropped heavily to the Zi'veyn.

His shoulders tightened. He could feel the sudden breath of expectation prickling the back of his neck, the inescapable approach of a critical moment. It was a familiar sensation, and an unwelcome one. The last time it had imposed itself on him he'd been standing over a foreign battlefield, waiting to give his regiment the order to break concealment and launch the first volley. The memories it summoned were just as distasteful.

He shook them off and raised the Zi'veyn, sending fragments of golden light flickering across the trunk. His mind focused, delving into the surrounding magic, whittling out the absolute centre of the magnetism as best he could while gritting his teeth against the doubt and distraction swelling in his skull, heart and gut. He didn't notice everyone else take a cautious step closer.

Slowly, he grasped it, as precise and minute as a pinhead, and released his tightly held breath. He had the centre, the point at which the pooling magic was at its strongest, where the amalgamation of spell fragments tangled back on itself, where their power looped and reverberated back against the magic in his own veins, humming perpetually in his chest. Infinitesimal chains of melody, solitude, anticipation; of sunset, lechery, perfection...and peace, present after all, if too small and weak to impose itself over the madness...

Yes, this was the magnetic centre, the point where the veil between their world and the gods' was at its thinnest, where the magic gathered, where it was drawn to. The best place to start...

The garden had been silent for a long while. Rathen shifted his weight. Glances were exchanged behind him.

Anthis cleared his throat delicately. "Hhhow...do you tell it where...to...?"

Rathen didn't respond. He turned the Zi'veyn in silence, pointing its golden lotus towards the tree so that its crown of thorns guided the trunk towards its centre, and extended it at arm's length. Again he focused his magic, driving it this time into the artefact and seizing the spell concealed inside, and began channelling his will and concentration to power it.

The local anticipation was finally pertinent; shared breath quickened and all eyes stared sharply from the oak to the relic as though they expected to see the intangible magic move, then to their surroundings, searching for the slightest change - for the ground to close up, the puddles of sunset to evaporate, the buildings to repair themselves, and the return of musical birdsong. No one dared to blink in case they missed anything, or moved more than an inch in case they distracted him.

But minutes ticked by, and impatience crept in. The local anticipation, it seemed, was prophetic, for nothing of what they waited for happened.

It was a long while before Anthis dared, carefully, to speak. "Maybe it's upside down?"

Rathen rotated it, turning the lotus towards himself and the jagged tip of the pyramid out towards the tree, and channelled his power, his focus, his will once again. But still nothing happened.

Petra frowned dubiously. "What if...it was the right way up, and you've just...sucked the magic out of yourself?"

Rathen paled further and moved one hand in a flurry, forming the signs of the first spell that came to mind. A ball of light, the very first taught to novice mages, promptly appeared before him. But his relief was fleeting. He hadn't missed, and as he'd cast, there came the subtlest flicker in the magic surrounding them - magic that hadn't moved or diminished in the slightest.

His jaw tightened and eyes dropped resentfully to the artefact. The others exchanged another series of doubtful looks behind him as the silence pressed back in.

"You said," Garon began rigidly, "that you'd fixed it."

Everyone cringed. Rathen straightened and fought against his own hideous smile. "I did."

"Then you don't know how it works."

"I'll figure it out." He spoke through his teeth and glared at the Zi'veyn, humiliation burning beneath his skin. *'I can't have missed anything, Kienza would have noticed it... It's the spell, it must be. I'm such a fool - as if it was really going to be so easy...'* He turned around, his frustration successfully masked, and levelled himself to Garon. "I'll have to analyse it further, but I *can* work this out."

"Eizariin's scrolls might have something that will help," Anthis added. "I'll keep going through them, see what I can find."

"I want to stay here in the mean time."

"*What?*" They turned to Petra, who looked quickly from one face to the next in alarm. "We can't! Just *look* at Eyila - we don't know what will happen to her if she stays in all this bloody magic for much longer!"

"Then take her away," Garon replied impatiently. "How will we know if it's working if we leave? And remaining among the magic may well help him."

"I understand your concern," Rathen offered with apology, "but Eyila will be fine. She survived the magic in Khry's Glory and that was far more potent than this."

Petra regarded him carefully. "...You're sure?"

He ignored what he was sure was the itch of lunacy creeping over the back of his mind. "I'm sure."

"Well...all right - but that's only *one* concern. Is it honestly wise for us to linger *anywhere*? Right now, we're close to several villages--"

"I don't believe we're being followed," Garon cut in, removing his jacket though the day was mild. "We haven't been for some time."

Petra looked then to Rathen as he nodded his agreement. "How can *you* be sure?"

"Magic. It's not sustainable, but while we were...away, I managed to make some adjustments to a detection spell. The Order uses it to detect and evaluate magic in people who have just awakened it. Using the elves' perception of magic as a base, I can use it to detect life."

"Like...bugs and stuff?"

"No - human hearts."

"Then it wouldn't detect *elven* pursuers?"

"*If* there are elves out here, then both myself *and* Eyila would notice their magic." He moved out of the sudden stream of warmth as the sun broke through the clouds and sat himself down beneath the tree, Zi'veyn in hand. "We're safe to stay."

Uncertainty further creased Petra's brow, but she left the matter alone. Then frowned at Garon as he fastened a thin, weather-stained jacket about himself and slipped his officer's badge inside. "Where are *you* going?"

"As you said, we're close to a handful of villages. Rather than waste time waiting around, I'm going to see if I can't find some information."

"From villages this close to the mountains? You really think it's worth bothering? Because I don't think collecting complaints about the local quality of cow dung for the farmland on the lower reaches is going to do much to stop a half-elven *psychopath*."

"When this place was evacuated," he explained calmly, "my informant chose not to follow. There's better business in the village - at least in war time - but their remaining in the region works in our favour: there's no distraction by the masses and the people we need information on will still be moving around out here. Their commands, royally sanctioned and otherwise, are above evacuation orders." He unfastened his sword and dropped it among the bags, mussed up his hair just a little, and scuffed his boots in the mud. Suddenly he was a vision of ordinary. He turned towards Rathen, and Anthis who sat down close by, rolls of parchment in his arms. "Good luck." He spared Petra only the briefest glance, then set off back through the ruins towards the eastern gates.

She watched him go in defeat, then looked to the others who already appeared absorbed in concentration. "I guess that's the end of that," she mumbled. She turned towards Eyila who hung at her side, her wide, pale eyes searching beyond the half-standing buildings, and sighed uneasily to herself. "Come on, then. Let's get you out of all this."

Climbing through the last of the wreckage that barred the city gate, Garon forced the knot of irritation out of his shoulders and settled the clench of his jaw. Petra had always been outspoken, but something had gotten into her, and just what was beyond him. But he hadn't the time to worry about it. There were more important things to turn his mind to, things that deserved his attention, his thought, his fret, more than whatever was bothering such an easily incensed young woman. Things they all had a stake in. Things far bigger than any one of them. Things that rendered everything else inconsequential.

He rolled his shoulder against the knot that tried to creep back into his muscles and caught himself clenching his fist in his frustration. He looked down at it, though he knew what he would see: only the third and fourth fingers were curling.

He stiffened and moved his hand to rest it upon the pommel of his sword instead, but it wasn't there. He managed not to growl.

Garon forced his mind to close against pointless thoughts and focused instead on navigating the sundered land, and after an hour and eighteen minutes, he crested a hill and descended into the shallow dale that veiled the village of Trinn.

Fendale's destruction was a ways behind him, and here the village lay untouched. But while Rathen had assured them that the magic wouldn't grow with the destruction of the arcane realm, its reach could still broaden, and Garon had overheard gossip in other settlements of depressed locations flooding, some from diverted rivers, others quite unnaturally. If Fendale's magic was so inclined, Trinn and its capillary of the river Suul could soon number among them.

But he'd closed his mind against what-ifs as well, and didn't entertain the concern for long.

The quaint buildings of since-reinforced drystone were dwarfed by the verdant slopes of the dale, and the stream that trickled through the weeds alongside the road was, by comparison, barely there at all. But despite appearances, Trinn was not a secret from the world. A quarter mile north the valley levelled out and opened onto a high road that skirted the thick Korovor Woodlands, used by neighbours, travellers, and traders carrying goods as local as honey and as exotic as the weaves and spices of the far-flung tribes. But, so close to the mountains, there were few places along this stretch of the road to rest out of the elements, and the village took full advantage of that fact.

The old inn that stood just inside the boundaries, visible above the other buildings from the narrow valley path, seemed to sprout a few more rooms with every passing decade, and a small brewery had been established further in. Its product was not excellent, but it was enough to smooth the journey, and for that the village was flourishing. And with Fendale's destruction and Orton's evacuation, there were even fewer lodging options for the weary and desperate.

Garon passed three guards as he neared the village and walked as openly as any man with nothing at all to hide. They paid him little attention for it, and as he crossed the ramshackle boundary walls, the villagers seemed to share in their disregard. But there was a collective nervousness in the air that was impossible to miss. Every village, town and city he'd set foot in over the past month had radiated the same, with fevered eyes surreptitiously checking every individual for the umber of eastern skin or golden insignias on the shoulders of even the most weather-beaten cloaks, even though any mage looking to make trouble would have surely discarded it.

But the atmosphere didn't get beneath Garon's skin.

He moved calmly through the village, his sights on the inn's broad chimney rising ahead as a point of bearing, higher even than the local Temple shrine. He nodded politely to almost everyone he passed, setting them at ease with a smile, but while his gaze was brief and his movements unhurried, his hearing had sharpened. He picked out every conversation through the jumble of afternoon activity, listening for even only a passing mention of anything that might be pertinent: war movements and closed roads, tribal incursions and traps, escalating arcane interference, new arrivals and anything at all out of the ordinary. Even hearsay had value, if one knew how to filter through the muck.

But everything he overheard was either old news or logical conclusions he'd already anticipated - which, itself, was also to be expected, and a fact that usually proved the value of knowing rooted individuals who couldn't keep their ears to themselves, especially when there was something in it for them.

Even without the chimney-beacon, the inn was not hard to find; a storey taller than any other building and at least twice as expansive, it would challenge even the simplest folk to miss it. Not to mention the noise, the tell-tale combination of ale, beef and smoke drifting from the open windows, nor the near-constant swing of the door with all the comings and goings.

Its creak announced Garon's arrival, and while half of the patrons looked up nervously, which they surely did on every occasion, it earned him little more than a cursory glance from the keeper behind the bar. It was clearly habit rather than interest. He probably heard it so often it had a place in his dreams.

With neither cloak nor tan, Garon was dismissed immediately and left to seek a table out of the way by himself. There were few to choose from that wouldn't invite strangers to fill the empty chairs, but he soon found a small two-seater beneath the stairs, far from any of the dusty windows and with a clear view of the entire public house.

He settled quietly and removed his jacket. To keep it on would suggest impatience, as though he was preparing for a quick getaway; it was all too easy to draw attention to oneself in such uncertain times, and to be noticed was the last thing he needed. Though the Arana was widely dismissed as stories designed to frighten people straight, the imagery of 'ghost' assassins, while ludicrous, was unfortunately apt: ghosts could pass through walls unnoticed, move among people unseen and unheard, while they would see and hear everything themselves. And that's precisely how the Arana operated. Looking around, Garon couldn't know if anyone present in that tavern hall was working for Salus, the leader of that shadowy faction. And he couldn't discount anyone from suspicion, either, for the Arana was even known to utilise children as young as seven years of age, if they were receptive to the basic levels of training. And who would ever suspect them?

But, after a careful survey disguised as collecting his bearings, the inquisitor decided that he was not being observed.

His shoulders eased only slightly, and he looked up with the same interest as the rest of the patrons when the door whined again. A young mother with three children and an elderly man stepped in, each carrying a bag on their backs, the children's almost dwarfing them. All faces were fatigued, exhausted by stress and fear. They, too, were shortly disregarded and hurried to find somewhere to sit. They ended up separating - the mother with two children, the grandfather with the third - several tables apart and craning their necks to keep each other in their sights.

Garon had seen many families like these in recent weeks, refugees who had left ahead of evacuations, fearing magic, tribes, and Doana's hidden camps; children whose eyes were haunted by worries they were too young to understand, sights they were too young to have seen, events no one of *any* age was able to comprehend.

He looked to the alemaid as she stepped in front of him - the daughter of the keeper, Garon surmised by the matching squint to her eye - and requested a draught of the local brew.

He looked across the tavern as she left. Children, elderly; loners, families - everything in between. *People.* All of whom he had devoted his career to protecting. And protect them he would.

The ale was as expected. Passable. But after the initial mouthful, he didn't touch it again. He was not there to drink, he was there for information, and he needed a clear head if he was to recognise the important details, let alone remember them. So he leaned back in his chair and waited.

He made a point of not checking the time, resting with his arms folded and chin on his chest as if asleep. He ignored the door, reading the reaction of the room rather than opening his eyes, and for the most part it was nothing. Only once did silence fall and the air grow denser than syrup, and he found when he looked up that it was no mage that had offended the collective, and, likely, no Aranan either. The woman had olive skin, an undeniably Antidian trait, and one difficult to miss even despite the poor tavern lighting. She seemed fully aware of that fact, for she tugged at her sleeves, too long for the season, to cover her hands and tried to hide her face in her dark curls. She seemed to debate whether taking another step inside was a wise idea, and when whispering picked up in a corner, she turned around and hurried back out. Another woman, certainly Turundan, called what was presumably her name and followed her in concern.

Garon lowered his chin and closed his eyes again. He'd seen plenty of racism circulating, too. With attacks coming from both the east and west, and residential foreign nationals being responsible for the success of a good many wartime conquests, it was to be expected. But dealing with it was not in his task description. He didn't condone it, of course not, but it wasn't a matter he could presently afford to take onto his shoulders. There were plenty of others in a better position to deal with it than he was.

Time passed through the buzz of unending chatter, and for a long while Garon was left quite undisturbed - up to the moment that someone rapped their knuckles brusquely against the top of his table.

He opened only one eye at the scrape of the chair pulled out from beside him and the dragging of the heavy tankard across the table, but received in return only an impish grin for the theft of his privacy and questionable beverage. He opened the other and raised his chin, regarding the young woman as she helped herself to his drink, pausing to make a sour face before raising the mug once again. She'd seen through his act; she'd known he hadn't been asleep.

"Eeesh," she sighed at last, placing the half-emptied tankard back on the table before dabbing at her rouged lips with a kerchief in a bewildering attempt at refinement. "It's no Eline Red, but it's better than water. Anyway, I'm surprised you found me - how'd you know I didn't follow the rest to Morton?"

"Because," he replied simply, "it doesn't conform to your business model."

Her slender, made-up face pulled into another suspiciously friendly grin. "That it doesn't. So: what is it you need? I can get it, whatever it is, you know I can."

"I know you can. And it makes me itch just thinking about where you'd 'source' it."

Her sudden offence was quite effective at erasing the deceptive amity. "Pardon me, sir, but I am a *respectable* business woman."

"Tess, you're a black market trader."

"I am a conveyor of hard-to-find goods."

"Purveyor."

"And anyway, when else but in a time of crisis is anyone truly in *need* of a little luxury? I'm just doing my bit to boost morale!"

"With a fourfold mark-up? That's once more than your rates during *peace*."

"'Peace' is a matter of perception." Her dark eyes shifted away and thin lips twitched. "And, anyway, no one's *making* them buy it."

"Not with steel, but your silver tongue is almost as good as magic."

"You don't know the half of it," she chuckled, "although," her sharp gaze returned to him while a suggestive smile crept over her lips.

Garon's eyes darkened immediately. "I have enough on you to get you put away until the day this ditchwater wins the Aleca Vitis award, so don't test my patience. Now," he sat forwards and fixed her severely, "what have you heard?"

She stared at him for a while, lips pursed, pensively gathering her thoughts. Garon chose to take that as a promising sign. Then, as expected, she shook her head. "Payment first." He handed her a folded piece of paper sealed with a hammer insignia, which she took listlessly. "An I.O.U.? Seriously?"

"Redeem it at any post; you know--"

"Yeah, yeah, I know you're good for it." She tucked the paper up into her sleeve, grumbling beneath her breath, every word of which he caught, then sat forwards as her attitude took a sudden shift. "The mages are planning something," she told him gravely. "They're going to strike Trinn. Why this little old village and not Morton while it's overflowing with terrified 'fugees? I reckon because they know we'd be expecting it. People here are frightened, but they reckon they're safe because they're insignificant, the mages wouldn't bother with them - which, I reckon, is precisely why they *are* bothering. Are you familiar with the term 'terrorism'? I take it from that smacked-arse look that you do. Well they don't want anything from anyone but fear. They want to sow chaos and frighten their way to the top, overthrow old King Thunan and sit in his chair, casting their spells willy-nilly at anyone who opposes them. Their attacks haven't had any sort of obvious plan behind them otherwise." She lifted his tankard again. "It'll be soon - in fact it's just as well for you you found me when you did. I'm out of here tomorrow, gonna set myself up in Kruuz or Nestor - they're stuck in a swamp, my services would be mightily appreciated there, I'm sure."

"I'm sure. How did you come by this?"

"I'd say 'the usual' except I've spotted a few things for myself as well. A couple of fellows walking around looking both high and mighty and shifty at the same time. No cloaks, though, so no one else really noticed them. They don't look further than that. There are no fanatic mage hunters here, though, so they wouldn't know the signs to look for - mostly the mage hunters have sprung up in the cities. Where they reckon they're most at risk."

"You said soon?"

"Next few days. No sooner than Thursday."

Garon nodded, mentally mapping the surrounding land. "Anything else?"

"I'm afraid I don't have their privy schedules."

"I meant have you seen or heard anything else - suspicious individuals, strange occurrences, or people who seem remarkably average?"

"Like yourself in your I'm-not-suspicious peasant jacket? No, nothing else. Oh, well, except the military moving further north to surround Doana's sneaky little camps, and savages making war on our doorstep, but I reckon you're familiar with that. It's not like it's a secret. Otherwise, that's all I've got."

He nodded silently, his thoughts hidden, but he found her suddenly frowning at him anyway.

"You look troubled. More than usual." Her eyes narrowed. "I reckon it's a woman."

He darkened. "Steady."

"That's a yes, then. Whatever it is, say you're sorry, take full responsibility, and give yourself an easy life."

"Speaking from experience?"

"Both sides," she sighed, draining the tankard. "And for that matter, men can be just as bad."

"Well, thank you for your advice, as unsolicited and uninformed as it may be, but things are far from being that simple."

"Yeah, that's usually the case where matters of the heart are involved, but sometimes women are worth the trouble."

He said nothing as she winked a smoky-lidded eye. His shoulder rolled, fist clenched. Then the atmosphere shattered and Garon's pondering was silenced along with the surrounding chatter.

A shriek pierced the air from somewhere outside. It sounded at first like a screaming horse, but it didn't whinny down, and it came again at a higher pitch before a third followed in quick succession. And then the situation was explained in a single word, one bellowed at the top of a guard's lungs, a warning rather than a terrified declaration.

"Zikhon's arse," Tess cursed as the tavern burst frantically into life, the two of them leaping from their seats with the rest, "they're early..." She glanced towards Garon, though she was already making her own exit. "Pleasure doing business with you - now get out of here and save that gruff, handsome face of yours before a mage replaces it with a donkey's."

"And you?"

Another flash of an impish grin. "As I said: Kruuz or Nestor. I'm sure you'll find me when you need me." Then she slipped into the frenzied crowd, managing, somehow, to remain untouched in all the pushing and shoving, and disappeared. "Good luck!"

Garon cursed, but with the burning casks of Stonbridge still fresh in his mind, he joined the crowd in their escape of the distinctly flammable tavern. Outside, he dared to pause in the middle of the road while everyone else crashed past him, collecting the scene with an attentive eye, sieving through the chaos of people running this way and that with no aim but to find shelter. But such was impossible in the face of riled mages. And he soon discovered something even worse. Even disregarding the single point further down the street from which everyone seemed to flee like roaches from a flame, he spotted the antagonist by light rather than deduction.

Crackling blindness, pops and flashes like localised lightning; threads of flame, arcing and spinning like a dancer's ribbons; multicoloured orbs of pure energy, bursting and imploding around the single figure trapped inside a cage of magic. And then, rising above the crying, yelling and shrieking and cursing, there came maddened chuckling, cackling, sobbing.

Garon's blood ran cold. Flashes of the accursed Ivaean desert invaded his mind.

This was no demonstration of discontent, no act of rebellion. This was something far worse - and an issue he could do even less about. Once it had started, it couldn't be stopped. The mage's mind had snapped.

In an instant, the ropes of fire swelled, and in that single pulse began lashing out from their hypnotic loops, snapping at the people who fled past in search of safety deeper in the village walls. The lightning, too, grew in its rage, penetrating the ground and provoking the earth to respond. The road cracked around the mage's feet as he cackled and wept in its grip, erupting shards of itself upwards and sending shockwaves thundering out around him faster than the blink of an eye. Buildings began to shake.

Garon's teeth clenched, shoulder rolled, fist tightened and searched for the hilt of the sword he'd left behind. He swore. But even if he'd had it, it would have been little use. The guard that attempted valiantly to put the aggressor down by leaping upon him from behind proved that, consumed near immediately by the full focus of the elements. He dropped as an unrecognisable black, smouldering mass.

There was no defence against this, nothing but distance. But the people were already enforcing it, their guard already raised against the potential arrival of dissentious mages. There was nothing more to be done. So, as the streets began to empty and walls and roofs began to collapse, Garon, too, turned and fled, ignoring the flash of white hot pain that blinded him as something very heavy fell and struck either his head, back or shoulder, and disappeared through the gates as facelessly as the masses.

His pace slowed only once he'd scrambled back up to the top of the slopes and into the cover of the trees, leaving the screaming village beneath and behind him, marked in the centre by a moving point of light that grew in intensity with every passing second, surrounded by plumes of dust. He made straight back for Fendale, his jaw knotted in anger, impotence and regret. His thoughts were focused exclusively on what the others had accomplished in his absence.

But he found, after a little while, that though he'd escaped the deranged mage, the magic had followed him.

The gashes that sprawled out from Fendale had stretched and snaked their way closer to Trinn, for he encountered them sooner along his route than he should have, and witnessed two in the very act of extension. But whether it was a direct result or a coincidence, he couldn't know; the only certainty was that the Zi'veyn could put an end to both, *if* they could get it working.

He didn't notice his pace pick up, feet pounding over the fields.

The matter grew worse as he neared the sundered town. The consistent tremor he'd first noticed ten minutes before intensified the closer he got to the boundaries, a disembodied wailing had replaced the gentle music, and the warm glow of fire illuminated buildings that still managed to peek over the walls, though just what could have caused them was more than he cared to think on.

The debris that had obscured the eastern gate had shifted, leaving it entirely blocked off, but the now violent quaking had also crumbled the wall beside it. He darted through with ease.

On through eerie pockets of stillness and others of cataclysmic seizures, he soon reached the old oak tree - whose boughs weren't even tousled - where the mage and historian were hastily slinging bags onto their backs with alarm in their eyes. They looked towards him with relief, but were disinclined to offer explanation.

"I'll go and get the others!" Anthis yelled over the mournful bays, but Rathen stopped him immediately and headed off instead, shouting something back about Petra and spite. The historian conceded, but Rathen had managed only four paces when the red-headed duelist appeared from around a corner herself. Her eyes were just as wide, brow furrowed with horror, and she looked across them all for explanation, her sword gripped tightly in her hand.

"Later!" Garon shouted. "We're leaving!"

She turned and raced off without a second to argue, dodging around a quickly spreading puddle of curious golden light. She returned in moments with the tribal girl in tow, rushing along on her own two feet with some kind of clarity in her blue eyes right alongside fear and the ever-present distraction, and the five of them fled with not a moment to waste.

"What's happened?" Two of them asked simultaneously once they'd passed through the inexplicably flaming stone walls, but no one answered until the town was well behind them and the quaking had diminished to a shallow vibration.

Then Garon slowed and turned to Rathen. "When did it start?"

"About...fifteen minutes...before you...arrived," he rasped as they finally stumbled to a stop, fighting for his breath in exhaustion. "It was gentle first, but...it got worse...steadily, there was no...warning..."

Anthis nodded his agreement, equally winded.

"I was in Trinn. A mage lost control of himself." Garon overlooked their apprehension. "I believe he was just close enough to Fendale for his magic to have an effect on it - like yours did in Khry's Glory, if delayed over distance. But if that's the case, this situation has suddenly become much more serious."

"What's wrong with your shoulder?"

Silently cursing himself, Garon dropped his hand from his neck and spared Petra a passing glance for her concern, as terse as her tone may have been. "Something hit me as I was leaving. A sign, I think. I'm fine." He turned and looked back towards Fendale, marked over the fields by a plume of smoke that rose into a strangely perfect cloud-like wisp. Then his attention slipped onto Rathen, but before he could even form the words, his question was answered by a bleak yet intense stare readily boring into him, begging him not to ask. Garon's jaw tightened again.

He turned away. "We keep moving," he declared, already heading southwards. None delayed behind him as the vibrations continued beneath their feet.

They moved on in silence but for Rathen and Anthis's quiet mutterings over a scroll Anthis had slipped back out of one of the bags, and Eyila's occasional murmur. But they were few, and soon stopped altogether as they trekked further from the magic's reach. When Eyila had recovered just enough, Petra led her to Rathen's side and left her there while she continued on ahead to walk beside Garon. He ignored her as she looked at his shoulder, even when she began gently probing it and cleaned it with her waterskin. He walked on as if she wasn't there. But he didn't shoo her away.

Chapter 7

The sky was perfectly blue; not a tuft of cloud marred its brilliance, nor the golden sun as it climbed leisurely towards its zenith. A pleasant warmth beamed down upon Kulokhar, bathing the capital city in a comfortable stillness disrupted neither by the bustle of late-morning business nor the birdsong in the surrounding forests and gardens, while an easy patience dulled and distanced troubles.

It was, in short, a perfect summer morning.

Which went entirely unnoticed through the Arana House windows, barely ajar, open purely for the exchange of stale air for fresh in the under-used drawing room, a space itself wonderfully equipped three kelicerans past for meals on just such mornings.

The large, bright, needlessly ornate room had been neglected for the eight years since Salus had killed and replaced Elina, as was the Arana's custom, and it was only following Taliel's recent suggestion that he get out of his office more often that he'd finally deigned to utilise it. But that morning, as he and Teagan took a late breakfast, neither paid any attention to the ambience - nor, indeed, to the food, though Salus had worked through two strong pots of tea.

Finally, the keliceran released a lengthy sigh into the pensive silence and rubbed his eyes with his knuckles.

"The trap?" Teagan asked quietly, since the stillness had been broken anyway.

"A bracelet," Salus sighed again, his eyes red, "or something like it, belonging to the earth tribe. Meant to lure them in, looking for their own. The earth was dug out beneath it at a gradient; as soon as someone got close enough to pick it up, the ground gave out and pulled more down behind them. The ditch was also cut asymmetrically to sprain the victims' ankles on the way down."

"The water tribe used an earth tribe trap against them?"

"They tried. They'd also lined it with sharpened reeds - one of their own tricks, I'd guess."

"Who tripped it?"

"Six children." He sat forwards and reached for the teapot, but only managed to shake out half a cup. He sighed and sat back, taking the cooling tea with him. "It's the closest trap to any settlement yet, but it wasn't nearby. The children ventured too far, well beyond reasonable boundaries. Makes you wonder what constitutes as 'good parenting' these days.

"But it does serve to prove that the traps aren't always so typical. Locating them all would be a challenge, and as far as patrolling goes, the Arana is stretched thin watching Doana, other lands and the Order. We can't contain the matter, and the guards, too, are occupied with evacuations and maintaining order over the refugees and mages."

"Numbers are too sparse to reinforce," Teagan agreed, "but another evacuation will be disruptive, and for more than our own affairs."

"And there will be more at risk if there's an attack, be it Doana, mages or Koraaz..."

"Alternative?"

Salus's neck twitched. "None. It's necessary. But evacuating a city as big as Rega is no easy thing; there isn't enough room. There will be more refugee camps springing up. And we'll lose a moth cellar which will degrade the chain of contact, and a critical outpost close to the Pavise mountains, Kalokh *and* one of Doana's camps."

"The lepidopterist will remain behind, and the city will be locked down, but only guarded by minimal watch. The moths will not be lost."

"I suppose not, but harder to reach and that means slower news." Salus sighed and peered down into his cup. "I suppose it's just *another* inconvenience..."

Teagan went on to say something else, no doubt infallibly logical, but Salus didn't hear it. He was too busy counting up those ever-accumulating 'inconveniences' and the substantial hurdles those niggling little matters built up into. And most of them would have been preventable had he been armed with the right intel. Just like everything else. But with limited eyes - the Arana numbered only so many - certain things had to be prioritised. Which meant allowing other things to happen.

His fingers tensed around the teacup, which he set back on the table before he could crush it.

Five days. Five days, and surveillance spells were *still* no closer to being a reality, even despite the work Erran had put in with the help of an apprentice who he'd *promised* was up to the task. He had managed to establish the observation point and allocate a feedback, but creating a stable link between the two was proving to be sickeningly impossible while absolutely vital. And he was frustratingly aware of the fact that this evacuation couldn't have been avoided even had they been installed the very moment he'd thought of it, because the very notion of such a spell had come too late. And that was his *own* fault.

How much longer was this going to take? And what more would be 'allowed' to happen in the meantime?

The tribes' squabbles were moving closer and closer to civilisation and there were no signs of either side backing down or thinning out; the mages were creating problems nearly every four days, and Doana was still sitting, waiting, plotting and presumably preparing for things no one seemed willing to venture a guess at. There were threats all around them, threats *within*; nothing was clear on any front - except the fact that things were certainly going to get worse before they got better. And he was sat there pretending to relax in the morning sunshine, his jaw tense, back rigid and shoulders knotted into his spine. Absolutely, unquestionably, incontrovertibly wasting time.

But at least he had the minuscule comfort of knowing that, at that moment, Erran was still working on it.

A servant stepped forwards from his position against the wall. He hesitated beside the table, looking from the two to the untouched plates. A nod from Teagan permitted him to clear them away; breakfast had long since turned cold. But Salus didn't notice him, nor the careful clatter of cutlery over ceramic, nor could he recall what had even been served. His attention wandered instead towards the far window and off towards Blackbrush Forest. The summer light illuminated its well-tended edges, but it was bleak inside, dark and private.

He didn't notice silence slip in as the tinkling of his fingertips across the side of the porcelain ceased, for his mind, too, had trailed off, and he stared and lingered thoughtlessly on a memory that hung from the boughs of the thick, broad forest. For a moment, his tensions eased just a little.

Taliel.

She'd recovered the records he'd wanted - which had contained nothing useful after all - standing right where they should have been in the chronologically arranged bookcase. Somehow, he'd missed them. But he could fathom how that had happened.

He rubbed his eyes again, absorbing himself in the strangely paralytic sensation.

He'd not slept in days. He hadn't seen Taliel in days. And he wasn't sure the two weren't unrelated.

He dropped his heavy hands into his lap and stared thoughtfully down at the teapot. His gaze then shifted slowly onto Teagan, who appeared equally lost in thought. "Is it normal," he began ponderously, drawing back his favoured's attention, "for a woman to have such sway over a man?"

"Based on observation, it would seem so," Teagan replied coolly, "but I couldn't say from a personal standpoint. I was twenty one when you elevated me to portian. Prior to that, I'd never found anyone worth the distraction."

"Mm..." Salus tapped his chin. "The only experiences I've had have been mission requirements..." His eyes narrowed further. "Why is it, do you think, that w--" A sturdy knock at the door both cut him off and startled him, enough, apparently, to call entry on reflex. But as a seasoned phaeacian of grave bearing stepped inside, he could only groan a further regretful curse. "It's too early for this..."

But they duly pushed themselves to their feet and braced for the report, at which Salus's weariness was promptly eradicated.

As quick as lightning, his face turned vermilion. "*They got away?!* There were *seven* of you out there! Why could no one stop them?! How did they manage to *kill* someone?!"

"It happened quickly," the grave man explained with a calmness more suited to a phidipan, "and the ground was unfavourable--"

"*Unfavourable?!*" Salus closed the distance between them in a flash. The phaeacian finally twitched, but for what ground he stood, he paled instead. Salus saw it, and it both pleased and sickened him. "For your sake, you'd better have another excuse ready."

Somehow he blanched even whiter, as though all the blood had drained down to his feet and out through his toes. "D-d-distance," he sputtered, "we were spread far, we couldn't know where they would reappear, and many of us were waylaid moments after it happened, I was the only--"

"*Waylaid?!*" Salus bared his fangs. "By *whom?*"

Suddenly, the phaeacian didn't seem so eager to speak. It was only the weight of Salus's black eyes that pressed it out of him. "Ditchlings."

The walls shook with the keliceran's helpless roar, and with the slightest, most effortless movement, he threw the quivering man aside and stormed out through the door.

The room trembled in the silence of his wake. Teagan paused to help the operative back up, and though he saw absolute terror in the eyes of the man who was only a fraction older than himself, the portian did not think little of him. He was only just able to suppress the same sentiment within himself.

But while the phaeacian could remain out of reach of the keliceran's rage, Teagan was obligated to follow.

"I should have known better than to leave this in the hands of phaeacians," Salus spat as Teagan caught up with him along the stairs. Everyone was quick to step out of their way, and as usual no one looked up at them, but Teagan knew on this occasion that it was not out of respect. After eight or more footsteps, curiosity began craning necks. "Ditchlings - this isn't the first time they've made such ridiculous excuses!"

"There were four phidip--"

"Yes, but they, at least, are capable. But three phaeacians..." He snarled. "This is my fault. I should have stayed there myself - I should have known *better!*"

He stormed to his office, all but ripping the door from its hinges, and immediately began tearing open assignment folders, muttering about knowing exactly how to fix the problem. Teagan waited patiently to one side, but the keliceran soon hissed a vile oath. "Only phaeacians are available. I'll have to trade them out. I don't want anything less than phidipans tracking them. It's too important to leave in the hands of agents who let themselves get overwhelmed by forest children." He shook his head to himself. "Three days. They could be *anywhere* by now..."

Another knock sounded. Salus looked up sharply, and Teagan saw with great relief that the whites had returned to his eyes, though it made their fury chillingly clear. He barked entry, and in stepped another messenger, a far younger phaeacian with a miniature scroll in her hand. Both stiffened at the sight of it.

Rather than wait for her to brave a step forwards or for Salus to snap at her to hurry, Teagan retrieved it himself and ushered the young woman back out of the door. The scroll, tied shut by a thin leather cord, was tiny, half the length of his smallest finger, and yet it seemed to weigh as much as a brick. But Salus didn't have the patience to entertain such sentiments and unrolled it with such aggression it seemed he sought to frighten the contents into favour. The tremor of a knot in his jaw as he read suggested that it hadn't worked.

He remained still for a long while. Teagan watched him closely from his peripherals, as he had long ago learned to do. Then, he screwed up the parchment and tossed it aside. It fell lightly while he sank into a chair. Teagan waited.

"I suppose it's not surprising that this should reach us now," he mumbled, disturbingly calm, as he had been all morning. His blue eyes, steeped in thought, turned up towards him. "Koraaz and Karth are already back with the others. Someone resembling the inquisitor was seen in Trinn before the Order attacked, and our plant followed him back to Fendale where the two were waiting. But," his lip curled, "she was in no position to intervene."

"They're back in Turunda - teleportation?"

Salus grunted. "What else?" He leaned back over the assignment folders with a more tempered patience and began crossing out the recent adjustments. "But why teleport to rejoin those three and linger by the mountains rather than go straight to the Order? And why flee the attack? ...Unless the attack was meant to establish a drop point... They're heading south, probably to throw us off and give Trinn a chance to empty out - nowhere seems to be safe from them, but people have been upping and leaving anyway, looking for some kind of refuge. Then Koraaz will go back to Trinn. Coincidences don't happen, not like this." A smile flickered. "We've got them. We need more out there immediately, Trinn and the southern roads, before the dust has settled - reroute nearby mages, get onto them, pin them in, get the Zi'veyn *away* from them!"

"There are no mages available in the vicinity, sir, nor available to transport."

But Salus ignored his clinically delivered case. He was already scrawling across numerous parchments, muttering beneath his breath, cursing and crossing things out, then rearranging the sheets and scribbling again. He thrust several pages into Teagan's hands without raising his eyes from the desk.

"Sir, we can't reassign--"

"We can. We have the element of surprise. It will be enough." Then his hand abruptly stilled. "Unless...unless the attack was just a distraction... What if--and we *are*, we *are* distracted! How many are *already* making their way to Trinn? And not just us - guards, and even the White Hammer will investigate!" He snatched a map out from beneath a haphazard pile of reports, dislodging them and sending them scattering across the floor. "They're heading south. The Korovor Woodlands..." his tone flattened. "And a cluster of places the Order has already ravaged. They're going to these places - they were in Fendale. But why? It has to have something to do with that relic, it *has* to!" His hand began moving urgently across the parchments again. "They think they have us fooled with the attack on Trinn. That gives *us* the element of surprise. Reroute everyone to the forest and surround the forsaken place - every crack, crevice; *anywhere* unnatural! We'll fence them in!"

Another growl rumbled free and he scratched the quill through the damp ink, snatched a sheet back from Teagan and similarly adjusted it, then cursed foully and kicked the leg of the desk. "Do we have control over *anything?!*" He slammed the quill flat on the tabletop, spattering ink across his hand. He cursed again. "We're too tangled up; Ivaea and Kasire, tribes - even our own military is getting in the way. Too many of our people are occupied with it all."

"Sir, may I suggest--"

He lifted the quill and returned to the alterations, muttering beneath his breath.

"Sir--"

"Phaeacians. They've served well enough up until recently, before things became so complicated. If they're given clear orders, they can manage. Phidipans can be replaced and rerouted to Trinn, and a few of those can replace mages. We don't need casters everywhere, a phidipan can recognise a suspicious mage and sound the alarm. We have a clue, now - we can handle this shortly and finally remove Koraaz as a threat. There are only so many twins our translocators are linked to, and few so far north of our borders - Dolunokh has never been a threat. But with Koraaz back in Turunda, we have far more resources at our disposal..."

His quill stopped scratching, and he stared into the ink. "But pinpointing him, keeping him in our sights...he's given us the slip too many times already..."

His fist struck the table, but Teagan didn't flinch, even as his mumbling rose to a bellow. "If we had these damned spells working--*it can't be this hard!*"

Another knock. Salus roared. The inkwell smashed against the wall.

But when the door opened, the crimson in his face turned to rose, his shoulders dropped, and he steadied himself against the desk as though his rage had only then dawned upon him.

Teagan's eyes flicked towards Taliel and he found himself, quite possibly for the first time, grateful for her arrival. Her perpetual distraction was perfectly timed. And she had brought a suspiciously heavy file box with her.

Teagan gathered the fallen reports and placed them back on the desk. "We are stretched thin, it is true," he began temperately, "and this is a delicate issue. But we must consider the possibility that the attack may be unrelated. There has been no clear contact between Koraaz's group and the Order even before we found them in Dolunokh, and we cannot afford to withdraw from our other duties on what is presently little more than a presumption. While I agree that we shouldn't let this opportunity escape us, I urge you to think it over. It will still be dealt with just as swiftly in an hour's time."

"Yes," the suddenly subdued Salus replied, head bowed in equally abrupt exhaustion, "yes...you're quite right... Thank you, Teagan."

He inclined his head and turned away, moving for the door on silent feet as Taliel stepped in and out of his path.

"...What if he's gone rogue?"

"It looks as though Taliel has brought you lunch," he said, stepping out into the hallway without casting a look back. "I suggest you eat it."

"But--"

The door closed behind him.

Smooth. Seamless. Perfectly structured. Entirely devoid of the force, compression and hard edges of human casting.

A force, compression and hard edge that had only been illuminated by identical incidents in the first place.

But these incidents were anomalous; enigmatic. The sudden spikes in the surrounding network of magic, the aura that pulsed from every mage with every spell they cast - neither followed the phenomenon. Even the poorly-understood magic that gathered at sites of magnetism emitted a near-constant disturbance. But this, whatever it was, was almost undetectable, noticed only by its shockwave, though the term was far too dramatic for what equated to the ripple of a raindrop in the ocean. It could be easily missed - and perhaps that was why the phenomenon was so little-understood, over centuries to its most recent occurrence two days past. Perhaps they caught only the largest of ripples, perhaps smaller spells slipped through their nets absolutely, along with anything that might identify it. But...surely such marks would be *greater* in these larger spells...

"'Preternatural arcanial phenomena'."

Startled by the voice beside his ear, Owan sat bolt upright and folded over his papers, staring with wide eyes at the woman who moved around from behind his seat and dropped elegantly into the luxuriously padded chair opposite, rolling her eyes with a weary groan. He sighed in what he squashed into mild irritation. "Don't sneak up on me like that," he grumbled, settling himself back down in the previously quiet corner of the lantern-lit study chamber. "And don't read over my shoulder."

"I apologise. But why ever are you wasting your time on *this* again? These anomalies pop up from time to time and always in insignificant places, they have done for...well, *ages*, and never once have they given us even a trace of substance to work with. Where was the last one? *Mosshorn?* Pointless." She shook her head, loosening her blonde hair, and smoothed down her bodice in her usual sign of dismissal. "They're nothing. Don't waste your time chasing after them."

"If everyone thought that way, we'd still be reeling from the disappearance of the elves."

"No, we would be further along than we are now because time would have been spent working on things that could actually move *forwards* and *get* somewhere."

Owan looked up from the parchment and regarded her with bemusement. "That's not how advancement works."

"I'm sure you would know." She waved her slender fingers. "Do continue with your vital distractions."

His eyes narrowed impatiently. "Shouldn't you be out repairing something?"

"No. I'm waiting for everything to degrade *just* enough that the city is on the verge of total collapse and everyone is sent into a panic."

"You don't need to neglect spells to do that," he replied regretfully despite her sarcasm, his gaze drifting out through the tower window, "just step outside."

She was silent for a while. Expectation drew him back to find she'd followed his gaze, staring out across the city bathed in the late evening light, her chin in her hand and a gentle crease to her brow. She spoke before he could begin to guess at her thoughts.

"Do you think they'll achieve anything?"

"Who?"

"The rebels," she replied distantly. "Do you think this uproar will actually get us the respect they say it will?"

He stiffened and looked back to his work, attempting to disconnect himself from the subject. "I think it will incite a greater aggression which will crush us out of existence."

"Really, though? I mean, we have *magic*. How could anyone without it pose a threat to us? What could they honestly do to stop us?"

"Magic can only do so much."

"And that is a great deal more than what we can without it." She raised her chin and sat back in her seat, but her gaze didn't shift from the city. "Surely the populace realise this?"

"I daresay that's exactly the problem. They're all equally disadvantaged and they're banding together. There's strength in numbers, especially when those numbers are enraged, and against which, as I've said, magic can only do so much." She didn't respond. He could have left the matter in that silence - his desire was pressing enough - but necessity, he found, had already turned his gaze over the top of his papers to hold her with veiled suspicion. "Why do you mention it?"

She shrugged. "I wouldn't mind a little respect."

"Respect?" He challenged, carefully. "Or fear? Because that's *all* they're going to achieve. Attacks on towns and villages, the razing of homes and businesses - there's nothing in that to endear themselves to *anyone*. And even if they were to succeed in frightening everyone into submission, the nature of that 'respect' would inevitably incite rebellion - and in such circumstances, I'm certain they wouldn't hesitate to spill blood in the face of magic."

"Mm...but don't you think--"

He all but lunged across the table, his work suddenly forgotten. His voice fell low and harsh, grasping for privacy against the other scholars nearby. "What is this about, Clarilla? Because you sound as though...you...as though you're actually considering *joining* them!"

"Well--"

"You know, you've *always* been irrational, but this--this is--*even for you*, this is--"

"*Owan*," she cried in a whisper, grasping his hand, "for the love of Vastal and all of Her *effigies* will you please calm down! I am *not* joining them!"

He stalled, face still twisted in alarm, heart still hammering in disbelief, and studied her eyes carefully. After a long moment, understanding settled and his shoulders sagged in defeat. "Orders?"

She smiled apologetically. "Orders."

Relief dropped him heavily back into the depths of his chair, from where he regarded her first with irritation, then evaluation. "Can I take it, then, that I don't need to subject you to the same round-about interrogation?"

She grinned. "You do not." But then her blonde eyebrows drew together in an almost familiar challenge. "I've 'always been irrational'?"

"Yes," he replied, unruffled. "Always. And your sister agrees with me."

"Well I suppose it's nice to know that I've brought the two of you together in more ways than one." Clarilla's gaze travelled back out of the window as Owan slipped absently back into his parchments, and the concerns that sat at the centre of every other mage's mind were quick to consume her in the lull. "Have you made any progress?"

Owan looked up at her distant tone, but found in place of the expected soft thoughtfulness an expression so grave it could have shattered the glass she stared through. It left no room for misunderstanding; anyone who glanced at her could have read it and empathised. "It's impossible without being able to get close enough to analyse it," he replied regretfully. "Stonton wasn't enough, and I've not been permitted field research since. And with the recent surge of power coinciding with the rebellion, we're all under even closer scrutiny. The elders won't risk letting *anyone* get close to it right now."

She shook her head hopelessly. "Our hands are tied by the very people we're supposed to be serving."

"The situation is arcane in nature, so it's not at all unreasonable for everyone to assume that mages are responsible. But if they see us gathering at arcanised locations, their suspicions will have even greater grounds and the tentative relationship we have with the populace will escalate even further. But something will be done about it. Of that I'm certain."

Her narrow eyes slipped onto him from the flickering lanterns of the still-bustling city below. He didn't seem to notice her calculating stare as he continued his reading. "You discovered something while you were out there. I know you did. Imelia won't tell me anything but since then you've been more hopeful about the whole thing. And more open to distractions..."

"I am a scholar--"

"You're boring, yes, I know."

"There's a difference between 'boring' and 'intelligent'."

"Only in a manner of spelling." She sat forwards, catching his eye. "What do you know? What did you find out there?"

He exhaled a deep, slow breath and considered her for a long moment. She stared at him pleadingly, her usually careless demeanour broken in her private desperation for some kind of reassurance. He sighed again, then, after glancing around and noting the distance of the nearest person, leaned forwards and lowered his voice to barely a whisper. She moved closer in response. "It's classified."

"*Oh!*" She moved to slap his arm, which he snatched out of her reach with a chuckle, and sat back in irritation. "You are so...*boring!* My niece is going to be boring, too, isn't she?"

"She'll be marvellous. And I'm sorry, but--no, don't try giving me that look. I can't, really. Nothing. Nothing...except that a handful of people are taking an active interest, and you didn't hear it from me."

"Hear what? There was nothing *to* hear."

He gave her a flat look, and she sighed wearily. "All right. An interest, you say. So they're boring, too?"

"An *active* interest, and no, not in the slightest. But they do know what they're doing."

She nodded slowly, absorbing his words. "*Active* interest - since Stonton to now?"

"I have no reason to believe otherwise."

"That doesn't sound reassuring."

"Perhaps not, but I'm certain in their dedication."

"...Why? You know them, don't you?"

"I...know the nature of one. And he's stubborn. He'll put an end to it, or die trying."

"Why are you smiling?"

"No reason."

"You're awfully confident in these people. From my perspective, the recent empowering of these places suggests they've already failed."

"And I would say it suggests they've made progress."

"Tell me, is intentionally making stupid conclusions just a scholar's way of providing work for himself?"

"For something to have changed, something has had to affect it. It may have gone wrong, or it may be part of some complex plan - the matter itself isn't exactly conventional - but the point is that something or someone has had an *impact* on it. Otherwise, nothing would have changed at all."

"...All right. But what if it's the rebels?"

"If it were, I daresay far more would have come of it by now and we would definitely have detected a greater shift in the network. It's not them."

She held him with calculating eyes while her fingers drummed thoughtfully on the tabletop, until she finally sighed in defeat. "You're boring, but you're smart, and I haven't the first clue about any of it. I have no choice but to trust your judgement."

"I'm honoured."

"You're agitating." She rose gracefully from her chair, smoothed down her dress, and moved around to kiss him on the cheek. "I'll never know what my sister sees in you. Anyway, I'd better go and change - I'm due for city patrol in half an hour."

"Be careful."

"I'll be fine. But in case I'm wrong, please make sure my niece knows that she had an aunt."

Owan frowned with sharp disapproval. "Don't talk like that, Clarilla. It's not funny."

She gave him a lopsided smile. "It wasn't meant to be. Good night."

The corner of the study chamber fell quiet again, but it didn't rest lightly, and the innate, warm comfort that guided concentration had been replaced by a cold, clawing and debilitating web of fret concentrated right above Owan's seat.

He believed what he'd told her - when Rathen set his mind to something, he made sure it happened. Eleven years may have passed since his banishment, and many more since they had been close friends, but one look in his eyes had assured him that that, at least, had not changed. And with a child in his care, that drive had been augmented. And he doubted that the inquisitor nor the celebrated historian in his company would let him give up on the matter either - not that defeat had ever been an option from Rathen's outlook. In fact, beyond the initial shock, it hadn't truly surprised him to find that he'd survived all these years, nor that he was breaking his sentence by pursuing a matter the Order was too shackled to address.

But...there was always room for doubt in such obscure or unusual things, and Owan was cursed to study that doubt, that question, from all angles by his very vocation. His very nature.

Just once he wished he could hand that analytical trait over to someone else, and then *he* could be the one to say 'I haven't the first clue about any of it. I have no choice but to trust your judgement.' And leave the matter at that.

He couldn't help a smile. *'What a boring life that would be.'*

His eyes dropped back to the parchments. Script of countless mages noted the sparse details of the strange magical occurrences, the little the Order had ever uncovered about the centuries-old phenomenon. A phenomenon, he was certain, that had nothing at all to do with any arcane torment that presently ailed either land or person, and that had indeed last occurred in Mosshorn, and four weeks before that near White Rapids.

He might be 'wasting his time' by studying them - though there was too little to study to waste more than an hour with the turning of every moon - but there was equally little he could do towards the things that mattered while the Order was forced to bend to the suspicions of the uninformed.

It was all on Rathen Koraaz.

For though Owan did have the first clue, he had nothing to extrapolate it with.

He had no choice but to trust his judgement.

...But...surely there was *something* more he could do...

The thought struck him like a four-horse wagon.

Study doubts and questions from all angles. As was his very vocation. He didn't need to leave the Order House to do that.

He scrambled together the parchments and left the study chamber in a frenzy, his mind bent on the matters the Order as a whole was too shackled to deal with - the things that would actually *get* somewhere.

He couldn't keep the fervent smile from stealing over his face.

Chapter 8

"He's rogue, I'm *certain* of it!" Salus threw open the office door and stormed out into the corridor, startling the meagre few with business in the surrounding rooms. "Koraaz has no intention *whatsoever* of taking the Zi'veyn to the Order. Drop points or no, he could have teleported it there in an instant, but instead he's running around with it like it's a new *toy*..."

"Perhaps," Teagan offered, unruffled as they made for the staircase, "the Order doesn't wish the relic within their walls. It would be too obvious - they know we want to keep it from them."

Salus growled. "It doesn't *feel* that way..."

"If Koraaz *has* gone rogue, what does that mean for his companions?"

"Well with Karth still with them, they're definitely up to *something*... Perhaps they need more than just the Zi'veyn. Or maybe the Zi'veyn *itself* needs more. There are places out there just *swimming* in magic. Whatever the case, they're not finished. Not by a long shot."

They left the stairwell at the second floor and swung around into another corridor lined with yet more pointless paintings. The two individuals they passed averted their eyes. The halls were emptier than usual.

"This is alarming. They need to be stopped before whatever plan they have can reveal itself. Whatever they were looking for in Fendale, they didn't find it. We can't let them get near Korovor... Reroute more to the southern roads, *everyone* nearby - and don't tell me 'to stop and think about it'. We don't know what the Zi'veyn could be capable of - if *all* it could do was stop magic, he would have it secured by now. He would *not* be running around with it at the risk of it falling into someone else's hands. And the Order - you're right, of course, Teagan, they know we've been hunting it - they would have wanted it locked up tight the moment it was retrieved."

"They could--" A growl of realisation silenced him.

"But even if we sent orders immediately, they're all still too far out and no one can leave their posts until their replacements arrive. No, no, no, it will take too long. We don't know what they're doing, what they're looking for or where they expect to find it - and even when we *do* uncover something, when we have enough information to launch a *precision* strike and stop them in their tracks, we'll *still* be too short-manned to make it quickly enough..." Another growl rumbled deep within his throat, but he was too absorbed in the cascade of counter-thoughts to hear Teagan's reassurances. "While *I'm here*, trapped in this damned place - I could respond the moment the reports come in, I could use the translocators, be out there in an instant and put a stop to them once and for all--"

"And what will we do when Doana finally gives themselves away and you're unreachable?" Salus spared him a brief, irritated glare. Teagan didn't waver.

"Forgive me for saying so, but you are underestimating the value of your leadership, as well as the capabilities of your subordinates. Everyone near and around Fendale and the southern roads have been alerted to his presence. They will be hunting him, actively, as dictated by their standing orders."

"But--"

"Rerouteing any more will sacrifice our position and endanger Turunda. The country will be exposed to the other elements and we will have to abandon this avenue altogether if we're to recover from it."

"That--"

"There are already a more than sufficient number en route - any more and we risk forcing them under one another's feet, then we'll lose Koraaz through our own negligence."

"*All right.*" Salus trudged to a stop beside one of the many elaborately gilded doors and sighed, rubbing the edge of his eye sockets. His desperation had culminated in another concentrated headache right behind his eyes. "Perhaps...you have a point. 'Too many cooks', 'patience is a virtue'... I--...*we* can't jump in without a plan, and the element of surprise can only carry us so far..."

He shook his head and opened the door, exposing the vast and sparsely furnished room beyond to the excessive torchlight of the halls. The great fireplace at the far end, one of the estate's grandest, offered only necessary illumination, but the glinting decor amplified its brilliance. The two mages hunched over a desk beside it, though certainly aware of his arrival, didn't look up from their work.

But Salus hesitated at the threshold, still in the grasp of lingering thoughts. "I had a feeling last Yule that this wasn't going to be an easy year."

"I recall."

"But I never could have imagined it would involve protecting the country from its *own* people. The borders, at least, are to be expected...but even though we chased Skilan out with its tail between its legs, there's already evidence that they're looking our way *again*, which is the last thing anyone needs. And Doana is actively tainting Turundan soil..."

"It's as if the country has the pox."

"The pox," he grunted humourlessly, "or a red-tail spider bite?" He chuckled drily, detachedly aware of the enchantments protecting the room from spells gone awry. "If only we could amputate the infected limb..."

A lilting chuckle drifted out from the darkness. "It's certainly a thought."

The room moved in a heartbeat. The very instant the two mages snapped around, Teagan and Salus stormed inside, and all eyes turned sharp against the gloom in search of the source of the voice. Not one looked at the other. The voice had been female.

Balls of light bloomed into existence, no patience for eyes to adjust to the dim, isolated glow of the fire, and their glimmer slipped immediately over a fifth figure - one who made no effort to escape discovery.

Instead, she melted out from the shadows where she'd been fiddling with a vase of flowers. She was already fixated upon Salus. With a slow, leisurely stride she approached him, her pale eyes sharp with scrutiny. They immediately sparked a rage behind his ribs.

She'd taken not even two steps when the mages sprung, forming the signs to snatch and immobilise her hands behind her back long before she was near enough to harm him. But the moment her left had been dragged back to join her right, her right rose to thoughtfully tap her chin. Another cast pulled it back around, and her left was suddenly resting upon her hip. It was as though the spell over her was as water over a duck's back. And she was still walking, leisurely, carelessly. Superiorly.

Salus's blood boiled, but as his hands rose to cast her back in her place, she was suddenly standing right in front of him, and grasped his wrist with a light and easy movement. Her grip was steel. She smiled at him far too cordially.

Seized entirely by keen, unreadable, pastel-rose eyes, a tangle of rage and irritation ran loops in his stomach, churning up a nausea that froze him. And...fear?

Cautiously, his gaze travelled over her shoulder towards Erran and his apprentice, both of whom were struggling against the bonds that had ensnared their hands. Then around to Teagan, who similarly battled against whatever had rooted his feet to the floor, just out of reach of the intruder.

His eyes crashed back upon her. She was still smiling. And still unreadable.

But then she dropped his hand and continued wandering, as though suddenly bored of him. Only then did he find his tongue. He kept his fingers loose while his fixed stare tracked her. "How did you get in here?"

She peered around at the wall-mounted trinkets, but merely shrugged in her distraction. "I was always here." There was an all-too familiar lilt in her voice. "I came in through the window. The wall. I wished myself in. I didn't 'get' anywhere, 'here' came to me." Her hand rose towards him at lightning speed as she peered passively up at a golden half-face mask. Salus flinched, but she cast nothing; instead she caught in her bare fingers a sliver of light.

Her gaze shifted sideways and eyed Teagan with amusement, then the light dropped to the floor with a soft thud. A small throwing knife, the length of a finger and the thickness of a nail. Her gaze slipped back to the mask. "Whichever you prefer."

Cautiously, his eyes narrowed. As she turned, he caught a hint of almost pure white skin and very dark hair. He glanced towards the others, but though they'd ceased their struggle, and Teagan's arms, it seemed, had also been immobilised and frozen to his sides, their hawk-like stares intensified. They'd each seen the same thing. But where they displayed clear mistrust and vexation, Salus found himself considered with curiosity. His attention slipped back onto her. "Who are you?"

She smiled again, inscrutably. "Liogan."

"Liogan?"

"That's what I said."

"Why are you here?"

"Oh just *full* of questions." She turned in what was almost a flourish, one that sent her dress and raven-black curls sweeping out around her. For a moment she appeared both wondrous and terrifying, and the room seemed to flinch at her presence. But Salus also saw the confidence in her bearing - the arrogance.

He suppressed his disgust along with his certainties and focused himself instead on the intentions of the person before him.

"I was just passing by and I overheard your troubles. Well, not *literally* overheard - not until I was in here - but I sensed your woes. And here I am."

"You speak as if you're a jinn."

"Well, if you prefer that interpretation, then I am a jinn." Suddenly she stood directly in front of him, just an inch taller, slight but noticeable, and her skin shone unnaturally ashen for a human. Her eyes, too, were bright, and the extent of their pale colouring was only revealed when his glowing orb struck her from just the right angle, a requirement which itself was also abnormal. They studied him critically for a very long moment. Then she returned to her wandering. "Turunda is in danger."

"From magic?"

"Among others."

"You still haven't told me why you're here."

"Mmm." She paused to lift from a pedestal a fine glass chalice enrobed in golden filigree, then a knife from another, equally ornate but certainly of human craft. Salus felt the room tense as she turned the steel in the firelight. A moment later, they were both returned carelessly to their stands. "Why do you keep all of these?"

She blinked as Salus suddenly stepped out in front of her. He, it appeared, had not been rooted like the others. Did that mean that she didn't see him as a threat? Or...that she saw him as an equal? Or did she simply want something from him and didn't wish to burn the timber before the bridge had been built? But...what could she possibly want?

What had *Denek* wanted?

Untroubled, she turned away from him and wandered slowly towards the fireplace. Salus followed cautiously.

"Magic, internal strife, foreign threats... You should move out of harm's way."

"I'm not the one in danger."

"Are you so sure?"

His footsteps stalled at her smile.

"Anyway, I was referring to your people."

"We won't be chased out of our own country!"

"I didn't say 'leave the country'. I said 'move out of harm's way'." Liogan pursed her lips in thought. "Magic is a powerful thing. It can build, and it can destroy - I'm sure I don't need to tell you. But magic isn't black and white."

"You don't need to tell me that, either."

She spared him a curious look. "...How *is* your training coming along now that Denek's out of your little picture?"

He stiffened. "Slowly."

"Mm. Well, keep at it. It'll come." She leaned against the mantle and peered down into the flames. They seemed to writhe in the otherwise darkened room, yearning to leap from the logs, to be free and spread their light and heat across the floor and up the walls, unstoppable by anything but their opposite. No one could rush in with bare hands on a whim and push them back, or they would be consumed like everything else that stood in fire's path. Fire had one purpose, and it was zealous in its execution. Fire, though violent, cleansed.

"Magic," Liogan spoke at last, her alien voice soft and entranced, "can do more than create and destroy. It can affect and influence."

Despite his own rapture, Salus couldn't help a stab of dubiety. "...What do you mean?" The firelight dimmed before him, though the flames were unchanged. His eyes flicked towards the mysterious woman but her gaze hadn't shifted. Neither had her body. Her arms remained folded, fingers relaxed.

"You cast a barrier around the flames," she said, no less softly, "filtering the light to your advantage - a distraction, or to mask your approach." The light intensified, and exceeded its original strength. Salus was forced to look away from it. "Or magnify it with a conjured lens for similar means."

Liogan turned away at an unspoken thought and resumed her flighty wandering. "But these are shortcuts, trickery cast by mages without such...purity."

"Purity?"

"She didn't cast--"

"Barriers?" She glanced suddenly towards Erran, who watched her with open and guarded confusion, and smiled. "Magnifiers? No, I didn't. As I said: trickery. But magic is not so black and white. It is far more than creation and destruction - as long as you have the pedigree to use it." She stopped beside the flowers she had been fiddling with, and though their stems had just begun to droop, their white and blue petals just begun to thin, they suddenly bloomed more vibrantly than they ever had in their prime.

She turned and squared herself towards Salus, ignoring the calculating stares of the others, and beset him with powerful eyes. For a moment, her skin flashed silver. "Fendale, Halen, Regiton, Loggerhead - the magic in these places and hundreds of others has torn deep into the earth."

"Why?"

"I couldn't tell you. But they dig deeper every day, and reach further with every disruption."

"What disruptions?"

"If you wish to hear what I have to say, you will be silent." She ignored the sneer that pulled at his lip. "Every crack in the crust - every perforation - can be made worse, the chasms longer, deeper. But they can also be guided."

"Away from cities?"

"Away from cities - or towards each other."

A dubious wrinkle marred Salus's face, already twisted in suspicion, and he analysed her even closer, searching for any hint of her true motives. But she remained unreadable.

Though when a sudden distance befell her eyes, dark, poorly angled from the light, he fixated on it until her focus returned half a breath later. Then she smiled, warm and mysterious. "Surely you played with jigsaw puzzles as a child."

"What does--"

"Snap the borders. Pop Turunda out like a puzzle piece and carry it away."

He growled as her hands fluttered about, but her gaze was unchanged. "This whole situation is a joke to you."

"Is it? I suppose you would see it like that - after all, how could it *possibly* be so easy? Oh, unless..." She thought for a moment, tapping her chin and peering up at the ceiling in yet another demonstration of condescension. Her plump, silver lips pursed, and she shook her black-blue curls. "No. No, you're right. I apologise.

It's impossible." Her hands dropped to her hips, and without a word began bustling past him towards the door.

In a heartbeat, Teagan, Erran and the second mage were upon her. Whatever enchantments she'd cast upon them had been broken - or, Salus suspected, released - but their every attempt to restrain her - their snatches, their grasps, their spells, their barring - all slipped over her again. And as Salus began forming his own attempt at a freezing spell, she vanished in her stride, leaving the four of them staring at empty space.

"Another elf?" Erran asked quietly, no doubt recollecting every detail of those few minutes, her every movement, her every word. Salus was doing much the same.

His jaw tightened. He felt Teagan's eyes slip onto him when he failed to reply.

"We can't trust her," the portian declared, his own voice equally hushed. "She could be another card in the Order's hand."

"You thought the same of Denek."

"She was speaking nonsense. She was trying to distract you."

"And I want to find out why."

"How? Denek remained here by choice. *If* this woman *is* another elf, she has made no attempt to conceal her power. She came and went as she pleased. I think it's a far higher priority that we raise some kind of barrier to prevent her from doing so again."

"And then we'll never learn a thing."

"And what is it you expect to learn?"

"Keliceran," Erran spoke up, "forgive me for speaking out of turn, but the things she said - they're not possible."

"...For mages without 'purity'..."

The three exchanged silent looks, each more ominous than the last. But Salus didn't notice them. He weighed her words, measured her knowledge - her superiority was justified. She was steeped in arcane wisdom, as only an elf could be, and though it made his skin crawl, he knew he could put it to use. She'd presented an impossible option, but when weighed against recent events, personal discoveries and her own sudden appearance in the middle of their stronghold, it seemed almost reasonable.

A smile that was nothing short of conniving momentarily pulled across Salus's lips, but he pushed it aside, straightened himself and turned purposefully towards Erran. "Don't we have some training to do?"

Chapter 9

An unnatural clearing pocked the edge of the village. Shaped by the violent collapse of Redgrove's outermost buildings and a swathe of the neighbouring forest blasted into splinters, little was left of either but scattered rubble and jagged trunks. Only the puddle of early summer rain that had gathered in the crater hid any degree of the wound in the road, feigning some small veneer of normality.

But the vast, empty acres of the village became a scar that could be seen from the top windows of the furthest houses, and the atmosphere that rose from that flooded pit cast a shadow so monstrous it was almost tangible. Even as Aria peered out towards it through the final hour of the evening, she felt its cold touch seep into her skin.

But it didn't rouse fear in her like it did in everyone else. Only sadness.

Movement drew her gaze from that dense emptiness four rooftops away. The woman across the road had taken up a vigil at her top window. She spotted Aria and smiled softly. Aria waved in response, and though the young woman returned it, Aria could see that her fear was close to the surface.

They both looked down to the road as a guard strode through the street, his hand on the hilt of his sword, head turning this way and that. But his presence meant little. When it had happened, there had been nothing they could do. Nothing anyone could. She hadn't been there, and old Ira wouldn't tell her a thing about it, but he didn't need to. It had surely been hopeless. Otherwise it wouldn't have been able to happen. And she suspected that she had a better idea of just what had gone on than anyone else in the village.

Her hands wrapped tighter about the perfectly carved piece of wood, but her ears pricked at a muffled call before her world-weighted frets could ensnare her. She hadn't caught the words, but she knew what they'd said and her stomach gurgled in response, snatching her back to the present.

She set the wood delicately upon the slender chest that stood beneath the window, filled, she'd discovered, with folded boy's clothes, blew out the lantern and hurried away through the bedroom, dancing between the shadows of strewn building blocks and leaping over the wheels of the wooden hobby horse that stuck out just a little too far across the floor. There was, of course, nothing she could do about that because he was in his stable, and if she pushed him any further against the cabinet he would bump his nose against the wall and be unable to reach his oats.

Opening the door, she was struck immediately by the fragrant aroma of onions. Grinning, she hurried down the dark and narrow staircase to the light and warmth at the bottom, swung through the door on the right and on into the kitchen. All her senses tingled.

The old man at the counter top waved her towards the table, one so big that five could have just about cramped around it. Only two chairs sat at it, though, which was preposterous, but she clambered eagerly into hers nevertheless, in front of which a glass of water and spoon were already set.

A plate was shortly slipped under her nose with a serving of shepherd's pie twice the size of her splayed hand, along with a needless warning that it was hot. The steam was already condensing on her face as she leaned close to take a deep sniff. Her grin broadened. It was her favourite, almost exactly how her father made it - though it *was* missing one thing.

The very moment she opened her mouth to declare it, a second plate with two toasted slices of bread were set down beside her.

Ira's wrinkled old face broke into a smile as she beamed and clapped, but he said nothing, took his seat opposite and joined her in the meal she was already devouring. When she looked up, his expression had slipped back into his usual frown - one she suspected was partly due to the sagging of his skin, but one that always swiftly curbed her enthusiasm. There was a familiarity to the downward turn of his lips, the lines around his eyes, the creases in his brow that always caught her off-guard and summoned, if she let it, an immense grief. It had come all too easily a month ago; every time she'd looked at him it had angered her. She regretted every one of those door-slamming instances now. She had since learned to push the familiarity away if just to find some comfort at night, and decided that it was not Ira's fault that he looked like her father. If anything, it was his fault that her father looked like *him*.

"Tomorrow," the old man began carefully between mouthfuls, allowing himself a smile as she looked up with big blue-grey eyes and cheeks stuffed full, "a music troupe is passing by - pipes, drums, fiddles and such. If you'd like--"

Her face lit up and she urgently swallowed her food. "I want to see them!"

Again her enthusiasm softened his features, and he raised his fork to his mouth. "Then you shall."

She grinned in excitement, but as she loaded her spoon with yet more mashed potato, Aria paused for a long moment and considered him as he ate. A silent debate began bouncing back and forth through her mind, should she, shouldn't she, but, as always, her curiosity was quickly victorious. She sat a little taller in her seat. "May I please ask a question?"

His white, wiry eyebrows slowly drew together. "Go ahead..."

"What happened to my daddy's mum?"

Peas tumbled from her spoon's starchy mountain, which she was quick to retrieve for a more rounded mouthful, and so she didn't notice his hand fall still halfway back to his plate, nor the heartbroken rend in his expression.

"She...isn't here..."

Aria nodded, still engrossed in pressing peas back into the potato. "I know. She died. My daddy told me. But what happened to her?"

"Aria..."

She glanced up expectantly, but her fleeting attention was seized by the sudden and intense hurt in his watery eyes. What curiosity had brimmed within her a moment before was immediately erased by shame. She lowered her spoon, her interest in the arrangement of peas lost. "I'm sorry, I'm so sorry - you don't have to tell me. I just...I wondered if what happened to her was the same as what happened to mine..."

"Yours? What's happened to Kienza?"

Her face lit briefly in amusement. "Kienza isn't my mum," she giggled. "She's my daddy's girlfriend! I don't know *who* my mummy is. And...she might not be dead, but...if she wasn't, she would be around, wouldn't she? Or come and see me sometimes?"

Ira stared back at her, lost for words beneath her curiously rational gaze. The silence quickly became stifling. He forced it away with a smile that didn't reach his eyes, and returned his attention to his food. "Yes. She would."

Aria continued to stare at him, then nodded slowly, uncomforted. He wasn't as good as her father at lying, and even he needed practise. But she smothered that eternal doubt, because she knew, in her heart, that her father was all she needed. And she was all *he* needed.

She straightened again and sought to change the subject, but a brief and distant clamour outside drew both of their attention towards the window.

Her wide eyes flicked towards the old man. "What was that?"

He didn't reply beyond a deepening of his frown.

Then it came again, stilling them both: a shout of panic in the street surely not six houses away.

"Mister--"

He rose to his feet as quickly as his aged bones would let him, silencing her with a gesture, and hurried to the small kitchen window. She held her tongue as he nudged the curtain aside and peered out into the darkness.

This time the words were almost intelligible, and they were getting closer. A shout, a scream, a crash. Laughter.

Aria's voice caught in her throat, trapped beneath her heart.

Ira dropped the curtain and staggered backwards just as a light flared outside. He turned with a deathly pallor to usher her out of her chair.

"What's happening?" She squeaked as he blew out the candle and rushed her out into the darkened hall.

"I don't know. Hush now, and hurry!"

She did her best to swallow her panic and focus on putting one foot in front of the other, but her legs were very nearly paralysed. She'd been in worse situations, she knew she had...but in this instant, she could recall none of them. This time, her father was nowhere around. Despite everything she'd experienced, she felt pure terror for the first time in her life, and she didn't know why.

Ira's hand tight on her shoulder, the two stumbled out through the back door and into the cramped garden. The screams were louder out there, and the laughing - the cackling, the whooping, the cussing. The crashing was close by, beaten doors and smashed windows, and the tiny, overgrown space she was thrown into played greater havoc on her senses, where the frenzied, writhing shadows sent phantoms darting all around them. And the heat, a dry heat...

Fire.

The hand on her shoulder steered her urgently towards the hedgerows and away from the rising commotion, where they forced their way through the thin yet rigid branches to the garden on the other side. They made for the narrow path that ran down the side of the house, but when another round of cheering followed the deceptively soft glow of fire at the head of that path, she was driven a sharp left. She almost fell over her feet at the old man's frantic pace, but she kept up. She had to keep up.

They pushed through thicker bushes and into another garden, one littered with weeds, roots and rocks that hindered their desperate escape. They made it only half way before the shattering of glass and terror-stricken cries erupted on the other side of the fence ahead of them.

They stumbled to a frantic stop, and in the brief moment Ira took to find yet another route, the whole world crashed down on their heads.

Firelight flared, blinding her, and she was shoved violently towards the thickened and convulsing shadows just as a heavy thump struck something soft behind her. It came again, and again, followed always by a ragged puff of breath. She tore herself around, pressing her back against the wall, trying desperately to disappear into it, and watched helplessly as another hit landed upon the old man's back, his frail torso pinned to the ground by the knees of the attacker. It was only then that she heard the stranger's howling, a wretched sound of joy and power that threatened to expel what little of her dinner she'd had the chance to eat.

The thug's cackling and Ira's haggard wheeze smothered her ears, and she became too numbed by another burst of fire to notice another villain move up on her left. And so she didn't truly see Ira grasp a flower pot from just within his reach and fling it around at his attacker, striking him in the head with little more than luck before lurching to his feet and throwing himself at the second.

"Run!"

The word drifted as though on a breeze, distant and languid, its urgency lost in her fright and confusion.

"Aria! *Run!*"

Light raged and flickered, leaving coloured shapes in her eyes. But she caught even through her blindness the flash of desperation in his as he was beaten back down to the knotted grass not two paces away from her. There was something familiar about it...

'Daddy.'

In a single, heart-shattering moment, courage seized her like her father's own protective grip. Her fright was banished.

With the greatest of will, she burst to her feet and darted away. But she didn't flee. She skidded to a stop at a short distance where the rocks littering the ground were smaller and plentiful, and began throwing them with all the speed and might she could muster. Most missed the thugs through her teary blindness and the constant shifting of the shadows, but a few struck, and one opened a nasty gash across one attacker's forehead that bled readily into his eyes. But despite the rain of stones, his assault upon Ira, who now howled in pain, didn't relent. And a knife suddenly glinted in his hand.

Before she could shout a warning, something heavy battered the side of her head and sent her crashing to the ground.

"The old man has fight in him!" A distant voice declared with sickening mockery. "It must be the girl - get rid of her and he'll crumble!"

Her blood surged while Ira croaked an oath she'd never heard before, and she shook her bearings back into place - but the immediate cry of shock and agony quickly dislodged them and froze her veins once again.

But it had not come from Ira.

The old man scrambled away from the black-clad bandit, who now staggered and clutched helplessly at the blood pouring from his neck as though trying to push it back in, and lunged for the first whose fearsome grip Aria was now trying to escape. Ira was a slight man, but the threat of the stolen and bloodied knife in his hand was enough to encourage the grasp on her dress to slacken, and she snatched herself free as quickly as she could. She stumbled backwards, allowing herself for one disconnected moment to stare in awe as the second bandit dropped and slumped, and Ira, shadowed by a vicious, rampaging fire, grappled with the first, ceaselessly jabbing the frightfully edged blade after the rogue's every dodge. This man, her grandfather, had gained the upper hand. And for a moment, she saw her father in his place.

"Run!" She heard her grandfather shout once again over the crackling of flames and shattering of glass. "I'll follow in a moment! But you *must* leave!"

Her astonishment crumbled. She saw the silhouette approach, saw the cold glint of steel, but even though she started towards him and the warning leapt readily from her tongue, she still couldn't stop it from happening.

The sword point re-emerged through Ira's chest.

Its blade glittered with crimson. The old man's rasp of shock was drowned by the cackle of the third bandit. The cackle was smothered by the scream that tore free from Aria's lips.

The original attacker slipped out from the broken grasp, but she didn't shrink back as his focus latched onto her. She stood her ground, small fists tight, eyes seething, burning so brightly with such rage, such hatred, that when he collapsed after two steps with eyes glazed and empty, she felt responsible. Though not regretful.

She looked back to Ira just as the blade withdrew from his body, dropping him to the ground as though he were nothing more than a heavy sack of vegetables. Her blood seared in her veins, heart hammered, but despite her rage, she was paralysed. She watched him so very closely, waiting for him to move, to push himself back up, to try, or at least to raise his head. But he didn't.

Only when the murderer's eyes fell upon her did she finally turn and run.

Right into another grasp.

Another scream shredded the walls of her throat, and she kicked and thrashed, clawed and pinched, her eyes stinging with unstoppable tears of pain, grief and the most intense malice she had ever experienced. But through her cursing, her pleas to be released, her pleas for Ira to get up, the soft hush of a familiar voice finally brushed her ear.

Disbelief stunned her. Her struggle stilled.

Her eyes flashed open while a croak and thud sounded behind her, right where the murderer had been. Her tears renewed immediately. Relief overwhelmed her. But when she spun back towards Ira, she found that he still hadn't moved.

Kienza observed him regretfully. But there was nothing she could do.

Fire seethed around them. She squeezed the young girl tightly as she shook in her arms, held her very close, whispered in her ear, and left the smouldering village behind.

Rathen spun quicker than the others at the grievous wail that burst into the night air, his heart swollen in his throat with immediate, unshakable foreboding. But while the ring of steel over lockets followed in that same endless instant, defence was the furthest thing from his mind.

He was on his knees and stealing Aria from Kienza's arms before she could grant him even a glance of reassurance, and neither had the others in their startlement yet lowered their weapons. "It's all right," he murmured soothingly in her ear, over and over, stroking her tangled curls while she sobbed and clung tightly to his shirt, "I'm here, little one, everything's fine now. Everything's fine." But the eyes he turned up to Kienza were fierce, and she met them with shame, mingling with that same severity. And sorrow.

His jaw tightened, and he held Aria even closer.

"What's happened?" Garon asked, sheathing his sword beside Petra while Eyila and Anthis both loosened their stance, and the latter returned his dagger to the scabbard concealed in his waistband. But though Kienza rose and stepped back from the pair, she was slow to regard them. Aria sputtered nonsensical words of relief between hyperventilation.

"Redgrove was attacked," she said at last, her eyes dragging heavily from the distressed little girl and the desperately furious gaze of her father as he discovered the swollen red mark across the side of her face. "By bandits. The village suffered the death of an afflicted mage a week ago; everyone was tense, their spirits frayed. The bandits knew they would easily give in to panic. They were right."

"I--ra s-save--tried to s-save m-me..."

Rathen hushed her and pulled her close again, looking to Kienza for confirmation instead. She nodded solemnly. His gaze shifted away.

"I was too late... Rathen...I'm sor--"

"Aria," he looked down at her, turning her tear-streaked face up to his to stare intently into her eyes, "you're all right, aren't you? You're okay?" She nodded but he didn't seem to notice, already engrossed in analysing the mark across her eye and temple that was certain to become a terrible black-blue bruise. "What happened?" She tried to explain through hiccups, but he had already stopped listening. He shifted and held her at arm's length, discovering the small cuts across her arms and hands from a fall, then turned her around and continued to look her over. Finding nothing more, he snatched her back into a tight embrace, whispering promises as she buried her face back into his chest that he would never let her out of his sight again.

Everyone else watched in silence as Kienza returned and enveloped them both in her arms. Middle of the road or not, no one was inclined to interrupt.

The sorceress spoke words too quietly for the rest to hear, and after Rathen gave a reluctant nod, she rose and turned back to the others, father and daughter following soon after. She smiled fondly, but it didn't come without effort, and she gestured for them all to gather.

The stars were suddenly extinguished, the night fell darker, the broad sky was replaced by the underside of a canopy, the ground was uneven, and a nauseous lurch invaded their heads and stomachs. Only Aria and Rathen were too preoccupied to notice.

"You can make camp here," she told them as they gathered their bearings. "I'm sorry to impede your travel but..." she looked towards Aria, and no one needed nor asked for explanation. Not even Garon appeared put out.

Her eyes hardened into steel as she watched Rathen's unending embrace, as though he thought he could reverse her experience if he held her tightly enough, erase her pain and terror. The guilt at arriving too late weighed heavily on her own heart. "These are not the first bandits to take advantage of such tension," she said with a softness that belied her fury. "With every disruption by mages or magic, the risk of such an assault rises, and it's happening all across the country. Security can only increase so much, and with people already frightened, such curs find little resistance..."

She turned away and circled around the curiously flat forest clearing, peering into the darkness and pulling their attention away from Rathen as she went. She stopped when they had their backs to the pair, and though he could still see and hear her, she knew he would try to ignore what weighty material she had to impart. But she didn't attempt to catch his eye. She also knew he would listen despite himself. "Dolunokh," she began purposefully, "is barely recognisable. The country has undergone mass evacuation, but more have died than been able to escape, and being at the concentration point, there are few places left for them to turn. Voiland, Hin'ua and Ithen have been almost obliterated; half the land has collapsed and crumbled as though the earth was a rotten apple, and those chasms have critically invaded both Kasire and Ivaea, aggravating tensions. They're blaming each other for the destruction and there are mages on both sides trying to work out how to increase the damage over the border. And among those forming of their own accord, those great gaping rifts are stretching their way down here."

"But Khry's Glory has been destroyed," Anthis reminded her dubiously, "imploded, with the holes in the walls seared shut. The magic shouldn't still be accumulating, should it?"

"The mage in Trinn exacerbated the situation in Fendale," Garon reminded him in turn. "It's possible that every such afflicted mage has some impact on the magic."

"It would seem that both of you are right. And while that magic is *not* still accumulating, it *is* now far more concentrated." She gestured around to the quiet forest. "The situation may not be quite so dire here as it is to the north, but Turunda is not untouched. There are chasms, you have seen them, and they are growing worse; countless settlements have been abandoned or formally evacuated, putting greater strain on those still standing to try to accommodate those they can, and just the *mention* of the severity over the borders is enough to incite a panic. Their assumptions of the magic's source have upset the populace without exception and created tension enough between them and the Order that factions have arisen on both sides, all of whom are prepared to take extreme measures against the other.

"Then there are the deep woods - kvistdjur are lamenting in a bid to send the trees to sleep, stendjur are rampaging, trying to close the chasms that cut through their homes with landslides and quakes, and uncountable birds and beasts are fleeing as far as they can. Seeds are not being scattered, plants are not being pollinated, and forests are not so...potently fertilised. Domesticated animals may be unable to follow them, but their distress is affecting the quantity and quality of the produce they're kept for."

"If you're trying to stress the gravity of our task, I assure you there's no need."

Kienza considered Garon for a moment. Then her eyes flicked towards Eyila. "The tribes are also affected. A few are even interpreting the physical effects as demonstrations of power by the earth and fire gods, and while some such aligned and distant tribes are ceasing their attacks under 'divine intervention', others are reading it as a sign of divine *encouragement*."

"How do they know when it's a god and when it's magic?" Aria's small and shaken voice rose from the back, where her father appeared focused upon cleaning her wounds despite the sickly pallor that Kienza had watched invade him as she spoke.

"They don't," she replied regretfully. "That's the problem."

"Those *disconnected* from the gods don't." All eyes fell upon Eyila, whose own were glacial, and shifted in discomfort. "Those that live too close to your cities, who have forgotten reverence and humility in the face of trade and material possessions. *They* are the ones who cannot distinguish the earth's fury from tripping over a stone." Her hand rose to the oryx horn amulet that hung about her neck, and they realised her tone was of sadness rather than anger. "We are not all so blind."

Kienza smiled humbly and inclined her head. "I apologise, my dear, I meant no offence to your tribe, and your own confidence in the matter is something to be envied, I'm sure. My point is: you're going to have a hard time reaching most of the afflicted sites. Never mind the fact that they'll be under observation, the routes themselves will be at times untraversable, and supplies short in most towns and cities."

"We've been managing, and avoiding towns and the main roads wherever possible."

"Which," her dark, sleek eyebrows rose thoughtfully, "might be a mistake. Things are chaotic the country over right now - no one will notice you. And it might be in your interest; with so many evacuees from so many directions, they're melting pots of information."

"We've not had much luck so far."

"Because, Inquisitor, you're relying on the things your contacts have deemed significant enough to collect and share. Use your *own* ears - the more, the better."

"What about Eyila?" Petra asked with concern, but the tribal girl straightened beside her and looked across them all with almost belligerent resolve.

"I do not want to enter your cities."

"That's probably for the best," Kienza sighed. "Nothing would draw attention like bronze skin and snow-white hair."

"But we can't keep leaving her outside. Could she not be disguised?"

"She would have to either be fully covered, which would be suspicious in the summer, or her skin darkened, which would mark her out as..." she smiled bitterly, "*different*. Xenophobia is popular at the moment."

"Could magic not--"

The dull thud of a foot stamping indignantly against dirt turned all their attention. Eyila all but glowered. "I said I do not want to enter your cities! I will not taint my culture, and I will not hide my skin! With magic or anything else!" Though she pulled the oversized cloak tighter about her small, cold frame as she said so.

Garon began to object to her logic, but Kienza silenced him with a sharp gesture. She stepped towards her, dark eyes narrowed thoughtfully, but the girl didn't shrink away. An all-seeing gaze gripped her, her soul read through her eyes, and the others watched as she straightened in defiance, laying bare her every thought and emotion where the others had fidgeted in discomfort and secrecy.

After a long, silent moment, Kienza smiled with satisfaction. "Yes. Something to be envied, indeed."

A flicker of bewilderment passed briefly over Eyila's unpainted features, but a smile shortly slipped into place, and she bowed her head. Kienza returned it, to everyone's surprise, with the wind tribe's own courtesy, sending the briefest waft of breeze from the tips of her fingers as she swept them sharply away from her forehead. "Saya'a lo toa."

The girl suddenly paled, and her eyes darted away.

Anthis noticed but said nothing.

The sorceress stepped back and looked across them all, certainly evaluating some conclusion or another, and when she spoke, Rathen, who was indeed still listening despite himself, couldn't decide if she sounded more curious or determining. "What do you intend to do?"

"We're heading south," Garon declared formally. "There are a few places in the Korovor Woodlands to check out."

"You're moving on?" Her gaze slipped onto Rathen at the back, who was still focused upon Aria and outwardly ignoring the conversation. "I see..." She returned to the others. "There are a handful; Korovor and the Eswolds are among the worst affected areas of the country. There are untold numbers of elven ruins hidden in those forests, and the concentration of the magnetism has drawn a great deal of power into them."

"It's no wonder the wildlife is so upset."

"Indeed, Mister Karth, indeed. And so I urge you all to be careful."

And then, all too easily, she moved away to join Rathen and Aria at the back, clearly if abruptly finished with her wisdom and without any intention of providing more detailed advice.

She knelt beside them, embraced them once more, but just as she was about to speak, they both interrupted in protest.

"Do you *have* to leave?" Aria's puffy blue-grey eyes glinted in the finest stream of moonlight, and Kienza felt her heart grow heavy. It all but dropped into her stomach when she found the same glimmer in Rathen's. She hesitated, then smiled fondly.

"No, sweetheart, I really don't."

Chapter 10

Aria was asleep within minutes. Listless, overwhelmed, and in the safest place the girl could imagine, she'd curled up beside her father beneath the shadow of a chestnut tree while the others had set up camp, her doll clutched tightly in her arms, and almost immediately succumbed to exhaustion.

Kienza set the child's bag down among the roots and smiled at the notched wooden sword Rathen turned over in his hands. But her perfect lips drew into a pout when she saw the sorrow in his eyes. "It's been on her hip the whole time."

The slightest breath of a chuckle slipped out as he nodded, but his dismal expression remained stubbornly unbroken. Then it seemed to grow even worse. "The whole time. Even...?"

Kienza nodded sadly and settled gracefully down beside him. "She must've looked so--"

"I can imagine how she looked clearly enough."

She bit her lip as he tossed the sword aside and buried his face in his knees, then looked up again a moment later in exasperation. She knew he was aware of her analytical gaze, and that he didn't like it, but rather than tell her to stop, he simply turned his head away to watch Aria sleep. The campfire slowly bloomed into life, revealing the constant knotting of his jaw. But she could have read him even had they been sitting in abyssal darkness. He was aching, distressed, and he was surprised by it, but he was making no effort to even consider the matter let alone face it. He pushed it away without even a glance, throwing his attention onto Aria instead.

Finally, her gaze slipped after his, and they both listened to the sound of her deep, rhythmic breathing, waiting for the giggle that always accompanied her sleep. It didn't come.

"Where did you rush off to before?" Rathen looked towards her, his eyes dark and resigned. "Weren't you supposed to be dealing with the source?"

"I still am, so to speak."

He bared his teeth in frustration, but shoved it aside. "Did I *not* destroy Khry's Glory?"

"No, you did," she smiled defusingly, "and there were things I had to see to regarding that very matter. The magic is still spreading out and magical interference is exacerbating it, and there are even *more* cracks dividing this already valley-riddled country - but you *have* cut off the source."

"And mages?" He surveyed the camp but found only Anthis sat beside the young fire, peering, as always, through scrolls and notebooks. "What about its influence on *them?*"

"It is still having an effect," she replied regretfully, following his gaze to find Eyila nowhere in sight, no doubt meditating while the duelist and inquisitor set to their usual if presently needless scouting. "And it may be worse since you've unleashed the magic. A flurry escaped each time the door was opened, but when you destroyed the place, a great torrent was freed as it compressed, until the walls drew together just enough to seal the gaps and take what remained with its own obliteration.

"Mages tormented by the loose, microscopic spell chains were initially being pulled towards Dolunokh - though they would never have reached it from here before its maddening influence got the better of them. But now that Khryu'vahz has been destroyed, rather than hypnotically following the trail back to the magic's source, they're gathering at affected sites instead, the lakes of magic, the dead ends. Places like Fendale hold traces of the lure, the beauty, even if it seems inappropriate. And the increased concentration is speeding their...breakdowns."

"But *why* is it affecting them?" He suddenly snapped. "And why only specific people?"

She hesitated. "I've not had the chance to look into it. It has something to do with blood, that's all I know so far."

He grunted and lowered his chin to his knees. The forest fell quiet but for Aria's deep breathing, the crackle of fire and the occasional rustle of parchment.

"I can't get the Zi'veyn to work."

She remained silent for a while. Finally, with a heavy nod, she shuffled up against him. "I figured. Otherwise Fendale wouldn't have been left in such a state. I know what you want, my love, but I can't help you. I can't find anything wrong with it, and the spell is so tangled... Oh, please don't look at me like that. Even if I could work it out it would take me just as long as it would you, with the added trouble of having to explain it all. You're the one who has to use it, so *you* must understand it right from its roots, and the only way to do that is to be the one to unravel it."

"Weeks I've spent poring over it. It should have worked... I've been looking inside and out of the accursed thing for any cracks or fractures I've missed but..." He shook his head in aggravation and ground the heels of his hands into his eyes. "I'm in over my head, Kienza. I can't do this."

"You can--"

"I *can't*."

"You *must*."

His eyes flared, and she matched his fury with affection.

"I am sorry, my love, but it's a truth. You are hunted, this is also true, but the fact remains that no one else has the freedom to pursue it, nor the blood to achieve it." She took his chin in her slender fingers and forced him to face her again. "You know this. And you know why you have to."

He snatched his chin free. "Don't manipulate me."

She snatched him back, her eyes suddenly cold. "I could say the same to you. We both know it doesn't matter what you say because you *will* keep working at it, and you will do it for *her*. Don't try to make me give you the answers to make your life easier when this is *all* you have to do!"

"And just what is it *you* have to do?!"

"Anything I must."

He swatted her hand away with a toothy snarl and stared off into the dark forest. She let him. They said nothing for some time. Rathen brooded; Kienza waited. Then he spoke, flat and irritated but with an effort to rein in his temper. "Do you have any advice at all? *Anything?*" He looked back around as she moved. He allowed her to take his hands in hers and her intense, heartfelt gaze to penetrate him, and though she said nothing for another long moment, she settled the flux of his tensions. And in place of his anger came a flood of something far worse.

She smiled sadly and brushed away the tear that rolled down his cheek. "Let yourself grieve."

The roll of the sluggish river made barely a gurgle in the thick, warm air. And yet the steady footfalls were still almost lost in the silence. Soft and quiet, expertly light even across the stark surface of the rock shelf - so light, in fact, that it could have earned a swift and paranoid knife across the throat. Fortunately, Garon patrolled so relentlessly that she'd come to recognise his gait.

Without even a glance towards her blades, though thankful she hadn't undressed for the shallow water after all, Petra continued ringing the water out from her hair before looking up at last from the river's edge. "We're safe," she said wearily, watching him walk by at a slow, observant pace. "Kienza wouldn't have brought us here otherwise."

"I know."

Her eyebrow twitched. She turned away to splash the tepid water across her face. "Of course you do. You're just so used to being on the job that you've forgotten how to stand still."

"In the same way you've forgotten how to be pleasant?"

She spun back around in surprise, her knee almost slipping into the river from the edge of the rocks, and stared at him as he came to a stop several paces away to stare off into the trees on the opposite bank. "...Was that a joke? Or an insult?" She scoffed when he didn't respond. "It's an improvement either way. Some attempt at colour and creativity. I am surprised."

He watched her from the corner of his eye as she rose to her feet, and saw, not for the first time, the brutal burns that wrapped around most of her right arm. She pulled her sleeves down over them, her asymmetrical blouse long since traded for something nondescript, and gathered her things.

"Water's all yours."

"I'm not here for it."

She frowned in suspicion as she pulled herself effortlessly up onto the shelf beside him and readjusted the bola at the back of her cinch. "Then what *are* you here for?"

He said nothing.

She rolled her eyes and walked away.

"Petra."

She paused and glanced expectantly over her shoulder, but turned fully when she noticed how slowly he turned towards her. His usual mantle of rigid formality had dropped - she wasn't sure it had even been there when he'd arrived. Instead, there was a discomfort about him. It held her attention, and a touch more patience slipped in with curiosity and a flash of foolish hope as she waited to discover whatever it was he appeared so hesitant to say.

"I need your help," he said at last, at which she deflated. "With Rathen. I have no experience with personal loss..."

"Then it *was* his father he left Aria with?"

He nodded. "They didn't have a good relationship--"

"It doesn't matter, he's hurt. It's clear enough to anyone..."

He watched her slender hand reach absently for her locket, then noted the disturbance in her eyes as she stared into space. He rolled his shoulder. "Make sure he doesn't get distracted. Don't look at me like that, I'm not being callous."

"It certainly sounds like it, but I understand. It's easy to..." She smiled meekly as she fiddled with the silver oval. "Easy to get lost in it..."

"Not without good reason." He forced his eyes back over the river. "How's Eyila?"

"She's coping."

"You're protective over her. Rarely away from her side."

"She's young. And she's been through more than any of us can imagine." She looked at him sideways, her eyes slight, but her tongue was provoked more by curiosity than a poor temper. "Why? Concerned for another tag-along?"

"She's been through a lot."

Petra stared for another moment. She didn't miss the fact that he made no effort to correct her. And neither did he. But pride prevented him from amending it. Then he thought better of it.

"Rathen will be fine," Petra assured him with a slight edge to her voice before he was able. "He doesn't need me or any of the rest of us looking after him. He has Aria for that. And Kienza's here, too." She looked to his shoulder, which he rolled again a moment later. The injury was still plaguing him. "How is it? Your arm, I mean."

He stilled and straightened, staring into the darkness. "It's still there."

"Another joke."

"It isn't slowing me down."

"No, to be honest I've noticed that much. But is it...getting any better?"

He looked down without thought and watched his fingers flex. He appeared to try to hide it around his side, but Petra could see it clearly enough to know there was no change. Still only his ring and smallest finger moved. But she had been aware of that for some time. He tested his fingers often, absently and when he thought no one was looking, but she rarely missed it, nor the lack of improvement. But she'd hoped that perhaps, despite her diligence, a detail had slipped by. If nerve damage could be overcome at all.

He dropped his hand and looked back up towards the trees. His expression was void. "It's fine."

"You could ask--"

"It's fine."

Her lips pursed at his sharp and insistent look. "It's actually difficult to comprehend just how stubborn and difficult you are."

He sighed wearily. "It isn't getting in my way," he assured her again, his stiff posture slackening, "and Kienza has more important things to do than play nurse."

"That sounds familiar."

"It's the truth, and you know it. It isn't getting in my way. I'm fine."

"Ooh, I *almost* believed you that time. Go on, try again, once more..."

He gave her a flat, unamused stare, but she only smiled and shook her head. It didn't appear to be sarcastic.

"If you're sure," she sighed, still plainly unconvinced, and rung the remaining water from her dulling red hair which was dampening her shoulders. "I'm going to..."

He nodded as she gestured away towards camp. "Yes. I'll--"

"Patrol," she smiled. "I know. Thank you."

He frowned as she turned away. "For what?"

"Always being vigilant."

"*That* sounds familiar."

"Which makes it no less relevant." She flashed him a smile and started on her way.

Garon watched her walk off into the forest, slipping gracefully between the trees, her blades flashing in the moonlight before she was swallowed by the night.

He rolled his shoulder, clenched his fist, and wondered just exactly what he was trying to do to himself.

"*Bah!*"

Anthis forced his racing heart into submission, then looked urgently down to the parchments in search of rips and tears from his suddenly tightened grip. There were only crumpled creases, which he regarded with defeat, and looked up to glare at whomever had startled him. But when he found himself staring into shockingly pale blue eyes set within a skin that appeared to shimmer gold in the firelight, he had to subdue his heart again.

"Sorry," Eyila smiled timidly as his gaze darted away. "I didn't mean to frighten you."

"No, no, no it's fine, it's fine. Really."

"I'm glad. I haven't had the chance to speak with you since you returned."

"Oh, y-you wanted to speak to me?" He was unaware of the childish grin pulling at the edges of his lips.

"Of course. I'm glad you're well."

"Oh, thank you...and the same to you."

She smiled peculiarly - pleased, but with a hint of unreadable thought. It was an expression unique to her, and while it had unsettled the others at first, he'd found it intriguing. Her eyes travelled down to the scrolls in his hands, and she shuffled closer to peer at the writings. He stiffened.

"Can you get the Zi'veyn to work?"

"M-me? No, *I* can't, I'm not--"

"I meant with your knowledge of the elves." She looked back up, stopping his heart, hope brimming in her eyes. "Your books - your research. Rathen believes you can help him."

"Oh, you...you spoke to him already?"

"Of course. Petra isn't quite so...hateful towards him. She seems to want to keep me away from you. But, clearly, she can't be with me *all* the time." Her grin turned impish. His smile renewed at the sight of it, and enthusiasm quickly returned to brighten her incredible eyes. Which, he noticed, appeared a little red. It was probably the firelight. "So can you? Help him?"

"Uh, well I mean, I'll do the best I can, of course, but how much help I'll actually be is another...matter..."

"You will be of much more help than you think. I have no doubt that Rathen will succeed. There's...something about him..."

The butterflies in his stomach choked and died. "Oh?"

"Potential. Or something more... Promise, perhaps. Or destiny."

He nodded. His smile was tight, teeth hidden behind his lips.

"He is our world's only hope."

"Yes. He does seem to be, doesn't he?"

The two fell quiet. Anthis continued staring at the parchments, reading the same few words his attention would permit him over and over again while she pondered the script she couldn't possibly decipher. Then her eyes travelled back up to him, and she considered him in silence for a while. "I liked the beard," she said finally, raising her finger to touch his shaven cheek. He flinched immediately and his skin turned rose. Fortunately, the firelight masked it. "I'm sorry," she chuckled, "I didn't mean to startle you - *again*. You're very jumpy, you know."

"N-no, no--I mean, yes, I am. I suppose so." He chuckled disparagingly before sighing in defeat, shaking his head at his own foolishness. But just as he finally found the courage to set his parchments down and for once try to have a normal conversation with her, to ask her the questions he'd suppressed first out of respect for her culture, then out of consideration for her loss, and now out of nothing but embarrassment, he was interrupted by a brusque voice from the trees.

The two looked up at the girl's name to see Petra emerge from the forest, her sharp gaze fixed entirely upon Eyila. But though her eyes didn't once graze Anthis, contempt encircled her like a tornado and dragged only him inside. "Would you help me fill the waterskins?"

Politely, Eyila smiled and nodded. But she was not blind, and as she rose and Petra turned away to collect them, Eyila flashed him a smile that stopped his heart once again and let in another foolish flutter of butterflies.

He watched her leave, three of the six waterskins in her arms, a number the duelist could easily have managed by herself, and sighed so heavily that his breath stoked the flames.

Then his eyes slipped resentfully onto Rathen, who sat stroking Aria's hair and staring far beyond the edges of the nameless forest. "Promise, huh?" He mumbled to himself. Another weary sigh slipped out. He couldn't fault the observation, as much as he tried, but neither could he help the bitterness.

Anthis turned back to his work before jealousy's hook could dig in too deep.

But as he squeaked in surprise and further crumpled his parchments, he found himself this time staring into the even sharper, frightfully keen emerald eyes of Kienza.

"I liked the beard too."

He grumbled. "You were listening?"

"Should I not have been?" The sylvan sorceress peered down at the parchments while he mumbled in abashed irritation, scrutinising the words with untold proficiency. Then her attention slipped down to the notebook that lay open at his feet. "How are you progressing, my dear historian?"

"I don't know..."

"A little bit distracted?"

"What?"

"Your voice rose too high, it's a dead giveaway."

He shook his head at her frustratingly knowing smile and once again attempted to find some distraction in his work. "Honestly, I don't have a clue what you're talking about."

"All right, all right, I'll play along." She propped her chin upon her hand and began quite openly to watch him. He shifted under her gaze, but she didn't relent. "So how does it feel?"

"What?"

"Being right. Recovering the Zi'veyn - though you were surely the only one in your field who could have done it."

It was subtle, but she didn't miss the curl of his lip. "You mean *Rathen* recovered it."

"Uh, no," she frowned, "I mean *you*. You think he would have gotten *anywhere* without your guidance? The Zi'veyn was your suggestion, they were your leads, your research - *you* found it. It may not have been where you thought it would be, but would you have tried to sail the Roquna at all if not for everything that led you to insist on Kasire?"

"But if not for Rathen, we would never have gotten to Khryu'vahz at all. Or found the elves."

"In both cases, he only opened the door." Her eyes narrowed. "And don't think that once you get it working you'll have outlived your usefulness. Garon may have the map, but you have the locations. Without your expertise, they'll be working with gossip, and they'll never manage to quiet the magic like that. There are far more arcanised ruins in the wilds than any of them realise. *You* know this well enough."

"I suppose..."

"You will see this through with him."

Finally, he put down the scrolls and turned towards her with guarded interest. "Why are you saying this?"

"Because," she replied quite easily, "I can see your jealousy in him, and I believe there is no reason for it. He isn't one to be envied by *you*. Elven blood or not. You've seen what it's done to him, and you can't imagine the pressure he endured in the Order from the elders who sensed something different within him. Don't envy him that."

"What's he told you?"

She raised a languid hand. "Absolutely nothing, Mister Karth--sorry, *Anthis*. But to my eyes, you are simply an open book. And you shouldn't let yourself be intimidated by Petra, either."

"I'm not intimid--"

"Open book. Now, I need you to do something for me."

His blonde eyebrows rose. "Me?"

"You. As I said, you will see this matter through together. And so I want you to watch him. Look for anything...different."

"Different?"

"Any changes. Magic, bearing, behaviour, enthusiasm - nothing is too small."

A dubious frown marred his young face. "Why? What are you concerned about?" His misgivings grew when she glanced towards Rathen and dropped her voice a shade lower.

"The elves did something to him, didn't they? So he could control his transformations - that's how he was able to subdue it in Khryu'vahz, wasn't it?"

"He did, though it wasn't a quick adjustment...why? What's worrying you?"

"Having met them for yourself, do you trust the elves?"

'No.' But he didn't answer right away. He gathered his thoughts, recalled all the details he could from that incredible encounter upon the mist-shrouded island, and considered them from every angle. Because it seemed that his answer mattered.

But he came to the same conclusion. "No, I don't."

"Though this Eizariin fellow is an exception."

"He's unlike the rest."

"I'll take your word for it. But he was not a part of...whatever it was they did to Rathen, was he?"

"No..."

"Which, by the simplest process of elimination in history, means that no one we deem trustworthy was present while it was happening."

"Kienza, what did they do to him? Why are you concerned? What do you know?"

"Nothing, at this point. But he feels different to me. His magic."

Anthis's alarm tamed at a thought. "The cuff, that band around his arm - it's a do'osos; the elves used to put them on their children. He said his mother gave it to him when he was young...to aid his human constitution, they said, but the spell inside was degrading, so they repaired it - perhaps it's just doing a better job keeping his magic in check."

She pursed her lips. "Perhaps..."

Her thoughtfulness subdued him, and he found himself able to offer a smile of reassurance. "I will watch him, of course."

She smiled back, her veiled ponderings abandoned, and patted him on the head. "I knew you would. Now, stop getting distracted and get back to work. There is a lot riding on you."

"You distracted *me*."

"You could have told me to go away. I wouldn't have listened, but you could have tried." She smiled fondly, an affection that always roused the same in return, and rose to her feet. But though she turned to rejoin Rathen, who now slumbered against the tree trunk, exhausted by the grief she'd unleashed, she paused.

"I have great confidence in you, Anthis Karth. Do not let me down."

Her words, though barely above a whisper, rung in his ears like a gong.

Chapter 11

By Rathen's estimate, it must have been only a little past six when his eyelids flickered open. The morning sun, though on its way up, hadn't yet found its way through the rolling slopes or thick, blooming canopy. And so the camp, set in a depression between the broad trunks of chestnuts, was still blanketed in blue-tinged shadow and the sparse clusters of grass carpeted in dew.

But the first thing to rattle his abstract awareness was not the damp, a chill, or the smell of the earth, but a heavy numbness in his arm. He grumbled, shifting to find some feeling, but quickly discovered not a root at fault, but the small, huddled shape of Aria lying right up alongside him, clinging to his arm with a grip so powerful that not even sleep seemed able to loosen it.

With one look at her peaceful little face, his bloodless limb was forgotten. He smiled softly, brushing the curls from her cheek, and a sigh drifted free at the release of the immense weight that had haunted him like a spectre for well over a month.

But another weight had thundered down in its place, a keening that stung his eyes, a loss he was surprised to feel any strike from at all. A weight he had faced, at Kienza's behest, and forced now into the deepest recesses of his mind.

With effort, he focused acutely on the rise and fall of her chest as she slept, the breath that warmed his arm - on that which was his sole reason. For whom his neglectful father had given his life.

But when a childish giggle bubbled through the air, one that had *not* come from Aria, he remembered at last what had roused him in the first place.

He sat bolt upright, sleep forgotten and immediately alert, and at the sound of a harsh, vulgar voice and an irritated snort, he discovered Eyila crouching behind a thick tree trunk eight paces away. But the girl couldn't have made those sounds, and after pulling himself out of Aria's iron grip, blustered to his feet and up beside her to find himself staring into the faces of five horses of various shades, tusks and patterns being clambered over by five children.

Five very pale, very scraggly, very large-eyed children.

Rathen's shoulders dropped as he groaned. "Oh good..."

"What *are* they?" Eyila whispered, peering around the edge of the tree at the child hanging upside down beneath a mottled grey, his bare feet in the stirrups, while another lounged on the neck of the dun, and another poked at the sharp points of the bay's perfectly straight tusks drawn forwards in threat. And though he couldn't see Eyila's eyes, he certainly heard her fascination, even if it was restrained by some small degree of caution.

He frowned for a moment in bafflement at her question, but quickly recalled the creatures' own intrigue at their last encounter at the edge of the Ivaean desert. "Of course...there are none in the desert... They're ditchlings--"

"Arkhamas!"

"For the love of--" He stepped out from behind the tree at the *Arkhamas'* loud and collective protest to stand over them with a shadow of disapproval, as though they truly were little more than mischievous children. "What are you doing here?"

"Checking in," the one poking at the tusks replied offhandedly, his keen stare unmoving from the ivory projections.

"'Checking in'?"

The boy that had been braiding the tan's mane slipped easily from its saddle and hopped towards him on light, calloused feet. He scrutinised the three, as Garon had appeared at Rathen's side, with oversized silver-green eyes - eyes that didn't miss a thing.

He puffed and blew a knot of lichen-speckled hair from his face before jabbing a stout finger past them in Aria's direction. "Why'd you leave her with some old man to go on yer adventures?"

"Excuse me?"

"I told Pip," Aria's sleepy but urgent voice rose as she clambered to her feet to join them, woken by her father's escape, "it was to keep me safe!"

"Pip?" Rathen's eyebrows rose higher as the ditchling stepped forwards and embraced her. He managed to restrain the impulse to snatch her away from him.

She was released soon enough, and the boy offered her a big, toothy grin. "Glad you're okay. We searched that village but we couldn't find no trace of you. But we did find--" He stopped suddenly, and all five looked towards Rathen in a very peculiar way. Until the lichen-haired imp glared at him in suspicion. "And we ain't seen sight nor sound nor smell of you buggers since just afore you booted her off. Where'd you go, huh? You better not 'ave been fixing up other places, 'cause you promised--"

"We've not fixed anything," Anthis assured them, suddenly among the group, "we haven't...gotten quite that far yet."

"Then just *where* have you *been?*"

"We--"

"We've been working on it," Rathen interrupted, agitated by the wild children's accusations so early in the morning, and further by the headache that came with such confusion. "And when we get somewhere, I have no doubt at all that you'll know about it. So don't worry your muddy little heads about it and leave us be."

The boy grunted. He didn't look around as his comrade who'd been hanging beneath the irritated grey dropped heavily upon his head. Instead, he wagged his finger across Garon, Eyila and Petra, who had also joined them without announcement, and only then did Rathen notice that Kienza was, once again, nowhere at all to be found. "You three 'ave been pottering about and doin' nothing at all of use for weeks. We seen you. But--oh, yeah, first of all, why's there a statue with you? And why and how's she movin'? And can they all do that?"

Eyila continued to stare, still half-hidden behind the tree at Rathen's side, with a distinctly familiar and dangerous curiosity in her eyes. Rathen glanced instinctively towards Anthis just in time to see his own gaze flick away. He frowned. For the briefest moment, he was sure that there was some trace of spite in his studious green eyes, but it was so fleeting and so unmerited that he decided that he'd surely imagined it.

"She's not a statue," he replied, brushing it off, "this is Eyila. She's from a wind tribe in the desert--"

"She's..." With more caution than any would have thought possible from such bold and impulsive creatures, the ditchling stepped forwards, raised a clay-painted hand and reached out to poke her bare arm. She didn't flinch or shrink away; his own wariness seemed to soothe her. Eyila stepped out from behind the thick old trunk and knelt with very open interest. The ditchling pursed his lips, and the others behind him, still entertaining themselves with the stoic beasts, glanced up with the same conclusion. "...'Intriguing' is the word, I reckon."

Then his great eyes snapped back onto Rathen and he straightened with a chillingly serious demeanour. The others, too, forgot their frivolity and hurried forwards to join him. "The forests are broked," he declared with more than a hint of accusation. "We're losing our homes - some have been swallowed by mouths we didn't know the ground had! And it ain't just the Lady doing it out of anger! She's been up and moving about like she's following a wasp, and her sisters are no better. Mostly we found 'em again, but not everyone's been so lucky. Some have fallen asleep forever without being nowhere near her!"

"But I thought the Lady looked after your dreams when you went to sleep," said Aria, timidly. "What will happen to them without her?" Beyond brief, grievous looks, the ditchlings didn't respond. Her little brow knitted in regret.

"Where?"

They each looked to Garon and puckered their lips in thought, then peered for a distracted moment at the white hammer insignia on the hilt of his sword before answering. "Ziili and Big Swing--oh, yeah, you call it 'Ellen's Drop', don'tcha? Ziili and Ellen's Drop. Oh and the High Dells, but that's harpy terr'try and no busyness of ours - fishally speaking."

"How is it affecting them?"

"Pff, *who cares?*" A girl with a delicately constructed crown of eggshells scoffed, and the others rolled their eyes with her. "Some've buggered off, which is good for us, but some've tried to drive us out of our setts so they can have the trees. It's made 'em even angrier, *that's* how it's affecting 'em. Good enough?"

"So your situation--"

"Still as good as having hungry ants in yer jimmies."

"...And that's--"

"Bad, yep."

"Harpies?" Eyila stepped forwards, frowning in concern, and five pairs of silver-green eyes immediately crashed onto her at the sound of her musical voice. "Ayuia? What is your business with them?"

The boy cocked his head. "Ayweeuh? Ayweeuh."

"*Ayweeeeeeuhhhh.*" The other voices chimed in.

The boy grinned. "That's a fun noise. And the harpies think we've got summit to do with all the hocus pocus going on, or that the Lady does, that she's ruining their nests by making other places more pretty, but that's a load of horse dung 'cause why would she do that unless she was already mad?! We don't really know *what's* got in their heads, but they been swooping in and trying to drive us off like a wren on an ant. First it was only if their trees got broke or all weird and our sett was too close to their nests, so they figured it was the Lady or whatever, so they tried to shoo us off thinkin' the *Lady* would follow *us*, but then it excallated when we showed 'em where to stick it."

"We ain't gonna leave the Lady on their say so!" A leaf-haired boy declared with the utmost conviction. "Stupid turkeys!"

"Yeah yeah! But 'cause of that, now they attack us any time a feather falls out. We're just defending ourselfs."

"And that, mind you, is *as well as* hooman attacks," the lichen-speckled boy continued with even plainer accusation. "Your folks are *still* burning our homes and killing us. We ain't even stolen that much lately, we been good, keeping our distance. But it looks like it ain't good *enough*."

"These people--"

"Oooh," the boy shook his head and leaned in closer. "Sneaky buggers they are. They miss all our traps, like they saw us layin' 'em, and follow us without being seen. It's weird. Scary. We seen people like them around a lot, but they never were no trouble to us. Now they're searching for us, though, and it ain't no accident what they're doing neither. But we didn't do nothing to provoke 'em all of a sudden. And they ain't working with the harpies-ayweeuh either, 'cause they're burning *their* nests and plucking *their* bums just the same."

Rathen passed Garon a meaningful look; the inquisitor's jaw tightened.

The ditchlings' eyes narrowed. "You know who it is, then. Can you stop 'em?"

"No," Rathen replied assuredly, "we can't. We can't even get them off our *own* tail."

"So it *is* the same people. We thought so. 'Course they're easier to mess with when it's you they're after. I s'pose 'cause they ain't looking for *us*."

Mischievous grins suddenly swept across their faces. "We drew footsteps in the mud and scuffed over yours and led 'em to all our poop ditches!"

Aria giggled, and even Rathen had to stifle a smile. Garon, however, was as ever unamused. "How did they not see *your* footprints?"

They blinked back at him. "We hung from the trees. Duh."

"Of course... Well, we're grateful for the help."

"Too right you are. So?"

"...Thank you?"

"No, '*so*' how much longer is this gonna take?"

"It'll take as long as it takes," Rathen replied shortly. "Longer if you keep stopping us."

A dramatic offence grasped the horde, and even Aria shot him a glare of disapproval. "And after all we done for you! Fine, we'll let you on your way and we won't interfere no more if we see some suspinachus people following your tracks."

"No!" Aria hurried forwards and immediately the ditchlings' expressions became amicable. "We're sorry, we don't mean it like that. I for one like it when you come to visit, and I'm grateful for you checking up on me. I don't know who is following us, and definitely not why, but I think it's *very* important that they *don't*. So please keep getting rid of them for us, if it isn't too much trouble."

The boy, who still had yet to introduce himself, smiled broadly and nodded. "For you." But when he shot an openly mistrustful glance to the others behind her, she gave him the same look of disapproval she had given her father. His pale cheeks turned pink, but he didn't lower himself to an apology. "Come on you lot," he said, though they were already turning around and preparing to move out, "let's leave 'em be." He gave Aria another hug despite Rathen's close watch, informed her that 'Nug says hi', then turned around and dashed off into the forest with the others on silent, muddy feet, leaving the adults blinking after them while Aria waved cheerfully.

Still bristling at the brazen creatures' expectations, Rathen was the first to shake off the surprise and place his hand on Aria's shoulder. She beamed up at him. "Well done, little one."

"Yes, quite. Now we should leave." Garon stepped away and began gathering his blankets. "Where there are ditchlings, there are harpies."

"We've neither seen nor heard from them since we got back," Petra reminded him, following his lead.

"Even so, the ditchlings have apparently been watching us throughout, but only once Rathen returned did they bother to approach us. They sensed his magic the moment we first met them in Wrenroot, and it could very well be the same for harpies." He gathered the remaining bags and followed Rathen towards the horses. "I presume these are for us?"

"They are," Rathen replied, already lifting the little girl up into the saddle of the mottled grey whose nose she'd been stroking, and once they'd strapped down their belongings, they mounted - Eyila with a little trouble, as it turned out that she'd never actually seen a horse up close before - and steered their horses away from the grove beneath the old chestnut and off into the tighter beechwood.

"Daddy," Aria began thoughtfully, stroking the horse's mane in front of him.

"Yes, little one?"

She peered up and around at him. "Where *have* you all been?"

"But can you really trust someone who just appears and disappears like that? Who walks through any attempt at restraint? What could we do against her if she's setting you up? Who knows what she's up to, or who she's working with, or to what end?"

"I understand your concern, Taliel, and I intend to exercise caution, but it's...how can I explain this?" Salus sat up from the blankets, eyes filled with tumbling, glowing thoughts. "She's provided me with a solution I could only *dream* of. One that could *truly* protect the whole of Turunda from any outside threats, from invasion *or* influence."

"Well, it sounds to me like nonsense."

"Nonsense perhaps to anyone without the ability to achieve it." He smiled placatingly at her frown. "I mean that it was beyond even Erran's comprehension, and he's one of our strongest mages."

Taliel sighed and rolled onto her elbow, the thin summer sheet draping perfectly about her torso. "I just don't want you to be led by the nose. I understand your passion to protect the country, all of us here are led by the same thing. But...I don't understand how you intend to achieve it. You've been working on surveillance spells, they could be incredibly valuable--"

"And I'm not giving up on them--"

"But you would have to achieve those and so much more before you could *ever* do something like *move the country*, if you could even do it at all! Why can this elf not do it herself? Why is she baiting *you* to do it?"

"Evidently, Denek is not the only elf out there - who knows just how many are hiding? But after finding not a *trace* of them for centuries, *something* has happened to cause two to appear in the space of just as many months. And look at what Turunda is going through! Magic, invasions, foreign spies - even the Order has been affected by outside influence! They would never have rebelled if others hadn't done it first!" A fire burned in his mind, and his blue eyes, usually touched only by fury or by passion, were alight and coloured in the greatest shade of confidence. "The elves are still here, holed up somewhere out of sight and fearing for Turunda's safety, the safety of their home just as much as it is ours, but if they come out and try something like this themselves, every effort they've made to conceal their existence will be undone, and there *has* to be a reason that elves have kept themselves hidden for all this time!"

"But--"

"I have magic, Taliel - Denek helped me to awaken it, it's clearly important - *pivotal*, perhaps. But what if I killed him too soon? Liogan could well only be here to see his task through! You know it makes sense."

"It--"

"You--"

"*Salus.*" She sat up and grasped his hand, the covers slipping from her bare skin, and gripped him with an insistent stare. "Stop. I understand. You've clearly thought this through. But perhaps you should focus on these surveillance spells before you try anything else. Assuming it *is* possible, it will take time, and we will need more immediate preventions and remedies in the mean time." She smiled to soften the blow of her poignant reminder, which he returned, subdued.

"Yes," he sighed, dropping back to the covers, "I know, you're right of course. I haven't given up on them - but establishing the observation and feedback points are easy, I managed that days ago. But creating the link between them, keeping the image complete and stable as it moves from one to the other is...it's..." he clutched his fists in aggravation, as if he could catch the elusive words. He shortly gave up with a half-barked snarl. "It's *exasperating!* After conjuring that fire, this should be easy! But it just... Erran said that it was fury or survival instincts that fuelled it, that it was from my very core, that the elf in me overrode the need for signs and just made it happen. But if that's the case, what would fuel *this?* What would make *this* happen? Because not even desperation is working..."

Taliel lay back down and shuffled up beside him, draping a slender arm over his chest and kissing his unshaven cheek. "Perhaps," she began softly, resting her head upon his chest, "you're under-thinking it. What you did to Denek was to save your life, it was immediate, but it was also simple. I don't know anything about magic, but I would think that fire would spring from the basic instinct to inflict pain in order to repel the attacker. But a spell with the requirements of sustained observation and relaying that information to another specific location, that would take more thought, wouldn't it? After all, anyone can make fire and light a candle, but not just anyone can make...spectacles."

"...Hmm..." Taliel looked up at the crease of thought in his brow. "That's a good point. This isn't a base need for survival, it's much, much more... It's not 'pain', it's sustained 'observe and relay'... You know, you might be on to something..." He pulled her close and squeezed her. They both felt his heart begin to race. "Taliel...I have to tell you...these last few weeks...they've been challenging, physically, mentally...but...I haven't been struggling as much as I should have been. I..."

"Hush, Salus, you don't have to say it."

"Yes, I do. I need you to know how...important you are to me. More important than I thought *anyone* could be. *To* anyone. Your advice, your thoughts...your presence...you have no idea."

Her fingers pressed against his lips. "Salus. You don't need to say it."

He kissed them, then she withdrew. "No. But...I suppose I need to know that you're not just doing this because you think it's an order. I'm your superior but this--"

This time, her lips pressed against his. He pulled her close again, enjoying her warmth, and felt his anxiety begin to melt. The single, blissful moment lasted forever.

"Quiet your mind," she said softly as they finally parted. "Don't create issues to fret about. Yes, you are my superior, and yes, I do believe that offering you my company is important to the Arana and to Turunda. But that is *not* why I am here with you."

"...Why, then?"

She grinned. "Because."

"...Because? That's all you're going to give me?"

"It is. Because I can already see by your smile that it's enough." She kissed him again, but this time it was all too brief. "I had better leave."

"Must you?"

"I must. Orders." She slipped out of the bed, brushed by the shaft of morning light that broke through the curtains, and began gathering her clothes from various locations about the room. "*Your* orders, in fact."

"Curses! What have I done to myself?"

Taliel flashed him a grin. He watched her as she moved, tracing her curves with his eyes. As she reached up high, he appreciated her narrow, limber waist and humble chest; reaching low, her firm rear and sleek legs, their strength belied by their slenderness. He smiled, until at last they too were covered.

"Look after yourself while I'm gone," she said as she turned around to face him, fully clothed and perfectly collected. "Don't you dare just run off to the office every morning, leaving your stomach to rumble until the sun sets. *Eat.* Keep up your strength."

He smiled from the bed. "Is that an order?"

"As a matter of fact, it is." She leaned across the sheets and kissed him, and he pulled her in closer before she could begin to leave. Only as his heart began to race did he release her, knowing that if he didn't do it then, he wouldn't do it at all.

She smiled softly as she walked gracefully towards the door. "Breakfast."

He nodded. "Breakfast."

And then she was gone.

He stared at the door, lost in thought for what felt like an age, though it couldn't have been longer than a minute before he finally found the mind to leave behind the night's bliss and turn towards the day's matters. But it didn't come as a trial; he was clothed and out of the door in no time, cutting across the wooded estate gardens from his comparatively small private home towards the grand Arana House, where his office waited on the third and uppermost floor. He caught a servant in the foyer along his way with a request to send something up. Because he was in a good mood. His thoughts were clear, his ambitions were plain, and he was filled with a crisp, focused determination to seize them. It was remarkable what a good night's sleep could do, and even more when Taliel exhausted him into it. It was the first he'd had in days, and that morning, that bright, fresh morning, he knew that whatever lay ahead of him would be no trouble. Anything that was thrown his way, he could handle.

Even the spell gave him a spark of hope rather than a punch of dread, because Taliel was surely right: in trying to approach it from another angle while Erran and his apprentice worked on it conventionally, he *had* been under-thinking it, drawing too much from that single moment in Dolunokh which, even after five weeks, he understood so little about. He was only one-quarter elf, descended by Denek's reckoning from one of his grandmothers, so he couldn't attempt to base his efforts on the use of *solely* elven magic. He wasn't so rich-blooded. But that didn't matter. He was still capable of so much more than the common mage - more than most of the Order - and that meant that it was an avenue worth exploring. But one that needed more thought. More tact. Intense emotion or desperation alone wouldn't be enough. Not for surveillance spells...nor for...

Yes, it was true, his efforts on those spells had waned with the distraction Liogan had provided, but while he didn't trust the she-elf as blindly as everyone else seemed to think he did - how *could* he, when she was as good as incorporeal? - his mind was readily open to her suggestion all the same. Whatever her true motives, if he *could* move Turunda out of harm's way...think of what he could prevent. His whole being was driven by a devotion to protect his people, a devotion so strong *no one* else could comprehend it, let alone share in it. If they could, more would surely have already been done to safeguard the country. Perhaps war wouldn't have touched them at all.

The door to his office rose ahead of him, and today it wasn't a prison he approached, but a seat of command and achievement. And he threw the door open gladly.

"Punctures would help."

Salus all but leapt out of his skin, and in a heartbeat his fingers rose to create the signs of the freezing spell he'd finally grasped. But he gave up just as quickly. He knew it would have no effect.

Liogan stepped forwards, clearly visible in the bright morning sun, her storm of black curls a deep shade of blue where the light struck them and her skin an unquestionable silver. Her lips were puckered and eyebrows high in approval as she watched him slouch in defeat, drop his hands and close the door behind him. "You have fast reflexes. And more impressive still is that those reflexes already encompass magic. You've only been training it for, what, a month?"

"Seven weeks." He stepped inside and approached his desk, outwardly ignoring her while keeping her at all times in his sharply trained peripherals.

"Oh," she smiled, chuckling in amusement as she followed him with her usual leisure, "I see what you're doing." She perched upon the corner of his desk as he took his seat and peered down at him knowingly. "But I know you're interested."

"In your information," he replied flatly with tactful distrust, looking over reports though he didn't truly see them, "not your games."

"Fair enough. Then I say again: punctures." Her grin broadened as he looked up impatiently and waved a careless hand. "If there were already breaks in the land you could push on."

"Push on with what? What could *possibly* be strong enough to break the ground so deep? A giant shoe horn? And what could possibly be strong enough to use it? Is there a race of colossal stendjur in the mountains I can coerce into helping me? Are they by chance the mountains *themselves*, hiding in plain sight all these years?"

She frowned in disappointment. "Now who's treating this as a joke?"

"You offered me nothing but cryptic statements yesterday, and you offer me little more now."

"All right," she slipped soundlessly from the polished walnut desk and stared soberly down the bridge of her elegant nose. "You want me to be straight? Strain the magic. Those rifts ripping their way through this beautiful land weren't formed naturally, it was magic, and that magic is folding into the elements themselves. If you concentrate on it, you can force it to your whim, and you can direct that destruction on towards the next."

"*What?!*" He erupted from his seat, stark incredulity sharpening his features, and stared at her in such open horror any would think she'd told him to disband the Arana, obliterate the military, open the borders and invite Skilan in for tea. She merely blinked at him. "You can't--that--*those chasms* have taken *hundreds* of innocent lives, and you expect me to make them *worse?!*"

"No," she replied calmly, "I suggested that you take control of and *steer* the magic. I don't recall saying 'crack open the land in every major city, bonus points for trapping children and elderly'. But," she sighed dramatically, "perhaps this *is* impossible for you after all."

His lip curled venomously, but he suppressed his bristling offence. "*How* could such a thing be achieved?"

"Ooh I don't know." She tapped her silver chin with a finger as slender as a pheasant feather quill and peered up at the ceiling, ignoring his stare. "It will take unorthodox magic, certainly, but it needn't be complicated." She pursed her lips, then nodded in decision.

The world turned upside down. His eyes burned beneath a blinding light, his skin prickled beneath a sudden warmth, damp earth assaulted his nostrils, but above all else his stomach lurched like a butter churn. He was grateful it was empty.

Salus raised a hand against the unobscured sun as another warm and strangely peaceful breeze wrapped itself around him even as panic pierced his heart. Frantically, he stumbled backwards and stared in shock at the expanse of black that lay at his feet. The abyssal rend stretched eternally into the depths of the earth, whole buildings and trees lodged deep in its shadows, its ends well beyond sight.

"Your village of Halen," Liogan said coldly as she surveyed the area. Her equally unaffected rose-coloured eyes turned onto him, and he did his best to regain his composure. She gestured out towards the rift. "The magic - can you feel it? Good. Then you can do it. Look closer."

"What am I looking for?"

"Anything more than its presence."

Confused and alarmed, he dared to open his mind and lean his consciousness forwards as Erran had taught him to do, closer and closer to the crumbling edge. But nothing stood out. There didn't seem to be any more or less magic in that black, empty space than there was around it. And while he found that that surprised him, he didn't really know why he had expected otherwise. Mages had done this, all for the sake of chaos, and left places saturated by rampaging magic to maximise the damage and prolong Turunda's suffering - and perhaps even to tap into later when their plans came to fruition.

Plans he absolutely had to stop.

He steeled himself and took a half step closer, dropping the sixth sense deeper into the earth. Carefully, he descended.

Liogan watched him closely, observing every twitch and furrow in his expression as they came. His frown soon creased harshly in recognition.

"Turquoise..."

Her eyebrows rose. "Turquoise? I'd have said carmine myself, but each to their own."

"And...ripples?"

The world turned again, his stomach lurched, and bile rose in his throat. He doubled over, fighting his body back under control, while Liogan waited patiently on the edge of the desk with a shadow of amusement on her lips. "And now," she continued once he'd straightened, rising to wander and nose around the room, "you've had a look at the magic. Ripples mean a surface, and a surface can be manipulated, yes?"

"Yes," he coughed, "but--" A map rustled and unrolled itself across the desk while a quill came suddenly to life, inking itself and trailing its fine nib across the parchment. He looked back around to Liogan as she opened the doors of the cabinet behind him. "Why are you helping me?"

"For Turunda's safety," she replied plainly, placing her hand upon his shoulder and nodding towards the map. "Halen is the most potent of these magically-charged locations - for the moment. So I suggest you start from there."

"But how?" He asked with frustration as she gave him the slightest push towards it. "You've shown me...*puddles* of magic and told me to push them. *How?*" He looked back around, but the silver woman was gone. He growled. "Cursed elves!" He snapped towards the knock at the door and gestured vaguely for the food to be left on a side table.

He sighed wearily as the servant obeyed and left without a word, then noticed the unbroken scratching of the quill. He frowned and leaned over the desk. The fresh scrawlings stood out immediately from the memorised cartography, outlining twelve locations on or near Turunda's borders through settlements, forests and mountains alike, and a number of them immediately struck a familiar chord. It didn't take him long to recognise that many were places reported to be corrupted by magic just like Halen, places where mages had been found snooping around - mages who would tell him nothing even once detained, before the Order secured papers for release into their own custody.

A snarl rumbled free, but Salus left those thoughts alone, choosing instead to chase almost desperately after that sense of tranquil bliss the day had greeted him with. He managed, as diluted as it was, and looked back to the map with a more critical eye.

The markings consisted of a number of lines - a scale of destruction, he surmised, as the highest count of six rested upon Halen. In fact, outside of the ravaged village, the next highest numbers remained in the northernmost reaches of the country, while those further south along the Pavise and Olusan mountains ranked lower. The smallest graced the southern coast, and those few were, he discovered, unknown to him. But that was not unreasonable; they were marked beneath the sea.

If the destruction - or perhaps, he mused, the strength of magic - was greatest in Halen, and Halen was to be his starting point, then by... *'pushing'* that destructive magic along, he could bring those lesser places to the same intensity, or close...and...

Suddenly, a laugh burst free, uncontrollable and absurd.

And, just as suddenly, it stopped.

How could he *possibly* be considering this nonsense?

But *was* it nonsense? *Could* it be so simple? Could it be *possible?* Magic was involved, and that very fact seemed to render the term 'impossible' worthless. And the chasm in Halen...it could have stretched into infinity. If they could all be so severe, so *deep*, and they could all be joined up...why *couldn't* it work?

He needed only to decipher how to push something intangible and he could crack the base of mountains, sunder the seabed - obliterate passage over the borders and rescue Turunda once and for all.

He needed only to figure it out.

A knock came at the door. Teagan. Salus rolled the map away and turned his attention, at last, onto the egg and cinnamon toast before getting down to the day's work.

But even as he read over the reports his favoured had brought with him, of successes, failures, and trivial interruptions from the movements of tribes and evacuees notably reported by phaeacians, his mind remained upon that map, and upon the magic surging in his veins. For it had the potential to do so much.

So very, very much.

Chapter 12

"He could *never* achieve it. Magic, elves, *whatever* - it isn't possible! If the elves really wanted this to happen, *they'd* be in a better position to deal with it than he is!"

"That's what I said, but he's rationalised it in a way I'm struggling to dispute. For *centuries* we've believed the elves were dead, and yet here are two individuals using magic in an impossible way - a way *only* elves could use it. One of them awakens Salus's magic and teaches him how to use it, and no sooner has he been removed from the proceedings than another comes along, another single elf, to put that very magic to use. He thinks they're trying to save the land through *his* magic rather than their own so they don't reveal themselves. Why they've been hiding away all this time is anyone's guess, but if they're hiding *here*, then Turunda's fate affects them as much as it does us."

A wave of uneasy looks rippled among the group. No one seemed able to argue or agree.

The oldest among them, an elegantly robed man with a bearing deceptive of his advanced age, soon sighed in deliberation. "Salus is an intelligent man," he reminded them slowly. "It's not surprising that he'd reach such a logical conclusion. But that doesn't make it true. I'm unable to dispute that Denek and Liogan are elves, and neither can I dispute that they were working together and using Salus as a tool. But there is nothing at all to suggest at their motives. Perhaps they *want* to obliterate Turunda. Perhaps they intend to kill us all and reclaim the land for themselves and they're hiding to maintain the element of surprise. Or perhaps this is little more than one part of a much larger plan. We just can't know, and I don't think we would be able to get the truth out of them with magic, deceit *or* eavesdropping, whatever the case. But they've chosen to consort with the Arana, and for that fact they'll play their hand very close to their chest. They won't want to risk Salus discovering whatever they're truly up to, and who is more observant and duplicitous by nature than Aranan operatives? No offence intended, of course."

"You're not wrong, my lord," the blonde mage sighed, folding her arms across her chest, "on any count. But what can we possibly do against *elves?* He's driven to the point of obsession as it is, and with that kind of help and encouragement, how could he ever be dissuaded?"

"He claims not to fully trust her," Taliel assured them, "but how far that mistrust goes, I can't be sure. He says he's being cautious, but he believes her too readily. And, I think, after he took Denek out so...easily...he doesn't see Liogan as great of a threat as he should. He seems to believe he can handle her the same way. The difference is that she doesn't seem inclined to play the inferior role like Denek did; he disguised himself as a human and allowed himself to be imprisoned, but Liogan teleported herself right into the heart of Arana House on her own accord, and Salus said that no spell seemed to affect her. And she left just as easily."

"Perhaps she's looking to plant a seed of fear in him?"

Taliel's fingers tapped thoughtfully along her lips. "Perhaps. But if she's succeeded, he isn't showing it. He's too focused on what she's offering him. And as Vari said, I doubt there's any way to discourage him from this elf's influence, either."

On an unspoken thought, all eyes turned then onto the Crown's liaison. The singing in the tavern beyond the door rose raucously.

Malson dropped his hand from his chin and looked across them all. "I had a meeting with Salus yesterday. He's seeing to his tasks and he's getting results, so his official work isn't suffering, which means I can't accuse him of professional negligence to distract him."

"Only because he already set out on those tasks before the orders were given."

He sighed wearily. "I thought as much. So he's truly acting on his own, now. Turunda may not be paying for it yet, but it's only a matter of time." The wrinkles in his old brow deepened in thought. "Doana have still made no hint towards their intentions, correct?"

David shook his thinly-haired head. "Absolutely nothing."

"Mm..." Malson breathed a chuckle, earning him inquisitive frowns. "They should be commended, really. To keep their hand hidden under such close scrutiny and in enemy terrain for so many weeks is no mean feat."

"And yet, if they had, he'd have been forced to set his own ambitions aside - at least for the duration."

Marie's ever-serious and almost portion-like expression softened for a moment. "Perhaps," the phidipan mused, "we should provoke them." She surveyed the startled expressions, but didn't deign to explain herself. Instead, she waited, and one by one, they grew just as contemplative.

Malson eventually nodded. "I think I can take care of that. And--"

"Reports can be adjusted," Jora finished. Malson smiled. The usually doubtful young man seemed more sure of himself lately, but with Salus's increasingly erratic mood swings, independent orders and personal activities, the phaeacian appeared to have finally made his mind up about where the best course of action for Turunda's safety lay, and it wasn't with the keliceran.

"Of course," Malson continued, a little more dubiously, "I can't be sure how effective my pressure will be. I can't read my position any more; Salus is being too cordial. There's little hint of the irritation or disdain he usually greets me with. Perhaps because he feels as though *he* is the one in control."

"Well, he is, isn't he? Look at the situation he has us all in; none of us know any longer what to expect of him."

The old man sighed heavily in agreement, but the words didn't pass his lips. "We can only attempt to distract and delay him--"

"That's all we *ever* seem to do," Marie growled. "One would think a body such as ours, dominated by phidipans and aided by a liaison to the *Crown*, would be able to do more than forge reports, run interference and stand back, chewing our nails, hoping that one morning Salus will wake up and decide it's too much trouble, reject his magic and return to traditional measures for defence."

"One would think," Malson agreed, but the smile on his lips suggested that he did not. "But you forget that it is not just the thirteen of us." His gaze slipped onto Taliel, and while Marie's followed, scrutinous, she didn't see the hint of apology flicker through his. Taliel did, and braced her reactions. "Tell him what we've learned."

"I've already been deployed. Information has stopped coming in from the resident spy in Adeliene; I've been ordered to find out why. I'm leaving after this meeting."

"A suitably low-risk operation..."

She smiled grimly. "You noticed that, too? Whatever the case, I'll make a deviation."

"The tail lost him," David frowned. "He knows he's being hunted. How will you find him?"

Her smile became impish. "I have my ways."

Awkward, hostile, brooding and thoughtful, silence in all forms was a thing of the past. Once Rathen had informed Aria of their encounter with the elves, the recovery of the Zi'veyn and their subsequent separation and entrapment, every waking moment had been filled with questions. Many were anticipated, and a number of those that coaxed frowns of bafflement or surprise from the others didn't faze Rathen at all - though there were, in her true fashion, a few that were either too clever or too strange even for him. But every question was answered to the best of their ability and it quickly developed into a group activity, passing the time while they rode along on the horses Kienza had left them. The atmosphere lifted for the first time in days, and even Garon seemed to relax a little. He didn't join in, but he didn't ride on ahead.

When the darkness fell and Aria finally drifted off to sleep, the usual dispersion of the camp came more slowly, and even Petra's hostility towards Anthis was slow to rear its head. But despite the near-pleasantness of it all, Rathen and Anthis wasted no time in throwing themselves back into their work. They were exhausted by the time they retired to their blankets, and slept deeply, harried in their dreams by thoughts and theories. Then, come sunrise, it all started again.

Drowned by a flood of new questions, their route continued to wind south towards the Korovor Woodlands. The trees began to thin on their approach, as though whole copses had decided to uproot and move on ahead into those thick forests with the rest of their kin. But despite its extent and density, it didn't house the same dangers as the Wildlands. And if it did, the beasts kept rigidly to themselves.

With every beat of the horses' hooves they drew nearer to the ruins concealed in those woods, and the breath of expectation brushed hotter down the back of Rathen's neck.

Between staring closely at the shape of her father's quite human ears, Aria noticed his distraction. But she didn't point it out. Instead, she directed her questions towards the others, and he soon buried his attention back into the open scrolls balanced precariously on the mane of Anthis's mare. The pair remained engrossed for the rest of the day.

By the dawn of the following morning, four days after fleeing Fendale, Rathen's shame in his failure hadn't dimmed in the slightest. He still felt ridiculous, ashamed, embarrassed, frustrated; angry at Kienza for not giving him the help he knew she could provide all because she'd decided that he had to do it all himself. And he was bitter over the fact that he knew she was right. Again.

He'd studied the Zi'veyn and blundered his way through the illegible scrolls for a month, secluded from distractions, helpless and with little else to do. He'd thrown himself into its workings, pushed his mind to the brink of its scholastic abilities. And it hadn't been enough.

'You're the only one capable of achieving it.' The wretched words seemed to chase him even in his dreams, which themselves had long since lost any trace of tranquillity since the elves had tampered with his cuff. But he was no academic. His magic may have been superior - a fact for which he sat taller in his saddle - but his mind was still quite limited, to the point that the whole situation was just a twisted joke. One which even Kienza seemed to relish in as she left him to struggle.

His single hope was Anthis. The man he'd originally mocked for his suggestion that an elven legend could be the answer to Turunda's problems. Because while Rathen could recognise a handful of words, Anthis was the only one who could truly read the scrolls. If anyone, besides Kienza, could provide the clues he needed, it was him.

But as the land dropped into another valley and the gathering trees imposed an early evening, their progress waned. Their minds were frayed and wandering, and Aria, too, had succumbed to weariness. By the time they made camp, the whole group had fallen quiet. They ate in reticence, and the stifling animosity was slowly creeping back in.

Eyila could take it no more. Despite the glassiness of his eyes, when she noticed Anthis fiddling absently with the chain about his neck, she eagerly shattered the silence. "You still wear it?"

"Hm?" His eyes brightened as he returned to his surroundings, and he looked down as she nodded towards his hand. "Oh...yes. Of course I do."

A snide grunt rose from beside her. "You still have *some* sense, then."

"Our beliefs aren't wrong, Petra, they're just misinformed." He managed to restrain the tired tone for fear she'd take it as condescension, but as he looked back to Eyila to grasp the opportunity to speak with her, she made another venomous noise.

"You're so gullible."

"Petra."

"What? It's true and you know it, Rathen - he'll believe anything he's told if it involves gods, and he rationalises it with *insanity* so it all fits together as neatly as a sword in a sheath." She shot Anthis a look of contempt over the fire. "How can you live like that? *You! An academic!*"

"Have you considered--"

"All right, fine." She slammed her wooden bowl on the ground so hard that Aria woke with a jump. "Your way. We learned of the gods from the elves, right?

Then how could the *elves neglect* to speak of *three* of five gods for the *whole* time humans were their slaves? Or leave them out of all documents and archives? No historian has ever uncovered or even *suggested* such a thing, despite all their research - not even *you* came across this until a few weeks ago!"

"Long post-magic elves indentured humans," he replied as coolly as he could, if only because Eyila was still watching him, "and they were concerned *only* with wealth and status, living luxuriously and in high standing, and it being taken away in death. They *never* used their hands, *never* philosophised, disregarded the natural order in favour of magical advancement, comfort and control over everything around them. Doru, Mind; Feira, Nature; Nara, Hands - They were ignored along with what They represented. They only spoke so reverently of all the gods *before* they were gifted their magic, but they never differentiated between Them specifically enough for Them to have been entirely different *beings*, it was all balanced and intertwined." He continued calmly, despite her attempt to interrupt. "What few occasions long post-magic elves mentioned Them was always in line with Vastal, never Zikhon unless being referred to as a loss. But the elves never taught humans directly, it wasn't the business of slaves and servants - even *irreverent* elves wouldn't have tolerated humans bearing such knowledge of their gods! Everything we learned, every connection we made, every bias we developed was from observation and what little of the elven language we understood. It would have been all too easy to get it wrong! And when the elves suddenly and tracelessly vanished and someone suggested that Zikhon, tied to death as they understood Him, had destroyed the elves while Vastal had swooped in just in time to save *humans*, *all* of whom were untouched, why would they question anything? They'd thank Vastal for saving them and consider it justice for the tyrannous elves!"

Petra blustered, her face surely as red as her hair, but appeared in her rage to have lost her tongue. But while the others remained silent, eating their supper quickly so they might flee the impending carnage, Rathen viewed the whole ordeal with calm and lazy disconnection. "How *can* you fit it all together without batting an eyelid?"

"I suppose I'm just not as close-minded as some people."

Petra still seemed unable to retort.

Brave or foolish, Anthis continued, though none were sure for whose benefit. "None of it is mutually exclusive. The Temple teaches of Vastal and Zikhon, but neglects Nara, Doru and Feira. But the *tribes* don't spread their efforts across all *their* gods, they dedicate themselves to the one element most relevant to their lives - correct?" Eyila nodded. "It's all intertwined. And, I suppose, having my mind opened to Vokaad has encouraged a less rigid view of divinity than most. The Sulyax Dizan concentrates on the Craitic prophecy of the end by Zikhon's hand, it doesn't work *against* the Craitic teachings of the Temple--"

"Except for murder, personal gain--"

"You're out for *revenge*."

"Against murderers like--"

"*Stop it,* you two!"

At the joint bark of mage and inquisitor, Anthis, finally bristling, quickly bit his tongue. But while Petra thundered to her feet, she did not fall silent. "Handle this cultist, *Inquisitor*," she snarled. "We have the Zi'veyn, he's outlived his usefulness. Why hasn't he been locked away yet?"

"You know, you throw that word around a lot, but have you ever seen me lighting candles? Drawing signs on the ground? Smearing blood on my face, rolling my eyes to the back of my head and speaking in reverse with three voices?"

"I've not *seen* you do *anything*."

"Oh, no, of course not, you're just flinging conjecture and judgement based on nothing but *other* people's assumptions. Why are *you* here, anyway? What exactly do *you* contribute?"

"*Enough!*"

Silence penetrated the camp like a frost.

The pair stared daggers, daring the other to be the first to defy the officer's demand. But when the tension came to a head, Petra turned and stormed away, chillingly voicing neither word nor snarl.

Regret finally barrelled down and snuffed out Anthis's ire. "Petra, wait," he called, kicking dirt over the flames in his hurry to rise after her, "wait, I'm sorry!"

But she didn't wait. She didn't cast him a glare or even curse him out beneath her breath. She vanished in silence into the trees.

The camp remained rigid until Eyila rose to follow her, silently regretting having spoken at all.

Anthis puffed in defeat and slumped back to the dirt, where he found Garon's steely gaze boring into him. He braced himself for a reprimand.

"We cannot afford to make a scene," the officer informed him glacially. "Pull yourself together and keep your distance from her."

"I know. I will."

"Good. Perhaps you should get back to work." And then Garon left, too.

Aria peered after them for a long moment before turning her confusion upon the others. "I don't understand. Why did Petra get so upset?"

"Because," Rathen smiled sadly, "it matters to her."

"What does?"

"All of it."

"Why?"

"Because."

Her big eyes narrowed in thought, slipping slowly back into the trees. "...I see..."

A breeze passed through the camp. Rathen poked at the half-covered fire, drawing the flames back to life while the young man's head dropped heavily into his hands. He dropped his voice low. "I wouldn't worry about it."

"Oh?"

"She's just confused. She doesn't know what to believe. According to the Temple, there are two gods, one good, one evil, and the elves were killed by Zikhon because Vastal grew weak when their faith in Her waned, replaced by a high opinion of themselves, apparently. Yes, don't look so surprised, I do know the stories. I didn't always live in the woods. But according to *you*, there are *five* gods, *all* of whom turned away because of that very arrogance and obliterated them, bar a handful saved by the god we know as Death, and now *no one* is left to listen to *any* prayers or grant *anyone* strength. And you have far more evidence to support your claims than the Temple does theirs."

"And yet that's been the case for *centuries* and nothing terrible has come from it!" Anthis protested wearily, watching the flames come back to life. "Because everyone's strength is their own. *Especially* hers... But, I suppose none of it really matters, does it? No harm *has* been done - and we could never tell anyone what we've learned, could we? No one would believe us. We could even be *killed* for it, and certainly ruin our careers - even a duelist's. Either no one would want to fight her, or they'd try to kill her instead. There's no harm being done with things as they are..." But the wistful sigh that followed betrayed his desire for the contrary, a desire to share the truth, to enlighten the world, to correct their beliefs and put strength into their own hands rather than relying upon gods who, it seemed, were no longer there. Or perhaps it was for professional credit. Rathen decided to favour the former.

The mage tapped the scrolls that lay open in front of him.

"Yes, yes, of course, of course." Anthis sighed and moved them over where he could clearly see them, safe from the reach of drifting embers, while Aria moved around to wriggle in between them, refusing to miss anything else. "You've tried pointing it, willing it, and powering it with magic - something you worked out for yourself, but I've also found written in these scrolls. Is it possible you're giving it too much?"

Rathen shook his head. "I worked over something similar when Kienza helped me affect the magic in Halen. If I was over-feeding it, I'd know."

"All right, so we'll assume you're not over-powering it. In which case--"

"Can I hold it again?"

Rathen fished the palm-sized relic out from the bag beside him without a second thought, while Anthis, startled by Aria's sudden and enthusiastic outburst, looked on in concern. Rathen heard him wince as she dropped it a few harmless inches to the ground. "She's fine. Go on."

"...Right...yeah, uh...so if you're not...over-powering it, then it's fixed, it's fuelled, but it's just not responding. So...how do we...turn it on?"

Rathen watched Aria rotate it in the light of the fire, hypnotised by the reflections that danced over the deep black surface. His eyes dropped purposefully to the scrolls, but of course he still couldn't read them. "There's really nothing in these? Or in your notebook? You found so much in the Wildlands and Ut'hala - what if--"

"If it's anywhere, it's in these scrolls." He chuckled sardonically. "I suppose that's something. Despite the mass of information Salus stole from us, none of it is of any use to him..." He fell silent for a long moment. Rathen waited. Despair flickered briefly in his eyes. "No. No, forget the rest. *This* is my priority. It's too great for anything else to compare."

"Too great indeed. Uncovering the Zi'veyn, proving a myth a reality...I owe you an apology."

"...Actually I meant the *situation* is too great, but thank you. Though you're not the first to question my methods. I'm used to it. My peers often mock me."

"And yet your name is spoken of highly in intellectual circles."

Anthis smiled, either modest or careful. "Pardon my asking, but how could you know?"

"Because Kienza is an intellectual circle all by herself."

"Ah, yes, of course she is... She's something else."

"She really is. And she knows it. Which makes her impossible. She has all the answers but makes you work them out yourself."

"How could something ever be an achievement if it were just handed to you?"

Rathen grunted. "It must be an intellectual thing. I remind you that I'm not looking for achievements, only a solution."

"Of course. To work, then." They both fell silent and watched Aria stare at the artefact's crowning lotus. "Maybe you have to will it differently."

"So 'please work' isn't enough, then?"

"It appears not."

"Suggestions?"

"Well I don't know much about the technical workings or application of magic..."

"I do, and I'm stumped. I'll take any help I can get."

"Maybe you need to show it where you want it to go. Direct it. Lead it."

"I've tried that, but *where* do I lead it when there's nothing to lead it *to?* The magic isn't in anything, it's all-surrounding."

"Well perhaps you need to...*not* steer it, then. Just let it be."

"Which I have *also* tried."

"All right...well, what happens to it when you power it?"

"Nothing. It just swallows it."

Something flickered over his face. "It just swallows your magic? ...You--"

"The thought had crossed my mind, but I doubt it. Otherwise victims would have to volunteer to have their magic stolen, and I just don't see that being an effective weapon."

"...Well then, perhaps it's because the magic is sedentary. Try encouraging that power out, give it a nudge, let it know you want it to move...?"

"It's magic, not a goat."

"A goat?"

Aria giggled.

"Never mind. But...perhaps you're on to something... Nudging it..." His mind trailed away, back to another evening when he'd peered over the edge of the rift that had freshly split Halen in two, when he'd assaulted the tumultuous magic with his own, first drowning it, then focusing the stream, finding the edge of the chaos and pushing, finally pushing, until the magic moved. A smile almost twitched, and he sat a little straighter. "I can do that..."

But as he snatched out his notebook and lost himself in his pondering, Anthis to his reading and Aria to the intricate onyx brushwork revealed in the writing light, none noticed the lightest of footsteps approaching from behind. Nor indeed when they increased with the effort of a stomp. In fact it was only after the impatient clearing of a throat that anyone looked around, and they were even slower to leap up in alarm. But the figure didn't move to take advantage of their sluggishness, and as Rathen loosened his fingers and Anthis withdrew his dagger, each closing Aria behind them, the mage quickly discovered why.

"Elle..."

The woman - beautiful, slender, pale skin warm in the firelight, a head of dark brown curls through which shone a gentle yet focused gaze - smiled.

Rathen's dark eyes widened and his guard dropped in an instant. Anthis cooled only a fraction, but his grip on the dagger tightened when another form stepped out from the shadows and broke the stillness with the drawing of his blade. Despite the inquisitor's vigilance, it seemed the Aranan phidipan had slipped all too easily behind him.

But Elle ignored Garon's arrival and returned the fierce embrace Rathen surged forwards to deliver. Only then did Anthis lower his dagger. Garon, on the other hand, remained rigid, while Aria peered around the historian with the greatest curiosity her eyes could possibly display. They observed the pair warily for a long and increasingly uncomfortable minute.

When Rathen finally released her, any smile he'd worn had vanished. He regarded her then with solemn resignation. "You didn't come all this way for a social call. The stakes are too high and you surely know the Arana is after us. Our marriage might not be on your records and you may have tampered with mine, but if you're seen...you're putting *yourself* in danger now, Elle. You shouldn't be here."

"I know," she mirrored his sobriety, "and if I thought I was at risk, I wouldn't be. But I know that the nearest of the operatives converging on Korovor are still half a day away - and," she added, glancing past them towards the beasts pegged on the far side of the camp, "they don't know that you have horses. They won't be looking for the tracks, and you can easily outpace them."

"How did you get here?"

She turned her attention briefly upon Garon, whose stern, fixated eyes had turned to steel with suspicion. She straightened. "Translocators. I was sent out from Headquarters on a mission, and no, this is *not* it. This is from Lord Malson. A delay due to the weather, *if* I were to record it."

There was no telling if the inquisitor believed her or not. His sword remained poised. "Speak."

"Fair enough. But first..." Ignoring the glint of his sword, she stepped forwards and dropped a bag from her shoulder, a worn, old, leather satchel which she handed to the cautious historian. The light had barely fallen over it when his eyes erupted in the sheerest joy. He snatched it keenly, caution forgotten, and hefted its weight in delight. "But the Arana--how did you--"

"Salus has finished with them. He has little care any more for elven ruins and relics. He's focused on other things..."

She then told them everything, and though they listened, some more sceptically than others, little she divulged came as any true surprise. News of Salus's efforts to create spells of surveillance, though extreme, seemed unfortunately appropriate from the head of a faction of spies, and his suspicions that Rathen had first been working with the Order and had now gone rogue also seemed suitably paranoid. His continued hunt for them and the confiscation of the Zi'veyn wasn't really news at all, and confirmation of his vicious campaign against non-humans and his hand in the stirrings of growing racism were equally inconsequential.

But when she reached the final item in her catalogue of bleak tidings, jaws dropped at last.

They looked at one another for a long, dreadful moment, until Rathen was the first to speak. "He was clearly planning something," he mumbled, though still lost in thought, "but...surely you're joking?"

"I wish I was. But this is only a recent development."

"He possesses elven magic and some degree of elven blood, and has an elf - and *not* the first, it seems - helping him to wield it. He..." Rathen sighed dejectedly. "*If* a thing such as *moving Turunda* is possible, he's quite possibly in a position to manage it. Vastal save us."

"I wonder if that phrase is still appropriate..."

Rathen brushed aside Anthis's passing remark and fixed the woman with severity. Her face, even with its somewhat bewildered wrinkle, would have enraptured him and frozen his heart had circumstances been even remotely different. "*Is* Salus capable of this?"

"I really don't know. He's driven enough. Presently, he's making slow progress despite training his magic obsessively, but once he starts to get comfortable with it, it will no doubt speed up. And with an elf's guidance..." She could overlook her confusion no longer. "Why are none of you surprised by this?!"

"Rathen is also half-elf."

"*What?!*"

He shot Anthis an unappreciative glare, and despite Garon's immediate command to tell her nothing at all, shared an obligatory summary of their experience on the mist-enshrouded island.

"Then Salus *wasn't* just guessing..." For the briefest moment, her startlement fled and her eyes transformed into wells of fathomless sorrow, seizing Rathen's heart with an aching regret, longing and fury. And as they turned upon him from their gaze through the ground, he suddenly felt nothing but shame. It lingered long past the forced return of her composure. "It was only following Denek's transformation and attempt on his life, which I admit I didn't see, that he came to the conclusion about you - but how did *you* come to--"

"Salus transformed in Dolunokh." Rathen's lip curled and eyes glazed for a moment in chilling recollection as the inconceivable sight crashed back to the front of his mind. "Just outside the doorway. It was far from complete, but there was no way I could miss even that little after what I saw on the island. Bone-white skin, thin cheeks, sharp teeth, black eyes. I don't know what he usually looks like, but no *human* could look like that..."

"What can we do against this?" All eyes turned onto Garon as he returned them to the matter at hand, and Anthis quickly gave voice to the only idea to present itself, the thought they were all reluctant to speak and exactly the last thing Rathen wished to hear.

"Turn the Zi'veyn against him."

"Do *please* tell me how."

"Moving the land," Garon looked towards the historian. "*Is* such a thing possible? Could the elves at least have done it?"

"The notes the ditchlings gave us in Tarun say so," he replied, earning a bewildered frown from the phidipan, "but just how, I can't imagine."

"How much trouble would it be to expand on their findings?"

He sucked air in through his teeth. "It's awfully specific, and probably too small a thing from an elven perspective to have documented beyond the event itself -

they were more interested in results than the science and workings behind their intuitive abilities. We can *try* if we find out where they got them from, but I think even then it will be an enormous waste of time..."

"Then he won't find anything easily, either. Otherwise, we're back to the Zi'veyn. Is there anywhere we can find more information about it?"

"No. Not quickly, anyway - we lucked into it on a number of accounts, and now we have the Zi'veyn itself, we have no leads even with these books back unless we turn tail and try to head back to Kasire. Otherwise, I can go over everything again and see what I come up with..."

"Did Eizariin give you nothing?"

"Not on this, no. I doubt he has any idea how it works either - why would he? It was made and sealed away centuries before he was born and their history covered up with it."

"Except for those caches. The rebels. There could well be more."

"Yes," Anthis replied with increasing hesitance, "there could, but *where*, and how long would it take to find them? And what would happen in the mean time? I can't believe I'm saying this, but I don't think it's worth it." He gave Rathen a passing look of apology and tried to ignore the meaningful and menacing look he returned. He returned to the inquisitor. "I'm confident we have all we need. We *can* do it. We just need to think."

"This all feels impossible," Rathen grumbled. His eyes rose back to Taliel's and his misery-lined face creased in desolation. The corners of her lips pulled downwards. "Is it still all on us?"

"I'm sorry. We've seen no trace whatsoever of anyone else moving against it. Even the Order is keeping its distance. They're already under immense suspicion." Her heart dropped as his gaze sank to the ground. In an instant she was teleported back fifteen, twenty years to his ordeals under the weight of the Order's expectations. She didn't speak, and as his every increasingly resigned thought passed over his face, neither did anyone else.

Finally, he straightened, armoured in resolution. "Then we'd better get the Zi'veyn working."

"From what Taliel has said, he won't succeed so soon."

"No," she agreed, considering the inquisitor, "but he has an elf with him again. It seems they're seeking him out."

But Anthis was already vigorously shaking his head. "I don't believe that." He ignored their dubious looks. "Just think about it: elves wouldn't need him, anything they wished to do they could do themselves. The first elf to help him was a *prisoner*--"

"Who, as it turns out, stayed *willingly*."

"The elves on that island weren't to be trusted," Rathen declared. "Eizariin *seems* different, I grant you, but that doesn't mean they're all either as friendly and inquisitive as he is or as frosty and self-important as Tekhest. Some could be far more dangerous.

"We know what he's trying to do. If we knew *how* he intended to do it or what the elf has told him, we could get in his way."

Anthis blanched. "In the *Arana's* way?!"

"The stakes are high enough," Garon mused. "We have to do what we can - but we will need more information. I'll continue reaching out to contacts, but otherwise..." It clearly took a great deal of effort for the inquisitor of the Hall of the White Hammer to swallow his pride enough to turn squarely towards the curly haired Aranan operative, trim his scowl and, with what was *almost* a degree of tolerance, speak the words: "we need your help."

But while eyebrows rose in surprise, she merely straightened and inclined her head. Not even a whisper of astonishment or satisfaction touched her lips. "I will do what I can."

"Beyond that, we keep focused on the magic. Salus aside, the matter has become no less important. We can't let its lack of sentience distract us."

All nodded in reluctant agreement, and upon the conclusion, Elle's demeanour abruptly shifted. Just as it had the first time, her attention settled entirely upon the black-haired mage and everyone knew that her matters with them as a group were finished. And Rathen had no feud with that at all.

Until the others turned away, a touch confused, and her eyes softened in sadness. He understood the moment she embraced him, in grief and in comfort. "I'm so sorry," was all she said. They remained that way for some time.

Her eyes had changed again when they released one another, and though she surely saw the remorse lingering on in his own, she didn't point it out. She smiled warmly instead, and absently reached out to draw his hair back from his face. "Well. We finally have answers. I have to admit, I'm glad. It's been so long that I'd...forgotten how deeply those questions had burned themselves in..."

"We have one answer," he corrected her, albeit softly, taking her hands from his temples. "And it doesn't make anything any better."

"Actually, it does. It just doesn't give us the last eleven years back." She smiled again, melting his resentment away - then she straightened, grinned cheerfully, and tucked her hands behind her back. "Now, I think there's someone I'd like to meet..."

Chapter 13

Aria stared at him from the saddle for a very, very long time. It soon reached the point that Rathen no longer had any clue of what she could possibly have been thinking, nor if her imagination hadn't departed with her entirely and skipped off into the hills.

Finally, her lips pursed, slowly and tightly. "Why?"

He cursed himself. He should have expected that. But as he inhaled to answer even while still gathering his thoughts, her sharp eyes hooked his and stopped his voice in his throat.

"No, don't tell me. I don't want to know."

They both sighed and looked away across the tall, sickly forest. The light was low, made gloomier by the mid-morning clouds, and the skeletal trees' crowns appeared more as leafy wigs than any sign of vitality. The others were scattered amongst them and waiting, just as they were, for Garon to return from scouting, and for the first time since Rathen had tucked the weary child into her blankets the night before, they had the privacy to speak. Which was turning out to be more difficult than he'd anticipated.

He adjusted the grey mare's bridle for distraction as Aria's penetrating eyes bore back onto him. "You love her, don't you?"

Once again an answer eluded him, and in that same moment the adulterous guilt he'd shut away for years caught up with him. He fled it in a desperate moment and focused again upon the bridle, but her stare wasn't so easily escaped. Though he frowned at what she said next.

"You're a lot older than me. You didn't always live at home - *our* home, I mean. In the forest. You lived with the Order, once, in the cities. Kienza doesn't. She's like we are now. She has been for a very long time - longer, I think, than either of us think."

"Sweetheart--"

She leaned out from the saddle and hugged him. "I won't say a word about her. But I don't think Kienza would mind. Actually, I think she'd understand. But I still won't say anything."

Rathen sighed and squeezed her, feeling that same guilt and cowardice creeping back into his gut.

"Elle is very nice," she said as he let go and attempted to kick off the mud and what he hoped was algae from his boots before climbing up behind her. "And funny. And pretty. She said I'm pretty, too, you know."

"I know. You're quite alike."

"Am I funny, too?"

"Looking."

Her eyes flashed impishly. "No wonder," she replied with tightly reined intensity, "look at *you*."

"Yes, very alike indeed," he smiled.

"...You've said I'm like Kienza, too."

"Yes. You are."

She nodded slowly, no doubt further piecing the matter together.

She soon turned away to watch for Garon's return, but upon no sign of him, she directed her attention upon Anthis and his beige dun several paces away, where he appeared to be reading over his scrolls. The drooping top edge of the parchment gave away his distraction. Eyila was waiting the same distance from him, studying the grim surroundings with even greater distaste than she had tirelessly regarded the forests. "Will we see her again?"

"Don't be sly, Aria," he sighed, "you know we will. You overheard everything we said last night. "

"Of course I did, I was right behind Anthis! Even with all your new elfyness, Daddy, you didn't even notice I was there."

It had only been a note, a fleeting touch, but the hurt in her voice pierced his heart. She'd tried to hide it, pretend she spoke in jest, but those very efforts gave it away and this newest wave of guilt she'd managed to strike him with was paralysing. It was only through impulse that he managed to embrace her at all.

Mercifully, it was then that Garon reappeared in the distance of the sodden forest, though he didn't appear particularly enthusiastic.

"It only gets worse," he announced as he returned to his horse. "It's not a fluke. The marsh has expanded."

"How could it when it was such a mild spring?"

Rathen groaned. "I could hazard a guess..."

They urged their horses after Garon's bay and ventured further into the marsh, the thud of every gingerly-placed hoof softened by the damp ground. With no clear path, the beasts were left to pick their own way around the labyrinth of puddles, some pierced with so many weeds they would be entirely hidden if not for the reflective glint of the clouds, and they soon began snorting poignantly in revulsion when the puddles became too vast to skirt and a smog of bitter stench was discovered gathering in the air above them. But as prudent as the horses were being, progress was still faster than had the riders been on foot. No doubt that had been Kienza's intention, even if she hadn't seen fit to verbally inform them.

The Korovor Woodlands had always been scarred by marshes, the result of the Grey Lake's frequent flooding, but as the sun hit its zenith, the nearest and most westerly marsh should still have been another six hours away on horseback, not already long beneath their feet. But as the afternoon aged, none were in any doubt as to the cause of the expansion. The magic toppled upon them as suddenly as it always did with the same aura of curious, almost disturbing beauty, and a peacefulness that still only Rathen seemed aware of. And it felt stronger this time; he found himself actively fighting to keep his head.

Despite the others' trepidation, Aria was not so unsettled by the change. She began to fidget in the saddle, twisting and peering all around them to be the first to spot their destination. But whatever ruins she'd expected, she was disappointed. There was nothing to see but a few old bricks grown over with moss, half-submerged in the muck.

Rathen drew in the reins as she slumped defeated in the saddle, and slipped down from behind her to rummage through a bag.

"This is it?" Petra mumbled doubtfully as she and the others came to a stop beside him, looking around very carefully for any of the usual abnormalities. But there were no gale-force winds, no puddles of sunlight, no phantom music or unexplained presences. Aside from the swollen marsh itself, nothing was out of the ordinary. But she wasn't so easily fooled. Quietly, she dismounted to the sludgy ground and placed her hand on her sword hilt, scanning the surroundings with a sharp, predatory gaze.

Aria tried to follow as Garon and Anthis did the same, but Rathen quickly stopped her. "You stay up there," he said, and though she inhaled to protest, the abrupt sightlessness of his eyes suddenly stilled her. She nodded and made herself comfortable. Only Eyila remained otherwise seated, but her eyes had become glass. Aria watched her in concern.

The thorns of the Zi'veyn glinted in the slivers of late afternoon sun, sending fragments of light scattering across the emaciated tree trunks and glittering across the water. But Rathen didn't notice them, nor the puddles he managed by chance to step around, nor even the foul miasma that dragged a sudden choke from Anthis as he followed more tactfully behind him. Battling to keep his focus, he stared beyond the visible world and into something draped over it, enshrouding every rock, tree and reed, and followed a trail that lay beyond human senses. Then, finally, stopping at the edge of something no one else could see, he looked down at the artefact in his palm. He stared for a long while, lost in thought, wrestling with decisions. No one dared interrupt him.

The marsh was silent; no birds sang nor insects chirped. There was nothing and no one around. But Petra and Garon continued to patrol with mindful footsteps, refusing for a moment to ease their guard while they knew hunters were converging on the forest from all directions. Within moments, everyone had grown skittish.

Aria managed not to scream as she saw something silver yet fleshy moving around in the water beside her horse's hooves, but her sharp gasp brought Petra running all the same. And she, too, looked down in horror.

"What is it?" Aria whispered as more appeared around it, breaking through the water surface to peep back at them with enormous, goggly eyes.

Petra stepped back and grimaced as one of them hopped away. "Frogs, I think. With rosy lips and women's legs..." She shook her head. "It must be the magic. That place was full of nak--" She paused and cast her an awkward smile. "Full of strange things."

Another movement and glint of pure sunlight sent her staggering backwards with a gasp. The silver frogs scattered but for the largest, which was already in the mouth of a grass snake that had burst out from the reeds, its long, sleek body quite impossibly solid gold. She swiftly flicked it and its meal away from the child's horse with the tip of her sword. "Aria, you stay up there."

"I was gonna," she squeaked.

Slowly, steadily, magic channelled into the relic, filling it like an ancient jug whose every crack had been painstakingly repaired, cautious of re-opening the old ceramic wounds. Don't pour too fast, don't over-fill it; be conscious of every drop.

Then the stream stopped. Reshaped, tapered yet blunted, it began probing the edge of the spell, the intent of the charm. Magic swelled, gradually, carefully, to match the opposing strength, then pushed, gently; a nudge. A primitive order to move, directing the purpose out of the artefact and into motion.

He felt it: the shift of intangible weight, of the slightest vibration of heat, of life, of activity. His heart was in his throat.

The spell, the power, discovered the edges of the relic's scopic black interior. With another gentle push, it permeated into the unnaturally forged metal, trickled between every particle of ore, every trace of mineral, every grain of dust and motive that composed such a vessel. Deeper and deeper, until the microscopically ridged edge of the brush work gave way to its pressure.

His heart jumped.

The magic seeped through, channelled along the brushwork like water through a runnel, but only for a moment before lifting away from the surface where the detail coiled, breaking free like a samara seed sent spiralling off into the wind.

The magic was unleashed, the spell, intent.

And nothing.

Rathen's heart stopped. His breath escaped in a single ragged puff and he returned at once to the marsh - and again almost slipped beneath the unnatural tranquillity. Battling it back into submission, he found Garon and Anthis watching him intently. He bit back the caustic oath that burned on the end of his tongue.

But it seemed neither of them felt the need to ask. Garon dismissed him and turned away in a moment, drawing the curse back up. "We can't stay here," he declared as he headed back towards the horses. "We need to find somewhere safe before nightfall and keep ahead of pursuers."

"We only just *got* here--"

"No, Rathen, you've been standing there for half an hour and you've gotten nowhere."

'Half an hour?!' The mage growled. "I came close--"

"It can't be 'close' if nothing happened. We move. Now."

His eyes burned daggers into the back of the inquisitor's head. Anthis clapped him gently on the shoulder, and at the historian's own identical grief, Rathen sighed and followed along, casting a brief and resentful glare down towards the pyramid in his hand. He tossed it into the saddlebag with nothing less than loathing.

"Did Kienza not shake them?" Petra asked as she mounted and tethered the enthralled tribal girl's reins to her own saddle.

"She did, but these weren't following our trail. Somehow Salus worked out where we were going and sent agents out this way. Once they get here, they'll start looking for us. The deeper into the forest we are, the better."

"And here I was under the impression that ending this magic was important."

He sent her a short sidelong glance. "We can't do a thing if we're captured." Then he snapped the reins and started off around the pools, leaving the others no choice but to smother their objections and follow.

As the horses renewed their trudge, Aria spun suddenly at a low rumbling close behind her. But Rathen didn't notice, nor that the rumbling was coming from his own throat. He was preoccupied by the anger, shame and embarrassment that came with this newest failure, and while he resented the defeat, at that moment he wanted nothing more than to be away from the magic and the compulsion to try again, for it would only fail and embitter his mood all the more.

He felt utterly useless, and the presence of that tiny black device in the bag strapped just beside him kept dragging his attention like a magnet, twisting his neck and setting his heart thumping.

Finding himself staring yet again, he snapped his head away and squeezed the reins until his knuckles turned white.

And discovered both Petra and Aria sending him meaningful looks.

"She needs you," Aria whispered as the duelist waved him over for what it seemed was not the first time, but as he steered his horse towards her, he drew up beside Eyila at her gesture instead.

The tribal girl, half-slumped in the saddle, lurched at his arrival, firing him a gaze both sharp and lucid. But it lasted only a moment. She soon stopped seeing him.

His frown softened in understanding. She'd been the same in Fendale, and far worse in Khry's Glory; distracted, muttering incoherently, and apparently even seeing things - or searching for something - that not even his magic would allow him to see. And he had no doubt as to the cause.

As brief as the experience was, the mage in the desert had seared herself into his mind to the point that he'd woken in sweats from lurid mirror nightmares three times so far. Here were too many similarities - they were thin and weak, but they matched up.

He chose not to consider his own struggles beneath the influence.

He handed Aria the reins, which she took eagerly, and lifted her bronze wrist carefully to keep from startling her again. Eyila didn't react in the slightest, but that only served to hike his concerns. Finding her pulse with his fingers, he extended his magic as Kienza had guided him while Eyila's own explanation of healing rolled through the back of his mind. He counted her heartbeat, brushed her aura, and seeped his magic in between every cell within her veins, both blood and arcane.

While he wasn't sure what he was looking for, it didn't take him long to find it.

In the first year of the Order, every mage was taught the tedious business of magical biology, lessons that had been drummed into Rathen often enough, even as a soldier, to recall the matter easily. Magic entered the blood from a fifth chamber in the heart, moving through vessels at the same pace as though it was blood itself - or, he'd come to note, as though it was merely riding along with the current. When utilised, it heated by one eighteenth of a degree, vibrating slightly and subtly, but otherwise continued to stream through the body leaving the blood undisturbed. As far as a well-balanced body was concerned, the magic wasn't even there. As for not-so-well-balanced bodies, they compensated well enough by a slight and unnoticeable heating of the blood, which itself served to prevent clotting and kept the magic from speeding on ahead and upsetting cardiovascular rhythm. Ultimately, it kept the blood and magic flowing together. That ability to compensate was directly related to resilience. It didn't matter how much or how powerful a mage's magic was alone - if they didn't have the resilience to keep up with it, the magic couldn't be used to maximum effect, and if their resilience was low enough, the magic couldn't be utilised at all. And the ratio of one's magic to resilience never changed.

Lately, however, that which was considered natural law was beginning to slip into question.

Eyila's magic was vibrating, and her resilience was struggling to keep up. It was as though she was in the middle of casting a spell and yet was giving off none of the usual arcane disruption while doing so. It was isolated inside her, moving yet motionless, as though manipulated like a puppet on strings. And it was stronger than it should have been. Slowly, but steadily, her body was buckling to its influence.

Rathen's jaw tightened. Kienza had said it had something to do with blood.

He lowered her hand back to her roan's mane, and though he felt Petra looking patiently back around at him, her fair face wrinkled softly in fret, he didn't dare look up. She expected him to do something, and once again there was nothing this disgrace of a half-elven mage could do.

He pretended to continue concentrating on something beyond anyone else's notice for a while, then finally steeled himself, swallowed his pride and urged the horse forwards. He told her everything he knew, but with no solution at hand, it amounted to very little. She said she understood, but she did a poor job of concealing her disappointment.

Falling under even greater shame, Rathen rode on in silence, staring into space with a weary mind, unaware of the scowl Anthis was firing his way.

Aria pirouetted, clumsily, though she was sure it was perfect, and jabbed her wooden sword at the air. Then she turned, jumped, slashed, and tumbled to her knee. She pretended that it was deliberate and rolled to complete the act.

"Don't lock your elbow," Petra said from time to time, observing from nearby upon the largest of the rocks that studded the low, dry ridge. "Keep your knees soft."

She corrected herself at every input, and for a while they came less frequently, but as the veiled sun set and the fire cast long, ghoulish shadows out from the surrounding trees, she started tripping more often. When she grew frustrated and tried to compensate for fatigue with force, sweeping her sword so hard she knocked herself off-balance and crumpled to the ground with a yelp, a hand came to rest gently upon her shoulder. She looked up as Petra crouched beside her, smiling softly, and ruffled her curls. "Very good."

"No it wasn't," she huffed, ceasing her struggle to rise and slumping in defeat instead. She stabbed the wooden sword into the dirt beside her, but it toppled and landed with a pitiful thunk. She groaned and dropped her face into her hands.

Petra smiled sadly and wrapped an affectionate arm around her. "Yes, it was. You have natural grace and a wonderful energy, Aria, you should be proud. You have surprising potential." She frowned and leaned closer as Aria mumbled something into her palms. "Yes, but everyone does. What counts is that you picked yourself back up every time. ...Yes, because you've worn yourself out. ...No, you didn't fail, you're *tired*, Aria," she lifted her chin and looked gravely into her huge, disappointed eyes, "listen to me: you did well. But you're not going to be perfect immediately. It took my father years to train me to this level, and I still have a long way to go before I could ever match up to him, so I practise all the time--"

"Why?"

Petra hesitated, startled by the question. "Because I want to serve his memory well."

"No," Aria shook her head, a sudden solemnity pushing her frustration aside, "there's more. Revenge. That's why, isn't it? For your father?"

She said nothing. Only smiled sadly. "That is part of it. And it's not an example you should seek nor follow. Aria, I know why you're doing this. But being protected isn't a weakness. Being able to protect yourself but *not* doing so out of fear *is*. No, hush. Having a sword on your hip, wood *or* steel, and being *unable* to wield it is as good as being unarmed. And it would have been foolish to try."

Aria fell silent. She didn't move. She didn't look up from the ground or loosen her tightly pursed lips. She didn't even sigh. Petra considered her for a moment, then shuffled around to sit in front of her. She lifted the toy sword and turned it over in her hands, brushing the dirt from the blunt wooden edge. "This kind of skill isn't for vengeance," she announced. "It isn't for showing off and should never be taken lightly. Every time you lift a sword, you're handling a weapon - something intended to defend, to deter violence, and yet exquisitely designed for the physical purpose of causing harm. Do you understand that?"

She pursed her lips and narrowed her eyes in careful consideration. "I do."

"Good. And do you understand that such a thing should *only* be used to defend and deter, and *never* for its physical purpose?"

"Yes...but *you* fight, and not for defence or deturn - we saw you in the city."

"Another example you're not to follow," she said quite sharply, "but I wasn't wielding it to cause pain. The purpose of a duel is to disarm or disable; I never aim to draw blood. I know my way around a blade, so I can afford to bend the rules, but *only* because I truly understand the intention beyond the physical function. Do you understand that?"

"I do, I understand."

"Good." She extended the toy sword, laid across both palms, and stifled a smile in favour of ceremony as Aria looked down at the hewn wood with new eyes. "Protect what's close to you. And practise. Expect to slip, anticipate it, and learn to recover from it. Work it to your advantage, and strengthen your balance against it. Don't try to be perfect. If you're perfect, you can't grow, you'll never be able to learn, and you'll fall against the first new tactic."

Aria nodded and took the sword. Carefully. Reverently. She stared down at it for a long while. Petra watched her, and when she finally looked back up, her eyes were alight with a misty blue fire. But when she spun around to look eagerly towards her father, sitting beside the flames, her enthusiasm wilted. His back was half-turned and she could see the glint of the Zi'veyn in his hands. Of course. He wasn't watching. He hadn't seen any of it.

Her shoulders rounded with a deflated sigh.

Petra's brow furrowed sadly. "He has a lot on his mind."

"He doesn't even realise I'm back. I *hated* being away from him, it was the very worst thing in the world! I didn't know what was going to happen, if I would even *see* him again...a-and I thought it would be the same for him..." She looked down at the sword through foggy eyes and all reverence vanished. She saw only a piece of wood. A toy. Her father's from when he was her age. Her bottom lip trembled. "He blames me for Ira's death."

"*No*." Petra grasped her shoulder more fiercely than she'd intended, but she didn't loosen her grip as Aria let her curly locks slip and shadow her face. "Absolutely not. You *know* that isn't true. He missed you so much and he's over the moon that you're back, we *all* are, and *no one* blames you for anything. And neither should you. He has the weight of the world on his shoulders right now, and he's struggling with it, that's all this is."

"He has Anthis's help," she mumbled, "how can he be struggling?"

"...Because," she began, stifling her spite, "they're *both* struggling. Those two are the smartest among us and they're both working as hard as they can, but they're stuck. That's how complicated all this is. He *is* glad you're back, but this is also very important."

"Yes. It is, isn't it?" Petra saw her lips twist into a lopsided pout. "I wish I could help. But I really don't know how."

"Have you tried?"

"What could *I* do?"

"I think you'd be surprised. In any case, you should talk to him. Interrupt him. He could do with a distraction." Movement in the marsh beyond the ridge gripped Petra's gaze, but it was only Garon. She smiled sadly and looked back to the girl. "Grown ups have a habit of not knowing when to stop working. Then their brains either get frazzled and don't work properly, or they live for nothing else."

"Really?"

"Oh yes." She rose to her knees and pulled Aria up to her feet, then took her sword and slipped it through the belt she'd taken to wearing for such a purpose, catching the cross guard over the leather. Then she tidied her hair, held her at arm's length, cleaned a smear of dirt from her forehead, and grinned. "Now go. You have a job to do."

Aria's enthusiasm waned. Slowing her approach, she peered around at him from the shadows instead. He didn't move, he didn't see her, and he had a peculiar look on his face as he stared through the elven artefact. She studied him for a while, debating whether or not it was a good idea to interrupt his thoughts after all, but one glance back towards Petra and her expectantly cocked eyebrow silenced her doubts.

She stepped forwards and brazenly forced her way past the Zi'veyn, through his arms and down into his lap, where she leaned against him as though he was as comfortable as the armchair back home, making it quite impossible for him to miss her arrival.

But thought was loath to release him; his eyes cleared as slowly as if she'd tapped him on the shoulder. But once they'd focused, the confusion in his questioning look fled. He sighed, set the Zi'veyn somewhat roughly on the ground and enveloped her tightly in his arms. "I've been ignoring you."

"You have the weight of the world on your shoulders," she informed him, sinking contentedly into his embrace. "You and Anthis are the smartest among us and you're struggling. I understand. But you should expect to fail."

"...Why thank you, little one."

"That way," she continued obliviously, "you'll be able to grow and get better."

"What are you talking about?"

She wriggled out of his grip, and his confused smile slackened at the maturity of her eyes as her gaze levelled gravely. "You're frightened by the Zi'veyn."

"I am not!" He blurted.

"I don't mean scared. I mean imitidated. And you're an *elf*, Daddy, you *can't* be imitidated by it."

"Intimidated. And I'm not - and neither am I an elf."

"You are," she informed him again, speaking far too surely. "But you can't let it push you around. It's like Oat: she trots around a lot, holding her beard high, but she's not as clever as she thinks she is. She's all bluster. But if you tell her what you want to do, she does it eventually, you just have to keep telling her and be really clear. Like sitting in her hay yourself, first. Or kneeling by the milking stool. Because she doesn't get it if you just sit on it and wait for her."

"She does."

"No, she thinks you're just sitting down. But she understands what you want her to do when you take the extra time to show her. It's just one extra step, but it makes all the difference, and makes her very un-intimitidating anymore."

"You shouldn't keep playing to her whims."

"I'm not - she's playing to *mine*. I get her to do what I want her to far quicker than she does for you."

He grunted. "That's true. But even so, you let her push you around."

"That's just what *she* thinks." Rathen laughed and ruffled her hair, and she smiled contentedly. She settled back against him. "I missed you. And also, the house was strange. My bedroom was *up*stairs. But there were lots of toys."

"There were?"

"Mhm. I liked the horse. Don't worry, I took good care of him."

Another smile crept over Rathen's face as he recalled the stuffed canvas horse head stuck on the end of a polished walking stick and all the wildly unlikely adventures they'd had. "Artera."

"His name was Beans, actually. And he had six feet. He made a lot of noise. Clippity-cloppity-clip, clippity-cloppity-clip."

"That's seven feet."

"Well...then *seven* feet! So he was even faster than I thought!" She grinned up at him, but his white face wasn't smiling. Hers slipped in disappointment. But just as a pout began to move into its place, she saw his eyes begin to widen and flick suddenly towards the Zi'veyn. Her jealousy was given no time to set in; something glittered within them, something that wasn't the flickering of the fire, and she jumped quickly aside as he lunged for it.

"One extra step..." He muttered to himself, looking feverishly about and across the camp. "Magic," he said only a little louder, "I need...something..."

Without a word, Aria scrambled away and hurried to the bags, returned in a heartbeat, and showed him the old stuffed doll she'd had for as long as she could remember. "Dance," she said as Anthis looked up from his scrolls at the commotion, and not a moment after she'd set it on the ground and Rathen had flexed his fingers, it moved. Its stumpy little arms pushed its stuffed little body to its stocky little legs, balancing well enough despite its oversized head and heavy, floppy woollen hair, and then, with surprising grace for such a rotund form, began dancing silently by the campfire. Thick shadows moved chaotically over the dirt and tufts of grass with every arabesque, sissone and cabriole, and Aria delighted in its weightless movements. Even Anthis peered closer in wonder.

But then, all too soon, it ended. The doll fell limp and dropped lifelessly to the ground.

Aria did not complain.

She looked up and around to her father. Anthis followed her gaze.

And Rathen stared, with eyes as wide as the moon, at the thorn-covered, onyx-gold, lotus crowned pyramid that hovered mutely between his hands.

Chapter 14

Moments after Petra's frenzied call, Garon appeared at the edge of the ridge, hauling himself swiftly up into the firelit camp, his blade at the ready. But his preparation crumbled to confusion when he discovered not a beast nor a stranger, but Rathen and Anthis each climbing onto their horses in the last brush of evening light, while Aria already sat keen in the front of the saddle.

"What are you doing?" He demanded in a caged hiss while his eyes flicked about through the enshrouding darkness for whatever had provoked them. But the child, he quickly noticed, looked far too excited, and Anthis seemed to wear the same giddy expression if only slightly more restrained. Rathen bore nothing but urgency. Garon slowed and hesitated, his heart in his throat. "What's happened?"

"He's done it."

He stared, dumbfounded, as Petra grinned in disbelief. "*What?* How?"

"He made Isabelle stop dancing!"

"Who?" His frown creased deeper as Rathen tugged the reins and turned his horse about. "Where are you going?"

"Back to the ruins."

"Rathen, it's--"

"With or without you, Inquisitor." Urging his horse into the closest thing to a gallop the treacherous ground would grant, the mage offered no other word nor chance as he sped past him to leap the three-foot ledge with Anthis close behind him.

Garon cursed as they splashed into the marsh below and hurtled away into the night. He turned to fetch his own and race after their impulse with as much dignity and authority as he could, but found Petra already handing him the reins.

"Go," she said, outwardly ignoring, as he did, the brushing of their fingers. "I'll stay here. Eyila's not far."

He bolted straight off after them. It took only a moment to catch them up; their pace had been quickly hindered by the expansive puddles. "What happened?"

"One more step," the mage replied, his eyes fixed ahead as hooves splashed through water and skeletal trees tried to snatch at them. "There was a missing link in the chain, the spell - I wasn't specifying where it was supposed to pull the magic from."

"How could you overlook something like that?!"

"I thought you said you'd tried that," Anthis said far more tactfully, but Rathen shook his head.

"No. I'd tried telling it where to *go*, but I was too vague; I told the spell that the magic was there, but I hadn't specified where 'there' was. I'd assumed it would detect it since it was all around us, and why would I try to activate it if there was no magic around to use it on? But I tried the same thing on the doll while it was dancing and nothing happened - *until* I told it where the doll was. One extra step; kneel by the stool, lead it by the hand."

Anthis and Garon exchanged a silent, quizzical look.

They thundered on for twenty minutes before they reached the edge of the disembodied magic, and Rathen was quick to relocate its centre, refusing this time to be knocked back by its power. He dismounted before his horse had stopped, had the Zi'veyn in hand before his feet hit the ground, and as a look of concentration gripped his hard features, Anthis and Garon were behind him.

Then he fell perfectly still. Their joint breath stalled in anticipation.

No music wove through the dark forest, no pockets of light or strange activities. In the hours since they had last been there, nothing at all had changed. But still they searched while the mage remained a statue, hunting for anything that might hint at success, anything that might give them some means of measuring his progress. They heard sounds - the songs of nightlarks, the rhythmic movement of creatures in the water, the croaking of frogs - felt the brush of wind, saw shafts of ever-dominating starlight shift through the gathering clouds and thin canopy. Their hearts jumped whenever such phenomena ceased. But they were natural; they'd been there before the arrival of the magic, and announced themselves after their own.

Truly, there was no way of knowing how far Rathen had come. The removal of so much magic surely wouldn't be quick, but they were left with not even a hint of how long they could expect to stand there, out in the open, in the dark of night, surrounded by shadows that could conceal any number of dangers, beast or human. Garon soon turned away and stared ardently through the blackness, hand resting readily on the hilt of his sword, and even Anthis put his acutely erudite eyes to use.

It was only at the deepening of Rathen's breath that anyone returned him their attention, and found his eyes closed tightly beneath a fiercely knotted brow. His knuckles, Anthis noted, were white, and the moon-bathed Zi'veyn was certainly not floating.

The historian's shoulders slumped in disappointment, and Garon frowned between them. "What is it?" But neither replied; Rathen continued to strain against the relic, and Anthis merely shook his head.

Garon grunted. So short and imperial, it was as though he'd expected the failure. Rathen bristled. The inquisitor turned and stepped back up into the saddle. "Let's go."

"It should have worked."

"Garon," Anthis stepped forwards, glancing carefully between them as the mage growled through his teeth, "it *did* work back in camp. Didn't it, Aria?"

"It's true, Mister Inquis'tor, it did! It really did!"

"But it hasn't worked *now*. When it counts." He met the black gaze Rathen turned over his shoulder. The danger didn't shake him. He held his stare with the same infernal authority. "Petra and Eyila are still at camp. We need to get back. Make no mistake, Rathen, I congratulate you on your victory. You've made progress. But it's clear that there are still kinks to work out and you're not going to succeed tonight. We will head back to camp, and you - *both* of you - will rest. You can continue work in the morning. But not here."

Long black hair flicked in a whirlwind as Rathen snapped around. "How am I going to get *anywhere* if we keep leaving these places behind?!"

"Need I remind you we are being hunted? We can't remain still. There are, unfortunately, *plenty* of places you can test your theories along the way, but we *must* keep moving. From one to the next. Otherwise, if Salus catches us, we're finished, and it won't matter any longer if you can stop dolls from dancing or not." He jerked on the reins and turned his horse away, brushing off the searing glare. "We're leaving."

Puddles had turned to murky pools and the soft, squelching, spidering ground interlaced between them had become like the threads of a fish net, forcing them into single file. Wherever they broadened enough to ride two abreast, ghostly silver birch trees had taken root to ensure the way remained obstructed, while grey-skinned frogs and small, swift rodents disturbed the countless sky's reflections as they fled the hooves that slipped into the muck with every few steps.

The marsh had become a swamp, and the summer storm brewing above them was certain to make the going worse - it had already started drizzling, and the air was already sticky and unpleasant. Even Eyila had removed her cloak, brightening the grey, lacklustre environment with her striking bronze skin and still curiously lush sash of leaves and phials. But there was nothing at all around them to see, and time dragged, every second punctuated by the rhythmic thump of hooves and what fleeting excitement manifested as a jolt of panic each time their horses faltered on the slippery ground.

Anthis sighed deeply, watching the hypnotic sway of the bay's rump as it trudged along in front of him. "I've been staring at that horse's backside for so long I've forgotten what the other end looks like." He dragged his eyes towards the newest copse of paper-white trees to grace their path. "Where are we? I don't recognise anything."

"We're not following any road," Garon replied. "Nestor isn't far. We'll be there in an hour."

That hour passed twice as slowly. It was eventually eased by the discovery of a road which the horses visibly delighted at, trotting with a definite bounce in their steps even if it lay beneath three inches of water, and the old village eventually rose from the misty grey flood. Cloaks were reluctantly returned to shoulders, shielding them from the sweet, cooling rain, and as they drew close to the first of the quaint if shabby old buildings, Petra led Eyila on a branching path that veered away from the village towards one of a few denser clusters of trees.

Rathen rode a little closer to Garon's mare. Eyeing the approaching building, he dropped his voice and pulled his hood lower. "Is this wise?"

"Kienza was right. Things are too hectic right now for anyone to notice us, even in a village."

"Even in a village just spitting distance from one *very* recently--"

"Yes."

The road emerged from the murky water as the ground began to rise, the village itself built upon a small hillock both higher and firmer than the surrounding marsh and out of reach even of its recent expansion.

"We're being tracked," Anthis reminded him quietly as they passed the first outlying home.

"Taliel was also right," Rathen replied. "He shouldn't know we're on horseback, no one will be looking for the tracks."

"Unless she's told him."

"She wouldn't do that. We can trust her."

No one gave voice to their doubts. They passed a second building, and a third built closer, and just like that, they were in the village.

"Regardless," Garon murmured, drawing his horse in at the hitching post beside what was presumably a herbalists' shop, "we need supplies and an ear to the ground, and Nestor is ideal."

"You have a contact here?"

He thought for a moment. "Kruuz is more likely. Even so, a small village relies on traders, and traders bring more than wares. And being in 'spitting distance' of Trinn, they'll absorb any and all gossip that passes through."

Lifting Aria down from the saddle, for which he was scorned, Rathen considered him with a wary cock of his brow. "Gossip?"

"It may be exaggerated, but it's usually born of truth. You just have to know what's worth following." He looked sternly across the three of them, then removed a pouch of coins from his saddlebag and handed them to Anthis who was slinging his beloved satchel over his shoulder. "We need supplies."

"I know, I've got it."

"Keep your head down." He looked to the others as the historian departed. "I'm going to see what I can learn. As for you two: don't wander, don't draw attention, don't--"

"You've told us *all* of this before," Aria sighed.

Garon rolled his eyes, turned, and walked away.

"Come along, little one," Rathen chuckled, taking her small hand in his, and together they walked through the drizzle towards the centre of the village. But while he hid his face and felt his skin prickle nervously in the presence of other people, going about their business despite the weather, Aria stared up openly at their houses, awe clear upon her face. In recent months, she'd discovered that houses could be more than hollowed-out boulders. They could be cut from far larger stones, even into cliff faces, and they could also be made from far smaller rocks, stacked carefully into straight-sided structures. But while each example had captured her attention, here she seemed lost in enchantment. It was true that this village looked like something out of one of her many fairytale books, surrounding marsh excluded: its houses were slightly wonky, old and grey, their roofs a mixture of thatch and shale, and the walls of a few were being slowly enveloped in moss. But beyond the obvious features were the far finer details, ones almost impossible to see without the sharp sight and curiosity of youth - above all else, the impossibly fine engravings in the stones themselves. They were weathered and in many cases impossible to tell from careless masonry, but few of these stones had been cut by human hands. The engravings - those that had survived - were elven.

Despite Nestor having stood for a few hundred years, Rathen suddenly understood where the ruins in the marsh had gone.

Lost in a world of whimsy, when Aria spotted the little well at the centre of the square, enchanting in its ivy and storm-beaten grey stones, she all but dragged him towards it. It was from there, as he held her back from leaning over too far as she peered inside, that Rathen observed the village with the greatest of caution. Favouring his hearing, he appeared first to be admiring the well, then tending hidden damage to his boot on the bench beside it, but all the while he tuned into the conversations of passing villagers and the minutiae of their lives.

He learned nothing at all, discounting "ooh, a storm'll hit soon, and mark my words, mark my words it'll be a beast."

Just as the village had taken root upon the hillock, naturally so too had the trees. The thickets that surrounded the grove were more vibrant than those that speckled the rest of the swamp; their white, papery bark seemed brighter, their leaves lusher and broader, and they grew taller and tighter together, their seeds having tolerated close neighbours to take advantage of the good fortune they'd landed in. The inescapable moss that clung to every studding stone thrived just as well as the birch, and the rich, emerald cushions made the stunted forest seem almost cordial, if one could overlook the insects, humidity and heavy scent of damp wood.

Eyila peered closely at one perfectly rounded green tuft. After a long moment, she poked at it with a careful bronze finger. It was firmer than it looked. She ran her touch lightly over the moss's bobbly surface, then pinched a piece and rubbed it between her thumb and forefinger, crushing the buds under gentle pressure. She sniffed the residue, then, tentatively, brushed it with her tongue. She spat immediately and considered the lingering taste.

A small pouch appeared from beneath her cloak from which she withdrew a pinch of what looked like thick, dry grass. She ground it between her palms and it quickly turned to dust.

Pinching and crushing another nub of moss, she rubbed it into the powder, mixing it as thoroughly as dye into clay. Then, as she had the first time, sniffed, tasted, spat and considered it again.

Petra watched, brow furrowed, as she withdrew a small sickle-shaped knife and began zealously gathering full clusters of moss from the stones. "Dear healer," she said lightly, "you'll make yourself sick doing that."

"You forget that my training goes beyond the use of magic." She extended one of the clusters towards her with a spirited grin. "Smell that?"

"Damp?"

"No, eresthal--...um...look." She tossed a piece towards her, where she stood watchfully between the trees. "Nutty and sour. It's found in plants with anthni--...it stops blood from clotting."

"All right. And what is that?" Petra asked, tossing it back and gesturing towards the dry grass she was grinding between her palms again, her expression still screwed up against the sourness.

"Noha root. Most plants I know with this ability are dry and activated through burning, but this...sponge thing is wet. But noha root has hot-drying properties - it's used as a dressing after searing a wound, but Liaha, my teacher, once used it against a moist herb to dry it out almost immediately." She extended a piece of shrivelled moss.

"Dry," Petra frowned in surprise. "And it will keep?"

"It should," she grinned. "We'll find out. It's nice to finally find something of use in these forests of yours."

"Besides fruit, nuts and game?"

Her smile became lopsided. "Besides that, yes. I admit the sands are harder, but their medicinal plants are boundless."

"Plants? Boundless?"

Eyila's lips pursed and curled. Petra had come to decipher some degree of the tribal's unusual expressions. This was a playful snarl that often met her own sarcasm. Petra grinned.

"Anyway, I have the feeling that I will soon need them."

"Oh? Why?"

"Because if things keep going as they are, Anthis will wind up with a few puncture wounds." Eyila sent the duelist a sidelong glance when she didn't respond, and found her expression tight and brooding. She looked back to the shrivelling moss, continuing to powder the most vivid, and settled herself lightly on the ground beside her. "Forgive me for saying so, but you behave like a child around Anthis." She saw Petra's head snap towards her, but she didn't look up. She fished out an empty pouch from beneath her cloak instead and began tucking away her prizes. She continued quite unapologetically. "Why do you seek confrontation with him? It does no one any good, especially yourself. You will exhaust your heart. If you hate him so, why do you let yourself get so worked up?" She didn't raise her eyes, though she felt Petra's burning upon her. They did little to unsettle her. "I think - in fact, I *know* - it's because you care. You fretted for him just as you did for Rathen while they were trapped in that place. Don't deny it. You're hurt, I understand that, especially after all you've told me of your father, and you're a fighter - you're aggressive and defensive in the face of anything that might try to knock you down. We've both lost our worlds at the hands of murderers. But they were not him. I know this, and so do you. And instead of transferring my...feelings onto him, I've tried to understand him and his motives."

Finally, Eyila closed the pouch and looked up, meeting the bewildered outrage that consumed Petra's face. "I realise it may seem strange, but in understanding and then forgiving him and his ways - ways I do not believe he can help - I can find *some* kind of...what was the word? 'Catharsis'? You understand. But keeping me away from him because of your *own* mistrust is making it impossible. I appreciate your care, Petra, but in this case it is neither needed nor wanted."

Petra turned away as she rose to her feet, and though Eyila recognised the purpose of the gesture, she ignored it. She rose and stepped around in front of her, back into her line of sight. "Perhaps you should try the same."

"He," she growled through her teeth, her gaze shooting past, refusing even to brush her, "is a cultist. He may dress it in honour and integrity, but he kills for personal gain. I admire that you, of *all* people, can look past that - clearly you are a better person than I am - but it confounds me also. And I...am not ready."

"Or are you simply unwilling?"

Petra's eyes dragged heavily onto her, catching her sad smile before she turned away to gather more moss.

Aria swung her legs playfully from her perch upon the well-side, her face turned up towards the sky, pattered by the endless drizzle. Her hood slipped down every few moments, which she quickly snatched back into place against anyone who might be watching her despite her cluelessly audacious presence, and she kept her humming to a minimum.

But she was bored. Here was this pretty little village made from the strangest of stones, surrounded by mystery, consumed by moss, inhabited by goodness only knew what, and she was unable to wander it. Her lips drew into a pout and she sighed wearily. She hadn't even her father to talk to, though he sat on the worm-eaten bench right beside her. He was leafing through his notebook with a bitter twist to his lips. In fact he'd looked like that for most of the day. And he'd been moodier than usual, too. Several times he'd looked ready to throw the book into the dirty water and be done with it, but something kept his nose among the pages.

Now, however, he just looked tired. He'd definitely over-worked his mind.

She straightened. She recognised her duty - but in trying to enact it, what came out from her mouth was not what she'd intended. Not that she was sure what that was, but it was far too close to the source of his troubles than it was a song about a goat.

"It didn't work," he replied with a drawn sigh, still staring sightlessly into the pages, "because I am a fool." She began immediately to dispute his claim, for which he smiled gratefully, but he was far from swayed. "Where Isabelle was concerned, I was directing it at a tangible vessel - a vessel you can see and touch. But the magic in the ruins *has* no vessel. I'd become so caught up in the details it needed to work that I'd walked right into the same obvious mistake I'd made the last time. And I don't have a clue how to get around it..."

She pushed her sad frown aside and shuffled closer, attempting to reassure him with a smile, though his eyes were still drawn into the book. "You made Isabelle stop dancing. You made the Z--" her eyes widened and she glanced about them, dropping her voice lower. "You made *it* work. You did, Daddy, we all saw it."

His shoulders fell with a deep, slow exhalation. He didn't look up, and this time her confidence didn't win a smile of any kind. If anything, his lips turned down further. She felt useless. But she didn't give in to it. Because he needed her.

She looked back up into the rain instead, pondering the matter. Countless drops of water fell onto her skin, making her blink erratically to keep it out of her eyes, but she enjoyed the cooling sensation and so didn't shield her face against them. But when she finally brushed a myriad of big, round blobs of water from her skin with one wipe of her arm, an abstract thought began to form. "Perhaps," she said slowly, following the thought as it took on a life of its own, "it's like marbles. They bounce and roll away and scatter all over the floor. In a bag, you can pick them all up in one go - like the magic you put inside Isabelle to make her dance. But once they're loose, you have to pick them all up one at a time or you'll stand on them and fall."

"Puddles!"

Rathen jolted in shock and spun around in his seat. He'd forgotten that Anthis was sitting beside him, silently reading through one of his notebooks as he, like they, waited for Garon to return. But the young man seemed unaware of his fright and continued urgently with a deeply pensive frown.

"You said the magic had gathered in puddles, not as one expanse, correct? What if your mistake was trying to draw *all* the magic up at once? The elves were all about context, so targeting a vessel - a body or a doll - is required to complete the spell, as you proved, to fill the missing part of the chain. But the elves were also extremely *specific*. They could have used this against an opposing faction, but they would have had to distinguish one faction from another, especially if they were intermingled. No doubt they had some elaborate way of doing this quickly enough for the weapon to be used to maximum effect without hindrance, but if we overlook that for the moment--"

"You're saying I should be targeting the puddles of magic, specifically, not the magic as a whole."

"...That's the jist of it, yes. One, three, five at a time; the lot when you've gotten a feel for it."

Rathen nodded slowly, his lined face creasing deeper as he mulled the suggestion over. One eyebrow twitched in a decidedly acceding manner.

"*Oh!*"

Anthis and Rathen froze in fright at the sudden and shrill exclamation, while Aria spun to discover an older woman with grey streaked hair gazing back at her over the top of a jug with bright, enchanted eyes. "Oh, what a pretty lass you are!"

Aria grinned, her cheeks immediately turning a vibrant crimson. "Thank you, missus..."

"Oh but this rain! Whatever are you doing in this marsh in such weather? You don't live near - I would remember a face like yours."

"We needed food," she smiled shyly, "we're travelling."

"Oh," her wistful eyes became steeped in sorrow and her lower lip quivered like a bowstring. "Refugees, hey? Such sad, sad times. Where are you heading?"

"West," Anthis replied, rising and turning as Aria pointed to the far southern end of the village. Rathen kept his head down; the historian was, to their fortune, surprisingly forgettable despite his reputation. "To White Heath."

The dramatic woman's eyes became grave as they lifted to him, and the well wheel creaked mournfully as she worked it to lower her jug. "You'll be passing near Eddon, I wager. You should find another route, and not just for the sake of your youngster."

"He's not my--"

"Why?" He frowned, interrupting Aria's protest. "What's happened in Eddon?"

"Well it's what *almost* happened, really. Bandits attempted to take the town a few nights past - I expect they were encouraged by the evacuations, decided they would be more likely to run away than stand firm. Well, they were chased off, thank the stars, but as sure as the sun rises, they'll be lurking around in the trees like ditchlings around an orphanage. It was surely by Vastal's grace alone that only one person was killed - a Kalosian, you know." Her eyes suddenly slighted in the greatest of suspicion, and her voice dropped in secrecy. "Out late, she was. Some suppose she was the one that let them in."

Anthis frowned. "Then why did they kill her?"

"Well she chose to work with bandits. What beyond trickery can anyone expect of them?" The wheel stuck as the sloshing jug hit the cross beam, and she dragged it towards herself with practised effort. "No, sir, I suggest you find another route."

"Yes, thank you, truly. We will."

The old woman nodded in satisfaction, either at his agreement or at the weight of her jug as she detached it from the hook, and after bidding them luck and farewell, she turned away to leave. "Oh," she threw back as she started off into the finally waning drizzle, "and keep an eye on the clouds! Mark my words, this storm will be terrible! Terrible!"

Anthis sighed as she walked away, while Aria clambered from the well to sit possessively in her father's lap. "One death. It could have been much worse..." His eyes dropped sympathetically towards the pair, but while he found Aria expectedly lost in an all-too-fresh memory, Rathen appeared only suspicious. Anthis frowned. "What is it?"

"Nothing, I hope. But my hope has been misplaced before... Don't you think that just one death - of a foreigner, no less - in the dead of night is a bit...convenient?"

"You don't believe it. ...Do you think...?"

"Like I said: I hope not. But Salus seems paranoid enough to take such extreme measures. I doubt there were any bandits at all..." He looked up as Garon finally joined them, finished at last with his intel-gathering and feigned friendliness among the locals. "Welcome back. Find anything?"

He shook his head, eyes quickly scanning their surroundings. "Not much. Numbers of mage hunters are growing in the larger towns, there's been a sudden absence of ditchlings, complaints about the marsh, and the incident in Trinn is being blamed on the Order. The only thing of note is a supposed bandit attack on Eddon, wherein--"

"Only one Kalosian was killed. We heard the same. It stinks to you, too?"

"Absolutely."

Anthis nodded, as though it had been immediately obvious to him, too. "Local supplies are thin. The flooding has ruined their stock. No one can say where it came from, but they're at least not blaming the Order - although one merchant did mention that a travelling priest put it down to Vastal's fury at the lack of a chapel, but the merchant seemed unconvinced. After all, there's *never* been a chapel in Nestor. But more than that, a few trade routes have been cut off and rerouted by a chasm to the south west. That's all."

"Nothing, then, to suggest Salus's progress nor his intentions. Though that's no surprise." He glanced down to the loaded bag sitting at Anthis's feet, then turned and started back down the road towards the herbalist's shop and their waiting horses. "We should move on."

"To where?" Rathen whispered roughly, grasping Aria's hand and hurrying after him. "Nothing but Korovor lies ahead of us. Horses or not, we *will* run into an ambush sooner or later."

"Which is why we have to keep moving. We'll head for Mokhan - I have contacts there, we should have more luck."

Rathen surged ahead and stopped him in his path, his voice as low and dangerous as the urgency in his eyes. "We were *chased out* of Mokhan not three months ago. It is also a *city*. A city a *stone's throw* away from Kulokhar. I heard what Kienza said, and I heard what Taliel said, but there is a line, and Mokhan is it."

"And what do *you* suggest?" Garon grunted when he failed to reply. He stepped around him as he bristled and walked on with his usual commanding air. Until a shout stopped him dead.

Everyone - the four, the nearby locals, even the two dogs that had been cocking their legs at the door of an out-of-work carpenter - turned and stared silently towards the furthest end of the village. For a moment, everything fell still. Nothing moved, until another shriek of alarm kicked life back into the air. All of a sudden, a crowd of people appeared running down the village road straight towards them, ensnared in a blind panic. Five figures followed them, but calmly, their every step brazen and confident as they tracked their wake, daring anyone to try to stand their ground before them, black cloaks billowing from their shoulders.

Rathen's blood boiled in his veins; he scarcely managed to compress his rage into a growl. He felt a hand on his shoulder; the rough tug told him it was Garon, and his cold orders to follow him away confirmed it. But as fire flared and blinded him, bursting into life around the intruders, his feet held fast. The flames erupted into the air, encircling the five mages in a furious, twisting inferno, a shield of heat and cinders that lashed out wildly to sear all stone, moss and wood within reach.

Had it been any ordinary fire, the damp wood and saturated moss would have been unscathed. But this fire was born of magic, shaped with the intent to harm. A glancing contact was all it took to leave a burning trail behind them. And the five young mages within its protection, each surely only recently graduated, appeared to relish the screams and destruction.

In the seconds since the heralding panic, roofs were already aglow and spreading fast. The most distant shortly collapsed, and a wail of despair rose around it.

Rathen ignored the tightening grip on his shoulder. He watched, veins burning in outrage, as the mages manipulated pots, stones and rubble into the paths of those fleeing, cackling joyously while young and old tripped in their haste; as trellises and thatch toppled and bellowed more embers over the gardens; as those embers took root against wooden doors and burned houses from below while the roofs above stood as bonfires.

"Daddy, what's happening?!"

"Rathen, there's nothing we can do. We have to leave." The inquisitor's grip tightened, but Rathen shrugged out of it, his fingers already twisting into cryptic tangles faster than any human eye could follow. But as water rose in a geyser from somewhere on the outskirts to quench the furthest and greatest inferno, Garon grasped the mage's fingers and wrenched him around to stare another blaze into his eyes. It was met bitterly. Rathen tried to snatch his hands free, but Garon was already dragging him along and through the frantic crowd attempting to barrel their way out of the village while the now roaring fire overtook the arsonists.

"We can't leave--"

"*We don't have a choice!*" Garon thrust him roughly towards his horse, but there was no room to mount and no time to try. He didn't say it, but each of them were sorely aware that the uproar would draw any and all of their creeping pursuers. So they unhitched the reins, slung loose bags over their backs and led the skittish horses out of the village and off towards the right of the flooded road all others were taking.

The creaking collapse of burning roofs travelled all too clearly through the trees.

"We shouldn't have left," Rathen growled. "I could have stopped them!"

"And *then* what?" Garon hissed, spinning towards him. "The village would remember us, *blame* us - we would become a part of this, and when people came asking, they would tell! Now, all they'll remember are those five mages; it's as if we were never here."

"How can you call yourself a protector if you're willing to stand by and just *let* that happen, right in front of you?! They weren't there to intimidate, they were there to *harm!*"

"Garon--"

Anthis was ignored. "And your intentions would mean nothing after that exposure! For these people, all mages are now painted with the same brush!"

"And by not stepping in, we've justified it! But that *assumption* is no reason to *let* people get hurt!"

"Rathen, we--"

"And if we're caught by--"

"We need to move. *Now.*"

The bickering stopped at Anthis's firm tone, and was forgotten at the fervent flicking about of his eyes. There was no need to ask. They hurried on in silence.

Then everything happened at once.

There were no footsteps, no splashes; nothing more than a presence confirmed by a shadow almost missed in the darkness of the overcast sky. Then a figure appeared, two arms' length away, a stranger whose eyes bore an unmistakable purpose and keen focus that left little doubt to her intent. Her arm was already poised, a piece of silver glinting between her fingers, its point aimed unerringly at them. Understanding took too long to fall.

But before it had the chance to land, Eyila suddenly stood in her place, rubbing her knuckles while the woman crumpled to the ground at her feet. Garon shouted while they stared at the girl in surprise, and his words cut a fever through their hearts. And through the woman.

She leapt quickly and nimbly back to her feet, and another flash of steel electrified their bodies into action.

But she didn't strike.

A ragged gasped escaped her lips. She dropped more slowly this time, hitting the ground with blood trickling down her chin, and a blade protruding through her back.

Petra tugged her sword free, flicked off the blood, and swung up onto her horse. She gestured into the trees and set off, Garon mounted close behind and Eyila following suit.

Rathen and Anthis stared at the suddenly lifeless and crimson-stained phidipan for a long moment. Neither thought in their shock to cover Aria's eyes.

Chapter 15

Tall, white and slender, drawn in smoothly half way up the body and rounded perfectly on top, one sleek arm bowed and resting upon a shapely curve, the other raised and extended, prepared and willing to serve at a second's notice.

The teapot shattered beautifully against the wall.

"*How*," bellowed the keliceran as steaming tea trickled, "could this be able to *happen?!* Scouts and patrols have been stepped up, from guards all the way to our *own!* Are we stretching ourselves thin for *nothing?!*"

But while Teagan provided a calm and no doubt well-considered response, Salus wasn't open to hearing it. He could think only of the fact that his surveillance system, had it been in place, would have completely shut out any possibility of this occurrence. But while he was close to a breakthrough, 'close' presently amounted to nothing. He'd improved upon his previous achievements of observation and feedback points, and just yesterday had succeeded in forming a link between them for all of two and a half seconds, surveying the other end of the spell-shrouded practise room in perfect clarity before it all inevitably fell apart. It was a victory, on paper, but until that link could be maintained indefinitely, those few seconds were as good as total failure.

His eyes snapped back from his daydream. "When was the last report from the scouts?"

"Three and four days ago."

"On time. And they suggested nothing untoward?"

"Nothing; you would have been informed."

Salus grunted. Teagan stared past him. "That the Order hasn't been placed under house arrest yet is beyond me," he muttered. "What is the Crown thinking...?" His fist slammed suddenly against the disarray of parchments strewn across the desk. "*Damn it all!* Mages are slipping past us, no one is pulling anything in on Doana, nor on Koraaz - in fact, our tails *lost* them four days ago! Our only sodding hope rests on our agents in Korovor - assuming *ditchlings* don't get them first!" Suspicion stalled him. His eyes travelled slowly up to Teagan. "How many of the scouts in that vicinity are phaeacian?"

"Four."

He laughed bitterly. "Out of *six*. In that case, it's clear what has happened."

"Our phaeacians are not inept, sir."

"They don't seem to be very *competent* either. What about our convergers?"

"A little under half. Most are phidipan, as you ordered."

"Well, that's something." But his tone didn't subdue. "I want more phidipans watching the surrounding area, and especially on their tail; replace who you can, juggle it around again." He rose sharply to his feet, knocking the chair back behind him, and made towards the far end of the office. Teagan's brow flickered as he passed.

"Sir? Where--"

"To investigate the phaeacians' incompetence myself."

"In Korovor?"

"Where else?" He kicked off his comfortable shoes and replaced them with worn down riding boots. "There's a translocator in Morton; with a horse I'll be there in no time." He hesitated beside a cupboard, which he opened after a moment's thought and withdrew a slender black roll of cloth. Teagan watched him tuck the fine blades into his boot without expression. Koraaz had also been heading into those woods. His gaze returned to the wall as Salus looked back at him. "Get it done."

"Of course, Keliceran."

And the matter was gone from Salus's mind. But as he rushed for the door handle, weighing his choice of the various reprimands the lowest rank of bungling subordinates had earned for themselves, there was a knock from the other side. A set of quick, sharp strikes from two second knuckles.

Irritation prickled in his veins, but after a single breath - slow, through tightly clenched teeth - he managed to stifle his haste, summon with all his strength a visage of neutrality and open the door with a carefully measured tug. He feigned surprise at his visitor. "My Lord Malson."

The old man's eyes were even more cantankerous than usual, and dropped almost immediately to his boots. His eyebrow rose crooked. "Am I interrupting?"

"Not at all, my lord. I returned just a few minutes ago."

He considered him for a careful moment, but his stare was met calmly. He soon pursed his lips in acceptance. "Very well. May I?"

Salus half jumped aside as the Crown's envoy walked in without pause for response or gesture, and again forced back his annoyance. He closed the door, preparing for whatever had ruffled the old man's feathers enough to drag him to his estate. "Is there something I can do for you, my lord?"

"Myself, and the rest of the country." He stopped beside the desk, eyeing Teagan very briefly, who appeared not to be listening, and turned to face him with an expression even darker. Salus maintained his composure, which seemed to visibly rile him. The keliceran took quiet pleasure in that. "The military *needs* intel. It needs it *yesterday*. Either Doana moves, or Turunda does - something has to give. Moore's soldiers are getting restless and he is about ready to charge in himself."

"They are under constant watch--"

"And you've found *nothing*. Step it up, Salus. Reposition, move closer, *something*. Kidnap their scouts, force them to show their hand, a *hint* of their plans! Surely Doana can't keep their secrets from the *Arana*..."

A smile almost sickly in its tolerance graced Salus's lips. "No," he replied calmly, clasping his hands behind his back, "of course not."

"Then make it happen. This *cannot* go on indefinitely."

"I agree fully. And I can assure you that it's our top priority. But it has to be done tactfully - the last thing we want is for them to think they're getting under our skin."

"And yet--"

"Yes, you're quite right, it has gone on for long enough, but the fact remains that they are in *our* land, and if we're to bind their game to *our* rules, we cannot let them think for a moment that they have the upper hand."

"I hate to be the one to break it to you, Salus, but they *do* have the upper hand."

His smile only waned because the situation demanded it. "Regrettably. But they can never be one hundred percent assured of that. We need to cultivate that doubt and expand it, which means we need to be--"

"Tactful, yes..." Malson sighed wearily, his agitation abruptly doused by the keliceran's confidence, with and to whose surprise he appeared either disinclined or unable to argue. But as he bowed absently to the promises, his eyes travelled slowly towards the third body in the room. The portian continued to stand in silence, apparently not listening - but one could never be sure.

Salus noted the change that befell him as he returned; it was quite impossible to miss. His tone lightened, his weight shifted, and the newest tea stain on the frequently re-treated panelling seemed to fascinate him. But his poor attempt at nonchalance was ultimately betrayed by his blatantly deliberate obscurity. "The Order?"

Salus straightened. Nestor. He was in no mood for a reprimand. He had little choice but to resort to the liaison's own tactical vagueness. "Surely you're aware that the Crown is still allowing them to run riot?"

"...Regrettably. But surely you have thoughts? Inklings?" At the briefest flick of his gaze, Salus eased in understanding. He was probing for his own, private request - an off-the-record surveillance of the Order that Salus has already put in place months ago.

"Nothing worthy of your time, my lord," he replied with a smile most regretful, and after being spared another swift but meaningful glance, he watched the liaison nod and retire to his usual, infuriatingly elite bearing.

"Doana is your priority, above absolutely all else. Get me something by the end of the week - or I daresay the Crown will start to reconsider *both* of our positions."

The old man, brusque and dismissive, strode past Salus as though he was no longer there and left the office without even the most cursory farewell.

Salus's face darkened as the door clicked shut.

"'Our top priority'?" Teagan still didn't move his gaze. "Are you planning something against Doana?"

"Planning? Not as such. But that old coot is right: something has to give. And it looks like it's us. What a surprise." He moved silently towards the door and listened, but heard nothing on the other side. He nodded to himself. "Forget about it for now," he said quietly as he turned the handle, "see to the phidipans." He slipped out into the corridor like a shadow, unaware of the tension in his jaw.

What on Vastal's forest-riddled earth did Malson think of him? What did the *Crown* think? That senseless, unreasonable gaggle of geese, tugging the strings of each authority like puppets manipulated for the entertainment of the king. They expected everything at the drop of a hat, as though he'd just been sitting cluelessly on a mass of information rather than passing it on as soon as it came in. Despite his every success in his eight years as Keliceran, anyone would think they deemed him inept - surely none of the other authorities were treated like this. Perhaps he ought to kidnap the old fools and dump them right outside a few of Doana's camps, then they could gather for themselves all the information the Arana was apparently choosing to ignore and he could focus his efforts on more productive solutions.

He grunted to himself. At the very least, having the Arana rescue them after their inevitable capture would be a simple yet boundless source of amusement.

This wasn't the first time the Crown had issued such 'priority' orders, but they were certainly stepping up the pressure. Fortunately he'd already prepared his responses following Malson's last acrid visit, and they seemed to defuse the liaison's temper with surprising success. But the Crown didn't need to ride him on this matter. He was fully aware of the situation - whatever reports he didn't read, Teagan did and kept him apprised. And as little as they seemed to yield, he was already considering alternative means.

And yet...Doana remained a maddeningly trying ordeal. The country of mountains and terrace farmers was far too adept at concealing their intentions. Either they had outside help, or they had created the single most successful facade in history. And though he wished to favour the former, he couldn't afford to rule anything out. And given how easily they'd picked off his local agents, the latter seemed increasingly plausible. Not all countries had a web of spies, informants, assassins and thieves - and not all that *did* answered to their monarch. But Doana had always seemed too simple, too primitive to have developed such organisation regardless of loyalty.

Seemed.

Even so, he still knew better than anyone what was happening inside and out of their borders, and he was in the best position to manage it. He wasn't about to crumble to the Crown's demands nor cater to their deluded expectations; he had his job to do, and he was doing it, by his own wits and guile. Because they hadn't failed him yet. And by sending out more phidipans, he was already improving the watch on his *own* terms.

His bearing straightened.

He threw open one of the many doors studding the walls of the second floor gallery and swept inside. Once elaborately gilded, this room, like the rest of the house, had been repurposed to the point of leaving no trace at all of its previous intent. Instead of a boudoir or some such, there was little but a curiously varied selection of rugs. All laid out flat, without scuff or overlap, the oval, circular, rectangular and octagonal tapestries in a swarm of colours and contrasting patterns appeared to be the central focus; an eccentric collection that one could admire from the comfort of a few plain chairs set beside equally small tables bearing only a quill, inkwell and ledger.

But the purpose of the collection was not so vain.

Such a manner of teleportation was a feat, to be sure. The Order didn't use it - presumably because they hadn't yet worked out how - and it had proven invaluable to the Arana over the thirty or so years since its conception. With the aid of a single mage, one could be transported in the near blink of an eye across country and borders to wherever a similar device of receptive enchantment had been established. That link between devices was the foundation of his own surveillance project, and since beginning, he'd gone from sparing teleportation little thought beyond a convenient tool to marvelling at its complexity. To transfer an image was one thing - a whole person was quite another.

As he closed the door behind himself, he couldn't help wondering at the true depth of the creator's abilities - but as it had taken her almost twenty years to make it a reality and had long since died, he would surely never find out. Which was typical. She could have been a great help to him - and he wouldn't have had to go out and waste valuable time, time that could be better spent finalising the very spells that could have prevented the necessity of his use of her rugs in the first place.

He nodded brusquely to the mage on shift, a younger blonde woman he barely took the time to notice, declared his destination, and stepped over several rugs to stop near the back upon one in particular, deep red and rectangular with a loud mess of white geometric lines.

Her fingers flexed and twisted as she dutifully followed, signs he watched but few he recognised, and held the final form. Kneeling at the edge, she pressed her crooked fingers into the weaving.

Salus took a breath.

In the next moment, the room shifted around him; the light dropped, the air became stale, and the sudden and sour aroma of smoke, ale and burned soup made his eyes water. But his stomach remained settled - which, he realised, wasn't unusual. Use of the translocators didn't bring with it the same tearing nausea that either of the elves' direct relocation did. There must have been something in the weave of the enchantment. After all, why would an elf bother to have a care over his comfort?

The stifling air chased him quickly from the cramped, dark closet and out into the keg cellar. Barrels and drums of ales lined the walls beneath a blanket of cobwebs, some taps coated in a layer of dust so thick they'd clearly not been touched for decades. The sound of drunken frivolity thrummed from above, and with every step towards the door the burning concoctions from the kitchen became stronger and more pungent, until finally offset by the more delicate scent of bread. He shut the musk of aged wood and dust away behind another creaking door and ascended towards the source that, despite his better judgement, caused his stomach to rumble.

But that would have to wait.

Passing the cook, who barely looked up, Salus moved through the kitchen, snatching as he passed two empty beer bottles from a collection of dozens beside the basin, and vanished quite ignored through the back door.

The warm, early evening air coaxed a yawn. He bit it back sharply, but while he could turn a blind eye to his hunger, his fatigue wasn't so easy.

Over the past few days his dreams had become a constant torment. The yearning he'd been plagued with for longer than he could remember hadn't diminished in the slightest, it was there while he slept and when he woke, and was all the stronger when Taliel wasn't around. The peaceful elements of his forested dreams, which themselves had become elusive as of late, had begun to overlay all kinds of imaginings, soothing him in whimsy and tearing him in half through nightmares, calm yet terrified at the same time, unable to wake himself free.

He'd not slept for two nights, and he knew the next would be the same.

Only Liogan's suggestion had given him any kind of welcome distraction, but even that he'd been left with little clue about. Despite two appearances, she'd told him nothing of substance, just fanciful ideas, half-finished thoughts, a plan without foundation that seemed to start at the fifth step.

Fortunately, detail was his strong suit, and with capable mages at his call, he had the resources to fill in the blanks.

If only he could be so confident about the capabilities of everyone else. The Crown had always been a council of fools, but now his own subordinates seemed to be lacking. And when all they were being asked to do was watch, listen and follow, there was no excuse for their constant failure.

The phidipans, the middle and most numerous rank, were up to the job; those destroying the non-humans and those chasing out the tribes were perfectly capable. Those embedded in factions both allied and opposed were also doing their duties admirably. And portians, the highest and most elite, were so efficient they brooked no doubt at all. But regardless of being the lowest tier, even the phaeacians were trained for optimum success. So why were they suddenly slipping?

He would discover that for himself.

The stables behind the tavern were small but clean, and occupied by five horses. A chestnut stamped its hooves nervously as he appeared through the shadows, shook its mane and raised its head, tusks drawn forwards in threat, while another simply watched him with wide eyes, its ears laid flat. These two, unsaddled and sticking close to the bales of hay, belonged to travellers. The remaining three did not.

He approached the nearest, a bay, neither too sleek to be a target for horse theft nor so bland as to be ideal for a butcher's sleight - it was as plain as any Aranan rider. The mare barely raised her head as he untied the hitch, gave not even a snort of protest as he stepped up into the readied stirrups and tugged the reins back towards the gate. She carried him willingly on light, patient hooves through Morton's streets, passing unmemorably through the town gates and skirting the evacuees' shanty that spewed out beyond it. And the moment the trees engulfed them, she responded to the spurring kick in a heartbeat. Erupting into a gallop, she hurtled through the trees at Salus's direction, following the map seared like pyrography into his mind.

Drizzle fell like mist, the sky was bleak, the ground beyond saturated, but the shift of the swamp, arriving far too soon, did nothing to hamper his bearings. The trees and rocks hadn't moved, after all, and the sun, though low and concealed, still descended in the south west. Focused on such rigid details, they remained unerringly on course, and eventually began tracking along the scouts' routes.

Salus's eyes sharpened through the rain as he pulled in the pace, and soon footprints, shallow and light, skirted the flood-water, discovered only once right upon them. But they didn't last; pools had already overflowed to consume them and before long all trace of the scouts' presence had vanished.

Aggravation was quick to disrupt his focus, but there was a grudging awareness at the back of his mind that his expectations had been impossible to begin with on such soft and yielding ground - and even phaeacians would have chosen more phantom paths.

He urged the horse on, his distraction slipping aside as portian training reasserted itself. The tracks continued to appear at close range and disappear just as abruptly, but after six more occurrences, his ire crashed back in. This time, the footprints appeared from a full six paces. Something was not right.

The horse snorted at the sharp tug on the reins, and Salus slipped quietly from the saddle despite the sludge.

Even before he reached them he could see that these tracks were deeper than the rest, heavier on the toes and twisted. As he followed them, the event of their creation was plain. The Aranan - he could tell by the evasive choice of route - had been startled by something. He'd turned sharply to discover it and taken two quick steps, turned away, then another few--

A grunt, bewildered and frustrated, escaped his throat in a puff when the tracks abruptly ceased. No murky water nor fallen leaves were present to obscure them and there were no additional prints to betray a pursuer. But something *had* been following him.

His eyes lifted discerningly to the boughs of the alder. No limbs were damaged, no branches bare of leaves - not a twig was out of place. And yet it was the only possibility. Unless...

Unless magic was involved.

The mages would've had to take a route like this to reach Nestor...

He rose sharply and turned back for the reins, restraining the curses that sought to fly from his tongue, until a curiously smooth mound a few yards off among the trees caught his keen eyes. Caution descended. His steps became as glancing as a vole's, and though he approached with an open mind, he'd already surmised the truth.

The body was bloated and discoloured, the face unrecognisable, its decomposition sped by the moisture of the bog despite the passing of no more than three days. But Salus had little doubt that this man was one of his phaeacians. A quick search of his boot confirmed it. He forced aside his irritation to focus his mind into an analytical silence.

The hair at the corpse's neck was matted with blood. A strike to the base of the skull. With a knife. From above. The trees. But the cut, despite the insects and dried blood, was too clean and precise. Steel had made it, and a subtle weapon at that - not something ditchlings would be capable of fashioning from the forests nor utilising with such deadly effect had they pinched one from a man, and neither was such finesse possessed by the tribes. And though there were no clear signs of how the body had managed to teleport from its footprints several clear yards away, his guts told him that magic had played no part in it either. Had it done so, the body could just as easily have been incinerated beyond a scrap of evidence as it had been simply abandoned.

And poorly concealed. *Deliberately* poorly concealed.

Tension convulsed in his jaw. Doana. There was a camp nearby. They were playing with him - and they had helped the mages slip by unhindered. Was that part of their plan? Or just his bad luck?

His teeth were clenched so tightly they hurt, but again he suppressed his curses and set to stripping the body of any link to the Arana. The evidence - thin but not worth the risk of leaving behind - was tucked away into a satchel, from which he dropped the two empty beer bottles to the ground beside him, disappointed that he'd needed them after all. He returned to the horse, making the slow and steady signs for fire as he went, and though the trained beast stamped uneasily at the blaze, it was too small and sputtering to truly consume the corpse. Which Salus was counting on.

He moved on, returning to his hunt without a backward glance, and after just fifteen minutes found another far-flung and discarded corpse that had again been struck from above. He stared up into the trees for a long while, searching for any evidence of direction, but these Doanans moved like squirrels. There was nothing to find.

The second corpse received similar treatment, but rather than an unfortunate drunk, this phaeacian was merely scorched - attacked from behind by lashes of fire.

His route remained certain despite the thinning of the scouts' tracks, so few and far between that the murky light had diminished and what surviving shadows had merged together into twilight by the time he discovered anything more of consequence. But these newest tracks, observed now by a shaded lantern, were unlike the rest, and loosed a childish wash of hope behind his ribs. Careful treading, light and certain, but ready to dart away at a moment's notice. Which they did, several times; abrupt course adjustments that maintained a south-eastern path. A tracker - and she'd been here only hours ago.

Salus's heart hammered like a stampede of horses in his chest. His eyes began flicking feverishly over the darkening forest, scanning every shadow, the edge of every pool, and missed twice in his haste two sets of hoof prints. He fell upon them like a hound in his third pass.

They were parallel to the tracker's, a few yards away and just as fresh, their pressure even and steady - untroubled. Unaware. The tracker had stayed close and unseen, remained alert and unwavering, trekking over the firmest, driest ground while her quarry stamped an unwitting trail. Was it arrogance, or stupidity?

The tracks diverged. His worry was forgotten.

He traced the horses, ignoring the distant weeping and stinging odour of smoke and dead fires, weaving his way in a phantom silence between birch trees and puddles, eyes never wandering from the prints, never once losing them in the shifting lantern light. Where they intensified and collected at the edge of a hump in the land, upon which grew broad blades of healthy grass ripe for grazing, footprints appeared and led away. One pair booted, the other bare, both undeniably female.

"The duelist and the tribal..." They were hardly key individuals, but they were a part of Koraaz's company and one of them had some kind of rudimentary magic. They had to know something.

The beat of his leaping heart threatened to shatter his sternum, but his focus was too steady to allow it any notice. The footsteps moved further up the mound, among tightly-knit trees overgrown with moss, and meandered senselessly. They were waiting, most likely for the rest of their party. They could only have ventured into Nestor...

The prints deepened. Toes suddenly twisted, screwing into the soil. Something had seized their attention.

Salus looked up. They'd turned towards the village. The cries. The mages. His alarm settled.

The footprints broke away, ball and heel deep in flight. They'd returned to the horses, but they hadn't mounted.

Salus abandoned them. The tracker had kept her distance, the pair too insignificant to break her cover for, but had moved after them when they'd fled. She'd bowed around, daring to near in the pair's distraction, keeping close, allowing them to lead her to more vital targets.

And then, quite suddenly, she branched away.

Salus followed urgently, recognising the pressure of the movements. She'd found them.

But a doubt rose in the back of his mind as he spotted new tracks and hoof-prints, and began to elbow its way to the front: if she'd succeeded, why had he not heard of it?

The doubt grew louder as bare and booted prints converged on the tracker's, and all the more so when something made him look up and ahead along the trail to spot the smooth form among the rough bark and knotted grass, caught by chance in a brief bleaching of moonlight before it slipped again into the sheath of the clouds.

A body lay where all tracks met. A female, plain, and dressed for mobility and stealth in this most bleak of Turunda's forests, if not for her bloodied rends and crimson stains.

The remaining prints scattered but all fled in the same direction.

His focus collapsed and a boiling rage flooded in to dissolve his composure like lye over an inconvenient corpse. The tracks were enough, he needn't have checked the wounds, the clumsy strike to the back of the head before being run through with an arming sword. Closer she had gotten to Koraaz than any other agent, but she had also failed, and in doing so had alerted them to the Arana's proximity. Phidipans were better than this! Whether they were against duelists, inquisitors, mages or not! Surely it had to be just this one, this single woman who was so inept, and Teagan had, under pressure, made a damned poor choice. Or perhaps it was his own fault for expecting results from hands other than those he could personally guarantee. Or...perhaps he should have been taking care of the matter himself...

No, he snarled, of course he couldn't. He was Keliceran, as Teagan relentlessly reminded him, and he had other duties - duties that were just as important, duties that simply *couldn't* be handled by anyone else. Though the tracks lay clear before him, only a few hours old, he had no choice but to leave someone else to chase them down. If he began following those tracks, even for a moment, he knew he'd not stop until he had them, and Koraaz had surely teleported them away by now. There was no telling how severe this phidipan's blunder had been.

Of course he was forced to remind himself, though it seemed only to further provoke his ire, that there were countless contingency plans a phidipan was trained to enact in such a situation, some of which could only work successfully on a target that had been spooked. A cheetah, after all, relied on provoking its prey to flee if just so they could trip them up.

No. The matter was irrevocably out of his hands.

He snatched the blades from the woman's corpse and rose back to his feet, eyes scanning furiously through and beyond the darkened forest. His scouts were dead; two had fallen by Doana's hands, as, no doubt, had the rest, while Koraaz's lackeys had felled another, and a phidipan at that. But though the afternoon-old tracks were surely now a week's distance behind them, Koraaz's magic couldn't hide them forever. Salus didn't understand it, but if the semi-elf was capable of such consistent concealment, he'd have done so from the start, at the first hint of pursuit...

A grim smile crept across his tightly knotted face with a grunt of abstract amusement. Evidently, Koraaz was simply not elf enough.

His eyes dropped back to the failed phidipan. His smile scarcely flickered. Like the others, she could still serve one small, final purpose.

She was lighter than he'd expected, and her lifeless body was easily moved, thrown into a more authentic position than those he'd arranged larger, heavier corpses into throughout his twenty-two-year career. Her knees scathed the ground, her back arched, and she dropped chest-first to the drowned mud. He dug his boot tips into the ground behind her with calculated pressure, a simple trip among a mess of fleeing prints, and after hauling himself back up into the saddle of the all-too-experienced mare, he cast a quick but astute survey of the surroundings, then formed the signs.

Fire exploded from his palm, streaming towards the corpse like a flurry of wasps. The sodden garments steamed on contact but the arcane flames easily took hold, while a second flare to the birch beside her scorched the bark, moss and lichen with even greater ease. The heat immediately dried the muggy air.

Then he cried at the top of his voice, rattled with panic and compelled by helplessness: "mages!" He snapped the reins and urged his mare west. "The rebels are back! *Mages!*"

The nearby village of Nestor burst into chaos; terrified screams rose from among the ashes of homes, weeping descended into hyperventilation. But Salus and his phantom assault were riding hard through the swamp, his eyes fixed on Morton, mind on his duties and the promise of swift messenger moths. The remaining hunters would be informed of the situation, the scouts and spies in the surrounding vicinities would be notified and all, he hoped, would act accordingly.

In the mean time, he had Doana to deal with - a matter that seemed to grow ever more tortuous and further beyond his control with every sweep of the wind.

Chapter 16

Rain fell as hard as arrows. The trees, too broadly spaced, offered little cover to break up the deluge, leaving hoods and cloaks weighted until the riders appeared as drowned spectres and surely just as miserable. Over three days the depressing mist of drizzle had transformed into hourly torrents that ended as abruptly as they began, while the bleak, unending clouds, when weather permitted them to look up, promised their imminent return.

Even the horses trudged with heavy hearts, meandering through the thick and sprawling swamp to avoid where they could the clouds of mist, fog and goodness knows what else that hung low over the pools, which themselves were now so vast and numerous that it was difficult to tell where one stopped and another began. Their every step was a mixture of caution and resentment.

With the fear of ghostly hunters on their tail they'd ridden hard from the reach of Nestor, and though over those three days there had been neither sight nor sound of pursuers, not one dared release their guard. Each time they stopped to rest the horses and dry what clothing they could beside a weak and shielded fire, the atmosphere was brittle, and the choice of suitable ground didn't help. Every night the risk of pneumonia grew.

But there were other factors to strain the tension.

A yelp, splash and equine squeal burst from the rear of the company, dragging them all to a sharp stop. It didn't take long to see that the brown had lost its footing; its rear hoof slipped from the slick and trampled mud to land hock-deep in the murky water, where it stuck without a hope of freeing itself.

Garon had already dismounted and rushed from the lead to help as Petra clambered, cursing, out of the saddle.

"Is Bark okay?" Aria called as her father moved to join them, warning her to stay where she was as he went, but she turned red and shrank as the duelist snapped a tart response. "Why is she so angry lately?" Aria murmured, hurt, but her eyes quickly flashed wide in panic at the thought that she may have overheard.

Rathen smiled sadly. "You'll understand in time. Leave her be."

While Eyila attempted to calm both Petra and the alarmed horse, who was slowly but steadily sinking deeper into the mud, the others pushed, pulled and lifted the heavy beast, acutely aware all the while of the strength packed into those rear legs. After minutes of struggle on all sides it was eventually freed, and calmed enough by the waving of Eyila's crushed herbs only to rear and whinny rather than attempt to bolt.

Finally, Garon turned to Petra who, despite having a knot of irritation in her jaw and a spark in her eye, stood still and silent. "Are you all right?"

"*Fine.*"

"Good."

The corners of her lips turned down as he looked away, and she seemed, for a moment, to resent herself. But she didn't apologise, and neither did the knot loosen.

"The ground is only going to get worse," he declared, screwing his heel into the soft earth. "We'll have to pick our paths more carefully, which is going to slow us down." He looked up across the vast and unbroken mire that surrounded them, then glanced sideways towards Rathen. "Can you do anything?"

"I can," the mage replied tentatively, "but as I've told you, I'm not comfortable using sustained magic with the Arana so close. And if Salus has an elf in his ranks, there's no knowing what he's capable of tracking. If Kienza had appeared and teleported us all out of their reach then I might have been willing to risk it, but as it is..."

"And as for tracking," Anthis added, shedding his sticky cloak during the brief spell of dryness, "the ghost could have reported back before attacking us, in which case Salus may know we're on horseback. The horses are struggling as it is - would we not be better off it we left them and continued on foot?"

"You can't leave us!"

Silence fell at the sound of the gruff yet squeaky voice. All eyes shifted slowly towards the horses, two of whom were looking back around at them expectantly, flicking their ears about.

Anthis blinked. "Did...?" He looked doubtfully towards the others, unable to loose the words, while Eyila and Petra each nodded slowly, sharing the same clear bewilderment.

"We've been out here too long..."

"You can't leave us!" The desperate voice rose again, at which another of the beasts looked around and began stamping its hoof with agitation. "It's wet here! And cold! We'll never survive on our own! Kienza summoned us but--"

"Aria, you devil, stop it."

Only then did the others realise that the small child was no longer in the saddle, and not even Petra could help a smile of amusement as she stepped out from her hiding place among the beasts' legs. The girl grinned impishly as Rathen lifted her back where she belonged.

"Anthis is right," Garon declared, brushing the matter and especially his own foolishness aside, "but unless Salus is following the tracks himself, it's also likely that he thinks we've teleported away. I doubt he has any idea about Kienza's help; he'll have naturally presumed that any magical measures were executed by Rathen. And in this terrain, our prints won't be clear. In fact, if this storm continues, they'll be covered up in a few hours."

"We're exposed out here," Petra reminded him sharply, but Garon shook his head.

"Our exposure is their exposure; any trackers would be as easy for us to spot as we would be to them. And when we reach the other side, the horses will give us distance. However," he walked away to rejoin his beast, but didn't return to the saddle, "they wouldn't struggle so much if they weren't so heavily burdened. We walk from here. The exercise will do us good against the weather." He looked around expectantly. "Come on."

Anthis's ability to read and walk in any terrain seemed a continuous source of surprise, and so Petra was not so reserved about loosing a cackle at any time he slipped. He didn't react, though, and Rathen suspected it had little to do with trying to ignore her hostility. This tattered old book, a journal from one of the hidden caches by Rathen's recollection, though he was unsure which, absorbed him more deeply than any of the parchments Eizariin had given him. He wanted to ask him about it, wondering if what had gripped him so was helpful, but he presumed that Anthis would have let him know if that were the case.

And anyway, he had his own angles to ponder, and as he negotiated a particularly narrow stretch of ground between two vast pools, he set to doing just that - if just to escape the monotonous trudge.

A cool and not unpleasant splash against his leg snatched Rathen out of his thoughts, and he shook his head as Aria glanced cautiously up at him from a shallow puddle. "Good to see you're making every effort to get as muddy as possible." But his humour vanished as an abrupt peace entered his heart and eased his senses, allowing him in the moment it took to recollect his bearings and steel himself against its immense power to realise that the terrain around them had changed. He tripped almost immediately, his toe catching on a stone, at which he recalled doing twice already.

Outcrops of rock broke through the ground which plants and fungi had taken full advantage of; trees, moss and lichen clung and sprouted from every hold they could find. Small cracks and narrow openings beneath them led down into limestone caves surely flooded by the rain, which seemed at present to be gathering itself for its next assault. Apparently the swamp had transformed some time behind them, though wide pockets of wetland still dominated between the miniature cliffs.

Lost in thought, he'd mindlessly followed the body in front of him, which he could have sworn had been Garon but now turned out to be Eyila. Her eyes were already distant and unseeing. Anthis was close in front, his reading forgotten as he kept a close watch on her, and his own face was creased with the same uneasiness as the rest.

Garon grunted. "We're almost there."

Rathen felt the claws of anxiety seize his gut.

For twenty minutes they navigated the labyrinth of pools and rocks, keeping close to the shelter of the looming trees, listening close and staring sharply against the thundering rain in search of hidden dangers. Discovering nothing didn't settle them; with a beauty so artificial, the air itself seemed to shake with danger.

Rathen could feel the Zi'veyn's presence hanging like lead in the saddlebag beside him. He focused himself on fighting the tingling in his veins and lure of the ethereal peace instead, though it proved to be even more difficult than the last time. Every time he stepped beneath the veil of magic it seemed harder to guard himself against it.

The trees' perches soon receded, spitting the group out into the rain's onslaught and the sudden glare of an ancient site. From the marsh rose a ring of stones like a maw of broken teeth, within which the ground had sunk, overhung only at the easternmost edge where yet larger stones were embedded within its face.

Barrows. This swampy realm seemed an all too appropriate haunt. And it would indeed have been eerie had a central plume of soft, golden sunlight not been radiating across every rock despite the thick and shrouded sky, had fingers of fog been anywhere to be seen, and had the ground not been at its driest in days.

But the sudden abatement of rain under the shell of the magic's influence seemed to escape the young historian's notice even as he stepped beneath it and lowered his hood, staring at the arrangement in awe instead. "Borer's Teeth. Barrows, short post-magic... I've never seen one so exposed..." He glanced about, noticing at last the absence of water despite the perfect depression. "The earth must have been washed away when the marsh drained..."

"Anthis," Garon snapped, but the young man ignored him, hurrying excitably on ahead with his flagging and irritated dun dragging along behind him. The inquisitor shook his head and picked up his own pace. "Keep together."

"I have a bad feeling about this place..."

Aria looked down questioningly from the saddle at her father's murmur, but when he only looked back with a smile, her expression saddened. "You'll do it this time, Daddy. I know you will."

"Thank you, little one." But that wasn't what was troubling him. In fact, despite everyone's expectations and the drive to prove to Garon that he *was* a capable mage, this time he felt something almost akin to...confidence?

Passing beneath the unseen shell and into the reach of the sunbeam, they stopped just short of the rings, and while the horses visibly delighted in the chance to rest on firm, dry ground, everyone else fell into their long-practised roles. While Anthis busied himself with the stone faces, Garon took up his watch on the far side and well within his reach, while Petra manned the other end, sword drawn and in sight of Eyila who sat on the ground and stared off in a trance.

Rathen, meanwhile, was trying to split himself in half, fighting away the sluggishness that kept trying to wrap itself around his mind while attempting at the same time to isolate the surrounding magic. He removed the Zi'veyn from his horse's load and belatedly noticed Aria sliding gracelessly out of the saddle. "Aria--"

"I just want to see the ruin!" Her muddy feet, bare, of course - what else for jumping in puddles? - touched the ground and she grinned at him appeasingly. "I won't go far - I promise I'll stay with Anthis."

His eyes shifted towards the historian for a long, evaluating moment. But as he watched him focusing as intently upon a menhir as a child might a butterfly, he felt a sudden pang of guilt at his lingering mistrust. Anthis had explained himself. And he did believe him. But...

But Garon was near enough.

"All right," he said with difficulty. "But stay where I and Garon can see you. And stay alert."

She beamed. "I will, I promise! Thank you!" And then she scurried away quite carelessly.

Rathen smiled, shaking his head after her, but his mood faltered as false sunlight glinted back from the Zi'veyn to catch the corner of his eye. He dragged his gaze away and out across the ruins. To normal eyes, there was nothing to see of the magic but its glowing manifestation. But to Rathen's, even in his distraction it was all-surrounding and pulled ever stronger at his senses, trying harder and harder to lure him into its bottomless well of lifelessness. It was a tug that grew stronger with his every exposure. It had succeeded with Eyila, the reason for which he only just grasped though certainly couldn't combat - but he was also stronger than she, and he had no doubt that it was for his elven blood. But he was still the only one aware of the peaceful undercurrent, though it seemed at that moment like a tidal surge, and he felt that, this time, he might just slip...

How he'd managed to steel himself against its potency in Khry's Glory was a thought he hadn't the strength to spare for.

Again, he thrust it out of his mind. He concentrated utterly upon his magic, focusing to touch on that which surrounded him, seeking out the centre of the magnetism. With trouble, he found it - unsurprisingly at the centre of the light and the stone circle, marked by a small altar. The burial chambers most likely extended a ways directly beneath it.

His eyes sank back to the Zi'veyn. He stood, pondered and fought in silence for a very long while.

Aria watched her father with measuring eyes. He was nervous. It was obvious. His knuckles were white. And yet, standing within the column of light, he seemed to her like a vision of hope.

She pursed her heart-shaped lips and turned away, not wishing to deter him by staring, and peered up at the enormous stone instead. Its face, like so many others that had grasped Anthis's attention, had been carved with all kinds of pictures, most of which she couldn't make out at all.

"What's this a burrow of?" She asked, looking about from one stone to the next and the dark cracks that opened between them.

"No, *barrow*," he chuckled, and paused his scrawling to trace a few particularly worn lines with his finger over the stone. "It's a...graveyard, of sorts."

"Oh." She looked back to the rock in front of her. Anthis glanced down at her before resuming his copy of the etchings, but noticed no discouragement in her eyes. "Of elves?"

"Short post-magic elves. They're still exposed to the earth, but the locations were marked by family. Before magic they were buried naked except for a thin shroud - like a blanket - and at a place that was important to the individual, usually unmarked."

"I remember."

"Only those with a strong relationship would visit the site, which would keep it quiet and untouched. Their bodies would feed the earth." He glanced down again, expecting confusion, but instead a sparkle of interest had settled in her eyes. He smiled and looked back to his work.

"Feed the earth how?"

He winced. "Uh, well..."

"They would turn into soil?"

"...In a manner of speaking."

"And animals would pick at their bones?"

"...Well..."

She traced her fingers over the lines just as he had, and moved just as carefully, but it was clear she was unsure quite why. "What happened to them when they died? Nug says Arkhamas go to sleep forever, and that the Lady takes their dreams and keeps them safe. I know what he means, but...I also don't. Do we dream when we die?"

His hand stilled; words eluded him. "Perhaps these are questions your father should answer."

"I don't think he would want to," she mumbled. She dropped her hand and moved on to the next stone. "Well, what happened to the elves, then? Did they go to their gods and dream?"

"Well, actually, before they were gifted their magic, they didn't seem to have any ideas of what would happen. They knew that death was inevitable, just another stage of life, but more importantly, they knew it would bring them peace. So they trusted the gods with their spirits."

"Didn't they wonder what would happen to them?"

"Undoubtedly." He smiled at her bewilderment. "But the gods weren't telling and they knew they'd find out for themselves in time. When they got their magic, though," he moved slowly after her, having finished with the previous menhir, "that started to change. This place is proof of that. Short post-magic, they were still buried in the ground, but they marked their graves so they'd be remembered even by strangers. It wasn't enough to simply pass on into the next stage anymore, they marked the ground and in some cases disturbed animals' habitats and hunting grounds with their barrows. In time they grew even more narcissistic - selfish - and started having prized possessions buried along with them, and eventually weren't buried in the earth anymore but in coffins and caskets and sealed inside tombs where nature couldn't--...where they couldn't give themselves back to the world." He shook his head. "Long post-magic elves feared death and tried to protect themselves even when there was nothing left to protect."

Her little lips pursed in thought. "I see. So they didn't turn into soil? And animals couldn't eat them?"

"No."

"Well...I don't really want to be eaten by animals, or turn into soil - not if I'm still alive. But..." she cocked her head, her young brow furrowing in bafflement. "I don't think I understand. If they're dead, why do they need their bodies if all they're going to do forever is dream, with or without it? Animals need it much more."

"Well they'd stopped caring about anything but themselves."

She grunted and turned away from the stone. "They sound horrible. It seems like all they did was take." She wandered back to the previous face and touched the etchings again, then soon found her way back to his side. She rose to the tips of her toes and peered over the edge of his book. She pointed to a few lines, told him they weren't dark enough, and he duly corrected them. "Where did *their* spirits go? Are they still here? Like their bodies?"

"No, I doubt that..." The tomb in Tarun snaked back into his mind, a memory he'd been trying to forget, particularly in the dead of night. But he could still recall that chilling feeling, a furious presence following them through the darkness - recall it so clearly it was as though he was back in that awful place. He cast a short glance over his shoulder as the hairs on his neck stood straighter. This place...it wasn't the same, but there was *something* here...

His skin prickled. He shoved his attention back onto the stone. "Uh...no. No, *these* elves were buried not long after they'd gained magic, relatively speaking. No coffins or possessions; they'd have been given back to the earth and moved on to the next world with this site alone serving as a memorial. They're at peace. There's nothing here..."

She dropped suddenly to the ground and sprawled over a spread of spongy foliage, dotted with small white flowers, where she stared dreamingly up at the sky. Anthis chuckled.

"What's the world like, do you think? Is it like when you dream? Your body stays put but your eyes and your feelings go somewhere else?"

"Mhm. Perhaps it's just like that."

"Then Nug is right?"

"He could be. None of us can know for certain until we get there ourselves."

Her lips curled into a small, soft smile. "I hope we do... Yes. I'm sure it will be fine. As long as my daddy is there."

Anthis's smile waned. He looked back to the rocks to find something he could use to distract her from her melancholy thoughts, curiously grown up though her outlook may have been. Or perhaps she really didn't understand as well as she thought she did. But death surrounded them; on every face the carvings told the story of the family who had been buried here, and of the embrace the gods had greeted them with. Zikhon was the dominant figure. Of course He was. He was the God of Death. And Eternal Peace. Acceptance. How could he and his peers have read Him so wrong?

"You have a different god, don't you?"

He blanched for a moment. "I...love Vastal. And the others."

"But you believe in one Petra doesn't. Will you go into a different dream world like Eyila will?"

He felt her eyes on him. He glanced; they were sad. He smiled softly. "My spirit will be put to good use. Of that, I'm certain. But," he looked back over the ruins, and then to the sunlight. He smiled at its presence, real or not. "It's all a long way off. For all of us."

"I hope so..."

Silence fell. Aria seemed not to notice while Anthis was simply relieved, but as he resumed his study and Aria continued to stare up at the unrelenting clouds, their downpour landing silently on an unseen roof far above them, a slight muttering gradually drifted their way.

Aria frowned sadly and sat up, her eyes falling upon her father. Anthis paused beside him as he made his way past to another stone. "Can I help?" He asked, though he already knew the answer.

Unsurprisingly, Rathen shook his head, and his pale face remained twisted in a knot of fret and indecision as he stared down into the depths of the relic that glinted in his hands. "No," he murmured distantly, "...just..."

"He's imit--*intimidated*."

Anthis hushed her, but Aria only looked back with assurance.

Rathen didn't deny it. Instead, he sighed and dropped his voice a shade lower. "I have an idea. But if it doesn't work..." His fingers drummed against the black, brushed metal in increasing doubt, then his eyes lifted suddenly to the historian.

Anthis faltered at the force of their concentration. "The elves were very precise, yes? But they made this thing, and it wasn't to remove specific *people's* magic. The doll proved that; it was made to remove *targeted* magic - from a host of elves, an enchanted item or even, in theory, all this. The vessel itself isn't relevant.

"Every time I've tried to use it, I've fuelled the spell with the assumption that it would just act on the magic around it, but because I didn't tell it where to go it just built up and fizzled out. But when I affected the doll, I was concentrating on the magic inside it and unwittingly directed the spell to the 'magic inside the doll', not the doll itself. That was more luck than judgement, but my mistake when we went back was falling into the same trap: omitting that part of the spell because there was no vessel." Aria saw the sparkle in his tired eyes and smiled. "That was *wrong*. The doll provided a point of focus, and by omitting that part, the spell remained *broken*."

"You said you'd fixed it."

Rathen straightened as Garon looked down on them from the high ridge of the overhang. "It isn't a breakage, it's intentional. The spell is so detailed and so unique that among *hundreds* of chains defining the element and structure of magic as a target, it's easy to get overwhelmed and miss that single fact."

"It's not unreasonable, Garon," Anthis agreed.

"All right - but what does that mean?"

"It means I've found the switch."

Silent looks were exchanged. Aria hopeful, Anthis cautious, and Garon, descending to join them, was unreadable, though Rathen knew doubt was prevalent. He didn't allow even a flicker of hope across his own face.

The inquisitor stopped and straightened. "Do it."

All eyes followed Rathen's down to the relic, but Aria was the only one to notice his knuckles turn white. She rose from her sandwort seat and strode around between her father and the two onlookers and began, quite without apology, to push them both away from him. "Maybe you should all go away and leave him alone. Petra and Eyila are over there - I'm sure you would enjoy talking to them."

Both denied the suggestion a little too readily. "It's fine, Aria," Rathen smiled, but his amusement barely landed. His gaze plummeted back to the pull of the relic, and as he took a deep, resigned breath, the others held theirs.

No one moved. Not a sound was made. All stared between Rathen and the Zi'veyn, watching, waiting for any hint, wondering in the back of their minds what he was doing, how it would work, and would they know it if it did. Once again, they turned towards their surroundings, paying acute attention, waiting to spot any change just as they had the last time, and the time before that. But after a long minute, in keeping with custom, nothing at all seemed to happen.

But just as disappointment began to set in, a soft gurgle caught Anthis's attention. He looked down at the cold touch that reached him even through his boot. His heart jumped at the sight of water, and for a moment, he smiled.

But the water quickly covered his toes, and continued to well up from the soil that not a moment ago was bone-dry. Alarm set in as it rose towards his ankles and Aria began huffing in a panic beside him, lifting her bare feet one at a time while doing her best not to distract her father. Anthis looked towards Garon, who wore identical hesitation, but was quicker to break it. "Is it him?" He asked the only witnesses to Rathen's previous success in a ragged whisper. "Is he doing this?"

"I don't know..."

"Rathen--"

"No," the mage grunted with great effort. "Shut up..."

They bit their tongues hard, watching the water rise from nowhere and faster than the tide. Anthis lifted Aria out and up onto the altar when her lip started to tremble.

The sky began to grow darker, and the threat of night pressed onto their hearts. It took a long while before realisation set in. Night was not descending.

The sunbeam that illuminated the marsh-locked ruin was shrinking slowly around them, and the rain was stalking readily after it. But before either could voice another distraction, a childish gasp snatched attention right back onto the mage. His twisted expression had grown sharper, and his eyes were shut tight.

The Zi'veyn floated silently between his hands.

Surprise knocked their fret aside.

At the far side, the darkness and encroaching rain stole Petra's attention away from the outlying swamp, and at the sight of the water that swelled now beneath her own feet, she immediately set to hurrying Eyila up and into the saddle. But when she spun towards the others to shout a warning or demand explanation, she witnessed the plume growing steadily thinner, the expressions upon the others' faces and the glint of metal hovering in the air before the caster, and a smile stole in instead. "Rathen! It's working!"

But he said nothing. His focus was rigid; sweat formed on his brow.

As the bleakness marched down on them, so too did the unnatural beauty begin to fade, and behind it flooded the same ghastly paranoia that lingered in any other graveyard.

Every aspect that set the site off balance began to diminish, even those they hadn't noticed - the silence but for the rainfall, which itself had become crisp in the absence of a low and insistent hum. Until finally, one at a time, they vanished, leaving the company standing in a damp, flooded ruin beneath thundering rain, the sun once again hidden behind the iron-clad clouds and a dank misery slipping back into their hearts.

Everything fell still.

Rathen didn't open his eyes, and neither did anyone move nor speak. It wasn't until his shoulders finally relaxed and a sigh of completion escaped in a ragged puff that their suspended breath was released, and his strain against the treacherously serene charm came to an end.

Aria leapt from the altar and embraced him fiercely. "I told you," she said as the small, unassuming relic descended gently back into his palm, and though he staggered a half step back and smiled feebly, he managed to return her enthusiasm. A hand clapped his shoulder as Anthis added his congratulations, while Garon merely nodded his own in silence. "How did you do it?" The historian asked, smiling broadly.

"Puddles...no vessel, but the edges..."

"The edges of the puddles were your targets."

He nodded as he steadied his haggard breath. "It's not as easy, but it works the same way...but I have to keep track of the edges...at the same time...and they shift..."

"How did you work it out?"

"Goats, puddles, marbles..."

Garon frowned, but Aria and Anthis's grins were explanation enough.

But when Petra's voice rose from behind them, there was no hint of praise.

"Turn around!"

Petra was already in front of them when they spun, her sword raised and guarded. Garon's was alongside it in a heartbeat, and only through the barred steel did the rest of them finally see the threat.

Rathen held Aria even tighter.

An immense, bestial shadow broke away from a broad crack in the barrow-face, and even at its feral hunch loomed at least as tall as a man. Otter-like in form, but gaunt and angular, and armed with savage claws on webbed hands and feet and a mouth filled with terrible, draconic teeth. And black eyes, wild and bloodthirsty, fixed like a hunter's arrow on every one of them at once.

It lurched forwards.

They didn't need Garon's order to flee.

A mournful howl bellowed after them through the trees.

Chapter 17

The weak reach of the campfire did little to help the careful, meticulous business of untangling branches from Aria's blonde ringlets. She hadn't been hiding in the bushes and neither had she been climbing through the tightest heights of the trees. In fact, as it turned out, they'd not gotten there by accident at all.

Rathen didn't approve of her attempt at an 'ummage to Arkhamas', but he kept that to himself, strained through the gloom and struggled to unravel the mess as painlessly as possible, acutely aware all the while that after the transformation of Borer's Teeth, they were almost certainly back in the Arana's sights. A quick arcane solution was not an option.

He glanced up as Aria winced and noticed her bottom lip poking out further and further. "I'm sorry, little one, but you did this to yourself."

"Mmm. That's not it..."

He frowned in question as he retrieved the knotted jumble that had slipped from his hand as she shook her head, and continued his attempt to tease a comb through it. He rolled his eyes when he worked it out. Of course. Whatever else had been on her mind since?

"It just sounded so sad!"

"I know, sweetheart."

"There must have been *something* we could've done..."

"It was a rushkin," he replied, moving on to another tangle. "Aside from handing it a knife and fork and lying down on a platter, it was out of our hands."

"But if it was going to *eat* us, why didn't it *chase* us?"

"You saw how thin it was. It didn't have the strength."

"And we damned it." She turned rigid with conviction.

"If we didn't, we'd have damned ourselves. And anyway, now the magic has gone, animals will return and it'll be able to hunt again."

She frowned. "How do you know there were no animals?"

"Because we didn't hear even a bird chirp for over an hour."

"Oh... So it *will* be okay?"

"I'm sure."

"Are you?"

His eyes slipped from her hair to regard her with a soft and quizzical smile. Where ever did she get this caring streak? It wasn't from him, he was certain about that, and even Kienza was self-concerned by comparison. And it couldn't have been from Oat...

He freed the final tangle with three strokes, fluffed her curls and embraced her fondly. "I'm sure, little one. Now come on - smells to me like dinner is ready."

"What is it?"

"Chicken."

Her eyes widened. "There are chickens out *here?*"

'Heron-shaped chickens.' "I know. I was surprised, too."

She hurried off to drop the comb back into her bag and smiled as she saw how tall her father walked. His bearing had changed since she'd been gone, as though he'd finally found the confidence he'd been missing all his life, but tonight he seemed to own the camp. He radiated surety. She felt a tremor of near-uncontainable excitement.

She bounded ahead of him to join the others, flashing a grin at Anthis as he glanced around at their return. He had an excited glint in his own eye, too, and it only fuelled her spirit. "What's happened?" She blurted, leaping into a spot by the fire.

"Anthis has made a discovery about the Zi'veyn!"

Aria's big eyes widened impossibly further, just as Eyila's had, so it was fortunate that the firelight rendered invisible the flushing of his cheeks at the tribal's musical enthusiasm.

Rathen spared her a brief, evaluating glance. She'd not recovered from the magic's influence when the puddles had disappeared, and he hadn't been able to work out why. She was fine now, for the most part, but again it had been only time and distance that could subdue her. "Really?" He asked, far more tempered, sitting down beside Aria and noticing as he handed her the dish Petra passed his way that he'd missed a knot.

Anthis presented the tattered and water-damaged journal recovered from the drowned ruins of Ut'hala; the book that had so firmly ensnared his attention for the last few days, that he'd always handled with the greatest care, as though it could disintegrate beneath the briefest absent breath. And he tugged from it a handful of loose pages.

Aria stared in horror. "Anthis, you've *broken it!*"

"No," he smiled inexplicably. "I've *separated* it. This," he waved the book in his left hand, "is the journal of Drekath Svol, a high-ranking elf in the qu'ulas's court. But--"

"The what?"

"Qu'ulas," he blinked. "The king. The king's court. But *this*," he moved on quickly, waving the wrinkled pages in his right, "is written in a *completely* different hand. Do you know whose?"

"No, but no doubt you'll tell us." Eyila fired Petra a sharp look; she sighed and rolled her hand for him to continue, the closest he would get to an apology. But still, such an encouraging gesture surprised him enough that he stammered for a moment.

"Kruik Vuthal," he finally managed. But the name was met with blank stares. "The creator! The Zikrahlehveyn's creator! Look!" He raised the slender notebooks that were piled at his feet, showed them again the depiction of the relic and held the loose sheets alongside. The script on both pages were equally illegible, scrolling yet jagged, denoting by sight the harsh pronunciation, but it did appear to be written with the same considered intention.

Unfortunately, he received yet more unimpressed stares. He sighed and put the notebooks down. "All right: 'Zikrahlehveyn'. Kienza confirmed that it translates into 'Eternal Preservation', not 'Preserver of Eternity', and we presumed that that 'preservation' referred to elven superiority over humans and even gods, who we know destroyed them because of that arrogance, daring to think that their magic was stronger."

"...And you're saying that it wasn't?"

"As far as we know, that *was* more or less why the gods turned on them, but it *wasn't* what the Zi'veyn was trying to preserve - not originally, anyway. It was *peace*."

"Well, doesn't that sort of go without saying? A weapon as a show of power would deter--"

"No, it *wasn't* a weapon *or* a show of power. It was a last resort."

Rathen frowned. Even Petra raised her head.

Anthis's blazing smile widened. "There's never been any sign of war from the time when the elves disappeared. Nothing. No weapons, no bodies, not even any passing mention of wide-spread unrest in any uncovered writings. That's why their disappearance has been such a mystery. *But:* we've seen for ourselves that that isn't *strictly* true."

Rathen straightened in understanding. "The anarchists..."

"The eight-point star symbols that denoted caches of information, scattered across ruins ancient even in their own time." Anthis gestured again with the loose pages. "A small rebellious faction disagreed with the direction their culture was taking, individuals with the very unpopular opinion that the importance of material wealth and status had corrupted their people almost to the point of being irreversible. They acted out, killing, stealing, sabotaging anything they could from those who ranked above them to prove that a life lived magically, without respect for the gods or the world around them, would be their downfall. They were right, in a way, but it was a desperate and ill-conceived method and what they expected to achieve, I really can't guess.

"These pages don't reveal that much - they seem more like a confession, an attempt at catharsis. There's probably a lot more in the rest of his journal, wherever that is, but--yes, sorry. Ultimately, what they sought isn't important because they didn't succeed, there were too few of them, and their impact was so minor that it was never recorded. What *does* matter is that a few of these idealists were acquaintances of Kruik Vuthal."

"You mean he was working with them?"

"No, but he was worried for them and afraid of what might happen if high society decided to retaliate. So he hatched a plan."

Aria stared, enraptured despite being far too young to understand political struggles, and even Eyila seemed to miss the complexities. But the others listened with intrigue, eating the peppered heron-chicken slowly, welcoming the distraction from their overshadowing ordeals. Everyone but Garon, of course, who remained standing just outside the circle, eyes searching, hand on the hilt of his sword, his shoulder rolling and fingers attempting to flex.

"Vuthal was, by both social standards and historical records, a nobody, but he was clever enough to devise the Zikrahlehveyn. It was meant as a means of suspending the magic from any attacking force rather than harming them and fighting back, be they moving against his friends, or his friends themselves if they were about to attempt something too foolish. The thing was that its creation would involve activity that could never go unnoticed. So, rather than risk drawing attention to himself or, more importantly, to his friends and being stamped traitors together, he approached the qu'ulas, buttered him up with everything he'd want to hear - that he had the most powerful magic, was the grandest, the most handsome, the most intelligent and so on - and told him that he could make him a weapon so powerful that he could secure his status for eternity without ever having to use it. The qu'ulas accepted quite eagerly, apparently, and that gave Vuthal the clearance to put his plan into action without raising suspicion." He sighed then, and his smile faltered a fraction as pity edged in. "He succeeded, as we know, but the qu'ulas appropriated it as soon as it was finished. He paraded it in front of his people with a rallying and tactical speech, which was described here as a 'threat masquerading as wonder', describing its ability to silence in an instant the magic within an enemy's veins and declaring elves at the very top of the chain of power - and himself above *them*, no doubt. And while the qu'ulas didn't actually say it, Vuthal goes on to presume that it was right then that the suggestion of elves being greater than the gods and the Zi'veyn being the proof of it began to crop up, and that that was their next step. The idea circulated very quickly."

He absently tapped the journal beside him. "Drekath Svol, while not tied to the creation of it, was close enough to the qu'ulas to know of the Zi'veyn, if not its truth, and to know that he intended to use it. He was wrong, though, but I think that was more to do with timing - the elves were destroyed before the qu'ulas had the chance."

"So," Eyila frowned sadly, "Vuthal's plan backfired. Not only did the Zi'veyn encourage the exact behaviour his friends were fighting against, but the qu'ulas took it and there was nothing to stop him from using it against them."

"Nothing but the fact that the rebels hadn't been discovered yet. Apparently most of their activity had been put down to dissent among humans because magic wasn't involved. They used their hands instead to make a point."

"And I bet they made no attempt to alleviate the blame." Petra grunted in disapproval. "Well?" She asked tartly, feigning disinterest. "What did his friends have to say?"

"I doubt they were impressed. He'd just handed their king the means to oppress *anyone* that stood against him, and they stepped up their own activity because of it. Many of them were eventually rooted out and killed and the whole matter covered up for fear it would make the qu'ulas's authority look weak. He'd made it worse by trying to make it better. And while he didn't have the weapon, he did have the drafts for its creation and, subsequently, its destruction. But he knew the qu'ulas would be aware of that so he set out to scatter the information where he'd never think to look for it, so he couldn't strengthen it, alter it or make another, while *they could* make another to use against it if they had to. Then he fled with the remaining rebels."

Aria's bright eyes were as big as saucers. "And then?"

"No idea. But after seven hundred years, my money's on that he died."

Petra grunted again. "He was clever enough to make the thing, but it was pretty stupid to tell the king what it actually did."

"If he'd told him any less, he wouldn't have been allowed to make it."

"He could have lied."

"We've only met elves once," Rathen mused, "but I doubt it would be that simple. It's possible that they could not only sense magic in use like Eyila and I can, but also the intent of the spells."

"*Smudge* the truth, then."

"Well the qu'ulas's speech was probably all fluff anyway. He knew what it could do, but I doubt he understood the workings of it. They turned away from the God of Mind just the same as the rest, and that didn't just mean they abandoned philosophy; odds are they wouldn't have had much care to put too much thought into *anything* just to understand the intricacies of how things worked. As far as he was concerned, the weapon had been made, it was in his hands and, if Rathen's right, the magic sensed in its creation would have corroborated what he'd been told it could do. And after being told by all his adoring fans that he was the most powerful, he probably thought it would obey his command in a heartbeat. But in the end, without Vuthal's help, he probably *couldn't* have used it. Even the idea of turning it against the gods was bluster, not to mention that it was just that: an idea."

"Then it couldn't have done it?"

"I doubt it, but they never had the chance to test it."

"They had the *gods* worried, though."

"Worried, or offended?"

Rathen peered thoughtfully over at the pages, illuminated by firelight. "Why didn't you find these before?"

He blinked. "Well the book's old - I didn't want to tug at anything that was loose and they were matted into the other crinkled pages..."

"This is all very interesting," Petra sighed impatiently, setting her bowl, empty of any scraps from the meagre meal, a little too firmly on the ground, "but how exactly does it help us? This is pointless information. In fact, even if we *didn't* have the Zi'veyn yet, it would *still* be pointless information."

The atmosphere shattered. Anthis lowered his books in silence and turned his attention to his own bowl, its contents long cooled, while Aria shuffled nervously closer to her father. Eyila fired the duelist a sharp look, but this time she didn't acknowledge it. Though she was very aware. Petra's lips formed a hard line.

"It could become relevant," Garon replied from the edge, quite unaffected. "We're moving against the Arana and Salus has elves at hand, not to mention that we don't know whether or not we're being tracked by Tekhest."

"I don't see how knowing *why* it was made will have any impact on that. If it was a technique for using it against them, fine, but this is just pointless."

"Garon's right. In knowing why it was made, we know what it was originally designed to do, and that *could* help us against them. And anyway, he's a historian; he's not had to put his work on hold for this."

"No, he hasn't, but now that we have the Zi'veyn and we've got it working, the matter is all on *you*, Rathen. He's not going to discover anything of use to us anymore." She actively avoided brushing Eyila with her gaze.

"If he wasn't still needed, I would have dismissed him to resume with his life, not keep him in harm's way out in this miserable place." The inquisitor turned away to leave the matter and continue surveying the area. His tongue, however, had other ideas. "I've tried to dismiss *you* countless times."

Her cheeks flushed suddenly in anger, and burned all the brighter as each pair of eyes fell mutely upon her. "Yes," she snapped, "of course. Because I'm just a tag-along, aren't I?"

"Petra, I'm sure Ga--"

"If you were needed, you would have been recruited."

"Garon, she *has* been needed," Anthis reminded the back of his head. "As has Eyila. Even Aria has pulled her weight and I doubt you wanted her to come along, either." He sent the little girl an apologetic smile. She smiled back, but her eyes were wide beneath a furrowed brow as they flicked nervously back onto the seething duelist.

"Rathen," the inquisitor began shortly, "is Aria's only family, and Eyila's was killed. Neither of them had any choice but to come with us."

"Yes but Petra *volunteered* for it, and she's taken up half of the watch without ever having been asked."

"She wasn't asked because it wasn't wanted. I don't need anyone's help."

Aria flinched as Petra rose sharply to her feet, and indeed the rest of them froze for a heartbeat, too. But she didn't shout. She didn't lash out. She didn't even snarl. She turned around, walked away from the circle, snatched her blades from beside her bed roll and vanished into the night-drowned swamp.

All eyes returned to the back of the inquisitor's head.

"Well done."

He glanced around as Rathen rose to his feet, an intense disapproval shadowing his dark face. Garon straightened against it and squared himself towards the others' matching expressions. "If she wants to indulge hurt feelings, she shouldn't be out here," he declared. "You *all* seem to have forgotten that we are being hunted by the *Arana*. They almost *killed* us three days ago, and they won't have lost our trail just because we've ventured into a swamp."

"People skills aren't taught in the White Hammer, are they?"

Rathen left to follow her trail. Garon turned his back coldly to the fire once again. "You should all get some sleep. We move on in the morning."

"To Mokhan?" Anthis frowned doubtfully. "You're sure--"

"No! To Wrenroot!" Aria looked around at the confused looks Anthis and Eyila shot her, the latter of whom appeared about to make her own interjection, and the growing irritation of the inquisitor. Her eyes widened with regret. "Well, we promised Nug that we would fix Wrenroot second..."

Garon was already shaking his head. "No. Wrenroot is--"

"You're quite right, Aria." Anthis ignored him as he spun. "We *did* promise. And we'll keep it. There's no use turning more friends against us." He glanced up at the inquisitor's grunt and watched him march away to indulge himself in a solitary patrol. He smiled slightly to himself, grinned at Aria, then tightened as Eyila leaned closer between them, her young, unpainted face striking in the firelight even with its wrinkle of confusion, and dropped her voice low. "Who is Nug?"

173

Chapter 18

Rathen stopped short when he found himself suddenly staring down the length of a blade.

A sigh of irritation came from the other end, and Petra returned it roughly to its sheath - after taking a moment to think about it, first. She then grunted an apology and turned curtly back to the lake. The dismissal was plain.

"It's all right," he replied despite it, "and I'm sorry, I didn't mean to frighten you."

"You didn't."

"...No," he agreed mildly. "No, just being cautious." She didn't respond - in fact her silence was down right hostile - but he leaned against a tree anyway, folded his arms and stared leisurely out across the bleak body of water.

She knelt down at its edge and waited. Her patience didn't stretch far. "I'd like to bathe, Rathen."

"Should I leave?"

"I would prefer that you did."

He nodded and obeyed. Slowly. He barely managed a full turn before the expected groan of defeat.

"Wait."

He stopped and turned in feigned surprise, but when he found himself suddenly facing someone else, he started as if she'd returned the point of the blade to his nose. Her face, a moment ago so harsh, was now creased in the most hopeless dismay, and the proud and rigid line of her shoulders had dropped into a slouch. She appeared younger - helpless. Her walls, so recently reinforced, remained, but it appeared that she'd at least pulled aside the gates.

"Why..." her weary expression twisted further. "Why did he say all of that? He didn't *need* to say it..."

Rathen leaned back against the tree and resumed his observation of the clouds reflected across the water surface, sparing her the discomfort of his gaze. "He's a difficult man," he replied musingly. "But I don't think it has anything to do with his position, I think it's him. I think he likes to stay in control - of us, of the route, of the situation. Of himself. He's guarding himself against something, and forcing this distance is how he does it. He never lets his walls down."

"Mm..."

"And it upsets you." His gaze didn't touch her even as she whipped around in startlement.

"What?! Of course not. Why would it upset me?"

"Ah. Then I must be imagining your irritation every time he brushes your help aside. Otherwise you wouldn't keep trying, would you? Though you'd think you'd have learned better by now." He grunted in consideration. "But, then again, Elle wasn't quite so warm when I was trying to catch her attention, either."

"What?" He didn't need to look to know that her eyes were wide and coloured with the same blanket of clueless innocence Aria attempted whenever she knew he'd discovered she'd brought Oat into her bedroom to play. She sighed, beaten once again. "Is it that obvious?"

"Only to people who care." This time he did look, for she jerked in surprise. First he thought it was at the fact that he cared, then considered it was just the fact that he'd said it. Neither sat well. "I'm not heartless," he informed her.

"I never said you were. You'd have to have quite a *big* heart to win *two* women..." She answered his flat look with a lopsided smile. "I'm sorry."

His gaze returned to the lake, and he stepped forwards from the edge of the trees to stop beside the water. A pair of nightlarks swooped overhead. They watched them dance and dive through the air, the bluer of the two making impressive loops and flits while the smaller and duller seemed to scrutinise the movements closely. Neither spoke for a few minutes.

"Have you considered," he began, startling her out of her rapture, "that it's you he's trying to protect?"

"Me?"

"His job is a dangerous one."

"I can handle myself. I have so far. And he knows it."

"Of course he knows it. But that wasn't what I meant." She frowned, bemused, but he retained his distant pondering, watching the blue bird dart close to the surface of the water to repeat his ballet with a perfectly choreographed partner. "Say the best were to happen - that it all worked out and you, being the strong-willed and capable young woman you are, decided to follow him out on a mission one day. I presume you would do so without asking him because he would never allow anything to compromise his work - so what if, when you found him, you got tangled up in whatever he was dealing with? That things got out of control all of a sudden because you didn't know the details and you got hurt, or killed?"

She said nothing. His gaze travelled down to her. Her eyes were absorbed in thought. "I wouldn't--"

"We may only have known each other for a few months, but I know you well enough to know that you most certainly *would*."

She turned away with a snort. "This is just conjecture anyway. He's not interested."

He looked back across the lake. "My point is," he continued mildly, "that he thinks hard, he thinks deep, he considers every possibility. His walls are up for a reason. Perhaps he doesn't want to let you get close. Or perhaps you're just irritating him. Who knows what's going on in his head? He certainly isn't going to tell us."

"No, he isn't."

"No. He'll just brood over things. Storm off. Then release it through tart remarks. Throw up walls, thicken the atmosphere, make this whole ordeal even more difficult--"

"*All right*." She folded her arms tightly, disguising her embarrassment as annoyance. Again, neither spoke for a while. The birds had disappeared.

Her voice, when it came, was small. "What should I do?"

"I really don't know."

"Well...what did you do with Elle?"

A smile flickered. "I chased her. Endlessly. Then I threatened to cast a love spell over her."

"*Really?*"

"*No!*" He grinned. "I just kept chasing her. But," his tone softened as sobriety returned, "she isn't Garon. With him..." He grappled for the end of the sentence, then soon shook his head. "He's a closed book. Tightly locked, in fact. I couldn't begin to guess. Nor would I want to."

"Well, what if it was you?"

"Me?"

"If someone was chasing you."

He thought for a long moment. "Me, personally...I suppose I like to cause myself grievance. A woman who will take command even if I know better, and then prove me wrong. So, if I was being chased, I would want her to confront me and tell me exactly what she wanted. And not give me a choice about it."

Petra smiled, mixed between amusement and fascination. "Really?"

"I was chasing Elle, it's true, but she stopped running, turned around, told me exactly what she thought and gave me one chance to change her mind."

"Which you did."

He chuckled. "Only just. But it was enough."

"What about Kienza?"

He faltered, struck for a moment by guilt, brief but intense. Petra didn't miss it. "Kienza...she just happened. She saved my life after my banishment and wore me down. Make no mistake, I didn't give in because I was lonely or desperate. She's...truly, she's wonderful. Powerful, confident, affectionate - how could I *not* fall for her?"

The conflict in his eyes was clearer than daylight. She looked away. "But you still love Elle."

He sighed mournfully. "From the bottom of my heart. That has never changed." He turned towards her and took her hands, a gesture that surprised her, but she didn't withdraw for the pressure in his eyes. "But: I am not Garon, either. He may well not like an ultimatum. So I will just tell you this: you need to tell him how you feel. No force, no confrontation, no expectation. Just lay it out there. Then walk away before embarrassment gets the better of either of you."

"But *how* do I talk to him?"

"Open your mouth, exhale loudly and move your lips. You were just doing it."

She dropped his hands. "You're funny."

"I am known to be, on occasion. As for how to approach the topic, I don't know. But he isn't telepathic."

"No. He's oblivious even to his own actions, in fact. He kissed me, would you believe it, and has ignored me for weeks ever since."

Rathen hesitated. That explained a few things. "Words and actions aren't the same thing. In many cases, action solves problems, and that's what he's good at. But...this kind of thing...it runs too deep, there's too much room for second-guessing, over-analysing, and Garon's nature is to analyse. And to come to the most logical conclusion, based on the evidence. And fleeting looks can be imagined. Your position might be obvious to me, but evidently it hasn't been loud enough for him. He needs words. Clear, direct words."

She nodded slowly. "You're right."

"...But you're not going to do it."

She bit her lip. "I need to think about it first." She shot him an urgent gaze. "Don't say anything to him about this."

"It isn't my place."

They looked back out across the water.

Rathen felt her presence diminish as thought enveloped her. His work was done. So, with a gentle squeeze to her shoulder, he turned around to leave.

"Have you worked anything out for Eyila yet?"

He stalled as his heart sank. He didn't look around, wishing to at least avoid the expectation in her eyes. "Not yet," he replied, his tone guarded. "It's complicated." He heard the sigh. It was brief, but heavy enough to crush him.

"I'm worried about her. Those mages...they lost control of themselves. And they had this crazy, far-away look--"

"I remember," he said flatly. "I'm doing my best."

"Yes. Sorry. I know you are..." There was more, but she didn't voice it. He was glad; he didn't wish to hear a plea to encourage him to try harder, to find a solution to yet another dilemma that had come to rest upon his shoulders.

And yet...

He slumped. He knew he had to stay. Regardless of topic, Petra simply wasn't ready for him to leave.

Rathen returned to the lake, but this time sent her a curious look. "You worry about her a lot. Why is that?"

"She's been through a lot."

"Of course she has. But so have you. And your sister is a mage. Is she older or younger?"

Her eyes slighted. "What's your point?"

"Answer the question."

She didn't. Instead, the lake stole her attention. But the sadness in her eyes betrayed the distraction. "Younger," she replied eventually. "By three years. She's twenty six. Not as young as Eyila, but... Yes, of *course* I worry about her. I worry that...the other mages, they were part of the Order, but nothing could be done for them or it *would* have been, wouldn't it? What if she..." Her voice caught. She shook her head, eyes shut tight, shooing the thought away. "But I worry about Eyila, too, and not just for the magic. She's lost everyone she's ever loved. She needs support, people around her who can help her, who *want* to help her. So she can heal."

"...Did you have many around you?"

"Why?" She asked, prickly.

"Just asking."

"...A few."

"The man in Carenna. The blacksmith."

A sad smile whispered across her lips. "He was one of the few."

He nodded slowly, watching the clouds roll over the water. Clearly, love had not ranked high on her list of priorities back then. She was a fighter, someone capable of seeking revenge. So she had thrown herself into it and regarded love as a hindrance.

But she was not Eyila.

He watched rings form as the first raindrops of the latest deluge began to fall. "Eyila seems to have an eye for Anthis."

She grunted. "She's just intrigued."

"Because he's different?"

"Because he's *very* different."

"Which is why you don't like him."

A sleek eyebrow cocked. "*You've* certainly become quite chummy with him all of a sudden."

"We've...hashed it out. Yelled, fought, reached some kind of understanding. ...Can I ask you something?"

She hesitated. "Go on."

"Do you have a problem with me?"

Panic, bewilderment and the faintest touch of insult mixed into a very unusual frown. "No! Why ever would I?"

"*I've* killed people."

Her alarm was replaced by discomfort, and she took the opportunity to step back among the trees and away from the suddenly torrential rain to distance herself from the matter. But his eyes were fixed on her as he followed, calm and patient. "Well..." she gave in, seeing no escape, "your...situation...isn't voluntary."

"Would it surprise you to know that neither is his?"

"What do you mean?"

"It's not my place. But I understand why you would hate him. He seems to take...well, he seems willing to do what he does. That's not the truth of it, but it's natural that, after your father's...well, you would take even greater offence than most others. Than I did."

"But..." For a moment, words eluded her. Incredulity and the sheerest confusion warred in her eyes, a thought in place that she was simply unable to grasp. "*How* can you tolerate him so easily when you have Aria--"

"Because he would never touch her. And if he did, it would be the *last* thing he ever did."

"And you can *really* be so sure?"

"I have to. Listen to me, Petra: Anthis did not kill your father. He *only* kills villains. Scoff all you like, but I believe him."

"He's already admitted to Eyila that that *hasn't* been exclusive."

"As he has also admitted to me, though not in so many words. And I've seen the withdrawal symptoms. Far too close. Anthis...he has no choice. It's a darkness he has no control over, like my own. The magic he gets back from it...I can't fathom how it works, not in the slightest. Perhaps it's the ceremonial dagger, enchanted in some way. I probed it when we were inside that place and found nothing, but...well, aside from this 'Vokaad' being real and *actually* granting him with magic, it's the only thing that makes sense. The knife is always with him, it carries some kind of influence, he thinks it's connected to his god somehow and the magic he's repaid in gets under his skin. But it's not magic like we know it, it's...more like a ready-made spell just waiting to be directed."

"Then get the knife away from him!"

"I've already tried. He almost killed me for it."

"If we let him keep it, we're *all* at risk - as are countless others."

"I doubt it." He turned towards her, fixing her with purpose. "Eyila needs people around her if she's going to get through this, but she needs their care, too. Not bodies, but heart. And she seems to want Anthis's company. But if you keep creating this animosity whenever he's near, you're going to destroy her chances of recovery. It will drain her and she'll give up trying. Who knows, maybe it's already happening, maybe that's why the magic is affecting her so deeply. Maybe she's not trying to fight it as hard as she could be."

Her hazel eyes flashed. "You're saying this is *my* fault?"

"I'm saying you need to let go of your hatred for him. For Eyila's sake, if not your own. Or anyone else's."

"My hatred for him is *justified*. I can't fathom how *any* of you can look past it - *especially* you and Eyila. He *kills people*, Rathen! He would kill every one of *us* if he could! In fact, every one of us *especially!* We're *valuable* to him! Even Aria! And you can look past it so easily?!"

"*No,*" he bellowed, "I *can't*, but I *have* to! And I *do trust* him. Every word he said to me was the truth. How many times has his mind collapsed around us when we've been out in the middle of nowhere - even in the *desert* - and didn't raise a hand against us? You know I'm right, Petra. Don't be a fool! You can't understand how I've looked past it, well I tell you: I haven't, not fully. But I'm trying! And Eyila seems to have done so with even greater ease, and she should have had the *hardest* time!" He barely noticed her frowning at him. "No matter what Garon says, you are needed, and even he knows it, but we need Anthis, too, and your constant digs at him are making it *impossible* to think! There's so much resting on the two of us, on *me*, and we can't possibly succeed with so much distraction! *Yes*, hooray, I've finally stopped the magic - in *one place!* There are still *countless* more to go! And if the magic is going to try to...try to destroy me like th-that every single time, we will need...need to find another way..." He exhaled and wiped small beads of sweat from his brow with a shaking hand.

Petra was still staring at him, a wrinkle of concern between her eyes. "Are you all right?"

"I'm fine."

"No, you're--" She lunged forwards to catch him as he staggered to his knees. Even through his clothes she could feel his fever. She cursed. "You're not. What's happening? Rathen, what can I do?"

The world tipped on its side. Nausea bubbled. The ground rushed towards him. He thrust his hand out to stop it and heard, despite his dislocation, the beginnings of a call for help. He felt an overwhelming urgency to stop her. He managed with a garbled grunt, but noticed only then that the grass around his hand had turned to flame. His panic rose.

And in its wake surged something dark and familiar, rising like a geyser from the bleakest, blackest depths of his blood.

In that moment his nausea was forgotten; he grunted an order for her to leave and focused his entire being into subduing it.

Breathe. Focus. Breathe...

Seconds passed like hours, but the spinning began to slow. The lake levelled, the trees stood upright, and his stomach settled. And the darkness slunk back into the abyss.

His breath was ragged and he found he was soaked, in rain or sweat he wasn't sure, and when he finally found the composure to look up, Petra remained, staring back down at him, sword in hand, eyes wide and cautious. But no one else had come. He sighed in cumulative relief.

"Rathen...?" She spoke carefully.

"Fine...I'm fine..." Slowly, he pushed himself back onto his knees, but it took effort. He had little choice but to accept her help to find his feet. "I'll uh...go and lie down..."

"Let me help--"

"No, I'm fine...I'm fine..." He ignored her protest, slipping his arm out of her grip, and began to lurch away back through the trees, bracing himself against the rough bark as he went. She watched him go. He was still shaking, the tremor she'd felt when she'd helped him up was too strong to pass so quickly. But she didn't chase after him. While she hadn't a clue what had just happened, she, too, knew him well enough to know that only the company of a certain few would be welcome after it, and only one numbered among them.

She sighed and turned hesitantly back to the lake. The ring of grass was still ablaze.

Chapter 19

The forest was black under various depths of darkness and shadow; distance obscured in that uncertainty, and the torrential rain fogged precision and smothered every sound. The night had them caged. Anything, man or beast, could be lurking mere feet away. Rushkins, hidden among the reeds of their lake burrows or lying still and flat in ambush in endless marsh pools. Näcken, watching from the deepest depths, priming violinic voices. Long-unseen harpies scouring through the treetops. Ghosts tracking in the shadows. They could be dead before they knew what killed them.

The diligence of Garon's patrol was painstaking, his attention dragged to the edge of his capabilities. So it had been for the past four nights. And in that time, he had found nothing. It did little to calm his tensions.

The swamp was beginning to thin; the Korovor Woodlands reasserted itself for one last clawing sweep. They would have been out of it in a day and a half had they not had to swing south west.

Promise or not - a promise he had *not* authorised - he resented having to return to Wrenroot. He disliked being out in the wilderness for so long. There was no news beyond private missives, and they had delivered little but the fact of increased activity of mage hunters, the state of the magic encroaching on settlements and the movements of the military. None of which truly helped beyond course corrections. But there were no rumours, no hearsay; nothing organic that may have slipped his superiors' notice, nothing in real-time, nothing for him to work with as and when the need arose.

A form took shape through the gloom on his right, one immediately familiar. It was Eyila, sitting still, straight and cross-legged upon a rock beneath the shelter of the trees. She didn't react to his presence. He doubted she noticed him at all. She was crying again. He was certain that her obsessive meditation every night was just an excuse to be alone and mourn.

He dismissed her and moved on.

Any information of substance was always passed on, but with what they found themselves facing, absolutely *everything* helped. And so he was grateful - though he wouldn't admit it - for Taliel's interventions, even if they put them all at risk. Information from the heart of the Arana was the most valuable information they could reasonably get, and the only thing that could keep them one step ahead of one of the most dangerous opponents they could possibly have.

...And then there were the elves.

His skin prickled.

The thought that they could be pursuing them chilled him to the bone. They could be capable of anything. And despite Anthis's confidence that the supposedly extinct race would rather wait and see what happened than reveal themselves and hunt them down indiscriminately, Eizariin's own certainties dogged his every step.

The Arana, he could deal with - even with a 'half-elven psychopath' at the lead. Because Salus was not fully elven, likely even less so than Rathen, and his mind was bound by the same rules and possibilities that limited all humans. Even with his extremist attitude and obsessive devotion, there were lines of thought that would simply never occur to him - just what those were, he couldn't fathom even himself, but it seemed to him that 'moving Turunda' still didn't really qualify among them. In short, for the most part, he was predictable.

But the elves had never been restricted by the concept of 'impossible'. Their minds were free. And their capabilities boundless. And that made them perilous. A power that could never be combated, only avoided. If even that...

He reached the edge of the trees and looked out across the lake. The water surface trembled with the last drops of the abruptly ceasing rain.

Past and future duties didn't matter; if they failed here, Turunda would fall. Perhaps the whole of Arasiin. And they held quite probably the *only* solution to the gathering magic. If left alone, it may well disperse like any other aged and crumbling spell in time, but not before it tore the world apart. Or before Salus could do it himself. The elves wouldn't jump in to correct their mistake, but it seemed a few were prepared to hasten the destruction. Perhaps they truly *did* seek the end of humans, to regain their land at long last and resume their reign now the gods had forgotten about them. And if they did...who could possibly stop them?

He grunted, catching himself.

No. He was going too far. It was a thought worth pondering - truly, the elves *weren't* limited by 'impossible' - but not one to be paralysed by. Otherwise, he was tired and his imagination was getting the better of him. *'An attempt at colour.'* He smiled. Then a sudden whisper of guilt snaked through his gut and devoured it, a sensation so abrupt and alien that it knocked him.

A small movement from further along the edge of the Grey Lake pushed his heart into his throat. Petra. It rose further. He had probably disturbed her. He forced himself to steady, forced his rolling shoulder to still, his voice not to call out to her as he watched her disappear into the trees, and only once she'd vanished did something familiar finally kick in to straighten his spine and beat the useless emotion back where it belonged. He grunted with defiance, though no one was around to witness it, and continued his patrol, discarding sentimentality and idle foolishness behind him.

Yes, what he'd said had been harsh, but it was the truth. He hadn't asked her to be there, he hadn't asked for her help, and as far as he could see, she had no reason to remain among them. She should have left long ago. He should have made her. But he'd presumed she'd have done so of her own accord once they were clear of Mokhan. He'd been wrong. And he hadn't tried hard enough to shoo her off when he'd realised it.

Then he should do so now. She was upset, she would be far more likely to finally give in, to leave in anger...

...But...not that night. They were all in a dangerous position. If she were to leave them amidst it, she would still be hunted down.

So it seemed he was stuck with her company again. Stuck with her brashness, her sarcasm, her ceaseless swordplay, the sound of her whetstone over steel what felt like every other night, her footsteps throwing off his own patrol, her spiced scent lingering in the air behind her, her laughter, which he hadn't heard in a few days... Stuck with it all.

He would do it. But he would do it another day.

Garon stumbled, over a root or his own foot, he wasn't sure. His mind was wandering. He was tired. He couldn't afford to lose focus.

But while he could turn to his duty and push aside distractions and keep childish absurdity like sentimentality from getting the better of him, everyone else was growing increasingly complacent, and Rathen's victory seemed to have distracted them from the danger all the more. And to top it off, now they were insisting on honouring a child's promise. It was an argument he could never win.

But there was, he noticed, a benefit. If they deviated back to Wrenroot, stopping at Red Heath for supplies and news along the way, they would have the chance to see if Rathen could replicate his success, an opportunity that would arise much sooner than if they were to head straight to Mokhan. He didn't doubt Rathen's ability, but the fact was that this ex-soldier had been the only mage he could have recruited if he was to keep the matter from the Order's attention - which, despite Rathen's initial insistence, did indeed shelter rebellious mages. The discovery that it took elven magic to operate the Zi'veyn was just a convenient detail.

But the whole matter had become unimaginably complex, a fact the others seemed to forget about all too easily, and while it had finally come together once, after months of toil, there was any amount of opportunity for it to go wrong on the second try. The crisis they were embroiled in went well beyond personal insult. And with Salus pursuing them...he may not have needed the Zi'veyn himself anymore, but his paranoia still wanted it out of their hands, and that meant his people were likely to be even less careful when they inevitably found them. The Zi'veyn's destruction along with them may suit him well. And quite probably the elves, too.

He battled back a yawn and refocused his attention.

He would get no help on watch tonight.

Chapter 20

"We know that they're minuscule spell chains of some kind, elven in origin, which appear to be weaving into the surrounding elements. But, more crucially than how, what we *don't* know is their *nature*. We have no idea what they're capable of. But, despite the evidence, I do not believe that they're intended to be destructive, the effects are too varied and random.

"They've also gathered here from somewhere, and suddenly; this phenomenon has been experienced far beyond our northern borders, which implies that it is not a result of neglected preservational duties, and unless there has been some international underground co-operation between subversive mages, the Order bears no fault at all. It also implies that the magic has a source, and if we can understand the chains' nature, we can locate their point of origin and, perhaps, staunch the flow.

"An opportunity to study the magic will provide us the chance we need to discover its nature, its structure, its source, and on then to whether or not it can be countered, deflected or relocated. It's also an opportunity to explore magical advancement - work has been done on dissipating magic, but never in such great concentrations--"

A hand raised. Owan fell silent. And waited.

The morning light was still obscured by the iron-clad clouds; instead the grand magister's office was illuminated by a few lanterns and a single obedient orb that glowed with the warmth of a tame and miniature sun. But the miserable temperament of the weather outside seemed to ooze in through the open window, stifling what little comfort those flickers could offer while the air, at least where Owan was standing, seemed so thick that it hummed against his eardrums.

The grand magister leaned back into his seat and turned his old eyes upon him. Owan fought the urge to shift and fiddle with his papers. "You say Rathen Koraaz has a plan?"

He deflated. His pretence had been shattered. "Yes."

"But you haven't a clue what it could be?"

"...No, *but--*"

"Then how," he asked calmly, "could your studies possibly help him? And should you discover something with potential, how could you possibly get the information to him? On your own word, I have given him the benefit of the doubt; should he, of all people, against all odds, succeed in finding some way to repair the matter, I will do what I can to keep the attention off of him. But I barely managed to dissuade Riken that he's out there at all, which means that, should anyone provide indisputable evidence to the reverse, the Order will appear to be working with him and covering it up. We will be under even greater suspicion."

"Then why," he began carefully, "if I may ask, did you lie at all?"

Arator smiled. It was a little too bright and mischievous for a man in his seventies. "I did not lie. Aside from your word, I have no evidence that he is out there, and neither does Riken." He rose, then, and wandered towards the window. He looked out over the city of Kulokhar, high enough in the tower to observe its three mile presence from wall to wall, from the artisan to the stately districts and everything in between. And high on the edge, overseeing all, the palace, a mixture of elven and common design, built entirely by the hands of humans.

Owan watched his eyes travel towards it, as they often did, and wondered once again at what he was thinking. Was he marvelling wistfully at the combination? At the decision of their ancestors to unite that which they didn't understand, even hated, with their own ideas and identity? Did he search for hope within that?

Or was he looking beyond the spirals, bartizans and tympana and pondering instead the people within - the king, the council, and their distrust?

He gave no hint. "Rathen Koraaz is not a tactless man," he said at last, his gaze unmoving from the distant palace. "He knows, with his circumstances, that he will have to keep himself hidden, and all the more so with the present unrest. And he is accompanied by an inquisitor, you say - a man whose very position requires finesse in judgement. But whatever they are up to, we cannot help them. I'm sorry, Owan. What information we could give them, they will have to discover on their own. We cannot have a hand in this."

"With all due respect, Grand Magister, we neglect the matter because we don't want to aggravate the populace, but they already believe we're responsible, and the magic is getting *worse*. It's snaking in through the Olusan Mountains and has already torn up Halen, Ausokh, Fen--"

He raised a silencing hand again. "I know, Owan. And believe it or not, I agree with you. But as I said: tact. For now, we must leave it alone." Now his eyes shifted, scanning the city as a whole while regret slipped in to mark his tone. "The people are riled - five over-eager graduates attacked Nestor not five days ago. They misunderstood the intent behind the rebellion, they were only looking for violence, and in light of it there have been four retaliatory attacks on mages across the country in just as many days, none of whom were involved with this pocket of extremists nor even resorted to magic to defend themselves. But that only seems to have added insult to injury." He turned away from the window and back to his desk, but he avoided meeting the scholar's gaze. "We have to focus our efforts on repairing our own situation before it is beyond our reach. Then we will be able to move more freely."

"And in the mean time--"

"In the mean time, you will stay within these walls. If you go out there and start poking around, people will lose their heads. The Arana will detain you in a heartbeat, and given the delicate situation we find ourselves in, it will not be so easy to transfer custody. King Thunan himself is wary of us."

"Yes but it's--"

"Our responsibility, I know, Owan. Truly, I am sorry. But my hands are tied. You must not try to help."

But then his eyes turned up to him, lit by something strange. A light frown flickered across Owan's face. "You have studies to see to. Perhaps you should focus upon them. Whatever they may be. Take no offence to my ignorance - we scholastically-inclined often have several projects in the air, do we not? It's quite impossible for the grand magister to be aware of them all." Coolly, he opened a drawer and withdrew from it a sheet of parchment and prepared the quill standing neatly beside the inkwell. "In the mean time," the nib began scratching across the paper, "I think I might check in with my nephew. His family lives near Mokhan, and Ziili has been adversely affected." Then he added, quite casually: "He's a member of the Hall of the White Hammer, you know."

"He is?"

"Oh yes. Very low rank, of course, but, I tell you, there is no such thing as an unimportant job."

"What is he?"

Arator didn't look up from his letter. "A sparrow handler."

Owan left the office defeated, wringing his notes in frustration. His intentions had been discovered all too easily, and while he supposed it hadn't been difficult after formally proposing field research twice already that week, he'd succeeded only in making himself feel further staunched and restricted. But his research simply *couldn't* move ahead without a closer look at the magic, and despite the apparent weakening of the elder's stance this time around - making contact with the White Hammer's communication masters and, at best, forming a channel to the inquisitor in Rathen Koraaz's company - he was still steadfast on his rejection. And what use was there in a messenger sparrow if they had no message to send?

He sighed and frowned deeper to himself as he descended the spiral staircase, paying no heed to the painted eyes of notable mages or ancient elven figures that followed his every move. His irritation was piqued even further by his own indecision. On one hand, he understood the grand magister's position. He was the head of the Order, and in such turbulence, their every movement mattered. But on the other, this *was* the Order's responsibility, and their lack of action didn't sit right with him at all. By doing nothing, they were giving the populace greater reason to accuse them of disloyalty.

But he hadn't a choice. He was under the Order's command and he had no wish to go against his superior's orders - though that didn't mean he wouldn't raise the subject again. He still had matters to present. Matters, it seemed, he needed to be reminded of. Because it wasn't just Rathen he was trying to help.

Just as crucial as stopping the manifestation of the magic was the health of his very own people. He was *certain* that this magic was the root of the affliction passing among a small number of mages, an affliction that compromised their sanity and killed not only them, but any innocents that happened to be around at the time. And it seemed that they were *not* actively seeking out victims. *Something* pulled them away from the safety of the Order, *something* dragged them off in apparently random directions, but what and to what end, no one could suggest, because none of the tormented ever remained long enough to be asked or followed. This affliction was giving the mage hunters just as much ammunition as genuine attacks; every case plunged the Order into deeper disgrace.

The worst case so far occurred only a week ago in the Green Hills, wherein the explosive death of a lone ex-sahra battalion major had diverted the river and caused a landslide, burying the low-lying village of Adeliene and all its occupants.

The singular upside was that no one seemed aware that magic or mages had been the cause. It was, on all accounts, simply a tragic disaster. But Owan couldn't shake the sense of responsibility, as hard as he tried. All it had done was reinforce his determination to bring the whole ordeal to an end.

But for now, all he could do was focus himself on his many varied studies. Whichever, given the present circumstances, he should find the most gripping. And if he managed to find anything hiding in plain sight, among the details he and others even more capable had pored over for months already, he at least had the potential means to share it.

He reached the bottom of the stairs, but his foot hesitated above the floor as a thought suddenly struck him.

What if he didn't need to send *information?* He was stuck in Kulokhar with every other scholar - but Rathen was not. Rathen was very much *out there*. What if he could send him a message asking him to take note of certain details and pass them back to *him?* Then he could apply it to his own work from the safety of the city and well within the grand magister's orders, from which Rathen himself was exempt. Perhaps he'd already uncovered the details Owan needed, but had no idea what to make of them! Whatever the case, as he'd said to Clarilla, *someone* had to have managed *something* for the magic to have gotten worse, and a presence in his gut told him that it had been none other than Rathen's doing. It just hadn't been enough.

Which meant that Owan could indeed be of use. Rathen would just have to help him first.

He hurried on through the corridors, past offices, study rooms, archives and vaults and on instead to his preferred space overlooking the gardens, his purpose bolstered, enthusiasm revived. His next task was suddenly quite simple: work out which details were the most important and translate them into a form that Rathen could make sense of without having to seek help.

He wondered in his haste, as his feet trampled fine carpets and polished wood, if this wasn't what Arator had intended in the first place.

Salus stared at the miniature report with a soft furrow in his brow. Upon his first read, he'd assumed he'd made a mistake. Upon his second, that the operative writing it had. Upon his third, that, somehow, the person to deliver it was at fault. After the fifth, he dropped it to the desk and held his face in his hands.

Teagan promptly dismissed the young boy and braced himself for the reaction.

But it didn't come for some time. Instead, when the keliceran's hands slipped to steeple upon the bridge of his nose, he appeared to be wrestling with a number of thoughts, trying to decide which should trouble him the most. Whatever the case, the matter couldn't have been severe, or the desk would have been upturned.

Finally, he dropped his hands and began to speak, but only a brief and disjointed noise managed to get out before confusion reasserted itself. Eventually, he shook his head in dismay. "He's done it."

"...Sir?"

"He's done it, and there wasn't a thing Andrew could do to stop him... And he lost him soon afterwards - a *rushkin* set upon him, would you believe." He shook his head again, eyes wide in search of understanding. He looked up at Teagan, but, of course, he didn't look back. "A *rushkin!* And for that, Koraaz got away..."

Understanding erased the wrinkle from Teagan's brow. "Koraaz. Then by 'he's done--"

"He's used the Zi'veyn. At Borer's Teeth. The thing floated between his hands and the magic faded, as far as Andrew can tell. Light vanished, water returned, and then out came the beast, they fled and it charged for him instead." But his perplexity remained, dragging his attention further onto the other matter that seemed to increasingly dominate his thoughts. "Why did a *phaeacian* have to be the one to find them? Why not a phidipan? Why not a *portian?!* There are too few of them - had portians been on their tail sooner, this whole matter would have been resolved already!"

"Not everyone can take the conditioning."

"No. But perhaps we need to find more who can..." Salus trailed off into thought. Teagan waited patiently. "We need to do something about the phaeacians--"

"They cannot simply become portians--"

"I wouldn't *want* them to be portians!" Embers sparked in his tired eyes. "They can't be trusted to hold a knife by its handle! They *continuously* fail at the simplest of missions, and consistently use non-humans as an excuse!"

"I doubt they are making it up."

"I'd prefer that they *were*. The very issue is that they're *not*. Harpies, ditchlings, *rushkins*..." he bit off a snarl and sank back into his chair. For a long moment, the ceiling engrossed him.

Teagan's eyes slipped onto him. He looked weary, sleep-deprived, but his mind was present. And yet, despite his relative calm, despite the room for rationality, he seemed disinclined to use it. His belief that the phaeacians were useless had only grown in recent weeks, and in that time, he'd convinced himself. It was true that phaeacians were not trained to the same depth as phidipans, and neither were they to portians, but no one brought into the folds and reaches of the Arana's web were incompetent. Not one. They just had to be assigned the right jobs for their skills.

Teagan straightened and snapped his eyes back to the wall with a self-disciplining frown. The keliceran was not to be blamed. Every one of them, phaeacian and otherwise, were accountable for their actions and decisions. Surely, if Salus believed it, the phaeacians *should* have been better than this. "What do you have in mind?"

Salus drummed his fingers upon the desk. "Get them out of the way," he replied at last. "Send them across the borders and have them keep an eye on things out there. Recall the phidipans except those implanted and have phaeacians take their place."

"All of the phaeacians? We will thin our numbers fiercely if we act indiscriminately."

"Mm..."

"And lose valuable skills."

"...You're right. Yes, you're right. There must be a few who are capable and possess skills we need to hold on to... And we'll need to renew our extermination," he added easily. "Phidipan or not, we can't have non-humans getting in the way like this; they've already hampered our latest efforts against spying on Doana, and the tribes may have moved off for now, but it's only a matter of time before they swing back around, dragging their squabbles onto civilised land." He glanced sidelong at Teagan, but this time, he didn't question the necessity. Clearly, he was beginning to understand.

He struck the desk in decision and a fire of enthusiasm flared in his eyes. "Yes. This is it. This is *it* Teagan! The Arana needs an overhaul - get the profiles, we begin immediately!" He all but leapt out of his seat, surging past the portian to retrieve them himself in his excitement.

"Sir," his favoured began while Salus dropped the folders on his desk, "what do you intend to do?"

"I already told you, we're rearranging--"

"I meant about the Zi'veyn." He noted Salus fall still. "If they have used it, should we not be addressing it? We have no idea what they are planning, but this is clearly progress."

He resumed opening up the folders and stayed quiet for a while. "This comes first," he replied at last, flat and resolved. "Phaeacians can't be trusted to do anything. We need to pull in as many phidipans as we can, and portians. Anything that can be handed to phaeacians, will be. Our priorities are within our own borders. We need mages on their tail. And at Borer's Teeth, we need to find out what they've done."

"Many of our mages are occupied. And one of those implanted within the Order has been caught by mage hunters." He didn't react to the flash of Salus's gaze. "She escaped easily enough, but they are increasingly disruptive. It's only a matter of time before our residential spies are hindered. We should consider doing something about them."

Salus looked slowly back to the agent profiles. "No. Not yet. They're keeping the mages on their toes. As troublesome as they are, they're no doubt preventing worse. They're a necessary evil."

"If they're left alone and unopposed, they will only grow in number and influence; the disruption will escalate. The guards are already having trouble keeping control of them."

"You forget that the White Hammer has been brought in to handle it. It isn't our concern. Our people may not be able to handle beasts, but city spies are more versed in human behaviour. They will be able to work around it."

"Only to a degree, and what will happen in the distraction? The Order, Koraaz, Doana; any of them could use the chaos to--"

The air rang. Salus lifted his fist from the splintered wood. His eyes were venomous. "You seem *intent* on looking for defeat today, Teagan. It's a problem."

"I merely offer counsel--"

"When it's wanted, it will be *asked* for."

Teagan's lips formed a tight and silent line. But Salus's stare didn't break.

"You doubt."

"No."

"You do."

"I am simply providing argument. An alternative side."

"That you think I'm unaware of?"

"Absolutely not. It is my job to ensure all sides are actively weighed; my mention of them is simply a means to ensure it."

Salus rose and fixed him with an ever harsher gaze. Teagan didn't move. "I am aware of *every* side," he pressed. "I don't make these decisions lightly, Teagan, but they must be made, and my choices present the best result in the long run. We're dealing with something *bigger* than mage hunters and unrest or inconvenience. We're trying to prevent the Order from *tearing* our home to *pieces*! *Foreigners* from moving in, imposing their ideals and eradicating us as a people and a culture! People can deal with inconvenience *now* if it means they'll still be alive in *ten years*! We're trying to *preserve* our *world*!"

"I understand tha--"

"*Do* you?"

"We're all fighting for the same thing. I apologise if I have upset--"

"*Upset?*" He scoffed. "You haven't *upset* me, Teagan. I don't *get* upset. I've been trained, just as you have, to suppress my emotions and keep them from dictating my actions. What I am right now is *confused. That* is not an emotion. It is a state, and one that can be rectified with reason. So I suggest you provide it, rather than 'argument'."

Salus watched him closely, but Teagan's bearing didn't change. He remained obedient, stolid but capable. He'd never presented himself with anything less. Even now, beneath the keliceran's burning stare. And so he shouldn't. For he was portian.

"I apologise," he declared just as steadily. "You are correct, of course. We are preserving our home and our people. Inconvenience is a minor price to pay for victory."

Salus stared at him for a long moment, then snapped angrily back to the desk to continue filtering through the folders, kicking the matter out of his mind.

He ignored agents' faces, ages, birth origins - some of which were unknown even to the individuals in question - and focused intently upon skills, strengths and achievements. High-profile assassinations, noted not for their results but for the tidiness and nature of their execution and the success of the act's disguise; intel-gathering, not solely for the information but the ease and speed with which it was delivered while avoiding personal suspicion; spying under a variety of identities and their ability to slip seamlessly from one to another and improvise without breaking cover. These were the most valuable skills, denoting individuals who could not only succeed at the task given, but maintain a position of trust in every scenario even once the job was done. Only these were worthy of keeping, and with a promotion to phidipan and the conditioning it entailed, the cruciality of their every task could increase along with their chances of success.

But there were so few to whom the honour could be extended.

A sudden sigh, airy and quite uncharacteristic, sent him whirling back around, and he started at the sight of the silver-skinned face, twisted in mock disapproval. He noticed only in passing that Teagan had disappeared as suddenly as she'd arrived.

"Tisk tisk, Keliceran," Liogan chided in her strangely lilting voice. "You're getting a little testy."

"Where is Teagan?" He growled menacingly, but though his hands were already instinctively raised in preparation, he knew his magic would slip just as easily over her as his ferocity. She merely smiled and rolled her pastel eyes.

"He's just popped out. Don't worry, he won't be long. Just long enough, I should think." She wandered around the desk, peering down at the papers he'd been so absorbed in a moment ago, and dropped casually into his seat. She ignored his bristling and extended a long, slender finger. "You're getting distracted."

"I'm doing my job."

"If that's what you call it. Looked to me like you were taking your inadequacy out on your faithful subordinate." She grinned as his face turned crimson with rage and waved it away with a languid hand. "There you go, getting distracted again. Would you please focus on my presence?"

"I would but I fear I might never eat again."

She laughed, then. He didn't like it. There was hatred in it. It sounded inherent, as though even her most genuine and joyful expression would be underlined with enmity. She rose back to her feet and meandered towards him in her usual leisurely way. "Oh I *do* like you, Salus." She slapped his cheek as they levelled - a little too hard to be playful, unless that, too, was inherent - and her tone dropped as she continued to wander past him. "But I'm not here to play. Tell me," her freezing eyes crashed back upon him, "of your progress."

"My progress?" He allowed the slightest curl of his lip to linger if just to demonstrate his own disdain, but kept his hand from rising to his cheek. He tried to stop it from turning red, but he had no idea if he was succeeding.

"Yes. Your progress. With the magic, the chasms and puzzle pieces."

"I haven't had--"

"The inclination? Drive to succeed? Strength of devotion to the safety of your people? To the 'preservation of your world'?" She smiled again at this most recent flash of anger. "Oh I did enjoy that little bit about 'upset', by the way. Very funny. Though I suppose that portian training you're so proud of is the reason you're so volatile. After all that suppression, when it finally snapped, you had no idea how to deal with the flood of spirit and passion that came with it, did you?" Again, she waved away his maddened bluster. "But we're getting distracted again." Completing her circle, she dropped back into his chair. "How about your magic? You train often enough, I suppose, but how are you utilising it? Aside from burning the corpses of your people."

"You're spying on me," he growled. "Why?"

"Because you are the key."

He blinked, then regarded her closely. He scrutinised her imperial eyes, eyes that saw everything, eyes that advertised knowledge of so much and yet masked every detail. Eyes that told him absolutely nothing, except that there was something to tell, but that nothing in any realm of human or elf could ever persuade her to reveal it.

He decided not to indulge her. "You're not here to play riddles."

"I might be."

"Get to the point. I'm clearly not working fast enough for you, so say what you've come to say and leave."

Liogan's eyes narrowed, but her insult was glancing. Instead, and certainly in retaliation, she made herself more comfortable, lounging across the chair, sleek legs entangled in the skirts of a dark and finely patterned dress resting upon the desk. "I'm sure it's exasperating. When fury, fear and the base need for survival powers a spell from your very core, it's impossible to revert to signs. I would assume, at least. Oh, they seem so *cumbersome*. How can you ever get in touch with your heart when your fingers are bending and breaking like that?" She made some coarse gestures and dropped her hands in abandonment. "Ugh!" She leaned back further, but her eyes had changed when her gaze returned to him, and they weren't searching for reaction. Though they were no less forceful. "However...you have made progress. You can't do much, but you're cunning in its application. You're smart, Salus, dear, which is why I'm here - but you're of no use to me until you can do more than boil tea--"

"I *can* do more than--"

"Oh you *really* let yourself get baited, don't you? For the very last time: stop getting distracted and listen to me. Magic takes concentration - I already told you, did I not, that magic isn't black and white? But while it takes concentration, it shouldn't be strangled. Don't focus so much that you can't react with your heart, but don't relax so much that it doesn't notice you're trying to use it."

"You speak as if it's sentient--"

"Don't interrupt. I've told you that before, too, haven't I? If you can't learn such basic manners, how do you expect to learn *magic?*" She sighed in torment and shook her head, then sat forwards, clasping her hands neatly upon the desk, and fixed him with intent. She looked every bit the figure of power she thought herself to be. A fact at which he bridled. "Do not over-think things," she continued just as importantly, "but do not be so deceived by your oh so wondrous blue fire that you *under*-think it. You've been told this by another intelligent woman, I believe. Fancy that. Such wisdom in so inferior a race. Oh don't snarl, you're not *quite* an animal. Perhaps you should apply to your practice what we both have told you. Instinct is one thing, but creating a spell is quite another, and you are not an elf. So very far from one that it's sickening, but you possess this ability all the same."

"You disdain me this much, and yet you seek my help."

"I do," she lamented, "and make no mistake, it sickens me as much as it sickens you. But it's the way things must be. And if you are to succeed, even to your own end of protecting this beautiful land, then you must tolerate me as I must tolerate you, and put your pride away. Your mages are not enough to help you. I, on the other hand, am far *more*."

"Then *help* me! Don't just appear in here as and when the fancy strikes you, deliver a few riddles and vanish without a word! It's no wonder I've made no progress if you don't stick around to make sure I've even understood a word you've been telling me!"

"Oh, my dear keliceran, you *do* understand. Don't insult yourself. But..." she squinted in thought. "Perhaps you're right. The original suggestion wasn't enough, and the rather thinly veiled hint at connecting the rifts wasn't either. Perhaps I really do need to hold your hand for your first few steps." She rose to her feet and straightened out her dress, a purposeful movement that made him take a step backwards and his hands rise in preparation, though the whole action, he knew, had betrayed his nervousness.

She was unaffected, of course, and strode forwards with her sharp chin held high, drew to a stop right in front of him, pursed her lips, regarded him harshly down the bridge of her nose, then raised her hand and tapped him lightly upon the forehead.

The world spun.

"There," he heard her say, and as a thought he was sure was not his own twirled around in his head, he saw through a haze that she had grinned and stepped backwards, "that should help to hurry things along. Now--look, stop gawping, pull yourself together and *listen*."

He tried, even as she dragged him dizzily back towards the desk and spread out what he guessed was the map, but it took a long while for the lines to sharpen enough to recognise that she was pointing towards Fendale. "The magic is reacting to spells cast nearby, yes? Well, it is - that suicidal fellow in Trinn triggered the chasm in Fendale to grow and quite unintentionally. By that logic, if you were to cast a spell of any description within the reach of such a place, you would be able to lengthen the chasm. Shush. Now, if you were to specifically cast into or against these streams of - what was it you said? Turquoise ripples? Then you would catalyse the magic and make the matter worse even if the spell's intention had nothing at all to do with it. *But*, if you could control the feed against that reactive magic and temper its response, then you could also control its angle, focus and epicentre, and direct the chasm wherever you wanted it to go."

His frown tightened as he followed a thought. "Push it..."

"Steer it towards the next. Link them up."

"...But these chasms are miles apart."

"Yes. But you can handle it, can't you, Keliceran?"

The door burst open before he could answer, his head snapping up in startlement as Teagan came barrelling inside and slammed to a short and sudden stop. With a single puff, he recovered breath and bearing, but confusion had settled firmly on his face as he stared back at Salus, who shared in his frown when he noticed that Liogan had vanished. Again.

"What did she want?" Teagan asked, closing the door behind him and looking deceptively briefly about the room.

"The usual. Where were you?"

"She sent me to the forest. I returned as quickly as I could." He studied the keliceran as he stared back down at the map. It wasn't difficult to see the distraction in his eyes, nor the idea unfolding behind them. He looked away. "Did she offer anything?"

He looked back when he failed to reply, and found that his eyes had grown even wider in rapture. Unease set in. And reinforced when Salus moved past him and made for the door. He didn't ask where he was going, nor to elaborate on what he'd meant by 'I can do it'. He left with urgency, and that told him enough: he wouldn't be held up, and wouldn't be dissuaded.

The door closed with an absent bang. Teagan's eyes travelled towards the map. Mistrust set his feet in motion, and he soon peered down at the familiar topography, at the marked locations dotted along the borders, and the new lines that were still forming like inky blood welling up to the surface to join every point, forming a bruised and deathly ring around the country.

The sight evoked a shudder of dread in the depths of his chest, and his eyes flicked dubiously back onto the door.

Chapter 21

Despite his immediate disdain, the contempt and loathing that rose as sharp and strong as instinct at the very sight of her, his heart had lurched almost buoyantly at Liogan's appearance.

The conceit, the self-importance, the knowledge that she was, and would always be, the most powerful person in the room seemed to be counter-balanced by the elicitation of hope that tailed her brazen arrival. But it was a peculiar hope, one that flickered like the shadows cast by a candle, first taking one form, then another, leaving him ever uncertain of its true shape. All Salus knew for certain was that the existence of that hope relied on him just as the shadow relied on the flame. It was his action to take; Liogan was merely providing the means, pointing the way - casting the shadow.

He had no idea how she'd done it, but he had no doubt that she had. With that tap on the head, knots began to unravel. Things began falling into place, connections so obvious that he felt positively sick with himself for not making them sooner. But before they had the chance to settle into anything close to clarity, his thoughts had billowed ahead so fast his fingers almost shaped the spells as he bounded through the corridors.

There were few figures within the gilded training room, all of whom were startled out of their concentration as he burst inside. Their attention quickly diverted, as was proper, but he paid them not the slightest notice anyway. Nor did he mark the fact that neither Erran nor his apprentice were among them. But Salus hadn't been searching for them.

He veered to the left where, among the paintings and ornaments displayed purely to make the room less bare, an ornate mirror was hung. With a golden frame flecked with onyx inlays and fingers of silver that rose out from its topmost edge like the tines of antlers, it was a piece as much to be looked at as in. But these details were lost as equally as the handful of mages who sent him brief and curious glances.

A mirror. It was the only suitable thing he could think of at the time. It was childish, in the vein of fairy tales, but vases, chalices, tapestries - none of them were right for the job. But a mirror was, by definition, a surface in which to view, but through which a gaze couldn't return. And it was this mirror he had marked as a receiver.

Every time he'd stared into the accursed thing he'd been filled with promise. *'This time,'* he had always thought, *'this time it will work.'* But it never had - not for long enough to call a success, at any rate. But now, promise disintegrated, and in its place had come something more robust. Was it certainty? In truth, he barely dared to name it.

He took a deep breath. Time slowed. His heart shuddered, but the determination didn't waver. His hands rose, fingers twitched, and slowly they began forming the signs he had learned well enough to shape in his sleep. But this time, things were different. He felt fetters of intricacy growing beneath the intentions, subtle links that anchored and multiplied eightfold with every twist of his fingers where before there had been only a single thread. But despite the complexity, the room for so much to go wrong, he felt no need to look closer and ensure he was doing it right.

The links were simple when taken on their own, each representing a single detail, coming together like a list rather than a description, a chain rather than a twisted length of string, and the very fact that they had formed at all was enough to assure him that he was on the right track. Even during his briefest magical victories, he hadn't experienced such certainty.

The fire flickered at the far end of the room. The mages at the desk beside it looked up, sensitive to the shift of his magic, and cast what began as careful glances in search of its results. But while Salus watched their interest fix and grow - the increasingly open turn of their heads, the deepening of their frowns, the lengthening of their stares - they didn't correct themselves beneath his gaze. For they were looking at him from his right and down the length of the room, while he viewed them directly in the mirror where his own reflection should have been.

But his breath was bated. There was no celebration. He waited for the spell to crumble. Every second dragged, uncertain, precarious. He re-assessed everything he viewed, shifting every few heartbeats to ensure he wasn't staring at his own reflection after all, blind to a sight so expected he looked straight through it. But nothing beyond the mages and flickering flames moved. A minute passed with no change.

It was only after another half that a flurry of butterflies burst into life and somersaulted in his stomach, fanning a sudden spark of triumph into a whirling blaze, and a smile tugged at his lips. A smile he didn't think to hold back despite a lingering breath of doubt. But it was born only of disbelief, and he couldn't deny what was laid before him. He had - yes, he dared to think it - succeeded.

How long had this taken? Two weeks? It was nothing. Twenty years had passed before the teleportation spells had been established. Two weeks were a drop in a bucket, and he was under no illusions that urgency and his own higher blood were behind it.

And the timing - what luck! Compensation for fewer pairs of eyes; the phaeacians' ejection wouldn't weaken the Arana at all. He needed only to set up these spells. It would take time, and no one else was capable of seeing to it in his stead, but he could do it. He *could*. He *had*. Doing it again would be nothing. He needed only gather vessels to focus his magic upon, something for the spell to centre around. Something that could be left unnoticed in the centre of a city and provide him a wide view. It would be far quicker than establishing them in person in every location.

And to think he'd argued with Erran when he'd suggested using the chandelier as a foundation, protesting on the forethought that it was restrictive, that, if he succeeded, he wouldn't be able to see closely enough to make heads or tails of what was going on in a space even only double the size of this room. But Erran in turn had carefully reasoned that the spell needed to be tied to something if the point wasn't to wander or shift, and that, once the spell was complete, it could be actively adjusted like a telescope to pan or magnify. Which, with the instructed rotation of his fingers, it did, and smoothly.

His heart fluttered again.

Yes. Vessels. And mirrors. And then the Arana would gain greater range than if the phaeacians had remained. No one would sneak past them again. No city would fall to foreign invaders; no plot of mages would go unnoticed; no individual arrival would be missed.

Salus's scheming smile widened. The Arana would be in control once again.

Taliel sighed deeply. The evening was ageing. The sunlight, welcome after so may days of cloud, was fading to rose gold and just managed to flood in through the window before the forest could swallow the sun. Birds still sang outside, perched openly on the ends of the brightest branches while a warm breeze tousled the leaves, chirping merrily into the final stretches of the day. The sight, the warmth, the sounds, all attempted to drag her beneath a blanket of sluggishness. Had she been anywhere else, she may have let it. But here, she needed to pay attention.

And Salus made it impossible, anyway.

She'd pressured him to get away from his office and clear his head, but even in his private house, he hadn't left his work behind. He was energised, racing around the sitting room, unable to sit down; any time his rear touched a seat he leapt right back out of it with another burst of enthusiasm. She was exhausted just watching him.

At last, Taliel rose from her seat by the window, grasped him by the arms and finally forced him to a stop.

"*I can do it*," he said into her face, "I *did* it! And I can do it again!"

"Calm down, Salus. You're going to wear yourself out. Sit."

"I can move Turunda, too!" He didn't notice her stifle a sigh, nor that she was trying to steer him towards a chair. "*Absolutely* I can! Liogan has told--no, she has *shown* me how to wield this magic! Better than Erran ever has!" But then he faltered, his expression abruptly slipping into confusion. Taliel took the opportunity to finally force him down. "Signs...but I still used signs..."

"And?"

"I used *signs*, not...*instinct*..."

"So?" She sat down beside him, watching his growing bewilderment. "Then you still need Erran's help. He's extremely capable, you know this - you'd not have chosen him otherwise."

"But why didn't she tell me how to..." He shook his head with a horrified realisation. "She expects me to do this with *signs?!* She thinks I'm incapable of anything more - where would I possibly learn them?!"

"Erran will teach you."

"And how would *he* know how to do it?!" He rose, this time in fury, but Taliel restrained him with a smile and a touch.

"As I understand it," she continued softly, pulling him back down, "signs are like letters, and just twenty six letters can form *uncountable* words. You need only learn them and put them in the right order. It's the same with signs, isn't it? How many different spells will the same one sign be present in? The sign for fire, for inst--"

"There is no sign for fire, it's actually a combination of hea--"

"Which only proves my point all the *more*. *Patience*, Salus. Learn the signs. It may take some time, but it will all be worth it, won't it?"

"...It will. You're right... Ugh, it's just so...it's..."

"It's important, I know. But you'll manage. For now, however, I suggest you keep your focus on surveillance."

"Yes...yes, of course. That's equally important. More so, in fact. There are threats all around us...and to think we will *finally* be back on top of it!" Again he rose in excitement, too quickly for her to catch him, and resumed his fervent wandering. She watched him closely, and he soon threw back a grin, eyes sparkling. She forced a smile into her eyes. An easy matter. "Then perhaps you might finally get some *rest* and I can stop worrying about you."

His smile softened. "I hope you never stop worrying about me. I mean...uh, well I don't want you to *worry*, you don't need to, I just mean--"

"I understand, Salus."

He laughed self-deprecatingly. He returned voluntarily, pulling her into an embrace, and she reciprocated, smiling as she felt him bury his chin affectionately against her. But, as it turned out, he was just shaking his head in awe. "*I can do this*, Taliel. I can! It's so simple!"

She sighed as he rose and wandered off again.

"I just have to stress the chasms, and that's easy - all it takes is magic! Liogan said..."

And he proceeded to tell her. And she listened. To all his assumptions, his logic, his excitement, his tangents that all looped back around to the beginnings in one seamless, obsessive circle. And she smiled, nodding, asking questions - simple questions, enough to keep him going and steer him towards the most paramount details, things she could pass on, that others could make use of.

But deep beneath her fond, supportive smile and bright, interested eyes, dread thrashed and boiled. Yes. Perhaps he *could* do it. *If* the elf maintained contact. Which she surely would. She believed he could succeed - she wouldn't have bothered interfering in his tutelage if she didn't. But this woman came and went as she pleased; no force could stop her, just as no force could deter Salus from following her pretty words and promises. Nothing could block her influence; nothing could keep her out.

She had his full attention.

But...so did *she*.

Taliel rose and caught him as he paced up and down the room in frenetic thought. "Salus. You have a lot on your mind. Make things easier on yourself and focus on the surveillance. Threats are all around us, remember?"

"Yes...yes, of course. Ah, you're right. I'm sorry, I'm just excited. But I have to deal with the agitators before Turunda can be moved or I'll only bring them with us. The ruins can wait. Koraaz *will* be stopped before he can reach them all. They're not going anywhere."

She looked at him. With his zeal suddenly restrained, he seemed oddly focused and considered. Reasonable. "It is...good to see you so confident."

"How can I not be?" He smiled easily. It was disconcerting. "I have magic, I have Liogan, and I have you." He turned himself towards her, took her hands in his, and peered into her copper-ringed eyes. "Thank you for keeping my feet on the ground, Taliel. If not for you, I hate to think what mistakes I might make."

"That's my job. I support you fully. You can rely on me." She embraced him then, if only so she didn't have to worry about the discomfort showing in her eyes. It took far too long to shove aside. "So, I was thinking," she continued tactfully as they parted, "you said you'll need the spell's focuses set up. You can't possibly do it all yourself, so--"

"No, but I don't *have* to if it's cast over an object, others can--"

"So I would be honoured if you allowed me to place the first."

He hesitated. She saw his eyes dull, and for a moment a jolt of panic at the thought of suspicion shuddered through her. She hid it perfectly, of course, and settled when he smiled wistfully.

"I've missed you, Taliel."

"I wouldn't be gone for long."

"No, but..." His expression brightened, a notion flashing through his eyes. "I have a better idea. I'll place the first - it's only right - but I want you come *with* me. We can do it together, just the two of us! I want you to be a part of this."

She said nothing as he stared at her, vivid, pressing, squeezing her hands in his enthusiasm. She could only smile and kiss him.

None of her irritation passed through, but it was more than simply present beneath the surface. She desperately needed the opportunity to get away and deliver this information, but instead she had trapped herself with him. She couldn't deviate and see to it on her way, and neither could she do so while he was gone and Vari was manning the translocators. But Rathen needed to know, and needed to know *soon*. Malson had already told her to report straight to them if she discovered anything severe enough, and his success under Liogan's meddling certainly fell under 'severe'.

"I would love to," she managed at last, controlling her eyes as they parted.

He smiled happily. "Good. In the next few days, then. I need to gather more mirrors."

The sun dropped behind the trees. Dusk fell in through the windows.

Chapter 22

Three days later, the air hung like lead beneath the thick cloud of tension.

Breath stifled, bodies rigid, hearts subdued by force, while a presence of danger stood boldly among them, grinning a charnel threat. But while the portian and phidipan stared hard at the wall, Salus paced, his eyes wild, dead to the atmosphere beyond his own skin.

Malson's pressures rang in his head. They echoed with every footstep. *'The military needs that intel!' 'This is your job, Keliceran!' 'You have all the resources you could need!' 'All your assurances, and what do you have to show for them?!'*

A small voice in the recesses of his mind wondered if perhaps he had acted rashly. But he couldn't afford to second-guess himself. Decisions had been made, action taken, and now all he could do was hope for the best. But his phidipans were capable. They would make the best of the situation.

So why were his intestines tangled in knots?

Footsteps approached outside. Salus stopped and stared towards the door. The footsteps passed and faded. He resumed his pacing.

Whatever their plan, one thing had been discerned: Doana's defences were not in place. So he had issued the order to attack a single camp head-on, to catch them off-guard and force them to show their hand, reveal a hint of their intentions. Just as Malson had wanted. He had stepped it up.

But he had spared only three for the task. A mage to cast the illusion of a company of soldiers, a phidipan to observe the response, and another to venture in and collect information from the heart of the camp in the chaos.

And now...now he waited.

Clouds shifted, casting changing depths of shadow through the window. Rain pattered against the glass. Time blurred beneath the soft, monotonous drone. The air inside shook with the continuous impact. The breath in their lungs seemed to join it.

Finally, a knock came at the door, unannounced this time by any footsteps.

Salus lunged for the handle.

The man on the other side barely flinched when the door was snatched open, and he stepped inside at the keliceran's silent order and took his place before the desk. Salus was immediately in front of him. Staring respectfully over his shoulder, he didn't see the fever in his superior's eyes. Nor the danger. But he was duly informed moments later.

Salus's temper snapped like a fine, dry twig. The phidipan recoiled as the tension shattered - the others had already braced themselves - and collected himself as best he could while the keliceran raged around him. The teapot narrowly missed his head.

"Get out!"

He didn't need to be told twice.

Neither Teagan nor Taliel watched the phidipan leave, nor Salus as he steadied himself over the desk, shoulders heaving, skin blanching white. Now, among the rain and growling puffs, the shaking air hummed.

"They figured it out too quickly," he spat after another torturous silence. "And we've lost a phidipan and a *mage*." Another deathly growl rumbled free. "They figured it out too quickly for any detail to be reliable. We've lost agents and gleaned nothing!"

"No," Teagan began calmly, but as Salus snapped around, he had to force himself to steady. He heard Taliel gasp slightly from beside him. "With respect, we've now learned that this camp was false. They had no defences - in place or in planning."

"Yes, *because* this camp was false. We can't assume the others are the same. So, in essence, we've lost agents, and gleaned *nothing!*"

"They have learned nothing from us, either."

"*Bah!*" He spun away again and fixed keenly back upon the map, as though he thought he could see the invaders within the grain of the parchment if he stared hard enough. "And we can't risk using the same tactics on another camp. Their communications can be intercepted, but they don't seem to be *using* any! Every camp is isolated, even *supply runs* haven't been witnessed for weeks! Something else is going on. Without a shadow of a sodding doubt, something else is going on...and we still have no idea what..."

He exploded again, clearing his desk in a single sweep. He had no patience for that small, wretched voice in the back of his mind, nor for its suggestions of his own impending reprimands.

He was *not* looking forward to Malson's next intrusion.

The thought ripped a snarl from his lips. That old fool. This was *his* doing. He blustered in with unending demands and no thought for logistics. While trying to work around the destruction of the land, the constant evacuations and the impact Ivaea and Kasire's petty squabbles were having on external observations, he expected him to deal with Doana, ward away the tribes, *accompany* those evacuations - he even had a *personal* request to observe the Order! Just how many *others* were unsanctioned? And not two hours ago had come in and pressed him to stop the mage hunters on top of it all! He'd agreed, just to shut him up, but he was firm on his original stance: the White Hammer would handle it. He had no room for anything else on his plate.

For days he'd felt the pressures sweltering up inside him, provoking sweats, nausea, sleeplessness; he was hungry but too tense to stomach anything, and distracted from the very work that haunted him. He was absent even in Taliel's company. A fact which sickened him all the more every time he realised it, always too late to correct.

A weight dropped in his chest as that very fact struck him again. His head pulled around and eyes fell immediately onto her. She didn't look back at him, but her eyes were a fraction wider than usual. His shoulders dropped with a stab of regret, which he chased away with a deep, composing breath.

"All right." He turned towards them, closed his eyes and tightly folded his arms, reining in his cascading thoughts, the pyretic thump of his heart, and let a bearing of rationality settle in their place. "By attacking Doana out of the blue and with only three individuals, we've cast an uncertainty into their plans. Even though two operatives were killed, it was still too well-executed for them to assume it was a result of restlessness. And as none of the three were marked by the military, there is now a new element they have to consider. No doubt they will assume that we were probing them, testing their reactions, and while they have long been aware of the Arana's existence, they still fell for this trick. Which means that, at the very least, they don't expect the *Arana* to attack them outright. We've set them off-balance, which means that, whatever their plans, they'll have to re-evaluate them in order to factor us in. And they don't know how we will respond."

"They will expect our actions to be unconventional," Teagan offered, "different from the military. They won't paint us with the same brush."

"Of course not, but they don't know how far we will go. All they've done so far is kill our scouts and residential spies. They've not encountered anything more than observers. Even those who ventured into their camps were never caught. Which means that this is the first real action they've witnessed on our part. They have nothing at all to compare it to." He breathed a concluding sigh. "We are back on top. This hasn't been a totally wasted effort."

"Malson won't be pleased."

His lip twitched. "When is he ever?"

The clouds thinned outside, casting the office into a paler shade of grey. Salus made a brief, checking glance out of the window. It was mid-afternoon, and the rain had subsided. The city would be at its busiest.

His attention slipped onto Taliel. Her eyes had returned to their usual alertness, but he still found himself hesitating behind the regret that tightened his throat.

But his frustration had been justified, surely she understood that. Perhaps she felt it, too, but hid it better than he had.

'After all that suppression, when it finally snapped, you had no idea how to deal with the flood of spirit and passion that came with it, did you?'

He squashed the foul voice out of his head.

It wouldn't do to linger either way. He straightened and returned to Teagan with his counter-actions, intent on dismissing him as soon as possible and moving on to something measurably more pleasant, but he was swiftly interrupted by another knock at the door. As was so often the case, all the news seemed to arrive at once.

But this report had set Salus's eyes gleaming.

And Taliel's under even steadier control.

"Red Heath?" He demanded ardently. "You're sure?"

"Long black hair, white skin, grim visage, travelling with a child," the phidipan confirmed.

"A hunter found them - who?"

"Beryn."

He nodded eagerly, eyes wide, thoughts crashing through them like an avalanche. "The refugee camp outside - what's the situation?"

"Stable."

"Few would come and go so close to Korovor," Teagan supplied while he continued to nod, "and there are only two mages stationed within eighteen miles of Red Heath. The village and the camp are fenced in by the forest, but they're safe."

"But why would Koraaz show himself there of all places...?"

It seemed more a thought than a genuine question, but Teagan replied all the same. "For that very reason, perhaps. A quiet stop for supplies."

"He couldn't conjure them? Summon them?"

"It seems to be beyond their abilities."

"He's at least partly elven."

"The evidence suggests that it makes no difference."

Salus leaned back against the edge of the desk, succumbing at last to his thoughts. The others waited patiently. Taliel begged her heart to quieten.

Finally, Salus straightened in decision. "I'll go."

"You cannot."

His eyes snapped hotly onto him. "Why?"

"Koraaz is a mage."

"As am *I*."

"I understand that, sir," he continued carefully, "but he has far more experience wielding magic than yourself, and he knows we are hunting them. There's no knowing what he will do when he sees you, regardless of recognition, and given the state of things as they are, we cannot risk you getting injured."

"Then *what* do you suggest?! Our nearest mage is in Attleton, *two days* away! They'll be gone by then, and a phidipan can't handle it!"

"Then a portian is our best chance."

Salus growled, but a grudging consideration was already edging in, and when he looked back to his favoured, he was shrouded by a sudden confidence. "*You* will go."

Teagan straightened without expression. "As you wish."

"Teagan is not a mage," Taliel protested a little too quickly, and silently chided herself for her panic. But fortunately, neither of them appeared to have noticed. "He may well be injured in your place."

"You underestimate a portian's abilities," Salus said with a softer tone, the slightest hint of a smile in his voice though his expression betrayed nothing. "He will be fine. And," he fixed the portian, "he will succeed. Go to Red Heath immediately. Meet with Beryn. Tail them until they're clear of the village. The women are of little consequence, but I want Karth alive. I want to know what they're up to. Seize the Zi'veyn. Kill Koraaz and the inquisitor."

Teagan nodded his acknowledgement and left. Taliel felt the blood drain from her face.

Salus stepped towards her as the door closed, and his voice became so soft that, for a moment, her heart jumped with the involuntary image of her husband's face. "What is it?"

"I'm..." she breathed into a smile and concentrated her shakes into the tight curling of her toes. "I'm just pleased. It looks like we're finally in a position to bring their meddling to an end."

"If I'm honest...I almost don't believe it."

Her thawing heart jumped in hope. "You don't?"

"No. They've been a thorn in my side for months. The thought that they will finally be out of the way, it's..." He smiled peacefully. Then shook it off. He returned to her with eyes suddenly as bright as when he'd first received the news, but she saw something else running as an undercurrent. Something that evolved her sickness into revulsion. And inhuman guilt.

He took her hand, she unable to stop him, and drew her close. He kissed her, untempered, unrestrained; his enthusiasm poured in, for her or for the removal of the thorn in his side, it was impossible to tell. His emotions were always unfettered, mingling together like white-water currents. Wild. Dangerous.

Cataclysmic.

She forced herself to melt into him.

She staggered when he pulled away. He was smiling; she smiled back. And then they left, taking the bag from the chair beside the archives as they passed, imposing a respectable distance between them as they made their way through the open corridors. Taliel followed his lead. Her mind had grown silent, her gaze unfixed; she suspended herself in limbo, unwilling to be too present nor withdraw into her thoughts. She didn't dare be alone with him. Or herself.

The rain had returned by the time they left the cover of the forest. It descended in a thin, fresh curtain that pattered softly against the city on the other side of the walls, through which they slipped via a well-hidden crack and into the back garden of a small and empty house at the edge of the lowest district. From there, they moved openly through the city.

Salus buzzed in excitement. Progress, on so many fronts. And Taliel was right beside him to share in it. And he wanted her to be, to truly be a part of what he was doing, to share in his protectorship, in the responsibility, and the victory when it all came together. Was that normal, he wondered? Past marks and conveniences had always expressed a desire to visit him at whatever kind of establishment he claimed employment to, and he'd allowed it, where possible, to allay them despite the inconvenience, but he'd never understood it. Now, though, he was beginning to.

But as he cast her an eager smile, he belatedly realised that she'd been quiet ever since they'd left the House. And as he took the time to look closer, it was clear that she was troubled. And she was trying to hide it. Which meant that it was personal.

Once again, he felt guilt swarm through his chest. Of course. His rage. He'd frightened her. What else could it have been?

For a moment an apology formed on his tongue. But it never made it through his lips. He didn't want to acknowledge it, he didn't want the sound of his voice at that moment to revive the memory that so clearly rattled her and nor did he want to see it come to life again in her eyes. So he said nothing at all, and the pair walked on through the rain in silence, matching the slightly hurried pace of those around them who had been caught short by the sudden return of the showers but continued stoically about their business anyway. Their shoes were quickly caked in the filth churned into sludge in the rain.

The density of bodies increased as they neared the trade district, where stalls, taverns, brothels and baths made their business, and among those many heading to work or to procure essentials with what little they had to barter with, there was a distinct and growing unease. The city was smothered by it. Every few minutes they passed someone with a nervous look on their face, but their eyes never met anything of another person but their shoulders, where a cloak would be fastened, or their waist, where a weapon would be hung, born of self-preservation rather than ill will.

As they moved deeper still, where the roads widened, the buildings separated, the light improved and the stifled smell of sickness and misery was finally replaced by that of spices and flowers, the populace changed again.

Thrice they passed mage hunters, groups of twos and threes wandering the city with the same self-importance as fresh-faced young guards, marking themselves out from the masses as vigilantes with white rags, kerchiefs and even silks tied to their upper arms. They surveyed the populace they walked among with keen, suspicious eyes, but no tact; it was clear that at least a few of them were present purely for the power. There was no doubt that these individuals would die at a mage's hands, and quite possibly get other people killed in their reckless provocations; the title and gratitude were all they sought, and the fact wasn't missed by everyone. While many cheered blindly at their undemonstrated heroism, others eyed them cautiously; children were pulled close to parents, customers concluded business at a hasty price and gadabouts made excuses to leave.

But the responses to the mages they hounded, never within their range by chance or design, were not so politely performed.

They walked in pairs, guarded and edgy; everyone avoided them, parting at the sight as though they were lepers, goggling at them as they passed, staring with open fear and disdain. The mages in turn regarded them with equal discomfort.

Salus found himself moving protectively closer to Taliel.

Their awareness heightened, they made for the centre of the city.

The trade district, the city's social hub, ringed the Order's towers that rose like three twisted beacons, an ever-visible point of bearing in the vast capital city, and was broken only by the mage district that splintered a short way into the north east. Here, people thronged despite the rain and proximity, and the pair appeared to walk as a couple, he leading her towards a private midday appointment promised in the luxuriant heart of the city. But despite their relaxed and leisurely gazes, he observed their surroundings attentively - the people, the buildings, the snatches of conversation, searching for anything suspicious or crippling to his plans. But there was nothing. The rain was prevalent; it hastened chores and discouraged lingering. No one would interrupt him.

They soon reached the edge of the shadow cast by the Order's spiralling ebon towers, the edge of relative ease in the city; the edge of the mage's district. Here stood the oldest and grandest buildings, the baths, wine houses, city hall, even upmarket tailors, all a mixture of elven and human construction that were both complimented and offset by the equally expansive and beautiful public gardens. Aside from the western temple, it was the only place in the city where the rich crossed paths with the lower classes - the lower classes who could just about afford the luxury of these central establishments.

But while the buildings bustled, the gardens in full summer bloom were almost empty; grass and benches soaked by the rain, those few who entered did so only for a habitual walk in the brief window between showers. And of those few they witnessed, each were well-known to do so.

The pair appeared to demonstrate the same intentions, making their way happily through four of the gardens until wandering into the third largest in the city. It, too, was empty, aside from the six-foot stone figure of a near-naked water nymph standing with playful demurity atop a fountain dais. Her feigned modesty was preserved only by an exquisitely sculpted fold of marble silk, while water spouted from the mouths of stone koi at her feet. Manicured trees served as a backdrop, casting dappled light over water and alabaster skin had the sun been out, and, more crucially, served as a far less exposed climbing frame for anarchistic children.

It was far from the most magnificent fountain in the city, and neither was it the most spectacular garden. Indeed, both were relatively ignored by the populace, who favoured either the largest for gatherings, or the smallest for privacy. All of which made this garden and its simple fountain the perfect spot: tall enough to be a stretch out of reach, familiar enough to be ignored, not so hidden as to attract suspicion, nor so open as to catch a passing eye.

And in the downpour, no one would notice his interference.

At his lead, the pair meandered towards it, and though their attention appeared fixed upon the last lingering purple ash flowers, their awareness of their surroundings rose.

No eyes were upon them - such had been the case for three and a half minutes - so as the path bowed around into a brief blind spot behind a tall, thick hedgerow, they broke into a dash for the trees. And waited.

As time hung still, Salus's gaze drifted towards Taliel. Her face glittered with raindrops, her gentle curls dark and weighted, and she didn't look quite so distant anymore. Instead, intrigue had begun to settle in and her eyes had brightened, though they, like his, continued to scan the gardens beyond, and her shoulders weren't as rigid. He found his own relax a little at the sight, and the knot of shame in his gut evaporated, forgotten now that she had. And in that instant, as she wiped the rain delicately from her face, he couldn't hold himself back.

She squeaked in surprise the moment he kissed her, sending him stumbling backwards a step as she pushed him away. Her eyes were wide and immediately regretful, and she whispered a hurried apology as he frowned back in confusion. "*I'm sorry*," she pressed again, smiling nervously, "I thought I saw something out there, I was concentrating and you frightened me!"

He followed her previous gaze, but saw nothing through the rain. When he looked back to her, his hurt hadn't diminished. "What did you see?"

"Nothing, just a bird, I think it was. A crow." She held his gaze, and though he scrutinised it, he saw nothing concealed in her eyes. He glanced back out into the rain, then back to her, breathed a laugh and smiled contritely. Then, the torrents came down.

In that moment, the edge of duty hardened his eyes. With a single look, he told her to stay within the trees. She didn't argue. As he slipped outside, the bag slung over his shoulder, she released a ragged breath of relief.

The instant Salus was clear of the cover he was pummelled by the deluge;

raindrops struck as hard as tiny stones, stinging the skin, hammering against his skull. But as chaos ensued and the populace in the streets began crashing around for sanctuary, he pushed the presence of the rain easily out from his mind. The strikes, though sharp, were so numerous as to become numbing and were easy as a whole to ignore, allowing his focus to fix upon handholds on the slick, marble statue. But Turunda's summer rain was fickle; he had little time to waste.

Years of nefarious practise carried him to the top in seconds, where he hung by one hand from the smooth, slippery lines of the water nymph's shoulders while the other plunged into his bag, and his eyes scoured through the creases and contours of the marled grey tresses. He picked his spot.

Withdrawing a small hammer and chisel, he snatched himself close to the stone, released his hold and struck into the hair with a single precise blow, grasping the shoulder once again before gravity could pull him past its reach. The smallest fragment chipped away from the inside of a crease; a little more than he'd intended, perhaps, but the damage wouldn't be noticed from the ground - even the man who came by to clean away the algae and moss three times a year wouldn't spot the difference when he was done.

Checking his grip, he returned the tools, oblivious to the battering rain, and withdrew another object - a splinter of wood from his own desk. It was no bigger than the tip of his finger, and yet had transformed from a consequence of frustration into a pivotal solution.

He dropped it into the chipped stone.

Next came a jar, which he opened with his teeth and grasped in the crook of his elbow. The smell was unpleasant, noxious, and seemed to intensify in the rain. But it would fade, and within seconds he stopped noticing it.

Working quickly, he scooped out a finger of clay and smothered it into the crevice, embedding the splinter and concealing the damage should anyone decide to take a closer look. The clay hardened in seconds.

He looked at the surrounding stone, noting the spacing between its darker grey flecks and their own varying shades, and flexed his fingers just as Erran had shown him. He executed the spell perfectly. Dark patches bloomed in the clay like bruises; the marble was unscathed.

He wasted no time admiring his work. He pushed away and dropped from the fountain to vanish back into the trees, where Taliel was waiting in intrigue. But there remained a crease of trouble in her brow. "Mages will detect this," she warned him as he returned, wiping away the rain, "masked or not." But she was silenced by the confident gleam in his eyes.

"It's too close to the towers," he replied, as if it was all the reason he needed. He proceeded to elaborate at her dissatisfaction. "The towers are saturated with magic, there's too much around here for them to notice this one tiny spell. They won't detect it."

"How can you be so sure?"

"Because when I asked Erran the same thing, he told me to take it into the tapestry room. I could barely detect it even though it was in my own hand. Among all their spells in this city, the Order won't notice it." His eyes were firm, as though trying to throw his own confidence into her, and for a moment she appeared convinced - until another wrinkle of concern marred her beautiful face.

"This won't be enough."

"Of course not. I'll place more in other towns and cities."

"And villages?"

He shook his head shortly. "Too insignificant."

"They've been attacked by mages."

"Who planned their attacks in towns and cities."

"And how will you conceal it anywhere else? These towers - there's nothing else like it in the country."

"No, but among all the magic running rampant, there are many spells at work in Turunda, spells keeping buildings standing. I can place it beneath them."

"Spells the preservers maintain?"

"Taliel, please, I *promise* you: they won't notice them. They're too subtle - they wouldn't find them even if they were looking for them." She still looked doubtful. His jaw and brow tightened in mounting irritation. "Taliel," he took her hands and smiled reassuringly instead, softening his tone despite the deafening downpour around them, "it will work. Trust me. I know you don't understand all of this, but I have given it plenty of thought. The Order is too arrogant to even think this is a possibility. We *can* hide these spells. And if a mage *does* happen to discover one, we'll certainly know if they try to disable them. There's nothing to worry about."

'And should they notice and simply move their activity elsewhere instead?' But she didn't voice that thought through the hope that Rathen might also see through it. She couldn't risk drawing his attention towards the fact that his plan wasn't as iron-clad as he thought.

Assuming Rathen escaped what was coming for him.

Her stomach twisted.

Salus was still looking at her.

With the greatest effort, she beat it down, smiled and leaned forwards to kiss him, distracting him from any attempt at reading her thoughts. "I apologise," she sighed with the perfect amount of self-correction. "You're right, I don't understand it, but you have clearly thought it through. I trust you, my love."

His eyes brightened at those two choice words, words she never often uttered - for fear, he'd concluded, that she might lose herself in public - and seized her by the waist. He kissed her hard, impassioned, empowered, and as panic, disgust and hate whirled in her mind, she savoured it all.

Chapter 23

Up beyond the rain that hammered the broad, dense leaves, the long-awaited sunlight peeked itself teasingly through the canopy. Bright, narrow beams glanced across bark and moss, freckling the ground with shards of gold. Even beneath the relentless patter of rain, the shining air exuded a peaceful silence.

But, in true form with the mischievous forest, that peaceful silence was studded with snickers and mutters, and those beams and freckles only deepened the shadows rather than brighten the path, concealing the roots and rocks that seemed to snake and rise up just inches from their feet the moment they looked away. Only the native escort that had appeared like spectres out of the tall, closely-packed trees avoided being caught by the tricks - though they were decidedly unhelpful in pointing them out, and cackled at their every stumble instead.

Rathen sighed quietly to himself as he adjusted his gait, narrowly avoiding one such rock he was sure he'd already succumbed to ten minutes before. The ditchlings were clearly leading them in circles, just as they had when they'd guided them out of Wrenroot those few months ago. Despite all the help the wild children had since provided, it seemed that they still didn't truly trust them.

Well, the *adults*, at least; Aria appeared to be quite welcome. They had greeted her before anyone else and even gifted her an elaborate tangle of flowers, both of which she had delighted at. But as they led them off into their muddled territory, she began looking around herself with increasing worry. Rathen had had little trouble working out why.

Nug hadn't been among the welcoming party. And she hadn't asked them where he was. So many had 'fallen asleep' - a charming term he was quite grateful for when dealing with the fates of such child-like creatures - and he could see by the growing haunt in her eyes that she feared the answer too much to ask. And by a far too prevalent memory.

The corners of his mouth dragged downwards as his own ideas of what had happened to her in Redgrove invaded, exaggerated and over-analysed, and he grasped her hand a little tighter. She looked up and smiled, preoccupied. He returned it with equal difficulty. Then he forced himself to look away just in time to avoid the reach of another long and winding root that rose, pierced and rose again from the ground like a breaching sea serpent.

He sighed dismally to himself. Wrenroot. What a tangled mix of thoughts it evoked. It was almost as treacherous as home, but distinctly inhospitable; it was like a mirror into another world, one almost identical and yet without one single detail to match. And he wondered, very tentatively, after all the strangeness they'd seen and the trials they'd been through, would his hollowed-out boulder be enough anymore? He had never stopped yearning to return to that familiarity, but he'd discovered, reluctantly, that he was almost enjoying his place in the world again, having a greater purpose for the first time in eleven years.

Being back in this strange little place, he felt almost a true sense of progress from a task that had not that long ago seemed beyond the bounds of possibility, never mind his own capacity. And yet here they were, coming back around, returning and repairing, just as they'd promised; retracing their own footsteps with but one enormous difference: this time, they had a solution. And it was a solution that rested in his own hands.

Rathen walked a little taller, and glanced down again as Aria squeezed his hand involuntarily against her own misstep. He smiled and put the thought out of his mind.

Yes. It would be enough for him. He could have this adventure, redeem himself, stick two fingers up at every authority by being the one to save the world that had rejected him, and return home content and safe.

But...would it be enough for Aria?

A brief and sudden yelp dragged him from his thoughts. Petra had not spotted the root.

A laugh rippled among the ditchlings, but aside from a somewhat embarrassed purse of her lips, she was fine. And in more ways than one. To everyone's relief, she had returned to her old self. She even appeared to tolerate Anthis. It wasn't natural, but it was at least an effort.

Unfortunately, the same couldn't be said for him. And Rathen had already worked that out, too.

He returned his eyes to the path as Anthis barked a none too delicate curse after falling to the same root.

It had been a little over two weeks, by his count, and it was set to get worse. He'd experienced that much first-hand. So Garon had astutely sent Anthis into Red Heath alone to gather supplies - but it was a small village. It didn't come as much of a surprise that he hadn't found any bounties with which to satisfy his needs, even among the neighbouring refugee camp. It had been a stretch to begin with. But if the unpleasant situation did anything, it was, curiously, reinforcing Anthis's honour. He had voluntarily returned unfulfilled, and it couldn't have been easy. It certainly wasn't for the rest of them.

Rathen's heart snatched into his throat as he stumbled in his distraction, and over-corrected onto ground that wasn't as firm as he'd expected. But as he grunted and unleashed a strangled curse, he found that the treacherous ground was suddenly the least striking of their concerns. The ditchlings had finished with their careening path; the setting began to change.

What had moments ago been damp soil was now slick mud, studded with cracked rocks and torn roots ejected from the earth, while one in every six trees had been uprooted and shattered sideways, allowing the last of the contentious rain from the dying storm to hammer in and attempt to wash away the unnatural destruction. Perhaps it was their knowledge of the denizens' beliefs and the importance this forest played in them, but this first glimpse of the carnage the magic had wrought was gut-wrenching. And they hadn't even reached the brink of its range yet.

Movement flickered at the edge of Rathen's vision; in that instant he heard both Garon and Petra draw their swords while the ditchlings simultaneously shouted, and he pulled Aria close even as he recognised that there was no threat.

A dozen or so more filthy-skinned, big-eyed children appeared from the shadows as suddenly as their escort had, the closest of whom sidled up to Aria and nudged her roguishly in the side. She grinned; Aria and Rathen frowned. Then a distinctly familiar voice rose above the din, its tone harsh but cheerful, and settled the confusion.

"*Nug!*" Aria tore herself from her father's grasp and hurried ahead to meet the scraggly haired creature, who seemed to have traded his almost tidy shirt for a pair of torn and tattered trousers whose single redeeming feature appeared to be an in-tact pocket. He beamed an inhuman smile, as did the rest, and caught her as she embraced him.

Rathen's dark eyes narrowed watchfully.

"Silly fool," Nug grinned with chipped teeth as he hugged her back, "nearly flattened me, you did!" But his mud-spackled brow knotted as they parted, and he stared at the top of her curly blonde head. "How come you ain't wearing the crown?"

"The crown?" Realisation sparked in her eyes. She darted abruptly back to her father, then on past him to the horse who stamped her hooves in agitation, and began removing the knotted twigs and flowers she'd draped into the mare's mane. A few adjustments to the white blooms and a quick retying of the ends and it was as good as new. She then turned, dashed heedlessly back past her father, dropped the circlet proudly upon her head, and beamed.

Nug nodded in approval.

Then his oversized eyes shifted past her and onto the awaiting party.

Every one of them tensed as his almost-silver, almost-green orbs drilled into them one at a time, noting everything, missing nothing, regarding each very, very carefully. The others, they realised, were doing the same. Upon Petra, they stared probingly, and Garon, they stared in understanding and disapproval. Upon Eyila, they frowned slightly in interest, and to Anthis they returned his cantankerous challenge. But Rathen received the most bewildering look.

Nug's eyes narrowed and his brow cocked suspiciously - it was only then that Rathen realised that not one of the ditchlings actually had any eyebrows. He straightened as a dirty, stubby finger jabbed towards him. "What's happened to you? You feel...different. Fuzzier. Not as clear..."

Aria turned quizzically, and Rathen felt everyone else's gaze land just as curiously on the back of his head. He shifted uncomfortably. "Nothing's happened..."

"What do you mean by 'not as clear'?" Garon asked over the top of him, and ignored the ditchling's returning disapproval.

"His magic. It stands out like a sore thumb or a poke in the eye - or it used to. Like the statue lady's. It's how we been able to track you. But now it's all..." he waved his hands about. "It ain't what it was, that's for certain. Summit's happened, there ain't no sense in telling lies."

"He's an e--"

"Look," Rathen interjected testily before Aria could finish, "do you want to stand here and debate the finer points of blood saturation, or do you want us to fix your tree?"

The ditchlings' reaction was peculiar. There was no cheering, celebration or relief - not even smiles. Not one of them moved nor adjusted their stare. It was as though the matter came as no surprise at all. And, if they'd already worked out why they were there, their present mistrust was rendered decidedly hostile.

Slowly, Nug reeled back his cynicism. "About time, too." Then he turned, gestured for Aria to follow him, and walked back off into the forest without another word, leaving the others to file in behind.

Eyila stared thoughtfully after the child as she encouraged her uncooperative horse to move. Her lips pursed, and she leaned closer to Petra, dropping her voice to a whisper. "Why do they submit to Aria?"

"She's a child; I think they just identify with her more than us." They then observed the distance between Nug and Aria shorten, and their eyebrows rose in speculation. "Although..."

"Stop," Rathen pleaded, casting them back a defeated look, "please stop..."

"Sorry..." He turned back, and after exchanging a single look of certainty, the pair walked on behind him in silence.

A growing twist pulled mournfully at Aria's features. Three months ago, this thick woodland had reminded her of home; it had been so green, so rich and vibrant, untouched and secluded. But now... She didn't have the words. She was sure they existed, but she didn't know what they were. 'Empty' wasn't it, though it was definitely missing something immensely important. Spirit, maybe.

The more she thought on it, the more sickening the dread that clogged her throat and stifled the excitement she'd felt at returning somewhere so familiar.

She looked to Nug, tearing her eyes away before some strange, primal compulsion made her start crying. "What happened?"

"The magic," he replied desolately. "Ripped it all 'sunder it did. All of a sudden the ground opened up from nowhere, chucked up rocks, pushed over trees--"

Aria gasped. "Your tree!"

"It's fine, for the majority part," he sighed dejectedly, "and the Lady's there again. She did a bit of musical chairs, moving off into the forest, but I reckon she couldn't find nowhere better and that's why she came back. But other Arkhamas ain't been so lucky. Lots of us are lost. But even with us knowing where our Lady is, our setts are still collapsing and we can't leave for somewhere safe 'til she does. There's nowt we can do. We're sitting ducks, we are, just waiting for the next rumble and tumble or for more hoomans to come in with their knifes and fire and get us while we sleep." He glanced around at the others, squinting in suspicion, but said nothing. Aria followed, but she saw the regretful look on her father's face and knew that there was nothing they could do about it. "*And*," he continued with even greater irritation, "the harpies are still flying at us. We're being assawted on...three fronts, we are! The ground is trying to eat us, the harpies trying to shred us, and hoomans trying to stick and fry us! And what can we do?! It's all this magic, I reckon - *none* of this was happening before the magic turned up."

Aria gave a sharp and sudden gasp, but as Rathen's head snapped up in attention, the world launched its onslaught, almost knocking him over long before he had a chance to make sense of what lay ahead through the trees. In that moment, all he could do was cling to the reins of his horse and focus his effort on erecting walls around his mind. His jaw gritted fiercely.

The group drew to a stop behind Nug as he and his cohorts released identically mournful sighs, and as they peered out from the edge of the trees, the sentiment spread.

The old grove sprawled out like a lost garden, overgrown and forgotten, peppered with moss-covered stones and fragments of unrecognisable structures as ancient as the trees that encased them. Sunlight cast its way through the canopy, tree trunks standing like pillars in a cathedral, and skimmed across the resting raindrop like diamonds. It appeared just as it had three months ago: an amicable merging of two worlds, each supporting the other rather than trying to smother.

But what had previously been a silent harmony was now a mutual struggle. Like a mortal wound, the all too familiar sight of rifts and chasms had riven the glade with crumbling and upthrust edges, and every tree and stone clung on to one another in a bid to keep themselves rooted on the surface rather than tumbling into the abyss.

And yet, among all that, it remained a sight of disturbingly beautiful tranquillity.

It took Rathen a while to notice that all eyes had returned to him.

His jaw ached as it tightened further. He swallowed hard, suppressing any sign of his internal battle, and turned to rummage silently through the saddlebags. Suddenly, his pride in his accomplishments seemed to weigh very, very little.

Light caught the Zi'veyn, and a whisper of awe rippled through the ditchlings.

"Can he really do it?"

"Yes," Aria declared proudly. "I've seen him."

"Mmm..." Nug scrutinised the mage and watched him shift uncomfortably. He sucked air through his teeth. "Well...if you say so... Come on then." The group, circled by muddy ditchlings, followed Nug into the clearing, where they parted at Aria's word to allow Rathen the lead. He walked on with eyes unseeing.

Nug cast Aria a wondering glance, and though she returned it with a smile of assurance, her brow quickly creased in distress. She didn't like that look.

He soon drew to a stop at the foot of the Great Tree, where ditchlings sat peacefully despite the surrounding chaos. But the Tree was not unscathed. It stood at a dramatic angle, weaver-bird nests hanging lopsided from the ladder-like branches, empty of life, and there was a strange silence within the hollowed knot of the trunk that revealed that even the owls had left. Aria's sorrow grew. Could the Lady truly still reside in such a thing?

But the softening of Nug's eyes as she glanced towards him gave her all the answer she needed. Something beyond the magic was still at work here. Surely it was the Lady.

They all watched Rathen for a long, expectant moment, but he had fallen perfectly still. "He might be like that for a while," Aria finally whispered.

"Mmm. Well, in that case," the ditchling turned to face the rest of them, the softness of his heart suddenly mixing with a new edge, one distinctly business-like, and an air of superiority which was neither successful nor out of place. "These hooman problems of yours are getting to be a mite troublesome."

"What do you mean?" Garon asked.

"I mean your war, and the sneaks what are trying to *kill* us all. *And* kill *you*. The first is cutting off our routes and hunting, and the second are...well I said it, didn't I, they're trying to kill us all. Now, we been interfering when they pass through on their way to make trouble, even bennyfittin' the harpies, but--...What's wrong with her?"

They followed his gaze onto Eyila, who stared around at the grove and the tree with a peculiar interest they recognised in a heartbeat. Petra was already standing protectively beside her, and even Anthis's foul expression softened.

"She's troubled," Garon replied evasively. "You were saying?"

"Looks it. And yeah, we been watching them, keeping tabs, interfering where we can, but they just keep coming, and they're getting vicious. These past few turns alone they been lashing out more often than the harpies. Used to be it was once or twice a month, but this past week we been unable to take a dump without having to dash off half way through. What do they want?"

"Why would we know? And how can you be so sure it's not just vengeful villagers?"

"'Cause they got a smell about 'em. And you would know 'cause they're after you, too. Is it 'cause we been helping you? Or 'cause you been helping *us?* 'Cause it if *is*--"

"No. If I had to guess, it's probably because you're getting too close to our settlements and you're upsetting people."

"Why ever would we upset 'em if we ain't stealing?"

"Because you're aggressive and...misunderstood."

"You mean 'cause we're *different*...?" He blinked. "Well that ain't a good reason for *nothing!* Snail's sneezes - just 'cause we don't have pink skin or tiny eyes, we gotta be *killed?!* The harpies at least can fly off like yella-bellies, but what--"

"I said I was guessing," Garon reminded him quickly. "How many of you have been killed?"

"Oh not many," he replied, suddenly subdued. "We can get away from them easy enough - it's just *insulting*."

"You also steal," Petra added, at which came a wave of protesting snorts and huffs.

"We've been good! We don't take nearly as much anymore. There's a war on, we get that. Not that any of you seem to be doing much of nothing about it..."

"What does that mean?"

"That your soldiers are marching to and fro like ants but not actually *doing* anything. The sneaky ones, *they* did, but it didn't come to much."

"What?"

"Yeah, just first thing this morning, 'fore the sun could brighten the tops of the Tree. Three of 'em went up to one of the camps, cast a bunch of spells and 'caused lots of trouble. Real noisy. Two of 'em got killed, but I don't recollect any of the rest getting sticked."

"Where?"

"Keep your britches on! Greentop, it was. Still a good place to hide, that, even with all the mess. O' course, all the newcomers are doing is sitting and twiddling their fingers or skulking about near your cities. They don't look like much to be worried about. Them ones from the west, they were beasties, but these--"

"And just how do you know what they're doing?"

"Oh easy," he grinned, "they're camped right next to some of our old setts, ones what didn't get ruined by the gashes. But they were getting in our way, so we moved anyway. Still go back to play tricks on 'em, but they ain't doing a whole lot of anything. Why do you even bother with 'em? Is it 'cause they're different, too? 'Cause they seem *just like you*. Ain't no grounds, far as we see."

"It's complicated."

"Must be. 'Cause it makes no sense to us."

A brief grunt pulled their attention towards the Tree, but while Nug first frowned at the sweat on Rathen's skin and the dampening of his shirt, his eyes widened inordinately as they fell upon the tiny black pyramid floating between his palms. In an instant, he and every other ditchling around them came rushing to the mage's side, heedless of Aria's warning for them to leave him be. But Rathen didn't seem to notice them.

Ever since their interference at Dolunokh, magic seemed intent on smothering him. Every detail Rathen had felt on their first visit to this forest had been enhanced, and it took every ounce of strength he could muster to keep it from burying him. Even as he focused himself entirely upon the spell rotating in his hands, he could feel its domineering presence towering over him from all sides, and an itch of panic at the back of his mind, a desperate worry that something *had* happened to him, being stuck in that unnatural place for so long. It was a burdening concern that had grown for weeks, that had swelled with his episode by the lake four days ago, and Nug's comments had only inflamed it.

He caught himself. If he dwelled on those thoughts he would slip beneath it all. He had to focus. The sooner the spell was complete, the sooner he could breathe...

While the ditchlings stared at the device in awe, Petra, Garon, Anthis and Aria looked closely around at the grove. While the Zi'veyn floated with eerie calm between the mage's hands, *something* had to change.

The ditchlings suddenly snapped around, startling them as their giant eyes swept across the forest in a mixture of panic and hope, but each nest-, lichen- and twig-matted head moved independently, peering around on their own whims rather than by the rousing of one collective thought.

The others looked even closer.

Then, as suddenly as the magic had first struck them, its resonating influence ceased. The grove became a site of destruction. The sunlight transformed into a brutal illumination of the battles of time and magic, the raindrops became the tears of the trees, the stone a crumbling remnant of an age and people long since lost, its modesty and honour never to rise again.

But in amongst that devastation, the crooked tree with its woven ornaments and incredible branches still took their breath away. In that moment, each understood what true natural beauty was, even in its imperfection.

A ragged gasp snatched free from Rathen's lips and he staggered forwards, crumbling to his knees.

Aria was quick to catch him, and one twig-antlered ditchling the Zi'veyn as it tumbled to the side. Anthis was just as quick to snatch it from him.

The grove hung silent for a long, dissecting moment. Every ear listened, every eye probed, and every mind considered, but the magic, it seemed, had truly vanished. The childlike creatures' collective sigh of relief eased the warm air, lifted the blanket of tension, and masked the rustle of leaves high above them. A welcome gust of wind brushed over their skin.

It was already too late.

A cry of rage erupted from the ditchlings, and the ground fell away from human feet. Alarm spread; Garon and Petra each tried to reach for their swords and Anthis his dagger, but the taloned grip that snared and spread their arms prevented any from getting close. Only the two mages could have provided any defence, but each were too addled by the magic to do so. Aria screamed, and while she could grasp her wooden sword, she simply didn't think to.

The ditchlings scurried across the ground beneath them like ants as the six were dragged sharply above the trees, whooping and bellowing and following as quickly as they could. But their abductors were moving too quickly, covering too much distance. In seconds, all sight of the clearing had vanished.

Those who were able struggled and shouted in the harpies' grasps, but they paid little attention; their enormous wingbeats were too powerful to be hindered by the writhing of prey even two thirds their own size.

"Garon," Anthis yelled venomously, "a plan?!"

But the inquisitor didn't respond. He stared hard into their heading across the green expanse of the forest, gathering what bearings he could. Wrenroot was at their back and left, while the trees thinned and stopped a ways to their right. Which meant that they were heading right back in the direction they had come. And with every wingbeat propelling them about ten paces a second, they would cover half a mile in nine minutes.

He looked back towards Rathen, but the awareness in his eyes was compromised by fatigue. He was thinking, clearly trying to bring himself to do something, but it wouldn't come soon enough.

Garon tried again to reach for his sword, and looked fleetingly towards Eyila. But to his surprise, the absence in her eyes was fading as quickly as Wrenroot behind them. She looked around them, looked beneath, looked above, and grinned.

"Huai'a ua Aya'u tai!"

With a startling jolt, their altitude began to drop, and the canopy surged up towards them.

"What are you doing?!" Petra yelled, kicking her legs in growing alarm as the branches rushed closer, but there came no answer from anyone, tribal or beast. They braced themselves and plummeted through the trees, scratched by branches, whipped by leaves, and were cast hard against the ground like rag dolls.

Anthis cursed as he landed on his shoulder, Petra grunted as she manoeuvred her legs and landed on her knees, Rathen hissed as he landed on his back; Garon staggered, grounding his heels, and managed to twist and catch Aria who had been about to crash head-first, softening her blow even as the impact finally sent him down. Eyila was the only one to land gracefully upon her feet.

Weapons rang free in a heartbeat, but as they leapt, spun and backed up tightly together for safety, shoving Aria and her frantic warning not to look into their eyes into the centre, the harpies alighted out of reach in the trees.

They found themselves suddenly ringed into an arena of sharp talons and sharper beaks, of savage yellow eyes that fixed each individual with a deadly consideration, watching closely, silently, weighing out who would should be dismembered first, and who should be saved for last.

They grouped up even tighter. Knuckles turned white over weapons, spell fingers flexed and loosened. Their hearts raced, eyes flicked about, and tried in their panic to work out where the first attack would come from.

But for all their readiness, when a sudden gale beat them down from above, all they could do was cower and watch as three pairs of long black talons descended from the treetops, rushing bared and open towards them.

Chapter 24

Death whipped sharply overhead. It thundered in their ears. The power of its single wingbeat was enough both to flood their lungs and snatch their breath away, and snap, should it wish, a delicately tethered lifeline.

But though they braced, paralysed by the blustering force, death did not pierce, nor puncture, nor rend.

One by one, as the zephyr abated, they dared to open their eyes.

The arena had changed.

Suddenly no longer sleek nor violently poised, the harpies that encircled them had become a curious sight of splayed feathers, bowed heads and tucked, inverted wings; a myriad of brown, red and beige quills spread out like ornamental fans in the midst of a sinister forest.

In spite of themselves, none could help but stare. It was only then that they realised they'd never truly seen these creatures, these expert hunters, these silent pursuers who had tracked them so relentlessly. In a fevered heartbeat, they discovered that they were not as bestial as they had thought. And that unsettled them all the more.

Beneath proud, raptorial chests, their torsos were strikingly human; their waists were narrow, hips wide, and their long legs and arms were as defined as any of their own. But those arms were sheathed in feathers, and those legs ended in avian feet adorned with seven-inch talons that promised a quick execution. Their faces, too, were a strange mixture of man and bird, with clear cheekbones yet mouths that hooked into sharp beaks, belying any ability to speak despite evidence to the contrary. And, though no one dared look at them directly, eyes both rational and deliberate but for a predatory amber colouring.

For the briefest moment, there passed the idea that they might just be able to reason with them.

Until the only harpy not to participate in the display caught their eye. And she had not been there a moment ago.

Instinctively, they each flinched back from her presence.

Larger than the others, in both size and demeanour, her feathers were brighter, perfectly preened and tended, and mottled with illustrious streaks of gold, copper and bronze that shimmered in the freckles of light seeping through the unyielding canopy. Perched tall upon the only bough to have been left unoccupied, flanked by two others who mirrored the brilliance of the rest of the aerie, she herself was a sight of deadly splendour.

A ruthless stare fired down the length of her menacing, rending beak. They shrank further beneath her scrutiny, and drew even closer together. Suddenly, the entrapping danger had swelled.

But still, nothing happened.

Garon was the first to steel himself. He took a single, powerful step forwards, his sword held firm in his left where his grip was still sure, right hand loose for support, and confronted the regal beast with such an unwavering confidence that, for once, his unreasonably relentless supremacy really had to be commended. "What do you want with us?"

But his words were met only with that same steely gaze.

Glances passed behind him. He didn't break his stance.

It was a long moment before the harpy's head finally twitched. It was a movement as sharp and halting as an eagle's, and her frightful eyes glinted in the light. A hissing squawk sounded in her throat. Her beak opened, and a voice both shrill and husky rattled eerily out from its depths, as though it did not belong to her. "Why did you calm the forest?"

"Because it was a hazard," he replied no less firmly.

"And those rodents let you do it?"

"Rodents? The ditchlings?"

"Of course they let us," Rathen stepped forwards cautiously, ignoring Garon's commanding look and Aria's squeaky warning, "it was destroying their home. That's all we've been trying to do since you--"

Another hiss, and in a flash of feathers her two attendants swept down from their perch to loom above them on the ground, beaks poised and wings splayed. Each of them recoiled.

She hissed again. "What are they planning?"

"Easy, okay," Rathen bared his hands appeasingly while the others raised their weapons, "calm down. We don't know what they're planning."

"You lie. Why did you get involved? Why did you choose their side? Why massacre us? What are the 'ditchlings' offering you? Or is it simply that they look more like you than we?"

"They're not--we aren't--we didn't choose--"

Garon silenced the mage's confusion. "By 'massacre', do you mean--"

She flared, her own magnificent wings bursting wide, huge and menacing in the confines of the forest, spanning the entire bough. Again, everyone flinched. "*Humans* skulking in the woods. Burning our eyries in the dead of night. Slaughtering us while we sleep, while we hunt; our old, our young. Our dronn'vaen." Her eyes burned with an inferno of accusation and hatred. It fell solely upon Rathen as he dared to step forwards again, ignoring once more the inquisitor's whispered command.

"If I may - do you have a name?" Nothing. He sighed and calmed the near-debilitating thudding of his heart. "All right. If we *had* allied with the ditchlings, and if we *were* responsible for the attacks on non-humans, why would the ditchlings *also* be falling to these massacres?"

"We cannot claim to know what the motives of such strange, private creatures could be. You hide and scheme behind walls and all that breaks free of those walls is violence, murdering anything you encounter, even one another."

"Hard to argue with that," Anthis mumbled. Rathen and Garon each shot him an ominous look.

"I assure you, our involvement in your feud wasn't intentional, it just happened. We were moving through Wrenroot to work out how to fix the magic there, and

218

other places besides. The ditchlings found us and wouldn't let us in because they thought we might make it worse, so they came along to keep an eye on us. When we'd finished and were already going on our merry way, we happened upon one of your kin attacking one of theirs and we simply stepped in to stop it - so *neither* side got hurt."

"You did not know what you were meddling in. You had no right to get involved!"

He braced against the shriek. "We realise that now. But why did that grant you leave to hunt us down if you knew we were uninformed? Forgive me if I'm wrong, but you didn't seem as though you were chasing after us to talk."

"We were not."

Rathen nodded slowly while a spark of dread rose in everyone else's gut. He attempted a placating smile. "If I may ask, what do *you* know about this magic?"

All around, the surrounding harpies looked uncertainly towards their leader. But she didn't acknowledge their gazes. Her yellow eyes were fixed upon the humans, keen and pensive, weighing out how much to divulge to these interlopers, if anything at all for fear it may be used against them.

Finally, she sat taller and lifted her head to look even further down her beak. "We know only that it is *their* doing."

"The ditchlings?"

"No. Their Lady. She and her sisters are trying to drive us out of our homes."

"Why?"

"We need not explain ourselves to you!" She shrieked. "Now tell us: how did you calm the forest?"

"You expect *us* to--"

"Anthis, don't." Rathen held out his hand and, after another silent look of urgency, received from the begrudging historian the onyx relic. He held it out towards her. "With this."

Cautiously, the creatures peered closer. Even those bent in respect leaned forwards from their perches. She above all sharpened in scrutiny, and stared at it for a long moment. "What is it?" She finally asked, though her tone revealed some understanding of its significance.

Rathen, too, replied with thought. "It's a...spell in a box."

"A spell in a box. Why?"

"Because the spell is too powerful to be cast at will, so it sits in here, ready to be used when needed."

"And what does it do?"

"It sucks up magic that isn't supposed to be here."

"And how do you know the magic isn't 'supposed to be here'?"

"Because I've analysed it. It has no purpose."

"No purpose to *you*. The Lady will put it back."

"No, she won't."

"How can you know?"

"Because I'm a mage, I know these things. And I know that the magic is destroying lives - not just human, but that of harpies and ditchlings too, and all kinds of other creatures."

"Yes. Many. More than you could know."

"Mayi'i," another shrill, husky voice croaked suddenly from beside them, "Rötternas Moder would wish to know about this."

They looked back to the chief harpy, but she offered no explanation. She merely twitched her head, presumably in acknowledgement, while her eyes remained fixed upon the captives. "You know how the Lady's magic works?"

"No, not at all, why would we?"

"Because you removed it. How could you remove it if you do not know how it works?"

"Why does that matter?"

"Because it is the nature of all things. To end, it must begin; to know how something begins is to know how to end it. A heart beats, and can be stopped."

"...That makes sense," Rathen conceded, "but in this case it doesn't apply. This isn't a natural occurrence."

"It is the work of spirits. Humans cannot know how such magic works, and so you say it is unnatural. Unless of course you are lying, and using your magical knowledge to make it worse for their benefit." Without warning, she swept down from the bough herself, landing as close to them as her escorts had, thrashing them with the force of another single wingbeat. She loomed, eyes ablaze, and shrieked into their faces. "*What are you planning?*"

"Nothing!"

"*You lie!* You have travelled from one ravaged spot to another, conferring with those mice, seeking one another out, exchanging missives, and fleeing or attacking whenever *we* should appear!"

"No! That's not--"

"*You* are the ones--"

"We've been trying to--"

"*Enough!*" Another stormy assault silenced the protests. The impossible strength battered them back, and in a single fluid motion she launched herself into the air and snatched the Zi'veyn in her talons. Rathen hissed as crimson blood trickled between his fingers. They were given no more time to react than that.

The surrounding harpies erupted into shrill cries and dove down upon them from the trees. Those two nearest immediately attacked Garon and Rathen, knocking them down with a stroke of their wings and pinning their hands to the ground with one foot while the other pressed their weight into their backs. Garon's sword flew from his hand as he struck the ground, and Rathen's were too far apart to form any spells. Petra was quick to attempt a counter-strike, but she, too, was struck from the back before she could bring down her sword, her wrists equally pinned. Anthis was thrown down easily, cursing, while Eyila pulled Aria close and lay voluntarily on the ground. The harpies were a touch more gentle with them.

Another wave of cries burst from the trees behind them, but these seemed to take even the attackers by surprise. And no wonder. These were not piercing avian voices. But rather than any sense of relief, the weight of dread in each of their stomachs doubled.

"Well well," she cawed in sardonic victory over the sound of the arriving chaos, her eyes falling accusingly upon the humans from her perch, "what is this? It seems your allies are here to rescue you!"

Half of their captors had already launched themselves off into the forest behind them, and there followed the immediate sound of rocks striking tree and feather, enraged screeching and rough voices bellowing and cursing - some quite clumsily.

The lead harpy glowered into the distance, the Zi'veyn ignored but still tight in her claws. The noise quickly drew closer, growing louder and more violent with every passing moment.

They felt the weight of their assailants shifting on their backs. They were distracted.

But before either Garon or Rathen could take advantage of it, the ditchlings burst in through the trees and the talons pinning them down pierced and contracted, eliciting howls of agony.

It was then that Eyila acted.

Propelled upwards by a phantom wind, she thrust her captor off of her back, held Aria close against her, whose big eyes peered around in a mix of terror and foolish fascination, and muttered a few alien words beneath her breath. In an instant, a rush of air expanded out around her in all directions, battering her pinned companions who could only turn their heads away, splintering bark, toppling their captors, waylaying airborne attackers and knocking down their would-be saviours.

For a brief and confused moment, time suspended and silence reigned. Then all eyes turned slowly upon the bronze figure and the awed child that clung to her.

It opened only the briefest opportunity, but her companions were the swiftest to take advantage of it. They seized their weapons in a flash and twisted towards the harpies, until her melodic voice rose into a sudden and powerful command.

Rathen growled, but he conceded after a moment, lowering his hands as the others dropped their weapons with equal hesitation. But while the harpies righted themselves and launched up out of harm's way, and the ditchlings jumped back to their muddy little feet, Aria wriggled free and charged off to the left.

Rathen made a quick dash to catch her. "Stay here."

"But they're--"

"They're fine. Listen to me: right now, we can't take sides."

"A bit sodding late for that," Anthis mumbled, but all ignored him.

Rathen returned Aria to the tribal's side and stepped forwards, positioning himself in the middle of the grove and directly between the two warring factions. The irony wasn't lost on him, but he had no patience for amusement. His expression was black, his eyes furious, and he cast equal scorn in both directions if just for the danger Aria had been put into.

Then, he turned decisively towards the ditchlings. "*What* are you doing here?"

"We ain't gonna let you get eaten!" It was Nug, of course, but now covered in so much camouflaging paint and mud as to be unrecognisable.

"They wanted to *talk*," Rathen replied impatiently.

"Oh, yeah, *looked* like it! And we're here to do the sweeping! Although I reckon we'll have a mighty hungerin' for a *turkey dinner* by the time we're finished!"

The harpies squawked in furore and raised their legs, baring their scything talons, and the ditchlings duly poised their weapons. Slingshots fired without warning; the harpies descended, and in a moment the battle was raging again. The glow of fire and a cheer of imminent victory went up near the rear of the ground assault.

Rathen's fury snapped. With a twist of his fingers, he unleashed his own waft of wind, extinguishing the sudden torch and flooring both sides again. "*Enough!*"

Each force retreated immediately to their defensive positions. Nug glared up at the harpy; the harpy glared down at him; Rathen glared at both. Petra noticed that the few on each side to brush their gaze over him withered back a step, and as she spared him a glance herself, she was quite relieved not to be its target.

"Why'd--"

"*Quiet.*"

The antlered ditchling pursed his lips.

Rathen shook his head in exasperation. How had this happened? How had he managed to get embroiled in this? Caught between one faction of unintended allies and another of accidental enemies, and while both sides had just as much at stake, they were at each other's throats! And *his!* These two peoples who had just as much to fear from a force almost beyond *mortal* measures, a force even he was dogged by, even he dreaded. And that was discounting the *Arana's* involvement. Both of their homes were within this forest, and they, like countless others of their scattered kind, were at its mercy. And they were trying to kill each other.

"*How,*" he asked helplessly, "*how* did all this start?!"

"They tried to kill us!" Nug declared viciously, jutting his jaw and his spear towards the huge raptorial figures.

"Why?" But he turned towards Nug. "What did you do?" He rolled his eyes at the collective offence, over-dramatised by a series of gasps, glances and agape mouths.

"What are you implyin'?"

"I'm implying that you are troublesome and are bound to have caused some mischief of another by your very namesake. So what did you do?"

"Well," Nug huffed, folding his arms and almost hitting another beside him in the head with his spear, "sorry to disappoint you, but we *didn't*. They stole from us, so we stole from them, then they tried to kill us for it."

"You stole our *eggs!*"

All eyes crashed onto the ditchlings in horror, but they merely straightened in defence.

"And you stole right out of our traps! We was just trying to survive!"

"You took their *eggs?*"

"Not until they stole meat right out of our traps *four times.*"

"*Liars!*"

"No, you just ain't got any fingers to count on!"

"*Stop.*" Rathen rubbed his temples. "From the beginning. With all this trouble, why don't you just move away from each other?"

"We will not leave our eyries," the harpy croaked intently. "We have been here beyond even your count; our dronn'vaen of ages followed the air currents to their strongest peaks. These are our ancestral lands."

"And we ain't going nowhere without the Lady!" Nug countered. "She and her sisters wandered onto your land for reasons we ain't been able to work out, but we're staying put as long as she does!"

"There is not enough hunting for the both of us!"

"And yet moving is apparently not an option." Rathen muttered cynically.

"Why did you start stealing from one another?"

"It was our only choice."

"Was it?"

"Of course."

"The ditchlings are much smaller than you. I can't see how their arrival could empty the forests."

"They are small, but they are many."

He glanced over those gathered; they numbered about the same as those in the grove, and he suspected they'd all left with Nug. Given their devotion to their feud, it was likely that this was at least half of Wrenroot's population. "Not *that* many," he decided. "And if that truly were the case, I think one of you *would* have moved."

"What are you suggesting?"

"That you attacked them first, passive aggressively, by taking more than you needed so they would have to move on. And whether you realised it or not, you started to do the same in return. Then you went too far and stole from their nests. They attacked you to protect their young and you attacked back to defend yourselves."

The expected protest didn't come. Rathen nodded to himself. "I thought so. And when did the magic move in?"

"Not long after."

"And you concluded that the Lady was responsible. An act of defence, or something."

"She and her sisters move on their own whims, but many have taken a liking to the mice that follow them. It is the only explanation."

"No," he groaned, "it isn't--look, it doesn't matter. In the end you're both being selfish and hoarding against the other because you don't want to share, so much so that you're prepared to *kill* each other and turn a blind eye to the *real* danger! Salus--the 'sneaky ones' are chopping away at you from the edges, you're both aware of this! And if you keep up this feud you'll *all* be dead, and by the hands of an enemy you can't even see coming! You need to stop! The forests *can* feed you both if you stop your petty hoarding and only take what you *need*."

"No."

"Never."

"Can't you see you're being *ridiculous?!* All of this boils down to you being *different* from each other! Did you even *try* to co-exist before you started trying to push each other out?! Before you started *killing* each other?!"

"That ain't what you big 'uns do, though, is it?"

He sent the twig-crowned ditchling a flat look. "We are not a people to be emulated."

"Then what could you possibly suggest?" The harpy challenged.

"Talk. Adapt. Learn to live side by side."

"With *them?!*" At least their disdain was in agreement.

"Yes."

"It don't come so easy for *you* though, does it? We seen you kill each other just 'cause your hair or skin or eyes is a different colour! Or 'cause you talk funny! We ain't killed Dappy just 'cause she can't say her esses!"

"The mouse has a point."

"Fanks, missus."

Rathen raised a finger. "Which proves that you're smarter than us."

"That was never in question. But we have *real* differences--"

"Differences that won't stop the sun from rising." Unbidden, he glanced around at his companions. They stood in a half circle, closely packed and covering a watch over both sides of the dispute, available weapons in hand. Ready to raise the alarm or defend each other in an instant. He looked back towards his difficult audience. "Conflict can come from more than just looking different. Beliefs can drive rifts between people who look exactly the same. But even that--"

"Their Lady--"

"*Is not responsible! She isn't re--*"

"Daddy."

At the firm whisper, he looked around towards Aria. She was shaking her head. A glance towards the others found both Anthis and Petra looking at him with equal concern.

"There is *something* in that tree," she told him quietly. "I'm sure of it."

The intensity of the others' stares suggested that they felt the same. Which irritated him. And, on Aria's part, surprised him. But he conceded if just to spare himself the trouble.

With a breath to settle his frustrations, he returned to the woodland court and spoke as calmly as he could. "All right. There is no divine presence at work here. The Lady isn't responsible for the magic, nor is she favouring one side or forcing you to attack each other. It's just the two of you bickering over exclusive rights to abundant space and food. And there have been deaths on *both* sides because of it."

"Not," the nameless harpy hissed, "by our hands alone."

"That ain't these guys' doing. They're hunted just like we are. *All* of us here are in the same ruddy hole."

The burning glare she channelled barely wavered despite a spark of admission flickering somewhere beneath her enmity. "...Yes," she said at last, "we have witnessed. This much, at least, appears to be true after all. But why are *we* being targeted? You little mice are a nuisance to them, and the rest of you are impulsive and aggressive and kill one another for reasons elusive to a rational mind. We, however, have always kept out of your way."

"Until, I suspect, your feud expanded into chasing each other into striking distance of our villages. My point is that if you stopped your petty squabbling--"

"Thought he was gonna say 'squawking'."

"--Then you could focus your efforts onto protecting yourself from *serious* threats."

Finally, silence. But was it consideration or scepticism?

Slowly, the ditchlings began muttering, while the harpies chattered on the other side. But the prime's hawk eyes only narrowed. "You speak fine words, white one," she declared, her measured tone seizing such attention that even the ditchlings paused to listen. "You cannot persuade them to leave us alone? Or yourselves?"

"They would sooner throw knives into our eyes, I think," he replied bitterly.

"Interesting. You seek to solve our problems and yet you are unable to solve your own. Tell me why I should not gouge out your eyes myself."

"*Because--*"

"Because theirs is a complicated culture, Mayi'i." Eyila stepped forwards, stifling Rathen's increasing exasperation, and stopped beside him to address the single harpy perched high in the oldest tree. But rather than meeting her with the same disdain she had Rathen, she regarded the tribal with a strange curiosity. And she listened, straightening, waiting for her to continue. "Among these five there are conflicting opinions on faith, and always at least two on the course of action in any single situation. And yet, despite their differences of spirit, they co-exist. It is true that a crowd is harder to convince than a single soul, but these five individuals of so confused a people live by their words."

Her head twitched, cocking to one side, and she leaned a little closer as her curiosity rose closer to the surface. "And why are *you* among them, little Ayavei? To offer direction to the hurricane?"

"I am with them because they wish me to be."

"You are a slave?"

While the others baulked at the suggestion, Eyila lightly shook her head. "I give them my presence willingly. My tribe was killed by the earthen two moons ago, and despite their own tasks and trials, they would not leave me where I, too, would be hunted down or destroyed by grief. So they took me with them."

"Because they could not find their way out of the desert without you."

"They are resourceful. They would have managed. And though I can turn around and leave at any time, should I wish, I do not. I count each of them among my friends."

"Your tribe was murdered."

The others cringed. Again, Eyila responded calmly. "Yes. It is also true that they are all I have, but that does not change how I feel. And I want to see them succeed with their ambitious task, and keep them safe - and I want to be there when they keep their promise to remove the magic from *my* people's sacred ground."

"And Aya'u approves of your association?"

"She trusts my decisions."

She examined the tribal for a long moment. Then she straightened and gently flexed her wings. "She does." Her yellow gaze turned thoughtfully onto the humans beside her, then back onto the tribal. Then fell decisively upon the ditchlings, who observed the proceedings with guarded stances and open looks of mistrust. When they saw her attention descend upon them, they straightened boldly and readied their weapons. But she did not react. "What do you make of this?"

Nug's spear slowly lowered, and he began to consider the humans. He sighed deeply, pursed his lips, and thought for a long, hard moment. Finally, he nodded. "They're complicated, all right. My head hurts from trying to keep up. But that's hoomans, I reckon, and from time to time they do spout some sense, like what that metal lady did. 'Course her voice was a bit distractin'. But, when the squirrel is skinned, we ain't really getting anywhere killing each other, are we? Least not while them sneaks is skittering after us. And they're harder to see coming than giant flying turkeys. I know who the bigger problem is - and I have to say, it would be nice to be able to eat that squirrel without having to try and bend one eye cloudward while the other 'un's spying out the bones."

"...It sounds like they're willing to try if you are."

But the harpy squawked in disagreement. "I never said we were willing to try."

Rathen groaned in despair, dropping his face into his hands.

"May I make a suggestion?" Eyila asked, to which the harpy inclined her head. But Nug interrupted before she could begin.

"Wait wait wait wait wait," he cried, stomping forwards. "Hang on one arse-scratching minute. She's too chummy with the turkeys - we don't trust her. What if she's trying to manipulate the situation to their bennyfit?"

"Nug," Aria spoke up, "she's with us. You can trust her."

"*Can* we?"

"Yes. You can." She stepped forwards despite Petra's warning for her to stay back, and approached the dirty ditchling with an appeasing smile, which she cast in the direction of the harpies, too, for good measure. "You trust me, and I trust her, so *you* should trust her. She's never done anything but good. She healed my daddy when he needed it, and Garon, and Anthis - she's special. She can do things with her magic that even my daddy can't. You shouldn't disrespect her." She looked to Eyila and gave her an encouraging smile, then back towards Nug. He'd fallen tightly quiet, but by the purse of his lips and fold of his arms, it seemed he was prepared, albeit grudgingly, to listen.

Eyila nodded the girl her thanks, then bowed her acknowledgement to Nug. He smiled and mirrored it clumsily.

"Matters like these aren't simple," she declared, turning to address the gathering. "As far as I've learned, to make it work, you need to make a compromise. Inconvenience each other and make common ground."

"No," Nug stated flatly. "That is a *stupid* idea."

"Actually," Rathen interjected despite his thinning sanity, "as unorthodox a take on 'compromise' as that is, it makes sense. Make an ultimately minor change to the way you live that will create a common problem and force you to co-operate. In co-operating, a trust or understanding will form. You claim that hunting is the issue. What about a limit on the number of kills?"

"Ooh! Yeah, great idea!" The brief enthusiasm in his giant eyes turned into a spiteful glint. "One rabbit each."

"That's not enough!" The harpy erupted.

"You're just greedy!"

"Harpies *are* much bigger than you..." Rathen pointed out.

The harpy released a sudden, mirthful trill. "No. One rabbit will be fine. One rabbit, and half a *ditchling!*"

"*Arkhamas!*"

"*All right!*" Rathen bellowed. "Forget hunting. What about territory? Boundaries? Give up *part* of your eyries and *part* of the Lady's range?"

She flared. "This is our ancestral ground! Would you accept us, or them, or even the *Ayavei*, moving across *your* boundaries and forcing you to leave half of your buildings behind?"

Rathen rubbed his forehead in a bid to dissuade the hammering of tension. "Yes," he sighed in defeat, "okay, I admit many people would have a problem with that."

"Perhaps if their Lady was removed--"

"You can't make her go *nowhere!* She goes where she wants, no force in the ground *or* the sky can stop her!"

"Neither can any force change the wind!"

"Blow the wind out of your backside!"

"Hunting ground, then," Eyila jumped in. "If you have lived here for so long, then you know where the richest areas are - divide them up."

"A wise idea. They can take the southern acres - it's closer to their holes anyway."

Now Nug flared. "The southern acres?! You know that's empty! Hoomans are too close to it! There's nothing in there but sparrows and caterpillars!"

She trilled derisively again. "You only have small bellies!"

"I appreciate the enthusiasm," Eyila said carefully, "but I didn't mean *try* to inconvenience each other."

"Well what do you really expect us to do, missus? Live in their nests with 'em? Roast our meat side by side? Cuddle up on biting nights?"

"What if," Garon began musingly from the back, drawing all eyes onto him, "you just kept an eye out?"

"What, like gouge them?"

"*No!*" Rathen bellowed. "What's *wrong* with you?"

"Keep a *look out,*" the inquisitor elaborated. "You're both being targeted by the same people, and both for the same reason. This much, you *do* share, and it's more than just a 'minor inconvenience'. So rather than attacking each other, turn your aggression onto *them.* Work together to save yourselves. They won't expect it - in fact, they're almost certainly using your preoccupation to their advantage."

"You mean like, if one of us sees something, we holler and let the rest know? They'll just fly away and save their *own* feathers! What'll we get out of that?!"

"They won't raise the alarm," she hissed, "they'll leave us to their weapons if they don't lead them into our eyries themselves!"

"Then one side will be killed while the other watches. These people will take advantage of *any* opportunity they can find, and betrayal is one such opportunity. For *both* sides."

"How's that?"

"One side panics, the other gets complacent," he replied simply. "Both become easy targets. So it is in *neither's* interest to betray the other. Whereas if you work together, you only stand to gain."

"...We ain't really being inconvenienced by that, though."

"You would have to work together," Eyila noted. "That means coordinating efforts, setting up some kind of signalling system; you will *have* to live in the same forests, but you'll be safer."

Slowly, the eyes of every ditchling and every harpy turned onto their rivals, and again a tentative silence descended. But this one was charged, buzzing with a multitude of unspoken thoughts, concerns and suspicions betrayed by expressions in eyes, brows and curling lips. Quiet chirps began among the harpies while the ditchlings no doubt conferred in silence - perhaps even with numbers beyond those present - and those caught in the middle watched each side with tension.

Again it was the lead harpy who broke the silence, her tone this time considered, hypothetical. "The magic," she began slowly, "whomsoever's it is, is tearing the forests apart. The prey has been frightened off and the hunting truly is thin; safe, thick acres to make homes within are harder to find. Things - all things - would be easier if the magic was gone."

"We can do that," Rathen assured them. "But will you cooperate if we do?"

Again, the two factions considered one another.

"I can speak for my kin," she declared. "We will do them no harm for as long as they honour the pact."

But Nug wasn't so quick to agree. He and the rest remained quiet, their eyes moving as one over their feathered adversaries. It took a long while before he shifted his weight, cocked his head and narrowed his enormous eyes. "We don't trust them," he stated bluntly. "*But*...if we'll be safe - from hoomans *and* from them - then...rashunly speaking, we ain't really got a choice, have we?"

"Not really, no."

"For this to work," Eyila reminded them, "you'll have to stop attacking one another - right away."

"Then we have a problem, don't we?" A dirty finger stabbed towards the harpies. "We can get word to our friendlies right now, but what can *they* do? It'll take a *month* for them to let all their kind know!"

"How long *will* it take?" Rathen asked, turning towards them.

"Six days."

"Really? Across the whole of Turunda?"

"Yes. Wings are faster than feet."

He looked back towards the ditchlings, all of whom seemed only vaguely more satisfied. "Then it looks like it will be on *you* to show the first honour by refraining from retaliation in that time. Consider it practise."

"We don't *need* practise, we know how to live peaceful, thanks very much."

"Then prove it. And you," he looked back to the harpies, "will also have to keep your word and make every effort to inform your kind as soon as possible. This feud ends *now*."

"At the say-so of outsiders?"

"To be honest," he growled, "*yes*, because we've been caught up in this too, and for no damned good reason. And because you *both* know it's the right thing to do, even if it's just to save your *own* skins - and, in fact, because you're making it harder for *us* to save *everyone's hides!*" He seethed, but as Eyila's hand rested delicately on his shoulder, he snapped it back. He straightened and turned away, abandoning his part in the matter at last.

"He's right," Aria informed them as he turned and knelt beside her, checking she was all right, and he smiled a weak note of gratitude. Suddenly, his exertion at the foot of the Tree had returned to thump in his skull.

Eyila stepped forwards and motioned for Nug and the harpy to come close. Garon and Petra baulked, and Anthis joined them once his jealous glare had passed; the two in question merely stared at her reluctantly. But a soft, assuring smile remained on her lips, and she gestured patiently to them both again.

Nug straightened; he was the first to step forwards, Rathen's words no doubt ringing in his mind, at least for the moment, and even returned after a few steps to leave his spear behind in the hands of a girl whose hair had been presumably painted with berries to approach his counterpart unarmed.

The harpy's elegant head twitched at this, and she, too, dropped to the ground with surprising grace for a creature so large. It was only then that any of them noticed how ragged her outermost feathers were, aged and worn, and wondered for a moment at just how old this crowned individual was.

They stopped several paces apart, so she encouraged them the final few steps by grasping arm and wing and pulling them together to stand side by side in front of her.

Then, her smile changed; her companions at her back, it was meant only for these two. And it exuded peace. "Ayuia," she began, looking up towards the magnificent harpy, "Arkhamas," she looked down to the appeased ditchling. Her hands pressed together at her heart, then rose to her forehead; as her left moved away behind her back, the fingertips of her right touched her brow. "Oluya toakan Aya'u tse," she whispered, and a cool breeze billowed from the downward sweep of her hand.

Nug's eyes widened, the harpy's closed, and her companions looked on in curiosity.

"You are measured equally; both of you are capable of honour, and both of you are capable of treachery. But only with your *combined* integrity can you save your people. Any action that puts one ahead of the other will doom *both* sides to fail. Know this, heed this, and you will only succeed."

While Nug stared up at her in awe, the harpy stepped back and stooped her head, flaring her feathers as her kind had done at her own arrival. "Saya'a lo toa," she said with a reverence that only further confused the gathered humans. "We will commit. You have my word, and that of the other dronn'vaen." She straightened elegantly, then turned her head to look directly at the ditchling beside her. "As do you, little mice. For the sake of all of us."

He nodded slowly, dragging his eyes from the tribal to the harpy, and while he stared for a moment, it was not in hesitance. He nodded again, consciously this time, and the amazement in his silver-green eyes faded enough for his usual liveliness to peek back through. But there was a solemnity there, too, and he straightened not in defiance but in virtue. "And us. It ain't gonna be easy, but I know I don't wanna be killed by these sneaky buggers any more than you do. We got a common problem, all right, and if the only way to beat it is to team up, then that's just the way it is. 'Course it'll take some time to take down our traps." He smiled sheepishly beneath the harpy's glare. "Awh, don't look like that, *neighbour*. You got your own traps to disbandle, I'm sure."

She didn't seem inclined to dispute it, but neither did she agree. Instead, her sharp yellow eyes returned to the tribal then to the humans beyond, over whom she cast one final scrutinising gaze. "It seems you are even more complicated than we had imagined. But also more intelligent. It is a shame your convictions are not shared among the majority of your people. But it seems you have just managed to convince *us*. That is no small thing." She stepped forwards, ignoring the weapons that flinched at her approach, and came to a stop before Rathen. He looked up with tired eyes, but managed to return the bow of her head. "You are lucky to have this one among you. Do not take her skills for granted."

"We don't," Anthis assured her.

Then, at a cue neither seen nor heard, the surrounding harpies took flight and began to disappear back into the forest. Despite their abduction, no one argued at their departure.

Nug, on the other hand...

"Oi," he snatched her wing as she moved to follow. "We ain't done! Just when are you gonna send this message?"

"One hour past noon," she replied with clearly restrained irritation, snatching her feathers free.

"*Noon? Tomorrow's noon?!* Why not *now?*" His eyes narrowed, and the remaining harpies stopped and turned, watching him and his band closely. "What are you planning?"

"We plan nothing. That is when the air is at its swiftest."

"*Sure* it is. How conveenyent. We ain't doing nothing until you do; we ain't letting our friendlies get killed so you can have one last hurrah!"

"*You are so infantile!*" She hissed, and whipped back towards the others. "This is *never* going to--"

"It will *have* to." Eyila gave each of them a firm stare. "Only together. Remember?"

A venomous glance exchanged between the two of them, brief, but hot enough to melt steel. They both snapped their heads away a moment later with muttered curses and predictions. But they then each looked back to Eyila, nodded with tight lips and beaks, nodded even more brusquely to one another, then turned and departed without another word to anyone.

The humans watched them go with raised eyebrows. Eyila returned to them and smiled victoriously. "That went well."

Chapter 25

Drizzle pattered. It was soft and constant, as reassuring as the babbling of the stream that rolled lazily through the hollows of the scowles. He could reach that river in five minutes should he wish - the walk would be quiet and invigorating. But it was late, dark, and he had little desire to leave the warm and familiar fireside chair. As old and patched as it was, it was soft, and perfectly conformed over the years to his shape and comfort.

He sank deeper into its folds as a cool breeze slipped in through the window. It tousled his hair and mixed the smell of the damp forest with the wood burning in the fireplace. Playful giggling nearby lightened his heart, and the strange voices of dolls chuckling in her enactment elicited one of his own.

A long, easy breath passed his lips.

Finally, the magic was gone. The job was done. And Aria would be safe forever.

A loud, muffled thump erupted in the centre of his head. His heart burst, the world slipped, and his eyes snapped open with a jolt.

To the dark forest, the campfire, and the four figures he knew and yet felt suddenly as though they were strangers.

His bearings were painfully slow to return. Each struck him like a hammer blow to the skull.

With a bitter murmur, Rathen cleared his throat and shifted against the tree trunk, sitting up from the slump he'd sank into, and smothered his choking disappointment. He would not be deceived like that a third time that night.

He looked hard about himself. It was growing dark and cool, the lengthy summer dusk stripped away at last, while the crescent moon hid beyond Wrenroot's treetops where the storm's last gasp was wheezing. The only light came from the small, flickering campfire, a sight that lately seemed to dominate half his life, and cast haphazard shapes across the tree trunks that only further confused his exhausted senses. And he still couldn't shake the scent of home.

Another wave of disorientation struck in his attempt to divide the two, and he quickly decided that the effort wasn't worth it. So he abandoned it, settled back against the bark, and let his eyes fall upon Aria who played with the ditchlings at the edge of the camp, gracious hosts who had led them back to their horses and permitted them to settle on the fringes of the forest. They were playing some strange game that involved throwing sticks upwards with a flick of the wrist to land inside a ring they'd drawn in the mud. At first he'd thought the point was to get the stick to land upright and stay that way, as he'd heard cackles of victory on every such occasion, but his understanding crumbled when the same outburst rose as one landed diagonally, dislodged another and fell on its side along with it.

But whichever rules eluded him, Aria seemed to grasp, and she laughed joyfully along with them, whooping in victory herself a number of times.

He smiled softly as he watched, and his eyelids grew heavy once again.

An instant later Aria was dashing past him, heading for the saddlebags. She snatched something, flashed him a grin, and hurried back to the ditchlings. He watched her give it to Nug. Even despite the low light, he knew what it was: a depiction of the Lady she'd whittled from the branch he'd given her. He'd seen her working on it over the past two nights, smoothing out the lines and rubbing down the splinters. It was a simple shape, and not at all unlike a ghost; it was quite a melancholy image, actually, but one that bore the grace of any entity of nature. As far as he would picture it, at least.

He smiled softly again. Nug seemed to like it.

Anthis watched Eyila smile at the mage's most recent crash back to his surroundings. His eyes narrowed past her bitterly.

So he hissed as she rubbed a salve of crushed leaves, sap and some kind of clay into the talon wounds on his wrist.

She snapped back to him in an instant, apology in her eyes while a smile persisted on her lips. But this, he could see, was for him. "Sorry - did that hurt?"

He smiled - genuinely - and shook his head. "No, I'm fine. It just surprised me." It hadn't in the slightest. But that didn't really matter.

Her smile broadened though the apology remained, and she returned her attention fully onto her task. Evidently, no one's wounds had been particularly severe, as she'd not once resorted to magic. She'd treated Petra, Rathen and now himself with herbal remedies, and it had to be said: her skill was adept. Not once had her touch stung or twinged; there had been a solution to numb, another to draw and weep out dirt, and now a paste to...well he wasn't sure, but it was sealing it, at any rate, and probably doing plenty more besides. And each had been applied with practised certainty and care.

His body tightened as she transferred his hand to her other, her fingers brushing his palm while she reached out to drag closer her mortars, and with an absent flick of her long, snow-white hair her scent drifted towards him. It was a scent he'd come to know as uniquely hers, strange but far from unpleasant: a mix of heat-dried leaves and something he'd finally come to place as damp sun-cured hide, which itself had taken on the essence of their trail through the forests.

He felt his palms turn clammy and his cheeks begin to burn as the aroma lingered and muddled his thoughts. Desperately, he sought any means to distract himself. "What did you call her?" He blurted the words so suddenly that he succeeded only in darkening his cheeks.

But Eyila's pale eyes were calm as they turned back up to him, composed and unaware of his blushing in the concealing light of the fire. She didn't seem to need any elaboration, either, as she answered his poorly delivered question before he could try, and with a smile so natural that his heart fluttered in spite of his efforts.

"Mayi'i. I suppose the closest would be 'matriarch', although that's not quite right."

Again, he fought the redness away. "She said dronn'vaen - it's elven, but there's not really a translation for that, either. How did you know how to address her?"

"It is the language of the Wind."

"Oh. I thought Rathen said your people spoke some kind of Ivaean..."

"Yes," she smiled, "but not exclusively. We speak Aya'u's voice when it's right to."

"I see..." Then the silence crept back in and she sank back into her work, tidying the salve and ensuring every break of the skin was covered. "Why did they think you were our slave?" He managed to prevent the words from tumbling out on their own this time.

"Because," she replied without any thought of offence, "my people are much more like them than you are, and they believe you think you're above them."

"That's ridiculous."

"Is it, though? Many of you hate non-humans - many of you hate *tribals*. And Salus is killing all the non-humans he can get his hands on. Their belief isn't unjustified."

"No," he shifted uncomfortably, "but it's a bit of a blanket assumption. We're not all the same."

"I know. Which is why I told them as much."

"...What did you say to them when we left?"

She smiled with amusement, entertained, as she often was, by his unending fascination. "It was a blessing."

"A blessing? Of Aya'u?" She nodded. "And you said they were measured equally..." He hesitated cautiously, and a moment further when she looked up in expectation. "Did She tell you that?"

Then her expression changed dramatically. Her bronze face screwed up almost comically as she regarded him as though he was mad, her eyes wide beneath a ridiculous frown and a slight puckering of her lips that looked like she'd either smelled something sour or was trying to hold back a hateful smile. She looked away, breathing either a laugh or a snort, and began covering the pasted wound with a broad leaf whose underside had been notched and scored. "Of course not. I'm not a priestess, why would Aya'u communicate with *me?*"

"No," he'd successfully embarrassed himself. "Of course not." He cleared his throat and straightened, attempting to cast it off as she released his wrapped hand. "Either way, it seemed to carry weight with the harpies. The ditchlings just looked...agog, I suppose."

"Aya'u is the Goddess of the Wind, and the harpies revere the winds as my people do." She faltered as she began gathering her mortars and pestles. "Did."

For the briefest moment, her face displayed an anguish so powerful it grasped his own heart and squeezed a lump of lead into his stomach. Then it was quickly locked away. Quite successfully. *Too* successfully. She turned him a smile, and though it was painfully close, he knew it wasn't real.

Then, she looked down at the waist of his shirt.

He frowned, confused, while an outrageously unlikely conclusion began flying around in the back of his mind. But that idea was quashed as her eyes rose, filled with a strange sort of consideration. One tainted, if only by a drop, with mistrust.

His mood collapsed immediately.

"How are you feeling?"

"Fine," he replied shortly, rising just as abruptly to his feet and tugging looser

233

his shirt, beneath which his daggers lay. "Thank you for your help. I appreciate it." He walked away without another word. He regretted it later, but he was in no mood for judgement or explanations.

Eyila sighed as she watched him approach the saddle bags and begin rifling through his own, a little too long to have been truly searching for anything in particular. But she brushed it off, stood up and turned towards Garon as he entered the camp from his patrol.

He took one look at her and adjusted his path to take him back out into the forest as seamlessly as he could.

Eyila didn't fall for it. "It's your turn, Inquisitor."

"I'm fine, thank you," he called back, gait unbroken, but when Petra spoke up, he stalled in spite of himself.

"You should let her have a look," she said mildly. "It could be worse than ours."

"If I'd sustained a serious injury, I would know about it."

"Unless your pride gets in the way."

"You have no right to talk to me about pride," he grumbled, resuming towards the trees. "*Or* self-preservation."

"And you have no right to put yourself so far above the rest of us. Your insignia only means so much, and it doesn't make you indestructible."

"I never said it did."

"No," she sighed patiently, rising, "but you act like it does." She reached out and grasped his arm before he could move out of reach. He glanced back into serious eyes. "Let her take a look."

He quickly snatched himself free and all but hissed as he turned away to resume his original, urgent pace. "I am *fine*." He was gone in moments.

"No, you're *infuriating*."

"Why even waste your energy on him?" Anthis asked, but she didn't respond beyond another exhausted sigh.

She returned to tending the food the ditchlings had given them - eggs and meat of some description, though all presumably too small to have once belonged to harpies - but looked up at a sudden high-pitched '*hyah!*'. A smile broke as she watched Aria demonstrate her sword techniques to the ditchlings, their game of stick-flipping forgotten.

She wasn't nearly as clumsy as she had been, but the few movements she'd taught her had been practised religiously ever since. The rest was all flair. The ditchlings, too, had retrieved their sticks from the pile and were copying her every movement. That may not have been wise, she thought, given the tentative truce they had only just managed to broker, against all odds, but she wasn't going to stop them. And as she glanced towards Rathen, who watched with half-closed eyes and an affectionate smile, she knew he wasn't, either.

"Did anyone notice," she mused, turning back to the fire, "that no one thanked us for ending their feud?"

"Are you kidding?" Rathen forced himself to his feet at the sizzle of flipping eggs and stretched himself as he approached to join them. "We're lucky they were in the mood to talk at all. Now at least we can forget about them hounding *us*." He sat heavily beside the fire, keeping Aria in his sights, and rubbed the drowsiness from his eyes. "We'll fix their homes as and when we pass. In the mean time, we should focus on Salus."

"And what do you expect to do about that?" She cocked a brow. "He wants to *move the country*. He's unhinged."

"He is, and if he has elven help, he could probably do it, too. They're malicious; whatever their reasons are for wanting Turunda moved, we can only assume that it won't be in *our* best interest."

"They're almost certainly just taking advantage of him," Anthis grunted from beside his own tree. "They'd have done the same to Rathen if Eizariin hadn't gotten to us first. They don't want to get their hands dirty so they're making someone else do it."

"Which suggests they think he's powerful enough to achieve it..."

Petra shook her head and shoved the tomatoes about the pan. "I say again: what do you expect us to do about it? We don't know how he plans to achieve it so we can't get in his way - if that's even *possible* - and we aren't in any kind of position to just go charging in and use the Zi'veyn on him or his elven friends."

"We need--"

"Information. Yes. I know." She sighed tediously. "Then it's still on to Mokhan?"

"I see no other choice."

"We'll be seen."

"I know we will."

"Then we'll need a plan."

A soft yet poignant clearing of a throat drew their attention towards Eyila, who was suddenly regarding them all with thinly veiled impatience. "I understand the position we are in," she announced, "with Salus, the Arana, and promises to the harpies and Arkhamas - but need I remind you of your promise to *my* people? To *me?*" Her eyes sharpened formidably, and yet the change was so slight, so graceful; it was as though a tempest had always roiled beneath her surface, its presence only now revealed. "When will we be returning to Ut'hala?"

"We haven't forgotten," Rathen softly assured her, "but it's...quite out of the way..."

"He means it will take us a long while to get there and there are other things we have to think about in the mean time." Petra smiled easily. "We *will* get there, but it might take a while."

"How long?"

They exchanged a look.

"Not too long," Rathen decided. "We just need to stabilise things here first."

"That could take months," Anthis grunted from the sidelines, which earned him sharp glances from the others. His lip curled, and he resumed his poring over large, loose parchments that certainly hadn't come from any of his books. No one wanted to look closer.

Eyila's eyes, however, had narrowed further. "He's right."

"Yes, perhaps, but last I checked, Anthis didn't have a crystal ball."

"That means he can't see the future," Petra elaborated, at which Eyila nodded in understanding.

"Salus is campaigning against non-humans, but it's only a matter of time before he starts targeting the tribes too, especially with their conflicts moving so close. It might not affect far-flung and isolated tribes like yo--liiike those out in...far-flung places, not right away, but it will eventually. He's devoted to his convictions - obsessed with them. If he begins to target the tribes along with the harpies and the ditchlings, there's no telling how far that will go. We need to stop him - or at least sufficiently hamper him - before we can travel so far out of reach."

"Where we would be safer."

"We're being hunted by the Arana, Anthis, *nowhere* is 'safer'. Don't be a fool." Rathen ignored the muttering and looked imploringly back up to the young woman, barely an adult and yet carrying and nursing the honour of her entire tribe with remarkable strength. "I understand your frustration, but this is bigger than any one place or promise - I don't suggest that anywhere sacred to your people or to anyone else is the same as a single carved rock in a forest, but even that doesn't compare when the lives of your people - of *other* wind tribes - are at risk."

She stared at him for a long, calculating moment. Rathen didn't blink. Finally, her shoulders stooped, her weight shifted, and she nodded reluctantly in concedence. "I hadn't thought about that."

"It's all right - it's not something that should have to occur to *anyone*."

She nodded again, her lips pulling into a sad smile, and apologised before walking off towards the spring that rose among the enormous roots of an ancient tree, rubbing her salve-coated fingers into her palms uncomfortably.

Petra leaned towards him with a baffled frown. "That was a bit grasping, wasn't it?"

"I don't think so." He watched her kneel beside the water at the edge of the light's reach and dropped his voice even lower. "He's already at it."

"What?!"

"*Shh!* Elle mentioned it when she was last here, but we didn't want to say anything in front of her. I only mention it now in the hope of preparing her in case we find any...evidence..."

"Why would he do that? To get to her? To *us?*"

"I doubt it. The popular consensus is that the tribes are dangerous, war or no, and Salus is obsessed with protecting the country from anything he considers remotely unsavoury. Or different."

They fell silent as Eyila rose, and Petra began dividing up the food as she took a spot by the fire, all the while sending the tribal girl brief, distracted glances.

Owan shifted under the scrutiny.

The sahrakh's gaze was particularly agonising. Cavalier, obstinate, self-certain; even the elite bearing with which he held himself rubbed him the wrong way. Owan had always found the soldier type unbearable but this was something else, and he had no doubt that his position as the highest rank to remain behind while the rest of the military wing had marched off to war had something to do with it.

He straightened himself against it, refusing to submit to the lieutenant general's pomposity.

Lady Delas, on the other hand, was a welcome presence. She, he had found, was always willing to listen, and while preservers were not typically called upon for tactical advice nor an intellectual point of view, she was a considered woman and had an air of command about her that was known to subdue many of the highest ranking soldiers and silence quibbling scholars. She alone seemed to balance out the soldier, and he breathed a little easier.

And between them both, like the pillar of the scales, was the grand magister, watching him with equal thought and patience that somehow only further settled and unnerved him. But while Arator was the only one among them that shared his academic calling and thirst for knowledge, his position as head of the Order enforced restraint over enthusiasm and a conservative approach instead. And it was his decision that mattered the most. The others could do little but advise.

Arator dropped his hands from his mouth. Owan seized up. "You've identified the source?"

"Dolunokh," he replied as calmly as he could, "as was expected - but it isn't that simple. I've been unable to identify *where* in Dolunokh it could have been; nothing correlates to any notable sites, and with everything shifting in its devastation, readings are even murkier. And the flow itself seems to have stopped for the moment."

All eyebrows rose. "Stopped?"

"Perhaps the source has been depleted," Delas offered, but while Owan shook his head, even Arator appeared unconvinced.

"We don't know where precisely it came from," Owan said, "nor how, nor why. We can't presume that those details are now redundant, and as it happened so suddenly in the first place, we also can't presume to say that it won't happen again. Someone could well have released it from something, either deliberately or not."

"From what?" The soldier scoffed. "A box?"

"Or perhaps it escaped. What could contain spells but another spell? Even enchanted objects are sealed. And even those spells degrade."

"I couldn't say to either. I've been unable to glean any clues from the spells themselves; none of them seem to share a purpose. In fact the sole commonality of each studied location is a disturbing, displaced beauty. Otherwise, from what information has been gathered, there's little else the spells have in common."

"And you're presenting *that* as a discovery?" Roane asked with even greater cynicism.

Owan didn't let it ruffle him. "Yes. They're so different, it's probable that they *never* had a link." He watched the soldier and preserver frown with varying degrees of doubt, but the grand magister, nodding slowly, appeared to appreciate the answer. "Above all of this, however, remains the fact that we still have no idea how it's weaving into the surrounding elements and causing the sheer destruction that it is. This is something we *must* focus on. But until someone actually goes out to study that particular detail, we can't possibly divine anything."

"You are correct, of course. But this isn't news. We are well aware of the situation."

"Not entirely, I suspect." He ignored the flash of insult across the soldier's face. "There has been a new development: two places - Wrenroot and Borer's Teeth - have suddenly gone quiet."

Delas shifted, crossing her legs and leaning forwards with a sudden sparkle in her blue eyes. Just as he'd expected. As a preserver, the practical applications of magic would intrigue her the most. "A cumulative effect? They've reached their end? The magic has lost its potency, perhaps?"

"I doubt it, my Lady. These two were nowhere near as bad as those further north, let alone those beyond the borders, and they're all continuing to grow steadily worse. There is something unnatural about the way they've ended."

She nodded slowly. Then her eyes changed. "Why have you presented this to us?"

He paused in confusion. "Because it's a drastic cha--"

"No, why have *you* presented this to *us*?" A suspicious smile was playing on her lips. "What are you scheming beneath all of this, young Owan?"

"He wants to go out there."

Roane grunted. "Absolutely not."

"I quite agree," added Delas, somewhat alarmed.

"Good Lords and Lady, we *can't* keep turning away from this..."

"Under other circumstances, you'd be right. As it stands, our priorities have been re-evaluated."

"Consider at least the personal risks," the old woman implored, "if you get caught by the Arana? Or by mage hunters? What then?"

"They'll do nothing more than imprison me - regardless of where custody lies, I can still think and piece together what I've found whatever cell I'm in."

"Assuming you get the chance to find anything at all before they pounce. You could get as little as two minutes before they snatch you off."

"Lord Roane is right, of course. I understand your enthusiasm, Owan, but things are not as simple as you might wish."

"No, they're not, my Lady, but these are just two sites while the rest are getting *worse*, and many of those have already resulted in evacuations, and others in *deaths*. We need to know how it's affecting the elements and we need to know as soon as possible so that we can prevent any further fatalities!"

"And what do you intend to do? The magic has dissipated - there is nothing left to see."

'Pig-headed brute,' Owan thought to himself as he bit down hard on his tongue and centred his efforts on keeping his sentiments from crossing his face. *'Not even Rathen would make so foolish an assumption.'* "It can't have entirely dissipated, not so suddenly. There will be remnants."

"And from those, you hope to see...?"

"An explanation. A cause."

"What do you suspect has happened?" The grand magister spoke up in a tone far too calm and collected, tripping Owan as he calculated how best to answer.

He settled for nescience. "I really couldn't guess." But he had taken too long. The grand magister fixed him with unchanged eyes, yet it was a stare that saw right through him. As it so often did.

"I don't believe you. You're an intelligent man, Owan. You couldn't observe all of this without developing theories, and neither would you even consider going out in the field without an angle on how to approach it, a plan of some kind."

The others looked at him expectantly. Ignorance hadn't worked, so he settled for the next best thing: vagueness. "I suspect that something has had an effect on it."

"'Something has had an effect'? Such as?"

Then Delas straightened, sitting tall, her elegant skirts shifting without a crease while a knowing smile played on her slender lips. She cocked a well-groomed eyebrow. "Something like a banished sahrot?"

Roane immediately flared. Arator sighed wearily to himself. "Rathen Koraaz is a *dangerous man*."

"Oh pish - you don't know what you're talking about, boy."

""You may be fond of him, but you all seem to have forgotten what got him banished in the first place! There is a reason he stayed away rather than appealing his punishment. Whatever happened to him, whatever magics he played with, Rathen Koraaz has as good as admitted his guilt!" In that moment, Owan was sure he saw him stand even taller. Like many from this soldier's class, a generation too late to know any better, Rathen was little more than a shameful footnote to the Order's recent history. But Owan suspected that Roane's present position of superiority of sahrakh over sahrot equally had a hand in his disdain - even if it was but a single rank's difference. Pride snaked its way into everything.

"He played with no magic."

"Then you have an explanation, Lady Delas?"

"I do not. But I would advise you, as politely as I can while you dance upon my wearing nerves, to hold your tongue when your knowledge on the matter extends no further than hearsay."

Roane's lips formed a hard line. "I apologise, of course," he replied, and it was almost convincing but for the tightness of his tone and the speed at which his acrid eyes shot back towards Owan. "What could Rathen Koraaz have possibly done to this magic? You're suggesting that a mage has had a *direct effect* on magic - not masked it, not counter-spelled, but modified the chains themselves - *elven* spell chains - and perhaps even removed them! The whole situation is *already* preposterous--"

"So why could a preposterous solution be so very unlikely?"

He flashed back onto Delas. "What?"

"Check your tone, young man. You heard what I said. An impossible problem requires an impossible solution. We don't know what Rathen has been up to, and in such unusual company. Who is to say he hasn't stumbled upon something in his freedom? Aside from his contradicting disposition." Her gaze turned fully onto Owan in that moment, an incredulous depth to the creases around her eyes. "You're *sure* it was Rathen Koraaz?"

"Positive, my Lady."

"I suppose it would be awfully hard to mistake him."

"If," the sahrakh continued impatiently, "against all odds, he *has* discovered something, why should that mean that he was also the one to execute it? He was a soldier, not a scholar; if he'd found something he would bring that information to someone with the know-how and the strength to--"

"If *anyone* among us has the strength for such an impossible task, it's him." The venom in the preserver's voice pealed the room into silence. Her eyes flared in a blue inferno. Roane's lips tightened. Even the grand magister seemed to shrink. "That boy had a fierce power buried within him, and to have survived his wounds without the aid of the healer granted to him shows, if nothing less, his stubbornness. He was *always* devoted to his duties as a protector, and I would *never* believe *anyone* who said he had given them up. For a man to fix this it would be neither safe nor easy, and if he *has* found a way, he would see it through himself if just to ensure no one else was put at risk. Then," she added with even greater acidity, "perhaps he might also be redeemed in the eyes of ignorants like yourself, Sahrakh Forlin."

Owan forced himself not to nod his fervent agreement. Arator, too, concealed his smile behind his hand. But as he dropped it to the desk, his visage was perfectly proper. "We are jumping to romantic conclusions. It may well not be Rathen's doing. It could, though I fail to understand how, be some of our own. We have some incredibly intelligent minds in the Order, but not all of them are predictable. It is possible that someone has worked out how to affect magic. For good or ill; they haven't come forth about it either way.

"Discovering why the magic has fallen quiet could be of use to us - should it be natural, we may be able to replicate it in other places. Should it be the work of mages, we are capable of the same thing. And failing that...discovering how it's winding its way into the elements *will* be key in combating progression."

Owan's heart all but leapt from his chest in anticipation as the grand magister's eyes turned wholly upon him. "Permission granted - but you must wait, just for a few days. We will try to find a window so that you can leave with as little attention as possible."

"If he goes out there, he will be detained and the Order--"

"I don't need to hear it, Lord Roane, believe me, I am more than aware." He continued to fix the scholar. "And utilise the sparrows."

"Sparrows?" But the sahrakh was ignored.

"Find out where he is and if he did in fact have a hand in it. And remember: he is a second pair of eyes. Do with that what you will, as I shan't permit a second excursion."

Owan reined in his excitement and bowed low. "I understand. Thank you, Grand Magister." He bowed again, to each in turn, not all of which were genuine, and spun on his heel to leave.

"Imelia."

He froze.

"She is due in two months?"

"Seven weeks," he looked over his shoulder.

Arator nodded. His eyes were shudderingly grave. "Be careful."

"I will." Then he left, enthusiasm duly shattered, a strike of solemn comprehension rising in its place.

The door closed. Roane stared after him, arms folded over his broad chest. "Is this wise?" He asked quietly.

"When all is weighed...I don't know." Arator sighed. "Only the results will tell."

"And you believe he can get them?"

"You don't?"

Roane's jaw tightened. "...I do. I just hope he gets sufficient chance."

Chapter 26

Though perpetually cool and still, Blackbrush's habitual solitude seemed infinite that night; the gnarled and towering trees shuttered out the weak sliver of moonlight so absolutely it was as though one walked beyond the reaches of the world. Space was endless in spite of the density, and the only evidence of living creatures were the ghostly hoots of unseen owls, guarding the forest from mice and moles. The air was eerie, but peaceful, radiating a calm and tranquillity impossible to find in the city.

Unfortunately, Taliel didn't feel it.

Salus had been quiet for a long while, brooding in silence beneath the cold light of a magical orb that turned the outlying darkness abyssal, his arms tightly folded and walking within the turmoil of his own private storm. Far from distancing his troubles, he'd seized nothing but the opportunity to fuse himself amongst them.

And this diversion had been *her* idea.

She sighed gloomily to herself, and in an effort to escape the ever-shrinking cage she'd trapped herself in, she forced a soft smile, moved up closer alongside him, and placed a hand gently upon his shoulder. "Salus--"

"This could have been avoided," he suddenly burst, shattering the stillness like the roar of a woken beast, "it could have been *avoided* if I had more than *one* sodding surveillance spell in action!"

"But would you have really put--"

"It was a grumpy old man and his mop-headed *son!*" He shook his head, lips curling into a mad and stupefied smile. "How can anyone make such a mistake?!"

"Mistakes happen--"

"Increasingly often! But this was by a *phidipan!* There's no excuse, Taliel! I can't--I can't--I can't--"

"Red Heath," she stepped around in front of him, grasping his frantic hands and blocking his path, "is surrounded by evacuees. Mistaken identity in grumpy old men isn't unreasonable."

But he was still shaking his head. "Among *common* people. And no one who answers to the Arana *is* 'common people'."

"Why thank you." But her smile was met with a distinct lack of amusement. She sighed and let it fall, stepped aside and allowed him to return to his trudge. His face was quick to collapse back into a pensive knot.

"These spells are a priority. This *can't* happen again."

"Then you'll need to send people out to place them for you," she sighed.

"I know. And I will. In every city and crossroad town. The more the better. Then this won't happen. If someone says they've seen Koraaz, we can bloody well make sure of it." He grunted to himself then, his eyes unmoving from the ground ahead. "And posters."

"Posters?" She frowned. "*Bounty* posters? We would be *bombarded* with mistaken identities - even deliberate fraud!"

"Not if the reports are sent to the guards."

"And if they're found, they'll have fled by the time it's passed on to us."

"There will be none to reach us. One sight of the posters and they'll avoid the cities all together. Separated from the populace, there will be no room for mistaken identity."

Taliel cast him a careful look. Her stomach turned at the rancorous curve of his lips. She looked away again, expressionless. "And if they're not as smart as you think and someone genuinely finds them?"

"Then we would have seen them, too. It's just a matter of getting these spells up. And quickly. They'll need to stop and get supplies at some point. Then we'll have them. Then we'll have them..." He descended into another silent frenzy. Taliel sank into fret. Then he returned with an abrupt and fearsome growl. "*What are they up to?!*"

"Hmm?"

"Wrenroot, Borer's Teeth - it's all gone quiet, like the magic has just *vanished*. Is he going around and gathering it up? Or is he suppressing it? Letting it build up to blow further down the line? But *why?!*"

"He is a rogue, you said so yourself. There's no knowing what he's planning. But, with everything else you're dealing with, why do you let it get under your skin?"

He dove suddenly in front of her, eyes wild, his sickening, incredulous smile unrelenting "*Because now he has succeeded.* And we *still, still* have no idea in what! I *can't not* let it get to me, Taliel!" A thought flashed through his eyes, luring his gaze into the endless blackness behind her as his mind tumbled away. An owl hooted vapidly. "Traps. If we trapped the areas, anywhere else affected, anywhere they could be about to go - magic, or ambush - anything that can stop them--"

"Salus, we have to deal with Doana, mages, mage hunters and...ugh, just *so much* more - you would *really* go to such an extent just for one man?"

"*Yes!* This 'one man' could be trying to undermine *everything* I'm trying to do!" Another flash, another haze, and a snarl snapped free. "And the *king.*"

"The king?"

He whirled away and stomped onwards through the forest, leaving her to hurry after him. "To think I have to protect this country from itself," he hissed. "He's ordered us to withdraw from the Pavise Mountain Pass. Apparently, the Crown has been 'reviewing our activity' and are 'dissatisfied' with our results. They want us to withdraw and redirect our efforts because they've decided that the border is quiet and too low-risk to 'waste' resources on!"

"What?! But Kalokh were under Skilan's thumb not three months ago!"

"That's exactly what *I* said, but Malson hit back with 'there's no hard evidence that Skilan are looking our way again, nor that Kalokh are under their control'. When I reminded him that we *did* have evidence he just scoffed and said it was only enough to encourage suspicion. *None* of them understand the importance of what we do! How *can* we uncover evidence if we're being impeded at every sodding turn?! He even shrugged off the tribes when I reminded him of the *three* different camps on this side of the mountains alone! 'They've not been seen in a month', 'they've long moved on'!"

"Surely the Crown can't be that uninformed, not with reports from the military and the White Hammer?"

"You'd think so, wouldn't you? But that's not all: when I re-issued my request for an audience with the Crown, Malson just asked if I thought dissolving the Order was really necessary. *Malson.* The man who has gone as far as to make his *own* requests of the Arana against that very faction!"

"Well it is an extreme step--"

"It's also *necessary.* They need to be broken up and imprisoned before they can do any more damage." But he waved that subject away. "But Malson's *ambition* doesn't end there - just today he countermanded the Crown's orders with the suggestion that we move further *north* of the pass and try to deflect Ivaea and Kasire's war back out of Ivaea and across into Kasire. The Crown isn't worried about it moving closer towards us, he says, but he can 'see further than they can', then alluded to sharing my own foresight. Which rankled, but didn't surprise me, the foolish old coot..." His pace had finally slowed, but his eyes continued reeling with notions and conclusions. Taliel drew him to another stop and slipped her arms around him. He didn't seem to notice. "The Crown's ignorance is increasingly surprising, though not unexpected. But Malson's dissatisfaction and willingness to move against it is alarming. He becomes more suspicious with every pass of the sun, and for the life of me I can't think what he's possib--"

She caught his lips in hers, and his rigid muscles dropped and loosened in a single satisfying instant. The atmosphere evaporated like mist; the chill serenity rushed back in. His hands finally unclenched and sought her hips, where they rested with intent equal to the sudden passion of his kiss.

He broke off without warning.

Taliel staggered and stared up at him, perplexed, then followed his gaze around to the left while her heart thumped up into her throat.

A woman, skin as silver as the moon, hair as black as a magpie's feathers, stared back at them from the trees in silence. Her eyes were biting, unbefitting their soft, blush colour, and they lingered on Taliel the longest.

Salus didn't even sigh at the intrusion. He straightened, released her hips, and stepped towards the arrival with resolution. "I might be a while," he said with a fleeting smile of apology, but she could see that some other matter had already consumed him. She nodded and smiled back. Her eyes returned immediately to the woman.

Salus didn't notice the stare between them. And a moment later, they were gone.

His stomach leapt into somersaults. He thought he'd been ready for the teleportation, but it seemed that even when he knew it was coming it still turned him inside out. "Did I interrupt?" He heard the elf ask, to which he gave the quickest answer he could while steadying his nausea with deep and careful breaths.

"I didn't think so. You were quick to dismiss her. I'm glad you have your priorities straight."

A frigid realisation pierced his heart. He whipped around, searching the darkness behind them, but of course Taliel was nowhere to be seen. A regretful sigh rounded his shoulders, but the moment was done. And he was sure Taliel understood.

Smothering the renewed wash of dizziness, he looked around himself instead. He quickly found nothing to see but grass dotted with scattered trees, clusters of rocks and dry straw.

And an abyss yawning open inches from his toes.

He blanched and staggered backwards. "I thought we were going to Halen."

"Yes," Liogan replied lightly, peering into its depths like a child into a bucket. "This is it."

He stared at her, searching for any signs of tasteless amusement in her foul eyes, but he found nothing but a chillingly detached observation. The abyss stole back his attention.

She was mistaken. She had to be. Though badly rent, the old village still stood, albeit in ruins, but here there was nothing but a few piles of stone and frayed bundles of what could perhaps have been thatch, and the chasm itself was much too wide. An ominous, burning glow even rose in the near distance. They were *close*, perhaps - the familiar scent of farmland, heat and the grass of the northern steppes coloured the warm breeze, as well as that same strange, familiar peacefulness. But this...

Even so, his eyes grew in averse comprehension. "It *can't* be."

"Oh but it is. Now come along." The elf stepped away and followed the crumbling line of the chasm, leaving him to trail absently behind her as he peered over into the depths. Slowly, the slivered moonlight revealed the trophies wedged in the endless darkness: first, the same weathered rubble and thatch, then whole fragments of wall, of floor; fractured doors and what could have been a wardrobe lodged where the chasm narrowed or turned. His blood chilled. And it was all still far too little for a village of three dozen.

He couldn't drag his eyes away, even as a burning fury set his heart alight. "When did this happen?"

"About three days ago. But that's not important." She drew to a short stop, folded her arms with both elegance and self-importance, and cast her gaze down the length of her fine nose towards him. "To business: stand here. Now concentrate on your turquoise ripples." She waited first for the ire to leave his face, then the struggle. "Push them." Her hand raised at the sight of the words forming on his lips. "You know how."

A growl rattled in his throat, but he squashed down his irritation and closed his eyes.

The magic hummed around him; he'd found the ripples in moments, and it took only a little more concentration against the turmoil to locate their edges. Now he had only to cast against it. Anything would do, the magic needed only a catalyst. It was simple. He just had to release his magic.

In that moment, the matter became infinitely more complicated.

Doubt bustled in, dragging the gravity of his task behind it to drown any avenue of sense he could make. His jaw clenched, his mind clouded, and his concentration twisted and thundered onto nothing more than trying to ignore it.

But all the while the voice grew only louder.

The sudden brush of the tranquil breeze coiled around him as softly as silk. Almost immediately, his tensions began to ease. He fell into its comfort willingly, his heart growing lighter with every slackening beat - until something foreign snatched him and evoked a sudden and unnatural warning in the depths of his gut. There was a sharp edge to the breeze, faint but sinister, and he realised that in the passing of his doubt, his attention had fled with it.

With effort, he dragged himself out of the lull, pushed the serenity away, and locked his mind squarely onto his impossible task.

No. No, not impossible. It was simple. Simple. He knew how to do it, and it had to be within his capabilities or Liogan wouldn't have brought him here yet...unless of course she sought to embarrass him in order to make a point. About distractions, most likely. She'd certainly picked her moment to arrive...

No. Now he really was letting himself get distracted. And the longer he took to act, the worse the burden became and the nearer that unnatural peace slithered back towards him.

A spell. He needed a spell. ...What spell? *Any* spell? Light? Fire? Heat? Would something so small and simple really work against such potent magic? Surely it needed something grander... A thought slipped in, an outrageous idea: could he possibly draw the land back together?

He stalled. As wrong as it felt, as heinous, though it grated against every thread of his principles, he knew that he needed these rifts left open. *Turunda* needed them. Sealing them wasn't an option.

But that in itself presented him with a route of action.

He steeled himself and silenced the chatter of his sabotaging spectre, raised his hands and began contorting his fingers. He did what he could with the signs he new, weaving pieces from the few relevant spells he'd learned and released them with as much confidence and focus as he could find. But he had no way of knowing if his attempt to break the land had succeeded, for the earth began to shake too immediately to follow the thought.

He heard the ground beside him crumble, felt the daunting chasm widen, and watched with his mind's eye as a new crack began to form, splintering away from the main body and snaking north-east at speed. His heart lurched in alarm.

"Temper it," he heard her command.

"How?!"

"You know how."

He snapped a strangled curse but immediately tightened his focus, refining the power, flow and intent of his spell to wall in the sides of the escaping ripples. There was no time to panic nor entertain his doubt.

"Now get ahead of it...that's it..."

The walls moved ahead, leading by an inch, paving a gulley that funnelled back into the chasm. Stubbornly, the magic tried continuously to regain its freedom, to spill over, surge back ahead and veer off to wreak its own destruction. Sweat rolled down his jaw and his pulse began to throb in his skull, but Salus managed to keep it in check.

"Now steer it."

"Where?" His voice was strained.

"Ausokh."

He barely managed to maintain his hold. "Ausokh's alread--"

"Which makes it perfectly receptive. Now steer it."

Dizziness gripped him, spinning behind his eyes. More splinters broke away from his channel, but there was nothing he could do. He could only just maintain his concentration on the main body, which, slowly, began at last to move east.

The tremors of the ground deepened beneath him.

"Weave your magic into it."

"Ho--"

"*You know how.* Encourage it, reinforce the momentum, create an undercurrent - anything to keep it moving."

'Weave it in... A command to keep moving...'

But his mind was slowing in fatigue. He could feel his strength waning - and in noticing it, it crumbled. A hot surge of panic seized him as he fought to get it back, and it took him a long while in his struggle to notice that the chasm had continued unerringly on towards the east without his guidance. Then, above the tremendous rumbling, came Liogan's grunt of approval. He wasn't completely sure what he'd done, but in that moment, exhaustion triumphed and his efforts finally shattered.

Time broke down to a crawl. Sound dulled, scent weakened, and even the tremors beneath his feet seemed to have grown distant. But as his eyes fluttered open, seeking grounding against disorientation, he was struck immediately by the ominous view of fire. The burning glow that rose from the bowels of the earth a quarter of a mile away had intensified and crept closer, and as his eyes focused with dread upon it, he discovered that the last few wretched remains of Halen had vanished.

It couldn't have been saved, he knew this well; there was no way to reverse the damage and nothing enough of anything left to repair. But...it had been his own hand to cast the final strike. His own actions had eradicated the last trace of Halen from the map. A rush of guilt chilled his blood at the notion.

And then a cold, calculating wonder moved in right behind it. His eyes dropped to his hands, and he pondered...

"Well," Liogan interrupted, sparking immediate soreness, "as much as it physically hurts to have the words pass my lips, you have done well."

He looked around in tempered surprise. "A compliment?"

"An observation based on low expectations," she corrected with a wave of her hand. "However, you've not been using magic all that long - had elven blood not streaked your ancestry, you wouldn't have even been able to distinguish the magic from its effects for at least another year. So perhaps I was wrong to presume so little." She flicked her blue curls over her shoulder and straightened, exuding a sudden supremacy that was in no doubt summoned to repair the damage to her ego. "Now: come along."

Salus wobbled as their bleak surroundings shifted again. But the ground was still riven, still shook, still rumbled; the night was still dark, the stars still bare. But the scent on the air had changed. It was cooler, moister. "East," he realised as his nausea settled, and cast Liogan a suspicious look. "Where are we?"

"Ausokh."

He'd suspected as much, but looked around frantically anyway, catching his bearings by the stars. The chasms were vast and the light even lower where the mountains hid the reach of the moon, but he was sure as he strained north-west that he could see something approaching.

"A trick of the darkness," she said as though reading his mind, "but it is approaching. It will be here in a few days."

"What do I need to do?"

"Nothing; it will come." She grasped him roughly by the shoulders, her long fingernails sinking unapologetically into his flesh, and turned him to face the imposing line of mountains. "Do it again."

He hesitated at the effortless drop of her words. "What?"

"Again."

"I *can't*."

"You can - strength and willpower are not exhaustible. You have as much of it as you believe you do. Now do it again." She held his head still as it began to shake in protest. "Do you want to keep Turunda safe? Then do it again."

He turned as she released him and again he surveyed her haughty visage for any sign of trickery. But, just as the last time, there was nothing but a cool expectation. He bristled. "Look," he snapped, "I might have elven blood, but - and as you *never* hesitate to point out - I'm *not* an elf. I *can't* do it again, not right away."

"Are you so sure?"

"Yes," he replied flatly even as he fought against a fatigued spasm in his leg, "I am." He didn't like the way her eyes narrowed in thought.

"I find you a very strange man. You have so much strength in your convictions and so much certainty in yourself, and yet when it comes to magic, you falter."

"What?"

"You heard me. You doubt, you stall, you weigh and measure beyond what you need to make a decision. What is it? Do you not trust magic? Or do you not trust yourself?" She cocked her head. "Or is it just me you're afraid of?"

His blood boiled.

She sighed emphatically before he could find his tongue, and pouted like a child which just seared his veins all the more. "Well, that really is a shame." But she didn't sound particularly sorry, and turned to wander a few careless steps away. "Because, unfortunately, we're not going anywhere until you *do*. And I," she dropped upon a méridienne that appeared from nowhere and lounged comfortably across it, "have all the time in the world."

Chapter 27

White; ice-white, bone-white. Black trails, streams, rivers of blood; sharp edges, thorns, spikes. Pain. Mind-numbing, consuming torment.

Fire burst, blinding, as bright and cold as the sun; skin seared, peeled, blood rushed to the surface.

Cries closed in, surrounded, screaming in the blackness, begging, why, why, why didn't he stop himself, why did he let this happen?

Agony. Thought obliterated, primal terror locked the tongue, strangled and smothered reason. Madness itched, scratching the edge of consciousness, clawing inwards, raking ever nearer.

Flickers of brutal, bestial faces invaded the flames, the darkness, the abyss of terror; of light; flashes of silver, of black, of blue.

Smiles, grins, grimaces; cackling, smugness, satisfaction.

Torture, blood burst, skin ripped, shredded by bone, by claw, by madness, by magic. Flames danced over black veins, searing alabaster skin, hotter than a pyre, cold and white.

Suspicion rode the madness, doubt followed the tracks.

Had they planned this all along?

Wailing, pleading, blame, betrayal, why, why, why didn't he stop himself? Why did he let this happen?

Death and fury; bodies blackened, hair smoked; eyes wide, white and heartbroken.

Aria's face.

Consumed by fire.

Rathen jolted back to the saddle.

Dusk remained, but the air in the fells was distinctly still. The few trees to dot the gentle slopes stood indifferently around him, the invisible eyes hidden within their branches passing over him in disregard. There was no fire, no screaming, not even the song of a nightlark nor the chirp of a cricket. Nothing. All was calm. Sickeningly calm.

A ragged breath of relief escaped his lips and his bearings tumbled back into place, but even so his heart continued to hammer so fast his stomach churned beneath it. His skin was soaked. And all from a memory. A memory as clear, fresh and chilling as the nightmare itself had been those two nights ago.

He glanced around at his company. No one appeared to have noticed his absence. Coolly, he tugged his shirt from his sticky chest. Then faltered as Aria looked up and around at him. Her beautiful skin was smooth, perfectly clear of blood, burns or bruises, but there was a concern in her saucer-sized eyes, no doubt summoned from his sudden jerk but one that shocked him all the same.

Instinctively, he reached out and embraced her. Concern dissolved into a smile and she recoiled with playful disgust, but wriggled back against him when he obligingly withdrew.

Darkness was falling. He'd either been daydreaming for a long while or he hadn't noticed how late it had grown. They would likely stop for the night before long.

But as noise rose in the near distance and firelight glowed as they crested a small hill, they knew their rest would have to wait.

Refugees had little mind for anyone but themselves, a fact not unreasonable given their circumstances, and so they surely wouldn't notice the passing of a small group beyond a quick measure of their likelihood to cause trouble, which a child's presence alone would deter. But it was unanimously agreed - barring Aria, who was growing restless - that it wasn't worth the risk.

Their course adjusted, avoiding the eyes of the refugee camp, they continued onwards for another hour before settling in the privacy of a deep but refreshingly natural gully somewhere between Red Heath and Attleton. Anthis vanished no sooner than they'd hitched the horses, which no one felt compelled to acknowledge, and Garon wasted no time in establishing a perimeter and seeking out whatever information that could be found in the vicinity.

Among those remaining, it was Rathen's turn to assemble the food, and after three nights of easy bread and salted meat, everyone shared Aria's desire for something 'wet'. And so he set to the task immediately, grateful for the distraction - until the warmth of the evening, joined with the heat of the entrancing flames, became more powerful than the obligation to turn, stir or cover, and he soon slipped back into daydream.

He returned with another start to find Eyila sitting quietly beside him, watching Aria with a smile as she thrust about her toy sword beneath Petra's watchful eye.

He played it off as though shifting his weight, but she must have noticed. The assumption was confirmed when she spoke a moment later, though it wasn't what he'd expected.

"She could be saving our lives in no time."

Rathen followed her gaze as the young girl thrust and leapt backwards in a single quick movement. It wasn't perfect, he could see that much, and Petra voiced it, but it was fluid enough that she maintained her balance and dove into another attack before parrying a phantom blow. He breathed a laugh, but his humour didn't last. "She doesn't need a sword to do that."

"I would agree," she replied lightly, "but you and I both have magic."

"And she has all of us. She should never be in such a position."

"Which she surely knows. But it's not necessarily what could be *ahead* that would stoke such a determination..."

His jaw tightened. "...No..."

Eyila sent him a sideways look, and her white eyebrows knotted briefly. She offered him a smile. "I'm sorry."

"It's all right, I can see what you're doing." He sighed as he looked back towards them, then returned his attention to the simmering pot. "I disapprove, but I'm not going to stop it. I just hope she never needs it - now, tomorrow, or in fifteen years."

"Don't we all..."

It took him a while to notice that her gaze had shifted onto him, and he stalled at the power of the concern in her pale blue eyes. And the speculation.

His brow twitched.

A curious thought appeared in that moment, and he then regarded the tribal mage with a speculation of his own, wondering if she could sense the depth of what was on his mind, if perhaps she recognised something - if, maybe, she'd experienced something similar herself and had kept it just as quiet.

He looked away as the pot began to bubble. "How have you been sleeping?"

She frowned. "Sleeping?"

"Yeah, any trouble drifting off? Fatigue the next morning? Any...dreams?"

"Why do you ask?"

Now he saw suspicion in her eyes, and this time it was not one that hinted at understanding. He smiled offhandedly to defuse it. "Well, we do have magic, but we don't seem to be any safer for it. If this chaos has shown us anything it's that it has its own power over us."

"It does seem to..." she sighed deeply and looked away in troubled thought. "No, I've been sleeping fine. Aside from being locked up in forests all the time. I miss the wind. The heat. It's cold out here. But no strange dreams. Nothing I...can't explain..." She looked up, then, and it was clear that her suspicion had resolved. "But *you* have."

He scoffed a little too suddenly, earning a smile of victory. "What? No, not at all. I'm just making sure *you're* all right - the magic is having a powerful effect on you, I'm just trying to understand it so that maybe I can find some way to help." He held her gaze in an attempt to persuade her, and after a long, silent moment, she looked away, unconvinced but unwilling to fight it out of him. He wondered, then, how she could know him so well.

"I'm fine," she replied at last, "while out of its reach. But when we draw close...I can feel something...*pulling* me. A promise of..." she hesitated, struggling to find the word, hindered by either language or her own comprehension. She soon gave up, and a distressed sorrow set in and coloured her voice. "A promise of all my problems and worries and sadness being taken away. And I feel a great yearning inside, but it's *maddening*, like I could never, ever run fast enough to keep up with it if I gave in."

"'If?'"

She smiled, but appeared only mournful. "What it promises is impossible. I know this. But in spite of that, there's something else inside me that responds to it, that desperately tries to reach it, but it's not...it *isn't* me. I've wondered if perhaps it's my magic, but I can't understand how that could be. It is its own being, but is it really capable of something like that...?" She shook the cascading thought away and hugged her knees into her chest. "It doesn't matter. But when I try to fight against it it feels as though I'm...surrounded by...*something*, I'm outnumbered and that it's only a matter of time before I can't fight against it any more...and each time I feel I become a little weaker. Or the yearning grows that much stronger."

"Do you feel anything else? Anything of the magic around you?"

"Yes." He straightened and tried to suppress his apprehension at the deathly drop in her tone. "I feel a frightening sense of belonging."

"Belonging?"

"That I should stay there. It's a...*need*, one stronger than I ever had at home, even before my magic surfaced, even when I was still in training. That I would be safe and happy there. Content forever. At peace."

"At peace..." It was too familiar. He shifted and again attempted to conceal his anxiety, flexing his fingers and reducing the cooking flames to a meagre glow. "And, otherwise, you feel assaulted? That the magic is trying to...I don't know, smother you or something?"

But her bronze lips pursed, and a thoughtful furrow creased her brow that both quashed his dreadful hope and fired his alarm. "No, no I wouldn't say that at all, just surrounded. Like it's all beckoning me close, and inching closer itself every time." Her frown turned onto him. "You look disappointed."

"Hmm? Oh, no no, just thinking. Just thinking..."

A light breeze rolled through the gully, rifling the embers. A gentle sigh passed beside him, as though the draft had swept away her troubles - something he deemed distinctly possible - but as she placed her hand on his shoulder, he felt his own diminish as well. "Thank you."

"For?"

Soft footsteps descending between the ridges snapped both of their attention, but neither rose at the familiar presence. Until a dark shape darted in from the other side and hurtled straight towards the startled inquisitor and his exhausted horse. But it didn't strike. Instead, it stopped quite abruptly mere inches from his face. And hovered there in the darkness.

"A sparrow?" Rathen frowned, watching the little bird flit impatiently to and fro. "I thought the White Hammer couldn't help us anymore?"

"No," Garon agreed, extending his hand cautiously for it to alight upon, but as he removed the message from the casing upon its back and moved towards the dying fire, his own bewildered frown set even deeper. Petra and Aria joined them from their tame duel and watched intently as he read.

Then, when his expression had settled into stark perplexity, he handed it to Rathen.

The mage blinked at the small fold of parchment.

The others gathered behind him as he took and tentatively opened it, reading it surreptitiously for themselves over his shoulder. "This isn't the White Hammer," Petra quickly observed, looking in confusion towards the inquisitor. "Who's 'O'? And why is a White Hammer sparrow coming with a message for *Rathen?*"

"What does it say?" Eyila asked while Rathen folded it with a grunt, and handed it to Aria who protested at not yet having finished. She proceeded to read it aloud for Eyila's benefit, but neither seemed to follow.

"I know who it is," he said with a strange smile, "the rushed writing - an active mind running five miles ahead."

"Anthis?" Aria asked, increasingly confused as she struggled through the abbreviations.

"No - do you remember Owan, the man we met in Stonton? Him. And it looks like *he* needs *my* help." Aria handed the parchment back, declaring, unsurprisingly, that neither she nor Eyila understood. But before he could enlighten them, both mages spun around, hands raised, fingers loose and ready.

Swords were ripped free of sheaths on instinct, and all eyes pierced the flickering darkness.

Anthis stalled at the edge of the emberlight and shrank beneath the stares.

A collective sigh of relief and annoyance eased the sudden tension, and Rathen was the first to glide past his return and the magical hum that surrounded him. "He wants me to analyse the magic," he continued, making room for the sheepish historian who approached with his usual compulsive interest even despite the euphoria in his eyes. "To find out just exactly how it's affecting the elements."

"The wind, the marsh, the earth," Petra nodded. "But can't he do that himself?"

"Given the state of things, no. And he wouldn't be asking *me* if he wasn't desperate." He frowned back down at the paper for a long, silent moment. "He must be trying to work on it from within the Order's walls..."

"*Can* you help him?" She asked delicately. "I mean, you weren't a scholar, and this sounds kind of..." she let it hang.

"Actually, for once, I think I can." He paused for another moment, until his eyes took on a cerebral colour more suited to Anthis if not for the touch of difficulty at the edges. "Magic is unique in its structure," he stated, clearly in the midst of gathering his thoughts. "There's nothing else like it in existence, just like rock, fire, air and water. And it's just as natural. But, unlike the rest, it's comparatively complex and should never form, nor be left, on its own... It *isn't* raw, like I'd first thought, but the chains have degraded in such a way that some of them are still powerful, they've just lost their subject, so they're replacing the original subject of their spell with something else around them, and it...from what we've seen, it seems that elements fit the bill...almost perfectly..."

They waited patiently while he lost himself in thought, though he seemed now to be speaking only to himself. "Khry's Glory was void of elements - void of *anything* but magic...could it be seeking the closest thing to itself to fill in the gap? Something equally unique and natural?"

"But he said it was weaving *into* the elements."

"Well for once I think he's wrong," a statement to which Eyila nodded her agreement. "But it *is* having a dire effect on them rather than just turning benign like any other degraded spell would. But the difference between these spells and any other is that these didn't necessarily degrade, but their subject *did* - and if that subject was a conjured...chair, for example, then should that chair spell degrade but an overlaying one for comfort *not*, that overlaying spell would be without a subject."

"And it's replacing the subject with the closest thing to itself..." Anthis nodded slowly. "Eizariin said something similar..."

"But why *haven't* they degraded?"

"They have - the effects they're having were never what they were intended to. But that whole place was made of magic, so everything in there would have been wrapped in preservation spells to make sure it held together, and they, by design, are supposed to last. These spells are just small fragments of larger spells that have retained just enough information to still function. Like if you were to tear a letter into pieces, you could have one piece with just two lines on it, but those two lines would still be legible and possibly still make sense even without the rest of it.

"Most of the surviving chains are benign - I think there are only two or three in any one place having an effect. But those, crucially, are more or less complete. And if one of them latches onto just the right thing, it could easily result in...well, everything it already has, and more besides. A spell for, say, warmth, could attach itself to a patch of forest and it will just get a little warmer than the surroundings. But if that spell attached itself to somewhere *already* warm - like a patch in the desert - it could be much more drastic. That patch would heat up much more quickly than the rest, then rise quicker than the rest, cool quicker--"

"And a great wind would be born. And moisture would be burned away and rise into rain clouds, while the cool air that moved down in place of the rising heat would heat up itself, rise itself, and more cool air would sweep in beneath it while yet more clouds form." Eyila's eyes were chilling.

"And if the spell had lost its temperature regulation, the cycle could repeat itself very, very quickly." Rathen sighed. "The results aren't something the world was ever prepared for. Even the chains of beauty have played a part. Loggerhead came to a standstill when everyone became entranced, didn't it?"

"I didn't realise it was so complicated," Petra frowned. Her hand shifted to rest upon the hilt of her sword as if it could offer some solution to an intangible problem. She looked across Rathen and Eyila, then to Garon, who appeared just as pensive. "It's getting worse, too, isn't it? Khry's Glory has been closed off but magic is still gathering and 'latching' onto things."

"Mmm...I'm just speculating now, but I think some might even be feeding off of each other. Chains with just the right remnants to compliment one another and form a more complete spell, and some of those may be enhancing *existing* spells. It would also explain why spells cast nearby exacerbates the situation..." He glanced up from the paper and across the dubious expressions. He smiled regretfully and folded it away. "But I could be wrong. It could just be slower-moving spells. Either way: as Petra said, Khry's Glory *is* closed. There's nothing new to come out of that accursed place. And I'll give Owan all I know, and find out whatever more I can...though...that may be easier said than done..."

"Why?"

"Because under that magic I can't--b-because, the Zi'veyn, I'll have to do it before using it or there will be nothing left to see. It will take longer..."

"What do you think he intends to do with the information?"

Rathen gave Garon a flat look. "Nothing as sinister as what's going through your mind, Inquisitor. He's just trying to do his bit, as we are. He's never been one to sit still and responsibility has hung over him just as strongly as it has me. He just chose a different direction to chase it."

"Yes. And he also wants to know if we have anything to do with the absence of magic in Wrenroot and Borer's Teeth." The officer's eyes darkened. Rathen straightened and matched it.

"Because he wants a solution as much as we do."

"I hate to feed Garon's paranoia," said Petra, "but we shouldn't tell him. Anything we can avoid falling into Salus's hands - this bird came by an official channel, he's probably monitoring them. We can't risk it."

"I know - so I'll tell him only what he needs to know. Which is nothing to do with the Zi'veyn."

Aria's eyes narrowed at the note of disappointment in his tone and the rounding of his shoulders as he tucked the note into his sleeve - a point that Anthis, too, didn't miss. But when the historian noticed Garon's gaze come to rest upon him, he was torn between standing tall in personal defence as Rathen had, or shrinking back under the pressure. His inability to do the first irritated him.

"Did you find anything in Attleton?"

"Like what?"

"News. Information."

"Would he have noticed a thing in that state?"

"Whether I would or not, I didn't," he replied shortly, though Petra hadn't spoken unkindly. "Did *you*, Inquisitor?"

"No," he sighed resentfully, "refugees don't really have access to current news. We'll have to wait for Mokhan, we're certain to find something there. We'll move on north in the morning."

"Actually," Anthis stepped forwards while the inquisitor turned to begin his patrol, despite Rathen returning to the fire and removing the lid from the fragrant pot, "Banmar Dells isn't far out of our way. We might do well to swing south for an hour or so first, take a look at the magic there."

But Garon was already shaking his head. "We can't linger. Kulokhar is only two days' ride away. It's too close."

"And it will still be two days' ride away from Mokhan," Rathen said as Aria handed him the first bowl to serve the steaming stew, which he'd privately decided was absurd given the warmth of the evening. "The difference is that Banmar isn't a city, and removing the magic is the only reason we came out here to begin with. And, as it seems that I now have even *more* to do, I agree with Anthis."

"As do I," Petra declared, and the rest nodded their concurrence.

The inquisitor's face darkened, upon her in particular, but, and much to everyone's surprise, he didn't offer any argument. Instead, with a sharp snarl of irritation, he snapped away and trudged back up above the ravine.

"What will the ruin be like?" Aria asked Anthis, twirling towards him with eyes almost aglow in excitement while the rest shook their heads at the inquisitor's see-sawing priorities. But the glum look he gave her as he took the bowl she handed him quietened that enthusiasm. She sighed heavily in disappointment. "It's just a few rocks again, isn't it?"

"It's barely even that."

"You sound disappointed yourself," Petra observed.

"Because it's little more than a large flat stone with weather-beaten carvings. And it's been studied to death."

"Well, it's just as well we're not here to study."

"And that means we should be bored?"

Eyila chuckled as she sat down beside him, at which he shuffled, smiled and immediately turned red. Rathen caught Petra's wrist as she instinctively moved to separate them.

The following morning, as they rode south through the warm, open fields, all eyes surveyed closely across the sparse and slender trees. There was no movement but for a distant herd of fallow deer and the flying to and fro of birds catching insects on the wing. But their exposure set a fire behind them, and even Eyila found herself missing the concealment of the forests.

But as Petra scanned the east from the rear of the company and noticed, purely by chance, the split stump of an ancient tree and the single limb that pointed along their heading, she suddenly realised the significance of that 'large flat stone'. She looked ahead to Anthis, who peered around with the same vigilance as the rest. "The stone - is that--"

"Rowan's Repentance." He looked back in surprise. "Yes, it is. You hadn't guessed?"

Aria frowned with curiosity between the two of them. "What is Rowan's Rip-rep--"

"Repentance - it's a Craitic parable about a thief who was punished by Vastal and chose this spot to ask for Her forgiveness."

"Would you please tell it?" Eyila also looked around with a quiet light of interest, which stalled Anthis's tongue. So Petra took over.

"It starts with a very dry summer. A fire spread through farmland, destroying a whole village's food and livelihood, and one man blamed the Goddess and strayed from the Temple in protest. For a month, he stole food and lied to try to get by, but things only got worse for him. One day, after he stole five loaves of bread that a baker had made for Communion at the Temple, he fled through the village and twisted his ankle on the dais of the Goddess's statue. In that moment, as he looked up at the statue, he realised that he was being punished. His initial misfortune had come from a fire that had burned the fields that the *whole village* had relied upon for food and work, but while they'd helped one another and rebuilt from the ashes, and their fields had become more fertile and crops more bountiful for it, only that one man had turned to crime and selfishness and preyed upon the people around him, all of whom were under just as much pressure to provide as he was.

"For nights he couldn't sleep, he was so plagued by nightmares, so he came out here, stood upon a large stone and remained there for twenty two days and nights to repent to the Goddess, one for every theft."

But Aria's face had slowly screwed up into a tight little knot, and she turned towards her father. "That doesn't make any sense. Why did he do that instead of apologising to the people he stole from and trying to make things right with them?"

"Because," he replied lightly, "some people feel the need to do things in a more round about sort of way."

"And what happened?" Eyila asked, riveted.

"Vastal spoke to him."

"He hadn't eaten or slept in three weeks," Rathen mumbled with a roll of his eyes. "I'm surprised a roaming deer didn't speak to him. Or a giant wedge of cheese."

Aria giggled, until another abrupt and pensive knot twisted her face again. "Daddy, wouldn't it take longer than a month for the fields to grow back?"

"We have a similar story."

Anthis looked up. "You do?"

Eyila nodded and cast him a wonderful smile. "About a priestess named Oluu'a. She'd been in Aya'u's grace for seven years but felt that her connection to the

255

Goddess was waning. Unlike the younger priestesses, when she meditated she heard nothing new on the winds. After three seasons, she began to believe that Aya'u had rejected her, so she climbed to the top of the highest butte in the centre of the Singing Sands and sat in meditation for half a moon to attain a greater connection with Her."

"And?"

"On the fifteenth night, she died."

"...Oh."

"Aya'u had taken her into Her wings. What she had mistaken as hearing nothing was actually perfect attunement. She was hearing constantly, but with nothing significant presenting itself, she hadn't noticed the ascension."

"You're sure it wasn't heatstroke?" Rathen cast Anthis an innocent look for the sharp nudge he'd received, but Eyila only smiled with the unwavering confidence of the faithful.

"Her m'yona amulet was gone. Her amulet and her spirit. All else remained as if in meditation."

"It could have been stolen."

"Yes - but it *hadn't* been. There were no footprints."

"The wind--" Anthis nudged him again, but still Eyila only smiled wider.

"The wind had been still that night. All but for evidence of a single brief whipping around where her body remained. The sand beyond was undisturbed, and there are too few qanats in that vast region for even a desperate or ambitious thief to risk the trek. Priestesses themselves rarely ventured so far."

But before Rathen could provide yet another possibility, Garon pulled his bay to a stop at the crest of the hill. The others drew up beside him and stared in equal surprise. Fog obscured the near distance, spanning the width of the shallow valley, penetrated only by the tops of trees. A chilling serenity reached out like ghostly fingers towards them, drawing them in with a deathly fascination. Instinct told them to turn away. But that was their route - and very likely their destination.

Garon urged his nervous mare onwards. With uneasy looks, the others did the same.

The edge of the magic hit half way down the slope. Rathen braced, but Eyila succumbed immediately, and the rest looked around in awe, their skittish horses moving tighter together. The fog seemed constantly out of reach, the hidden forest growing no closer despite every monotonous hoof beat, but the wisps had already encircled them, sneaking around to cut off their retreat and steal away their bearings. Soft patches of white light were the only fixed landmarks until they levelled with the first trees, but their origins were phantom, impossible either to see or guess at, while gentle tones of powder blue and lilac shifted about like glow flies. But all the while, their surroundings remained eternally bleak and grey.

Their skin soon began to prickle, goose-flesh spreading at a sudden chill that intensified as swiftly as a raging polar gale, and it took no one too long to notice that the land was not grey by fog alone. Unsettled glances rippled as the horses' hooves crunched on through crisp frost.

But Rathen had long projected himself beyond the confines of the ghostly web.

The fog had heralded magic; for the first time, he'd had warning, and the moment they'd passed the threshold he'd wasted no time in narrowing his focus into a search, probing the chains, their movements and anchors for anything he hadn't noticed before. But while he'd prepared against the swarming magic, it was merciless in asserting its dominance. Within moments, his armour began to thin.

Urgency redoubled his efforts. He could do nothing about the assault so far from the magnetism's centre without risking an oversight, and while concentration seemed increasingly impossible, his choices were limited: try, or succumb. Terror made the decision for him.

His mind surged onwards, tracing and retracing a haphazard path through every mark and detail, collecting and recollecting everything that stood out, anything of note. It wasn't long before discoveries began to diminish, but he didn't spare a moment to wonder at whether or not there was anything left to find, or if his focus had finally been exhausted. He didn't dare stop for a heartbeat.

It wasn't until a sudden pressure tightened around his arm that his desperate absorption finally shattered, but as his eyes bolted down to the cuff beneath the weave of his shirt, his heart burning in his throat, he found only Aria's hand and a quiet, worried look in her misty blue eyes. His relief was glancing. He spun in the saddle without even an assuaging smile, hurriedly fortifying his mind and noticing, at last, that they had come to a stop.

Then the magnetism tugged, and his eyes landed on Rowan's Repentance - and the figure seated upon the frosted ground behind it.

Each of them eyed the stubbled old man warily from their saddles, and the dark, official cloak he had wrapped himself in. No one was willing to approach the lone mage, ask him what he was doing, if he was all right; none would risk provoking or startling him. But neither could they leave him behind and move on. This was the spot; the magnetism always centred around structures like this altar. They'd all learned that much. But they were also sorely aware of just exactly what they were seeing.

And Rathen above all others.

Aria released her hold on his arm as he dismounted despite Garon's command, but the quietly snapped words didn't reach him. No one tried to pull him back. Everyone held their breath; hands hovered over sword hilts. Neither man nor mage reacted.

But for the slightest twitch of his lips, thoughts shaping on his breath, the man was deathly still. His aged and haunted eyes stared off for miles. There was a stark conflict within them. Confusion. Disappointment. Rathen saw it in a second even amongst his own struggles. Otherwise, they were empty. The man was completely unaware of his presence. And Rathen didn't announce himself - harried by his own alarm, he didn't think to say a word, but there would have been no use if he had. Trapped in her trance, Eyila didn't respond even to being shaken, and this man was much farther gone.

He lifted the wrist that lay limp upon his knee. Again, Garon's command didn't register, and neither did the others' gasps of alarm. But the man didn't react either.

Rathen's magic immediately penetrated his skin, probing carefully into his veins, and he reined in his focus before it could spill on ahead in a maddened frenzy. He tripped a few times, but even in his torment he located quickly what he'd both feared and expected: a terrible heat, the engagement of a spell with no intention in place, magic moving in blood too cool to keep up - magic moving, but by the will of neither itself nor its host.

All identical to Eyila's ailments, but far more concentrated.

But there was nothing he could do even had aid occurred to him. In that moment, as he gathered the last, faint details, his own struggles crashed upon him as though the sky had collapsed.

He launched to his feet, dropping the man's hand before squeezing his own against the quivering of his bones, and hurried back to his horse to dive into the saddlebag, muttering feverishly as he rifled through.

Aria watched in distress from the saddle, and Garon appeared quietly beside them, casting the child a reassuring gesture while watching both mages intently. She gasped in fright as her father spun away, the glint in his hand revealing his prize, and dashed off with an urgency rivalled only by fleeing. He fell perfectly still when he reached the altar.

A charge set in the air. Quietly, Garon freed his sword from its sheath. Petra appeared beside him in equal vigilance. Anthis moved closer between Eyila and Aria, ready to grasp the reins should either's mount spook. No one was sure just what they expected to happen, but they had no doubt that something would.

As they strained, their ears began to pick out the faintest sounds - breath, mutters, the gurgle of a stomach - and their eyes found the branches of the nearest trees. The beechwood soon began to gather through the fog, drawing slowly closer, peering down upon them in interest. They stared back with caution. It took a long while before they realised that the cloud was receding, and that the frost beneath their feet had begun to thaw.

All eyes drummed back onto the trembling mage.

Nervously, they waited. Minutes dragged as the fog crept away, the ice melted, the phantasmal lights diminished and the air returned to summer warmth, but, in time, the wooded slopes had finally returned to normality.

But Rathen didn't straighten. He didn't collapse. He didn't exhale in fatigue. Though his task had come to an end and the floating Zi'veyn descended gracefully into his hands, he didn't move.

Their earlier trepidation rose as the relic struck his palm and tumbled to the ground. But as they stared, trying to read his purpose through the shaking of his shoulders, another far more sudden movement ensnared their attention. The haggard old mage had burst furiously to his feet, surrounded by the popping and flashing of small, blinding lights.

It was then that Rathen crumpled, and the mage surged for him, clambering feverishly over the stone that divided them while he landed face-down in the dirt.

The two swordsmen were in motion in a heartbeat. Leaping between them, Garon struck with the flat of his blade, thrusting the crazed assailant back while Petra seized Rathen by the shoulder and dragged him away to safety. His fever was evident upon contact. She cursed none too carefully. "Not again, Rathen," she grunted, setting him down against the furthest tree, "not now..."

The horses bellowed in alarm behind them, and she turned in time to see Garon strike the ground beneath the pressure of a spell. The mage dove for him immediately. And she was too far to help.

Another force of windless power suddenly blasted by, clipping the mage mid-leap, throwing him aside even as Garon braced his sword across himself. Petra spared the briefest glance to its source: the reins of both mounted horses in one hand, the palm of Anthis's right was bared flat towards the mage.

She didn't indulge her shock, gratitude or disgust. "Keep clear of him," she called instead, and left Rathen huddled, burning and shaking, whispering for them all to flee while she leapt towards the rising inquisitor.

The mage scrambled back to his feet with a ghastly convulsion of weeping and whooping while she snatched Garon by the shirt, but as she dragged him away despite his protests, the mage didn't follow. It only alarmed them more.

He began staggering around as if in a daze, clawing his face and clutching his head while the lights popped faster and fire sparked like lightning. The smell of burning wood, cloth and skin began to outweigh that of the forest.

Garon stopped struggling. As another abrupt blast propelled the raving mage deeper among the trees, he and Petra hurried back to Rathen, lifted his limp body between them and carried him to safety while Anthis steered the panicking horses away, keeping his distance on Petra's command.

Mercifully, every back was turned when the explosion came. But the sharp, startled, agonised shriek carried for miles.

Anthis soon dismounted, his hair standing on end from that haunting sound, but he didn't venture far. Aria began to scramble down, but he pushed her back into the saddle. "Stay there," he ordered with an unnatural firmness. She cast her huge, glistening eyes upon him, and though they were filled in that brief moment with protest and fright, she heeded him. Her little knuckles turned white as she clutched the reins even tighter.

Garon cursed as he snatched his hand back from Rathen's forehead. "He's scolding." He looked across the shaking body towards Petra, and noticed immediately a strange colour in her eyes. He knew what it meant. "This has happened before."

Reluctantly, she nodded. "A week ago. He got control of himself in the end, but it didn't last this long. And this time he's exhausted by the Zi'veyn..." They watched him shake and mutter, warning them away on a thin voice. Her jaw tightened. "He wouldn't talk about it afterwards, I don't know what happened. But I don't think there's anything we can do..."

Garon rose. "Get your bolas. Stay with him." He ignored her questioning look and hurried towards the others, whose expectation he also discarded, and retrieved a number of waterskins. Then he approached Eyila, but it was clear in an instant that the girl was still enthralled. But he had to try. "Fever," he said, "do you have anything for a fever?" She looked right through him. "Eyila, listen to me, do you--" A pouch suddenly hung in front of him, extended from the sash hidden beneath her cloak. She looked down slowly, and while there was still a great distance in her eyes, there was also a spark of familiarity. He took it, bowed his thanks, and hurried back, realising only as he returned and opened it that he hadn't a clue what to do with it.

Petra, however, took it from him immediately and began rolling two of the small, fibrous red balls between her hands. They broke apart in moments and released a miasma that quickly cast a chill in Garon's eyes, reminiscent of mint but for its distinctly sweet fragrance and the lethargy that it induced. He leaned back and shook it off, watching as Petra pressed it against the mage's slick forehead.

"How did you know what to do?" He asked, tempering his surprise.

"I've seen Eyila do it. These are fur beetles. She used them in antiseptic - when we fell in that--"

"I recall."

She smiled apologetically, then chuckled as he shook his head in shame. He glanced up at the pleasant sound, and for a moment, their gazes locked. Until they both looked away.

Slowly, Rathen stopped shaking, his temperature began to drop, and within minutes was sitting up on his own, head in his hands, an empty waterskin at his feet, and Aria clinging closely to his side, her young face warped in grief.

Chapter 28

"What do you mean, 'it's not right'?"

Rathen squirmed beneath the expectant stares and tightened his folded arms. Half an hour had passed yet they'd remained uneasily close to the forest while he'd recovered, and in that time he'd made a rather distressing discovery. Even Eyila, who had slowly returned to her senses, seemed to detect the same thing. She was the only one not looking at him in dismay.

"Well...the spells have stopped--"

"We can see that much," Garon snapped impatiently. "The point?"

"The, uh...the magic is still here." The thickened silence seemed to have suddenly lunged for his throat. He straightened in defence. "The scrolls I'd read, with Anthis's translations and that elf's journal, all said the Zi'veyn suspends the magic in the blood, interrupting and blocking spell-casting. Magic *outside* of blood - which, I remind you, I managed to target despite the fact that this thing was *never* designed to do it - has also been suspended and the chains broken. The magic has completely broken down."

"...But?"

"...But it...hasn't gone anywhere. It's as good as raw now, truly, so it's no danger, but it...should have dissipated immediately." Again, silence. "I'm sure it will," he amended hurriedly, "now it's not doing anything, it's just going to take time. The spells haven't been countered, they really have been unravelled, so it *is* harmless...it's just going to take time to fade away..."

"Right," Garon shook his head. "So, ultimately, there is no problem?"

"Well, no, but...it's just not the result I expected."

"What does it mean?" Anthis asked, frowning between the two mages, both of whom clearly understood more on the matter than he did. "If the magic is still here, doing anything or not, that's still a problem, isn't it? If it *should* have vanished as soon as you finished--"

"Why didn't you notice this before?"

"Because," he bristled, "this is the first time we've not had to flee immediately after, or been carried off. Now, though, I can feel it. As for what it means, I don't know. There's no order to it, there's no way for it to affect anything on its own, but if it's still here, in whatever state, I can't help feeling like it could still wind up causing trouble - that someone, somehow, could still abuse it. Though I can't fathom how."

"Neither can I," Eyila agreed with a pensive frown. "But I'm also uneasy about it. It *should* have disappeared."

Rathen sighed deeply in frustration. "We'll work it out."

"What about mages?" He looked inquiringly to Petra. "Well...he didn't seem too pleased when you broke the spells. How far will that go? Was it just because he was here, or...? I mean," she chuckled nervously, "we're *really* close to Kulokhar..."

Worried looks were exchanged when neither mage answered.

"What about Owan's message? Did you find anything?" Anthis asked if just to move the matter on, but Rathen's expression became only bleaker.

"Yes. I did."

"And it's not good, I take it?"

"It depends on how you want to look at it. No, magic *isn't* 'weaving' into the elements, but it *is* complicating them, to the extent that they have become kind of saturated with it."

"And the difference is...?"

"Weaving is irreversible; saturating is separable."

"I'd have guessed the other way around."

"No - water and cloth, cloth can be dried out; thread and cloth, thread becomes a part of it. But *the point* is that the saturation makes the elements easier to manipulate magically."

"And the magic is still here..."

"No - well, yes, it is, but that *isn't* a concern in *this* case because it's not in any organised form anymore so it's not interacting with anything. As far as the danger from affected earth, wind and rain are concerned, it's as good as gone. Cloth only gets wet when you combine the two, when they interact, not when they're just next to each other."

"But it means that mages could change it." They looked down at Aria, who even now remained protectively close to her father as she peered back in worry. "And they could use it as a weapon, couldn't they?"

"Yes," he smiled regretfully, stroking her soft curls, "they could - but not by just *anyone*. They'd have to truly understand magic, which narrows down the risk even in the Order."

"But it could also mean that my people and I have difficulty if the elements don't react to our casting as they usually do," Eyila mused in concern. "Results could be violent. Or imperceptible. And Salus doesn't seem to be 'just anyone', either." She cast a severely thoughtful look across them all and found that Rathen had already come to the same conclusion.

He sighed heavily. "Potentially, he could use it to his advantage *if* he has the right guidance. If he were to...link up the chasms or something like that."

"That's absurd," Petra scoffed.

"My point is that it could *become* a problem." His gaze passed by chance over Garon, who he discovered had fixed him with hard eyes. He straightened beneath the rigidity.

"Are you sure?" The inquisitor asked concisely. "You've only tried once--"

"Garon, if I had never seen the magic before, fine, I would have a lot to pick apart. But now, there's little left to discover. This is the situation, the bare-faced truth of it."

"Everything is increasingly in Salus's favour," Petra groaned hopelessly. "Can we *really* stop him? Is there really *any* chance at all?"

"Yes." Again, all attention dropped to Aria, and she stared back at them with such ardent conviction in her young eyes that she managed to inspire a small flicker of courage in each of their hearts. "There *has* to be."

Garon, to everyone's surprise, spared a brief chuckle as he nodded his agreement. "There has to be."

Anthis, however, sighed with a weary smile. "As if we needed any *more* reason to remove it. Or 'suspend' it." He looked up from the relic he'd been turning over obsessively while they spoke. "But I suppose it makes no difference. On we go."

The end of the matter drew in sharply when a sudden gasp set them all on alert, and the immediate ring of steel from the swordsmen hiked their agitation. But as the lone woman appeared hurrying towards them through the trees, recognition set in and half of them relaxed, while Aria simply beamed. Her gasp, it seemed, had been in excitement. Clearly their nerves were frayed.

But so, it seemed, were the woman's. Her expression a twisted grimace of dismay, her pace as she stormed towards them on impossibly light feet didn't slow as she neared. She greeted them with an equally abrupt demand to leave, and continued past without even a backward glance.

Rathen frowned after her. "Elle?" But she didn't respond beyond a hurried gesture. Duly, with the others close behind him, he grabbed Aria's hand, retrieved their horse and rushed after her over the side of the wooded slope and down into the neighbouring riverbed. It was there in the damp mud that she finally stopped and turned, scrutinising the surrounding ridges.

He moved close and dropped his voice, searching for whatever had alarmed her. "What is it?" She silenced him sharply, and for another long moment, they waited anxiously for her attention to finally fall upon them.

"You shouldn't be here."

"You're one to talk. What's happened? Were you followed?"

She smiled suddenly. "Don't be a fool, sweetheart. It's you who is being followed. But I have information that can't wait." Uneasily, they gathered closer. "I know how he intends to move Turunda."

Everyone had turned white by the time she'd finished her brief explanation. Rathen in particular was like a sheet. "But," he swallowed, squeezing down his anxious tremor and controlling his blood as best he could, "you don't know where?"

"No. The borders. That's the best I can give you."

"He'll be using ruins." Anthis's musing tone earned him unanimous confused glances, but while it seemed that the impact of her words had missed him, he'd simply distanced himself in favour of a clear head. His brow furrowed as though he were merely pondering a translation upon a weathered old stone. "There are chasms all over the place but the magic is at its strongest in the ruins. The chasms are probably widest there." She confirmed that with a nod. "As for borders, there are a number of ruins in the mountains. There are bound to be chasms there, too." She nodded once more. Anthis sighed heavily and cast an abstract look towards Rathen. "'Someone could abuse it'?"

Again, everyone's blood drained. Petra's voice trickled out in a horrified whisper. "And by removing the effects, we've just made it safer to approach..."

"Will he still be able to push the magic if the chains are broken, though? If all he's doing is casting near it to exacerbate it and then steering the reaction--" The historian's eyes widened in sudden realisation, kindling a green spark of hope.

"Tha-that mage back there - nothing happened when he...well, nothing happened! The forest didn't collapse or catch fire - so casting around it *shouldn't* affect it! Surely, remaining or not, that magic won't be a problem now?"

"You'd think not," Rathen managed, attempting to push aside his dread as Anthis had, "but he has an elf instructing him. But what kind of instruction has he had?"

Taliel shook her head. A breeze passed as a unified sigh.

Garon, however, straightened stoically. "It doesn't matter. This is our only course of action. How long do we have?"

She held his level gaze, but Rathen saw her captivating copper-ringed eyes dim by the slightest degree. His heart sank. He knew what she was going to say even before the perceptive inquisitor could work it out. He turned away hopelessly. "He's already begun. Halen, Ausokh and Dustwatch. He lost control and the chasms snaked away on both attempts, but he did, ultimately, succeed."

Her words seemed to ring in the air. Heavy, dreadful, and yet they were as slow as feathers to settle. No one moved.

Until Rathen kicked violently at the damp mud, loosing a brief, furious roar. Everyone flinched, but even as their hearts pounded and eyes frantically searched the ridges, no one chastised him. Though Petra did prepare to reach for her bolas.

"What can we do?" Anthis finally dared as the air defeated Rathen's cry, looking around at the mage's back as he fell still and visibly seethed. "Can the Zi'veyn stop that much?"

"If *you* don't know," Taliel replied, "no one does. But the damage has already been done."

"Well, he's only one man; he can't possibly get to every area at once."

"No, and Doana has him distracted at the moment. And the elf hasn't been back, but there's no knowing when that will change."

"*How,*" again they flinched at the incredulous voice as Rathen spun back towards them, "could he *possibly* have achieved this?!"

Taliel was the only one to face into his fury, and she spoke smoothly, untouched. "He's bypassed the learning. The elf has...meddled somehow, planted the information or cleared the clutter in his mind so he can get to it, as far as he says. I don't know - but the fact is that he can *use* his magic now, though *not* with the best of them; he knows how, but he lacks the experience and application."

"And how long will it be before he gains that, too?!"

She held his challenge. Only when Eyila spoke up did she look away, her musical voice capturing their full attention, as it so often did.

"We need to block the magic along the borders. Or suspend it."

"If we hit his targets, we'll be back in his sights."

"Well apparently we're already being followed again," Rathen snapped bitterly.

"It's the only way."

"It will rile him up even more."

"A thought," Anthis stepped in, "can we not draw the land back together? Seal up the chasms? If the magic is making the elements--"

"I don't have the power for that!"

"But Salus does?"

"With precise help and *elven* guidance, yes," he hissed, "he probably does."

"Then, if you had the same--"

"Which I *don't*."

Eyila mumbled quietly in thought. "...Then we need..."

"...Yes?"

She hesitated under the impatient stares. "The...elves. We need the elves' help. Of course."

Anthis's bemused frown lingered, while Rathen rejected the suggestion before she'd even finished. "Absolutely not. Even if Eizariin could be contacted, I wouldn't trust his help. Anthis only had a couple of hours with him - that's not enough to know *anyone's* allegiance."

"Then what do you suggest?"

He merely stared back at the historian while he searched for an answer. Taliel spoke before he could discover one, her eyes once again scrutinising the hills.

"There's more: he's beginning to trap areas like these - ruins and anywhere else known to be awash with magic. He's also establishing surveillance spells in towns, cities and crossroads - they're already in Kulokhar, Pelas and Stoke Rass."

Garon narrowed his eyes, sensing she'd cut her report short. "And?"

"And," she obliged, "bounty posters. Of you all. You'll have to be very, very careful."

"He's put *bounties* on us?!"

"So much for Mokhan," Petra grunted, but Garon was already shaking his head.

"We now have our information," he declared. "Mokhan isn't necessary." He sheathed his sword and fixed the phidipan with another level stare. "When is he likely to move again?"

"I can't say. He's erratic. But your travelling is going to become harder, too. For *all* of us, in fact. He's just provoked Doana."

"This guy is becoming a serious threat to *everyone*," Anthis groaned. "A man so convicted and with that kind of drive and power is *dangerous*."

"Well we can't confront him," Rathen snapped. "We have no idea what he's truly capable of. He shouldn't even match a *novice* with what little training he's had, and yet look at what he's done! The *only* thing we can do is use the Zi'veyn to break the magic along the borders and hope it's enough to slow him down. And work out how to *remove* the damned magic once and for all."

"Remove it?" Taliel frowned, but Garon was quick to divert the subject.

"I hesitate to remind you all that it isn't *just* Salus we're dealing with. He has the whole Arana behind him, notably mages and portians. They are *also* a very real threat. We can't let one man distract us."

"Well clearly they're not *all* behind him," Anthis noted, but his gesture towards Taliel only earned her Garon's intense stare, shifting from its previous co-operation and almost willingness to trust into a deep and burning scepticism.

Slowly, his unspoken thought passed around the others. Fortunately, with a careful and observant approach, Rathen was the one to voice it. "Elle, how are you getting this information? Why would he divulge anything to you?" But then his heart knocked sideways and skin turned ashen as a thought ambushed him, striking him as hard as a hammer to the head. "Elle, please tell me you're still only a phidipan..."

Softly, she smiled, with a deep and sympathetic fondness. "Yes, my love, I am still only a phidipan."

"Would we even know if you were lying?"

Rathen sent the inquisitor a sharp look. Then another thought brushed him, and his suddenly pensive gaze searched her while he put it all together. "You're working with the go-between, aren't you? Lord Malson. He gets close enough to Salus, confers with him directly, and if he's working with you and probably others, there must be something set in place; you've taught him rudimentary snooping or something. Or you all learn little snippets and build it up together with his direct observations. That's it, isn't it?"

"More or less," she replied. "It's not perfect, but with thirteen pairs of quite underestimated eyes, we've been able to learn his plans. But it takes time."

"Which is why you can never tell us everything we need to know."

"Like I said: it's not perfect. But it's still the best any of us can do, and you, at least, are still armed with more than you would be without us."

"And what happens when Salus figures it out and starts feeding you false information?"

But the smile she gave Petra was steady. "There is only one of him. We will notice; things won't add up. Not even he will be able to pull the wool over our eyes so easily. We are of the Arana, and he has been the keliceran for eight years. He's out of practise. We are not."

"She has a point," Garon replied reluctantly. "Aranan operatives are all extensively trained, from phaeacian to portian. None of them should be underestimated."

"But are we not right now underestimating *Salus?*" Petra asked.

"No. For the simple fact that we recognise that we *don't* know what he's capable of. We don't even know what *Rathen* is truly capable of." The mage braced against the glances. "He's pushed the magic and lengthened the chasms. That should be beyond any mage's abilities. At the very least, we can trust that he will continue to surprise us."

"That's not as helpful as you think it is."

"But it's better than nothing."

"I'm not seeing the difference."

"Then look harder."

Petra snarled and snapped away. The others pretended not to notice.

"That's all I have," Taliel declared, dusting off her hands. "I'm sorry I can't offer more."

"It's more than you should be doing." She smiled as Rathen stepped towards her, and the rest recognised her abrupt dismissal - or, rather, the way her eyes had locked onto him and saw nothing else besides - and began to turn away and potter around, surveying their surroundings instead. Petra lured the reluctant Aria away with the promise of swordplay secrets.

"What you're doing," Elle said quietly after a kiss that Rathen knew Aria had scrutinised with a craning neck, "is incredible."

"Good to know I still have it."

"That's not what I meant," she chuckled. "I mean all of this. It's...beyond noble. After everything you've been through, to step up--"

"I didn't really have a choice. That man was going to hang on my door until the end of my days if I didn't."

"I suspect so - but I *also* suspect that you agreed before he managed even a third visit."

He grunted. "Or perhaps he simply made a good case. And I had something to gain."

Her soft, brown eyes narrowed and another smile played on her lips. "That may well be true. But it's not the whole of it, and you know it. Regardless, you are a hero. Again."

He kissed her firmly, and she leaned her whole self into it. But, more importantly, in that moment she wasn't calling him a hero. She sighed as they parted, and as their eyes locked, a familiar wash of heat passed through his chest. One he'd not felt since he was a much younger man. He pulled her close again and kissed her with a passion. This time, she was the one to break it, and her eyes shone with a heartache so strong and sudden that he felt the edge of despair creep into himself.

"Rathen, after all of this - when it's all over--"

"No, Taliel. I won't talk about this."

"But why not? Rathen, what you're doing - what you've *done,* clearly you've some kind of understanding of wh--"

"Understanding, control, present actions - nothing I do will reverse my sentence, Elle, you know that. Don't fool yourself."

"That isn't what I meant."

His eyes softened with regret. He looked down, avoiding her gaze, and took her hands in his. "I know."

"I would give it--"

"All up. I know. I haven't forgotten. I haven't forgotten *anything.* But I don't want to talk about it. I don't even want to think about it. I...I just can't, Elle. I can't risk jinxing it - getting my hopes up, or yours. We both know things aren't so simple, not with your profession." His gaze ensnared her. "People in your line of work don't retire."

A smile flickered. It was sad. Sorrowful. Heartbroken. It was rather more of a twitch, perhaps a quiver to keep from crying. But Elle wouldn't cry. She would grimace, but she wouldn't cry. Not with the others around.

She looked back up with sudden composure and nodded slowly. This time, she did smile. But it was not a phidipan's mask. It was still sad. "I love you, Rathen." Her hand slipped out of his. Lightly, her fingers travelled across his wrist, then up along his forearm. She stopped at the edge of his sleeve, beside the seam, then moved up one more inch. Precisely where, within the folds of the rolled up fabric, his wedding ring resided. "Don't forget it."

Then she turned and left, and Rathen couldn't bring himself to stop her.

Owan moved carefully through the forest. His every step was tempered, placed as lightly as it could be while he strangled back his haste. He was more than a little uneasy. He'd passed the boundary of magic a few minutes ago and had since been bombarded by waves of unnatural sensations. He discovered beauty in the smallest things, both wonderful and sinister, and felt a pervading sense of safety so artificial it was almost steeped in treachery. It was inescapable, oppressive, but as alarming as every peculiarity was, he forced his mind to remain steady and fixed upon the magic, probing it, analysing it, filing the details away in his memory and scribbling the most significant into his notebook. All the while the magic washed over him, he braced against its influence, even as every report of every ailing mage repeated themselves word for haunting word through his mind.

His heart lunged into his throat as his foot snagged briefly in a tangled knot of grass, and a startled oath barked free. He clamped his mouth shut immediately, and after casting a sneer at the offending knoll, he continued moving carefully through the forest. Very, very carefully.

Close by, the road meandered, veering eastwards to cross the river at its narrowest point which even now he could hear rushing by. The old bridge meant that there was no need for anyone to venture from the track, so no one ever did, which made this area, by chance, an isolated, inconspicuous location. And despite its insignificance, despite its emptiness, it was almost certainly being watched.

His footsteps became even more cautious as he spied the edge of a small clearing up ahead. A concealment spell or aversion enchant wasn't on the cards - not when nearby spell-casting seemed to so easily antagonise the already tumultuous circumstances. He was left instead at the mercy of his own stealth, and he was sorely aware that he was out of his depth.

The clearing was small, large enough for an oak tree to flourish had an acorn ever taken root, but was instead overrun with bluebells and delicate sweet woodruff, creating an unbroken carpet of blue and ivory but for a single rocky stump at the centre. But that stone was not a natural form. It stood too crooked and meticulously balanced, its faces were too smooth, and its underside was too abrupt and angular to be the result of natural weathering, especially in an area so unprone to flooding. Rather, it had been carved that way centuries upon centuries ago as an homage to Vastal, to intellect, philosophy and logic - to Doru, Her face of Mind.

Owan had learned that all such monuments were peculiarly shaped, though this was the only one he'd seen for himself, but while he'd visited this tiny grove uncountable times and become familiar with the stone's lines and corners, he had no idea what the tablet had once said. No one did. Its fragments were shattered and weathered smooth. But its presence and intent resonated with him - as did the unfortunate fact that the modest elven structure had long been broken, quite deliberately, by decidedly ignorant humans. But still, this remained one of his favourite locations.

Yet he entered it timidly.

Stepping through the trees with caution, a tight muzzle on his enthusiasm, he remained at the edge of the tree line only for his heart to take a sudden plunge. Though far from unexpected, the state of the grove was not as it should have been.

The most striking of the gathered travesties were the rends - narrow lines that scarred the sheet of bluebells like veins of poisoned blood - and the glittering puddles glowing between the leaves and blades of vibrant grass, the colour and luminance of the dusk sun. He stared at the magic for a long while, peering into its construction, before a precise and delicately built column of small pebbles caught his troubled eye from the edge. Like ants, as he noticed one, he discovered another, and then another would seem to appear from the trees. Each impossible tower was low, about knee-height but for the last to catch his attention, which must have stood at twice his own - about the same, he noted distractedly, as the height of his preferred study room.

His gaze tracked it up into the trees, and he noticed with a start that, beyond the roof of leaves, the sky appeared to be lower. He stared harder, certain despite impossibility that the clouds *were* closer, the sunlight brighter, and that even the azure of the atmosphere would be within his reach if he were to climb up to the highest boughs.

Sharply, he withdrew his gaze. The sight was enough to madden him and he couldn't afford the distraction.

The flower-riddled ground regained his focus and he dared a step away from the trees, casting a wary glance back over his shoulder before crouching quietly beside the nearest branch of the young rift. Nudging aside the grass, he found the rend wider than it had appeared, deep and black and harbouring a lake of undulating power, vast but purposeless. His blood tingled; he didn't dare stare at this for too long, either.

He looked then towards the pools of light and extended himself towards them. What he found surprised him, but it took only a moment of pondering before it began to make a curious kind of sense. *'A wash of light...and water.'* Here were two chains of quite certainly different spells, but whose surviving elements were compatible enough, it seemed, for the two to merge together. He frowned as the logic behind the impossible matter evolved. *'Elven context - wash or wash - bathe or sweep... A spell for a 'wash' of light merges with another for 'water'...to create puddles of light...'*

Lips pursed, his eyes flicked across towards one of the delicate pebble columns which he duly probed with equal diligence. Again, the chain was short and vague, but here its single instruction came as no surprise at all. *'Stack.'*

But as he turned his attention skyward, the matter became more complicated. It took far too long to decipher its purpose, but once he'd finally begun to grasp it, a new thought began to take shape. Until a rustle in the forest overrode it.

Owan snapped around beneath a hot wave of panic. Notebook discarded in the long grass, a spell already hovered about his fingers, and while his ears strained over the sound of the river his eyes scoured through the shadows. But though the thumping of his heart honed his senses to a point, he found nothing.

Slowly, his alarm receded, and he turned cautiously back to the magic with one ear dedicated to his surroundings. He extended himself again, and his train of thought resumed.

Rising from the earthen crack, he crept low back into the trees, but rather than probing for the centre of the magnetism, he reached instead towards the furthest edges of its influence. With an idea of what to look for, it took little time to find - but it still came as a shock.

Along the edges of the magic, where there stood no visible sign of its presence, he found precisely that: edges. Boundaries. Restrictions rather than instructions, a command to end, to stay and remain. The magic itself provided its own containment; the chains could gather, could pass the boundaries, but they couldn't leave once within its command.

He blinked as another thought hit him.

Walls. Stacking. Intentional construction - and a roof. He looked up at the lowered sky. Put together, these spells could build something, and the disquieting sense of safety pointed towards a homestead. A home - built entirely *out of* magic.

His head swam at the impossibility of it, but logic continued to stitch itself together. Had such a place been built with magic as a tool alone, these loose spells would consist only of commands for interlocking, angle and direction - phrases as specific as 'roof' wouldn't appear at all.

But these spells *hadn't* been woven to interact with materials and objects around them, they'd been created inclusively and from scratch. Here were far more specific instructions, thick and numerous spells that filled every role - tool, wood and nail - magic itself was the material! And with so much weight to lose on these vast spells, a few had apparently retained just enough of themselves to function as if they *had* been intended solely as an instruction from the start.

...But where could such a place have possibly been? And how had no mage ever discovered it?

Owan shook his head and squeezed his eyes shut tight. As tantalising as the idea was, he had to focus. He hadn't much time.

He looked back to the invisible boundaries and turned his mind instead towards their details - most notably in search of a hint towards whatever dictated their positioning - and shortly cast himself back to the hidden grove. It was almost certainly radial. But if that was the case, and there were remarkably efficient boundaries in place to keep the magic isolated once collected, how did the magic manage to escape with the chasms?

He grunted. The answer was obvious, and a quick search of the containment commands confirmed it. They didn't pass beneath the ground level. If a chasm grew long enough to reach the edge, there was nothing to stop it from burrowing below and leaving the surface to collapse under its own weight behind it.

But that discovery eased him. The boundary spells were simple but strong, and the greatest danger came from the growth of the cracks; boundaries meant containment, and that meant that affected areas could be evacuated and avoided. The cracks could not. But discover the nature of the reaction between magic and element and perhaps the chasms too could be contained.

Naturally, the fissure at his feet became his next priority, but as he peered into the magic that shattered the ground so readily, tempering himself against its influence, a chill passed at the edge of his senses, agitating his caution.

He spared no moment to turn and look. He dropped even lower and slunk into a huddle of trees and shrubs, peering back out into the forest from his hiding place. Far too soon, a figure appeared from the shadows.

Silently, she brushed past where he had been only moments before, drew to a stop and looked about the forest. But she didn't turn towards him. The blonde haired woman didn't appear to have seen him. He didn't sigh his relief. He sensed the magic within her, noted her attentive bearing and the even greater severity to her air, and the lack of any cloak about her shoulders. It was true that no such uniform presently weighed him down either, but while he'd illegally left his behind, he doubted she owned one at all.

Her back turned and she continued on. Quietly, holding back his tension, he slipped away in the opposite direction. He'd discovered the nature of the magic, and with it the very foundations of its interaction with the elements. But it was not enough to work with. It seemed he would be relying upon Rathen's unschooled expertise after all.

Chapter 29

For four days they'd travelled with eyes fixed over their shoulders, from sudden glances to open stares across the fields and sparse coppices towards the southern horizon, imagining Kulokhar hiding behind every hill. They'd swung wide and given the capital city ample space, but with no landmarks in sight, it was all too easy to confuse a yard with a mile, a matter made worse by the heat of summer. That very day the warmth made the tension almost palpable, even as they waded ankle-deep through fresh flood water from a diverted river - the fault, no doubt, of magic. But where Aria and Eyila seemed able to dismiss their inhibitions and wade barefoot quite happily, the rest were bound by adulthood, disgusted by the leak in their boots.

For the fifth time in as many minutes under the hot afternoon sun, Anthis's jittery eye was snatched by the abrupt spinning of the duelist. "Petra," he said as calmly as he could, "you're making me nervous."

Her attentive gaze didn't stray from the horizon. "We're too close to Kulokhar."

"I'm sure we're not."

"We are, and we're out in the open. We should have headed further north where there's cover and food."

"Cover *would* be nice right about now..."

A tight sigh came from the lead, short and abrupt enough to finally draw Petra's eye. "We are far enough from Kulokhar," Garon informed them for what must have been at least the tenth time, "pursuers will be seen long before they attack, there are no surveillance spells out here, and no one would *expect* us to be out in the open. We. Are. Safe."

"Oh, that's just as well," she replied tartly, "since we have no horses to flee upon..."

"It was necessary. Our hunter would follow the hoof prints over the bridge."

"And we lost a day doubling back on ourselves from that detour."

"Would you rather we *kept* our tail?"

"Are we so sure we even *lost* it?"

"There's been no sign of him."

"There's *never* any sign."

Garon spared her a brief, sharp and notably bitter sneer. "If you're dissatisfied, by all means, take the lead if you think you can do better."

"What, and deny you your precious command?"

"And yourself the chance to complain."

"Oh I'm so sorry, I forgot. Your judgement is so perfect that you have no need of a second opinion."

"I can value a second opinion, but all you seem to dispense are unconstructive criticisms and whining, huffing and groaning. It doesn't do much to inspire attention."

"I don't whine, huff or groan."

"Then you should pay more attention when you speak instead of acting upon the first impulse to grab you."

Rathen sighed wearily while Petra returned the remark. He looked down with some relief as a small, muffled voice whispered from beside him.

"Daddy, did something happen while I was away?"

"Like what, little one?"

"Well," she took another thoughtful bite from her apple, "Garon and Petra seem...well on the outside it looks like they hate each other. But they're always throwing little glances the other's way when they think no one's looking, so I don't really believe that."

"No," he replied quietly, "neither do I. Nor, I think, does anyone else. Least of all themselves."

"I see..." Slowly, she turned him quite a critical look, cheeks stuffed full with fruit. "You told me that I should tell someone when I like them. Why can't *they* do that? They're both so brave, they can't possibly be frightened..."

"Matters of the heart...take a different kind of courage. It's a kind of courage everyone possesses, but...lies hidden. Deeper in some than in others."

"Why?"

"I really don't know."

"...Were you brave with Kienza?"

"Kienza never gave me the chance."

"And Elle?"

Rathen looked away with a sad smile while she wiped the dribble of juice from her chin. "I wasn't given a choice. The courage rose on its own."

"Does that mean you love Elle more than Kienza?"

His tongue froze, and he felt her judgemental eyes burning rapidly through to his soul. He stared straight ahead. "Eat your apple, little one."

Another hour passed before there was a break in the monotony of the landscape, but the sight of the village didn't encourage any relief. The mood dropped even further when Garon announced that they were heading in.

"What?"

"The Wildlands are just a few days away. We need supplies."

"So close to--"

"We're *too* close to Kulokhar for Salus to waste time raising surveillance spells here. He'll spread out first."

"I thought you said we *weren't* too close to Kulokhar."

"Perspective, Petra."

"What about the posters?" Anthis asked as she turned away hotly.

"They won't be so close to home yet, either, and copies take time."

"Even for the Arana?"

"Even for the Arana. I suspect the posters are a deterrent more than anything else. He's relying on his spells and subordinates to find us. I know the general public - there are *always* a few in every town and city who will make up a report for some fraction of the reward, and Salus is no fool, he surely knows the same. I doubt the reports will even reach the Arana. Besides, I have a contact here."

"And what do you intend to glean that Elle hasn't already told us?"

"Anything. But you will all wait outside. It'll be safer if only one of us is seen at any one time."

Rathen grunted. "You'll get no argument from me."

"Are you sure we need to go back into the Wildlands?"

Petra wasn't the only one to cast the historian a surprised look. "I'd have thought you of all people would be jumping up and down to get back in there with all those unexplored ruins."

"And indeed I would be, if not for the bodiless shrieking and the feeling that eight thousand pairs of eyes were watching you as you sleep, working out whether it would be better to eat you toe- or head-first."

"Head-first would be smoother. Less friction."

"Thank you for that."

"Yes, we need to go through the Wildlands," Garon confirmed while Anthis shivered in revulsion. "Salus is targeting the sites along the borders and if we want to reach them and try to stop him in his tracks, we need to cut through the Wildlands or waste two to three weeks bowing around it, in which time he could do much more. It's our only option."

"And we have a duty to see to the magic there, too. Isolated or not, if it splinters it will be just as destructive as any other."

"Yes, I understand that," Anthis grumbled reluctantly, pausing to shake a tangled matt of grass from his boot, "but what about the *other* side of the Wildlands? The ruins in the mountains are inaccessible, to say the least, if not lost altogether."

"If they're lost then Salus can't get to them either, can he?"

"Unfortunately, Aria, if anyone can find them, an elf can, and it seems he has them queueing up to help him." He shook his head while a grimace touched his lips. "And then he'll destroy them before anyone can learn anything. It'll all be lost for *good*."

"Then we just need to get to them first - if an elf can find them, then--"

"Aria, hush."

She looked sadly up at her father.

Anthis cast back a sympathetic smile. "If only it could be so simple. But it's not blood knowledge. Your father doesn't know where they are any more than we do."

Her shoulders dropped and heart-shaped lips pursed, but a sudden idea sparkled in her eyes before her disappointed pout could take root. "The Arkhamas!" She cried. "Maybe they could help us find them!"

"I don't think there are any in the mountains."

"Well, what about harpies?"

"We have no way of contacting them. And anyway, they're not...they don't share one mind like the ditchlings do. They won't be very receptive so soon. Assuming there are even any out that far..."

"The ditchlings could find some local harpies and have them pass on a message."

Rathen frowned at the back of the inquisitor's head. "You're putting an awful lot of stock into their truce..."

For nearly half an hour they waited uneasily behind a hill while Garon ventured into the village, and when he finally returned, two full bags slung over his shoulder, the harder-than-usual edge to his jaw flattened the mood into the dirt. They scrambled to their feet. He'd learned something.

"What is it?" Rathen asked despite himself as the inquisitor slipped smoothly down the bank to join them, but his misgivings grew when he saw the urgency in his eyes. His heart skipped a beat. "What is it? Were you recognised?"

He shook his head, but their relief was fleeting. "Salus," he said gravely. "He's moved again. Fendale and somewhere east of Ferna, I suspect along the Olusan Mountains."

The air turned to lead. "When?"

"Two days ago."

"And?"

"Two days ago. The elf must be teleporting him around. The quakes happened close together."

"So much for that distraction. There's no way we're going to get to the mountains in time."

"No, I believe Doana's holding his attention. If it wasn't, he'd have done more."

"I doubt that. We might not know what he's capable of but something like that *has* to take its toll. Right, Rathen?"

He turned Anthis a blank look. "You would think."

"Doana is still an issue," Garon assured them. "There's been an attack on White Heath."

Another bout of dread struck them still. Petra was the first to shift in discomfort. "Doana's actually made a move?"

"No. Salus has."

She blinked.

"Framing, provoking, encouraging fear and decisive action." Rathen groaned and pinched the bridge of his nose. For a long moment they were lost in their concerns, and one by one came to look patiently between the inquisitor and the mage for a solution. They were the last to return, and both with the same look of resignation. "Was there anything else?" Rathen asked rather than acknowledge the others' expectation, and Garon seemed to be of a similar mind, though probably not for the same choking pressure that Rathen felt clawing in around him.

"Ivaea and Kasire's conflict. They're saying Ivaea's buckling, that Kasire is pushing back."

Eyila looked at him carefully. "But you don't believe it?"

"No. Salus would be redirecting his efforts towards them if that was the case."

"How do you know he isn't?" She pressed. "If he's being teleported around to meddle here and there then he probably doesn't need to free up much time in his day..."

"I know because he's fierce. Given everything going on right now, he's on high alert and under great pressure. If Ivaea really was losing and Kasire pushing this far south, we wouldn't be hearing about it at all. He would be doing all he could to tip the balance and turn it away."

"And yet Doana--"

"Doana was underestimated and snuck in; as for Skilan, the animosity is so great that even deer expected their attack. And I suspect the Arana's efforts against Skilan were intentionally lax to begin with. Some people won't learn until things are beaten into them, King Jalund among them. And perhaps King Thunan..." He looked back up the hill. The others followed his gaze. He retrieved his belongings and slung them over his shoulder with the rest of his burden. "We shouldn't stay."

"Were there posters?" Anthis asked as Petra all but wrestled one of the bags from the laden inquisitor, who of course displayed no thanks.

"No, but we shouldn't take any more chances than we need to. And, it seems, we can't afford to linger." He turned away, rolling his shoulder beneath his load, and led the way back out into the fields with the village pinned directly behind them.

Aside from a brief and blustery stop-over in Stonton, the landscape remained unchanged for two days. But, as evening crept in on that second day, a daunting black mass of leaves finally began to form in the distance, sprawling ahead further than any eye could see. Within an hour they found themselves walking within the confines of the trees at the edge of the Wildlands, and while they relished the concealment, anxiety stifled their lungs. They were finally hidden - but so was everything else.

While the others finished eating, Aria stood upon a rock and peered off into the darkness from their meagre camp within the trees, her gaze sharp and vigilant - not so much for intruders, though, as for wildlife. And while the eventual arrival wasn't one she'd been watching for, it was no less pleasing.

"Did you find the horses?!" She yelled suddenly, startling everyone else before Kienza had even reached the edge of the light. But the forest-clad woman was already beaming, and pounced forwards to seize her as though catching a wild rabbit. Aria giggled ecstatically, easing the alarm.

"Yes," the sorceress chuckled, "I did. And it was very clever to speed them away and wade down through the river." She looked up towards the others as Aria giggled in her tickling grasp, begging her half-heartedly to stop. "It worked, of course. You lost your tail." Finally, she released the child and embraced Rathen for a long moment before greeting the others similarly, albeit without quite the same affection. "I must say, I am very impressed," she said, turning back towards her lover. "Your efforts with the harpies and the ditchlings - very democratic indeed. I admit, I'm surprised."

"I'm not useless," he said defensively, though he smiled all the same.

"No, but you're not a diplomat."

"That much is true," Anthis said, much to Rathen's irritation. "He lost his temper a few times. Eyila was the one to secure the truce."

"And she did the best job any could have done. It's uneasy, but the fact that it's holding at all is remarkable. Whatever you said to them seems to have hit them deep." She smiled warmly at the bronze-skinned girl, who blushed beneath the direct and approving gaze. "Well done. Both of you." Then she looked back to Rathen and Anthis. "But I suppose the greater congratulations comes for the Zi'veyn. It actually works."

"Technically, but it's--"

"Yes, we'll get to that." She waved his words away. "First, however, I have a few things to tell you - but before all of *that*," she looked pointedly down at Aria, "you've not shown anyone yet, have you?"

They frowned in confusion, but while they missed the details of the matter, the eight year-old hung her head and her voice reduced to a mumble. "No, but he doesn't need it, so it doesn't matter."

"I think it matters very much. And I'm *sure* everyone would like to see it either way."

But she didn't reply. The ground held her attention. Rathen watched her stare at the dirt, wondering what he was missing, but when the pieces tumbled into place, a guilt powerful enough to knock his breath crashed down upon his shoulders. He knelt down beside her and took her in his arms, kissing the top of her head. "I'm so sorry, Aria. I was so happy you were back that I forgot all about it. But it *is* important. Please show us."

Petra caught on as Aria's eyes travelled past them towards the bags piled on the far side of the camp. She stepped away to collect the child's while the others continued to frown, and smiled just as regretfully as she handed it over. "I'd certainly like to see it."

"As would I," Eyila said, though she couldn't have known what they were talking about. But that detail didn't seem to trouble Aria who, with an excited smile, opened the bag and dug her hand inside. But she hesitated before pulling it back out. Her big eyes dulled beneath a shy furrow.

Rathen placed his hand upon her shoulder. She looked up into his dark eyes, meeting him with shame, but at the sight of his encouraging smile, she took a breath and at last withdrew her work. A small sphere of light bloomed above them by the sorceress's hand, outshining the weak fire, and revealed the child's carving in its entirety.

Cut from rich, dark elm wood and a hand's length in height, was a vague, almost spectral shape of a woman. She was beautiful, a notion certain despite the lack of detail, with a narrow waist, small ankles, delicate shoulders and long, flowing hair. The figure's hands were pressed together at her chest, and her unseen but surely dainty feet stood within a cup formed of sepal leaves from which five smooth tendrils rose, spiralling tidily to encase her and meet at the top in a point, like a young rose bud in filigree. The finish of the wood was smooth and precise, free of any accidental cuts or natural knots; the piece was, in essence, flawless.

"Aria," Petra breathed, reaching out to gingerly touch the wood, which was even smoother than it looked, and trace her fingers behind the impossibly whittled spiral, "how in the world did you do this?"

"With unimaginable difficulty." Rathen shook his head in awe, but beneath his admiration an even greater guilt was swelling for the simple fact that she had been correct. The piece was beautiful, unique, skilfully crafted, even from such hard wood - truly, it was her masterpiece...but he didn't need it. After all the work, all the time she had poured into it, having made it on his order, to complete the task he had set her as he sent her away, working to the very best of her ability to prove, no doubt, that she *was* useful...and he didn't need it.

His eyes dragged back to her, noticing at last that hers had not once strayed from him, but despite his shame, he found himself smiling proudly. And he knew why. No, he didn't need it - not for what it had been intended for. But in that moment it had become something else - a symbol of her confidence. He had never questioned her belief in him, she had always been the first to declare with whole-hearted conviction that he could do something, no matter how ridiculous it was, but here she had put that trust into form, and by doing so illustrated her own dedication to the crisis. Every one of them were turning their expertise towards doing whatever they could to bring the situation to a close, and in that moment, he understood how deep that truly went. Magic, academia, protection and cunning - and heart. Where he and the others worried about the outcome, Aria had absolute faith that they would succeed. And that counted at least as much as everything else.

He pulled her into a tight hug. "Well done, Aria. Well done."

She beamed and hugged him back. "It's not *that* good," she giggled modestly. "But I did my best."

"Who is the lady?" Eyila asked, kneeling down and looking more closely at the carving, her eyes curiously sharp with one single, mysterious thought behind them.

"She's...no one in particular, I think," she shrugged as her father let her go and had a closer look himself. "Just..."

"The embodiment of nature."

Aria nodded at her father's conclusion.

"Feira?" Anthis asked.

"Vastal?" Petra suggested.

"Aya'u?" Eyila breathed.

Kienza smiled to herself while Aria grinned bashfully. "I don't know. Maybe all of them."

"Maybe all of them indeed," Anthis smiled. He gave her a suddenly formal and approving bow of his head and her cheeks turned even redder. "You have outdone yourself, Aria. It's beautiful. And it...reminds me a little bit of..." he chuckled as her eyes widened hopefully. "Of the elves. The spirals, the stories--"

"Stories?" Garon looked closer. Now Aria's cheeks blazed, and Rathen's brow rose at the inquisitor's suddenly open interest.

"There." Anthis pointed towards the base, and they slowly began to pick out shallow, subtle carvings remarkably similar to those found on ancient elven ruins inscribed across the wooden leaves. A gasp or two shortly followed. "They look like..." Anthis's eyes widened. "A simplified version of the poem carved into the pavilion we found in the Wildlands last time - but how did you ever remember it? You only saw it once!"

"Because I liked it. I wanted to have the whole thing on there, but it...was too small."

"What poem?" Eyila asked in growing fascination.

"'The roots that burrow beneath our feet reach to the depths of the world, where Feira's heart beats, connected by wooden veins, all trees, all plants, all bushes; Her essence feeds all creatures from insects and fungus to the beasts that feed upon them. Sylvan glades, hidden in the tangles of Feira's hair, offer protection for those pure and in need, whatever form they take'."

Anthis blinked. "I...well, that *sounds* right..."

"She protects everything in the forests," Aria explained, "and we're trying to protect people, too. So I thought--"

"It's perfect," Kienza declared, squeezing the girl's shoulders fondly. "And, I jump to point out, she received no help from me."

"Well, that's not actually true - Kienza got me the wood." She smiled at her father. "It's from home. The big tree above the wonky hollow."

"Your favourite tree."

She beamed. And then her cheeks turned red again. And then her smile began to fade. She fought to keep it but shrugged disparagingly. "But Daddy got the Zi'veyn to work, which is really great...so we don't need it anymore."

But Rathen shook his head with fervour, and took a tight hold of her hands. "We *need* it, sweetheart. I promise you. There are going to be...difficulties...further down the road, and if nothing else, this figure and the inscription you so wisely chose will encourage us to keep going despite it - despite Salus, and whatever he throws our way."

Her big eyes hardened, and with a single, sharp nod of her head, her gloom suddenly halved. But despite her determination, he saw her lip quiver, and she didn't declare her acceptance. He pulled her close again.

"What did you have to tell us?" Garon asked, looking away to Kienza as a tear rolled down the young girl's cheek, and in an instant, severity descended over the sylvan sorceress's cheerful features.

In that moment her beauty shifted from wonderful to oppressive, and there was a sudden intolerance to foolishness in her eyes. "The Order has issued a decree," she informed them plainly. "Magic is only to be used where necessary. They've noticed that casting seems to exacerbate the situation and are taking measures to minimise it."

"That's going to hamper things," Petra pointed out. "War is coming closer every day, and, whether people like it or not, we *need* mages alongside our soldiers."

"Not to mention that the Arana isn't going to obey it," Garon added.

"They are only a few and their magic is minimal," Kienza assured them. "As long as the majority adhere, it will be enough."

"The rebels won't follow. They may well see this decree as a means of submitting to the populace."

"Any spells that cause such havoc will not go unnoticed. By *anyone*. If they aren't reasonably necessary, as indeed a rebel attack would not be, the Order is prepared to dole out severe punishment."

Garon's eyes narrowed suspiciously. "How do you know that?"

She flashed a grin. "Because I snoop, dear inquisitor." Then her sobriety returned. "The Order is also aware of the magic's strengthening along the north-eastern border - Salus's doing, of course - and they're looking for patterns, but they've also taken the opportunity while all attention was turned that way to poke around some ruins in the west."

"Owan?"

She nodded. "They're also aware of the Arana's efforts to trap the areas and are avoiding them easily enough. They know they're out there, so they're ready for them."

"He's been in touch with me - about magic and elements."

"And what did you find?" She nodded again as he told her. "On the nose. And I daresay the Order is familiarising themselves with the notion of a place built entirely out of magic - though they're a bit short of the mark. At the moment they seem to think it's a single house." She sighed and shook her head hopelessly. "It's just as well *you're* all out here, or I fear Turunda would split into smithereens by the end of the month." She turned, then, towards Rathen, and spoke before he could loose the question on his tongue. "Tell me what the problem is."

"The magic hasn't gone anywhere."

"Yes, and?"

He gave her a flat look. "Okay, so I jumped to conclusions. Forgive me for thinking that a solution *you* backed would in fact *be* a solution. But the magic hasn't gone anywhere, which means that it could still be a problem."

"In my defence, I never explicitly said that the magic would be *gone* after using the Zi'veyn."

"The word 'removed' was thrown around an awful lot."

"Yes," Anthis stepped in carefully, "but elves and their--"

"Don't say 'context'."

"Oh come now, he isn't to blame. Tell me: how far did you get on your own spell before you got that garish old thing to work?"

His dark eyes suddenly narrowed, turning almost black with suspicion. "Why?"

"Well you've grasped the Zi'veyn," she replied, untouched, "you've repaired it and understood it. You're the most qualified out of *anyone* on the subject..." She smiled apologetically as she watched the knotting of his jaw. Clearly, he knew precisely what was coming. So she obliged. "Now you have to use that knowledge to make a spell to *remove* the magic."

She waited for him to respond - everyone did. Among their grunts of hopelessness and irritation, all eyes turned to Rathen. But his protests didn't come. He didn't move. Even Kienza wondered if he'd been pushed to the point of something breaking inside his head.

"In the mean time," she continued when it became apparent that he was no longer among them, "keep using the Zi'veyn to suspend the magic and break apart the spells. It's not the end of things, but it *is* helping, and it may well stop Salus from being able to find some of the ruins if you can get there first. As for the spell, the work Rathen has done on the Zi'veyn's replacement will certainly form the foundation for *this* one."

"You couldn't have told me sooner?!"

She shuddered at his sudden outburst, just as the others did, while Aria even squeaked. Kienza smiled sheepishly while the girl slapped her hands over her mouth. "I didn't want to pile it on." She took his wrist, then, and excused them from the group with a vague explanation of 'magical matters' before leading him off to the side.

"I'm *sorry*," she told him as they stopped beyond the reach of the firelight, "but you know I have my reasons."

"Yeah, you know, it wouldn't hurt to let me in on your grand schemes *once* in a while." He glared while she kissed him, but it didn't take much for him to give in. "Fine. Forgiven - as long as you answer some of my questions."

"That sounds dubious."

"What is the magic doing to mages?"

"Really? You're just going to come right out with that? Jumping straight to the end of the game?"

"Why does it *have* to be a game?!"

"Because I've found that it's the only way that you will *learn*." She sighed in disappointment, then dropped down onto a perfectly seat-shaped root and waved him down beside her. "Eyila's suffering with it. Anyone can see that much. Have you had a look for yourself?"

"Yes. You said it was about blood, so I checked. When she was under the magic's influence her own was excited and her resilience wasn't keeping up with it. The peacefulness seems to calm the senses but leaves the magic open to attack. Her resilience falls behind with everything else. I found the same in another mage almost a week ago, but he was much further gone.

"I've also spoken to Eyila about it, and she says that it gets stronger every time, but it isn't attacking her, just surrounding her, like it's waiting or goading."

Kienza frowned. "Why would it be attacking her?"

"I just...well because she seems to be overpowered by it. She's not strong enough...she succumbs quicker and deeper every time...and it's getting..." He stared off into the darkness.

Kienza watched him carefully. "Getting?"

He looked quickly back to her. "Uh, getting harder for her to resist it. She comes back out of it eventually, but I've seen her lapse a few times days after the fact, especially at night."

"She's probably just tired."

"Yeah, probably..." He looked back off into the black forest and fought the worry from his tone. "Is this what's been happening to everyone else? Weakened resilience? Or strained?"

"Most likely."

"Even..."

"Probably."

He didn't have the strength to voice the name. The thought that Sivaan Rosh could be anything less than perfect struck him with a strange disenchantment. He looked back to Kienza to find her studying him closely. "What is it?" He asked with a flicker of alarm.

"Nothing. ...You look...older."

"Well," he puffed, "things are..."

"Stressful. But I wasn't looking to offend. You wear it well." She leaned over and kissed him, softly at first, but passion was quick to slip in.

"I'll take what good news I can get, I suppose." He held her close and quickly matched her vigour.

Kienza returned to the camp alone with a distinct purpose in her eyes. But though she quickly found whom she sought, she wandered instead towards another.

She knelt beside Eyila at the edge of the trees, who was staring away to the north for miles, and began gently stroking her hair without a word. The tribal girl didn't jump, nor did she seem surprised by the contact, but when she turned her a smile, Kienza could see in a heartbeat that it didn't reach her soul.

She stopped stroking and embraced her instead. Eyila returned it without question despite a furrow in her brow. "I am so, so sorry," she whispered softly, and for a few long seconds, neither of them moved, until Kienza felt the briefest shake of her shoulders and shudder of her chest - but no sound. No tears.

She took her cheeks in her hands when they parted, and looked firmly into her pale eyes. "Ut'hala *will* be repaired," she promised her, and though she said no more, she rose with the certainty that Eyila believed her.

"What was that?" Anthis asked quietly as Kienza joined him and his books beside the fire.

"Nosy, aren't you?" She sat down and dropped her voice, though she was quite aware of everyone's location. Despite being at the centre of the camp, they weren't about to be overheard. Anthis, too, cast an instinctive look around, and set his work aside as she turned hard emerald eyes upon him. "Tell me what you've noticed."

He hesitated, but after Kienza's confident if vague assurance that Rathen would be away for a while, he proceeded to tell her all about the events of Rowan's Repentance six days past.

Her brow had creased deeply by the time he'd finished. "Not the first time, you say?"

"No, but Petra was the only witness to the first." He watched her patiently, waiting for further questions or a clue of her suspicions, but her fingertip remained speculatively upon her lips. "What do you think happened?" He finally asked.

"Any number of things," she mumbled. Then she raised her head and smiled gratefully. "What else?"

"Well that's all, really."

"I don't believe that. Remember Anthis: nothing is too small."

He grimaced into the fire in thought. "The ditchlings," he said at last. "They said he felt different. 'Fuzzy' was the word."

"Fuzzy..."

"And he's...he's still playing himself down, but he's been holding himself taller at the same time, and not in defence. He's..." He trailed off and cleared his throat uncomfortably.

"His ego has swollen?"

"I suppose you could say that," he replied very carefully.

"Mm...he's inciting it himself..."

"Sorry?"

"Nothing," she smiled pleasantly. "Now, is there anything else?"

"Well..." he looked about again, to which Kienza repeated her assurances, but his indecision remained unsoothed. He gave in only for the unbearable pressure of her gaze. "It's not my place to say it, but he does seem...distracted from time to time. Concerned."

"Personal concern? Or...'professional'?"

"Heh, I think you would be a better judge of that than I am."

"Anthis, you know him better than that."

He chewed the inside of his cheek for a moment. "...Then, yes. I'd say it was a personal concern..."

"And you have an inkling of what it could be."

He nodded slowly. "Magic. But in that area, you would *definitely* be a better judge. He could be worrying about Aria. Or his father. Or..."

Her eyebrow rose. "Or?"

"Or...anyone. You, perhaps. Who else would there be?"

"Yes. Well, I think your first guess was right."

He looked towards her when she failed to elaborate, and faltered when he saw an ominous colour in her eyes. He straightened. "What is it? What do you think is going on?"

"I have my ideas," she replied quietly, "but I need more. So far, though, there's nothing I'm...*too* concerned about...but you must keep watching him. Remember: nothing--"

"Is too small." He nodded. "I know."

She smiled her gratitude, then embraced him. Startled, he hugged her back, and his confusion persisted when she withdrew and took a gentle hold of his arm. But as she turned it over, a sudden and instinctive panic seared through him. Frantically, he tried to pull his arm away, but though he tried, and tried so very hard, it didn't even twitch. Before he could find his tongue to beg release, she was already tracing a delicate fingertip down the length of his median antebrachial vein.

In an instant, his struggle ceased. Ecstasy throbbed like fire through his blood. His breath shuddered free, and the campfire blurred in his clouded eyes.

Kienza smiled and lowered his arm gently back into his lap. "A little refresher. You'll have no opportunities in the Wildlands."

Gracefully, she rose to her feet, and after peering about the camp once again, stepped away and left the young man staring into the flames in a stupor. Rathen needed rousing from his own. But as she made her way back towards the depths of the forest where she'd left him, her name rose from behind. She stopped, turned and smiled warmly as Petra hurried towards her, throwing her own cautious glances across the surrounding trees. "Yes, my dear? What can I do for you?"

"Uh," her enthusiasm dissipated as a shameful smile crept across her lips. "I have a...favour to ask, if it's not too much trouble."

"Mmm, it depends. If it involves suspending time then I'm afraid not..."

"No, it's--" Petra frowned. "You can do that?"

"No," she pouted thoughtfully, "I've not figured it out yet. Now, what can I help you with?"

"Well, it's not for me. It's Garon. He's--"

"Nerve damage, yes, I know all about it."

"Oh...well, is it the kind of thing that can be healed with magic?"

"Oh yes, absolutely."

"Thank goodness!" She beamed with relief as hope brightened her eyes. "So, could you?"

"Oh no. No no. Not at all. No."

Her smile collapsed. She watched, perplexed, as the sorceress shook her head far too conclusively. "Wh...why not?"

"Because he doesn't want my help."

"No," she sighed fractiously, "he doesn't want to *ask* for it. He's too damned proud - even though, and I'm *sure* of this, he thinks his honour is being compromised by disability." She shook her head hopelessly. "He says it isn't slowing him down, and it's not, but that doesn't mean he should have to make do, does it? He's...just...so *stubborn!* ...Why are you smiling at me like that?"

"You sweet thing," she cooed. "You're quite stubborn too, you know. You didn't listen to him when he told you that he's fine at least five times - I have no doubt about that count."

"Because he was *lying*. He doesn't want to look weak, so the only way to help him is to *force* it on him."

Kienza's enviable lips bowed into a soft, sad smile. She reached out and took Petra's hand, stroking it softly with her thumb. "I would help him, if it would be welcome. But as it is...he doesn't want to be healed."

"What? I-I don't understand - you're saying he *wants* to be injured?"

"No of course not, that would be silly."

"Then why doesn't he want to be healed?"

Her thumb stilled, but her smile persisted. "Because of you."

Chapter 30

Leaves of emerald, jade, peridot; a hoard of endless aeons' secrets cradled beneath sweeping sylvan crowns; roiling hills and rising crests frozen in tourmaline, Turunda's fair and stormy shape, a majesty in slumber to envy the stars; a home, a bounty; Arasiin's beating heart.

So Turunda had for centuries been proclaimed by poets and troubadours, afflicted as they so often were by an incurable and unyielding romanticism. But despite the beloved subject, it seemed that this not insignificant forest had been neglected from the innumerable verses for daring to break the popular mould.

Though the wild and tangled domain certainly harboured more secrets than the royal chambers, the perfection was shattered by dark and primordial shades of malachite, diopside and verdite, gnarled and invasive roots and vines that strangled out of existence any thought of tranquillity, and the blood-curdling, charnel wails of vaporous creatures one daren't even imagine.

Here was not serenity, humility or solitude; here was anguish, insignificance and isolation. Entrapment in a place where impossibility met the expected, a place unreal and yet pure on all levels - the very essence of what could happen when nature was kept free from the meddling reach of human or elf, and it radiated a magic all of its own.

And it was not friendly.

From the moment the sun crept up over the forbidding canopy, no one could shake the nagging sense of eyes watching them through the mist. They saw nothing, heard nothing, but there was no doubt that they were not alone, nor that they were unwelcome. And though there were no natural trails to be found, no evidence at all of any forest denizens, they were not eased in the slightest. In a region so virile, *something* had to live there. It just didn't leave the usual traces.

Somehow, the forest had become bleaker and more horrifying than the first time they'd ventured in - perhaps because, this time, they'd not followed a road. There was no hint of civilisation behind or ahead of them; they had entered from the wild and intruded on a whole other world.

Eyila's reaction to the restless paranoia was the worst of them. Spinning at the slightest provocation, jerking and jolting over noises, shapes and movements while muttering what could only have been curses in her native tongue - some of which Rathen was horrified to recognise - and she stuck as close to her companions as a midday shadow.

But they were no better.

Throughout the day choruses of strange hooting and trilling pervaded the air, changing with every shift of the sun as new creatures rose to hunt; otherworldly roars, growls and bellows rumbled through the ground without warning, shaking branches and snapping the company to a halt. When the limited light began to abandon them, their blood froze at sudden, piercing, nocturnal shrieks. At the screams; at the laughing and singing. The trees too creaked mournfully in the wake of every apparent breeze, though not one graced them with its touch. Instead the air became even more stifling, the same boughs that had offered them shade during the day tried to flatten them at dusk. The scent, too, had grown wilder.

"This forest is nothing like home," Aria whispered carefully as her saucer-sized eyes flicked feverishly through the darkness that walled in their camp. "It's wild, it's dangerous...and in some places, it's angry. At us."

Rathen felt neither the need nor desire to enquire further.

That first night in the Wildlands' grasp the atmosphere became so suffocating, so ominous, that individual tensions were forgotten. The need to study, to meditate, to theorise and create - all were lost to the overwhelming compulsion to scrutinise the roiling shadows. They were out of reach of the Arana at last, but they'd wandered willingly into a hunting ground of a whole other breed.

When their unflinching guard finally burned them down to their blankets, they tossed and turned in a plague of sweat-drenched nightmares and disorientation; hazy and uncertain, never sure if they were awake or sleeping, if their imaginations weren't trying to sabotage them with the creatures they'd feared since childhood, dredging out the worst from the stories that had terrified them as toddlers. The tales that even now remained chillingly close despite all the years that had passed. The hours were endless.

Then, when helplessness began closing its clammy grip, the morning light finally arrived to chase away the stupefaction. Led by ghostly wisps of fog, and hoots, trills and strangled cawing, it was the most glorious thing any of them had ever seen.

But it was over too soon. And then it all began again.

By the fall of the second long and wretched evening, when they at long last reached the open carpet of treetops and took a single, sweeping look through the waning light from the exposed cliff top, each of them felt that same petrifying desperation creeping back up their throats. It was only in that moment of benumbed majesty that they noticed the pockets of autumnal trees, the swathes of orange, red and brown scarring the vibrant green, but they were too exhausted to entertain it.

They peered instead over the edge of the precipice that dropped away inches from their feet, stretching off in either direction before being swallowed by the forest.

The desolate sight was identical to the one they'd faced on their last reluctant visit, but it became slowly evident that it was not the same spot. There were no roots for hand-holds, and no sign of the ruin. That sole landmark could have been anywhere. Minutes away, or days. Searching for it wasn't a risk they could take.

"How are we going to get down?" Petra asked tentatively, but no one replied beyond Eyila's stammer of protest. A rope soon appeared in Rathen's hands, gingerly conjured from thin air, at which everyone shifted.

"We have no choice," he reminded them, and moved to tie it resignedly around a thick tree trunk. He returned to the edge, loosening the length as he went, and gave it a sturdy tug. There was no give. His heart shot into his mouth as Aria peered much too far over the edge and warned her back immediately. Then he looked over for himself. "I'll go first," he said with deceptive confidence, and, against Garon's objection, began his descent. And despite the protests of them both, Aria was close behind him.

She wasn't as adept as her father at creeping down the rope while walking her feet across the sheer, dusty cliff, and dangled a few times before managing with stifled panic to wriggle her way back into position. But Rathen was keeping a very close eye, and in due time, they both passed through the tops of the trees and clambered back into the sinister tangle.

To their surprise, Petra was the first to join them, and moments later Garon appeared through the branches while Anthis's voice floated through the lull of wildlife cries, reassuring Eyila as she presumably began her own descent.

"It feels even worse down here," Petra was beginning to say as she stepped down and moved to stare cautiously through the trees, but a sudden startled yelp, crack of branches and quick lash of air behind her cut her off. She spun in time to watch Garon bounce to an abrupt stop, the rope coiled tightly around his body like a snake while his eyes bulged in alarm. She surged forwards while the rope lowered him safely to the ground and immediately began turning over his hands. He sharply snatched them away. She promptly snatched them back. "Rope burns. What a time to stop wearing gloves."

A billow of air and Eyila was suddenly beside them. "What happened?" She asked hurriedly, taking his hands despite his efforts to pull them away again, but her healer's grip was much firmer.

"Three guesses." Petra turned the defeated officer a disapproving glower. "You *have* to be more careful."

"Yes, yes, I know, thank you for your input, *helpful* as ever."

Rathen rolled his eyes while Garon hissed at the vinegary fluid Eyila rubbed into his pink palms, but he noticed as he passed that Petra, for the fourth time in half as many days, seemed strangely untouched by the tiresome hostility. She didn't even twitch.

"You *do*, though," Eyila reiterated.

Rathen frowned at the pair's commotion over the barely injured man. "What's the fuss? He just slipped. Accidents happen, you know."

"Don't they just?"

He frowned again, and watched absently as the officer's hand half-curled with a start and a wince.

"Where are we?" Anthis asked as he joined them.

"No idea. I can't feel the magic of the ruin."

"That doesn't matter," Garon said as the tribal continued to fuss. "We have no point of bearing in this place, especially in the dark. We're not going looking for it. Our immediate priority is camp."

"Camp? *Here?*"

"So close to the ledge, we're probably safe. There's nowhere to hunt, nowhere for anything to hide or run."

"And you can be so sure that that kind of logic will work in here?" Petra asked doubtfully.

"Do we have a choice?"

They didn't. So, as the unnatural shadow swelled, Rathen dismissed the conjured rope and they went out in search of a suitable site. It didn't come easily. Bones, faeces and unfamiliar tracks somewhat executed Garon's assurances, but following some unwilling examination, the bones were found to be free of gnaw marks, the faeces were dried out, and the tracks belonged, most likely, to some form of large goat. Even so, they continued on until the condensing darkness forced them to make do with a tight and shallow alcove in the cliff face.

That night, Anthis sat at the shielded fire, his back to the cave, eyes transfixed to an object in his hands. The glint caught Rathen's eye as he turned it monotonously over and over.

"The key?"

Anthis flinched in fright, and again as Aria leapt from a tree to the ground beside him. He shook his head in defeat as the mage sat down beside her. "Yeah, I found it in the cache the last time we were here. Never did work out what it was for... I'd thought perhaps we'd need it for the Zi'veyn - not that I was in any state to think about it at the time," he chuckled ruefully. He rotated it again. "But why else would it have been put away with the rest of it?"

"Maybe," Aria began lightly, leering at the ornate, black key, "it's for something out *here*. Why would a key be kept so far from its lock?"

"To avoid strangers unlocking it?"

She blinked.

"Though she's not wrong," her father continued. "It wouldn't be a stretch to presume it was for something nearby. If not in that very same ruin..."

"Yeah!" She almost cried. "You should have a look! We *are* trying to fix the magic, so we'll have to go back there sooner or later!"

He smiled meekly at her enthusiasm. "Believe me, I'd *love* to, but we have no idea where 'there' is. And fixing the magic or not, there are other--"

A sharp scream pierced the air, so abrupt and brief that it rendered them as lead while their blood turned to ice. Terror seeped in. But it seeped from the cry. There was nothing otherworldly about it.

Anthis flew from the camp only an instant behind Rathen, while Aria hurried back into the alcove on her father's command. Moments later they burst through the trees, knife and magic ready, and scoured the area around the frozen tribal in a frenzy. But they found nothing beyond the husk of an ancient tree.

"What happened?" Anthis whispered, backing up towards her while Rathen continued to hunt, but she didn't reply through the hand she'd clamped over her mouth. Instead she opened her eyes, stared sharply ahead, and pointed. They followed nervously towards the base of the tree which appeared suddenly bone-like in the arrival of the weak, thin shafts of moonlight.

Slowly, they stepped away, edging around the thick, knotted trunk, scrutinising further than their eyes could manage. On light feet they negotiated its grand and sprawling roots, weapons at the ready, until an aberrant shape in the depths of its shadow brought them to a stop. Anthis managed to stifle a curse.

Nestled within the roots, curled up in a dark hollow, a small form lay sleeping. The size of a child, but gangly - fully grown, whatever it was - its face hidden behind a mat of moss and spider silk, its skin covered in a layer of pallid lichen. It didn't move in the slightest, still in a slumber which didn't thin in their presence. It hadn't noticed their arrival at all.

And neither had it stirred at Eyila's scream.

Frowning, Rathen dared a step closer. Still it didn't move. It didn't appear to be breathing by any conventional means, either. Slowly he crouched, and began to notice that what he'd thought was lichen was in fact its skin, and it was as pale as the tree beside it.

He sighed in pity as Petra and Garon arrived from opposite directions, their blades equally in hand and each demanding in a whisper what had happened the moment they found them.

"It's dead," Rathen announced solemnly, rising to his feet.

"What is it?" Petra asked, looking closer.

"An askafroa."

"Askafroa - but they're a myth..."

"I'm afraid that kind of rationality is going to be turned upside down in here."

All looked around to Aria, who was suddenly standing beside Anthis and staring down at the nymph's corpse with eyes wide in a strange, keening sorrow.

"Is this what's been shrieking?"

"No. Askafroa are silent."

Rathen stepped forwards and turned her away, squeezing her shoulder consolingly. "It's all right."

"Is it?" Petra asked, careful to avoid upsetting the child further while thoroughly unsettled herself. "The last time we were in here, we saw nothing at all."

"We *heard* it all, though," Garon reminded her. "Just because we've seen something doesn't mean we're in any more danger now than we were then. It's dead, whatever it is; it *couldn't* have hidden from us."

Eyila looked searchingly around them while Anthis returned to her side. "Do we move on?"

"No." Garon sheathed his sword and started back towards the camp. "There's always a watch."

Even so, no one slept that night, either.

After another early start with breakfast eaten in blunt silence, they moved right along, keeping east to their best guess. They had all agreed: the mountains were their goal. They would do what they could for any afflicted place they found along their way, but they weren't about to go looking for them. Duty didn't assert itself to object. After the discovery of the askafroa, everyone was resolved to reach the other side of the forest just as soon as they could.

It must surely have been almost noon by the time Anthis's exhausted mind wandered onto the scattered orange leaves they trekked over so carefully. He looked up at the surrounding trees and considered the autumnal colours, and noticed at last that a few were completely bare. "Magic did this?" He asked, glancing towards the two mages, though neither appeared touched by any such evidence.

"No," Rathen replied bleakly. "Kienza said kvistdjur are lamenting." He pulled Aria closer as she grew a little too excited by the mention of the woodland sprites.

"What does that mean?"

"Stubborn trees," the child almost burst. "Kvistdjur sing to them! Their song encourages autumn by soothing any stubborn trees to sleep. Their leaves change colour as they get sleepy, and they fall with the rest, and that gives the bugs and creepy crawlies and mushrooms things to eat. Then the trees eat them while they sleep."

Anthis's eyebrows rose, and he nodded in much the same way she did when he taught *her* something - though everyone but she could see that he wasn't entirely convinced.

"It's true," Rathen assured him as his eyes dragged habitually into the trees.

"But it's not even midsummer. Why would they sing now?"

"The magic is probably upsetting them," Eyila replied. Her voice was distant. "It's upsetting everything else. Perhaps they want to put the trees out of their misery..."

Rathen noticed Aria nod sadly to herself. But his own attention was suddenly consumed by something Eyila must have already sensed coming. He didn't notice himself immediately stumble, nor Anthis hurry to catch him, nor the fact that the historian lingered close to his side. His mind had fallen under a violent assault; his focus was shredded to pieces, his blood surged and the band around his arm grew warm. Time, distance, the trudging of his feet, it all fell away. There was only the desperate struggle.

"You're muttering," Anthis warned in a whisper, but Rathen didn't hear this, either. The young man's lips formed a hard line, and curved into a far from believable smile when he noticed Aria looking up at him in worry. He realised in that moment what the young girl must have been thinking, for the thought had occurred to him a few times already. But if her father was succumbing to the lure of magic - for that's all it could have been, given how Eyila, too, was now heavily supported by Petra while her eyes surveyed a whole other realm - there was nothing she, he, or any of the rest of them could do. Anyone, perhaps, but Kienza. And she had tasked him with keeping an eye on the weathered old mage for a reason.

He made another attempt at a smile, more successfully this time, but though he managed to provoke one from her in response, it was just as feeble.

Rathen's steps soon grew urgent. Anthis struggled to hold him back, maintaining a grip on his arms as they contracted even tighter against his body. But he didn't relent.

"We should hurry up," Anthis said lightly to the others, letting go of him though remaining near, and gave Aria the faintest glance. She understood it in a heartbeat and attempted to take over the subtle restraint herself. "Kvistdjur could still be close."

No one needed encouragement. In a moment, the mage's pace was matched, and they all but ran ahead and into a sudden pocket of rain - or, rather, a heavy deluge they'd neither seen nor heard in their haste.

"Ugh!" Petra spluttered as she and Eyila stumbled into the luke-warm downpour only a step behind Garon. "Where did this come from?!"

"Rain does that," Anthis grumbled, shielding his eyes and peering carefully through his fingers, but he found only a peek of the sky between the towering ancient trees and it appeared to be completely blue. "Apparently..."

"No. It's too isolated to be rain..."

"Isolated? What makes you think--" She stopped as she stepped out into dry air. She cast a bewildered look behind her as a soaked Aria emerged, leading Rathen and tailed by Anthis, the latter of whom appeared just as confused. Aria, on the other hand, only beamed. "It's like a waterfall!"

"Isolated," Garon grunted. "As I said." He resumed his lead before Rathen could overtake him, and everyone fell in behind, their dripping clothes now clinging to already sticky skin. There were more than a few murmurs of discomfort, but their aggravation was forgotten when they happened quite suddenly upon what could only have been the source of the displaced magic.

Rooted amongst the thick, looming, time-worn trees, just as silent and careless, stood another wooden form, one intricate, compelling, but somehow absolutely untouched by the surrounding menace. The form - giant, fair and unnatural - exuded serenity, a sensation that washed over each of them as they stared, as readily as a breeze over plains. Even the trees were pacified, neither bending away nor attempting to smother. They stood as if the figure was one of them, and she as tall and regal as any ash, oak or checker tree. And it was a 'she'; with a form so ripely feminine, it couldn't be cast into doubt - even despite the aurochs horns that protruded from the top of her head.

From the roots of those battle-ready features, luxuriant hair spilled like water, washing over shapely shoulders and billowing clear of her neck and chest, baring the feathers that sheathed them like a gorget. Her breasts, however, were boldly exposed, perfectly shaped and quite human, so much so that a few of them blushed at the sight.

Framing her magnificent torso, her hair continued to roll and flow, draping over slender arms and gathering at last in her out-held hands. Long, thick strands of algae trailed from her cupped tresses, concealing the rest of her form while moss grew modestly across the hip and crotch which, no doubt, was equally as bare and attentively carved beneath.

The evocative and unnatural shape resumed at the curve of her hips, but only for a moment. Carven shelf fungus sprouted along the length of her left thigh while trumpet flowers and butterflies adorned the right, and below the knee each leg bent backwards, fetlocked, and ended in a horse's hooves. The chiselled figure stood lightly upon the largest of a collection of lily pads, carved as a whole from a single tree at the head of what had, until quite recently, been a stream, now dried and barren but for the bed of smooth, tumbled pebbles.

A few, they finally noticed, were floating a foot above the rest.

"A monument," Anthis murmured as they approached. "And a diverted spring..." but as his eyes traced what should have been the flow of water from the ends of her cupped hair down into the dried stream bed, he found instead that the flow of water *did* in fact persist - and flowed straight up into the air.

He frowned, bewildered, back towards the curtain of water.

Having fished the relic out of his bag while they'd walked, Aria hurriedly pressed the Zi'veyn into her father's hands. He didn't acknowledge it beyond taking a hold, and continued at his urgent pace towards the statue before coming to a short stop upon one of the lowest lily pads. He then fell perfectly still.

His unnatural behaviour formed a pit in Aria's stomach. She forced her eyes away and hurried instead to Anthis's side for distraction while Garon and Petra faced out into the woods, and Eyila stepped dreamily, free of tension's hold, to settle down silently at the foot of the statue. She didn't notice a rabbit hop timidly past her, silver of coat, human of face.

Anthis hurriedly sketched the giant wooden figure. Aria scrutinised his work as it unfolded, her big eyes flicking critically between example and depiction, and so she was quick to notice the tapered point of the woman's ears. "She's an elf..." She concluded, restraining her wonder for fear of distracting her father than for attracting unwanted attention, which was foremost in Anthis's mind as he responded just as quietly.

"No, it's Feira. Elves made it, short post-magic - it's how they envisioned Her."

"They thought She looked like them?" She watched him nod, his eyes flicking between paper and wood just as hers had, and pursed her lips. "Hmm...when I draw, I draw ears like mine..."

"Exactly. They knew nothing else. All of their work was like this - though their few surviving depictions have since been...*adjusted*."

"...I see...but I don't understand why."

"Because, Aria, hatred is a very petty thing."

Her lips pursed tighter, and she continued to watch him in silence.

Rough and haggard breath puffed as irregularly as the shrill and distant birdsong, punctuated by the slightest grunts much like the abrupt and blood-curdling avian screams. By comparison, Rathen's struggle was positively melodic.

But it still set Petra on edge, even against the local repose. She halted her patrol beside a broad tree, three feet wide at the trunk, and withdrew her waterskin from her bag, casting an uneasy glance up towards the mage. She sighed anxiously to herself. "Why does it have to take so long?"

"Consider what he's doing," Garon said from behind her, startling her as he passed on his own route. "It can't be easy."

"I never presumed it was. I just wish we weren't all standing around *here* while he's doing it."

"Don't we all? Just keep your eyes open."

"Oh I am, don't you worry..." She drank just enough to avoid both dehydration and the need to refill from wild water so soon, closed the skin and set it back among her belongings. Her hand immediately returned to its instinctive hold upon her sword hilt as she rose back to her feet, and cast a careful look over the forest.

Until Garon caught her eye, lingering to fetch his own water. The bandage Eyila had tied around his right hand loosened as he withdrew it, and she watched him tighten it with his left. It didn't go smoothly. He turned away from her to resort to his teeth. She obliged only as far as looking away. "How are they?"

"Don't get distracted," he grunted a moment later. "Not here."

She nodded and straightened, and movement immediately grabbed her attention. A benign hop of the peculiar leporine creature. The tension in her shoulders eased, but as the rabbit came to snuffle gingerly about Eyila's dirty bronze feet, the tribal didn't flinch. Petra's brows drew together again.

"There's nothing we can do."

She glanced towards Rathen, still embroiled in his struggle. "No, there isn't."

She looked about the confined grove, at the rabbit, the rising water, and whatever else had managed to escape their notice. She shook her head helplessly. "This magic..."

Garon sighed ponderously, tucking his waterskin away, and rose to survey the area in her stead. "What about it?"

"...Is it...I mean...is...all this..." she puffed in exasperation. "What the magic is doing to people, to Eyila, to all those others...but people keep...*using* it...and as a *weapon*..."

"Is it worth it, you mean? No. Though I expect a great many mages would disagree."

Her eyes shifted sideways towards him. "Do you think Rathen would?"

He continued rolling his shoulder without a word.

Out of nowhere, a shudder took hold of them. Fear and anxiety crashed like an avalanche, and whatever ambience had been hanging in the forest a moment ago was instantly replaced by a humming silence, vanishing along with the tranquillity. They grasped their swords on impulse, but their eyes turned skyward as thunder approached, snaking rapidly through the boughs towards them from the very path they'd come. Then they were soaked.

The wall of water surged back towards the chiselled statue in a swathe, narrowly missing Anthis and Aria who were quick to step out of the way, while drenching both Rathen and Eyila, neither of whom reacted. Its height dropped, its strength diminished, and it returned at last to its place in the figure's hands, spilling over and along the hair's length, following the threads of algae, and trickled at last down into the stream bed to gurgle tamely along its winding route. The pebbles, too, had given in and lay back down with the rest.

Their relief was short-lived. Immediately, eyes appeared between the trees. Pale green, like the flesh of an apple.

"Vakehn..."

Anthis pulled the enraptured child close while Garon and Petra hurried to their side, blades held ready, and herded them back closer to the two absent mages. They counted - at least six pairs of eyes stared back at them, faint enough that they could easily have missed others standing further back in the shadows. But those eyes didn't move. They didn't blink. They were fixed upon the six of them with malice. Or curiosity. Or simply observation. It was impossible to tell, and their owners made no sound or move to reveal themselves, hide themselves, set them at ease or attack. Which made the risk even greater.

Anthis jolted with a stifled murmur, and both blades immediately angled towards the forest ahead of him. Each of them stared harder through the myriad of gnarled tree trunks until a deep snort puffed from the darkness. Rough, but inquisitive, and distinctly marked by mistrust. A warning.

Then came a rustle, and they started and tightened. A snap of a twig muffled beneath a paw, and a face soon appeared through the murk. A new pair of eyes came to rest upon them.

Anthis sighed in relief and let his shoulders sag. "It's just a deer..."

But Aria tightened her hold on his hand, and Garon his sword. Petra followed their lead.

The beast moved out where the light could finally reach it.

Long-legged, sleek, lean and strong; tawny with brown mottled stripes and a narrow head that stood at the height of a man's, crowned with crescent antlers. Immediately, upon a mere glance, the beast was the picture of nobility; majestic, proud and healthy. A prize for the most skilled of hunters.

But the seconds ticked by, and the pressure grew. Beneath the unshakable threat of the creature's gaze and a second, far less patient warning snort, the majesty trickled away, and the assumed image of a grand stag began to correct itself.

Those long legs ended not in cloven hooves, but in cat-like paws concealing needle-sharp barbs. The strong, lean body was more muscular than a cervid's should have been, with thicker shoulder and rump muscles for attack rather than running. So too were its jaw muscles, a broader skull that promised a bite with power more akin to the crocottas of Ithen, as well as the bone-crunching teeth packed into its muzzle. And that wondrous crown of streamlined black antlers gathered at the lead into a frightful armoury of thorns. A bow of its head, a swift, powerful leap, and its target would be gored.

They dared not move. The now exceptionally ordinary rabbit froze. The green eyes didn't react. The raghorn surveyed them all with menace.

A quiet curse came from the back of the group, but a short, sharp hush silenced the wearied mage. Aria spared her father a look, checking the distance between them now that he'd begun to return to himself, and so she was the first to see the brutal stare of the tribal behind him.

Her shocking blue eyes burned, searing into the back of Rathen's head with malevolence, and her hands were slowly rising from her sides, fingers already preparing a spell.

Thoughtless and instinctive, even as heat flooded her little chest, Aria ripped herself free from Anthis's grip and seized Eyila's dangerous hands before she could unleash her intentions.

Swords flashed, heads spun, strangled alarm grunted. All came to stare upon the two in confusion. And no one missed the hatred, the condemnation, the hunger for vengeance in those usually so kind and astute eyes.

It was the very same look the maddened mage of Rowan's Repentance had burned Rathen with when he'd quietened the magic of those misty dells.

Another snort snapped their attention back to the raghorn. Blades promptly followed.

The beast had shifted. Its stance was hulking with front legs splayed, and its eyes appeared to glower as it dropped its head and angled its horns towards them. But still it made no move. And neither had their audience.

"If we are very, very careful," Petra murmured, "we might be able to get out of here..."

"As far and as fast as we can without provoking a charge." Garon nodded shortly. "Follow me - keep close, and Anthis, Aria, keep a look out behind us."

The group remained tight, so tight as to almost trip over one another had they not been so very slow and cautious, and as they followed the inquisitor's lead towards the bags, no one suggested that they weren't worth the delay. Instead, under intense watch, they each picked up a load, negotiated it so that weapons were always ready, and backed away through the grove, across the stream and into the trees on the furthest side, where the green eyes seemed to have vanished.

Nothing followed them.

They remained close and alert until the early hours of the following morning.

Chapter 31

The ground moved on its own. The roots were reaching out to trip them. Trees were living things, after all, and living things moved; there was no reason they couldn't attack intruders. The forest was wild enough, strange enough, full with all kinds of impossible creatures - some of these trees could very well *not* be trees at all.

The fact that such an idea seemed so very reasonable was, of course, where the problem lay. Their brains were addled after another night wasted chasing the elusive respite of sleep, and when they finally had managed to catch its tail, they'd risen feeling as though they may as well not have even bothered trying. They were so very tired, irritable, disorientated, staggering along across uneven ground where it was in fact their own feet that tripped them. But they tried their hardest to stay calm. They knew they couldn't give in to stress - not here. But that condition made it all the more difficult. Especially when injury kept finding them. Eyila patched up the increasingly common cuts and scrapes with salves and bandages, avoiding use of magic not out of respect for the Order's decree but because, by her words, 'a stumble isn't venomous'. A remark which only served to turn their thoughts towards the various levels of harm the sinister forest and its creatures may just be capable of.

By the time they happened upon the edge of another dome of magic, tensions were reaching breaking point. It was only by that same sheer necessity that they managed to maintain control of themselves, but yet again Anthis shouldered the additional burden of hiding the extent of Rathen's struggle from the rest. Kienza had asked *him* to keep an eye on him rather than any of the others; whatever was wrong with him - and he had his guesses - she didn't want them to notice. How the mage managed to handle the Zi'veyn in such a state, he couldn't fathom, but as long as he did, he surely couldn't be suffering as badly as Anthis feared.

Eyila, on the other hand, was another matter. Petra had kept her close since the near-incident at the statue two days past, but she had informed Anthis that she would be in his care when next they were forced to a stop. It was a duty that surprised and intimidated him, but one he intended to fulfil to his best capacity, even though it meant no 'wandering off, goggling at rocks or scribbling in that damned notebook'. Evidently, Petra was warming back up to him.

That afternoon, as Rathen set to fixing another, far less remarkable ruin - a shrine to the Goddess of Life, Vastal Herself, though since Anthis wasn't allowed to inspect it it may as well have been an ant hill - he sat nervously upon a rock beside her. But his fluster didn't last for long. She was thoroughly unresponsive, so much so that talking to her suddenly became much easier than usual, as well as an avenue of much-needed distraction.

"You must be comfortable," he said absently, tugging his shirt away from his sticky chest. "All this heat. I don't know how you can possibly live in the desert...though I guess if you grow up with it, you get used to it. It would be normal...although I suppose it's not as humid. I think it's the stickiness I hate the most..." He watched Rathen mindlessly while his thoughts trundled slowly along, and his gaze began drifting around the forest. "This place really is something else. It's so...*wild*...in every sense of the word..." he grunted. "Every sense... Last time we were here we didn't see any...eyes, or raghorns or dead nymphs. But this time it's as if they're seeking us out... Mm. It's a shame your first experience here had to be like this. I think you'd actually have liked it otherwise. Last time it was almost peaceful..."

A sudden shriek scattered his thoughts, neither too near, nor quite far enough. The two swordsmen burst back through the trees and Aria clung closer to her father whom she had taken to guarding. Silence fell for but a moment, then the birds continued crowing as though they had never been interrupted.

Anthis chuckled nervously while Garon and Petra warily resumed their watch. "Perhaps not *too* peaceful... Ohhh I would love to wander around in here, see the ruins, study them - I mean, *who knows* what all this is hiding? What we have yet to discover? What time-worn questions could be answered..." he sighed wistfully, staring past the mage and up at the shrine, tracing with his eyes the lines that flowed like water, the most common depiction of raw life. "But with everything *else* hiding in here, it's impossible. You'd be just *asking* to be...ugh, I'd rather not think about it. ...Though..." his brow furrowed softly in consideration, "I don't think I'd like them to go anywhere, either. They're part of what makes this place so wild, really - probably the very reason it's been left alone. Why it's so full of life. I mean, I doubt if even the strongest lumberman could fell any of these trees. Which means, at least, that everything stays in tact. The statues in here - well, they still all have pointed ears. And that's..." He smiled to himself, and his thoughts tumbled further until another pensive frown slipped in.

"This place is one of the last frontiers. If everything in here was discovered, what would be left? Once everything has been found and translated, there'll be nothing left to learn about the elves...what an awful thought... Perhaps we're not *supposed* to find everything. Perhaps some things *should* remain hidden forever - at least then no one could *actually* know everything, even if they presume to; there would always be something left...something to drive people...keep fascination alive..."

His eyes turned towards Aria, and a smile spread quickly over his lips. Though she kept a tight hold on her father's trousers, her nose was now mere inches from the stone. "Something to drive young minds. And so few of them care anymore. All my peers are so much older than me. If I'm honest, I...sort of thought that kind of passion would die with me. That sounds ridiculous, I know - it just seemed that no one else was likely to follow this path. All my friends wanted to be soldiers or merchants - anything with power or money. And there's no power or money in academia..." But a smile returned to his lips even while he shooed the romantic thoughts of freedom and enlightenment away. He looked instead back towards Aria and watched her brush her fingertips over the carvings. "Or perhaps I'm worried over nothing..."

Another shriek, and Anthis forced the invading tremor out of his breath. "This forest, on the other hand, seems particularly predisposed to kill us..."

But in that instant, the soft howling of the displaced whirlwinds behind them suddenly began to waver, and the leaves they'd whipped up, as foreign and unnatural as the currents themselves, drifted in the lull and faded into nothing before they could settle upon the ground. The light, too, increased, and only then did he realise that the previous overcast darkness had also been a figment of magic.

But as his eyes flicked from Eyila, who continued her unbroken stare through the forest, and onto the victorious mage, he found him neither rousing, stumbling, nor straightening with a long, relieved breath. Instead, with the Zi'veyn clutched tightly in his hands, he surged off abruptly into the trees as if his heels were on fire. Aria tried to follow, but doubt held her back with a searching look towards the others. Garon returned in an instant and gave the order to follow.

"What's happened now?" Anthis mumbled dubiously, hurrying to his feet and taking the near-limp tribal by the arm. "Come along, Eyila, we've another merry chase..."

She rose and shuffled emptily and obediently along beside him. He was pleased to see that attack hadn't yet crossed her mind. No change at all passed through her vague and subdued eyes. But while he'd initially been relieved, the reason revealed itself the moment they stepped into the trees. It was not some kind of sudden progress against the magic that battled so relentlessly down upon her, nor was it as hopeful as the naive conclusion of an isolated incident. In fact, it offered no insight at all.

Almost as soon as the shrine vanished from their reach, his lungs burned with the flood of dry heat and for a long, desperate moment breath itself eluded him. Even before the shock passed, he knew that magic was to blame. Another affectation thundered around them, one thick with an unnatural deathliness and stifling heat.

Two tainted areas; two gatherings of magic overlapping one another. This was a special forest indeed.

A forest whose canopy now grew starkly thinner with every step, and whose colour in the rush of light diminished.

Ash drifted through the air as listlessly as dust beneath a cellar's lamp; grass and weeds were indistinguishable from the roots, which themselves were as charred and brittle as the trunks and bare branches. And at the centre of the grey, scorched clearing, untouched but for a coat of soot, a stone pavilion, solemn, lonely and haunting. And so very silent.

While Rathen dashed ahead and stumbled blindly up its steps, the rest slowed restlessly. But there was nothing to be said. Garon shortly resumed his watch, Petra a moment later, Aria returned to her father, and Eyila remained in Anthis's care. And Anthis stared up at the pavilion while desperate argument filled his mind.

He chose his side. Taking Eyila first by the hand, then correcting hurriedly to her wrist, he set off towards the structure. "Sorry about this," he told her quietly as she dragged along behind him, "but I have to know..."

The pair moved around the wide stone base in circles, his fingertips trailing across its surface through the ash of the burned-away vines and roots, searching for any tell-tale bumps or crevices, anything that broke the perfect monotony of its construction; any buttons or trips or poorly-blocked alcoves. But he found nothing. Nothing to suggest at any hidden chambers. No doors. No locks. There was nothing there at all.

He circled eight times before that understanding finally began to dawn.

With a confused and beaten grunt, he stepped back and cast his eyes over the sides of the platform, up along the columns, their top arches and the sunshade they wove themselves into. Eyila sank to sit quietly upon the ground beside him.

He shook his head in bewilderment. "How can there be *nothing*...?" His eyes flicked quickly up towards Aria, but she didn't appear to have found anything to take her interest from guarding her father. "I don't understand...but...I suppose...it's not impossible..." Brow knotted, his hand slipped absently into his satchel and fingers immediately closed around the key. It was cold to the touch, and he could feel the etchings of long, intricate grooves as elegant as the brushwork on the Zi'veyn. But they didn't match the relic.

Even as he drew it into the reach of the sunlight, he knew there was no lock in this place that it would. He'd come to the conclusion that it was too big for a box, and too grand for a thing - especially if that 'thing' wasn't the Zi'veyn itself. No, it was to a door, one equally as elaborate, and if the key was contained with details of the Zi'veyn and locked away in a place like this, then perhaps it could be near that first site, or there could be yet more information to be found, scattered about the wilderness, needless but no less fascinating details about the relic's creation. Or maybe it concealed something else of equal power and importance, something that could help them even further - perhaps even complete Rathen's new task of *removing* the magic for him.

But...where *was* this door?

He found himself staring off to the side in thought, and jumped when his eyes refocused and met the gaze of another pair of apple-flesh eyes. He quickly found two more secreted in the trees, just as impassive as the last. He looked quickly towards Petra. Her sword was drawn. She'd seen them. And wherever Garon was, he'd no doubt spotted them, too. An assumption confirmed when he appeared a moment later, wearing the same ready expression despite his apparently calm and steady demeanour.

He pulled Eyila to her feet with apology and retreated closer towards them, tripping over a root as he went. He cast it only a cursory glare, but in that instant he couldn't help but notice how straight it was. And charred. In the middle of the clearing, it should have been burned to dust with all the rest. And it shouldn't have moved so easily.

A thought slipped in, an awful thought he couldn't overcome.

Gingerly, reluctantly, against all reason, he nudged the root with the tip of his foot, disturbing the dust that had concealed it. His lips immediately clamped to lock back his dread. A bone. He looked towards Garon and found the inquisitor looking back at him, shaking his head for silence. Something in his eyes told him he'd already made the discovery.

They waited together without even a whistle of a breath for what felt like an eternity under the inhuman green stares, watching for movement, disappearances or arrivals, and for the coming of any other forest denizen that should be

299

unconcerned by their audiences' presence. Finally, a sigh of relief drifted from behind, accompanied by the clatter of metal on stone and a shaken little voice trying to be brave. The grievous sense of death lifted from their hearts, leaving only caution and unrest.

Garon glanced back to the pavilion. Rathen had dropped to his knee, and Aria was already helping him back up. Anthis, on the other hand, looked to Eyila when he felt her hand begin to move, and kept her wrist held tightly in his. "It's all right," he whispered, looking around rather doubtfully himself, noting the gathering of yet more eyes, "it's all--"

The sudden drop of his feet sent his heart into his throat; nothing broke the silence but a single shrill and terrified scream.

Like a trap door, the ground had snapped open directly beneath them and pitched them all into a sudden black and yawning abyss. None were spared; Aria's shriek cast above them as she and her father were thrown from the pavilion and into the chasm along with them. But their descent was short. Roots snared out from the perfectly straight walls of soil and caught them roughly as they plummeted, snatching them back and pinning them safely to the earth. But their relief was stunted. The Zi'veyn tumbled past, falling as though it was nothing more than a dislodged rock. Nothing reached out to catch it. It was shortly lost to the blackness.

Desperation turned onto the two mages, but Rathen was still struggling against exhaustion, and Eyila's furious eyes hadn't left the magic's grasp. It was quickly apparent that neither of them were responsible for the roots.

Dreadful understanding began to slip in and the roots' hold grew tighter, smothering and strangling them as they struggled, squeezing up the panic from the depths of their souls. Aria choked and sobbed.

Necessity finally forced Rathen's bearings back into place, but though he fought, his hands were bound too far and tightly to form any kind of sign, and while Eyila thrashed in a rage, she was in no state to even realise what had happened. Garon couldn't manoeuvre his sword, though who knew what he intended to do once he'd cut himself free, and Anthis similarly couldn't get to either dagger. In their frenzy, it took a while for anyone to notice that Petra had fallen still.

"Petra?" She didn't stir. "*Petra!*" But though Garon yelled her name, Eyila bellowed senselessly and Anthis prodded her none too lightly with his foot, she still didn't wake. Blood soon trickled down her neck and collar bone. Her sword arm was also clearly broken.

Garon hissed a string of curses, and his struggle for his sword began anew.

"Give up, Garon," Rathen snapped. "You'll cut yourself free and fall to your death."

"And you propose we wait here until we're crushed or starved?!"

"No," he growled, "I propose we just *wait*. Do you think these roots just decided to catch us all on their own? This is wild magic. Something saved us."

"Or trapped us."

"Rathen's right," Anthis interjected. "Whatever the motive, something caught us. And it looks like we have no option but to wait and discover what."

Garon huffed in disagreement and continued his thrashing while the others rolled their eyes, but his struggle faltered moments later. His eyes came to rest vigilantly upon Petra instead, where he watched the sluggish trail of blood travel across her chest and its slow, faint rise and fall.

"What about Eyila?" Anthis asked worriedly between attempts to soothe her.

"She'll wear herself out. She's as bound as we are, she can't do any harm."

"What about to herself?" But he already knew the answer, and no one cared to voice it.

Rathen's grimace melted at the peep of the small, dismayed voice beside him. He turned and smiled as well as he could despite the small but sharp sting that burned in his cheek. But Aria's expression grew even more distressed as her eyes fell precisely upon that spot, and he knew immediately that the cut across his face was bleeding. "It's all right," he promised. "We'll be okay."

"There's nothing you can do, is there?" She choked. His heart grew even heavier at the fresh spring of tears in her eyes. With the deepest shame he'd ever experienced, with the greatest defeat, helplessness and impotence, he could only shake his head. "I'm scared, Daddy." Her tears fell, and his heart broke. "What's gonna happen to us?"

"I don't know, little one. But we *will* be okay. We were caught for a reason. As soon as whoever it is comes to get us out of here, we'll escape."

"How?"

"With magic."

"B-but you're not supposed to use it."

"If I have to destroy this forest to save you, Aria, I will do it. No decree is going to stop me, even if it came from the gods themselves." He held her searching stare for a very long moment, and for the briefest instant, she seemed about to object. But her mouth closed. She sniffled and said nothing more, accepting his determination. Her tears soon dried. And then her attention fell onto Eyila, and she watched Anthis continue trying to soothe her fit in horror. Rathen told her to look away. She obeyed immediately.

Worms wriggled out from the soil, falling over the binding roots and tumbling clumsily into the depths. Spiders proceeded with far more grace, skittering over shoulders and provoking distorted sounds of disgust, and earwigs writhed and twisted their way from one compact tunnel entrance to another. In the silence left behind when Eyila finally wore herself out, the brief appearance of a badger on the far side of the chasm denoted the interruption of a burrow system, and the hesitation of deer on the edge a disruption in a foraging route. But still nothing capable of trapping them - or freeing them - arrived.

As shadows lengthened and the sun began its descent to the horizon, Petra finally roused. Garon's eyes had barely left her. "Petra, listen to me," he said firmly as her eyes fluttered open, "you mustn't move. You've been hurt, but--" Her eyes flashed wide and panic set her into an immediate struggle against the snares, but even as Garon cursed and commanded her to still, she ceased almost as quickly with an agonised howl. She looked immediately to her arm, trapped against her body and bent into an awkward angle, swollen, bruised purple, and with one more kink than it should have had.

"What happened?" She demanded with a voice edge in fear, noticing briefly the trail of blood across her chest as her heart thumped harder, and looked up and around at their situation.

"We don't know. The magic left, then the ground opened, and then these roots caught us."

She wriggled her shoulders in an attempt to loosen the roots for breathing room, but there was no give at all, and she found that the rest of her body had gone numb beneath the restriction. "I take it we can't get out?"

"Not yet."

"Not yet? Then you have a plan?"

Garon snorted, earning a scowl from the mage. "More or less," Rathen replied. "We don't have much choice but to wait right now."

"No," she struggled carefully again, "we don't... How long have we been here?"

"Stop moving. About an hour."

Petra peered past Anthis and around to Eyila. She was staring down into the blackness with only a shadow of awareness in her barely waking eyes. She knew something was wrong, but working it out was beyond her. She frowned in concern, but said nothing. The magic had only been silenced; it was still here, and she was still struggling out of its grasp.

Her eyes lifted absently back towards the ground above them, and her furrow deepened with a thought. "The trees. If the spells were broken, shouldn't they have been restored?"

"Nothing but the atmosphere changed when the magic faded," Rathen informed her defensively, "but the Zi'veyn *did* work."

"The Zi'veyn..."

She looked around nervously at Anthis's crestfallen tone. "What? What is it?"

No one wanted to say it. Garon was the first to steel himself, after which everyone stared solemnly into the darkness below. No one had the stomach to ask what they were going to do next.

Dusk was falling when a magical presence finally invaded Rathen's senses. Carefully, he nudged Aria awake, who had fallen asleep in exhaustion and worry, hushed her and gestured towards the surface with a nod of his head. Her eyes widened in immediate understanding.

He then looked down the line to the others and spoke barely above a breath. "Ready?"

Garon and Anthis each nodded, while Petra looked back indignantly. "Don't make me sit this out."

"Just guard Eyila and Aria. Don't do anything you don't have to."

"My *left* arm is just fine, Garon."

"Even so, we don't know what else you suffered. I'd rather you didn't injure yourself further."

"You?"

"We."

"Shh..." Rathen listened more closely. Footsteps, soft and easy, approached from above. "They're coming..."

Wrists flexed, hearts raced, hearing sharpened. Seconds, at first racing, stood still. The footsteps stopped. No one moved to look up.

The roots that coiled around their chests suddenly came to life, tightening and lifting them away from the dirt, suspending them over the endless chasm where, for a heart-stopping moment, terror chased away their voices and they stared paralysed at what they were certain was their doom. But Rathen had been correct. While their hearts thundered like the hooves of a thousand horses, the chasm rushed away from beneath their dangling feet and ash-smothered ground drove in to replace it.

Among relief, two points of colour immediately stood out, neutral browns, greens and white, bleak but evident. Had grey wastes not surrounded them for fifty feet, the two figures would have certainly been mistaken for part of the landscape. But, as things were, they were exposed, and their six hostages patient and prepared.

The roots uncoiled and tossed them carelessly to the ground. They wasted no time in executing their intentions.

Rathen rolled immediately onto his back while Garon and Anthis each leapt to their feet, the latter with much less grace, and Petra, despite her inflamed injury, quickly gathered Aria and Eyila behind her, sword ready in her left hand. Rathen's fingers twisted and contorted with practised ease, releasing in a fraction of a moment a spell to stun their two advancing captors. Garon was already surging forwards to disarm them, while Anthis darted off to the side to search for anything hiding in the bushes. It was executed perfectly.

Until the three of them hit the ground.

Eyes glazed, they staggered and dropped to their knees, blades and spells rapidly forgotten as their hands rose to grasp their heads as if to stop them from spinning. In that moment, Petra, too, found herself unable to rush to their rescue, and though Aria had drawn her wooden sword, she didn't use it. Neither of them were able to shout despite their vehement attempts. It seemed that whatever had dazed the others had nullified them, too. Instead they felt only the helpless flood of dread.

The two figures, clad as part of the forest, continued towards them unerringly. They paused for only a moment beside the dulled inquisitor, from whom they took the sword without resistance, then Anthis, whose dagger had already been dropped. Rathen, they didn't approach, but Petra saw yet more roots sprout from the ground, wrap about his wrists and pull them apart, dragging him face-down to the ash.

Then they made for her.

Panic rose in her throat. Her fingers tightened desperately about the hilt, and while she tried to reassure the deathly-silent child, her own voice still wouldn't co-operate. Instead she focused all the strength she had into her grip and dropped her gaze to the ground in concentration, aware all the while of the nearing of the mottled, brown feet.

Those feet came to a stop before her. Still Aria didn't peep. And despite all of her effort, her sword was taken from her hand as easily as had she been asleep.

Petra turned up a scornful gaze. She locked with the apple-flesh eyes. The eyes that observed. That were empty of anything human. Empty of anything at all civilised.

Chapter 32

Three more figures emerged from the thriving forest as a frightful strength hauled Petra to her feet, and a sharp push to her shoulder gave the wordless command to march. Able at last to put one foot in front of the other, Aria made an impulsive dash for her father's side. Despite Petra's successful cry for her to stay, their captors permitted it - but not for Rathen to embrace her. All he could do while he was dragged to his feet and his wrists were wrenched apart was repeat his weak and failing promise that they would all be all right, and march on with a breaking heart while she clung desperately to his side. They were led sullenly away into the forest, and the ground rumbled closed behind them.

"What happened?" Anthis dared to whisper some minutes later while his eyes scoured the trees for traces of more wild adversaries.

"They reversed the spell," Rathen growled.

"Oh. *Wonderful.*"

"Sarcasm doesn't help."

"If you would just be quiet," Garon snapped, "perhaps I could *think.*"

While the inquisitor thought, Rathen turned his attention onto their captors. Vakehn, forest guardians - the eyes were unmistakable. But their form was chillingly human. A form they'd chosen on purpose for this encounter rather than any number of others - but why? Had they sought to intimidate, a bear would have been a wiser choice. So what did they have in mind? Empathy? Did they intend to negotiate for their release? Or was it simply for the ease of walking upright and opposable thumbs? It would be no trouble to change that the moment it was no longer convenient and devour or dismember them at their den.

His eyes narrowed in thought. No. He didn't believe that for a moment. If they were prey, there would have been no need to open the ground and trap them for three hours. Nor, with magic that powerful, would there be need to march them. They could have been carried by vines or passed from tree to tree. Or carried over their own shoulders.

Softly, he hushed Aria's nerves. No, there was more going on here. Something that required a relatable form, he was sure - not that they had succeeded. It was impossible to identify with something that had such unnatural strength, grace and inscrutable eyes. In fact, the longer he stared, the more he leaned towards the conclusion that, no matter how one looked at it, they were not human at all.

Their hair was dark, thick and shimmered green, among which twigs and climbers grew, and was woven midway into long, loose braids that swung down their backs and sprouted tiny, haphazard little leaves. Their eyes were perfectly almond-shaped, while their lips, straight and equally void of emotion, were berry-red. The only facial feature to distinguish the males from the females was the subtle difference in the shape of the jaw. Their skin was mottled and as brown as tree bark, but smooth, at least where the forest itself hadn't seized it; upon the shoulders of one, fronds and toadstools had taken root, and yet they were clean and meticulously tended, while another's was overrun by a carpet of sagina that cascaded over one shoulder like a fine and equally cultivated mantle.

But while other wild creatures had adopted the camouflage of their surroundings, these vakehn, he realised, were actually clothed. Intentionally-crafted garments of lichen woven into moss and spidersilk caught the light and broke up their shape, while at the same time concealing their modesty. It was a strangely civilised application for forest-dwelling creatures, but even ditchlings could appreciate a torn shirt. Unless this, too, was for the benefit of himself and his companions.

His eyes dropped towards Aria, who had grown ever more quiet but no longer clutched his trouser leg so fiercely, and found a quiet interest beside the trepidation in her eyes. He wondered if, perhaps, she'd seen what he had. But if that were so, a glance towards the others showed that they were alone. Ahead, Anthis and Garon walked rigid and guarded, heads turning just enough to cast surveillance towards the vakehn behind them without drawing attention, while at the rear, Petra seemed ready to jump to the group's defence in a heartbeat despite her broken arm, and remained protectively close to Eyila who herself had finally settled and seemed at last to be mending. That, at least, was a relief.

An angled face half-concealed behind curling green tresses suddenly filled his sight, and a blunt shove to his shoulder ordered him to keep moving. He bit back a snarl and did as he was told.

In minutes the forest had grown darker and denser. Ominous shadows retreated from the leaf litter only far enough to let them through before slipping back in to cut off the path behind them, like prison guards making way for the arriving condemned. The humid air had cooled, but what had been a relieving breeze became a breath of portents, chilling their skin and standing their hair on end. Hearts pounded harder, mouths dried, and fervent eyes searched the darkness.

One of the vakehn left the procession and hurried on ahead, moving with barely a sound over the fallen twigs and leaves, and disappeared almost immediately among the trees. Their prisoners stiffened. Wherever they were going, they were almost there. The air seemed to grow even colder.

But as Rathen struggled to handlessly negotiate over a long and elevated tangle of roots, Anthis's sudden, startled gasp sent his foot slipping heavily through a loop. Aria quickly helped him out of it, firing the vakah behind them a very open sneer for her chuckle, then rushed forwards to defend Anthis from whatever had unnerved him.

But the pair stumbled to an abrupt stop beside him before the historian's escort impatiently dragged him away.

The sight was not beautiful. The unshakable menace forbade it. But there was a majesty to the glade, one so potent that it shook their hold on reality for a moment, yielding instead towards the arcane. But if there *was* magic at work here, it was not that of Khryu'vahz.

Beyond the knotted roots stood a picture of pristine and ancient woodland, a pocket of Turunda's antiquated history preserved even as the centuries crawled by. Thick, gnarled oaks, the most time-worn they'd ever seen, hundreds of years old if not a thousand, stood about the grove like time-lost sentries, their branches laden with long, yellow catkins and broad leaves so vast and numerous that they closed out the light despite the great space between the trunks, casting a silent melancholy over the inhabiting vigour.

But the evening sun did slip through, gracing the earth with small puddles of light within which patches of wild garlic and yellow pimpernel grew and sprawled with enthusiasm, and butterflies flitted through the golden channels and up into the boughs. Among one particularly dense mat, a pair of weasels leapt and bounced, piping a little song in their war dance, while nestled between two others a freshwater spring gurgled to the surface and rolled away in a fine, lazy stream, trickling over smooth, white rocks in a subdued and miniature waterfall.

Cushions of moss claimed every scattered cluster of rocks, some of which were shaped and levelled as perfectly as stools, while at the foot of those that weren't stood the dark openings of burrows. Lichen crawled up the tree trunks, fungus sprouted from the bark, and claimed in abundance the single vast, fallen limb which itself served as a home to some creature or other, and which the weasels were now using as a jumping frame.

Rathen's eyes widened beneath his rising brow. By that single view, in that single moment, it was as though the world he knew beyond the sylvan borders had simply ceased to exist - a distant memory, or something yet to occur.

The pristine enchantment was rudely broken when a sharp tug on his wrist dragged him forwards.

They were pulled into a line in the middle of the dark grove while their jailers took up positions behind them, and all eyes turned onto the grandest of the oaks. The weasels were now scurrying across the rough old bark with ease, and a bird, dusty blue and about the size of an owl, poked its head out of a knot and squawked a warning. The weasels seemed unconcerned.

They, on the other hand, grew increasingly nervous. The vakehn were waiting for something. Or someone.

They jumped at movement to the left, but the forest guardians didn't react. It was one of their own, the one that had run off ahead, and her return didn't appear to mean anything. But at movement from the right, they each straightened, raised their chins, and the threat they emanated for the benefit of subduing the group tripled.

They held their breath as a figure stepped out of the shadows. On some divine cue, a breeze tousled the forest crown, shifting the thin beams of sunlight.

The woman had each and every one of them enraptured the moment the light brushed her.

On legs perfect enough to rival any effigy of Vastal, she strode slowly and confidently towards them over the uneven ground, negotiating every obstacle with flawless grace as her hips swayed with every deliberate step. Her waist was small and lean, perfectly curved and contoured by muscles that betrayed her strength, and, though as grey as fog, her skin glowed with health and potency, complementing the far darker shade of her hair which itself was long, loose, thick and voluminous. She could have hidden among the trees in plain sight whatever hour of the day, if she hadn't been born directly of it.

But her face, too, was a thing of wonder. Framed by her luxuriant mane, her lips were round and plump, so alluring that whispers of promise and affection could almost be heard by the sight of them alone, and pronounced cheekbones and a narrow, refined nose bestowed an air of regality, as too did the flaring crown of twigs perched towards the back of her head. She was the picture of resplendence. And she knew it. All but her breasts were bared and free to be admired.

But her eyes. Her eyes struck terror in their hearts. Elegant and angular, burning red, licked with orange flame, they harboured instability. There was an intense rage, and a keening love; empathy, and disdain. Passion. Volatility.

She walked slowly along their line. Even the trees seemed to bow in submission. Four hammering heartbeats to each step, she stared at each of them with those terrifying eyes, evaluating them, if not peering directly into their souls. No one breathed. Each felt she lingered on themselves the longest. Her gaze could have rivalled Kienza's.

But she said nothing. She gave them no acknowledgement beyond that invasive, mysterious glower, and came to a stop at the end of the line beside one of the vakehn after what had felt like minutes. He leaned in towards her and spoke in a hushed voice; Petra was the nearest and strained to hear, but she caught nothing. The woman didn't respond at all.

At the far end, Anthis dropped his voice just as low. "She doesn't look like a vakah."

"Because she isn't."

Rathen's disturbed tone drew his eye, and he felt the lump of anxiety rise higher in his throat at the sight of the blatant alarm in the mage's tight expression. Guarded, he looked back to their host. "What should we do?" But the curt, swift strike to his shoulder silenced them both.

The woman began to walk again, sightless steps backwards with no less grace than the rest. Her eyes hadn't once left them. Even now she continued to assess them as she sat upon the largest of the mossy seats in front of the grand old oak. The moment her rear touched it, the moss swelled and grew impossibly vivid, and the flowers at her feet bent their heads towards her. The weasels, too, finally settled and sprawled out upon a branch.

She sat there for a long while, watching them.

They began to itch. Impatience soon got the better of Garon. "What do you want with us?" He demanded, foolishly without the briefest waver of hesitance or caution. The vakah beside him seized his shoulder before he could storm forwards out of the line.

But the woman didn't flinch. She didn't even blink. She rose calmly and strode back towards them at her own leisure. But this time, they didn't hold her attention. Suddenly the Zi'veyn was in her hand. Each of them blanched.

"This calms the magic," she said in a voice so sensual that, for a moment, none but Aria truly heard her. Her eyes drummed choicely back onto Rathen. "It quiets it, but it doesn't destroy it. An elven creation. To suspend an opponent's magic. The Zikrahlehveyn."

Haunted, Rathen swallowed hard and braced himself as she stopped barely two paces in front of him. She shifted her weight, throwing one perfect hip out to the side, one small crease in her torso. "...Yes..."

Her chin lifted and the intensity of her gaze redoubled. He couldn't look away from her eyes. "You've been using it all over Turunda, calming broken spells. It has saved countless lives. But it has not secured them." She took the vine of his left hand from the care of the vakah and pressed the relic into his palm. He continued to stare at her, searching for the deception, but her eyes were too complex, too chaotic to read. His chance fled as she turned and walked away. A gasp rippled around him at the sight of her hollow bark back, though eyes were quick to fall onto her rear, even despite the long, bovine tail that flicked before it.

"Is she reading your mind?" Anthis asked, trying unsuccessfully not to stare, but his lips pursed when that throbbing voice rose up.

"Reading his mind?" She chuckled, turning again with a smile that could splinter a heart into pieces. "Of course not. I've been told all of this. As I said, you've been using it all over Turunda." But then her smile faded, and the joyous amusement in her eyes shifted to realisation. She looked across them all again, with a gaze far more clear in its hunt. "...You have no idea who I am, do you?" It passed over Rathen. "You have an inkling..." then down onto Aria, and her smile returned. "Ah, but *you* know, don't you, little chipmunk?"

The child nodded, eyes wide with wonder. "You're the queen, aren't you?"

She reached out and brushed long, slender fingers affectionately across her cheek, then stepped back with a powerful presence into the view of all. "Yes," she declared proudly, "I am - though not as you understand it. I am the ruler of this forest - of *all* forests - and all that lives within them. I am its spirit. Its protector. I am Hlífrún, Rötternas Moder."

"Root Mother..."

Her eyes flicked onto Anthis, who pursed his lips again. "Very good. Though perhaps I shouldn't be impressed. After all, you are a well-learned one. Though it is an obscure, ancient language for your tongue all the same. Older, even, than the elves you so glorify." She smiled as his cheeks burned brighter.

"You're a skogsrå."

Her eyes flicked back onto Rathen and burned in the most violent insult for the most fleeting moment. Then she smiled again. "I am not *a* skogsrå. I am *the* skogsrå. But I will forgive you. You are not a democratic one, despite your accomplishments among Arkhamas and harpies - and among your own kin, though long passed they may be. But your wits and command are suited to a different calling. And, my," she moved closer and trailed a fingertip down his chest, "*what* a command."

Again his eyes were transfixed to hers, but he could feel his cheeks burning.

"Excuse me, Your Majesty," Aria's voice piped up, pulling her attention slowly away from her father, "I mean no disrespect - but aren't there any other skogsrå?"

"Not within Arasiin. This land is mine; the other masses belong to others of my kin. I would presume. Your books have told you otherwise?"

"N-no...I just didn't think there *wouldn't* be others..."

She smiled and bent down towards her. "But there is no other Arenaria, my dear." She rose again and her dominance returned. "Yes, Arasiin is mine. Which brings me to you. And to that." She gestured towards the relic in Rathen's hand. "But...not yet."

"Pardon us?"

"*Quiet*, Garon," Petra hissed.

"Yes, *quiet*, Garon," the skogsrå imitated perfectly. "I should think you would like me to heal this fair lady here. And I expect she'd like it, too." She turned to the nearest vakah and spoke in strange, fluid words, to which the young woman nodded, released her hold on Rathen's remaining wrist, and hurried away with another. "I presume you're not about to turn your magic upon me - I would be so very, *very* disappointed if you did."

"He won't," Aria assured, "Your Majesty."

"Such manners. She does you proud, Rathen. Oh stop looking so shocked! I have eyes and ears everywhere. Now, please," she gestured languidly towards the two returning vakehn and the familiar bags in their arms, "follow my friends, here. They'll escort you somewhere you can lay your heads for the night. And we'll do something about that food."

"Uh, food?"

"Yes, those awful rations you've been eating. Wouldn't you like something fresh?"

Rathen flinched beneath the strength of her stare.

"We appreciate the offer," Anthis said tentatively, "but we don't want to put you out--"

"Oh *nonsense*. Now, follow them. Please."

He, too, shrank beneath those eyes and their sudden, dangerous flare.

Despite their better judgement, they had no choice but to leave Petra behind in the skogsrå's care, who permitted, after a fuss, Garon to remain as security, and Rathen, Aria, Eyila and Anthis were left to follow the lead of the two vakehn. They watched the forest guardians rigidly as they shouldered the bags they'd left behind at Vastal's shrine, but the two paid them little in the way of any concern, meandering silently through the trees as though followed by nothing more than an obedient scurry of squirrels. Beyond the occasional meaningful glance, no one spoke a word. It wasn't until the vakehn drew them to a stop beneath the reach of another impressive oak that their silence was broken by an utterance of astonishment. Here, there *was* beauty.

This venerable tree appeared at first rather short, but its twisted trunk was simply thick, and entangled in creepers that coiled all the way up into its crown. Its boughs, too, were just as broad and heavy, so much so that it would take just one to crush a man's body should it collapse under its own weight. And within the greatest of those branches, under the light of the gathered fireflies, were hollows carved like long, open nests.

Ferns with accents of spidersilk hung like drapery from the thinner branches, upon which the insects' flames glittered like little yellow dew drops and were reflected back from a small stream that flowed freely through the softest grass.

"Daddy..."

"Yes, sweetheart," he said even as his surprise turned slowly towards suspicion, "it's beautiful."

"They made this for us?"

He dropped his voice and sent a quick look towards the quiet vakehn. "Perhaps. But I doubt they get many visitors. Be careful."

"Actually," they each stiffened at the chime of the soft voice, one tinged with the strangest yet most familiar of accents they couldn't quite place, "they're our beds." The vakah smiled at them.

"Oh," Rathen replied carefully. "And, uh...where will *you* all be sleeping?"

"Open, among the trees."

The male of the two stepped forwards while she continued her unsettlingly placid smile, and he turned his own fully upon Eyila. "You may take mine, miss," he said, taking her hand softly in his and gesturing towards the second highest. "It's certainly the most comfortable."

"Oh...thank you," she smiled, blushing. "That's very kind of you."

"Yes, very kind," Anthis agreed tightly.

The vakah cocked his head at the young man, but deigned no response. Rathen closed his eyes to spare himself the tension. The two had begun to walk away when he finally opened them again, and he gave the historian's arm a brief, sharp backhand while the others watched them leave.

"I'll take the top," he announced, turning and looking up at their apparent lodgings. "Anthis, you take the middle."

"Am I on the bottom?"

"No, sweetheart, you're at the top with me. Garon and Petra can take the bottom. They'll be quicker to the defence; Eyila and I can cast from a distance if we need to."

Anthis studied him while he rubbed the sting from his arm. "You don't sound too convinced." But neither mage, he noticed, replied. "Rathen, what are we going to do?"

"We haven't much choice."

"We do." He stepped around in front of him, eyes burning with urgency. "Use your magic *now*."

"Not on your life."

"What about *Aria's* life?"

Rathen stared down at him. "You didn't feel it. She is...*powerful*. They *all* are, but her most of all."

"He's right," Eyila agreed. "I felt it, too. It's...terrifying..."

"Are you all right?"

She smiled at Anthis's sudden concern and nodded as his cheeks turned pink. She frowned in disappointment when he hurriedly looked away.

"A skogsrå is the spirit of the wilds," Rathen continued to spare himself again. "It's an ancient word – 'forest warden', I think. They're mostly relegated to legends and stories now. *Everything* in this forest is."

"Pre-elven," Anthis agreed tightly, "the creatures, the language...but how are they still here?"

"Hid themselves away, most likely. But a skogsrå is intertwined with the wilds, they're part of one another. But I didn't know that there was only *one* of them..."

"Yes, *one* - so where's the problem?"

"All the power to rule the forests and its creatures - it doesn't fall to many, it falls to *one*; all of that power and everything with it is consolidated into *one* individual. I can't stand against her...and I wouldn't want to go up against a vakah again any time soon, either..."

Anthis shifted at the two mages' nervous expressions. "So we're stuck here, then?"

"For the moment. We can't be the one to throw the first punch."

"Punch?" Aria frowned. "But, Daddy, she wants our help."

"She probably just wants to make sure we're going to keep doing exactly what we already are."

"Yes," Rathen replied, "but on her terms."

"What could they possibly be? If we remove the magic, which we're already doing, then we're both already winning anyway."

But again, Rathen didn't respond, and this time Aria looked more than a little concerned. Anthis's tongue didn't seem willing to obey his command to press the subject.

In short time, Garon and Petra returned, the latter moving her arm around somewhat excessively but clearly in perfect health, and the vakehn returned on cue with baskets in their arms. They set them upon the ground at the foot of the tree and began to hand out servings to their unwilling guests. They looked into the woven-leaf bowls warily.

"What is it?" Petra asked as neutrally as she could while probing the unidentifiable mass.

"Boar and rain tubers."

"Boar?"

The vakah flashed her a bright, amused grin. "None of us here are herbivores."

The impenetrable darkness that had suffocated them night after night was softened at last by the yellow glow of fireflies. And they'd have been quite welcome on any other occasion, but tonight they felt sickeningly inappropriate, almost mocking the distinct and tangible danger they found themselves trapped beneath. Rathen was not the only one to wonder if they weren't a deliberate joke. But they made do - they had no choice - and after their suspiciously delicious meal, most of them retired to their nest-like beds while Garon examined the perimeter.

Rathen stared up into the leaves, watching them shift lazily in the breeze to reveal the smallest pockets of stars while Aria slumbered beside him, lying across his chest. She hadn't begun to sprawl yet, so he was comfortable enough for fret and fatigue to lead him away into a world of irrational thought and self-pity that he had, until then, managed to hold at bay. And it all began with one, dangerous question: how did he ever get caught up in this?

He grunted softly. That damned question. It never did him any good. The magic, the chasms, the Arana, and now a - *the* - skogsrå. Queen of the Woods. Root Mother.

For a moment he pondered a brief flicker of wonder at just how far the hand of the Spirit of the Wilds reached. And just what within the scowles would bend to it. He let that thought drift away in favour of absently mulling over her title, and, inevitably, darker thoughts began to creep in.

She undoubtedly wanted them to fix the Wildlands. But she would have her terms. She'd have left them alone to continue as they were otherwise. If every creature in every forest reported back to her, she'd know they weren't about to stop. And she'd surely also know that the threat they were fighting against went beyond renegade magic.

So what did she want?

The books he'd read to Aria back in their safe little hovel began once more to reverberate through his skull. The stories, the lore, the myth, and eventually the third-, fourth- and seventh-hand accounts. The source of the average man's knowledge on the matters of the romanticised 'wildlings', from harpies to lindworms (ditchlings were almost always excluded for being a nuisance and a menace rather than anything exotic). But while most accounts were, no doubt, exaggerated, embellished or outright fabrications, it took just one look into the skogsrå's eyes to see that she, at least, had been underestimated.

The protective arm Aria had fallen asleep within tightened around her, and he looked down as she stirred. "Daddy," she said quietly, her eyes still closed.

"Yes?"

A smile spread across her sleepy face, and her dirty, bare foot kicked out to the side of the hollowed branch. "I want one."

"I'll see what I can do," he chuckled, and kissed the top of her head. But as she began to drift back off to sleep, he heard the exasperated tone of the inquisitor further out in the woods. Carefully, he lifted himself up to peer over the edge of the bed.

"You would be better off."

"No, thank you, Your Majesty."

While Garon continued his march back towards camp, keeping his eyes firmly on anything that was not her, the Root Mother fixed him with a boundless stare. "...It really hurt you to say that," she surmised - correctly, by the curl of his lip - and smiled in amusement. "You are a curious one, aren't you? Your convictions - they mean so very much to you. I'm not human, therefore I cannot be a queen. And your work--"

"Don't go there."

She cocked a black eyebrow. "Yes, your work." Her eyes drifted towards the tree as it fell into sight, and rested upon the second branch from the ground. "And your heart. But you deny it." Her eyes returned to him. "Why? For the sake of your pride?"

"You know nothing about me," he replied flatly, and fired her a look of fury for her sudden, blisteringly delightful laugh. "Oh, no, I know plenty. Too much, perhaps. It makes me feel dirty."

"Then turn around and leave me alone."

His arm was suddenly seized by a steel grip, and he found himself staring into vehement eyes framed by lines of glee. "Be careful, Inquisitor Brack," she said dangerously, "you forget who you're speaking to. I might not be a queen in your eyes, but this is *my* domain, and you *will* respect *me*, *and* it, or you won't live long enough to regret it."

Then, just as abrupt and seamless, her demeanour reverted to its previous ease. Garon freed his arm and spun at the sound of footsteps to find Rathen joining them outside of the tree's earshot, looking between them cautiously. "What's going on?"

"Oh, my dear," she cooed affectionately while he already began to regret getting involved, "your friend here is a difficult one. I only offered him my help and he all but bit off my hand!"

"Help?" He frowned carefully. "With what?"

"Noth--"

"Why, to heal him, of course!" She interrupted innocently while the inquisitor stiffened further in anger. "I fixed up young Petra's arm without breaking a sweat - it really would be no trouble at all..."

"What? Why? What's wrong?" Rathen demanded, hurriedly searching the officer up and down for whatever injury he'd missed from their brawl with the roots, but he found not even a rip in his shirt. "Why does he--why do you need healing?"

"Oh, well, aside from a pesky disorder of character, there's the matter of nerve damage."

Rathen's eyes flashed wide. "*Nerve damage?*"

"It's nothing," Garon replied gruffly, stepping past him to escape the interrogation and resume his survey in peace. "An old injury, I've learned to live with it."

"Oh, pish," she said, moving quickly in front of him to block off his path, nailing him again with her strange, cruel stare. "It's not *that* old, is it? Two months? Three?"

"...I've not noticed anything..."

"No," she turned towards the troubled mage, "I don't suspect you would have. He's been hiding it from you, my dear, albeit not very well."

"Why?"

"Well because--oh," her hands quickly covered her plump lips, "no, I've said too much." She smiled sweetly. "You're sure you don't want my help?"

"Positive."

"Oh well. Good night, then." She left with a languid wave, and both of them felt themselves ease. Until Rathen's attention returned inquiringly to the officer. "Garon?"

In true form, Garon walked away.

"Oh, there you are." Rathen stopped and peered up into the highest boughs of a tree just out of sight of the oak. "Ah--oh...sorry if I've...interrupted..."

"No, no, not at all." Eyila quickly threw an animal skin over her own as she rose from her perch and began descending the rough old trunk to join him.

"O-oh," he stammered, averting his eyes. "You didn't have to come down..."

"It's fine. You need something?"

"I-I just wondered if you knew--" He frowned as she reached the bottom and turned at last to face him, the light of the moon glancing across her bronze skin and the unmistakable streaks of tears. He realised then that the music had dimmed in her voice. His tone softened. "Eyila, what's wrong?"

She smiled and gathered the skin tighter, shaking her head and wiping her cheeks as surreptitiously as she could. "Nothing."

"Eyila--"

"No," she continued to smile, "really, I'm fine. Promise."

He observed her closely, thoroughly unconvinced, and she held his gaze with puffy eyes. He didn't ask again. He stepped forwards and embraced her instead. Rathen had learned long ago that there was more than one meaning to the word 'promise'. She sought comfort, not questions, and to avoid the latter had resolved to turn to her own company. And, as a gentle, consoling breeze invaded the impenetrable forest, he guessed at another's. He confirmed in that moment the source of her despair.

He held her tighter and kissed the top of her head, and she shuddered with a wheeze as another potent wave of bleeding anguish burst free.

Anthis stormed back to the entangled oak with his teeth clamped tightly behind his lips, gave the trunk one swift, sharp kick and squeezed his ire into a dense and stifled growl.

"What's wrong?"

"Nothing!" Startled, he looked up and found Aria peering down from the highest bed. He made his best effort to smile. "Nothing, I'm...." He sighed smiled apologetically. "I'm fine. Promise."

She pursed her lips, then began climbing over the side of the branch.

"Aria, *no*," he told her firmly, "stay up there, you'll hurt yourself." But she ignored him, and with the skill of a squirrel she clambered down the vines, turned around, pulled him by the hand down to her own level and embraced him.

He smiled softly and returned the gesture.

"I know what that 'promise' means." She looked up at him, and though she seemed about to say something, it didn't pass her lips. She squeezed him tighter instead.

Chapter 33

Slowly, the soft trill of birdsong eased away the euphony of sleep, and morning's gentle chill caressed the skin to goose-flesh within the comfort of silken sheets. Unhurried, untroubled, eyelids fluttered open to face deep emerald, and a peaceful sigh slipped through a smile.

Then Rathen remembered where he was.

He sat bolt upright, startling Aria who had sprawled across him in her sleep, snatched her to safety though she was far from tumbling out of the branch, and jumped again with a stifled cry when he found the Root Mother perched upon the end of the bough, watching him with a disconcerting level of attention. Her perfect lips curved into a smile. Unnerved, he did his best to return it. "Good morning..."

"Yes," she beamed, "it is." She rose and leapt from the branch, the thin, flimsy gossamer she'd now clothed herself in flowing like water behind her, and landed lightly upon the ground some thirty feet below. Her voice carried back up in a song much too exuberant for first thing in the morning, and the birds' gentle warbling was replaced by a sudden, squawking chorus. "*Rise and shiiiiine!*"

Startled awake, the others glared at her over the edges of their nests.

A gaggle of vakehn served a breakfast of some kind of wild egg and a selection of equally questionable fungi, all of which they'd eaten with hesitance through a desire to avoid insulting their host. While the vakehn waited upon them, Hlífrún watched them closely, further uneasing them after their unnaturally rich sleep. Then, once they were satiated and suitably disturbed, she declared, before they could excuse themselves and finally make an escape, that there was something they needed to see. Under that fearsome gaze, they had no choice but to cooperate.

And so it was that they stumbled nervously through the forest behind her, speaking their concern through silent looks but for the grunts of surprise when they tripped. Unlike they, Hlífrún and her vakehn had no trouble navigating the tangle, and it transpired only once a particularly tricky knot of roots and briar unwound itself from Aria's path that the struggle was deliberate. Another glance of irritation breezed through the group.

"You're showing us the magic," Rathen spoke up to distract himself. "That's what you need help with?"

"Well it's hardly about a mouse problem." The skogsrå ducked beneath a branch, and a sudden, keening heartache invading her silvery voice. "The magic is ruining the forests - an understatement, of course, but you've seen it for yourselves - and my creatures are dying. It's blocking foraging routes, separating hunters from their prey, collapsing and exposing their homes and outright killing them. Most of the 'wildlings' as you call them have fled for safety, which, ironically, puts them now in the danger of humans." She bit off a sharp snarl. "All your kind know of them is what your books and stories tell you, and so they die at your hands instead because *you're* frightened of *them*. Because you think they're monsters that *only* belong in books and stories. And that every word you've read and heard regardless of source is true. Just as many of my creatures come to believe that all they need to know of humans can be learned in the two minutes it takes for one of you to loose an arrow."

"We're not all--"

"No," she replied firmly, returning her eyes to the front. "No. And neither are we. But how often does either side get the opportunity to realise that?"

"But this is besides the point. With every crack in the earth, my connection to the forests is being severed."

"Your connection? What do you do for it?"

The Spirit of the Wilds cast back a straight and unmistakable look. "Everything." Steps faltered while they calculated the depth of that answer. "The Wildlands is the last great stronghold, deep and thick enough to be protected from humans, to be able to thrive in safety. It is also the seat of my power. And it is at risk. If the Wildlands goes, so do I."

"So you want us to keep on doing exactly what we are?"

She answered Anthis with little more than a cryptic smile.

A rumbling sound soon pervaded the warming forest air and the shrill, intermittent birdsong they'd become woefully accustomed to. But as it presented a new concern, the all too familiar touch of magic rushed over them and chased it away. Dread boiled in Rathen's stomach and he felt himself begin to fall to the assault in a heartbeat. But then, for no reason at all, it passed, and in its place came the enthusiastic embrace of relief.

But he wasn't deceived for long.

The magic hadn't gone anywhere. Its pull and guidance was still present, he could feel it luring him forwards, closer and closer towards the rumbling while peace remained a permanent undertone - but the aggression, the desperate compulsion to follow that pull, the inability to block it out of his mind...those had evaporated.

Bemused, he looked around to Eyila only to find that her eyes had already turned to glass. It was only as his gaze chanced to brush the vakah beside her that he noticed the feather-light spell that enshrouded him. His eyes became incredulous. "What in Zikhon's name are you doing?!"

She smiled for a moment in amusement. "A barrier," she simply replied. "To stop the magic from affecting you."

"Do you have *any* idea what...could have...?" He listened. He looked. But nothing had changed. The rolling sound had grown no louder, the ground had not cracked beneath them, and the magic that remained had not come unhinged. His gaze dropped back to her, bewildered while the others continued to search in a frenzy. "*Your* magic doesn't affect it..." He looked back towards the absent. "Can't you also help Eyila?"

"Of course they can," Hlífrún replied with a laugh. "But so can *you*."

"No, I *can't*, my magic--"

"Did I say anything about your magic? Anyway, she's not your priority right now."

"No, but--"

She cast him a frightfully impatient look. "She is not your priority right now."

Eyila continued to trudge along at Petra's side, leaning heavily upon the duelist's aid, but though Petra sent him an urging look, she knew just as he that if there was truly anything he could have done, he'd have done it by now. And if the vakehn didn't see fit to protect her as they had him, there was little any of them could do to change their minds. They were doubtlessly under orders, and the skogsrå's volatile mood swings rendered negotiation out of their favour.

But while Rathen had control of his own senses, he could at least try to work out what she had meant.

The rumbling was growing steadily louder, and the inappropriately cheerful music sought without success to distract them. But it was the sudden aroma on a shift in the breeze that struck the final blow to their guard. Burley, vanilla, perique tobacco and mulberry. An arcane scent they'd only ever experienced in one place and now sent a jolt of dizzy terror through all who recognised it.

"What is this place we're going to? Uh--Y-your Majesty?" Petra amended, pushing herself past the shock, but again the skogsrå simply smiled and held aside a brush of foliage to the fully sunlit clearing on the other side.

"See for yourself."

Hands rose against the blinding light. It was the clearest view they'd had of the sun in what felt like months, but now it only added to the assault on their senses. The rumbling grew to its loudest, the scent intensified and came in wafts on the breeze, and the music continued its delicate and untouchable melody as though it was tinkling inside their skulls.

Rathen clenched his teeth. He'd forgotten how chilling the magic could be, and he dreaded the impending experience of silencing it with a clear head. He would feel the beauty vanish, the peace, all the disquieting wonder. It had chilled him at Borer's Teeth, and again in Wrenroot, but where the magic's assault had grown at every exposure, so too had he been spared that distress in his exhaustion.

Now, though, he would feel its full force, as well as the spear of hopelessness it was sure to fire through his heart. The only thought that gave him any comfort was the possibility of learning something from the process that could help him with the newest task he'd been coerced into - but the spell was a trial for another time.

A cool spray of water against his skin stirred him from his frets, and as his eyes finally adjusted to the brightness, he found himself gazing up at a thundering wall of azure water crashing down from fifty feet into a white, lily-studded lake. He gasped despite himself. But while it shook the ground and shook the air, even this vast and powerful thing could not outmatch the forest, dwarfed as it was by the trees that grew on either side like drapery, rooted even to the face of the cliff.

But mouths hung open nevertheless, and for a long moment they each stared in silent wonder.

Light danced across the grass from the shimmering falls. Birds flew low over the surface of the pool and snatched dragonflies on the wing. Reeds swayed rigidly in the breeze. They smelled the lilies and the damp earth, they heard the bird and insect songs, the bubbling of fish and splosh of frogs. They counted the haphazardly formed rainbows that streaked unnaturally in all directions up and down the waterfall.

Enraptured, Petra took a slow step forwards. The spray brushed her, but the sensation in the wake of what was already becoming a warm morning was too pleasant to retreat from. "I had no idea Turunda had anything like this..."

"*Petra!*"

The tranquillity was broken. A strong grip about her arm dragged her sharply backwards. Her hand immediately seized the hilt of her sword, but where she'd expected to find a vakah holding her back, she found Garon. Protest forming on her lips, she followed his gaze towards the right of the water's pool and gawped at the shimmering white stallion that stood on the furthest bank.

Anthis eased in relief. "Relax, Garon, it's just--"

"No, it isn't." Rathen pulled Aria close. "It's a näcken."

"Actually," Hlífrún sighed tediously, "it's a bäckahäst. Näcken don't bother to disguise themselves." She approached the water's edge and stepped one delicate foot onto the surface. It dipped and rippled, but held like a spider's web, and she strode across it with confidence, her gossamer flowing around her like a royal gown. The stallion froze and watched her closely, but the moment her toes touched the grass on the other side, it nickered and bowed its head, affectionately muzzling her outstretched hand in greeting.

They watched the queen smile. It was an honest expression, full of heart and contentment, and one that became more ravishing the longer they looked. Petra turned her eyes away. The others were slower to do so. Aria hadn't broken her captivated stare at the horse.

The bäckahäst lifted its head as she scratched its chin between its tusks, baring for a moment its thorn-sharp teeth as its lip curled in interest. She rose up onto the tips of her toes and kissed its forehead, then ran her hand along its flank and gave its buttock a firm and dismissive pat. Obediently, it turned and walked into the water, vanishing into thin air long before it had submerged.

They blinked in astonishment. Until Garon shook Petra by the arm he still held fast to. "*What* do you think you're doing letting your guard down like that?!" He demanded in her ear, but she pursed her lips and snatched herself free, turning her attention upon Eyila instead.

"Garon, leave it," said Rathen as he pressed. "It's done." With a nervous breath, he turned to face the waterfall. "The magic is focused here. ...No..." he frowned miserably, "*beneath* the falls. At the...at the bottom of the pool." He looked vexedly towards the Root Mother as she returned across the water. "What exactly is down there?"

"Old things," she replied, smiling briefly towards Anthis, but rather than elaborate, she settled herself on the reedy bank and ran her fingers leisurely through the grass. "But for the moment, the door is locked. We must wait."

"Door?"

"*Oh--*"

"No," she giggled as Anthis plunged his hand into his satchel, "it takes a different kind of key. I told you: we must wait." Then she turned her eyes towards the water, lay back on her grey elbows, and sighed in contentment beneath the warmth of the morning. The three vakehn separated to take up their own meditative positions around the water, and they settled just as easily.

The others looked at one another in doubt before uncomfortably following their lead.

An hour passed and the sun was just edging in above them when Hlífrún finally stirred. Her painite eyes fluttered open as the light graced her cheeks, her lips bowed into a smile, and she rose elegantly to her feet. The others scurried impatiently to join her.

With the laziest wave she signalled to one of the vakehn on the far side of the water, and he was quick to respond. With an extraordinarily high leap, he rose from his spot beneath a tree to grasp a branch some ten feet above his head, pulled himself up as though he weighed nothing at all, and promptly disappeared.

A moment later they winced against the blinding light that shone out from between the leaves. It shortly dimmed, then another flare appeared opposite, in a tree close beside them. In quick succession a flurry had lit up, four on each side of the water, bouncing from one to another until the ninth appeared on the cliff face right beside the waterfall.

Their breath stilled in anticipation.

A new rumbling began to shake the forest, and they watched as the water itself began to part, spreading like curtains, folding and crumpling like cloth, yet continuing to flow unhindered. And on the other side, where there had surely been rock, it bared now an arched doorway.

But while they observed in wonder, Rathen focused himself on keeping his feet right where they were. The vakah's spell may have eliminated the pressure, but the magic was still coaxing him forwards, and now that the doorway to its source had been opened, its call had grown that much stronger. But this time he had the power to deny it, and deny it he would.

Hlífrún turned and smiled, starting backwards towards the falls, bidding them to follow. They did so warily but for Anthis, who equally tried his best to keep his feet under his own control rather than run on head in excitement. He failed in his restraint to notice that they had stepped out onto the apparently solid water, and scrutinised instead the smooth cut of the arch. "This is elven," he said, oblivious to the spray.

"What else would it have been?" Rathen asked blandly.

Levelling with the glint on the cliff, he spun around and surveyed the ricocheting light. It was a perfect stream, making its way from sun to falls by deliberate and subtle design, a notion only pre-magic elves would have conceived. But, as he marvelled, a dreadful thought slowly began to take shape. He stepped beneath the arch and spun back around to avoid a trip. "Wha-uh, what is it reflecting that light?"

"Stones. The elves set them in the bark to catch it."

"That must have been a long time ago," Aria mused. She cocked her head at the grey-skinned spirit. "I know how trees grow. Shouldn't they have been swallowed up by now?"

"Feira wished them not to be. I ensure it stays that way."

"But how can light unlock--"

"We've found stones embedded in trees before..." All eyes turned to Anthis at his suddenly agitated tone. His eyes were wide beneath a deeply knotted brow, and his young face was creased with torment. "But no one...no one has ever..." His hands floated helplessly to his lips, his head, to the air for answers while his eyes stared at some distant horror. Aria searched ahead into the darkness. "How many of these have been *missed?!*"

He began to shake. Petra took him gently by the shoulder and steered him forwards as she did the enthralled tribal.

They descended into darkness over treacherous ground. Light formed slowly above them, a dance of gathering fireflies flickering softly in the wake of the queen, and within moments had illuminated the staircase, spiral and constructed of woven roots. The light was stronger than it should have been, and they began to doubt that they were typical fireflies at all - but no one wished to look close enough to find out.

The staircase levelled out into a tunnel riddled with hanging, rising and intersecting roots, but this time their guide coaxed them away, and they stepped freely into a chamber no larger than eight feet across. But while its size matched that of the last chamber the Wildlands had sheltered, this one was decidedly empty. Only a few small tables stood along the left side of the room, atop and beneath which were only a few pots, boxes and other inconsequential items. But they were no longer searching for information.

Rathen swallowed hard as his eyes dropped to the Zi'veyn. This was the spot.

"Pre-magic," Anthis muttered, his troubled whisper amplified by the cool air and compact walls while he looked across their carvings, already analysing the details the others had yet to notice. "Another holy site to Feira...things happened here..."

"Things like what?" Aria asked in her own attempt to be quiet.

But Anthis could only shake his head, the wonder that should have been in his eyes denied by his anguish. "I...don't know... The other crystals were found by nothing significant...either... Oh...Gods..."

Aria smiled sadly and wrapped her little arms around him.

"Well, it doesn't matter anyway," Rathen stated absently as he turned the Zi'veyn over in the fireflies' glow. "We're here for the magic." He straightened and turned to Hlífrún, who was once again smiling at him with eyes that burned bright with fascination even in the darkness. "I don't mean to be rude, Your Majesty," he began very carefully, "but there's not very much room down here..."

Her eyes narrowed, but her stare didn't break. He swallowed hard again. Then, as sweat threatened to form on the back of his neck despite the cool if stale air, she smiled sweetly and turned away, spreading her arms wide. "Out!" But, of course, Garon immediately protested. She rolled her eyes impatiently. "Oh you *do* like to be a nuisance. Fine. The *rest* of you: out!"

But this time Anthis stammered.

"You're supposed to be watching Eyila," Petra reminded him, but he only looked back at her with wide, empty eyes as he struggled to find some kind of answer. She shook her head with a scoff. "Good to know where your priorities are. Fine. *I'll* look after her while you go gallivanting around. Just don't get in Rathen's way."

"*Oh for goodness sake!*" Dust fell and rock crumbled as the queen's rich voice reverberated about the room, striking them all stone-still in fright. Then she huffed and sulkily folded her arms. "Now there's no room for me." She turned sharply and looked down at Aria instead. "In that case, we must play a game."

The child's face lit up, until apprehension slipped in. She hid it well, however, for the skogsrå only smiled. She glanced past her to her father, but he was already looking towards Petra, who gave him one subtle nod and lifted Eyila gently to her feet, declaring that they would be outside. He turned back to the child and smiled reassuringly. "Go ahead."

Hlífrún beamed with joy and grasped the little girl's hand, leading her right on out of the chamber. Rathen's smile collapsed as he watched them go, but his shoulders eased a little when they stopped and sat on the ground just outside the door in the middle of the short tunnel, joined by a replacement flare of fireflies.

Garon took position in the doorway and gave him a nod of assurance, leaning against the frame where he had an easy view into both chamber and tunnel, while Petra took up a post at the far end. With his magic out of the question, Aria's safety was left in their hands.

Rathen sighed and looked down again at the unassuming relic. "The sooner I get started..."

The atmosphere in the chamber quickly thickened, but the silence was at least occasionally broken by light hearted giggling and accusations of cheating.

"Little chipmunk," the Root Mother sang gleefully some twenty minutes later as she tossed the rock up into the air and snatched three knucklebones from the ground, "what fun is there in cheating when I can win so much more easily by simply moving *faster* than you?" She handed her the rock with a mischievous grin as Aria poked out her tongue, and waited as the girl took her turn to toss the rock. It rose notably higher this time, and she snatched three pieces herself before it landed back in the palm of her hand. Hlífrún narrowed her eyes at the collection of eight bones, and the seven in her own possession. "Now I think *you* might be cheating."

"May I ask a question?" The girl began as they gathered the scattered pieces for a fresh game. "Are you the Lady?"

"She can't be, Aria, the Lady is a group of sisters," Petra reminded her softly from beside the stairs, still smiling at the girl's infectious joy.

"Actually, I am they, and they are I. My presence in the trees is stronger in some than in others."

Petra's eyes widened as a sense of sudden inferiority kicked her in the head. It seemed to miss Aria, however, who continued her rather brazen questioning thoroughly unperturbed. "In that case, if you're a god, why do you leave them and make them follow you?"

"Ah, but I am *not* a god, and I don't leave *or* make them follow me." She scattered the fifteen knucklebones. "I'm always there. But as seasons change and life grows, the strength of life in the trees change. Some go to sleep sooner than others, some don't sleep at all, and so my presence shifts to whomever is most receptive."

Aria nodded a little too easily. "And looking after their dreams?"

"They believe what they will," she sighed. "I don't know what lies in the next life any more than you do. But I would wager that, should they live as they're supposed to, whatever comes next will be kind to them. And as long as 'the Lady' continues to live in their hearts, they will do just that. Watching over their dreams is just a comfort."

"So it's not real?"

Hlífrún smiled at her knot of concern. "It's as real as they believe it is. That's why it's a comfort."

"...So *do* you look after their dreams?"

She pursed her lips thoughtfully. "Perhaps. I've no idea what I get up to while *I* sleep. Perhaps I do gather them up and that's why so few of my own dreams make sense. Listen to me, chipmunk," she leaned forwards and fixed her with a gaze that exuded a sudden, endless wisdom, as though she were much, much older than the ruins in which they played. "Some things you should never try to understand. Knowledge can be a burden. In mystery, there is freedom."

"But Anthis--"

"Does not wish to know the answers to faith. If I have learned that much of him, you must know it, too. It's tangible knowledge he seeks. Not metaphysical."

She blinked slowly.

"The nature of reality, of existence - the kind of questions that only serve to feed the ego of the one who can finally answer them. Things that don't really matter."

She nodded slowly, and her eyes drifted slowly onto Petra. The duelist appeared lost in troubled thought. "I think I understand... So that goes for knowledge that will make us sad or angry too, doesn't it? If it changes our hearts in a bad way, but doesn't really have anything to do with anyone else, or anything around you, we don't really need it."

"...I suppose..." Hlífrún frowned and followed her gaze. Then she understood. She turned back with a smile and dropped her voice beneath even a whisper. "Very astute. Vengeance too, in a way. Live happily, chipmunk, and live well. Some things you don't need to know, others you need not to."

Anthis slowed his enthusiastic rush as he passed Garon in the doorway. Frowning at the unusual look on his face, he followed the officer's riveted stare towards a table just inside the chamber. The question forming on his lips quickly evaporated.

The moment he caught sight of it, his heart lurched. Sweat beaded on his skin as suddenly as if the floor had caught fire, and he swallowed hard past the quickly-forming lump in his throat. His heart thudded, his collar felt tight, the skin prickled on the back of his neck.

Both of their gazes urgently snapped away.

Garon turned his back and leaned against the opposite side of the doorway, clearing his throat with a light, unassuming cough while Anthis stuffed the dried herbs and their erotic magic into a jug. Eye contact was avoided, and they returned to their own business without a word.

Beyond the magic, the world didn't exist. There was only the arcane. Order within chaos, simplicity within intricacy; a structure to be probed and dismantled while its products enticed, lured and distracted at every step - self-preservation, if magic were so capable.

But he was above it. He had beaten it before, this legacy of a formidably mighty people - a people who thought themselves so far above him and yet had driven themselves to the brink of extinction for such foolish use of it, who even now hid in the mists and forbade themselves life's freedom, paralysed by the fear that it may happen again.

But he had beaten it many times. And he would do so again.

Another controlled breath; the final threads of the web began to tear.

Snap.

The music silenced.

Snap.

The scent diminished.

Snap.

The peace relented.

And nothing.

The cold touch of metal only complemented the emptiness which itself began to suffocate him, just as he'd known it would. He spared it no moment to set in. Immediately, he sought his safety line. Like a wisp of smoke from the hearth, Aria's giggles gathered and drifted, circling around him to slow his breath, ease his senses and quiet his mind but for one all-important thought. And only once he had that thought firmly centred did he take a deep, sedating breath and open his eyes.

The mural of trees spread across the wall before him was awash in a weak yellow glow, and the stale, dusty air was silent in the lull of laughter but for a gentle rustle just behind him. Rathen turned, steadying himself against the wall as the chamber shifted sideways beneath a wave of exhaustion, and he found Garon staring out into the tunnel with his back turned and Anthis sitting quietly upon the floor, surrounded by papers and the glow of hovering fireflies. He was looking up at him expectantly.

"Well done," the historian smiled. "You seem calm."

"As do you."

Anthis nodded, subdued. "I think I've worked it out. This place is locked behind light - which means that, once closed, it can only be opened at a certain time the following day, at the earliest."

"And what does that mean?" Rathen asked, sitting down before another spell of dizziness toppled him over, grateful for the unimportant subject. "It's a safe?"

"Not so much for keeping *things* in, as *people*."

"So it's a *prison?*"

"No - a place of contemplation and penance."

Rathen frowned speculatively. "How do you know that?"

"The stories on the wall."

"What stories?"

"Well," Anthis smiled, rising to his feet and stepping excitedly over the dry old papers, further exhausting the mage, "well actually the story itself is...a discovery, of sorts. It's rather familiar..."

"If it's familiar, how can--"

He raised that lordly informed finger. "Source." Rathen watched drowsily as he gestured right the way around the room. "All of this is about the importance of nature, of preservation, relayed by a story of someone who ignored Feira's rules. Look here: a woman had been on a pilgrimage through the wilds for weeks when she grew tired and stopped to rest mid-way up the tallest hill. When she turned around she found herself looking out over a landscape so beautiful that she stayed right there for three days until the full moon. She was enchanted, convinced that it was the greatest example in the world of Feira's power, and she wanted to share it, but there was little room for more than a few people to catch the view at any one time without the trees below getting in the way. She believed her intention was noble, so she went ahead and uprooted a number of those trees to open up the viewing site and replanted them somewhere else. And people *did* come, and the sight *was* beautiful - but it all came at a price. Wildlife was driven out, their homes removed, food sources from the sparser trees lost. And then, after a summer so wet it had been hailed - and I remember reading mention of it from a few different sources already - as 'Feira's Tears', the world fell."

Rathen's weary brow creased. "The world fell?"

"So far as I can see, it was a landslide. No trees, no roots, nothing to bind the soil. People were killed."

"And that's a discovery?"

"No, but its nature *is*. This story is one that survived even into long post-magic times."

"I thought the elves had rejected all their gods and nature and balance by then."

"They had. The surviving version: they removed the trees to open up the view and draw people in to see it. But, rather than replant the trees, they built an inn with the wood. People flocked to see that view and stay in that inn, just as they knew they would; it became popular, prices rose, the inn expanded, and they became rich."

"And the landslide?"

"Conveniently omitted. Happily ever after."

"Right. And all that means that this is a place of contemplation and penance?"

"The isolation, the depth, roots everywhere you turn, and the story itself serves as a more direct reminder of Feira's importance. As well as the very fact that it's right here, where the veil between us and the gods is at its thinnest if the magic is any indication. So yes," he declared, returning to his spot inside the ring of papers, "it does."

"...Fair enough. What have you got there?"

"Ah - just bits and pieces I found in the crates. Otherwise it's just common spiritual things, pots, incense burners...herbs..."

"Nothing to fit the key?"

"Not a thing. And all that I *did* find is just more information on things we already knew - 'we' as in...*my* 'we'."

"I'm with you." He watched him glance back over the papers while a grimace of disappointment slipped in. "We have the Zi'veyn, remember, Anthis - we don't need anything else."

"I know that but...surely we can't have gotten *all* the pieces of the puzzle..."

"Probably not, but we've managed just fine with the ones we cut out and scribbled in ourselves."

Anthis gave him a sideways look. "You did that, too?"

"Of course - but, I'll tell you: Aria's a master. Sometimes I hide pieces just to see what she'll come up with. Half the puzzle once. It was a horse originally, standing in that typical proud-horse stance, front hoof raised - in fact I actually left the hooves in there, they were part of the border and if the *border's* not complete, she won't touch it."

"Reasonable."

"Absolutely. Anyway, rather than a horse, she wound up with two fauns, one running away from the other because the one at the back was trying to tickle him."

Anthis burst out laughing, at which point Aria herself came running in, barrelling past the smiling inquisitor, and leapt upon her father with a look of faux indignation. "How *dare* you have fun without me!"

"From what I heard, little one," he grinned as he returned her tight squeeze, "I think you're just as guilty as I am."

"It's done?"

Garon straightened and stepped aside to let the skogsrå pass, and their merriment crashed to a halt. Rathen rose to his feet, wary against dizziness, and gave her a nod. She smiled beautifully, but just as her lips pursed to form words of gratitude, a withering look took over.

A hollow voice rose above the thrum of water in the distance. A crushingly mournful song reached into the chamber like the claw of a cold, helpless spirit, stroking skin to gooseflesh in its unending search for eternal rest.

A sigh no less forlorn slipped from the Root Mother, and she turned and fled the room. Rathen saw the foolish wonder spark in Aria's eyes, and was immediately on her heels as she chased after her. The rest had no choice but to follow.

Squinting against the onslaught of dazzling light beyond the falls, the harrowing dirge was at its peak. A canticle, tempered and patient, it wrenched the heart even in its horror.

Rathen caught Aria by the wrist just as her foot hit the water and scolded her firmly, and at the skogsrå's curt gesture, the rest stopped short just behind him. They tightened together. Slowly, Garon drew his sword, and they watched closely as the skogsrå crossed the pool.

The song drifted from the furthest bank. Straining against the light, their keenly attentive eyes began to discern a figure standing in the shade. Tall and slender, with arms outstretched as if about to embrace the whole forest, and legs that seemed half a length too long. There was motion about its feet. But it was not earth. It was air. It wasn't standing at all, they realised, but floating, raised a foot or so from the grass by a miniature vortex of leaves and twigs.

The same perilous mixture of fear and intrigue that had shadowed them through the forest bade each of them to stare harder, and while the creature's details came slowly to most, Rathen and Aria were each acutely aware of what they were seeing. And where that recognition filled one with joy, it burdened the other with alarm.

Roots and twigs bent into a cadaverous humanoid shape, eyes glowing like fireflies from within a woven head shaped like the skull of a bear, and a foxfire heart visible through the ribs of gnarled branches. Her voice echoed within that chest, seeping out between the weaves as it rose up through her wooden throat, head and horns of sprigs and sprays thrown back in full devotion to her song.

"What is it?" Petra asked, appearing beside them, sword drawn and ready.

Rathen held Aria even tighter as the word shaped on his lips. "A kvistdjur."

The song rose in a hopeless crescendo, and dozens of trees began to wash from verdant green to sickly yellow right in front of their eyes, leaves fading from tip to centre across a great stretch of the bank.

"It's lamenting, isn't it?" Anthis asked, torn between horror and fascination. "It sounds so...heartbroken..."

"To us," said Aria. "To trees, it's a lullaby."

The creature made no reaction to the footsteps that came to stop behind her, nor the grey arms that enveloped her body or the untamed mane that slipped between the gaps in her weave. She remained as still as the tree she appeared to be, her aching voice flowing freely in ardour. But that lullaby began to wane, diminishing on the air like a closing music box until the lid was shut.

Her head and arms lowered, the vortex evaporated, and twig-like toes touched the grass leaving her standing subdued in her queen's embrace.

"Aria, *no*--" but she'd already pulled herself free. Rathen muttered an oath and rushed after her once more, restarting the chase. She made it to the far bank before he managed to catch her again, but as he seized her shoulders at last and pulled her backwards with a scolding, she'd already come to a stop just a handful of paces behind Hlífrún. She stood staring openly at the wooden creature in her arms. And they both noticed immediately that she wasn't well.

"Rotten..." Rathen straightened and cast the queen a sober look. "How many...?"

"Too many." She released the kvistdjur, whose bark had chipped and peeled away to reveal dark and gritty hollows, and watched her shamble, entranced, back into the woods. "She, at least, is still among her senses. There are others who are much worse off. But...they don't sing anymore."

"Why *are* they singing?"

She turned and smiled sadly. "Because they're afraid."

"Is there not something you can--"

"If there was, Anthis, I'd have done it." She turned away testily and looked back into the forest, tracing the kvistdjur's path with her eyes as she wrapped her arms about herself. "It's happening everywhere. They're delicate. I can only soothe them in person, but I've found no way to halt the rot. But it is no disease. It's the magic - it's *always* the magic." Then the injury faded from her voice, and she returned to them with the air of regality that had vanished in the chamber. "The Wildlands is riddled with this taint. *My* Wildlands. If it isn't stopped, my influence will fade away and nothing in here will be safe. There will be little to stop enterprising humans from coming in and felling it all, and my creatures will wander out of bounds and into human land.

"But it goes beyond the simple yet ceaseless threat of your kind. The soils themselves are already sterilising, streams and rivers diverting, carrying away their water and sediment - trees are falling, the earth is opening. The organic network between every living thing is disintegrating. Unless something is done, and done *soon*, this forest and all others are doomed. And your own hunting grounds will go with them."

"We understand that," Rathen assured her, sensing the demands that were coming, "there are a lot of areas affected all across the country--"

"And well beyond. My reach has been completely cut off from Hin'ua, Duakhul, Ithen - too many others. Dolunokh only survives because the magic ravaging everything else is holding it together."

"I assure you, Your Majesty: we are working on it."

Slowly she regarded him with another of her disconcerting scrutinies, until something beyond the clearing stole her attention away. Her eyes became razor-sharp, and she whipped around to stare deep into the woods beyond the falls as another distant, gloomy melody rose over the thrum. Her lips formed a hard line, and she looked back at them fleetingly with that same hard edge. "Go with Birk. I'll return soon."

"Wait," Rathen cried, "go where?" But she'd already dashed off into the trees. They exchanged helpless looks while the three vakehn joined them.

Chapter 34

Rathen's teeth grated at the crack of thunder that threatened to finally obliterate his patience. He dug his fingers deeper into his ears and stared even harder at the scribblings in his notebook, blocking out the forest and trying to focus himself onto something useful. But his eyes only continued to sink right through the pages, and his tightly-wound thoughts worked assiduously against any effort at progress.

They'd followed Birk as commanded, whichever of the shepherding vakehn that was, and were led to a new sleeping tree to rest against the heat of the day while they waited for the skogsrå to return. But even once the distant lamentation had ceased - and they'd been listening intently - Hlífrún was nowhere to be seen. And neither, they'd finally realised, were the vakehn.

Finding themselves suddenly abandoned in an unfamiliar encampment, their anxiety plunged deeper, and their eyes drifted ever more frequently towards the small rocky pond that sat unassumingly just within the edge of the clearing. More than once they'd roused from fretful daydreams to find themselves staring towards its depths in search of anything that could be lurking within.

Garon's patrol about the trees became more urgent, and Aria, though wary, was bold enough to sit at the edge of the water and guard over it to 'do her bit for the group'. No one had missed it. Her contribution of the arty-fact no one needed was still firmly under her skin.

But even while Petra kept watch over her in turn, stating when challenged that she had merely chosen that spot to rest, no one saw anything beneath the water but marimo, perfect balls of algae spinning peacefully at the bottom. No horses, no 'näcken', no sprites of any description. Nothing at all otherworldly. And so they'd continued to watch the water until whatever certainly called it home finally reared its head.

Their restlessness only grew. But while they knew that leaving without Hlífrún's say-so would most likely incur her wrath, the strength and reach of which they didn't dare to guess, they entertained the notion with increasing consideration with every passing minute. And as clouds began to gather and the light began to fade, Garon finally took matters into his own hands.

But, while the vakehn were indeed absent, it appeared they were still steadfast in their charge. He'd tested their reactions by walking as far as he could, but where they'd expected the woodland nymphs to reappear and turn him around - peacefully, guessed some; aggressively, warned others - he found only a barrier. And he hadn't gotten far. They were indeed prisoners, abandoned, forgotten, and completely trapped.

Night was slipping in, and a storm had coalesced from nowhere. The odds were stacking against them. Now, there truly was no option but to stay.

And Hlífrún had still not returned.

Rathen growled in tension and shook his ceaseless thoughts away. Then another burst of light erupted through the trees and another crack set his teeth on edge. His notebook snapped shut and he slouched against the tree trunk in seething defeat.

He looked up at footsteps a moment later and smiled as best he could. "Is she all right?" He asked quietly, looking past Petra to see Aria staring vigilantly over the water and Garon leaning surreptitiously against a tree beside her.

"She's just fine," she replied, sitting down beside him. "Her patience is remarkable. I don't think she's blinked more than three times in ten minutes."

"I'd swear she doesn't blink at all while she's whittling." He glanced about the trees. "All clear?"

"Seems to be. Which is as good as we're going to get." She considered him warily. "I hesitate to ask, but...why were you so worried about kvistdjur? That one back there seemed fine..."

"Because it was preoccupied," he grunted. "Make no mistake, they're vicious. Hlífrún is the queen, but kvistdjur are the forest guardians. She watches, thinks and commands; they act."

"Not the vakehn?"

"Kvistdjur are the *primal* guardians. They're more in tune with the forests, but they're closer to animals than humans."

She bit her lip as she wrestled with the decision to voice her next question. Finally, senseless curiosity got the better of her. "...What could it have done?"

"Did you see its fingers?"

Long, tapered, sharp - at least those that hadn't been claimed by the rot. She shuddered. "Yes."

"Now imagine them ripping--"

"Yes, thank you." She leaned back sullenly against the tree. "Did you get all of this from books like she said?"

"Some of it, I admit – I have an eight-year-old with an unhealthy interest. But most came from Kienza. The rest...experience." She sat up with a jolt but he waved her questions away. "I live in a forest. What do you expect?"

"But Aria was acting as though she'd never seen one--"

"And may this remain her only encounter."

A gentle rustle among the trees set an urgent fire beneath the camp, but it was only Eyila returning from meditation. There was no puffiness to her eyes, he noticed. But there never was when she returned. His expression softened in pity. "How is she?"

"She's fine..."

He watched Petra's expression twist sadly, then drift briefly onto Anthis. The young man appeared not to be paying the tribal any attention, but though his eyes were pointed towards the key he was turning over in his hands, they weren't looking at it in the slightest. Petra shook her head to herself.

"She seemed better this time. After the magic." His eyes drifted back to her. "What did you do?"

"Garon suggested a way to subdue her. I tried it. It worked."

"Subdue her how?" He noticed that she was deliberately avoiding his gaze.

"The same way he does you."

"...Which is?" She said nothing, but he didn't miss the speed with which her hand rose instinctively to the side of her neck. He stared open-mouthed in disbelief and no small touch of insult. Not even the flash of lightning and near-immediate crash of thunder rattled it out of him. "You *knocked her out?*"

"Look, I didn't want to do it," she snapped defensively, "but it didn't hurt her and she was only stunned, and for *seconds*. It did the trick. Don't look at me like that. If she doesn't hurt *you*, she's liable to hurt *herself*. And you know it."

He sighed heavily. "Needs must? Sounds like Garon."

"What did Hlífrún mean when she said 'you could do it'?"

"I don't know."

Now she studied him. "But you have an idea."

"Nothing I'm ready to try."

"Then in the mean time...?"

"...Needs must."

Another rustle stole their jittery attention and two vakehn finally appeared. They set their baskets down in silence at the foot of the tree and began sorting portions of food into bowls of woven leaves and distributing them about the camp. Rathen and Petra looked down at their offering nervously. More meat - a bird, perhaps - rain tubers which tasted like a strange combination of potato and lemon, and yet more of the peculiar fungi they'd been served at every meal so far, off-white, vaguely yellow and with multiple heads on a single stalk. It didn't look healthy, and its burnt caramel taste struck them as notably deceitful. But they ate them, as usual, to avoid insulting their host. The vakehn assured them that they were equal to spinach. No one could quite see how.

Anthis reached up from his spot in the grass and took the bowl while another flicker of light washed out the clearing. "Aahst."

"Zeymakrah." The vakah smiled in surprise. "You speak it perfectly."

He stared at her for a final fraction of a second, then straightened with conviction. "You *are* an elf."

What little quiet muttering stopped as all eyes crashed upon the pair. The air rapidly turned to lead, and suddenly that niggling sense of near-peril that had followed them around since coming into such strange company took on a frightfully marked form, guided by the voices that had only a moment ago been so mysteriously familiar. But while they stared in fevered calculation, Aria gawped from the edge of the pond. She took the bowl handed to her by the second vakah and stared up at him in open wonder. He smiled back. Garon tensed further between them.

"We used to be. But Feiruikanax saved us."

"Feira," he nodded slowly as pieces began falling into place. "Just as Zikhon did. Devouts."

"Yes," but there was a distasteful shape to her berry-red lips, "but those He saved were not worthy. They were - and remain - a part of the problem. I take it that you've seen them? Hiding away on their islands and denying all responsibility? We, at least, have attempted to reform, and for that we have become one with Feira's forces. But...there is no reversing our actions." She turned away solemnly.

"So you can't do anything about the magic?" He asked after her, but she shook her head with a sad smile.

"If we could, we would already have done so."

"Why does your magic not affect it?"

She turned then towards Rathen, who stood in guarded challenge. Petra was already rising beside him, hand ready to snatch her blade. But the vakah sent him the same smile. "We know how to work around it. Rötternas Moder has guided us and over a thousand years, our magic has changed. But it is not the same as hers. She was able to extinguish the fires - but not even she can do what you can. They could have caught alight again at any moment."

"A *thousand* years?"

She smiled back around at Anthis. "A number of us lived in the wilds long before our kin's downfall. 'Devout', as you called us. There are some among your kind who seek to do the same. Your druids. They don't grasp quite the same concepts, but it is good that they try." She turned again and started away, then chuckled as he called after her once more. "We have much to do before midnight."

"Yes, sorry, I know, I'm sure. But," he presented the grooved black key, and she took it with a frown. "Do you know what this is?"

"The key from Reyn'lehfeik, in the southern forest. But as for what it unlocks, I do not know. There is no locked door here. The vines and roots could help us open them if there were."

"You're sure?"

"We are. We've looked. We know all that resides within the forests, and there is no lock that would fit this key - now or before." She pressed it back into his hand with another apologetic smile and finally walked away.

While the others watched the two brown-skinned non-elves slip back into the trees, he sank back to the grass, staring down at the mysterious key in growing disappointment.

"What's wrong?"

Despite the gentle tone, he jumped in surprise and snapped around to find Eyila's bronze grin radiating right beside him. "Sorry."

"I-it's fine, it's fine," he chuckled belittlingly. "Just...well, this place. On edge." And now even more so. He glanced sideways and found her watching him patiently, then gestured emptily with the key before tucking it back into the paper-stuffed satchel. "Can't work it out."

A flutter arrived beneath his ribs as she made herself comfortable on the ground beside him and began rifling through her bowl. "It's that ruin, too, isn't it? Aria told me about the light-locks, and that you were frightened you'd missed others like it because you didn't know what they were."

"Frightened? No, no - it just...bemused me, that's all."

"Like the key is bemusing you?" She cast him an aslant smile, then popped several stems of fungi into her mouth. "I thought you said some things should be left undiscovered."

After a moment, blood filled his face and his eyes widened in horror, betraying his much too quick smile of puzzlement. "Whe-uh-when did I say that?" He asked in a fluster, hurriedly looking away in an attempt to conceal his embarrassment, but the sudden shriek as she threw herself against him roused him into sheer panic.

The rest of the camp leapt to their feet.

The blood-curdling cry came again, closer than the first. Any and all weapons were bared as they instinctively tightened up together around the base of the tree, but a third shriek rose, even closer still. Fervent eyes scoured between the trunks, the boughs, the leaves; another flash of lightning, another peal, another shriek, this time right upon them. Their throats tightened, but not a shadow moved. Then the terrible cry pierced the air once again, far to the other side.

They stilled and sharpened their panic to a point, focusing at last on listening over the rain that drummed down onto the thick, impenetrable canopy. When the lone shriek came one last time, it was almost as distant as the first.

A unanimous breath of relief eased from tight lips, and slowly they returned to their previous positions without a word to each other.

"What was that?" Eyila asked in a strangled whisper.

"I don't know," Anthis replied as he calmed away the catch of alarm in his breath. "It happened last time, too, but nothing came of it..." He looked down at a dull pressure in his abdomen and found the bronze girl huddled in his arms, bent elbows pressing into his ribs while his own fingers pressed white marks onto her skin.

He let go of her immediately, apologising clumsily as the heat flooded back into his face, and looked about the camp at the others, none of whom appeared to pay them any attention. He turned back and matched her embarrassed smile.

But then her lips pursed, and she regarded him with a quick, thoughtful look. He frowned as her expression flashed into a smile, and she seized him suddenly by the wrist. "Let me show you something."

He was given no opportunity to make an excuse before she'd dragged him out of the clearing. "Where are we going?" He asked, not daring for a moment to allow himself intrigue as his eyes pulled warily back over his shoulder.

"I found something while I was looking for somewhere to meditate - I wanted to know what it meant." She grunted in disgust as she ran out into an abrupt column of rain let through by a break in the trees. "That got me last time, too." She threw him back a smile in apology, but continued to drag him through it all the same. And with every step a smile crept across his own face.

Finally, they came to a stop beside a small boulder, one tangled in roots - just like everything else in the forest - and half concealed in liverwort. But there was clearly something etched into its surface.

Anthis crouched in front of it and traced the visible lines with his fingertip while Eyila waited behind him, then nodded to himself. "It's an Eyn'feik - a mark of equality, between elves and nature. Neither are above the other; they're one in the same. There's probably quite a few dotted about through the forest." He waved her down beside him, momentarily distracted from his nervousness, and pointed at the lines. "The trunk of this tree carved in the middle here is a person, see? And the ground is another, lying down on its side, and the very top of the leaves is another, reaching up into the sky." She nodded, peering closer, and for a moment her earthy scent - dry herbs, cured hides, chestnuts and dew - tickled his nose against the damp of the rain. It was lost as he turned back to the stone. "They, uh...it's...a symbol of equality."

"You said that."

"Yes, sorry. Uh...yes. Look here: this body lying on the ground represents the nutrients left in the earth upon decomposition. The tree grows from that and is tended and supported by this next body, who in turn is nurtured - fed and shaded - by the tree. Then, upon death, the person's spirit climbs the tree which lifts it towards the gods, while its body is returned to the earth to start the cycle again."

"They rely upon one another. They're all born as part of one entity, not as a single being..." She smiled softly; he didn't look. "Knowing your place in the world, in life and in death. My culture has something similar. That's partly why it caught my eye. But instead of a tree, it's a gust of wind. The other tribes, too - a plume of water, a mountain, a flame. We look after the natural cycles and thrive when the elements thrive, then the elements carry us up and into the Winds to reach the Frozen Gates...while..."

He looked around at her weighted pause and offered her a nervous smile. "You know an awful lot about the other tribes' faiths," he said in a bid to distract her.

"I've told you already: they're intertwined. They need one another. My people dedicate themselves to Aya'u because we live where Her influence is strongest." But the sorrow only continued to creep into her eyes, and he could see the words 'or we used to' scrolling through her mind.

She must have felt him looking, as she pushed it away and turned him a smile before glancing up and around at the trees. "This place is so confusing," she said, finally ringing the rain out from her white hair, though he doubted it really bothered her to have taken her this long to do it. In fact he couldn't help thinking in absence that her bright, often so mischievous face looked that much sweeter in its frame. "It's such an assault on the senses. I should have noticed the shift in the wind, the coming of the storm, but I didn't."

"You're assuming the storm is natural." His eyes returned to the stone. "But no one expects you to give us running updates on the weather. And here, I doubt it would have mattered anyway. We're not leaving until Her Majesty decrees it."

"Still... I don't like these forests. They're pretty, in their own way, I suppose, but...the air is so...heavy. It's wet, it smells, it's loaded with spores and seeds, none of which are even going anywhere, they're just...*hanging* there, waiting for a wind that never manages to reach them. No wonder the trees are all so tight."

He breathed a helpless laugh. "Sorry."

She frowned at him, puzzled. "Why are you apologising?"

"Oh, well...I don't know... It's not always like this, it's just this forest, and the time of the year..."

"Mm. But then when it *isn't* the forest or 'the time of the year', it's cold."

"I...I suppose it is..." He laughed again. "I suppose you're used to a different world. We light fires then, though."

"Yes - but in your own buildings. And then you're cut off from everything and everyone else! And the heat is so isolated...it must get suffocating with all that smoke!"

"We have chimneys. Oh - uh, hollow pillars built over fireplaces so the smoke goes up and out through the roof."

"But the heat surely gets too much."

"Fire guards. They protect the flame and catch the heat."

She nodded slowly. "And what does he do with it?"

"He? Oh, no, it's a panel--a sheet of metal netting that you stand in front of the fireplace."

"...And what does *that* do with the heat?"

"...Nothing..."

She blinked in confusion, then shook her head and continued ringing her hair. "What a waste." He couldn't help smiling in his bewilderment. "You cityfolk are very strange," she continued before a thoughtful pause. "But...you're not as bad as I thought you'd be. You five, at least, I like. You most of all."

He spluttered and gawked in surprise. "M-me?"

"Mhm," she grinned impishly. "If not for you, I wouldn't know that my people's ideals were ever represented outside of our tribes. It makes me feel a lot better. Like maybe some among you also believe the same things. Like the vakah said - druids! And perhaps, in time, it might spread to the rest of you. And then the world will be a better place. And perhaps...perhaps then our people could mix..."

His giddiness trickled away in a steady stream, leaving him with a smile as hollow as a rotten log. "...Oh...yes, maybe. Well, you're welcome..." *'Faith. It always comes back to faith...she must have more in her heart than that...'* Unbidden, Petra's accusation of priorities began ringing suddenly within his skull and chased his sickeningly callow hesitance away. *'Priorities. All right, what else does she like? What else does she do? There must be something else we could talk about, something that won't remind her of home... Healing? No, certainly not... Herbs...plants...oryx...'* His eyes flashed with the clattering arrival of an idea, and the word tumbled unstoppably from his lips. "Books."

She stared back at him in surprise. "'Books'?"

"Yes, books. Stories. Do you read very much? I can give you something to read if you'd like, keep you busy, take your mind off of the forest..." He noticed only then the confused crease between her eyebrows, and another thought, one much too late to save him, announced its arrival with a cold rush of self-loathing. "Oh...you can't...*can* you...read?"

"Yes," she replied slowly, "I can read."

"...Words?"

"Oh."

"...Well, in that case," another thought spoke for him before he could find a reason to flee from it, one that set a nervous heat across his cheeks and forehead, "w-would you like me...to...?"

She cocked an eyebrow "...Teach me, you mean? To read cityfolk books?"

"Oh - no, no no, don't worry, nothing you wouldn't enjoy. Elven stories - I'm sure we could find something in the cities - you won't have to come in, Aria can help me pick some things out..."

She shifted with a doubtful puckering of her lips, and he realised how pushy he was being. "Sorry," he said while silently chastising himself, "it's not important." He rose hurriedly to his feet and gestured back to the rock. "Yeah, so...well...I'm glad I could help."

He turned to leave, quite certain that death by embarrassment was a possibility after all, until he felt an abrupt grasp around his wrist. He looked around and found her smiling back at him.

"Yes, please."

A smile seized his lips while relief silenced the debasing voice in his head. He nodded his agreement, and the two continued to smile at one another. For much too long. Discomfort duly set in.

Anthis looked away hurriedly and pulled his hand free as smoothly as he could, though it came out as a snatch all the same, and turned again to leave. This time, though, a small figure bursting through the trees stunned him where he was.

Rathen stepped in barely half a pace behind Aria and very nearly tripped over her as she stopped far too suddenly in front of him. He frowned, once he'd steadied himself, at the strikingly guilty look on the young man's face. His dark eyes shifted onto Eyila, who looked only a fraction less awkward. "Sorry... Keep moving, Aria."

"No no no," Anthis said almost frantically, quite obviously avoiding any and all eye contact as he set off at a rushed march away towards the trees, "I was just leaving anyway, Eyila just wanted me to translate something, which I've done, so I'll be on my way."

The pair watched him in confusion as they stepped out of his way, then cast Eyila another questioning glance. But she suddenly appeared just as baffled. "He's very peculiar," she said once he'd vanished hastily from sight. "He seems so sure of himself until you get him alone, then he's jumpy, he stutters, and he either stares or doesn't look at you at all..."

"Nooo," Aria giggled with a roll of her eyes, "that's just your effect on him. He's actually quite elenquent."

"Eloquent."

"Elegant."

"My effect? Why?"

"Because he--"

"Aria."

She looked up and around at her father, and understood in an instant the strange, innocuous look. She turned back to the clueless tribal and shrugged, smiling simply. "Because he's strange."

"Yes," Eyila smiled slowly as her eyes drifted back after him, "he is..."

She allowed Rathen to escort her back to camp. After the shrieking, she wasn't about to refuse him, and he wasn't about to listen. But just as they returned to the great old tree, Rathen glued to Aria's heels all the way, Garon stepped away from the pond and fixed him with intention. One look at the severity in the officer's grey eyes seared away Rathen's good humour.

"We need to talk."

"But we only just started playing a game!" Aria protested with a huff.

"And what game was that?"

"Shadow-hopping. Daddy has to be my shadow and stay as close as he can while I go whizzing about."

"It sounds like fun," Garon said with only the slightest degree of sincerity - though even that came as a surprise, "but I think it's time you went to bed."

"I can't. I'm too awake."

"Hence the game," Rathen whispered.

"Well, perhaps Eyila will play with you instead."

All looked hopefully to the tribal, but she was already grinning with anticipation. "Absolutely." She took the equally enthusiastic girl by the hand. "Teach me how to play shadow-hopping!"

They watched them leave, then, at another flicker and wail of dying lightning, Garon moved quickly into the middle of the camp, searching the trees all about them. Rathen, Petra and Anthis followed, stopping only at the most central point where they could keep the greatest distance between themselves and the forest, the sleeping tree included. They dropped their voices low, and eyed even the grass with suspicion.

"We need to leave."

"No need to panic, Garon, your affinity for stating the obvious is alive and well."

He ignored Petra's snide remark. "Hlífrún is wasting our time. Every hour we're in these woods, Salus is moving, and he is training."

"What exactly do you want us to do?" Anthis asked crisply. "We have demands for help coming at us from all sides - ditchlings, harpies, and now Hlífrún, though she's not come right out and said it. The difference this time is that she has us *trapped* here until we do what she wants."

"Well it's not going to happen. We're not here to serve this 'queen', we're here for Turunda's people."

"She and her wildlings *are* Turunda's people."

He sent him a measured look. "You understand full well what I mean."

"Garon," Rathen sighed wearily, "you said all of this last night."

"And the bad feeling I had then hasn't died at all."

"I have a question," Petra began carefully, "why hasn't Kienza come to get us out?"

All eyes turned onto Rathen with the same sudden expectation, and he straightened defensively. "Because I suspect she knows more than we do about Hlífrún and that's enough for her not to get involved - which also means we're not in danger."

"Yet."

"...Yet."

"Well we need to get out before we *are*."

Petra frowned as Garon's hand rose to his forehead for what must have been the eighth time that day. "Is that another headache?"

"No. It's nothing."

She rolled her eyes. "Well, he's right on the *first* count, at least: we do need to leave, and soon."

"And you've concocted a plan in the last day, I presume?" Rathen challenged impatiently. "Because otherwise there's no point to this at...all..." He noticed that all eyes had fixed onto him again, and they were no less expectant than the last time. More, perhaps. He shifted uncomfortably. Then an unpleasant understanding dawned. His shoulders sagged in sufferance. "Why?"

"Because she's taken with you."

"All the more reason I should stay *away* from her."

"She'll listen to you."

"No, she really won't."

"Explain what we're doing, make her understand that this magic isn't the *only* threat, that time is of the essence."

"I'm pretty sure she already knows that. Look, she has her reasons for keeping us here, and until we know what they are, all of our 'explanations' are going to fall on deaf ears."

"So we should wait until she sees fit to tell us?" Petra countered. "Call me crazy, but she doesn't strike me as all that direct."

Garon nodded in agreement. "Fear and uncertainty have us on edge, and she knows that. She's not going to clear the matter up and lose one of her advantages, she's going to keep them all in play for as long as she can and string us up like puppets. *We* need to manipulate *her*. And you are how we do it."

Rathen was shaking his head in disbelief, but they continued to watch him with that same pressure and expectancy until, finally, he found himself just beginning to agree. He caught himself and shook it away. "And just how would you presume I even find her? She's not back yet - unless she's decided to ignore us."

"Like I said: she's taken with you. Wander out of camp alone. The best the rest of us would get is a vakah to turn us about. Hlífrún will come to you herself."

"*None* of them need to come for us, Garon, there's a *barrier*."

"Yes, I haven't forgotten that, thank you - my point is that she wouldn't pass up the opportunity even if she *has* decided to ignore us."

"*Just* what I wanted to hear." He looked to Petra as she placed a hand on his shoulder, but he found little comfort in her strange smile.

"Rathen," she began with an encouragement and support that also struck him as just a little too sweet, "just tell her what we're doing - tell her about Salus and his mad ideas. She knows about us from creatures in the forest, as I understand it, but all she knows about Salus is what those creatures have overheard *us* saying *about* him. Assuming there were any around at those points to hear it. It's a gap in her knowledge. And if the cracks are cutting off her link to the other forests and Salus is out there making them *deeper*, she'll see that *he's* the real threat."

"That's a really good idea, Petra, you seem to have a very solid grasp on the matter - perhaps *you* should go instead."

"No," she grinned playfully, slapping him a little too firmly on the back, "I came up with it for *you*. Don't insult me by rejecting it."

He looked helplessly to the others. "That is *exactly* how Hlífrún is going to be. Sweet and venomous at the same time."

"And I daresay you'll spot her deception just as quickly." Garon gestured towards the trees. "Go on. No time like the present."

He stumbled backwards at Petra's gentle shove, and studied the two suspiciously while Anthis grinned openly beside them. He shook his head in defeat as the trap closed around him and trudged off into the woods, muttering under his breath.

Darkness slipped in around him. The camp fell away, and his breath began to shake. He was painfully aware of what he was walking into. Even if all the books he'd read to Aria were riddled with misinformation, everything Kienza had told him was true to a word, and those words were ringing in his head like a chorus of bells. He could only hope that what he'd said in her defence was just as true. Otherwise, why *hadn't* she come to their rescue?

He shook the useless thought away. It wasn't the time to worry about that. He needed his wits about him.

Cautiously he walked on, doing his best not to stare around himself in alarm, straining his ears over the crashing rain as he wove around trees and rocks until he was finally swallowed by absolute darkness. His eyes took far too long to adjust. By the time the shape of trees returned to the abyssal landscape, his heart was beating a thousand times a minute, his palms were hot and clammy, and his breath was sharp. How he managed to prevent his anxiety from bursting forth as a yelp at the sound of the throbbing voice close behind him, he didn't know.

"Looking for me?"

He spun around and watched fireflies coalesce from the blackness, illuminating tree bark in their painfully weak glow as he struggled to find the face the voice belonged to. But of course he knew, even before he spotted the two chestnut ovals that burned as intense as fire.

Her face emerged from the tree, bark-skin smoothing as her lips curved into a succulent smile. Her hair rolled free, her crown rose from beneath it like sprouting saplings, and her shoulders, breasts and arms followed, breaking free from the trunk as her perfect and powerful torso took shape. Roots retracted into toes, and she stepped as a being towards him, naked, brazen and formidable.

His eyes finally darted away and his lips bowed into an embarrassed smile. "Oh-uh-um...looking? No just...going for a walk. Stretching my legs before bed."

"Mhm. Like you do every night, you mean?" She stopped close enough for her wildflower breath to brush his chin, and she stared at him with hungry eyes, calling his own back to meet them. "I'm sorry I didn't announce my return. I was...troubled."

"Troubled?" He stumbled backwards over a root, eradicating his casual attempt to find distance. "The-the kvistdjur? Was that what we 'needed to see'?"

"Ish."

He looked at her very carefully, but still she gave nothing away. She just continued to smile with that all-knowing look. A look that rattled him to his core. A look that, if not for its distinct element of danger, could have belonged to Kienza. Or to Taliel.

He laughed nervously again, turning away to escape her suffocating stare, and tempered his voice into humility with the greatest of effort. "Look, Your Majesty, *please* don't think us rude--"

"Never."

He swallowed hard as she closed the distance in a single, feather-light step. He forced himself to stand taller. "But, uhh...we need to move on. In the morning."

"I know." Her hand slipped gently up his arm, across his collar bone and back down his chest. He didn't move, focusing all his might on ignoring it.

"You know?"

Her hand rose again and stroked softly across his cheek. Her lips parted in a sensual smile. "Of course. You have things to do."

"...Then...you'll let us go?"

Her flaming eyes grew hotter, her smile even more voracious, and his throat tightened as a confused hope began to roil in his gut.

But then her hand suddenly trailed away, and she wandered back towards the tree to investigate a knot. A resentful pit opened in his stomach at his own foolish disappointment, and stability reasserted itself as he focused on the sight of her hollow bark back and gently swaying cow tail, making a point of avoiding everything around it. "Sure," she said offhandedly, "I don't see why not. I have things to do, too."

"You do?"

"Of course. Plenty. More than I care to think of, actually - but such is life. You may leave in the morning. I'll provide you with food - I'd rather that than have you kill my creatures." She finally looked back and smiled mischievously at the bare-faced panic fuelling his surging thoughts. "Oh relax, you've not killed anything I couldn't stand to let go. Just leave my wood-grouse alone and all will be well."

"W-wood-grouse?"

"Yes," she grinned. "Adorable, aren't they?" She puffed out her bare chest, pressed her wrists back into her rump, fanned out her fingers, and made strange, hollow, rattling and clicking noises as she raised her face skyward.

Rathen found himself so confused as she straightened and grinned that he didn't dare react in case he offended her. He was unaware of the bemused smile already curving his lips. "Wood-grouse. Yes. We'll leave them alone - you have my word."

"Good." She nodded with satisfaction and turned back to the tree she'd emerged from, gesturing off vaguely towards the camp hidden somewhere in the swirling darkness. "Well, on your way, then. The others will want to know how this went. Oh, but..."

He looked up from the path he found his feet already tracking along and faltered as he discovered her suddenly standing before him once again, close enough for her breath to stir him. And stir him she did. Her lips pressed softly against his, and though he knew he should be startled, his mind drummed emptily, as though she'd removed all capacity for thought in their contact. It was...blissful.

Slowly, much too soon, she stepped away, her hand slipping reluctantly from his neck, and retreated once again towards her tree, flashing him a devilish smile. "Don't tell them about this. We wouldn't want them to get jealous." Her long fingers curled into an alluring wave, growing longer still as she stepped back into the wood. "Nighty night..."

She vanished.

Chilled and confused, panic rushed at him from all directions. He all but ran back to camp.

Chapter 35

For the first few hazy seconds of the day, everyone awoke feeling perfectly calm and rested. Cool dew had gathered on their sagina moss sheets, there was a subtle chill on the air, and the whispering breeze drew a lazy rustle from the highest boughs.

But even before the blood-curdling squawking could correct that feeling of serenity, agitation came stampeding in. Again they had slept too well - *unnaturally* well - and the absence of any trace of the past night's storm cast the morning into an even deeper shade of doubt. As did the lack of anyone to greet them, rudely or otherwise.

They rose quietly, keenly attentive to their surroundings, and quickly discovered a basket of food set at the usual spot between the roots. Two full sacks sat beside it. It seemed that even the vakehn had lost interest in them.

"You're *sure* you didn't offend her?" Petra asked dubiously, but when Rathen reiterated for a third time the entire meeting - but for a few very minor, quite needless details - they were left with an even fouler taste in their mouths.

They ate what had been left for breakfast, which of course included even more of the off-white, knobbly, burnt caramel mushrooms, and began gathering their things. But still no one came. Even when they'd shouldered the bags and made cautiously into the trees, no one appeared to intercept them. They began to wonder if they'd actually been permitted to leave after all, if the barrier wasn't still rigidly in place and no one had bothered to come and see them off because they weren't, in fact, going anywhere at all. That doubt faded with every step after the three minutes it should have taken to reach it. It seemed they had the Root Mother's blessing after all, she just hadn't deigned to inform them.

No one was sorry to put the whole perturbing encounter behind them. Though neither did their abrupt return to shambling through the forest with one eye glued behind them fill anyone with a giddy sense of excitement.

Routine came crashing back around them and every shadow was once again thick with hidden threats. They hadn't trusted Hlífrún, nor the vakehn, but at least beasts and wildlings would be discouraged from attacking in their presence. Now, though, they were exposed to every element of the savage and perilous forest, and group tensions were stretched dangerously thin.

But though they spent that whole day walking blind, as Rathen hadn't thought to ask for even vague directions in his haste to escape, they encountered nothing at all along their clumsy path. No shapes, no sounds, no movement beyond the usual unsettling ambience.

Which meant they must have missed something.

They rested only briefly, ate on the move, and stopped for the night's camp only when they had to, making do in patches where the trees were spaced only slightly further apart when no suitable sites presented themselves. Guarded, they lay above their blankets, and sleep evaded them no matter how desperately they hunted it through the darkness. Whatever cost their recent restful nights had come at, every one of them would have gladly paid it if just for a single hour's reprieve. Instead, they watched between glancing dreams as night thickened, reigned, then slowly gave way to leaking indigo light. Familiar birdsong announced the arrival of another day of tense and doubtful progress. They rose and met it with resignation.

The mood remained unchanged until the evening of the following day, when the forest was permeated by a captivating beauty. But as their guard rose yet higher against the magic and they searched even harder through the suddenly enchanting trees, they found nothing otherwise unusual.

Surveying the mediocrity, Petra's eyebrows drew into a slow knot. "...That's it?"

"I guess so...unless it's inside the trees..."

But Anthis's jest was met by halting silence. It was a possibility no one had considered. They looked to Rathen but he provided no insight, and Anthis alone saw the clouding of his eyes. It seemed that their freedom had come with the collapse of *all* the vakehn' spells.

The ruin they found themselves ambling into was beneath even the description of 'meagre'. Little more stood among the overgrown woods than a strangled and crumbling structure of stone. It appeared at first like a table without its middle, but the two furthest legs overshot the hollow surface which itself was set at a slight incline, and rose half their height again. There was evidence of thinner stone rods once running between them. But that, truly, was all.

Rathen immediately took up position in front of it, Zi'veyn in hand, Aria at his side, and the wary patrol began. Carefully, Anthis peered around him at the construct, his green eyes alight with intrigue.

"Nara," he said very quietly after only a moment, and with more than a touch of surprise, "the God of Hands..." He shifted to get a clearer look. "A verein - kind of like a loom, but made of stone. Immobile. It would have served as the framework for their pieces...which..." again he shuffled around, careful not to distract the mage nor earn a hush from the child beside him, though she was watching him in measured interest, and looked around at the base of the structure before the land around it. They offered him nothing.

He frowned and looked instead to the stones themselves. They were thick - thicker than a typical verein - and sturdy. Needlessly sturdy for cloth threads or even hide strips. And...out here? With so much to Feira, to nature, he hadn't expected to find anything related to handiwork or manipulation...

The idea came in carefully, but it was all that seemed to make sense. "Vines and roots. Not even wicker would need a station this strong. They wove vines and roots here, into tapestries, dream catchers, baskets...no, no, more likely just tapestries. This place is soaked in magic; all the pieces made here would have been blessed...and no one needs a blessed basket..." He observed the stone for another quiet, pensive moment before shaking his head in awe. "I can't believe this is here. Standing or not, workshops were *never* made in places like this. The kiln in Wrenroot was there before the trees were... This forest really is remarkable... I...wonder..."

Finally, his thoughts straying even as they tumbled from his tongue, he caught himself. He sent a quick look down to Eyila, sitting entranced upon the ground, but one glance at those distant eyes told him she couldn't possibly be listening.

And yet her repetition of the words he'd foolishly blathered in that same assumption a few days ago had shaken him. They were things he could easily have mentioned in passing before and just forgotten he'd said them...he didn't pay attention to *everything* that came out of his mouth, especially in the presence of history...but...if she *had* been listening after all...what else had he said?

The return of that question, one that had pealed through his skull at least once an hour since the fact, sent that familiar chill of panic down his spine.

His lips pressed tightly shut. He reached into his satchel, retrieved his notebook and a pencil and sat down in the dirt to sketch the verein in silence. To his knowledge, he said nothing again until a sigh, 'daddy' and light clatter of metal came from the structure, and a sharp intake of breath from beside him. His studies were forgotten in an instant.

"Eyila," he began slowly, lowering his book as scorn flared across her face, and reached openly towards her despite the alarming instinct to recoil, "Eyila, it's fine. You *agree* with this, remember?"

But her unblinking eyes were chained with malice to the back of Rathen's head. He sighed in conflict, but he acted anyway. Seizing her arms, he pinned them to her sides and held her body firmly in place. She struggled immediately, and he discovered just how powerful her deceptively slender frame was. He couldn't help wondering if magic had enhanced it while muddying her mind, or if it was all hers, brought to the surface by rage. He knew he preferred the latter, but restraining her and being in her line of violence suddenly put the young woman in a very strange light. One he couldn't decide upon. But, if nothing else, its strange, discordant familiarity intrigued him.

Those thoughts that flashed through his mind for an incomprehensible moment were chased away as she began her wild thrashing, and he held her even tighter, calling a warning out to the others.

And then, just as quickly, she fell still and slumped heavily in his arms.

Petra was suddenly standing beside her. A question burned in his eyes, but he had no time to give it voice. Rathen - breathless and teetering over Aria's support - moved forwards to meet them. The Zi'veyn was held purposefully in his hand.

She was lowered back to the ground, her rage passing like a puff of cloud over the sun, and she returned to her trance as seamlessly as had it never ended. Anthis watched her, a dubious knot in his gut.

"Rathen," Petra started as he straightened with slow composure, "you had an idea?"

His heavy nod did not inspire confidence. "It's not perfect, but her condition is getting out of hand. We have to do something, and soon. I've been giving it some thought, and I've come up with something that...might work."

"Might?" Garon had joined them.

"Humans aren't designed for magic. Our physiology isn't suited to cope with it. We're not elves. For us, it's a matter of the degree of resilience we inherited from them along with that magic - it's all that allows us to use it. Too little means a weak constitution and eptibility, regardless of the amount of magic produced, because it can't flow properly or be trained. 'Too much' resilience means that even lower amounts of magic can be used with great skill because they have the capability to control it, and control it finely."

"You've told us all this," Anthis reminded him impatiently, keeping one eye on the tribal girl in case she began to agitate.

"Oh. Well, either way, mages are being affected by this magic - but not all of them. As far as I've been able to tell - at least from between Eyila and the mage in Borer's Teeth - it comes down to resilience. Blood. Both of their resilience is just high enough that they can use their magic acutely, but all this *loose* magic, I think, has been influencing their own. How, I don't know, but it's riling it up. I don't know if it's trying to affect their magic like it is the other elements, if it's seeping in and mingling and increasing the amount of magic, or if it's doing something else entirely, but it's only under exposure that it gets this severe. Whatever it's doing, the resilience can't keep up."

"And what about the mages we find wandering in a daze, nowhere near any magic?"

"We've been to Khry's Glory, yes? Remember that place?" Their expressions soured affirmatively. "Peace and beauty; a sanctuary, a place that, *by design*, alleviates stress and concern. But the spells were made by elves, for elves, *not* humans. We don't have the constitution to handle it. Even *you* all fell under its charm, it was so potent. And the spell chains that have gotten out - the smallest, simplest and most numerous - describe the very essence of the place, and I think for some, even one exposure is enough for it to get under their skin. It pulls them, shadows them, haunts them, and they follow it because something in their magic is telling them to. It's how Khry's Glory was designed."

"To the point, Rathen."

He bit back his irritation. "I've analysed Eyila's magic a few times under these conditions, and both times I've found it going crazy and her resilience flagging behind. She's being affected by the magic around us. I can break those spells and their interaction with the elements, but if it's interacting with *her magic* then, *maybe*, its structure has become just that little bit different from the rest. Or maybe it's being protected by something inside her that can't tell the difference between what belongs and what doesn't. Either way, it needs a bigger push." He cast a serious look across them all. "With the Zi'veyn."

Everyone blanched. "The *Zi'veyn?*

"So, earlier, when you said 'we have to do something', you meant 'take drastic action'?!"

"Rathen, she doesn't *have* elven magic."

"I'm well aware of that," he declared quickly over the clamour, "but perhaps whatever the *elven* magic is doing *to* her will stop and her own will calm down. This isn't something I threw together in the last five minutes, and I don't see anyone else offering suggestions."

Indeed, as doubtful looks passed among them, they were sorely aware that no one else was qualified to offer a second opinion.

Rathen nodded decisively and knelt down in front of Eyila. "Petra, be ready. Just in case." With a careful breath, he lifted the Zi'veyn between them and closed his eyes. A small voice rose quietly beside him, small, but sober. He opened one eye with a gentle smile. "I wouldn't risk it if I didn't have the strength, little one." Then focus stole over his face once again, rendering his expression hard and deeply lined, and everyone watched in nervous silence as the relic began to float. Garon instinctively drew his sword, but at Anthis's look of shocked disapproval, promptly returned it to its scabbard. Two thirds of the way.

The Zi'veyn seemed to hover forever - far longer, it felt, than when he turned it upon their surroundings - and his expression, too, contorted into new shapes of struggle. But Eyila remained a picture of wistful calm, so far removed from her own awareness, and her young, bronze face grew only softer. Until, finally, she blinked.

Relief eased a collective breath as her ice-blue eyes focused onto the Zi'veyn floating close before her - and was erased just as quickly when she lunged rapidly out towards him. Petra and Anthis reached after her in a heartbeat as the relic tumbled lightly from the air, but Rathen was in no state to retreat. He teetered helplessly on the spot until he collapsed forwards in exhaustion, and into her outstretched arms.

She held him tightly.

Only he heard the words of gratitude delivered barely above a whispered sob. He smiled meekly and managed to return the embrace with a shaking hand.

The rescue faltered. Petra sighed and shook her head witheringly. "Well done, Rathen," she smiled, while Garon tucked away his sword and Anthis stifled a jealous sneer beside her.

Gently, Eyila released him and transferred his weight to Aria, who was waiting beside them and hopping in her desperation to help, and instructed her to sit him against the tree. Ardent concentration had suddenly fallen over her face. One bronze hand came to rest softly against his chest, the other over his forehead, and after an evaluating moment, she withdrew, twisted her fingers into magical gestures and returned her hand to drift over his heart.

His breathing soothed almost immediately, the deep rise and fall of his shoulders relaxed, and his body straightened from its slump. When he finally raised his head, his eyes renewed and invigorated, he found Eyila looking back at him with a soft, confident smile. His own slowly curved and his brow knotted suspiciously, but he said nothing beyond nodding his thanks.

"What does this mean?" Garon asked more than a touch sceptically when the two mages rose. Rathen had expected the question, and he hesitated as he finished putting together the answer. Especially when he caught the doubtful look in Eyila's eye. She knew what he was going to say, and his hesitance, he realised, had confirmed it. She turned away with a tremor in her jaw.

"It's no permanent solution," he replied ruefully, avoiding a glimpse at her disappointment. "I treated the symptoms, not the cause. She'll be at risk with every re-exposure. And...she can't be left anywhere alone. Even if she were to want to leave, or we wanted to get rid of her," his eyes flashed towards Garon, but the inquisitor's face was expressionless, "she couldn't. Not unless..."

"Unless I'm prepared to lose my mind like the others." She stood tall and lifted her chin defiantly. "It's just as well I'm not going anywhere, then. If nothing else, you need a healer. What you seek to do - against the magic, against Salus - you are likely to get hurt."

"You don't need to defend yourself," Anthis assured her, "none of us want you to leave."

She smiled gratefully, then turned a little too sharply back to Rathen. "How did you do it?"

"It's your resilience, as I thought. It's not strong enough to keep your magic in check *and* the invasive magic *out*. But I was able to use the Zi'veyn to break the bonds between your own and the rest. It was...trying to merge with yours. To empower itself."

Eyes widened, but a terrible comprehension screamed in her own - a sentiment only he could appreciate. "It wouldn't have managed - human magic is too different. But it will keep trying, and without the Zi'veyn to break it all up...it'll continue to work in the background. And every exposure will hasten it." His heart softened as her face began to twist and unstoppable thoughts tumbled through her eyes. The rest looked on in silence as they considered the implications of his words.

Her arms folded tightly across her chest, all trace of her previous resolution dissolved, and her fingers pressed white marks into her skin. "So," that fearful understanding invaded her voice, "with every exposure...I'll get closer to...and there's no way to stop it?"

"Not yet - but now we have a clue, something to work with, and the Zi'veyn can stop each bout much sooner which will slow it down a great deal."

"But how can you be *sure?*" She was hugging herself now, and her white eyebrows almost met in her distress. But Rathen was suddenly standing right in front of her, closing the distance she'd put between them and herself with one quick and exact movement, and grasped her firmly by the shoulders. She stared up at him with a doubt that lingered despite her surprise, but the fearsome determination with which he locked her gaze stalled her rampant thoughts.

"Because *you* have shown me how to see the magic in my own veins as clearly as you do. It's not hard to see it in yours, and I can see *exactly* what it's doing. *That's* how I can be sure - and why you also know that I'm right."

She continued to regard him sceptically from beneath a furrowed brow, and it was a long while before that doubt began to buckle. Finally, her expression softened, and she sighed a breath of defeat. But she continued to hug herself. "All right..."

"Good." He squeezed her shoulders, then looked critically back out into the forest. "Now, if we're all fit, we *really* should move..."

"You might be on to something big, here," Petra told him quietly as they shouldered the bags and set off at a hurried pace. "For everyone."

"That doesn't seem to be very different from the norm," he replied drily. "But, perhaps I am. I hope so."

"So do I..."

He flashed her a consoling smile. "Your sister probably isn't even affected."

"Well," she sighed without the dare to hope, "we can't know for sure." She looked on ahead and scanned the surroundings with the usual degree of misgiving, and dropped her voice even lower. "Doesn't it trouble you that we've not see a single creature since we left two days ago?"

"'Troubling' doesn't begin to cut it."

"Do you think it's Hlífrún's doing?"

"That's *why* 'troubling' doesn't cut it." He shook his head as his lips formed a hard line, and caught Aria's hand as she tried to slip past him and rush off ahead. "I feel like I've accepted a deposit on a service I never agreed to do..."

Both sentiment and circumstance persisted well into the night; the camp patrol began a perverse shift from the hope of finding nothing to finally locating something malicious lurking in the darkness, if just to justify their paranoia, while the others dove into their own business to escape it altogether.

Rathen stared hopelessly into his notes while Aria set upon a piece of wood with her frighteningly dexterous knife skills, and Anthis read through the papers he'd retrieved from the ancient chamber a few days ago. Or so he tried. His eyes drifted unceasingly towards the spot where Eyila had slipped away as silently as she did every night.

She hadn't said very much since the magic had been lifted, but it was no great leap to guess what was consuming her thoughts. Anthis couldn't imagine what she must have been feeling, knowing that to stay with them meant that she would fall into the line of fire time and time again, her magic attacked within her own veins until she slowly lost her mind, and yet to leave and escape it would ultimately be nothing short of a death sentence while it took its toll quietly in the background. The knowledge that they had been responsible for her initial exposure in the first place - a fact she was no doubt equally aware of - set a shame in his gut so rending that he wondered if his knife wound hadn't opened back up.

He wanted to go after her, to speak to her, to comfort her. To apologise. Rathen had been much too firm, too direct. Eyila was too young for that kind of handling. She was strong, it was true, wonderfully so, but there was a great delicacy hidden beneath it, and one that harboured a broken heart.

Someone had to go after her...but...what could *he* say? No doubt something stupid that would make her feel worse. Or she wouldn't want to talk to him at all. Rathen would be accepted, he was sure. Because they had that crucial detail in common. But he...he had nothing.

He cleared his throat against his monstrous disappointment and shuffled his back towards her exit. He didn't notice himself return not two minutes later, and when a flush of wind picked up, he steeled himself, dropped his papers and slipped away before he could change his mind again.

Anthis trekked quietly through the woods, mindful of every step over fallen leaf and broken twig, moving like a shadow with his eyes glued to the treetops. It didn't take long to locate her unmistakable form and the colour of bare skin in a thin shaft of starlight. But the sight stalled him, and again rattled the doubt of what he could possibly say, and again echoed the certainty that it was another's company she sought. One who could understand well enough to be able to set her at ease.

But, though he felt compelled to turn and leave, he didn't. Because someone needed to watch over her in her distraction, whether she knew he was there or not.

Anthis turned to the side and settled down against a tree, tuning his mind to the wafts of rustling breeze, the movement of small, nocturnal creatures, and the occasional shudder or gasp of the young woman's sorrow. And he felt, in her heart-rending presence, some sense of comfort in knowing that she wasn't truly alone.

Watching Anthis sit down and fold his arms lazily across his chest, making himself comfortable for what was sure to be a long wait, Petra turned with satisfaction and stalked back into the trees. "Find anything?" She whispered when her path crossed Garon's, but he shook his head with the same foreboding. She sighed dubiously, her fingers turning white around her sword hilt. "I don't like this..."

"Neither do I. I understand what Rathen meant. I feel...indebted." He glanced towards her hesitant hum. "What is it?"

"...I have to wonder if we shouldn't be taking advantage of it." She met his disbelief directly. "Indebted or not, it's been done. We should rest and recover - because Eyila's right: Salus is dangerous, and when we get out of here, we're going to be right back in his sights. It won't do us any favours if we're in bad form."

"Any form is fine as long as we're *alive*." He rolled his eyes at her persistent look. "What did you have in mind?"

"Well, for starters..."

He frowned and followed her gaze to his shoulder. His expression withered. "No."

"I'm not talking about healers. I mean exercise. Move it more - besides rolling it."

"Such as...?"

"Sparring."

"Sparring..."

She ignored his flat tone. "Why not? We've been cramped in here for over a week, we're all getting frustrated. A bit of back and forth would help *both* of us loosen up. And I could really do with it."

"No," he stepped past her and resumed his patrol, "thank you."

"It would also sharpen our focus..."

"By exhausting ourselves?"

"By unwinding." She hurried forwards and blocked his path. Her eyes were hard, and this time she ignored his groan of frustration. "We're jumping at shadows."

"By what proof? Don't drop your guard, Petra."

"For goodness sake, Garon, would you please drop *yours?!*" The flicker of insult in his eyes did little to impede her exasperation, stifled to a harsh whisper though the outburst was. She took a half step towards him to draw it even lower. "You *can't* be so tightly wound *all of the time*. When we *do* come by a threat, you're going to be too exhausted to see it! You're *always* too pre-occupied with being official, being in charge, keeping everyone moving - have you considered that we would all keep moving *anyway?* That the *rest* of us have eyes and ears, too? Even *Aria* stands guard, and do you know why? Have you given it any thought at all? It's because she fears for *the rest of us*, not just herself. And her eyes and ears are no less keen."

"This speech," he growled, "*again*. Stop concerning yourself with my well-being."

"Why? You're certainly not going to do it."

"It has nothing at all to do with you."

"That's a lie, and you know it."

He stalled in his attempt to find a way around her. "...What do you mean?"

"You won't let anyone heal you, and for the *stupidest* reason I've ever heard."

"Which is?"

She stared at him, studying his carefully tempered look, but his level gaze gave nothing away. There was nothing at the surface, and nothing beneath it. It was as though he felt...nothing. At all.

Her jaw tightened as her certainty began to waver, but she hid that much from her eyes.

"Whatever reason you've concocted," he said in a low, dangerous voice, "abandon it. I won't be healed because it is needless. I've been trained for worse, and I've been trained to adapt. If I turn to a healer for a little thing like this," he continued over her protest, "then how will I be able to adapt when the damage is...more permanent?"

"And you know that this *isn't?*"

"It's getting better."

"I'm not seeing it."

"You don't need to."

"I'm looking close enough." She followed him as he finally managed to slip by. "It's not getting better. At all. It was for a while, I watched you exercise it with swordplay. But you gave that up the minute you saw progress."

"There is no opportunity for it in here."

"A month ago." Again she hurried around and in front of him, earning herself a very sharp snarl. "You can lie to yourself, if you want. But you won't fool me."

His eyes gripped her. Grey eyes. Aged eyes. Troubled eyes - eyes that held...nothing, sometimes, and intense passion at others. Finally they had shifted into the latter, but the power of their ferocity stilled her, and for that her challenge faltered.

"Leave." He spoke through his teeth. "Me." His eyes burned. "Alone." He stared her down.

Heat rose in her cheeks as she felt herself shrinking, flushing red in the darkness. Resentment rose as sharply as her insult. Her tongue swelled and mouth dried in anger, words failing her when she needed their defence the most. And yet her lips moved anyway, and the useless, infantile words came out on their own. "Why can't you be brave?"

He straightened and turned away, dismissing her in favour of his patrol.

Frustration began to rattle her bones, and her body took over. Impulse snapped her away, and she stormed off through the trees before he could notice the furious tears in her eyes. They rolled down her cheeks, and she bit her lip hard in self-loathing, asking herself yet again why she bothered trying.

Kienza, as wise and all-knowing as Rathen deemed her to be, was simply wrong. Garon was fuelled by nothing more than stubborn pride. He was consumed by his work. It was all that mattered to him. It had to be, for what few occasions he'd spoken to her as a human being were overshadowed by the innumerable times when he had been nothing and no one more than Inquisitor Brack.

And she...she was a fool. A blind, whiny, mulish child.

No, that wasn't fair. Even Aria was cleverer than she was. Aria learned. She didn't. She just kept hammering away at him, and he dismissed her every time. Rejected her. Cut her down and spit on her.

How many times had she given herself *this* moth-eaten speech? How many times did she have to get herself hurt before it finally sank in? Perhaps she should take a page from his book and protect her pride. Leave him alone, if he wished it. It was probably for the best. For her, if nothing else.

...So why couldn't she stop her tears?

Chapter 36

On the eleventh wretched morning of their arboreal confinement, they awoke to find two more bulging sacks placed unsettlingly close to their heads. They leapt up with a start, checking over themselves and their belongings, but nothing appeared to be missing, added, changed into wood or goodness knows what else their fevered dreams could concoct. And so, they checked again.

"We're being followed," Garon had stated ominously just as they'd begun to settle down, but sorted through and handed out the sylvan rations all the same.

Anthis's lip curled as he eyed the stalks of the tiresome fungus. "We're going to start sprouting these soon..."

"I wonder if they're useful."

He cocked an eyebrow towards Eyila, and watched as she took a handful from her bowl and stuffed them into a pouch on her sash, which she'd kept stored in a bag to avoid offending the Root Mother. Quite out of nowhere, she'd begun taking a strange interest in the forest. Some kind of professional curiosity had pushed out her disdain, and she had begun meticulously analysing various leaves, barks, fungi and lichen, and not only with her eyes and fingers. A few were subjected to a taste test, and others were combined with bits and pieces she carried with her, occasionally leading to spontaneous combustion right in the palm of her hand. But while the others had panicked and spun around for enraged vakehn, she had only hummed in intrigue.

"Well, we'd better get used to them."

"Why?" Anthis blanched in alarm, snapping back at the inquisitor's regretful tone. "Have we still got that far to go?"

"I didn't think so..." Rathen looked up and found Garon observing him. He privately noted that it was a little too early for the purpose in his eyes.

"No," he agreed, "we don't - but I've had a thought. Hlífrún must know what we're doing - *all* of it. Salus has been attacking harpies and ditchlings and who knows what else. That won't have slipped by her. But she's keeping us here anyway, even though we could be out there stopping it, which means that she wants our help with something bigger. I don't think this magic is a matter as simple as we - or Salus - believe."

"What are you getting at?" Rathen asked carefully.

"Hlífrún is the Root Mother. She said she's connected to all the forests, and that every chasm weakens that connection. But perhaps that connection goes beyond just her - perhaps all the forests are linked to *each other*. This forest right here, the Wildlands, is her seat of power. It's the heart of Arasiin's nature. If they *are* all connected, and this is the heart, then perhaps fixing this place will have echoing effects."

"Yes, a good point - except the magic isn't coming *from* here, it's come from

Dolunokh, and it's gathering all over the place, in forests *and* villages, and the chasms themselves are destroying far more besides."

"Wildlife homes are suffering more than humans'. Most sites of magnetism are in unpopulated areas."

"It's true," Anthis conceded, "what elven cities we still use are long post-magic, they have little significance to the gods. The magic doesn't gather there."

"Even so--"

"Rathen." Garon's eyes were burning. "We're trying to protect Turunda, and *everything* in it. Do not forget that."

"...Turunda's people, you mean."

"Everything and everyone."

He nodded slowly, coolly studying the officer's fervour. "And you say she's 'keeping us here'."

"She is."

Now Anthis blinked, and the realisation that had slipped over Rathen finally crashed onto everyone else. "He did say that, didn't he? Garon, I thought we were on our way out. Do you know something you're not telling us?"

"No..." But all eyes turned onto Petra. Her foot had slipped backwards into a readied angle, her fingers curled around her sword, and she regarded the inquisitor with open mistrust. "Something's wrong with him."

They knew in an instant that she was right. They recoiled immediately, ushering Aria back behind Rathen and Anthis, but Eyila moved forwards with a scrutinous frown.

She stopped beside the duelist, allowed no further by a warning arm, and studied the inquisitor closely. But Garon didn't shrink. There was no alarm, no denial, no attempt at allaying them. He merely stood and waited, his face a mask, uncharacteristically void even for him.

Despite Petra's sharp discouragement, she reached out and bared her palm towards him. She nodded a moment later, her lips setting into a hard line. "Magic. Wild magic."

Rathen quickly spun away, snarling violently. "Hlífrún."

He scoured the forest, between the trunks, across the wood, searching for those loathsome eyes of burning painites he knew were observing them from the shadows. "*Hlífrún!!*" His bellow shook the air.

The others formed up together, splitting their guard between Garon and the trees. Petra drew her sword, Anthis freed his dagger, Eyila loosened her fingers and Aria turned to watch their back, her hand grasping for the wooden sword at her hip which she knew couldn't possibly do a thing against creatures of the forest, if she even wished it to.

But it mattered little, because their weapons were rendered immediately useless. The ground lurched opened beneath their feet and they dropped and jolted into a dreadfully familiar snare. But the roots that had held them fast against the earthen wall for hours that first time now rose and lifted them out, casting them sharply back onto the surface above. While the others staggered, bruised, and collected their balance, Rathen stormed forwards unfazed, summoning the Root Mother with another seething call.

More roots erupted from the ground in answer and coiled around wrists and ankles to drag them to the dirt, but again their hold faltered before it could take.

A form flashed out from the darkness.

The roots returned in an instant, and this time they held true. But Rathen was not in their grip. He was frozen ahead of them, his arms raised, wrists apart in the grasp of long, grey fingers, and Hlífrún - Root Mother, Spirit of the Wilds, Queen of the Woods - stood before him with eyes ablaze and her perfect, terrible face twisted in wrath. Her voice seeped like a poisonous fog through her teeth. *"Enough."*

"Garon," Rathen hissed, his dark eyes burning as black as coals, meeting her scathing stare levelly, "what have you done to him?"

She didn't grace him with an answer. Her acridly curling lips closed, and her harrowing gaze continued to drill its way into him, daring him to persist in his challenge and promising a swift and decisive punishment should he do so. But where he had once shrank from those eyes, now he all but matched them.

The others held their breath. Kvistdjur, healthy and monstrous, emerged from the surrounding trees. His companions willed him with all their power to stop.

But the skogsrå made no motion to her sentinels as they formed a patient ring around them, waiting for her order to attack. Her bare chest rose and fell sharply with outrage. Then her fine chin lifted and her brutal features hardened. Her fingers slipped away from his wrists.

Rathen's arms dropped heavily. Neither made a move for the other. Instead he watched her warily as she took a step back, rubbing his raw skin, and she, too, maintained the lock of her gaze even as she knelt and plunged her hand into the earth. It vanished as easily as had the ground been sand, and when it withdrew, a tangled, fibrous mass came with it. He blinked at the vaguely yellow, multi-capped stalks and everything fell horrendously into place.

His eyes flicked back to her, thick with accusation - but her throbbing voice rose first.

"Mykodendrit," she said, almost conversationally. "Spindle fingers, as the vittra call them - yes, you met a pair of them on your first visit. It grows in and around the roots of trees, plants and grass, passing information, sharing nutrients. Mother trees use it to feed saplings. Smaller plants use it to warn others of predators. The kvistdjur use it. *I* use it. This is the network, and it stretches beneath all of Arasiin. And, when the mature stalks are carefully harvested and eaten, one will, for a short while, become part of that network. For humans, though, it is a weak connection - just strong enough for manipulation on a subconscious level." She plunged it back into the ground, the grass and soil wholly undisturbed, and rose to wander slowly about them. He turned and tracked her carefully. "But this fungi is sensitive. It relies on balance to survive, and the magic is upsetting that balance. It's interrupting connections, it's mislaying information, it's stealing nutrients and changing the network's shape.

"The network is at its strongest in forests, and the forests are at the greatest risk. This is how my connection is being severed, without which the natural balance will shift; wilderness will wane first, then your crops and hunting will suffer, too." She stopped beside Garon, and with a gentle brush of her fingers through his hair, his eyes suddenly cleared. He looked around in a panic, only now aware of their circumstance, but his struggle ceased when she squeezed his shoulder. He looked up at her in confusion, then followed her gaze towards Rathen and his guarded bearing. "But it's here where it is at its strongest. And it's challenging my seat. I can afford pockets to be cut off - the land will heal, as will the network. But *not* without me. If the Wildlands fall, all hope of repair and renewal is lost."

"We understand that," Rathen replied mindfully, his previous fury finally tempered into consideration as his eyes flicked briefly over the watchful, rooted guards, "but there's more you're unaware of. Salus is *dangerous*, and with magic he's an even greater threat. He wants to *move Turunda* - he wants to split it away from the rest of Arasiin and move it away to 'safety'. He's stressing all the chasms *right now* and *deliberately* making it worse!"

"I am aware of this," she resumed her predatory circling while the band of glowing foxfire eyes impaled the captives. "You spend more time talking in the forests than you realise. But as I've said: I can afford to be cut off from a few pockets, and even if such a thing were truly possible - and I am forced for the sake of my kin to assume that it is - it will not happen quickly. He is not an immediate threat."

"He's also killing wildlings - *your kin!* You know this, you said it yourself! Through Garon! He sees you as a threat to the people of this country - how long will it be before he decides to direct one of those chasms through here and clear you all out of Turunda for good?!"

"You will stop him before then."

"Not if you're going to keep us in here, we won't! He has *elves* helping him, elves who *want* to see him succeed. All it takes is for one of them to step in, take over or say 'I just had a thought' and progress could speed on ahead so fast that we have no hope of catching up."

"I repeat myself again: it will not happen so quickly."

"Would that we could all be so confident about the actions of a mad man."

"Or indeed the people that let him rise to power." She stopped, reassuming an air of supremacy, and regarded him coolly down the length of her regal nose. "No."

"...No?"

"No. The priority of the Wildlands remains paramount. You will stay and repair every site within it. Then, and only then, will you be free to chase down your 'ghost'."

She observed him unmovingly as he appeared about to burst, his ashen face flooding crimson and hands clawing at the air. Her eyes didn't stray from him as Garon's voice rose to step in from behind. But whatever case he wished to make, and to whomever, it was silenced by a brusque gesture.

Faster than she could blink, Rathen flashed in front of her. She didn't flinch, having felt his movements in the ground, but the cloud of menace that darkened in his wake billowed out around him like a toxic shadow. For the briefest instant, she was betrayed by a flickering of her brow.

"Listen to me, *Your Majesty*." His breath was hot across her face, tone low, bitter - dangerous. And the dark, perilous promise in his eyes was meant unmistakably for her. "Whether you care to hear it or not, the magic is affecting *far* more than your forests and your 'network', and we - the *six* of us - are out here to put an end to it. We're the *only* ones putting an end to it. For the sake of our people *as well* as yours. We already have arrangements with the ditchlings and the harpies, and your demands will go right along with them - but, and if I'm going to be completely honest with you, *my* home *isn't* affected, and I don't care *one whit* what goes on in the cities. I could *easily* return to my chair beside my fireplace and abandon this whole situation. And without me, the rest of these fine people will be stuck. *You* will be stuck. And the world will fall apart around my home - which itself will remain untouched because I will have poured *every* ounce of my power into shielding it. With magic that you do not possess. Magic your vakehn no longer possess." He took a step closer, but she didn't retreat. "I am out here for *only* one reason, and she is standing back there, wrapped in your roots. So, *O Root Mother*, I think that you should probably let her go before I revoke my services altogether and leave you and your precious forests to fall, and your kin's fate in the hands of a mad man. And he needn't even resort to magic to wipe you all out. It wouldn't take many cinders to set this whole twisted forest ablaze - your singing kvistdjur have already made a start on laying the kindling, and the dry months aren't far ahead..."

The forest hung as silent as death. He ignored the shocked stares and centred his deliberately brazen defiance squarely upon the skogsrå. He kept a tight rein over the victory that came with her hateful scowl.

"Yes," she hissed, "that command..."

His eyes shifted past her at the slight sound of moving earth and watched as the roots finally receded, freeing Aria first, then the others. Anthis was quick to catch her hand in case she tried to run to him.

Satisfied, he returned to the skogsrå. "We are going to continue as we were. We will correct every site we pass, but we are not going out of our way. Our priority is to impede Salus until we can find a way to stop him. Then, and only then, will we be free to eradicate the magic - here *and* in our own homes."

Hlífrún's lips pursed, and her grey, gossamer-shrouded hip kicked out as she shifted her weight. She stared at him for a long while, assessing, calculating, regarding his steadfastness with the consideration of a ruler, weighing the chance and fate of all her kin in the face of something neither could truly know the outcome of. But though he carried the same uncertainty, he wore only confidence.

Finally, her head snapped away with a bark of agreement, and a good many of the kvistdjur melted back into the forest. "I hope you know what you're doing, Rathen," she warned him as the few that remained stepped forwards to join their queen.

"To your credit, Your Majesty," he said a little more easily, "you know the forests well, but not the cities nor the people in them - nor what sudden power can do to a man. But I know *something* about forests, and I know cities, I know power, and I know the magic plaguing us - probably better than most."

"Yes, you do. But I hope all the same." She turned, then, to vanish back into the trees with her sentinels, but Rathen gently caught her wrist. One of the kvistdjur snatched out at him as fast as a scorpion. He released her in a hurry, and the sharp, wooden talons stopped as still as a tree just inches from his arm. Hlífrún turned with an expectant look.

"There is one more thing: you've been poisoning us."

"It is no poison."

"Call it what you will, but these mushrooms of yours have left us vulnerable. What else have you done to us?"

"Nothing. The mykodendrit was a precaution. I've not needed to resort to engaging it until now."

"You could have told us outright what you wanted, you know."

"You would have declined."

"We've still declined."

"Perhaps. But at least now you understand how serious I am."

"And look what good it's done you." He sighed and stepped back, then bowed his head graciously. "You have my word that we will do all we can, Your Majesty, but we will do it *our* way."

"And if the Wildlands fall before you succeed?"

He smiled abstractly. "We wouldn't let it happen. If nothing else, my home is in the scowles. I can't afford to lose those woods."

Her eyes slighted thoughtfully. "Yes, it is, isn't it... In that case, while I have you, allow me to apologise for the incident--"

He waved it away. "It was a long time ago. And it was my fault, I startled her."

"You did, but she was young, and overzealous in her care of a colony of swiftlets. She has since learned."

"As have I. But I would appreciate it if you could keep your kvistdjur away from Aria when we return home."

She turned and considered him, then her gaze trailed slowly past and onto the child who watched the pair with a mixture of fascination and caution. She looked back to him. "Are you sure? She isn't like other children. She could bond well with them."

"Or she could startle them like I did and have no magic to repel their attack. Kvistdjur are swift."

Again she paused for thought, but shortly nodded her head, her wild black hair bouncing around her perfectly-sculpted shoulders. "Very well."

He bowed his head, deeper this time, and rose to find her smiling fondly. All trace of her fury had passed but for the volatility inherent in her eyes. "I thank you. Now: are we free to leave and continue as we intend?"

"You are."

"And you won't keep us here?"

"I will not. The way is open to you. You'll reach the border in five days."

"Thank you. Oh, and, we won't be eating any more of those mushrooms."

"No, I imagine you won't." She smiled beautifully, freckled with affection, and, to his surprise, turned with her entourage and stepped away into the trees without even the briefest inappropriate glance.

The others joined him the moment their captors were out of sight.

Garon grabbed him roughly by the shoulder. "You," he growled, "play a dangerous game."

"Yes, I do," he cast his hand away from him, "and it worked. We're free to leave."

"And it'll take us five days to get out." Petra rubbed the tension from her forehead with a sigh. "But I suppose that's something..." She returned her sword to her sheath at last, though she didn't relinquish her hold, and adjusted the bag upon her back before stepping forwards with more than a little urgency. "The sooner we move, the better. No stops unless we have to." The others grunted in agreement and she pointedly ignored Garon's look of protest as she stepped past him. They all fell in behind.

Eyila shortly hurried up beside her. "Do you think Rathen meant what he said?"

She smiled sadly at the fret in her brow, but she didn't need to consider the question for long. She looked back to their heading. "I think he wishes he did."

Anthis, meanwhile, was more vocal with his concerns, and it earned him a sharp, unanimous look of warning. He promptly glanced about the supposedly empty woods and lowered his voice to a hoarse whisper. "Everyone wants us to fix their homes - are we really going to go all across Arasiin and do it one by one? There *must* be an easier way..."

"If there is," Rathen grunted in a manner that suggested the thought had occurred to him far too often already, "only Kienza can give it to us."

"Couldn't the elves help?" Aria asked. "Or the vakehn? They're elves! Or, were..."

"The vakehn lied to us - there's a surprise - so I wouldn't trust them or any other elf as far as I could throw them. And regardless, we have no way of contacting them should there be one we *could*. It's Kienza or no one."

Anthis shook his head. "And what if *she* can't help?"

"Then my promised payment is going up."

For two more days they continued unmolested, and a sense of progress finally began to brighten their path. They abandoned all the mykodendrit and every other species of fungus at the first opportunity and continued with the tubers and meats, albeit warily. Aside from some brief if excessively powerful cravings for sweet mushrooms - cravings they each kept worriedly to themselves - they experienced no more unusual turns.

But no sooner had the collective mood began to rise than another helpless issue rose to trample it back down. It was one they had expected, in truth, and much sooner now they spared it thought, but the ensuing tension had slipped it their minds. Not that there was a thing they could do to help it. Willingly, anyway.

They'd not been near a settlement for three weeks, and Anthis's foul temper was just beginning to broil. Manifesting as impatience and snapped responses, it was only going to get worse, and he knew it as well as they did. But while he'd begun keeping to himself - perhaps for their sake, perhaps for his, or maybe through the simple desire to avoid taking their lives to satisfy a number of his needs - on that, the thirteenth night, the accumulating pressure finally reached breaking point.

Chapter 37

"No, Aria, look, like this:" Rathen tightened the blade of grass between the edges of his palms and thumbs, raised it to his mouth and blew. The whistle was perfectly pitched.

Aria, her face screwed up tightly, moved around and scrutinised his hands even closer before adjusting her own to match. She raised it to her mouth just as he had done, blew hard and hopefully, but the resulting sound was just as blunt and muffled.

"You're too low." He adjusted her position, she tried again, but instead came the sound of the grass flapping loose between her fingers. "Now you're blowing too hard. Gently, Aria, you're not trying to shoo off a fly."

Movement caught his eye, and he glanced up across the fire as Eyila rose from her lonely spot just within the light's reach. Despite the heavy shadows, it wasn't difficult to see the preoccupied look that shrouded her face, nor the mournful distance in her eyes. Her gaze brushed no one as she ghosted into the trees.

Sympathy bowed his lips until a rough, inconsistent whistle brought him back to Aria. "You've almost got it," he smiled, tousling her hair. "Keep trying, I'll be back in a minute." She nodded, adjusting the grass again as he rose and stepped quietly away from the camp. Anthis, sitting across the fire with elven texts in hand, watched him darkly.

"Eyila," Rathen called softly, catching up with her among the black and ancient trees. "Are you all right?"

"I'm fine," she beamed back at him peculiarly. "I'm just going to meditate..."

He'd recognised her lie even before she spoke. She'd used that smile too often. But he didn't challenge it. "I'll walk you," he said instead. "Just in case." With her reluctant nod of thanks, they proceeded in silence. A heavy, burdening silence that neither addressed until Eyila turned at last and looked at him with another peculiar expression. She must have felt him staring at her; he only noticed it himself half a moment before, but at the haunting in her eyes - something he may have imagined, he privately admitted - he decided to carry his see-sawing debate through.

He smiled lightly before turning his gaze towards the trees. "Aria lost her family." She didn't speak, but he hadn't expected her to. The trivial and almost conversational way in which he'd made the statement had no doubt confused her even more. "She was too young to remember, fortunately, and I've never told her. Her village was razed by bandits, you see, and she was the only one to escape. I think they hid her away somewhere and she sort of wandered off when hunger got the better of her. I found her in my garden a few days later, and she's been with me ever since. She was two years old, I think." He didn't spare her a direct glance. He didn't need to see how it landed. "My own mother died when I was three. And when my magic surface when I was seven, I was carted off to the Order. I never really had much of a family. And, of course, my...father died not long ago."

"Petra's lost her father, too," he glanced around at a chirp of a bird, the songs of which had become increasingly ordinary over the past few days, "and Anthis...well, it's not my place to talk about his family. And who knows about Garon - I wonder sometimes if he didn't spawn off the back of a frog." Finally he looked, and she stared back at him with eyes as big as eggs, glittering like starlight over a lake. His lips slanted apologetically. "My point is, while we might not know *exactly* how you feel, we're not without some idea. Don't suffer in silence. Use us."

She appeared to think for a moment, but, to his deep disappointment, nothing came of it. Instead the glitter abruptly vanished, her strange, belying smile clattered back into place and she spoke with a voice so strong and certain it would put Garon's denial to shame. "Thank you, but, *really*, I'm just going to meditate..."

His heart sagged in his chest, but he kept his sigh trapped behind his lips and nodded. The defeat hadn't been entirely unexpected. "All right," he smiled. "Good." And they walked on for another silent minute until she slowed them at last to a stop.

Closing her eyes, she turned her face up towards a tree. The slightest breeze disturbed her hair. "This spot feels right."

"All right - shout if you need anything."

"I will. Thank you, Rathen." She caught his hand as he turned away, but this time the smile she gave him was soft and open, and it set him at ease, if only a little. "Really."

He inclined his head, then left her to climb up the trunk as he made his way back towards camp. But a dark shape flickered out of the forest when he was only half way back.

Rathen abandoned his spell as his hands dropped in relief. "Anthis, you scared the *life* out of--"

"Leave Eyila alone."

He blinked at the abrupt tone, and strained a little harder through the blackness to regard him - and ensure that it *was* him after all. "I was escorting her, Anthis, and reminding her that she can talk to us. She's fine."

"Talk to *you*, you mean."

His dark brows drew slowly closer together. "What are you talking about? She needs a friend, I'm just tryi--"

"She doesn't need your kind of friendship."

"My *'kind'* of friendship?"

The shape scoffed bitterly, sparking Rathen's irritation. "You just *have* to have every woman tripping over you, don't you? Do you think you're entitled to them? Is it because you're so far above the rest of us? As a mage? As an accidental hero? Or is it just a game of notches on the bed post for you?"

A blinding mix of confusion and insult propelled Rathen forwards before he could think, but Anthis stood his ground with a powerful sneer. "*What?!*" he hissed, dropping his voice against being overheard, by human ear or otherwise. "What in Zikhon's name has gotten *into* you?!"

"I'll tell you: I am *sick* of watching you fawn over her. It's disgusting. She's not interested, and she's hurting - *leave her alone.*"

"You think--" Sheer disbelief dazed him for a moment. "*Eyila?!* She's *nineteen!* She's a *child!*"

"And young enough to be your *daughter.*"

The debilitating perplexity threatened to burst something inside his skull, and a familiar, terrifying turmoil started to rage in the blackest reach of his consciousness.

He stamped it down.

He knew what this was, what had truly stoked Anthis's ire, and he was as helpless to it as Garon had been to Hlífrún's mushroom-manipulation. But that did little to offset the monumental offence. "Anthis," he said as steadily as his insult would allow, though it came through his teeth all the same, "she needs help, and she isn't going to ask for it."

"She doesn't need *your* help."

But upon the slightest lash of that venomous tone, his efforts snapped. He fixed Anthis cruelly, whose green eyes he could see in the shift of moonlight bore an identical sentiment. "*She* doesn't?" He growled. "Or *you* don't want her to have it?"

His lip curled. "*She* doesn't."

"And you know what she needs? Really? *You?*"

"I've got a better feel for people than you do."

Rathen's voice rattled caustically. "Oh I don't doubt that. A very *special* 'feel'. So special that I'm not sure she'd like your 'kind of friendship' either." He watched Anthis darken with anger and felt no small pinch of satisfaction. But it didn't last for long. Sense was all too quick to kick back in and encourage him to abandon that avenue of resentful entertainment. Antagonising him wouldn't achieve anything, and though he was loathe to admit it, in this state, the man was dangerous.

Rathen straightened, composed himself, and tempered his voice into a tone of persuasion. "Anthis, whatever ideas you've concocted, you're wrong. Look, Eyila is right along through there, and we *both* know she doesn't want to be alone. *Go* to her."

"Oh, so you're going to stand back, how very *generous* of you."

"Vastal's *Blood*, Anthis! I have no interest in her! At all! Are you really so frightened of your own feelings that you have to find excuses to avoid them?!"

"*What* excuses?"

"For someone with such a 'special feel' for people, you've not got a great read on yourself."

"And you know me so well?"

He sneered. "Regrettably."

"Then allow me to apologise for sullying your magnificent presence."

Again the fury rose, but again he breathed it away, and finally remembered that he was not in fact chained to the spot. He shook his head in helpless exasperation and turned to walk away, sparing them both the blisteringly familiar confrontation. "I'm not doing this with you again. You're not yourself."

"We're not finished."

He snapped back around as Anthis's fingers closed sharply around his shoulder and impaled him with a brutal look. The boy's eyes were alight with foolish challenge. "No," he snatched himself free, "we're finished. If you want to pin all of your inadequacy onto someone, look somewhere else. I won't be party to your self-pity. But that girl is out there right now, crying in the trees, and despite everything, she won't talk to any of us. Myself included. And I've not tried to wring it out of her because I know who she *really* wants to talk to, and I've been hanging back just *waiting* for you to shed that yellow stripe of yours and step up, to stop sitting around and watching her from the shadows, but your cowardice is just too deep-seated. Which is remarkable, really, considering how easily you raise your blade against murderers, rapists and bandits. And yet you can't let a girl cry on your shoulder. You really are *pathetic*."

Something inhuman pierced through Anthis's eyes. "Pathetic, am I?" His tightly balled fist thumped him sharply in the shoulder, but after the surprise flickered away from Rathen's face, he only laughed.

"You really think *pushing* me is going to prove otherwise?"

"It certainly makes me feel better."

Rathen staggered half a step backwards at another heavy shove, and again his anger began to swell. But this time, he was disinclined to suppress it. He speared him with a dangerous focus. "You had better stop and think about what you're doing..."

"Should I?" He struck him again, much harder now, whatever meagre restraint he'd had dissipating like fog, but he was met only with another mocking cackle.

"Yes. You really should."

Rathen saw the enraged strength gathering behind his knuckles as he pulled them back even further, and stepped aside just in time for his fist to hurtle past his face. He felt its power as a lash of air across his cheek.

Stunned eyes crashed onto Anthis, but he was already moving in for a second swing. Rathen sighed witheringly. "I gave you fair warning."

A second later, Anthis was on the floor.

Petra tutted as he hissed and flinched away from the damp cloth. She pressed it firmly to the side of his face and gave him a chiding look for his irritation. "Don't," she told him pointedly, "pick a fight with a soldier."

"He's a mage," Anthis growled, "he was never a real soldier." He winced again at the slap she imparted to the side of his head, and subdued if just to spare himself more injury. "Right, your sister, sorry. But you know what I mean. He never uses his magic so liberally...never *used* to, anyway..."

"He probably never had need before."

He watched her closely as she reached for a dry cloth, noting the amount of blood on the other. He twitched his face, testing the pain, and regretted it the moment a deep and pounding surge of heat flashed from the edge of his brow and down into his jaw. He kept his face still after that. "Have you noticed it?"

"His magic? Yes, but each time it's been necessary."

"Really? Even this?"

"I dare say so," she smiled wryly. "Assuming that this *was* magic. What are you getting at, anyway?"

"Nothing..." He stifled another hiss as she wiped away the last of the bloodied water from his face, then handed him another cloth, as clean and damp as the first had been, and left to tidy the rest away. He looked up as Rathen entered the camp, and both turned sharply away from the other. Petra sighed and shook her head.

Her despondency hiked further as Garon stepped out from the trees and cast them both curious looks. Predictably, as position dictated, he turned then to her, his face its usual hollow shape of authority. "What's happened?"

She shrugged disinterestedly and continued wringing out the cloths. "Nothing important."

"Really," he grunted doubtfully, then cast her a sideways look. "Conversational tonight. You've been quiet lately."

"Surprised you've noticed."

"Hard not to when you're not chirping in my ear."

"Glad you've been enjoying the silence."

"Blissfully."

Her expression was stone, betraying not a hint of her fight to keep her reaction suppressed. She turned away with perfect composure and walked off into the trees; he barely glanced at her parting.

Rathen glowered at him reproachfully. When the officer's gaze fell then onto him, sitting at the foot of the tree, he turned away icily.

"Well?" He demanded, stepping out into the middle of the tight little camp between the two guilty parties, looking from one to the other as a parent would two naughty children. But where Anthis turned, pulled in his leg and leaned his elbow on his knee, forming a wall of sulking defiance as he pressed the cloth to his face, Rathen replied with a brusque snap.

"'Well' what? It's like she said: nothing important." The way Garon folded his arms, sighed and shook his head grated at him monstrously.

"I expected better of you."

"Sorry to disappoint."

"*Hey,*" he stepped aside and grasped him by the shoulder, but Rathen immediately snatched himself out of it. "I've had enough of the attitude from all of you. Remember who you're speaking to."

"Oh, who *am* I speaking to?" He rose to his feet as Garon loured, and squared off at him with a rancorous scowl. "A man? Or a *badge?*"

The inquisitor's face darkened. "*What?*"

"You know, you might command more respect if you gave a little out in return, but as it stands, you *barely* pass for a human being. How you weren't drowned at birth the moment they saw your forked tail, I'll never know." Garon's furious eyes widened, and Rathen took some small satisfaction from that. Which he made no attempt a hiding. "Lost for words? What a novelty."

But, to his disappointment, the outrage suddenly dropped from his face. Rather than reach for the bait, the officer took a step back into his usual infuriating composure. "Whatever your problem is," he said calmly, "sort it out. We need to get out of here with our wits in tact."

"*You* are my problem."

"And what did I do to earn the honour?"

Rathen bridled at the flat, disinterested tone and the poor, so very poor choice of words. "Honour," he grunted. "*Honour.* It always boils down to that with you, doesn't it? Honour. Pride."

"What?"

"For someone who pays so much attention to his surroundings, you can't seem to see what's staring you *right* in the face. Or perhaps you just choose not to - I don't really care. Maybe you're just that inept." Garon stormed back towards him, and Rathen met him squarely, thriving on the quick return of his anger. "But you could learn a lot if you just opened your damned eyes."

"And what," he spat, "am I supposed to be seeing?"

"Oh, I don't know. That it's possible to live without your pride in absolute pristine condition? That you might even be *happier* if you muddied it a bit?"

"What are you talking about?"

"I'm sorry," Rathen suddenly laughed, "I'm not doing a very good job of explaining myself, am I? I suppose that's because I can't truly fathom it myself - or perhaps it's because I'm not sure how fine a point to put on it to make sure it actually drills through your skull. I think it's a little of both, though, so I guess I'll just come out with it: for reasons *completely beyond* my comprehension, Petra *feels* something for you. But, instead of being even *remotely* civilised towards her, you treat her like the shit on your shoe. And why? To protect your pride. Don't make faces, Garon. I know how you really feel about her, we can *all* see it - your authority slips, your rigidity falters, and then you double it all and reinforce it with an extra layer of jackassery to compensate."

For an endless moment the two impaled one another with contempt, each challenging the other, daring them to say exactly what was on their mind despite being fully aware of the blows it would come to if they did - and yet each almost willing it to happen. Even Anthis looked around at the charge in the air.

But, finally, Garon's blazing eyes dulled. "That's quite the imagination you have."

"Don't be ridiculous. I don't have one."

"I'm not here to worry about people's feelings or make friends--"

"Well that's a relief--"

"*None* of us are. We're out here to do a *job*, Rathen. A job I *only* need you and Anthis for - so if I'm being 'uncivilised' towards her, she's well within her rights to leave. No one asked her to come and no one's *keeping* her here. She's tagging along and putting up with my 'incivility' entirely of her own accord."

Rathen barked an acrid laugh. "She is *far* more than just a 'tag-along', and you know it. But I warn you: she *is* going to give up on you to protect herself, and if you don't want that to happen, you had better do something, and fast."

"Why would I *not* want that to happen?"

The clench of his jaw was so rigid at the sight of the heartless indifference in the man's eyes that he felt his teeth might crack, and he wanted so *very* dearly to hit him. But Garon wasn't the type to surrender to brawn. So he managed, somehow, to restrain his rage and the offence he felt on Petra's behalf - though he knew she would not be so inclined - and moved a tight step closer, dropping his voice to a snarl. "All right. All right, fine. Continue to deny it. Protect your pride at the expense of everything else. Heart and health - just like this injury of yours. You can keep that to yourself too, if you must - I *really* don't care - but don't make the rest of us suffer for that ego of yours. And if not us, *her*. Because she cares, Garon. She *cares*. And I don't doubt that she's the first since your own mother to do so."

"You don't know what you're talking about."

"No, Garon, I know *very* well, just like I know you're not worth my breath--"

"*Then cease!*"

"*But that poor girl is!*"

Garon whipped away from him with a scoff, but Rathen was quick to reach out and spin him back around. His hold was immediately reversed and he was seized in turn. Anthis watched them stare another hail of daggers at one another. "You had better decide what matters to you, *Inquisitor*. Your pride and your badge, or your humanity. Because if you keep ignoring it and shutting it away, you're going to turn into nothing more than a uniform with a tongue. And I dare say the transformation has already started."

The officer released him tersely and stormed away without a word, vanishing back into the trees whose company he seemed to favour. He spared not even a moment for Rathen to read his response.

An infuriated growl rumbled in his throat. "I'm surrounded by *children*." His eyes snapped towards Aria, who sat still beside the fire, watching the confrontation with a mixture of fear and fascination in her big eyes. "Arenaria, come here." He turned and stalked off in the opposite direction. "I need some adult company."

Every step they took away from the brooding camp became easier. She was sure something had laced into the air back there - such anger just couldn't be natural. But while Aria wondered what had happened to upset everyone, she found she was a little afraid of asking. She decided eventually that she didn't need to know - though when she looked up at her father and saw the deepened lines in his face, the need rose anew.

But still she chose not to address it.

A few minutes later, however, and she found herself smiling. "I'm enjoying this."

Removed from his thoughts, he looked down at Aria in surprise. "'This'?"

"Adventure." She didn't notice the pondering look he sent her mature and considered smile. "What will we do when we leave the forest?"

"Go where we think Salus is most likely to try to cause chaos."

She nodded and pursed her lips, and the thought that so frightened the adults came back to claw at her. She decided to voice it before it grew too big. "*Can* he move Turunda?"

"I really don't know, little one. But, like Hlífrún, we have to assume he can, for the sake of everyone else."

"...I wonder if someone will write about all this when we're done..."

His eyebrow arched as he looked down at her pensive pout.

"Like all my stories. Important stories - heroes stopping villains."

"We're not heroes, little one."

"Good people stopping bad people, then."

"I'm afraid we're not important enough for that," he said softly. "We're just a few very *small* people. No one will notice we even had a hand in it. They'll all think the Order was responsible for the magic's end, just like they do its start. Little people never get noticed. Not for good deeds."

"Well, we don't really *need* to be noticed, do we? As long as we do the right thing. And...I don't think I'd like to read the story if it was written, anyway."

"Why not?"

"Because I would already know the ending."

"That doesn't usually stop you."

"I also think, once this adventure is over, I'll miss it. Reading it will make me sad." She pushed the encroaching disappointment away - it was foolish, since the adventure wasn't over yet. But, still... "Can we have another when we finish this one?"

"Oh, not right away, I don't think," he replied evasively. "But...in time, maybe. Probably. Who knows what life has in store..."

His breath was almost snatched away by the onslaught of images he could do nothing to stop. His old life - how simple it had been despite the trials of his superiors and everyone's expectations; Taliel - what happiness they'd shared, though that had *not* been simple, and it remained as such even then; of the future they had planned, the life he'd had, what it should have been...and what it could now become...if he really could be pardoned...or if she really could leave the Arana...

He blinked when he realised Aria was speaking, and offered her an apologetic smile. "Sorry, little one, I'm very tired..."

She cocked a pale eyebrow and her face broke into a far more impish grin. "Thinking about our next adventure?"

He couldn't help smiling despite his heartache, and pulled her close beside him. "I dare not."

Mercifully, exhaustion struck quite abruptly, so they turned about and made back for camp, seeking the tell-tale light of the fire through the darkness. Aria was asleep in his arms by the time they returned, and everyone else had retired to their blankets, their backs turned away from one another but for Eyila, who appeared to be the most peaceful. But while his eyes stung with that same desire for sleep, his mind had set itself aflame.

He settled Aria upon her blankets, across which she promptly sprawled, and sat down beside the fire with only the company of his relentless thoughts.

Anthis's insinuation still stung. Garon's pomposity still grated. The ideas that had exploded from Aria's innocent words were still swirling ruthlessly in his head. But though he was too tired to even consider finding a distraction, he didn't think on them at all. They swilled and mingled, but nothing progressed; no new worries formed or grew, no old ones resolved or weakened. They were nothing more than an unpleasant mass, a dull cacophony that drowned itself out into a constant, tolerable hum.

His heavy, fading focus drifted onto the fire. He was lulled easily into its calming flickers, soothing waves and almost predictable rhythm, his eyes moving with its tongues a fraction ahead of each undulation. The smoke stung with every breath and he blinked against its dry heat, but he remained transfixed nevertheless.

Before long, the sensations vanished.

The scent of sap and scratched bark began to slip in, and damp soil churned up by foraging nocturnal beasts. It smelled homely. Safe. And when the chirp of a nightlark, both distant and close at hand, cast a thread of brightness through the gathering familiarity, he felt his muscles loosen and his body disconnect. It was as though his hands, feet, legs, arms, head were not his own - but it didn't alarm him. Fatigue was drawing his mind away like an old friend.

His frustrations, too, began to dim, appearing trivial now that he sat apart from them, and as moments trickled by, the darkness about him deepened. He became distantly aware of the strangeness of the disembodied sensations. He'd never noticed them before. Or perhaps he had, and the fleeting moments before sleep remained vague mysteries in waking, experienced only in the descent. He found he enjoyed it.

He watched as the shapes around him vanished, the light softened, and the face formed above the flames. Regal, beautiful, *perfect*. He watched the enticing lips curve into a smile. Was it Taliel? Or Kienza? No, neither. The face caused him no anguish - and yet it stoked a fire in his heart and a lurch in his gut just the same.

The fire dropped beneath his sight, but the face endured, with eyes of flaming chestnut, of painite. The light drifted behind him and the darkness reigned, but the face, the body, they never melted away. He felt soft fingertips run over his palms, over his wrists, feeling his pulse, and his fingers closed around hers, feeling the same rapid rhythm. It was supreme, the clearest sensation when all else felt slow, muffled, numbed and disjointed. But still there was no alarm. Her pulse echoed the dance of the flames.

But the fire was lost. The darkness engulfed him; arms and legs intertwined, soft lips, hungry lips, hers and his, brushing the other's skin, smooth and rough, like the bark of a tree.

And then, euphoric haze.

Chapter 38

It was only when Petra startled Rathen out of his confused and sluggish bout with waking by sitting bolt-upright that he finally realised there was a problem. She spun around upon her blanket in an attempt to find the bearings she hoped she'd simply misplaced, but every narrow tree trunk and wide space between them dropped the pit in her stomach even deeper. "This isn't where we made camp!" Her eyes crashed onto Rathen, who shot up in belated alarm. "Where are we?!"

"Where's Aria?!"

"Eyila's gone, too!"

The pair scrambled, waking Garon and Anthis in the process, and set immediately upon a desperate hunt until a giggle fluttered from the direction of the sunrise. They steered sharply and tracked it to the edge of an overhang. Standing over a collapsed and blackened old house and its broken well a short way from its foot, there, among the trampled planters and splintered food barrels, sat Aria in a ring of ditchlings playing a merry game of pat-a-cake, while Eyila sat upon a rotten bench with two more ditchlings fussing through her hair.

Their shoulders sagged in relief, but an anger of disapproval was quick to flood into its place when all the ditchlings paused to look up and cast them great big innocent smiles. Aria and Eyila promptly followed, though the former was the quickest to realise what trouble they were in.

Fortunately, Petra spoke first. "You shouldn't have run off like that," she chided far more calmly than Rathen would have as she made her way down a shallow gulley, driving her sword into the dirt for stability if not also to make a point. "*Anything* could have happened to you out here."

"Not with us around it wouldn't," one of the ditchlings chimed, but Rathen shot him a sharp look.

"We weren't talking to you." He turned to the rest as Garon and Anthis appeared at the ledge above. "Are you responsible for this?"

They each blinked giant, silver-green eyes and looked around at one another for a clue, but they appeared only more surprised when they returned. "Why would we be responsible for *this*?" A girl asked from beside Eyila, who had, it seemed, been braiding her hair. "It was like this when we found it - someone *else* burnt it down. One of you hoomans, I reckon. Ain't no such thing like we'd have done. It could've scorched the trees!"

"Not the house," he sighed. "Our camp has moved."

"You're sure you didn't just forget where you were? It's dark at night."

"There's no sign of our fire."

"Just as well." She gestured a dirty hand back towards the house.

He sighed and squeezed his eyes shut tight. It was too early for this. "Never mind. Where *are* we, then?"

"Wildlands," a boy replied unhelpfully, then added, "about a day's run from Rul."

Rathen's eyebrows rose in astonishment. "Rul? I thought we were still three days from the border..." Then a thought occurred to him. An obvious thought - and a thought that brought with it phantom stirrings that he couldn't place for the life of him. Even so, his eyebrows dropped low. "Hlífrún."

"We're as good as out of the forest," Garon declared. "I have no intention of questioning the means nor the motive. Though I would like to know what *you* all want."

"Why should we want anythin'?"

"Because you're here."

"We're here 'cause we *live* here, geenyus," the boy rolled his oversized eyes. "Why are *you* here?"

"We don't know - and, I notice, we didn't see any of your kind in the Wildlands at all. Why is that?"

"Are you mad? It's *wild* in there!" But then his eyes suddenly turned to glass and he stared off for miles for the briefest moment. He stood when they cleared, and his naturally devilish demeanour was quite suddenly set aside in favour of an unsettling sobriety as he approached them. When he spoke, they shifted promptly in the same direction. "We had that fella, Salus, for a while, but we lost him 'cause magic snapped and shuddered and crumbled the ground. We reckon he was on his way to Fendale, but we dunno what he was gonna do there."

Rathen's gut turned over. Fendale. If he'd just had the Zi'veyn working back then...

"Also, his toadies are bein' more aggressive with us than before. They been leavin' poison out - it ain't been gettin' us, nor the harpies really, but that's what they been tryin', along with smokin' us out and trappin' us when we try and scurry away. It used just to be fires and scattered traps, but now they're gettin' right up close to our setts, and while we ain't much ones for toleratin' trespassin', none of our usual deternments work on 'em."

"I'm sorry to hear that," Rathen said, honestly, "but there's really not much we can do about it right now."

"We ain't askin' for your help," he almost laughed, "we're just lettin' you know what's been up. We got our *own* plans - we can be nasty, too, and they're gonna find out! And, no, you don't wanna know - not with ladies in your company." Petra stifled a laugh at the bold and extravagant wink he sent her.

"The harpies," Rathen said, untickled as he returned Aria's hug of apology with a squeeze of her shoulder just soft enough to let her know that she was forgiven, but that there would indeed be words. "How are things...?"

"Eh, they don't try to hurt us no more," a girl with a remarkable crown of dusty white mushrooms replied from the circle, "and we been holding back on 'em, innit - but they *did* come screeching in to one of our homes not two days ago and start accusing us of stealing..."

"...And I take it you were guilty?"

"Not me *personally*, but in our defence we thought the turkeys - harpies, right, yeah, 'no more descriminatinery terms' - well, we thought they didn't need these shiny knifes and forks, and 'cause we're all friends now, we ought to share, innit.

But they got mad and took 'em back." She fired them a spiteful look. "What? Just 'cause we ain't hooman we can't use cutterly?"

"Cutlery, and that's not what I was thinking. If I'm honest, I was wondering why *they* had them..."

"Well 'cause they're shiny, innit? But we weren't gonna eat with 'em and dirty 'em up, we wanted 'em to make better weapons - ones this Salus wouldn't expect us to have."

"Well, that is in their interest too, I suppose. But what happened when they took them back?"

"...We couldn't make the weapons..."

"He really is!"

They looked towards another ditchling, and Rathen frowned uncertainly at his cryptic outburst. "But," he looked nervously back to the girl, "did they attack?"

"No, admittedly, so we didn't do nothing to 'em but call 'em names. No one wants to be the reason the harpies leave us to die. Not that I reckon they're really gonna save us, but it doesn't hurt to have eyes above, does it? We're all crossing our fingers and toes for it to work out."

"And has it? So far?"

She pursed her grey lips, then, slowly, they all began to nod. "We been working on a few traps together, and we've caught a few, but they always get out. Hoomans are big - we're not sure where to start with 'em."

"'Start'?" Petra dared to ask, but she received only calculating looks.

Chillingly, the eyes simply fell back to Rathen. "We're muddlin' through."

"So it's been an improvement, then?"

"Yeah, I'd say so," the boy answered Garon, eventually.

"Then we've helped you."

"Yeah, I'd say so."

"Good. Then you can do something for us." Each child-creature regarded him with caution, while the rest frowned in surprise. "We've been in that forest for two weeks. We have no idea where Salus is, where he's been nor where he intends to go. We know his plans, and it's *imperative* that we stop them - but we need to know where best to direct our efforts."

"And you want us to find out? How d'you expect us to do that? We can't follow him *every* which way, y'know."

"He's targeting sites in the mountains and along Turunda's borders," he explained evasively, "but we don't know precisely which. But there's method to his actions, and he *will* have a map."

"And you want us to get it? He'll keep it in his castle, no doubt."

"He's not a king."

"No, but that big grey house is guarded about as well as. We know. One o' the cooks makes a scrummy gooseberry crumble, but we can't never get close to it! The one time we *did*..." They all shuddered.

"Well, this isn't a gooseberry crumble."

"No, that it ain't..." The boy turned away and the ditchlings' eyes focused onto a collective thought. They watched the creatures in silence, watching some nod, others shake their heads, but for the most part they remained perfectly still. Until, at last, the boy turned back around. But it was the mushroom-crowned girl who spoke.

"We'll do what we can."

And with that, they rose and left without so much as a nod of farewell.

"...Do you think they thought we meant *they* had to do it?" Petra asked quietly as they disappeared into the trees, but Rathen merely shrugged, then turned a stern look down at the little girl beside him. She smiled back sheepishly.

Though so close to the edge of the Wildlands and the road back into their own world, they didn't rush to move out. Instead they had the usual breakfast of rain tubers and strange, conical fruit and redrew the outline of their plan: head east, towards the mountains, and make straight for the nearest of the most likely ruins. Anthis had already pin-pointed two locations before his 'ailment' could cloud his judgement, and Garon had decided that it was unlikely that Salus would waste time trying to find and affect places that may not even exist. Therefore the most well-known of the two - or, rather, the only one that sounded passingly familiar - became their goal.

But after a lengthy reminder of the need for anonymity and that, for the moment, it still fell to Anthis as the least recognisable among them to gather food and supplies from settlements, a brusque hail was all that announced the arrival of yet more ditchlings.

Or, rather, their return.

The boy laid a torn canvas bag across the ground, and they all peered down at its grubby charcoal marks in question. Garon was the first to recognise it as a map, and Anthis noted the circles around the edges. Around Halen, around Fendale, around Ausokh, around White Barrows, Gennith's Point and Víla's Rest, and countless more besides. Some, he'd never seen before. Some were under water. And some had already been struck out.

The weight of their task landed like a mountain that had been uprooted and dropped upon their heads.

Eyes fell disheartened as Garon shook his head, and though he spoke with that same steadfast certainty he always did, it only crushed them further. "We can do this. We stop him at the others before the rest can become an issue."

No one offered him their sarcasm if just so they didn't have to hear it themselves.

"We know where to go now - and White Barrows was our heading." He looked to the ditchlings. "Has he struck it yet?"

"Not that we're aware of - mind you, the turk--*harpies* would know more about that. It ain't our area. Now," his eyes became shrewd, "what're you gonna give us for our trouble? We put ourselfs right in the line of danger for you, y'know."

"What happened?" Aria asked keenly, and the boy's eyes brightened.

"*Oh!* Well, we - well, *they* - scurried through that black forest o' theirs, through the gardens, dodgin' the dogs, the guards, the traps, and clambered up the ivy on t'other side of the house. 'Tweren't no problem, o' course, I reckon they thought no one was gonna break in in the mornin', and they definutly had the right place 'cause we been followin' a few of the less careful ones back. Anyway, up they clambered, peered inside that window he's always peerin' out through - all clear - jimmied it open and tumbled inside, and *there was someone in there!* She weren't in sight inishully, but she certainly was when they was in!" His audience stared on in concern. "*But*, when they was hangin' in the window, lookin' at her, her lookin' at them, she just turned around, picked up the teapot and left. She didn't seem in no hurry but it lit fire under their backsides, I tell ya. Fortunely, the map was already lyin' open on the desk, so they got a good long look and sent it all back this way as quick as they could, and we drew it out for ya."

"Did they get out?" Aria asked before the others could, her voice strangled in her throat. But to all their relief - and surprise - the boy nodded.

"No one else showed up, so once they had what they was after, they scarpered."

"I wonder if we can trust it..."

Rathen sent Garon a very sharp look. "He won't have expected *ditchlings* to rush in there and copy it, no matter which way you look at it. This is *all* we have. We have no choice but to run with it."

"*They* certainly did." Then the boy's craftiness returned. "Well?"

"Yes, fine. What is it you want?"

They wasted no time in pointing towards Petra, who immediately staggered backwards in surprise. "Me?"

"You want her to teach you something, you mean?"

But they shook their heads, and the boy jabbed his finger towards her again. "The others, they want what's 'round her neck."

While the others frowned, her eyes grew into saucers and stared back at them in horror.

"Her *locket?*" Garon asked in disbelief. "No. No, last time it was *braids* you wanted--"

"And this time it's that lockitt. We can always take this back..."

"We don't need it, we can remember--"

Petra stamped her foot down onto the canvas sack before the ditchling could begin to drag it away, and snatched her elbow out of Garon's hand as he tried to stop her from unclasping the chain. "We won't remember it."

He stepped back with a rough, dissatisfied sigh, but didn't protest. They watched her drop the fine chain into the small, dirty hand without hesitation, then bend down and scoop up the map. There was no trace of hurt or anger on her face. It was there, certainly, but she didn't let it show. How much of that, Rathen wondered, was for Garon's benefit?

The boy swung it around, dangling it from his fingers, and he and his companions watched it glint in the light. "Blindin'." He beamed and clasped it around his own neck. "Thanks very much. Now, I reckon that about concludes our busyness, so we'll be off - you all be careful out there. Oh," he glanced towards Aria and smiled as the others began to scamper off ahead of him. "Nug says hi."

Rathen sighed in defeat as Aria grinned and returned the greeting. "Why does Nug always have to say 'hi'?" He grumbled, then looked to Petra as she handed Anthis the map. "Are you all right?"

"I'm fine," she replied with a brief, weak smile. "It's nothing. It got us this map."

"You didn't need to hand that over."

"And what about the *next* time we need their help and they withhold it out of spite? No, whether we like it or not, they've helped us out more than a few times.

They even tried to rescue us - twice. We can't afford to lose their willingness to help. And they *did* put themselves in serious danger for us just now." She smiled emptily again and stepped away for her things as the others began gathering up to leave. "It's fine."

Garon looked over Anthis's shoulder as he ruminated over the map. "White Barrows." He didn't apologise for startling him. "Do you know where it is?"

He hesitated, then shook his head with an irritated growl. "Not precisely..." But then his head snapped up and he shouted something after the ditchlings, the sour bite that now permanently coloured his tone ringing in his words. They returned in a moment, a snubbed look on each of their faces, and all but yelled *'Arkhamas'* back at him before waiting irritably for whatever he had to say. "We need to get to White Barrows as quickly as possible. Get a message to the harpies and ask them to scout it out. We need directions."

"Oh, that all? O' course, *Majesty*, whatever you say. We'll get right to it, and have it delivered on a silver platter with a gold ribbon and eight iced buns, on the back of a snow-white weasel." They all bowed with an excessive flourish, which was a very bizarre sight, and scurried off again while Anthis growled at the offence. Then, they raised their bags, slung them over their shoulders, and made at long last for the tree line.

Fragments of warm light peeked through the leaves above, penetrating the forest here far more easily than it had in its depths, and before long they began to catch glimpses of the wild emerald fields beyond. Minutes later, they stood at the threshold.

Sunlight rained down on them. Its heat was almost tangible, pleasant in its freedom, and then smothering and inescapable. It ushered in a sense of hope, then immediately snuffed it out with the path and duties it illuminated before them.

But behind them was nothing but confusion and danger and compromise that sat out of their favour, and a threat they had no hope of understanding. In the sun lay their own world. Behind them was quite another.

But as the others stepped out in resolve and began their return to a familiar world, Rathen found his feet rooted to the ground and a sense of grief hanging heavily from his shoulders. There was a deep and desperate compulsion to stay within the cool shade of the trees, among the threat they didn't understand in the knowledge that it, at least, was natural, and had a purpose. And it was wonderful for that alone. And yet more wonderful still were elements that even now faded from his memory, things he couldn't quite find a grasp on but things he knew he desperately wished to keep, remain within and hold forever.

A mournful desperation rose in his chest, and a lump formed in his throat.

And then a hand slipped into his, and he looked down into Aria's radiant face.

She squeezed his fingers and kissed his arm. "It will be okay." She stepped forwards, carefully, cautiously, and crossed the edge of the tree line. "I promise."

With a deep breath, he followed her.

Chapter 39

The eyes that so casually observed him from across the desk were, Salus noted, strangely adept at concealing the strength of the old man's condemnation. As far as anyone else was concerned, it may not have been there at all. *For* anyone else, it probably wouldn't have been. But he could see it, and he knew the old man's face and bearing regrettably well enough to know exactly what was going through his mind.

His own face, however, was the picture of neutrality. A lie that had become so well-practised for the old man's benefit that not a trace of his insult and anger made it through his eyes. Which only pierced his opponent's with increased suspicion. He found himself enjoying it.

Malson sat taller, no doubt in an attempt to retain his imagined superiority - how deeply that rankled. "Explain."

Salus bowed his head in perfectly feigned obedience. "While General Moore moved to reinforce the east, Doana made the mistake of sending a few camps to give chase - which gave *my* people the opportunity to slip in behind them. In doing so, we discovered what appears to be their standing orders, which we're in the process of decoding, and have done what we could in the small window to sabotage them. We poisoned the water supply of a few and framed the commanders from others. Their numbers are thinning as we speak, from which we'll be able to observe which camps are bolstered by absorbing the men left over from the implicated commanders' and which are abandoned - and, above all, from which direction they truly intend to attack."

Malson nodded slowly, chewing over what Salus had claimed to be the fruits from poor intel suddenly working out in their favour. He'd left a few things out, of course, for prudent measure. For example, he didn't need to know that Doana's standing orders had already been decoded, nor what they contained, nor, in fact, that it appeared that *every* Doanan camp was a decoy. As far as the evidence pointed, Doana's armies were there purely to hold Turunda's military in place while covert actions occurred instead, and it was crucial, to Salus's far more tactical mind, that it be allowed to happen. Turunda's partial withdrawal to needlessly reinforce the eastern border had already confirmed his guess that if the military abandoned the stalemate, Doana would strike to provoke, razing a few towns and cities to regain their attention. It was far better in the end to keep the information quiet and the Crown out from underfoot. While the armies occupied one another, Doana was no doubt already sending individuals into Kora - and so was he. Better to let them think they remained in control and focus instead on disrupting their true task. It was a job made for the Arana.

And, neither did he need to know that, in cracking said code, they'd discovered that Doana had left something behind in their first meagre victory - a contingency plan buried beneath spells in Bowden.

Nor did he need to know that refugees had overrun the translocator room in White Heath, hindering their mobility in the western reach of the country. But that was only a temporary matter.

Finally, Malson raised his chin haughtily in spite of his acceptance. "I suppose that's something - though we have yet to see if it has *truly* worked in our favour. They may not be standing orders, but prior instructions for their arrival here, or even a letter to a loved one. Now - Ivaea and Kasire."

"We've managed to deflect them again, but war is dynamic and we have our own conflicts to attend to. Despite what you may believe, I can't *truly* have eyes everywhere.

"That said, Ivaea is now pushing Kasire back across the steppes and towards their joint border. They won't be a problem for a while."

He didn't need to know that their conflicts had obliterated one of his outlying watch points, effectively blinding him to a good stretch of the grasslands, though that was also temporary. Nor that a subordinate had died - also temporary, as far as replacements were concerned.

"Fine. And the tribes?"

"They're moving away."

He didn't *want* to know the means.

Malson sighed sceptically. Salus knew he was weighing the likelihood of the Crown's satisfaction. Then, once again, his oh so noble chin lifted and his strangely youthful eyes turned down his nose before proceeding to issue a few choice commands. But they were the same old things: move here, more eyes there, listen hither, follow thither. The same, worn out, senseless rubbish. He was increasingly convinced that the Crown was deliberately trying to distract him from the things that mattered, sending him nonsense tasks he knew would yield no results 'just in case we've missed something'. And all because they thought, in their comfortable discussion chambers with their fawning servants and fine, gold-trimmed robes, that *they* knew best on every subject under the sun.

Not that it really mattered to him anymore - he was ignoring most orders and handing over the usual reports, and they had no idea at all. He *already* had people moving, watching, listening and following, because he had never pulled back absolutely when he'd been ordered to, just in case they *did* miss something. His people weren't a flowing river, constantly moving and ready to be diverted. Some of them were lakes - steady and constant, guarding the same spot until a mighty force decided otherwise. And he had not decided otherwise.

In the end, the Crown wouldn't be 'satisfied with the results' even had he obeyed their every misguided whim like a desperate, starving child. Because each of them, to a one, had the wrong idea about the Arana. 'Crown's Fang' it may have been - but not that of a dog, but of a spider. Untameable. Venomous. Something to be feared rather than conquered, for anyone who tried to bend those fangs to their will would only get themselves bitten. And Salus had many fangs, each more deadly than the last.

But rather than the Crown, as Malson sat there parroting his orders, he found himself pondering his suspicions towards the regal old man. He'd voiced no more personal requests, and indeed, he didn't ask about those he already had. Which was strange. Perhaps he trusted Salus to report when and if he had anything, or he was satisfied just knowing that a matter the Crown was continuing to handle poorly was being taken care of by someone who was not a politician. But somehow, Salus doubted it.

If he'd been discovered and reprimanded, his people would have known about it, and that in itself was suspicious. His own dissatisfaction with the Crown had suddenly fallen quiet, and it wasn't because the Crown had done something to remedy it.

So what was he playing at?

"And your request has been denied, again."

Even as Salus nodded his understanding with only a mildly disappointed frown, an obscene lash of fury boiled his blood. Despite everything, despite knowing better, he was *still* trying to play by at least a few of their rules, but the Crown was refusing to acknowledge him. It was as if they *wanted* him to take matters into his own hands but were too afraid to ask and risk casting themselves into disgrace should the public turmoil that would come of it be linked back to them.

In a way, it was just as well that he was taking one step closer towards that end every single day. And if the Crown continued to bury their heads in the sand and deny his requests for an audience to persuade the dissolution of the Order, he would wind up handling that, too.

He rose from his chair and bowed as the liaison turned and left.

The moment the latch clicked into place his last fragile hold on his decorum snapped.

He'd been ducking Malson about this for a while, but that morning he'd been in the most tolerant mood to deal with it - and, thanks to his code-breaker, had armed himself with more than enough information to be able to give him only what was needed in order to smooth it over. But still the old fool remained critical and pompous. Infuriatingly pompous.

He knew if he held onto the teacup he'd grasped to steady his nerves any longer, he'd crush it. So he threw it instead. And once it had shattered against the wall with a satisfyingly shrill peal, he collected the pieces with a negligent flex of his fingers and floated them into a pile on his desk, which promptly received the next lash of his rage.

Fortunately the need to bellow into his hands passed with the bone-cracking clench of his fists, and he whirled back behind his desk to begin poring furiously over reports and plans, if just for some sense of progress and control.

All key tactical locations were manned; there was not a back alley or window left ajar for anyone to slip through and into the country, and not a rat hole or bird's nest in which anyone could hide anything in within their fair borders. The incompetent phaeacians were gone, each and every one of them, promoted where appropriate or cast out of the way, and the phidipans had taken up their old jobs well.

Well. But not perfectly.

They'd found little to reinforce his suspicion on Malson, which was a result of failure rather than there being nothing to find. Malson was doubtlessly careful - his position towards the Crown was a precarious one, and if they suspected him of dissent he would be cast out, and then Salus would have to deal with someone else - someone with even *less* clue of how the Arana worked. Malson had been here for years, and for that, Salus had to concede, he was the lesser evil. But that didn't mean he could be trusted.

The single thing they *had* discovered was that, very occasionally, he had been seen going somewhere at night, in the trade district of the city rather than the royal or stately, but anyone who had spotted him had been observing something else at the time and were unable to determine his destination. And while his surveillance spells now hung in every city, most towns and a few crossroads, Kulokhar was ceaselessly busy and pulled the spells in all directions. He needed him followed, on foot and discreetly.

And, looking down at the most recent report from an accomplished phidipan, he knew just who to send.

But the Order were still solid, too. He needed his spells around the towers - and inside them. The mages were still rebelling, and in the last week it had reached new heights, with attacks in the larger cities and, devastatingly, the port in Roeden, which had killed sixteen people, five of whom were self-appointed mage hunters just bold or stupid enough to think they could stop her, as it was so often the lone mages who were the deadliest. But how to get those spells inside those twisting spires was another challenge.

Non-humans, too, were proving a trial, but in this case he wasn't sure he could blame his people so heavily. It may have been his own fault for under-estimating them. Because the beasts were wisening, and wisening fast. Fortunately they took out great swathes of them before they could catch on, but there were still too many ditchlings, harpies and the like scurrying around on their doorsteps. And yet, while they were nothing more than vermin, *animals*, the phidipans seemed as yet unable to handle them. Perhaps that very perception was the problem. Rather than seeing them as rats and pigeons, perhaps they should consider them among weasels and eagles - smarter beasts. Hunters rather than prey, but animals all the same. That kind of simple adjustment always yielded results.

But while he scribbled that down in a hand still trembling with pent-up rage, the final matter that weighed so heavily upon him at night began to parade around the front of his mind with a fanfare of trumpets. He was loathe to face it, even had his mood not begun to deteriorate. Koraaz hadn't been seen for two and a half weeks. Not since he'd been heading towards the Wildlands. And he didn't like that one bit.

Perhaps he'd died in there - it was a notion he entertained from time to time - but he found a sickening confidence against it. And a sickening helplessness to follow. All he could do on this matter was trust that his people would spot him. There were enough looking, and there was nothing in that wretched forest but trees and the things that so often went bump in the shed at night or howled savagely at the moon. He would *have* to come out at some point. Unless he really *had* died...

A long-drawn sigh breathed out some degree of the tension knotted between his shoulder blades, and another blue, flocked teacup floated out of the open cabinet to settle in his steadied hand. But as he poured out the last contents of this newest pot, his mind drifted towards another individual he'd not seen or heard trace of in a very long while. But Liogan's absence, while troubling, at least wasn't a hindrance. She'd been an uncontrollable element from the beginning and he'd decided early on to disregard her as a blessing - she was not to be counted upon, and he was making great progress without her help anyway.

He'd already joined Halen to Ausokh, Ausokh to Dustwatch, Dustwatch to White Barrows, and only a week ago turned west before all of Halen's magic could drain away through those channels to the east. He wasn't sure if it actually worked like that, but he wasn't prepared to take the risk. But no sooner had he pushed from Halen to Fendale than the military moved and Doana gave chase, forcing his attention away. It was excruciatingly frustrating, but it was progress. The only concern he had on that matter was that these delays gave the Order the chance to ruin his progress or usurp it - if not the elf herself.

That frustration returned the rapid boiling in his veins, and he quickly put the cup down. He took a few deep breaths, concentrating on the bergamot of the tea that writhed in every inhalation, until his temper began to settle and the many-pinned map and various report papers fell mentally back into order.

Then snapped up at the composed and lacklustre knock against the door. Teagan entered at his tight grunt, and the pair filled one another in on the past two hours' occurrences.

The portian looked down at the assignments he was handed while Salus dropped heavily into his chair. "So," the keliceran sighed, "they've abandoned Korovor and Hoarwood. And they're reinforcing the west - Greentop and The Ghost Patch." His eyes dropped briefly to the map. "They're keeping Kora in their sights."

"Your reinforcement of Splintertree and Eening are almost portentous." Teagan replied, to which Salus grunted humourlessly. "By keeping an eye on the approach, we'll notice should they begin to move more individuals towards the city."

Salus snarled beneath his fingers. "We can't let them find whatever they think is kept in there. Dusty maps, royal bloodlines or ancestral records, *whatever* it is..."

"Their claim wouldn't go through, whether they find it or not."

"And then they will attack us zealously because we support a supposed usurper! They *can't* find those documents! I will *not* bow to some muddy-blooded *queen* on *our throne!*"

"I dare say you will find no argument."

Salus began to eye his favoured closely. He was no quieter than usual as he continued through the papers, but he could see a thought buzzing around him. "What is it?"

He looked up without surprise. "Fair allocations. It's a shame Hower and Moroes are unavailable, they would be well-suited. But those you've selected in their place should do well enough."

Salus's eyes narrowed. "But?"

"Taliel's speciality. She's one of our most adept at coaxing information."

"Yes...?"

"She's easy to trust. And she's inconspicuous. All valuable attributes when time is of the essence. Roviin is only four hours from Kora; she would be better suited than David for picking the place apart."

But Salus was already shaking his head. "No. Roviin is a very small village;

they probably haven't seen all that much, and she's too beautiful to slip in under their noses. An attractive woman appearing alone like that? She'd be noticed."

"At which point she would be able to weave a cover in a heartbeat, if she allowed herself to be overtly noticed at all."

Salus's eyes narrowed again. "Is there something you'd like to say?"

"Only that you are not utilising her to her full potential," he replied smoothly, the portian's face thoroughly unchanged. "You've not sent her outside of the grounds in over a week."

"I need her here."

"For?"

Salus bit back his frustration and began busying himself with the nonsense on his desk. "She's intelligent. She provides a third opinion."

"I see."

His eyes shot towards him. "You think I'm being protective. I'm not. She's more than capable of handling herself. But right now, given every sodding thing that's going on, she is of the most use to me *here*. There is nothing more. Is that understood?"

"Perfectly."

"Good." The teacup clattered as he set it roughly back on the desk, dark droplets leaping out and staining the strewn papers, and he rose sharply from his seat for the cupboard across the room. "Get those assignments in motion. I'll deal with Bowden."

"Sir--"

"*What*, Teagan? You have objections, do you?"

"Sir, with all due respect," he spoke calmly even while the keliceran proceeded to change his shoes, "while many avenues may be going well, you are still needed here. You know how dynamic conflict can be, and this situation is far from conventional. Doana snuck in right under our nose, and we still haven't clarified whether or not Skilan is looking our way again."

"What do you expect to happen? That Doana are going to launch an attack on all sides in the hour or so that I'm gone? What's the military there for if they can't hold them off?! And there's the standing, overriding order that any intel crucial to the urgent defence of the country is given first to the person most capable of putting it to good use. Which, in the case of a sudden attack from another direction, would be General Moore, *not me*. The only thing at risk right now is Kora - and as you have already advised me against getting involved in that myself, there are eleven *other* agents working on it instead!"

"We can't know what will happen--"

"Which is why I leave *you* in my stead, Teagan!"

"Let me--"

"*You can't!*" The cupboard door slammed shut and in a flash Salus was before him, his eyes burning, face twisted into impatient menace. But the portian didn't flinch. "It's been left under *spells*, which means *you* can't do a thing about it. I *can*. And if I can't *break* the spells, I can, at least, *find* them. Whatever catastrophes occur in the next hour, they're *yours* to deal with." He snapped away and threw the door open. "I need to get *out of here!*"

*

377

Stepping out through the back exit of the cobbler's shop, Salus's skin prickled at a sudden chilled breeze. Cool air swept in from the east, carrying with it the crisp, clean scent of the Olusan Mountains that stood glowering in the distance, and offset the midsummer heat which was now only set to get worse. For a moment, he stopped and breathed it deeply. He'd always preferred the assignments that had sent him into colder climes in his youth, and though it was only a handful of degrees cooler here than back in the city, he felt his tensions evaporate. It smelled so...*free*. It was only on occasions like these when he truly appreciated how stifling and imprisoning that office was.

But there was no time for disconnection or yearning for simpler days. What Teagan had said may have been melodramatic, but it wasn't incorrect. He couldn't afford to be away for long - especially if Doana realised that the existence of their contingency plan had been discovered, left here in their first wave of brief occupations three excruciatingly long months ago.

So he scuffed his boots in dust from the alley, mussed the knees of his trousers, dropped a flatcap upon his head and softened his scowl into the look of trivial bother that any other man would carry. Then he stepped out into the wider streets, a perfect example of ordinary.

It was late morning and suitably busy, thick with the sights and sounds of commerce and sociality while guards looked on, mostly alert, though the eyes of a few drifted tavernwards, anxious for the coming of lunch time. Dogs barked at passers-by for warning or attention, another caused chaos while it chased down a cat, heedless to its surroundings and its own enormous size, and children played and thieved just out of vendors' sight until one clumsy individual sparked a similar chase and awoke the attention of two drifting guards.

It was, in short, unremarkable. But while Salus scanned each and every face for any sign - expression, twitch or colour - that set them apart as suspicious, a number of the more quiet and subdued individuals paused at the rise of cheering to the west, close to the town walls. Salus heard it, too, moments before the rest, and he didn't miss the distinct thread of malice laced through its core.

It took all of half a second to work out what it was, at which point he promptly disregarded it, ceased his own examinations and turned his sights upon his task.

The town square; the hub of sociality, where the tavern, ever-changing travelling merchants' stalls, tea and wine houses and other such establishments had long since gathered, accompanied by simple wooden bandstands and fountains all within easy reach of the well, auspicious tree or whatever else had encouraged the settlement to take root there those many forgotten years ago.

But the sounds began to change from bustle to merriment as the square opened ahead of him; with laughter and gossip came the sound of warm, seasonal music from the wandering players, and beside it the scent of bread and ale from the inn and sweet, fruity festival cakes from the red- and orange-hued stalls. But while he appeared to smile and enjoy the surrounding festivities as much as anyone else, Salus paid them no internal attention as he melted seamlessly into the crowds. Carried by the current, he made his way casually to the farthest side, and the very moment a fire-breather astounded the crowd, he slipped away into an alley.

A few light, hurried steps later, he arrived at the back of the bath house.

It was busy inside; he needn't have taken a moment to listen against a window, the laughter and chatter could be heard even over the music, and the smell of fresh rose petals and damp contended easily with the pitch and fragrant sweets.

He paused to work the matter out.

There was no question over whether or not Doana knew of the Arana. They had taken out his residential spies at every site they'd struck, and they'd done so tidily. They knew he and his people were the greatest threat to their activity, which seemed to be recovering some kind of archaic evidence that would put their *own* queen on the Turundan throne where she'd supposedly belonged all along, so keeping all of their plans, orders and intel in-hand was foolish. The Arana would doubtlessly make it into their camps sooner or later - as so they had on several occasions - so it was far better, if they had to keep any plans in writing at all, to secret them away somewhere else. Somewhere out of thought. Somewhere in plain sight. Somewhere the public would overlook, and somewhere Salus's subordinates wouldn't gain access to without drawing attention.

That most recent and most successful raid on a random handful of Doana's camps had uncovered in one their intentions in the ancient city of Kora, and in another, with great pains, the code to decipher it. In fact, the very existence and location of the contingency plan he was presently on the hunt for was discovered within the code-breaker *itself*, disguised as a part of the key. Hidden in plain sight, as, it seemed, were those secreted plans - but only for a mage who was looking for them.

The bath houses were some of the oldest structures still standing in cities, riddled with dark corners and loose stones, and the elven spells that powered a few necessary details were maintained to this day. No ordinary person would notice anything hidden away, and a mage would not notice the appearance of a new and subtle spell without knowing precisely where to look for it.

But Salus was no ordinary person, and neither was he blind to its location.

But there were, just as Doana had planned, people in his way, and he wasn't prepared to wait for the baths to close that night and risk a Doanan slipping in and recovering it in the mean time. So his first move was simple. And one he'd now decided upon the means to handle.

Quietly, he hurried further along the alley until he was a suitable distance from the festivities but close to one of the wider roads. He could hear relaxed voices talking of work and trade, and, to his satisfaction, the sound of hooves over stone and wooden wheels rattling along behind them.

He wasted no time. With a practised twist of his fingers, a torrent of fire, bright but harmless, erupted on the other side of the buildings that shut the alley in. Voices rose in a sudden rage of shock and terror, and two horses screamed. Another sign and another flare rose on the opposite side of the road, seemingly out of nowhere, and then another, for good measure, towards the head of the road.

The panic spread quickly, and Salus was all too ready to direct it. "Mages!" He yelled in flawless hysteria as he made his way coolly back down the alley. "Mage attack! *Run!*" The alarm spread in moments; the nearby merriment collapsed into terror. And he slipped into the emptying bath house.

The heat within was stifling, and the pungent, floral miasma was laced with cedar wood which dried and choked the breath. It took Salus a few controlled breaths to overcome it, but at least he hadn't to waste time for his eyes to adjust.

Like most bath houses, the main halls were bright - the elves had known what they were doing when they'd built in the windows - and even though newer structures had been built up around it as the over-sized town had sprawled, the light that leaked in through the fogged glass was still plentiful.

He moved quickly, lightly, avoiding the puddles the clientele had left in their haste to escape the phantom threat, and sent his mind out to the magic. He was suddenly awash in spells, but simple chains for simple matters, and he could tell even at a glance the old from the new. They had their differences beyond age, too - some were distinctly less elegant than others, and it wasn't difficult to work out why. But when he found one particular spell, as small and insignificant as a mouse in a room of dogs and wolves, he knew he had found what he sought. And it was the most inelegant of all.

He grunted a laugh. That didn't surprise him. Doana were not known for the same tolerance of magic as Turunda - eastern mages were oppressed and taught only what their military needed of them. There was no room for fine-tuning, no opportunity to practise and learn. They were as good as slaves.

And look how Turunda's mages repaid their own country's benevolence. With murderous rebellion. Give them an inch, and they try to take the country. Perhaps Doana were on to something...

He knelt quickly beside the ornate cedar wood bench and pushed the matching screen away. No sooner had it shifted an inch than he heard the hollow tilt of the flagstone. A victorious smile flickered. As the chaos continued outside, he prised it up with one of the fine, flat blades he withdrew from his boot. And there it was. The lockbox.

It was small, about the size of a book and just as deep, half the size of the flagstone, and constructed of steel to protect it against the moisture inherent in a bath house - or the flooding of a field, or the damp soil of a lake or river bank.

Victory surged - until some nagging voice at the back of his mind pointed out somewhat belatedly that he had encountered no resistance in freeing the box.

And he could still feel the spell.

It was locked conventionally and he hadn't the key - that was a problem that could be overcome. But breaking the spell that shrouded the box itself rather than the hiding place, that would be another matter. One that could also be beaten, but certainly not here. He had no time. He had to get it back. His heart was racing in anticipation.

A warm light flared through the window above him, and he lightened on his feet. It was time to leave before anyone returned.

It was only then that the atmosphere struck him.

The screaming outside - it was still lively. Too lively. And his fires hadn't moved - in fact they should have diminished - yet the light through the glass was that of flame, he was sure.

Clutching the lockbox, he scraped the flagstone back into place and returned the screen before hurrying back down the private hallway and out through the rear door.

Heat rushed over him the moment he stepped outside, and firelight rose from the wrong end of the alley. He rushed towards it, the screaming, the chaos, adopting as he went a look of panic that was not entirely false, and skidded to a halt at the edge of the square. His heart roared. *Mages.*

Then it lurched, and a shattering understanding kicked in.

His own ruse had triggered an attack. Perhaps they'd been ready, awaiting a signal and his distraction had come first, or perhaps they were merely opportunists. Both were equally possible, and it sickened him to the point of dizziness as he watched three figures with zealous looks upon their foul faces, twisting their fingers into strikes of fire and lightning, that he had been party to this...*this.*

But as a lash of light crackled into existence and whipped out towards the fleeing crowd, his eyes dropped unbidden to the lockbox in his arms. Quick calculations brought his moment of monumental struggle to an end. The trio were not likely to kill. Doana were.

He turned and bolted back towards the cobbler's shop.

Chapter 40

Aria breathed the latest mindless sigh of relief as she skipped along barefoot beside her father. For three days, they'd been free from towering trees and ominous shadows, and for the first time in two weeks could see more than ten paces ahead of themselves. Spirits were high even in spite of the rough terrain; the earth, first soaked into mud, had been trampled and churned by horse, deer and cattle before being baked dry by the barren heat into all kinds of treacherous lumps and holes. But it was a small price for being able to see any and every enemy coming, and not having to remain on their guard against the very bark of the trees.

Even so, they steered towards thickets and dells all the same, and otherwise trusted their concealment to the assumption that other travellers would have more sense and stick to the roads. As a result, they encountered no one along their way.

But their luck, by its very nature, soon ran out.

At the slackening end of the final valley, a sprawling array of tents and wagons had entirely consumed their destination's approach, stretching well into the surrounding woods. Any hope of hiding within those trees was shattered.

Stopping at the edge of the dell, the group crouched low and surveyed the encampment.

"Refugees," Garon observed. "From Toakh, I'd think. They would be most at risk if Doana brought in reinforcements." He sighed and shook his head. "What a sorry state of affairs this country is falling into."

"It can't be helped," Rathen grunted remorsefully. "What do we do?"

"We need supplies and information. And there may be someone in there who can help us. I'll go in and see if I can find them. Petra, you wait with Eyila and Aria - keep as far from the camp as you can."

"I'll handle the supplies," Anthis declared quickly, his voice still tinged with the unrelenting bite.

"Be careful," Rathen warned him. "There are more eyes out there than there should be." He ignored the young man's unappreciative grunt and turned towards Garon. "I'll wait with Petra."

"No. You're coming with us." Rathen baulked, for which the inquisitor merely cast him a sideways look. "The refugees will have stirred up chaos. No one will notice new arrivals, and no one will be looking for us, *especially* if we split up. Taliel mentioned surveillance spells and I want you to look for them. If you can find them, you should be able to ward against them - correct?"

"I suppose...but even so, those bounty posters will be everywhere by now--"

"And among the refugees, we will only add to the sea of unfamiliar faces. No one will notice us."

"Can't you cast some kind of illusion?" Eyila asked.

"Illusions, yes, but I can't *conceal* us. Only those among the diz'al in the front- and rear-guard can do that."

"What about masks?"

He looked down at Aria. "Masks?"

"If you cast an illusion of a mask, we would all look different but we wouldn't be *hidden*."

Rathen blinked at the simplicity of the thought, but the idea quickly frayed. "Any mages wandering around will see right through it, and Salus's surveillance spells might be able to as well."

"It's not worth the risk," Garon agreed. "Not yet, at any rate. We need more information on those spells of his and on the state of the Order before we can go casting anything ourselves. For now, we'll trust the upheaval the refugees will have brought with them." He rose slightly from his crouch and made his way down the slope. The others reluctantly followed.

They kept to the thin, sparse trees as best they could and soon began to divide. Petra led Eyila and Aria away into the denser folds of the woods, Garon and Rathen made themselves as inconspicuous as they could and approached the camp from the edge, while Anthis moved brazenly head-on, empty bags slung over his shoulder and a rustle of parchment inside his sleeve. They'd seen him filtering through the less savoury contents of his satchel the previous night. They each privately hoped he succeeded.

Rathen's shoulders grew increasingly contracted as they neared the haphazard camp, full as it was with people and all the noise and smells that came with them. By the time it swallowed them, he'd rounded so nervously that he appeared crooked and much, much older.

Garon, too, had taken on a transformation, but his had been voluntary: his hair mussed, his shirt untucked and untidily laced, one trouser leg lying lower over the top of one boot than the other, which themselves were already dirtied from the fields. He shuffled along no more or less downcast than anyone else around him. Together, the pair appeared merely to be going about their own unfortunate business.

But above the general chatter and occasional groans of pain, from injury or illness or fatal insult at the loss of status in such a ramshackle setting, there came a more fevered ruckus. Something about it struck them both unpleasantly.

Neither made any outward show of noticing, but they each sharpened into it as they made their way around tents and wagons, moving unfortunately closer to its source all the while. They soon distinguished cackled insults and accusations, curses and slurs, then the air began to prickle dangerously. A few more moments and a crowd fell into view beyond the disorganised refugees, in a spot they'd vacated beside the old walls. Most had turned their backs; a few looked on in horror.

Rathen knew what he was about to see, but he couldn't pull his eyes away from it even as his blood ran hot with rage.

A man, tawny of skin but where it had bruised, swollen and split, was lifted by three men and stood upon a barrel. His hands were bound, as his ankles probably were, but he made no attempt to writhe, jump or struggle.

A woman, pleading between her wails, was cast suddenly from the group. She'd also been beaten, the evidence far more obvious on her much paler skin, but she rose and threw herself right back into the crowd, scratching and clawing and ripping her way back towards the man upon the barrel, the man who continued to deny every accusation being thrown at him with perfect conviction, even as a noose was drawn about his neck, lashed to the strongest bough at the edge of the forest.

'Why doesn't he run?' But Rathen knew the answer. Even had he not been bound, they'd have caught him easily, and it was more than likely the woman would also suffer for his escape.

Just as she would if either of them were to get involved and break their own cover.

But still Rathen argued the point internally. Unfortunately, he ran out of time.

The barrel was kicked out from beneath the man's feet the moment they drew level, and a righteous roar erupted from the crowd, drowning out the heart-wrenching cries of the bereaved widow.

They turned their eyes away, and shame engulfed Rathen's soul.

On the other side of the walls, the tone contrasted with sickening cheer, and the fiery colours of red, orange and yellow hung as pennants and bunting from building to building, suspended above the streets. Rathen's tightly knotted eyebrows rose at the sight of them. "It's Midsummer already?"

"Just about," Garon replied, sparing them a passing glance between surreptitiously eyeing the locals. "You were in Khry's Glory for a month."

"I guess I've not recovered quite as many bearings as I'd thought..."

They continued on and made towards a tavern, where Garon stopped and appeared to inspect the noticeboard outside. He dropped his voice low as he lingered on an advertisement for carpentry services. "We don't have much time. Walk around, stay out of sight, and see what you can find. We need to know *exactly* what these spells of his can do."

But they both froze, their blood turned to ice, as a hand clapped Garon heavily upon the shoulder and a strong, authoritative voice rose at his back.

"A word, sir, if you wouldn't mind."

Warning and quickly-devised instructions passed to Rathen in a glance, even as his expression softened into the confused but amicable look of any innocent and high-spirited stranger. But when he turned at last to face the man, it dropped into genuine surprise. "Taric?"

Rathen turned to discreetly hide his face, but he listened closely to their movements, torn between dread and relief as he processed his glimpse of the familiar black and white uniform, and the White Hammer insignia on the hilt of the formidable sword hanging at his hip.

But despite Garon's recognition, which he realised had been whispered, the man didn't smile. Instead, he regarded him firmly and gestured towards the garden seating of the tavern. "It's a hot day - perhaps we could discuss matters over an ale. It would make the situation easier for the both of us."

Then, Garon's flawlessly obedient and amicable smile returned, and he bowed his head. "O' course, sir. Anything to help the constabulary."

He didn't pass Rathen another look as he followed this inquisitor beneath the tavern arch and around to a small table just within the shade, and Rathen wasted no time in leaving. Trying not to appear ruffled, he moved on casually and around the side of the tavern as though attempting to find some shade of his own while he checked over his boots, but all the while he listened intently, watching the pair out of the corner of his eye, certain that Garon would find some way to give him a signal if action was needed.

But instead, and much to Rathen's surprise, the officer - *both* officers - appeared to relax.

Taric gave Garon a careful look as the maid turned away to fetch a pitcher and glasses. "You don't look as smooth as your poster."

"A regretful situation," he replied dismissively.

"And vague. I can't seem to find any substantial reason behind it. I take it things aren't as straight-forward as you'd hoped?"

"When is *anything* straight-forward?"

"Quite." He leaned forwards seriously, appearing to any onlookers as though he were about to begin his questioning of this unfortunate refugee. And, in a way, he did. "How is it coming, this self-enforced mission of yours?"

"It's...progressing." He watched Taric nod woefully, personally familiar with the true meaning of that tight-lipped statement. "But, the Order has no hand in it."

He sighed deeply through his nose. "A shame that news has to come so late. But is magic truly responsible for all this destruction? I find it hard to believe..."

"Then you'd best adjust your faculties. I would tell you more if I could, Taric, but the matter is painfully complicated. All the more so now we have the Arana on our backs. They're the reason our faces have been emblazoned throughout the cities. Fortunately, they've yet to hinder us, but they're not making things any *easier.*"

"No, I imagine not..." His dark eyes became suddenly shrewd, and he regarded Garon with open suspicion. It was hard to tell whether or not it was for the benefit of onlookers, but it didn't break when the maid returned with their beverages. When she left, his voice dropped even lower, and he spoke but two words.

Unaware that Rathen had turned white in the corner, Garon didn't flinch. He poured the pitcher and raised his foaming tankard to his lips, then bobbed his head as though flicking his untidy hair from his eyes before taking a sip at last.

Taric's expression didn't change. "Petra Dalton and Anthis Karth's posters came up at the same time as his. 'Disorderly conduct' and 'trespassing', as I recall. I could believe that, but hardly worth a bounty. Are they yours, too?" He raised an eyebrow as he nodded. "Strange band."

"They weren't all planned. But they have their uses." Garon's eyes widened as he noticed the sudden intensity in his colleague's, and he lowered his tankard slowly. "What is it?"

"I don't believe it. Garon Brack: you've got a thing for your duelist." His smile widened in amusement as Garon rolled his eyes and denied it.

"For the love of Vastal and all Her effigies, would you turn your analytical brain off for the moment, Taric?"

"Not a chance. I might miss something important. And I dare say, old friend, that this is one such thing - but I won't pry. We both have other matters on our minds..."

"Yes," he turned a frown at his companion, ignoring the lingering smile. "What are you still doing here? I thought you'd have left a month ago."

"Ah, well," he smiled, "'when is anything straight-forward?' The counterfeiters I was tracking were just one part of a vast collaboration conspiring to flood the opiac market. I just got back from tracking down a few others, and the whole thing seems to tie up here. I've almost got them."

He raised his tankard with a grim smile. "Well done. Then perhaps it'll free up some guards to bring these lynch mobs to an end. I doubt the one outside on our approach was the first to have happened."

Taric's expression became sullen. "That's all part of it, I'm afraid. There are elements encouraging it as a distraction while they transport materials and 'goods' to their various holdings, and it gets out of hand. The guards can't keep up with it - and I get the sense that not all of them care to. I've issued my reports and it's being handled, but it's happening across the country. People seem to think they're 'safer' when they take justice into their own hands. The trouble is, they have no idea that when they run out of one minority to condemn, they'll just look to find another, and then another, until finally they begin to use it as a means of exacting vengeance for personal wrong-doings and then inevitably get snared by it themselves. They won't know how to stop."

"An unfortunate truth..."

The pair were silent for a moment, brooding over their ales, until Garon pushed the tankard away and rose to his feet. Taric followed so swiftly, anyone would think he'd risen first. "Thank you for your co-operation, sir," he said only a little louder.

"Not at all, kind constable. Always happy to do my bit. And thank ye for the ale."

"Don't thank me," he replied quietly, "thank expenses. And I'll handle the posters. You'll get an official pardon and the rest will take some doing, but they should be gone by the middle of next month."

"Thank you." He bowed, then, and left the inquisitor beside the table.

Standing in the shadows, Rathen shook his head to himself, somewhat baffled, but satisfied, and turned away at Garon's momentary sideways glance to begin his search for the spell.

Eyila straightened abruptly in her spot upon a rotten tree stump and looked intently off to the right. Petra's hand tightened around her sword and Aria shuffled closer to the pair, but they all eased when Anthis came hurrying through the trees.

"You're back quickly," she said, forcefully restraining her disgust as she noted the liveliness to his eyes, though the biting tone, which had been creeping into her voice ever more frequently these past few days, managed to slip through.

"Yes, I am." He ignored her manner about as easily as the others had come to ignore his own recurrent fits. "I had some luck." He dumped the full bags on the floor and looked purposefully towards Aria. "I need your help."

"Her help?"

"Is it about what you said before?" She asked eagerly, to which the rejuvenated

Anthis nodded, and she looked hopefully up towards Petra.

She regarded the pair very carefully, and Eyila particularly focused her curious-cautious frown upon Anthis. A moment later the duelist appeared about to speak, but the words didn't make it past her lips. Her eyes narrowed only further until, finally swayed by the urgency in Aria's eyes, she nodded - though she was clearly still far from convinced. "Keep her safe," she said, confident at least in the fact that he was presently in a position to do so, though the means truly sickened her. "Be back before the others - Rathen will kill me if he finds out. And in any case, none of us want to stay here longer than we have to."

"Be quick," he said, already moving back towards the trees and waving Aria after him, "got it." They disappeared, leaving the two exchanging confused looks behind them.

"Do you have any ideas?" Aria asked as they made for the edges of the refugee camp. "Because I think she might be a bit old for fairy tales."

"She doesn't want to read 'cityfolk books', which I think means anything that would reinforce her already poor opinion of us."

"We're not all that bad," Aria protested, somewhat hurt.

"No, *we're* not, but greed and hate aren't accepted as easily in her culture as in ours. As far as I can tell, the tribes' current conflicts are unusual. So best to play on the safe side and not to get her anything that normalises that kind of thing, which only leaves us with fairy tales."

"But there's hate and greed in fairy tales - my daddy always pointed it out and told me never, ever, ever to do it."

"Yes, but fairy tales aren't as...*murky* as other types of stories. Greed and hate are never condoned or accepted as a normal detail of life."

"I don't think her people have *never* felt greed. They must have. Someone had a bigger share of dinner than another, and they wanted to even it out, *at least*. That's normal, isn't it?"

"Yes, but that's not the kind of greed we're talking about. We're talking about the kind of greed that pits people against one another, family against family, all for the sake of personal gain."

"I see..."

"I hope you do. Now come here." She giggled as he lifted her up onto his shoulders, and he pointed as they walked towards the striking array of fiery flags billowing over the old walls, and away from the tree on the other side of the road and the body swinging from it.

The narrow alleys did little to calm the race of Rathen's heart, but at least there were fewer eyes, and on such a bright day, the shadows were even darker.

There were probably fewer people gathered than it seemed, but every settlement across the country and likely beyond would be bustling and spirited for the next two weeks, growing steadily more boisterous as each day passed. Midsummer, he'd learned as he walked around, was twelve days away, and celebrations of the sun, life and fertility would be at their peak on the First of August, complete with dawn prayer, midnight fire dancers and all the sanguine experiences that followed. It was, in short, an exhausting occasion, and one that seemed to start sooner and last longer every year. But it was a spectacle all the same, and he usually entertained Aria with a few fire spells and his own attempts at the seasonal flaming tarts - though he never could manage it without burning the whole thing to a cinder, so he amazed her with the wonderful cheat of magic instead.

But even if the crowds were but a shadow of what they would become, they were still much too great for Rathen's nerves. How dearly he missed the Wildlands. He'd managed to make it a whole month without stepping foot in a village, town or city. *'And the last time I did,'* the thought rose undesired, *'the Arana almost had us.'*

But he had a job to do, and he decided it would be easier, quicker and much more distracting if he just got on with it.

He extended his mind and searched for magic. It wasn't hard to find; a few masses of elven spells conjoined with the Order's repairs, in which there was nothing unusual or out of place at all. And so he knew he could discount them. Either Salus's spell would stink only half as much of arrogance as the elven spells, or its construction would be clumsy and uneducated, elven tutors or not. Magic wasn't something that could be learned in a month - nor, in fact, a year. Not if it was to last.

He wandered from alley to alley, taking backstreets and empty roads as he searched with his mind's eye until, at last, something began to take shape.

It fit in far too snugly - a testament, he supposed, to Salus's teachers - but it wasn't perfect. It *was* clumsy, and it *did* have a strange pseudo-elven arrogance to it, but it was also simple enough to function - and simple enough to read.

The closer he could get to it, the better.

He followed it like a bloodhound. He knew he was drawing nearer when its chains became more tangible, and he began to make out the commands, ignoring as he passed all other spells that hung like a smog around the town. He shifted around corners, detoured around busier streets, but it seemed to be leading, ultimately, to the town centre. That didn't really surprise him, he supposed - where better to survey all around than from the very middle?

He stopped at the edge of the square, hidden in another shaded lane. He didn't need its exact location, he was close enough to get everything he needed.

Once he'd made certain that he was out of sight and out of reach, a part of the very shadow itself, he focused in on the spell once again and began the tedious business of picking it apart.

He'd been at it for only two minutes when the sudden sensation of magic engaging tugged at his senses from the far side of the square.

Rathen spun just in time to see a plume of fire erupt into the air.

Blood thundered in his ears, and he swallowed his heart back down before it could leap from his mouth. The concentrated silence in his mind reverberated with a single grievous understanding.

"No..." He watched the plum with wide eyes as a scream shattered the merriment. Then another plume burst into existence, followed immediately by yet more screams. Then another. Then came a cry that froze him to his core. *'Mages! Mage attack! Run!'*

In that moment, Bowden's square had transformed. Where people had only seconds ago been enjoying music on keyed harps and wheel fiddles and the ridiculous yet remarkable performances of fire-eaters and -breathers, they now scrambled, wailed and careened all around. The square had set itself alight in frenzy, and the festival banners themselves appeared like a suspended inferno.

Horses screamed and squealed in the chaos, startled and stampeding, dragging their carts or pulling them over; people fled in all directions, knocking over things, stalls and one another as they raced over the stones made slippery with spilled and trampled stock.

A fire-eater's flame was lost from her hand as she tried to save a young boy from the path of a terrified horse, and so another fire began to grow, and much without the aid of magic. It spread rapidly, torching the wooden stalls, their fruit, cloth, spices and toys, and among it all rose an acrid, toxic stench as things that should not have been burned were consumed the quickest.

And then came the mages. Three figures from the north, two from the west, and two more from the south-east, their faces twisted in foul enjoyment, all weaving their fingers into signs of destruction - designed, he could see, not to injure a living soul, but to strike terror instead, to burn homes and businesses and leave innocent people with nothing. Nothing, but an equally burning hatred.

He felt that terrible primordial force rising from deep within his being, and knew immediately that this was not born of helplessness. It was born of rage. Just as it had been four days ago in the presence of Anthis's insults.

His fury rose further at the thought of losing control of himself and escalating the carnage to bloodshed, so he squashed and stamped it back down with all his might. Whether it was 'gifted' as a means of deterring or ending violence, or as a means of causing it, he didn't care. That beast could not surface.

He snuffed it out as easily as he had the last time.

Rathen shrank back into the shadow as mages drew close, but they neither saw nor sensed him. Of course they didn't. Even had they not been so focused on their onslaught, they were too used to the presence of magic and the sensations of other mages casting their spells. He could have been a talentless beggar as far as they were concerned.

But...*he* could feel *their* magic. He could feel their power. And he outmatched them.

He could stop them.

His hands rose, his fingers began to twist, but before his spell could take shape, they were gripped and stilled by another pair of hands.

His eyes jerked up into Garon's and he read the overwhelming force of their reprimand. And he knew, in the same twisted way that stopped him from saving that poor tan-skinned Ivaean, that he couldn't help them.

'We're not heroes, little one.'

No. They weren't heroes at all.

Reluctantly, but obediently, he followed Garon back down the lane, away from the square, and out through the gates to vanish with the rest of the city amongst the panicked refugees. And rather than rage over the foolishness of these hot-headed young mages, he found himself fretting silently instead over the most recent bout with his affliction. The transformations suddenly seemed much easier to suppress - but they also seemed to have become equally as reactive.

And what he could have done with it, single-handedly among that catastrophe...it didn't bear thinking about.

Like many others, they fled Bowden without a backward glance. It wasn't until they'd crested the eastern dell that they spared a moment to look, but the terrible majesty of fire and lightning crackling and flaring well above the defining walls, and illuminating the rising smoke like a bleak theatre curtain, only made them feel sick with hopelessness. Knowing that the general opinion of mages being to blame for the roving magic had driven a handful to act out like this struck Rathen and Petra the hardest.

But while Petra took it on as personal motivation, it only added to Rathen's distress, and his recent conversation with Aria began repeating itself even louder in his head.

It wasn't difficult for the others to notice how shaken he was. He was quiet and withdrawn, he offered no input on Garon's brief account of occurrences, he shared nothing of what he'd learned in Bowden, if anything at all, he didn't seem to notice Aria's slip of the tongue that revealed her own presence in the city, and when they finally came to a stop for the night he absorbed himself eagerly in his notebook despite it being a frequent source of exasperation. But no one wished to interrupt him or his brooding cloud of distraction, for it was clear he preferred its company.

After they'd eaten the fresh cheese, boar and bread - Rathen seemed to have forgotten about his own in what appeared now to be genuine concentration - they each went about the same post-supper ritual of patrol, meditate, watch and read.

But this time, Garon found himself distracted.

Perhaps it was the meeting with Taric. He'd not seen his colleague since the White Hammer had granted him permission to tackle this issue, which had turned out to be far more serious than their commander had presumed after all. But the encounter seemed to spirit him back to simpler times, and for that he found his mind wandering and his patrol less than effective.

When he spotted Petra up ahead, climbing nimbly onto a rock with the aid of a tree branch to peer deeper into a ravine without risking exposure at its edge, his feet came to an involuntary stop. She must have heard the slightest scuff of his boot.

She whipped around sharply, first with readiness, then with disappointment, and the vague and fleeting pang that came from that increasingly common look lingered with him a moment longer than usual. He realised that it was his own strange kind of disappointment.

It bit a little deeper as she looked back along the length of the ravine indifferently. "Yes?"

"Nothing," he replied quickly.

"Good. Keep walking, then." She looked up again when he failed to do so, but the cutting edge of her eyes convinced him.

He sighed to himself and continued his patrol, and this time a small and ridiculous voice rose from the depths of his being. It was a voice he'd not heard in years, and yet it had somehow retained the same power to bait him. "Your hair," he said, surprising himself as he surprised her, and she whipped around in startlement again. His pride reasserted itself, quickly hiding away his own perplexity. "It's faded. The colour."

Her brows drew together slowly, and she glanced at the lengths of copper that fell over her shoulders. She turned him a strange look. "So? It stands out too much. It's better this way."

"I suppose you're right."

"Mm." She stepped down from the rock and turned to resume her course.

"Petra, wait." He ignored her bristling impatience as she turned back around. "I've been...unfair to you. I apologise - I didn't intend any hostility."

Her eyebrows, high just a moment ago, dropped into a deep knot, and her lips curled into a bitter smile as she folded her arms in her decision to entertain him. "Yes you did. You're smarter than that. ...What is this, anyway? I finally back off and keep my distance from you, and now you're seeking me out? Why? So I might drop my guard and make myself a target again?"

"No," he replied earnestly, "not at all."

"What, then? Or does it just suit you now? You witnessed something in that city and now you need comfort?"

"No, it--"

She laughed sorely. "Actually, I don't care. You won't find it from me. I've tried to be the better person, but I'm physically tired of it. I'm not playing any more. So go and bother Eyila if you want someone else to crush. I'm sure she'll put up as good a fight as I have - you should get *endless* entertainment."

"Petra, will you *stop* it?"

"Sure. The moment you leave me alone."

He stood there for a helpless moment, racking his brain for the best thing to say or do to calm her down, the best way to persuade her to accept his apology - to *force* her to, if he had to - but her cold, scornful hazel eyes stalled and obliterated his every thought until, finally, he simply walked on past her with a frown of defeated confusion.

Anthis watched from a distance with pity - though he wasn't quite sure who he felt more sorry for. But before he could decide, a terrifying idea was already weaving itself together in his mind. Watching Garon's beating should have shut it down immediately, but instead the inquisitor's sheer incompetence only spurred it on, and he found himself arriving at a simple conclusion that he decided not to delve beneath the surface of. In short, he could also be brave, and as he found himself quite averse to being compared to Garon, he decided he could also be more successful.

Clutching his papers tightly, he turned away from the bags and headed off into the trees, his pace quickened either by excitement or dread. It didn't take him long to find Eyila; he spotted her distinctive form up in the sprawling boughs of a hornbeam. Despite leaving the Wildlands, she seemed to have developed a habit of seeking her refuge in trees rather than upon rocks whenever she had the chance. Perhaps she was growing fond of the forests, at last, or perhaps the wind really had just been stronger up in the canopy over these past four evenings. He wasn't exactly in a position to know.

Seeing her now, though, her torso bare, her hides and cloak draped over the branch beside her, his previous resolve quite suddenly evaporated.

He stood staring up with reddened cheeks at her dimly silhouetted back for a long, doubtful moment. He couldn't see if she was crying. Perhaps she really was just meditating, in which case he really shouldn't intrude. He wasn't sure how much her faith played a role in it, or whether it was her own personal way of winding down, like Petra and her whetstones or Aria and her climbing. He couldn't presume it was more or less of either, but it was important enough to her to maintain the habit. He had no right at all to interfere.

He sighed quietly and turned away, moving off silently back through the woods.

Then turned around and came right back, clamped his papers in his mouth, and began climbing the tree.

Eyila flinched above him, and she sniffed and fidgeted and threw on her cloak, hurrying to compose herself as he pulled himself up and sat wordlessly on the branch beside her. She smiled at him. It was the least convincing smile he'd ever seen. But he returned it all the same, and looked off ahead into the night. They sat in silence for a few minutes.

"Y'know," he said at last, startling her, "something's been bothering me." He turned and met her quizzical expression with one of suspicion. "You seem to know an awful lot about your gods. All the ins and outs - more than any normal worshipper or devout reasonably should."

"Among my people, everyone is involved," she explained rather readily, and his eyes narrowed ever so slightly further.

"No, no it's more than that...you're almost consumed." An uncertain look flickered across her face, but it leaned in an instant towards offence. He realised his mistake. "I mean dedicated," he amended quickly, "very dedicated. And the wind seems to...actually...*respond* to you."

"Nonsense." Again it was too quick.

He turned in his spot and regarded her with increasing speculation. "You saved us in the desert through *prayer.* Rathen felt no magic - he said so. None at all. And you've done it since. And blessed the harpies in the same sort of way the priestess did to us in your village." He saw a wash of heartache dull the stubborn denial in her eyes and regretted the mention immediately. But he pressed on anyway. "Wind magic, too, without any signs. Even Kienza seems to know something - she said...sss...saya'a...lo toa... The harpy matriarch said the same thing."

She smiled at him curiously. "You remembered that?"

"I'm an academic," he shrugged. "I know how to mentally file things. What does it mean? If you don't mind."

"It...I wouldn't know how to translate it. It's a phrase of reverence. To a priestess."

"A priestess?" Then it all clicked elegantly into place. His eyebrows rose and inferiority began railing ferociously at his confidence. "I see..."

Dejection dulled her sigh as she cast her eyes back out through the crooked tree trunks. Anthis knew in that moment that the walls he'd never noticed were about to come down, so he turned her his full attention. "It was all I ever wanted," she said after a moment, almost to herself. "To dedicate myself to Aya'u - I was so sure I'd been *born* for it. I studied and trained with the other girls for five years, and it all came so naturally. I progressed quicker than any of them - people said I had the heart of a priestess, some that I was destined to succeed the Sayaah, our head priestess. But I was only an acolyte at that point, I had to gain attunement with the wind first; only once I could hear every word and warning that glided upon it could I finally take my oaths and become a true Priestess of Aya'u. I could decipher the coming of the most dangerous sandstorms, detect the strength of the turning seasons, encourage the winds if they are needed...guide the spirits onto the Winds..." She paused wistfully; Anthis waited. But when she spoke again her musical voice had a cutting edge. "But then my magic rose and ruined everything."

"Ruined?" He asked carefully.

"The Sayaah took me to Liaha, our village healer - a mage - and she confirmed with such...*certainty* that it was magic. There was no room at all for misunderstanding. And from that moment on, I was the pupil of a healer, *not* a priestess.

"I'd thought at first that it was a gift from Aya'u, a means of serving Her all the better - I thought, if I could master it, that the other elements would come more clearly and I'd gain attunement with the wind that much more quickly. But Liaha told me that I wouldn't have enough time to train as a healer *and* as a priestess, and as the magic *was* a gift from Aya'u - a means to serve Her people - I had no choice but to put that first. And she was right, of course: training my magic took up all of my time."

He watched her shoulders round beneath the thin cloak, and her eyes gleamed in heartbreak as she reflected on her lost dreams. Anthis was almost afraid to speak, because, in truth, he didn't fully understand. "But you still have a connection to Her," he said very carefully at last. "Everything you've done - you've not lost Her..."

"...No," she admitted quietly, "Her voice feels distant sometimes...but it has never faded like I feared it would. But this...this isn't what I expected of my life..."

"There are two sayings among my people: 'life is made of broken expectations', and 'the unplanned moments are the most meaningful moments'. Eyila, the ability to *heal* - that's no small thing. I know of no other mage who can do it. Except Kienza, I suppose, but...I'm not too sure she's any ordinary mage..." He observed her for a moment, watching her pull at the cloak's fraying hem. "You were called away from becoming a priestess, but Aya'u hasn't abandoned you for it. And I'd say, somehow, you've found some way of balancing it."

She smiled, and for a moment it shone with nostalgia. "Truth be told, I never fully gave up on my practice. I found moments to slip away - Haya, my best friend, was also training to be a priestess, and she found me in meditation on a mesa one night. Priestesses are forbidden from meditating for more than seven hours a day, but she was sneaking in extra training, anyway, and she...helped me. Offered advice, techniques, passed on anything she'd learned that could be of use to me. But when she reached attunement and became a full priestess, she couldn't spare the time any more. And with my own duties as the village's healer, I...couldn't spare enough time, either. And so I never reached attunement."

"...Does that matter?"

She looked at him in surprise, her eyes maimed. "What?"

"It sounds as though you really *couldn't* have done both. But Aya'u never abandoned you when your duties changed, just as you never abandoned Her. You *still* haven't. And isn't that what counts?"

"...Haya said my 'heart was Hers long ago'."

"I think she was probably right." Eyila smiled very briefly, but her gloom quickly shooed it off. He sighed to himself. "Well, if it means anything at all, I'm glad you didn't become a priestess. You wouldn't be with us if you were."

He smiled as she breathed a laugh, and cast him another glancing smile. But her gaze lingered, and he felt his cheeks, obedient and cool for so long, begin to flush. "Thank you," she said, to which he shrugged meekly.

"You're welcome."

"No," she turned further towards him, as well as she could upon the branch, "not just for that. Petra told me that you...that you laid out my people by our customs."

"Oh...well...it was the right thing to do...anyone would have--"

"No, they wouldn't. Had you not been there, no one else would have done it. Even if they'd thought to, had they been told of those customs beforehand, they wouldn't have done it."

He disagreed, shaking his head despite her own impassioned tone, but he couldn't bring himself to mention Rathen's name. His voice outright abandoned him however as she leaned over and placed a soft kiss upon his cheek.

"*Thank you,* Anthis."

He didn't notice his foolish smile, and he couldn't have helped it if he had, just as he could do nothing about the burning of his cheeks but turn his head away and try to keep his giddy surprise under control. Which didn't work because he didn't turn his head away in the first place. In his loss for words he gestured instead, waving her gratitude away, and successfully knocked his assembled papers from his lap.

She laughed heartily as he threw a futile hand after them, and quickly pulled him back before he could slip and follow them. She chuckled again at his defeated smile, and when her own embarrassment began to colour her face, she at least managed to turn away. Looking over the edge, she summoned a wind - with signs this time, Anthis noticed - and the scattered pages lifted from among the old roots and fluttered back up towards him.

As he reached out to take them, however, he saw something that hit him so hard he thought he'd fallen out of the tree after all.

Each sheet floated, as tattered as the last, suspended before them in a haphazard spread, and under nothing more than perfect, impossible chance, the overlapping edges of four insignificant pages connected insignificant ink stains. A near-perfect circle was created. And around it, and with a tilted head, the ragged edges and corners of those pages formed an eight-point star. A distinct eight-point star whose top limb was longest, the bottom, left and right half its size, and its four diagonals, little more than meagre flares, were no less intentional.

Anthis blinked twice, snatched the papers, and scrambled down the tree leaving Eyila frowning after him in disappointment.

Chapter 41

"Impossible."

"What is?" Rathen asked absently, squinting at his scribblings in the waning light of the fire as Garon trudged heavily back into the hollow of the hill they called camp.

"Petra! How am I supposed to make amends if she won't listen to apology?!"

"Well you know what they say...'even thorns have roses'..."

Garon fired him an unappreciative look until the sound of urgent footsteps rushed clumsily in their direction. He tensed and reached for his sword, then grumbled in irritation as Anthis blustered out of the trees, holding aloft a handful of old papers.

"I was wrong!" The historian declared, stumbling frantically into their hovel while Eyila stepped after him with much more grace. "I was wrong...what are you doing?"

"Savouring the moment." Rathen opened his eyes and dropped the book into his lap. "Continue." But the three of them frowned when he presented the tattered papers in answer, and proceeded to watch in confusion as Anthis knelt on the beast-worn ground and began scattering them with meticulous precision. Rathen cast Eyila a curious look, but she could only shrug.

"There."

They all looked over, but no one made sense of the arrangement until Aria got up, shuffled around at an angle, and examined it with far more open eyes. They snapped up quickly, suddenly beaming. "The anarchists! There was something in the Wildlands after all!"

"Why wasn't it painted across the walls like the others?" Garon asked as Rathen moved in an attempt to locate the shape himself.

"Perhaps it was and we missed it. They haven't all been obvious." Anthis knelt closer and began poring over the collection. The others waited - for quite some time - but he didn't speak again. Only once they began to scatter and return to their own business did he finally rouse, and he beckoned Rathen over curtly. "Notes - the Zi'veyn - experimental--"

"If you would just calm down and breathe you'd make it a much easier time for the both of us."

He tapped the paper excitedly. "*Read it!*"

And, to the best of his ability, he did. His eyebrows rose gradually, he made himself more comfortable, he shuffled the sheets and tilted them into the light, and eventually took them back to his own private spot beside the fire despite Anthis's strangled noises of possessive concern.

"Well?" Garon asked impatiently after they'd waited in clueless silence for nearing twenty minutes.

"Experimental notes," Rathen replied without looking up. "Anthis, this elf, he wanted to suspend the magic to stop his friends from getting hurt or hurting anyone else, right? Well, there's sort of a problem with that - I never gave it much thought because it wasn't relevant to what *we're* using the Zi'veyn to do, but I did wonder about this elf... That suspension is only enforced upon another person while the Zi'veyn is actually being used. As soon as he put it down - or if he was stopped - the magic would be unleashed back into the blood again and whatever he was trying to keep from happening would go ahead and happen. Well, here it looks like he was trying to find a way of prolonging it - trying to encourage the spell in the Zi'veyn to sort of...'cast' another spell itself, or trigger one that would produce a second layer of suspension for a time, even when the Zi'veyn wasn't being actively used. A safeguard for if the wielder was incapacitated."

"But he couldn't make it work?" Anthis guessed before Garon could voice a hopeful comment, and Rathen promptly shook his head.

"He tried approaching the magic in different ways, and it looks like he came *close* to rendering it inert and even disabling it altogether, but the results...frightened him, it looks like, so he abandoned it. I guess he was going to try to use the Zi'veyn as-is, but discreetly."

"Are there any details?" Garon demanded suddenly, at which point Rathen finally looked up and flinched back as he found all five of them staring at him in anticipation, including Petra, who stood otherwise facing out over their surroundings. "Anything that can help us?"

"Um," he flicked quickly back over it all. "Yes, but not a lot. Approach with intent to calm, not destroy...that didn't work. Come at it hard and fast, a shock attack to break the magic, again that didn't work...then there's something similar but aiming for the heart - and even if that *did* work, it's useless to me since the magic is loose...wrapping a spell around it to suspend it and...and modify it to *dissolve* it?" He looked closer at the paper. "It would only have been temporary while the heart was still in tact, it would have continued to produce magic, but it would have taken a long time to replenish..." his voice descended into a mumble until he lowered the papers and stared off into the fire, lost in thought.

"*Rathen!*"

He snapped back to them. "Uhm? Right. Yes. Well...ultimately the Zi'veyn calms the magic by suspending it in the blood. To do that, something must pass through the blood and come into contact with every mote of magic in it in order to affect it as a whole. The spell in the Zi'veyn is like a net, but it doesn't catch and hold, it just passes over; it screens the blood, detecting everything in it...so if we tightened the net...no, if we replaced it...no, *coated* it with--if we did *something* to that net so that each mote of magic wasn't just noted but also *tagged* by some kind of...parasitic spell, something that could...drain every mote...destroy it..."

"Can you do it?"

Now Rathen's quick eyes dulled with hesitance. "I can't modify the Zi'veyn. If I damaged the spell, I couldn't reverse it, and if I tried to reconstruct it, odds are I'd get it wrong, no matter how much Anthis has collected on it. It would need to be a whole new spell." He looked cautiously across their dubious faces, and turned to Garon last. He was just as intense as he'd expected. "I'm trying. And this will help. But more than that, I'm not prepared to say."

"I have other notes and papers that this might shed some light on," Anthis offered, to which Rathen nodded gratefully. Then, he handed back the papers, avoided the inquisitor's gaze quite deliberately and directed his attention wholly upon Aria and the doll in her hands. It was clear as he seized his notebook, rose to his feet and abruptly declared that she and Isabelle were both in need of a bath, that he had no interest in entertaining their many remaining questions.

Half Turunda's breadth away, however, there was no such mercy.

Shadows writhed in the stuffy darkness of corridors and stairwells, reaching away from the pockets of torchlight as though trying to escape the heat rather than through any natural laws. The sconces that had for so long housed gentle and expansive arcane lights now held only fire, and the flames added offensively to the summer warmth that grew only more stifling with every flight of stairs.

The decree against unnecessary magic was being taken very seriously, even to the point of the grand magister's own discomfort. And yet Owan had pulled a uniform robe over his plain clothes anyway. Temperature aside, anything less would have been unseemly when answering these late-night summons, and the matter must have been serious. Any normal person would have been asleep at that hour.

Owan, however, had just been pulled away from his work.

For the last two weeks he, among a select number of trusted mages, had been observing the increasing concentration of magic across various areas in north-eastern Turunda. It hadn't taken long at all to discover an unfortunate pattern, and that in turn had enabled the educated prediction of sites most likely to follow suit. But though they'd dispatched a few to investigate those sites, they'd found nothing and no one unusual - except, of course, the spells the Arana were using to trap such areas in a crude attempt to catch the guilty mages. But they were easily overcome.

Unfortunately, besides a few key locations to keep an open eye on, they'd learned little at all of consequence.

His contact with Rathen hadn't yielded much to extrapolate with, either - in fact he'd offered very little; no more or less than what Owan needed in order to confirm a few things he'd already worked out for himself. He was certain it had been a tactical move. Rathen hadn't changed all that much. Born no doubt from concern toward the rebellion, he hadn't wanted to risk anything more than necessary falling into the wrong hands.

But that tight-lipped response had only lent further credence to his own private suspicions that far more was going on than his old friend would have him know. *Had* Rathen had a hand in the sudden reduction of magic at other saturated locations? A sparrow could only carry so much paper; he'd likely decided that it wasn't important enough to include. If he was responsible, even partially, he'd probably concluded that the Order didn't need to know. And if he wasn't responsible...well, then there was nothing to tell.

Assuming of course that Rathen had actually read the entire message properly and didn't just skim over it or only answer the first or last thing he'd read...

Reaching the door of the eminent office, Owan took a moment to recover from the heat before knocking, and entered at the distracted call from within.

Aside from the anticipated heat, the first thing to strike him was how old Arator looked. His lined face was twisted in the grips of unpleasant meditation, and his usually neatly combed and tied grey hair was loose and vaguely dishevelled, as though he'd run frustrated fingers through it a few too many times. He did just that as he looked up at Owan's arrival, and though he tried to appear his usual amicable self, gesturing to a chair and offering a glass of water, he was unable to keep the severity from darkening his eyes.

"I'll get to the point," he said as he dropped heavily back into his own seat. "Earlier today, mages attacked Bowden. There's regrettably nothing unusual about that, and a few still loyal to us and the Crown apprehended them before it could go too far...but..." the old mage sighed. "They've been questioned. It seems there was a little confusion at the onset of their...activity. They were awaiting a signal - the finalé to the fire-breathers' performance. Instead, plumes of fire rose from the centre of the city some ten minutes sooner, and they took that as a modified signal. They thought that something had gone wrong and they should act immediately if their strike was to go ahead."

"...But it hadn't?"

"It depends on how you wish to look at it. The Arana were responsible for those plumes."

Owan's confusion deepened. "The Arana? Were they trying to frame us?"

Arator grunted a short, humourless laugh. "If they had been, there was little need; the rebels incriminated themselves almost immediately. All the Arana did was hasten them into it. But it's not as simple as all that. It was no mere Aranan mage. It was the keliceran himself."

"The...the keliceran? That's the...the *head* of the Arana, isn't it? *He* has magic? Should he even--should that be *allowed?*"

"I can't comment on that," he replied, waving a tired hand, "but for the head of a powerful authority to possess magic - myself excluded, of course - well...suffice it to say that it's everyone's problem."

"But how can we be sure that it *is* the keliceran?"

"Through our own good fortune - though that is again a matter of perspective. One of our own was in a building overlooking an alley; the activation of magic drew her attention, she looked out, noticed right away that he was not one of us - rebel or otherwise - and so could only have been from the Arana. She witnessed his magic in that moment. Then, she sent me this." He handed him a roll of parchment from his desk and waited as he studied it. Naturally, Owan could only shake his head in ignorance despite the perfect realism of the image. "I know this face," Arator declared. "I met him only once at a Crown meeting, years ago - but, knowing his position, I felt compelled to commit his face to memory."

"The keliceran...that's..."

"Impossible." He smiled at Owan's strange look, though he'd known that that wasn't the word on his tongue. "But for all this magic and late awakenings, it has happened. He possessed magic no one - not even himself - knew about until recently, and he has been trained, I would guess, by those among his ranks in order to keep it hidden from the rest of us. His spells were sloppy but they worked well enough, and given that the Arana have developed all kinds of ill spells we can't even *begin* to guess at...we have no idea what he could be capable of. Or what he would try to do with his new-found power. Power he neither respects nor understands."

Owan's eyes dropped back to the face of the remarkably nondescript man. He'd always fancied that he'd know a spy when he saw one, but this man's face - kind, almost, with a strikingly regular nose and soft eyes, framed by hair that was neither too long nor too short, too tidy or too unkempt - well, he found himself quite suddenly doubting his own life-long acquaintances.

Paranoia began creeping in, and the longer he stared at the portrait, picking those normal features apart, the darker the man's eyes grew - until, finally, they appeared to stare straight back at him, picking apart his own thoughts and secrets while disarming him with a friendly look.

Alarmed, he rolled the parchment away and cast it back on the table.

"But he wasn't the only rogue present in Bowden this afternoon." He returned quickly to the grand magister who had roused from his own simmering thoughts. His eyes were suddenly sharp, and he studied the younger man closely. "Rathen Koraaz was also there."

"Rathen?"

Arator nodded. "He wasn't involved. If anything, it seemed he was about to try to stop the rebels when they launched into their attack, but he was stopped himself. By a companion, I would guess. He fled with him, at any rate."

He continued to watch him, and Owan felt as though his thoughts were being assaulted now by his own superior. A man he'd always believed he could trust. "He hasn't been in touch with me since," he replied, forcing away his dubiety. "I haven't the faintest idea what he's truly up to, only suspicions."

"And you've shared them with me to no end." He sighed and rose from behind his tidy desk to stare out through the window, searching, as he so often did, for solutions across the lantern-spotted, banner-strewn city. "There's too much magic running rampant out there, and we haven't the first clue how to stop it..."

"We're trying, Grand Magister."

He turned him an apologetic smile. "I didn't mean anything by that, my boy. But, I fear, no matter how you go about it, control over the matter will continue to elude us."

A soft and pleasant whisper of breeze slipped in through the open window. The two savoured its brush, and stood a little easier as they felt it tug away some small thread of worry.

Arator turned back to his desk and cast him another weary smile. "I'm sorry, Owan. It's really quite late. You should be sleeping - though I take it from the look you wore as you came in that you were still at work. *Rest*, Owan. You'll have enough sleepless nights ahead of you."

"M-my lord?"

The old man nodded gravely. "And so you *should* look alarmed. It's only three or four weeks away now, isn't it?"

"Oh..." he smiled with some relief. "Yes, yes, it is."

"Then make the most of the freedom you still have. A child is a wonderful thing - but it's also the greatest test of endurance. Be sure you're in the best shape for it. Good night, Owan."

"Yes, thank you - good night, my lord."

The door clicked shut, and two deeply troubled sighs heaved.

On the western side of the city, secreted at the furthest edge of the stately district, equal unrest clouded the night.

In a room that was a touch too small for its fireplace and luxury, several particularly warm and expansive lights hung whimsically beneath the vaulted ceiling. Their glows were cast back brilliantly by the vast collection of mirrors, and the room appeared as though it were full of a thousand miniature suns. But while the light bounced from their silver surfaces, the opulence did not stretch endlessly into their depths.

Instead the mirrors presented pictures of dark streets lit by lanterns, surrounded themselves by moths; of people both alone and in small groups moving on towards their homes on quick or staggering feet, and of the occasional cat or mouse scurrying about its own vital nocturnal business.

But these mirrors showed more than just pictures, for the sound that accompanied them was not imagined. The shift and shuffle of travel-weary horses filling the stables of several inns, the drunken singing and raucous laughter inside the emptying taverns, the hushed giggles and promises of couples visiting empty squares and grounds in the most private depths of night.

But even pushing into the blackest hours of the morning, from some of those elegantly framed windows came worry. Distrust. Anger. The overwhelming frets of people who were all afraid for their lives, who doubted their safety from the camps of hooligans and barbarians on their doorsteps while their own military were too busy picking the dirt out from between their toes to do anything about it.

'Useless,' hissed some, while 'trust in the general,' soothed others; 'we'll do it ourselves,' vowed a few as they picked up formidably-edged work tools, and 'it's all a conspiracy to raise taxes', slurred others over four empty tankards.

Salus had heard it all too often, and though it vexed him, he was more concerned with what he *wasn't* hearing. Across thirty six mirrors, there was no sight of the subject that so distressed them. Across thirty six mirrors, not one of them watched Doana's camps.

As that fact floated about him like a thick cloud of flies, he began to feel deserving of those words, even though they were not aimed towards him. The Arana, after all, was a myth - which in itself meant an imperfectly-kept secret - but no one gave them any honest thought. And so it was only natural that the public held Moore to blame for the inaction. Martial scouts were only trained for gathering tactical knowledge and intercepting messengers; it was *his* people's job to get into the enemy camps and gather the truly sensitive information they needed in order to lay out timing, priorities and fortifications.

But the longer the people complained about and lost faith in the military, the harder the Crown would come down on *him*. And while he couldn't care less what the Crown thought, the people's dismay was unpleasant. It needed to be corrected, and fast.

As fast as yesterday.

That afternoon, Doana had moved again, and this time without the military's provocation. They'd proceeded as though they were preparing a three-pronged attack on Turunda's forces, reached the cusp, then aborted just one *step* before

Moore could give the order to meet them. It was like running to the end of a jetty to dive into the water, then stopping suddenly at the very last moment to stare into the depths while the dust kicked up behind carried on over the edge.

But the unlikely action was no mistake; there was no deterioration of his chain of contact this time around. Doana were baiting them. They wouldn't make the first move, but their food supply was thinning thanks to General Moore's efforts, and they were no doubt growing restless. But even so, Salus had other suspicions: their sudden activity could also mean that they were making progress elsewhere.

His eyes travelled towards the dark streets of Kora, framed in lavish golden filigree. There had been no word from the city. But that meant nothing.

It could also have meant that they knew he'd discovered their lockbox - and that in turn suggested that it may well contain more than just a contingency plan.

Regardless, whatever their goal, whatever their motive, Doana remained a threat as long as they had a foothold in Turunda. The longer the stalemate lasted, the more time they had to search, and there was nothing to stop them from storming Kora altogether if things fell out of their favour. The damage they could cause while the military stood around umming and ahhing at their intentions could be catastrophic. And *he* would get the blame for it.

All of this lead him neatly to one further, irritating conclusion: Doana *weren't* just baiting, they were attempting to confuse. With every feint Turunda's prudent general *didn't* fall for, Doana gained the upper hand, and the moment they *did* finally strike, no one would move until it was too late.

And that in turn produced yet another: Moore had no choice but to make the first move. Far better to hit them hard and fast than wait and see what else would happen, and rattle their scavengers in the city in the process. If their back-up was suddenly engaged ahead of any schedules, that would set a fire beneath them and evaporate their focus.

But while their most recent bluff would have alarmed the good general, it would not have been enough for him to make rash decisions. Moore would need provoking...

Salus shifted in his seat. His stiffness reminded him that he hadn't moved for quite some time. But with such a perfect position to oversee the hidden goings on of the country, why would he go anywhere else?

He chose not to acknowledge the answer his own body presented with the overpowering arrival of yet another yawn.

The few spies he'd had within Doana's camps had been murdered weeks ago - it was something he'd come to expect when he began to recognise Doana's own sly competence - and he hadn't bothered to replace them. It wasn't a trick he could pull twice. But while he had others watching from outside, it wasn't enough; their movement was sudden and they hadn't been close enough to hear the plans.

But with spells, he could see and hear it all as it happened, and he could act upon it immediately. That was why he'd created the spell in the first place...

Then his next move was simple: establish surveillance inside the camps, and as soon as possible. It would be a challenge, but it was achievable with the right people.

Otherwise, provoking Moore would be easy. It was no trouble to stage an attack by the opposition - countless wars had been triggered by a third party's meddling, and in the end, the sooner a brooding war began, the sooner it was over, and the better then for everyone. And doubly so in this case, since his own country was directly involved.

A soft knock came at the door, a familiar knock that made his chest flutter, and an identity confirmed when the door opened before he could grant permission. He looked up as Taliel stepped in, her soft face marred by a look of concern. It looked that way increasingly often these days. He was busy - perhaps too busy. But she understood. She must have. She *had* to.

"Salus," she said in that achingly soft voice, "come to bed. You need sleep."

His eyes drifted back to the mirrors even as his mind processed a response, but it never made it out. It took him a long while to finally rise to his feet, and even then his gaze continued moving from one image to another, just in case he'd missed something. He didn't pull himself away until another, firmer knock sounded, and he looked up at this new arrival beside whom Taliel now stood with perfectly trained composure, staring at the opposite wall.

"I apologise for the intrusion, Keliceran," the young man said formally, his own gaze fixed to the fireplace, "but the box is open."

The sag of Taliel's shoulders was barely visible, and indeed, Salus didn't notice it. His eyes brightened, though they were still edged in fatigue, and with one final sweep across the mirrors, he followed the young man out.

Chapter 42

Rathen release a long, deep breath as his eyes roved the veiled sky, his notebook open and forgotten in his lap. A thick sheet of iron clouds, laden with the scent of promised rain, diffused the sun and cast a pleasant coolness through the air. Like the shield of a colossal knight in one of Aria's story books, the sloping fields were guarded from the worst of the summer's heat and all life seemed to slow down and breathe in the respite. Birds looped and cavorted without fear of exhaustion, and jackalopes and deer alike ventured out beyond the safety of the trees to graze in the open meadows.

But, despite being so often at the mercy of the elements, he did not relish the lull.

Though the clouds were far from breaking, each of them continued to search the sky, but the location of the sun remained in the realms of guesswork. Such had been the unchanging case since they'd stopped what felt like hours ago, and with no way of knowing one way or the other, they were left with little choice but to continue watching and waiting for noon, when the winds were supposedly at their strongest, at the foot of the High Dells right where the ditchlings had told them to, eyes pinned to the clouds in search of the harpies' approach and wondering all the while if *they* were any wiser to the time.

Rathen watched as restlessness crept in over the others, until only Eyila and himself, as a long-suffering father, seemed to have any kind of patience. While Aria kept herself busy climbing the trees, Anthis stared off in the opposite direction, up towards the mountains, and it was plain that his anticipation was for the impossibly isolated ruins above. Petra stood and strode, then stood, then strode, sending irritated glances back towards Garon who himself paced unendingly back and forth, setting everyone else further on edge. Lost in a cloud of thought, his hand was balled at his mouth. His fingers were only half-curled, Rathen noticed from his seat at the foot of a tree, and he dwelled on that for a time rather than on Anthis's translated papers.

Finally, a familiar shriek pierced the cool air.

All eyes snapped towards the north, their guard rising on instinct though the six avian shapes sweeping down towards them from over the conifer treetops were sorely expected.

Eager for progress, their bags were over their shoulders before they could distinguish the colour of their feathers from the bleak grey of the sky, but any gratitude they'd prepared for their temperamental allies was dismissed before it could be offered. "Come," was all the leading harpy said, and not one of them alighted. Instead they bared their menacing talons, as long as the length of a full and open hand, and eyed them one by one with menacing yellow eyes they still found difficult to meet.

But despite more than a few misgivings, Rathen steeled himself and stepped forwards. Aria kept close to his side. Eyila followed, and Garon an instant later, until they were all standing within frightful reach of the gleaming black talons. Rathen ushered Aria forwards; she took a little more encouragement than he'd expected, but he found she was rather occupied with staring up at the raptorial figure in awe. He turned and met the leader's sharp, yellow gaze directly. "Be careful with her."

The harpy's feathered head bobbed once, hopefully in understanding, and her legs stretched out towards her. Aria extended her little arms out to the sides and the talons clamped snugly around them. Rathen winced at the perfect fit, but chose not to dwell on the designs of predator and prey and instead stepped bravely towards the next. The others uneasily followed suit, but before anyone had a moment to brace themselves, there came a sharp and unyielding pinch, a powerful thrash of air, a lurch of their stomachs, and the ground beneath their feet was suddenly replaced by the surging rush of treetops.

And then flooded cold, instinctive terror. Thought shut down as their feet attempted to tread on empty air and every cell in their body screamed that it was wrong, that the most important thing in the world was for their feet to return to safe and solid ground even sooner than humanly possible. But once they forced themselves past that ancient fright, through helpless necessity if nothing else, there came the most shocking, most wonderful thrill.

Their breath was snatched away from their lips, their hair roiled and whipped violently across their cheeks, grasps adjusted and pinched a little deeper into their arms, but not one of them cared. A few, unaware of the activities of their vocal chords, even howled in elation as they rose higher into the chilling air and watched the conifer forest rush by like a raging green river. They saw for miles so vast it challenged belief, as far even as Bowden, three days behind them, and the sloping meadows seemed as flat and easy as a slackened sea. They thought they could even see the dark, imposing edge of the Wildlands.

But of them all, Eyila delighted the most; tears of wonder blown from her childlike eyes, lips dry in their exuberant smile. And Anthis beamed in joy for her.

The harpies had made the effort to be far gentler with their holds this time around - it was still dismally uncomfortable, of course, and as miles flashed by in minutes, Rathen found himself wishing, if only for a moment or two, that someone had thought about slings or harnesses.

They soared higher and the air turned frigid. Thinning trees gave way to bare rock, cracked from the touch of winter immemorial. And as the mountains filled their sight, their spirits abruptly shattered.

The air became as cold as death, the sound of wingbeats became as monotonous as a charnel clock's pendulum, and what had a moment ago been a marvel was now an omen.

A river of black - a rend of darkness; the chasm had carved its way through the mountains like an axe through flesh. It tore up the valleys, skirting the largest peaks, and sundered brutally straight through the younger, leaving their faces massacred in its wake. It was devastation, cataclysm - it was worse than they could have imagined. And yet, now faced with its magnitude, no one could recall their expectations.

And it was splintered, they noticed dreadfully. As though two separate rifts had met, one from the north towards Dustwatch, and the other from the east, from Ivaea. Their true sources were unknown, hidden well beyond the secrecy of the mountains, but they each hoped dearly that it was but one single, indecisive rupture.

The rush of air began to slacken and the wingbeats became measured and irregular, and the snow-patched ground began reaching up towards them. Purpose set in to override their hopelessness, and they prepared to land. It was only then that they realised they had no idea how. A few began treading air in the hopes of hitting the ground at pace, and others drove their feet out ahead of them to aid in the deceleration. Instead they were dropped a foot or so from the ground, and none had a graceful landing. Rock had never felt so hard.

Eyila was the only one set down gently, but she hadn't her feet to stand upon, and despite their outwardly callous conduct, the harpies all sent the Ayavei girl looks of concern. The others were quick to notice the glaze of her eyes, too - all but for Rathen, who had succumbed to the raging magic in the same urgent manner he always did. He was left to Aria's care while the rest recovered their bearings.

Settling his reeling head and stomach and pushing aside his own grudgingly shaken awe, Garon began to study their surroundings.

They had alighted within a sunken ring of tall, jagged menhirs set within the snow of this brief levelling of the mountainside. Facing the peaks, the furthest edge of the ring sloped upwards into a gentle hill, and more stones could be seen embedded within the middle of the elevated face through the ice. Aside from the thaw-cracked stone, the barrows were identical to those at Borer's Teeth, if more frozen than sodden.

And frozen it certainly was. Garon was already shivering. He steeled himself stubbornly, refusing to be affected. It didn't take him long to still.

But it seemed much colder than it ought to have been. Surely the snow should have been thicker. It was certainly cold enough...or was it? He resentfully had to admit that he was still disorientated, and having just ascended from summer meadows to the perpetual winter of the mountains left his perspective somewhat biased. There was no knowing if the intense cold was a result of magic or not.

But he had no such doubts over the ribbons of looping ice.

Coiled and rolling, it was as though a stream had loped through the air and been frozen immediately in place, and the cold, iridescent blue-purple light that slipped across those crystalline tongues as though water still flowed was just as suspicious. Beautiful, certainly - enchanting, even. But ominous. The allure was, as always, nothing less than disturbing.

He glanced around and caught Petra looking just as uncomfortable, her fingers indecisive in reaching for her sword, though steel would do nothing to help. He noticed a pocket of diamond dust shimmering silently in the air behind her, and then another closer to where Rathen stood, clutching the Zi'veyn which itself looked remarkable in the pure white setting. But, surely, it was nowhere near cold enough for that...

He decided to avoid stepping near those frozen clouds, just in case. It was little more than chance that he happened to turn around when he did and see Aria about to reach into one. She leapt back from it with eyes as big as saucers at his suddenly barked warning.

Garon's mind turned immediately to defence. There was unlikely to be anyone up there - even Salus - and should he be wrong, they were high enough and isolated enough to see them coming. He could afford to watch from beside a fire. And as his teeth resumed their previous chattering and the hairs on arms began to stand up beneath his sleeves, he knew he had little choice.

He was given no time to ponder over firewood, however, when a bundle dropped into the snow behind him and a sudden rush of wind forced him a step forwards. He turned and found the lead harpy as she alighted on the frozen ground. If a bird could look disgusted, her face was the perfect example. He wasted no time in lighting the logs with the tinderbox in his bag.

"Three days ago," it announced shrilly from somewhere in its throat as he sparked the firesteel, "there was an attack of flames in one of your cities. Its glow was seen from our eyries."

"We know," Petra sighed heavily, stepping up beside Garon. "Bowden."

The harpy bobbed her head, then looked off in the direction of the chasm. It couldn't be seen, but its presence loured just behind them as obviously as had the sun been stolen. "The western mountains have been rent, also. Two days ago. An earthen tribe has been obliterated. A water tribe was just missed."

"A water tribe in the mountains?"

"They most likely built around a spring," Garon replied as the wood began to smoke, and he blew the embers into life.

Her brow further knotted in concern. "The White River..."

"It still flows. But the Northrage has been cut off. The Grey River survives, by chance. The forests have not yet been affected. Green Hills still feeds from the flow of the White."

"I wonder if Hlífrún had something to do with that..."

"Perhaps," Garon said, straightening after warming his hands over the small flames for far less time than he'd have liked and stuffing them back into his uniform gloves. "Or it's just dangerously thin chance. Either way, Salus is aiming for the borders. The forests aren't an issue. It's the loss of her connection that worries her."

"They're very active," the harpy continued, speaking, they presumed, about the rest of the Arana. "Moving, scurrying. They're like busy ants rather than watchful spiders."

"How do you know it's them?"

"Because," she fixed Petra with her sharp, certain gaze, "they have an unnatural air. Can you not sense it from them?"

"They wouldn't be very effective at their job if we could..."

"What of your own safety?" Petra asked, crouching to the flames, unable to keep away for any longer. "And the ditchlings?"

"The...Arkhamas? We have...a system. We have a way of communicating so that we do not alert our attackers. We can move them into a trap the other has set up. It thins them out well enough."

"A system?"

"Trills and ruffles; whistles and rustles. The mice--the *Arkhamas* are more useful than they would appear, ground-ridden as they are."

Petra's lips pursed distastefully, but she held back any retort. Her temper had mellowed over the past few days.

Suddenly, the harpy spread a single wing, and the edge of a single silver feather glinted on its underside. Strangely, she reached down with her beak and plucked it. And even stranger still, it rattled. Only when she tidied her wings away with practised grace and offered it out towards them did Petra see that it was a necklace.

"The Arkhamas requested we return this to you," she said in a perfectly unchanged voice despite the clamp of her beak, and dropped it into Petra's outstretched hand.

She stared at the oval locket in unvarnished surprise, tears quickly springing to blur her sight, but she had no time to thank her before she rose into the air with a buffet of her wings and began to fly off with her kin, casting back the advice to simply 'call when they're finished'. They descended into the trees far below, and Garon wondered if they would actually hear them when they did.

He, Petra and Eyila sat in silence around the warming aura of the fire while Rathen and Anthis each busied themselves with magic and the ruin respectively. Aria leaned with arms stretched wide into a wild and relentless current of wind that blew up over the shelf, sweeping powdery snow up behind it. Her clothes billowed, and there was a tremendous look of joy on her notably pink face. They both kept a very sharp eye on her, ready to spring up and catch her, but before long the tension finally forced Petra to her feet and she turned the girl around, sending her away to 'help' Anthis instead. She was more than happy to oblige.

The slightest flicker of movement drew Garon's gaze towards the sheerest edge of the mountain. It took a moment of hard staring into the thin and dangerously slanted trees to see the two huge eyes staring back at him. He stiffened, becoming acutely aware of the inches' distance between his hand and his sword, but the thickly-furred, dog-like face watched him with subdued curiosity while its four feet - more like hands than paws - clung to the rough trunk and its long tail coiled about a branch for extra support. It was not alone, Garon noticed, and had spotted three more when Petra gasped beside him, having followed his gaze. But the four and any others besides did nothing but stare. They left them be in return, but kept a constant note of their location.

In the end, though, the tension of being watched so keenly and the rapidly swelling silence became too much, and that ridiculous yet persuasive voice in the depths of Garon's subconscious began goading him again. Watching the glint of the locket turning over in Petra's hands, the thoughtless words came out before he could stop them. "Why did your father train you?"

A sleek eyebrow cocked, and she looked at him with speculation. "Why?"

"Did you ask him? To follow in his--"

"No, why are you asking? You know who he is, you know he trained me for the Crucible. You know it was so I could succeed him."

"I meant...well, he's important to you."

"Whose father isn't? Yours?"

"No, he is," he replied lightly. "He's a cobbler. Taught me the importance of a good pair of boots."

A smile flickered, but it was all too brief. She turned back to the locket and ran her nail along the seam. "But you didn't answer my first question."

"I think you'll find that I did."

"No, you didn't, you brushed past it with an obvious statement. Why are you asking? In fact, what are you even doing?" Her eyes flashed with sudden venom. Her temper was mellowing, but it was still volatile. For a loathsome moment he stammered foolishly. She waited for him to present an answer, but he was too slow. Disappointment dropped as she scoffed and rose, the snow crunching beneath her feet as she walked away. "I am so sick of your yo-yoing."

Garon blinked, and as if his mind had vacated him for the duration of the exchange, he suddenly returned to himself and frowned in the sheerest confusion.

...What *was* he doing? What had he expected to achieve with such a stupid question? And why had it mattered so much?

The cold must have rattled his senses as well as his bones...

A resounding splash seized his attention and he spun to find the ribbons of ice collapsing and spreading out over the snow, their ephemeral blue-purple lights nowhere to be seen. But in that same instant came a familiar foreboding, and he turned immediately towards Eyila.

Her eyes were raging even before she spun in the snow to stare vehemently in Rathen's direction.

Garon seized her in a harmless restraint before she could launch into her irrational attack. Rathen was quick to turn and hurry to her side before Garon had the need to subdue her, the Zi'veyn once more floating between his hands.

Her eyes began to soften, then cleared, and as Rathen sagged with the effort, she caught him and cast her own spell in payment, returning a degree of his strength.

But Rathen's relief at the surrounding stillness and returning normality was fleeting.

'Just how much will silencing this magic really do?' The all too familiar question rang dubiously in his mind. If the magic was still there, what was to stop Salus from affecting it? Unless his rudimentary, half-baked instruction didn't cover the sensations of magic...if it stayed still, kept quiet, he just might miss it...

Rathen doubted it. He couldn't know how much of that chasm had been Salus's doing, but the fact that he was capable of it at all suggested that his hopes of thwarting him by such measures were futile. But what other option did he have?

...Well...perhaps there was *one*...

Tentatively, he turned and faced the others. Garon looked back so tightly he must have heard his thoughts. But he said it anyway. "We need to go to the Order." While Petra and Eyila gawked in shock, Garon was already shaking his head. "I know, but it looks like he really *could* move Turunda - or he'll completely obliterate it in the process. Turunda *needs* magical defences, and they need to know what--"

"No." Garon's voice was firm as stone. "Going to the Order defeats the entire purpose of having sought you out in the first place. Not to mention the very imminent fact that it would take us *into Kulokhar.* No, it's too dangerous. Far better--"

"*He's* too dangerous!"

"*Far better* to keep to the current plan, *for now*. We interfere with his plans, slow him down, while we work out a *permanent* solution."

"I am only one person," Rathen reminded him darkly, "only one *mage*. The Order numbers nearly two thousand - *they* could work out a permanent solution *much* faster than I can!"

"They don't understand the Zi'veyn like you do, nor all this magic! It would take them weeks, if not *months* to come to grips with it before they could even begin *working* on it, and they would distract each other with foolish suggestions or experimentation! You *know* this! And who is to say what could happen if a malcontent got his hands on it all and managed to do something with it?!"

"You *can* do this, Rathen," Petra said, looking at him pointedly. "And...if we *did* need the Order's help, we couldn't just waltz into the capital city, not with the Arana looking for us. If you need to confer with one or two of them, we'll need a plan." She held Rathen's gaze, deliberately avoiding Garon's. "*If* you really can't do it yourself."

"Of course he can do it," Aria announced, somewhat confused by Petra's doubt.

"Well, *maybe*," she pressed with a heavy sigh. "It's elven magic, an elven spell, the Zi'veyn is an elven construct. But your father...well, he's only *half*-elf."

Aria's young, pink face pulled into a slow, doubtful pout, and she regarded her father carefully. Her big eyes grew increasingly sceptical.

Rathen growled and snapped away from them, muttering defeatedly beneath his breath.

"I think we're done here," Petra declared with a look about the ordinary ruin, and ignored Garon's subtle look of approval to locate Anthis crouching on the far side of the barrows' altar, examining some mark or other very closely. His head popped up somewhat dejectedly when she called him away, and though he said 'one moment' three or four times, she ended up having to trudge over and drag him away by the blanket he'd wrapped about himself when the harpies finally answered Garon's doubtful call.

They left the watchful, dog-faced creatures behind them, who hadn't once strayed from the trees, and descended the mountain in another jarring yet astonishing flight. Once again they were all dropped unceremoniously to the ground, and the harpies left without farewell.

"They're rather rude, aren't they?" Petra observed tartly, watching them vanish above the trees as she climbed back to her feet and dusted herself off.

"*Is* it rudeness?" Anthis pondered. "They're not people..."

"They set Eyila down gently enough. It's all deliberate."

But Garon's attention was still on the mountains. His eyes narrowed. "Ferna." The others searched out over the meadows from the edge of the forest, but he ignored them in his pique. "They've left us at the *opposite* end of the forest - the next site was south of White Barrows. They've just added *four days* to our journey!"

"Let it pass, Garon," Rathen sighed, rubbing his head which had begun to throb half way through the bracing flight, "it can't be helped. It is what it is."

He looked up towards the sky. It was growing darker, but it remained impossible to determine the hour. "I doubt we'll make any progress today, anyway.

We should move into the trees and find somewhere to camp. We have the cover of the dells, we should use it."

He was quite right, though Garon still took a moment to consider it before agreeing. But as they trekked into the forest, Rathen found himself having to restrain his pace. He was tired and eager to rest despite Eyila's help, but he felt some sensation in his soul that reached out for something more than sleep alone. The forest exuded such comfort and care; hidden from prying eyes, shielded from the elements, but also wilfully hospitable. It was as if he was back in the warmth and familiarity of the Scowles, but here, the trees themselves seemed to welcome him.

Rathen found a wondrous peace that night while the others fretted over the howl of wolves and the shift of vengeful shadows moving in to kill them for their interference. In fact, the possibility of the Arana's presence hadn't occurred to him at all until it was pointed out the next morning. It cast a rather unpleasant pallor over breakfast.

Confusion chased it off, however, when Garon announced that they were to continue west and into Ferna despite their goal lying somewhere in the mountains to the south-east. "After what the harpies have told us," he explained as they looked at him as though he'd gone mad, "we need to know what the *people* are saying. But above them, I want to contact the Hall and see what *truths* they can shed on the matter. We've been out of touch for too long; we need to find out what's been happening."

"We're close by," Anthis mused, "we may as well make use of it. We're fine for supplies, though."

"Good - then wait outside. The fewer of us in there, the less chance we have of catching anyone's eye."

"Or worse," Rathen muttered. The quality of Salus's surveillance spell had grown in hindsight to trouble him.

They were on the move by mid-morning, only too happy to put the mountains and their meddling behind them, and made quickly for the city of Ferna. They avoided the road, though it ran flat and parallel a short distance over the hills, and soon spotted the immense grey walls from across the rolling meadows. As they drew nearer and Anthis launched into an enthusiastic and largely undesired history lesson, it was clear that they'd been modified from their original build untold centuries ago; aside from certain reinforcement, the uppermost third was a few shades lighter than the rest, its stone masoned far more meticulously and laid far more precisely, and projected out near the top to form a suitable parapet complete with bartizans and battlements. Once merely the boundary of a thriving elven city - short post-magic, Anthis assured them - and defence against beasts when it needed to be, now it was an impetuous guarantee against siege and attack - if not perhaps an open invitation to try.

But despite the needless tampering with the walls, the city itself was still a sight to behold. The best view came of course from the road, but the river approach was far from blind, and above those menacing walls, rising with the slope of the land, stood a mass of drystone arches and domes with lines that flowed like water; homes and halls, parks and baths, bell and aviary towers, crowned as a whole by a vaulted temple and its two stone sentinels, each clad in thick, chiselled armour. More modest than Tarun or Kulokhar, without a trace of onyx, gold or silver to be seen, and yet no less impressive - and its every building was still in use to that day.

It was just past another clouded noon when Garon broke away and the rest stopped beneath a towering overhang at the edge of the river. The water ran pitifully low, but it made for a perfect place to hide while they waited, and was far enough from the walls that no one would happen to spot them, especially while the festivities outside the gates occupied everyone's attention, citizen, guard and wayfarer alike.

Unfortunately, it also occupied Aria's attention; sat atop the overhang, hidden among the bushes that surrounded the vast old willow, she stared longingly towards the gathering, watching the flags and the flames waving in the breeze, infused with lively music and the aroma of seasonal toasted spices. Rathen kept a close eye on her though he ignored her every wistful sigh, each one a little stronger than the last for his benefit, until finally she gave up and spoke. Rathen shook his head immediately.

"It's all right," said Petra, "I'll take her. There's a ridge a little ways on, she'll have a safe view of the fire-breathers from there. It's a solid hiding spot."

"How do you know?"

"I've utilised it once or twice," she replied evasively. "Some people just can't take losing."

"Yes, I imagine some people are just like that..." Reluctantly, Rathen gave in, and the pair shortly vanished around the riverbend to follow it upstream, closer to the ancient city. He climbed up beside the willow tree to take up the watch in her stead, while Eyila washed some of her spare skins and Anthis pretended to read. But, within five minutes, as he watched the dance of the distant flames and the billow of fire-like banners, his mind was consumed by his daunting task yet again. He barely noticed the approaching footsteps.

"You're missing all the fun."

Chapter 43

Rathen whipped around as quick as a loosed arrow. But though his heart threatened to burst out of this throat, he forced his primed fingers to still and studied the approaching man as inoffensively as he could. It wouldn't do to cause a scene so close to the city, not with what they'd left behind them.

He was quick to notice the amicable look in his eye as he neared the willow, and the pleasant smile about his thin lips. But the sword at his hip unsettled him. He had to forcibly remind himself that it wasn't unreasonable to bear such a thing given the recent turmoil, and neither was the confident, purposeful way he carried himself. In some cases, bearing alone could keep one safe.

And yet, in the next chilling moment, he felt the blood drain from his face and his fingers itched even more urgently to contort into spells. The voice at the back of his mind seemed dulled as it spoke, assuring him that, had this truly been one of Salus's agents, he would never have presented himself so openly.

Unless, of course, he was counting on exactly that assumption.

At Rathen's sharp response, the man slowed and raised his hands, eyeing him cautiously in return. "Sorry, I didn't mean to startle you. But - if I may - what are you doing all the way out here?" He gestured back towards the fair. "If it's mages you're worried about, they wouldn't dare attack Ferna. It's the safest place to enjoy yourself. There are old elven defences folded into the stone, and the mages can't undo them. If they hit, they'll be snuffed out before they can torch a barrel."

"Yes," Rathen replied slowly, though he didn't meet his easing smile, "I've heard the same..."

"Well, why don't you join in, then? You look like you could use a distraction, if you don't mind me saying."

"Actually, I was just looking for some peace and quiet."

"Ah," the stranger persisted, disquieting him even more. "A distraction *from* the festivities. I see. Well, that's a shame. I really don't want to add to your problems..."

Rathen didn't need to ask what he'd meant. The numbing moment in which some kind of understanding began to dawn hung for an eternity. Then, as a warning rose from behind him, time stampeded forwards and everything happened at once.

The dull snatch of the sword as it was freed from a leather ring, the rise of Rathen's hands, blood surging in his ears with the crackle of hungry magic, the rush of footsteps as Anthis dove forwards ahead of him, dagger bared to meet the blade, and the thud and whoosh of forcefully vacated breath as he struck the ground, kicked backwards by a well-placed boot as Petra's sword rang against the stranger's instead.

The man pushed into his blade and jumped backwards, holding the honed tip out towards her. "Come with me quietly," he began with a chillingly reasonable tone, casting a look of honest persuasion across the three before him, "you *don't* need to get hurt."

But while the others watched him in calculation, Petra delivered a swift response, knocking his blade to one side before rotating to strike him from the other. He parried the blow with ease.

"Aria," Rathen shouted urgently, but Anthis was already moving back down into the river. He heard her frightened voice, heard Anthis tell her to stay out of sight, and Eyila too, though she protested violently. Rathen added his own command, yelled sharply, furiously, but even while he watched Petra engage this stranger, he found himself unable to think or act.

His magic was surging, roaring in his blood - but what could he do? So close to the city, so close to the fair - to any onlooker, these were two duelists partaking in an agreed contest a safe distance from the city, and people were surely beginning to spectate. But as soon as he unleashed any kind of magic, there would be mass panic, and it would only take one clumsy flame to torch the dry grass...

But if he did nothing, and Petra was defeated...then Salus would finally have them.

He could feel that monstrous power rising in his gut and he pushed it down on instinct. This time, however, his efforts were shadowed by an obscure hesitance. He knew he could suppress it, he knew he could keep it from coming out, but it *would* try again, and the concentration it would take to maintain it beside the inability to think of anything to help would render him entirely useless. Everything would be in Petra's hands.

The girl was skilled - if he'd had any doubt about that, her alarmingly swift sequence of pirouettes, parries, feints and ripostes obliterated it - but her opponent matched her at every swing and step. It wouldn't be over quickly. And if he managed to get in just one lucky hit...

His eyes burned as he watched them.

He knew he could suppress it. But he also knew he could recover. He'd healed from his last bout without a healer's aid and even within its grip he'd wrestled it to an end himself. Perhaps, this time, he could control it...

A glint of hope flickered at the back of his mind. He'd been stopped before. By Petra, as he understood it. And Garon had shown her how to subdue Eyila. *'The same way he does you'*. She could stop him...

If she won.

With every 'if', 'or' and 'but' they fell quicker into the Arana's hands.

Amongst the din of expert clashes, Rathen's body began to shake. Adrenaline, excitement, terror, power. He couldn't believe he was even considering it - he couldn't believe he had the *time* to - but even as his mind raged against the encroaching haze in this crucial debate, he wished desperately that he could confer with Kienza. This was too sudden; it felt impossibly wrong to unleash it here and now - there had to be another way.

But his mind was slowing, and he realised too late that he'd wasted all of his time.

He had only a moment to yell his warning before his decision was made for him.

"If you stop this and come with me," the stranger spoke calmly between deflecting the quick and precise barrage of her sword, "you'll be given mercy." He managed his own lunge, but she rotated away from it. "I don't have to tell them about this."

Petra snarled but refrained from any sarcastic comment. She had no desperate questions and the man's skill was too sharp to waste time talking. They had to be away from him as soon as possible, which meant she needed to be able to leap upon the briefest opening the instant it appeared. But as she parried a quick string of overhand strokes, failed to succumb to a feint and riposted his low stab, her heart sang. It had been much too long since she'd crossed her blade with one of such skill, and while the situation itself was unfortunate, it was bliss to finally release weeks of frustration.

But then, after only a minute or so, the opening she'd been waiting for arrived, and it was very obliging.

While their blades locked under matching pressure, she freed herself with a firm boot to his gut. He staggered backwards, winded, but was quick to catch himself, and with his own flashing grin of enjoyment he rushed to recover the advantage. But as she readied herself, something passed over him. Just out of the reach of her sword, his feet stumbled to a stop, his eyes flashed wide, his poised blade faltered with a sudden hesitance in his shoulder, and his lips moved to direct the distraction. She didn't fall for it.

She kicked his legs out from beneath him and raised her sword for a swift, crushing and necessary stroke. And then a tight, agonised, guttural sound choked up behind her. She stalled in fright. It was shaped almost into the word 'run'.

Then came the sickening crack of bones.

She spared only a single shuddering glance over her shoulder. Then she returned to the man and struck to kill. If nothing else, it would be a kinder death.

It didn't land.

The man jumped back to his feet with his sword in hand and avoided the blow by throwing himself into her. The ground shook as they landed, but before Petra could wrestle the bounty hunter away, she saw what stood hunched over in the spot they'd been standing in just seconds before.

A form tall, lean and white, streaked by scrolling black lines beneath the skin, with sharp, jagged shoulders and elbows and matching protrusions down its spine. It turned its head in a storm of onyx hair and its black, whiteless eyes seared into them with the most intense malice.

A fear as deep and ancient as the first breath of man gripped their muscles and squeezed their lungs. They stared back, paralysed.

With unnatural speed, the beast launched itself towards them. They managed by the skin of their teeth to roll out of the way just in time. Anthis called up from the riverbed in alarm, but Petra warned him to stay where he was. It was only as blood-curdling screams rose from the city beyond that Petra realised the ground's shaking hadn't ceased.

Where before the picturesque city had been marred only by the adjustment of the walls, sinister thorns of stone that exceeded even its elevated height had erupted from the earth, encircling the aged city with a barricade of deadly pikes. Revellers fled while the stone pierced through every tent, flag and stall that had been erected closest to the walls, and their terrified screams renewed as six armoured, stone giants dug themselves free of the dirt.

Petra stared in horror, and she realised in that moment that if Rathen saw them, he may well lose his fickle interest in her. Or, rather, in the stranger.

"*What is that?!*" The man yelled, torn between the beast of alabaster and the beasts of limestone.

"Forget it," she growled, gripping her sword and moving herself around between Rathen and the river, dragging his frighteningly sharp eyes with her, "just don't let him see the city or he'll slaughter them all!"

She struck at him mercilessly, throwing all of her might into each attack, knowing that she would do little to harm him but enough at least to keep his attention. Sure enough, the chalk-white skin was as tough as steel and not even her strongest blow did more than scratch it. She pushed her agility to the edge dodging the swift swipes of bone-armoured, elongated fingers, and when she faltered under the inescapable speed, the stranger, the fool that he was, stepped in and took over.

"We can't kill it!" He warned in a panic as he almost stumbled in his attempt to dodge three quick slashes.

But Petra was already reclaiming his attention. "We don't need to." Even while she did her best to keep out of his reach while remaining close enough to provoke him, her eyes worked quickly. Again she searched for an opening, a way around his claws and hooks and thorns to reach his neck without injuring herself. Garon's wounds were at the forefront of her mind, and she knew that, in this state, Rathen was capable of so much worse.

She faltered again when her heel hit a root, and as the bounty hunter stepped back in, she was given the thinnest chance to notice that they were much too close to the river. A few steps more and she would certainly see Aria's terrified face or the glint of Anthis's dagger. Rathen wanted the stranger, but the beast wanted anything that moved. *Anyone* that moved.

She dashed forwards and stole his attention with a series of strikes at his flank, then began leading him downstream and away from the overhang. But she knew she wouldn't be able to get to him like this. He was too dangerous, his own body an armoury of weapons. He needed to be downed or stunned, only then could she get close safely, and her bolas were the only way to do it. And for that to work, he would need to be running.

She clenched her jaw in decision, turned her back to the beast, and ran. She didn't need to look over her shoulder to know that he was following; his footfalls were fast and heavy, and his ragged breath uncontrolled. So when they stopped and fell behind, she was just as quick to notice.

Panic gripped her heart. She slowed and shouted, waving to draw his focus, but something had shifted. He'd stopped and turned, fixated on the stranger yet again.

Petra yelled once more, but still Rathen ignored her. She gritted her teeth. This was her only chance.

The stranger sent a glance her way as she reached back for her bolas, but it wasn't a look of desperation. It was understanding.

His expression darkened, he gave her a single nod, then he turned and sprinted away. Rathen gave chase immediately.

And Petra's bolas wouldn't come free.

She cursed and tugged harder before fumbling in an urgent frenzy for the problem in the chain, until a blood-chilling howl joined the screams of the revellers. She looked up in sickening horror as Rathen leapt, pinned the stranger to the ground, and swiftly raked him into pieces.

Tears of fury pricked into her eyes. A yell tore free from her burning throat.

Then, finally, Rathen stopped.

The white beast swayed for a moment, growled as if to itself, and shook its head as though a fly was buzzing around it. Petra yelled animatedly, finally discovering the twist in the bolas' chain, but Rathen ignored her once again. His sights were now fixed on the city, the shrieking, fleeing people and the giants that snuffed every flame and life that lay outside the walls.

That summer's day, the approach to Ferna was the scene of carnage.

And it was about to get worse.

With a howl, horrific, rasping and pained, Rathen charged towards it.

Her bolas came free, and without a thought she swung, threw, and raced on behind them.

It was a poor throw, an angry, desperate throw. A throw that would have missed had he not staggered, stopped and swayed again. But as it was, they caught his ankles by chance, and he tripped as he tried to continue. He hit the ground like a horse; she was on him immediately, and delivered a single well-placed strike with the butt of one of her daggers.

He fell still in a moment.

Then the world slowed.

Petra sank to the ground beside the beast's body, her rapid heartbeat rattling her bones, aware, distantly, that the ground's shaking and the boom of stone footsteps had ceased. When she thought to look around, she found that the giants had made towards the walls and now stood guard as still and imposing as the statues they appeared to be. What people that had survived the sudden and unexplainable massacre had vanished.

Her eyes drew then towards the stranger. Slowly, she began gathering her bearings to approach him, but stilled when she heard her name called from behind. She looked back towards the city to find Garon running towards her. He spared not even a glance for any of the bodies. He was fixed on her.

Detachedly, she steadied her shakes and wiped her sweat as he skidded to a stop in the dust, then he knelt and stared at her critically. He checked her wounds - she hadn't been as careful as she'd thought - he checked her eyes, he asked how she felt, and only when he'd confirmed that she was truly unscathed did he turn at last to Rathen.

He looked now as much a victim as any man lying around them. His skin had returned to its usual pale tone, his ribcage and shoulders had narrowed to their original shape, and every sharp, bony spike and hook had receded back into his body. He was instead covered in cuts and bruises, and blood, not all of which was his own.

Garon shook his head with a long, reproachful sigh, but he didn't give Petra any kind of chastisement. Instead he squeezed her gently on the shoulder, then moved to lift Rathen, bloodied and beaten, and carry him away beside her.

But the three were snatched from the ground long before they could make it back to the compromised safety of the river.

They flew for quite some time, the distance tumbling away behind them at impossible speeds, and were eventually set down in a dense and familiar forest. The harpies told them only where they were - the Eswolds, the tamer, northern reach of the Wildlands - before flying off again.

"Now we're even *further* from the mountains," Garon had growled as he watched them depart the unnaturally vigorous forest.

"And far enough from Ferna," Anthis pointed out. "We'd have picked up a tail or three after all that - now, at least, we've lost them." He grunted to himself as he stared off after them. "Perhaps we *should* go to the Order."

"The wind does seem to be carrying us that way..." Eyila agreed.

Rathen was semi-conscious while Eyila worked over him with magic and herbs, expertly considering each case and applying only what was needed. But she wasn't the only one to notice how quickly he recovered. The fact that he was awake at all was surprise enough, but that so many of his wounds had closed up already and without any help all but stunned them. He passed out eventually, but Eyila assured them that it was just fatigue and that he was better off that way.

Anthis watched him thoughtfully for a while. "Kienza said he was gaining some kind of control," he said at last, breaking the silence as they sat around uneasily in the middle of the afternoon. "He stopped it himself, before."

"He did?" Petra frowned. "When?"

"We were in Khry's Glory for a month," he replied flatly, "things got tense." He ignored their aghast looks. "He healed without anyone's help, and stopped it by himself."

Petra frowned as she recalled that afternoon's event. "He...he paused a few times, today. He was swaying, shaking his head..." She looked at him with a hopeful light in her eyes. "Do you think he could have been trying to fight it?"

"Only he can tell us that. But he's stubborn enough. If he's capable of fighting it, I have no doubt that that's what he was doing."

"Shame it came too late."

"He was a bounty hunter, Petra," Garon reminded her firmly. "Anthis recognised him right away. Don't mourn a stranger."

"Don't be so callous," she hissed, "he *helped* us."

"Because we were worth more to him alive."

"No, it was *more* than that. He was *honest*."

"So honest that he simply *forgot* to introduce himself as a bounty hunter?"

"He gave us the chance to come quietly, he didn't want to fight."

"For his own sake. He knew you were dangerous."

Petra shook her head, rose, and left in silence. Garon frowned after her, irritated and confused. She'd been upset since he'd found her, but he'd presumed it was because she'd been shaken by Rathen's power. But she'd stayed quiet. Troubled.

"Can't you see that she doesn't *want* to instantly believe the worst of people?"

His eyes travelled to Anthis. "You're saying I do?"

"I think your profession demands some degree of scepticism, but it's a sorry way to live. She's only been able to tolerate my faults because of her desire to see the good - or try to. And to forgive Rathen. And, dare I say it, *you?*" Anthis frowned as Garon scoffed and walked away without a word, far more easily than usual.

Eyila's eyebrows rose as she pressed a leaf over the final smearing of salve on Rathen's shredded shoulder, and she cast Anthis a smile. "I think we're wearing him down."

Their attention turned back to the mage. Aria sat quietly beside her slumbering father, her young face twisted in consternation as she wrestled with a thought that had been plaguing her for some while, until finally she lifted her head and looked both the historian and the bronze healer square in the eye. "Why," she asked in a tone much too adult for an eight-year-old, "would the Order keep a spell like that alive?"

"They wouldn't have known what it was," he sighed regretfully, pulling the girl close into an affectionate hug. "Your father's told me that they only have a vague understanding of most of the spells they maintain, and it's considered safer to keep them standing than let them fall apart because they don't know what else could come down with it. They patch holes, they don't re-cast the whole spell. They'd have analysed it as far as it being something for defence and left it at that." He chose not to voice his surprise that disasters like these didn't happen more often.

The girl nestled against him, her brow knotted and eyes fixed on her father. "That's irresponsible."

"It is, a little. Perhaps you should take that up with the Order."

"Yes. Perhaps I should."

He gave her a gentle squeeze, then a thought occurred to him. He looked between the girl and the tribal, then smiled. "I think you need distracting. Would you like to hear a story?"

She looked up at him with big eyes. "Yes."

"Go and fetch one, then."

She stared at him for a further moment, a question in her round face, but when he nodded, she looked around to Eyila, beamed, then scurried off. Eyila frowned after her while she rifled through her bag, then pulled out two books and considered them both very carefully. With a decisive nod, she stuffed one back inside and returned in a rush, presenting a book with a picture of three children in a forest on the cover.

"What is it?" Eyila asked, peering at it curiously.

"It's a book!"

"She can see that," Anthis chuckled, then looked a little more tentatively towards Eyila. "I thought, perhaps, you might want to read to her."

"*M-me? Read* to her?" A thick shadow of intimidation clouded her ice-blue eyes. "Anthis, you *know* I--"

"I know, I know - I'm going to help you. She needs distracting, wouldn't you agree?"

Her eyes flicked sadly to the little girl, then to her father, lying wounded and unconscious on the ground beside her, dotted with bandages and notched leaves. "Yes," she sighed grievously, both for the child and her own impending strife, "yes, she does. All right. What is it?"

"It's Old Gruel!" Aria declared. "There aren't any cities in it, and only a few children, and an old lady - she's Old Gruel. She--"

"No, don't ruin it!"

Anthis grinned at her enthusiasm, then patted the ground for Aria to sit down. Eyila shuffled up closer beside her and sent Anthis a confused smile. "Why didn't you tell me you'd found a book?"

"I...well, things have been a little hectic." He opened the book on Aria's lap, and Eyila immediately shrank back from the first page. "It's all right. Look: you know the meaning and the sounds of the words, you just need to learn their shapes. Follow with me: *'Once upon a time...'*"

"Once upon a time..."

"*'There was a little house...'*"

"There was a little house..."

"*'Shaped like an acorn...'*"

"Shaped like an acorn... I don't think this is working."

"You're doing perfectly."

"Because I'm just repeating everything you're saying!" She huffed and slouched. "I'm never going to learn."

"My daddy made me write the words when he taught me to read." They looked towards Aria, whose heart-shaped lips were pursed in thought. "Maybe if she does that, she'll learn the shapes better because she'll have to think about them rather than just look at them. It's easier to forget things you've seen than things you've *done*. It's the same with Petra and swords - she told me it's no good watching, you have to feel the sword. Maybe Eyila needs to feel the words."

Anthis blinked at the eight-year-old girl, then leaned over, snatched his satchel from beside the tree, and withdrew a notebook and a pencil. "Thank you, Aria."

She beamed proudly while Eyila eyed the pencil in doubt.

Garon stood among the gnarled and tangled trees and watched Petra from a distance.

The last time he'd tried to talk to her had not gone well, and in three days he'd devised no new ideas on how to approach her - nor any real understanding as to why she'd reacted the way she had. Or, he had, but was disinclined to accept that it was a result of his own doing. So he kept an inoffensive distance and pondered the matter that troubled him so unreasonably.

She sat alone beside the stream which reflected the purple light of the setting sun like a mirror, freshly filled waterskins piled beside her, and examined her locket with suspicion. No one could work out why the ditchlings had returned it, and that fact seemed to trouble her. It meant so much, that little piece of silver, and yet she'd given it up in payment for a map that could have been sheer nonsense, knowing she'd never see it again. It was worth it, she'd said; she'd trusted that the map was good, and trusted the ditchlings with her most cherished possession even though they'd have done nothing but fill it with mud and let it tarnish.

He adjusted his shoulder against the trunk of the chestnut, shifting away from a knot.

She did seem to want to see the good in people. It was a failing. Had she been more reserved or suspicious, she wouldn't have gotten involved with them in the first place and she'd be free of this mess. And yet, somehow, at the same time she wasn't all that naive about it; she'd jumped immediately upon that bounty hunter and only began to doubt him after the fact, she'd fought off bandits along The Ghost Patch's road while Khryu'vahz had divided them, she'd attacked the phidipan outside Nestor without hesitation, she'd come to their defence in Mokhan even when the whole city was charging against them, and more besides.

It was foolishness, there was no question about that, but she had saved their skins too often for it to be bald-faced luck. And yet, despite it all, she seemed to know who was worth a second thought. And the bounty hunter's death seemed to plague her.

Not for the first time, he thought she was ultimately too gentle to pursue a course of vengeance. She had a harshness to her, but it was only a stroke, and she carried her heart's scars well on the outside. As for inside, he had no idea what was truly going on. She was difficult sometimes and open at others, and it seemed to change with the winds because, beyond a certain point every four weeks, there was certainly little sense to be made of it.

Quite suddenly a voice spoke up in his mind, one of reason he'd come to rely on in his professional years, and he listened to it intently. *'Why does any of this matter?'* It asked of him, and he couldn't find a rational response. *'You have a job to do. An* important *one. Nothing else matters. The whimsy of these people is getting to you - shake it off.'*

He straightened, as if his senses had come crashing back down on him. What was all of this? If his superior could see him now...it didn't bear thinking of.

And yet, even while these very reasonable points presented themselves, he lingered beside that tree, watching her open the locket, stare at the pictures and lose herself in her thoughts.

It was only when she put the locket aside with finality and began to disrobe that he finally turned away, seeing as he did so a flash of the horrific burns that enveloped her right arm and stretched about the side of her torso.

The camp was quiet when he completed his patrol. Anthis and Eyila sat together around the fire, a book laid open between them and parchment on the girl's leg, which she wrote upon with the greatest care and concentration while Anthis supervised. Petra wasn't yet back, and Aria had fallen asleep at her father's side. But Rathen's eyes were open and turned darkly towards the trees he emerged from. They were quick to shift onto him.

"Garon," he said in a mildly rasping voice, to which the inquisitor approached to spare him the need to speak loudly. He knew what he would ask, and even had his throat not been shredded by those terrible, spine-chilling howls, he wouldn't have wished to conduct the matter from across the camp.

Garon crouched beside him and nodded for him to go ahead.

"Did I kill anyone?" He asked the question quickly, and closed his eyes in disgrace when Garon nodded.

"The bounty hunter."

"And others?" His tone remained harsh.

"No. Not by your hands. But your transformation triggered something. Anthis believes it was the spell the elves set into the city when it was built. It was supposed to be some kind of protection from elves who were getting too confident with their magic, so it was designed to react to a Zikhon devout."

"A Zikhon devout." His eyes opened and he stared up into the leaves overhead. His gaze was black with insult. "Someone who changes, you mean?"

"That's what he believes. The sentries took your transformation to mean that your people were in danger in the city. They only attacked what they determined to be threats, and only from outside the walls. Unfortunately, they weren't very sophisticated creations..."

"So they attacked anyone waving lanterns or torches..."

"It wasn't your fault, Rathen."

"It would *never* have happened if I hadn't been there." His voice was acid.

But Garon had no answer for him. It was the truth. There was no sense in denying it to make him feel better, and he wasn't foolish enough to believe such a falsehood anyway.

Rathen turned his head away and stared back into the trees, a hard set to his jaw and the threat of fire in his eyes.

Silently, Garon rose and stepped away, leaving him to his shame, and Anthis and Eyila returned their pitying eyes to the surface of their parchment.

Chapter 44

The evening hung heavily, though it seemed to Salus that he was the only one to feel it. All around him the city was abuzz in the light of celebratory fires and frivolous, unceasing melodies; Midsummer was still a week away and yet already the more decadent of people were gorging themselves on the festivities and throwing all care to the wind, and the lowest of the populace were taking full advantage of it. No one was paying attention to anything but their own enjoyment, and that made it only that much easier for insidious plans to crash into action. And at present, Kora was prone to more than most.

Closing himself off from the offensive mirth, he stormed through the blithesome city, his eyes catching on anyone who may not have belonged even as he abandoned his vigilant purpose, making straight for the city's library. The agent who had been tasked with fetching him was left in his dust.

He wasted no time in feeling out the dark, secreted cellar entrance and all but leapt onto the unassuming rug cast into a corner inside. He was back within the confines of Arana House in a moment, and continued directly for his loathsome office. As usual, no one stood in his way, and he threw the door open without breaking his gait. "Report," he demanded of the portian behind his desk. "Now."

Teagan coolly handed him the miniature scroll and paid no attention to the frustrated fumbling and cursing of his superior while he struggled in his rage to open it. Salus's teeth clenched while he read, but he made not a sound. His jaw must have been ready to shatter.

His eyes were very nearly aflame when he finally looked back up. "*How* did Koraaz get out of the Wildlands without *anyone* seeing him?! How did he get into *Ferna* without my *spells seeing him?!*"

"They know we're tracking them," he replied, unaffected by the glass-shaking yells, looking straight ahead towards the door, "they would have waited for a window. And the incident in Ferna occurred outside the walls."

"And they stopped *nowhere* after getting out? They needed no food? No supplies? *Nothing?!*"

"If they had, your spells *would* have detected them."

"*Would they?!*" Salus's seething eyes searched the dim office for some kind of answer while his mind raced to make sense of it all. "No, they *must* have stopped somewhere...Koraaz is a mage - perhaps he knows about my spells. He must have sensed them - it's the only way he could get around them like this. There's no other explanation. But to go through all the trouble of circumventing them..." His expression dropped, and his eyes widened into near-perfect circles. He looked towards Teagan as the helpless thought took perfect shape. "He's half-elf. What if he's in *league* with them? Destroying the world and paving the way for their return - we know they're still out there, we know *first-hand*. But...what would they get out of it? Koraaz would get protection by blood, and, no doubt, a promise of some seat of power - but what about the rest? Safety? Or are they just that gullible? The inquisitor is a rogue, the historian a psychopath, and the duelist...she's had her brain beaten out of her...

"No, no - half-elf or not, it's too much to think he could do all that by himself...no, it was too big, too spectacular. He had help. And it was *showy*...what if it was all an elaborate distraction? Ferna's defences are *still* up, yes? And this happened hours ago. The stone creatures, the golems, they're still standing there and attacking anything that moves outside the wall - goodness only knows what else is there. And why?!" He whipped back around to Teagan, the wheels in his mind turning so quickly that he could hardly keep up with them. "Phidipans - *portians!* Get them after him - find out what he's doing, why he's working with the elves, what he gets out of it - this is *my* world he's trying to destroy! I want intel! By *any* means!"

"His accomplices - if indeed--"

"Accomplices," Salus spun away with the thought. "Yes accomplices - the child would be the easiest to break, but she wouldn't know anything. She wouldn't have made sense of anything that's going on. The tribal is a mage, but a savage - she won't know how to wield her magic properly; if her hands are bound she can be overpowered, and she's young enough to be broken. We can push on her easily - it was her tribe we massacred, we have a way in. The duelist is hard-headed, she would be too much trouble to break for what little she knows, and the same, no doubt, goes for the crooked inquisitor. Karth is weak, armed but only dangerous at certain times...and he would know a great deal...while Rathen is untouchable. He would need distracting..." He levelled towards Teagan. The zealous fire blazing in his eyes had steadied into terrible, cold decision. "I want Karth."

"Sir," Teagan offered calmly, "Rathen Koraaz is not a full-blooded elf. We know from your dealings with them that they don't think much of anyone with less than 'pure' elven blood. Why should he be an exception?"

"Because I am *also* an exception. Liogan and her kin are working through *me* - it's possible that Denek was trying to bring me over himself before I killed him. He was an elf, and he didn't *have* to tell me I had any kindred blood... This is it. This *must* be it - it's the only thing that makes sense. We're *both* pawns, with the single difference being that I *know* they're manipulating me. I have no intention of fulfilling my part in their plans; I'll take as much from them as I can get and turn it to my own needs, but *Koraaz*...oh, Vastal's Blood...what if Koraaz *himself is* an elf?! What if he's not just *part*-elf at all?! He's powerful enough, and Karth is with him - they've been together *all* this time, Koraaz and an expert on the ancient elven world, a world he never saw but wants to bring back..."

"Sir, forgive me, but this--"

"And perhaps they have no intention of using the Zi'veyn to gather up the magic to use for another purpose after all - an elf wouldn't need it! Perhaps they *will* use the Zi'veyn against mages and are still searching for the means to do so much more..." A sudden snarl ripped free of his throat. "'Perhaps perhaps perhaps' - we need *certainties!* We need to know what they're doing, once and for all - we need to stop them *before* I can rescue Turunda! Otherwise, what's to stop him or elves from hitting us once we've moved?! Nothing! Nothing except more elven--...except more elven magic..."

"Sir, I must protest," Teagan managed at last, though he couldn't be sure it wasn't because Salus had lost himself in his rampant thoughts again. "Your magic is powerful, but you cannot possibly stand against elves *alone*. You destroyed Denek because Denek made a fatal error and underestimated you, but an elf won't make that mistake again, and neither will Koraaz."

"I need to get stronger..."

Teagan's heart sank in the briefest stab of hopelessness.

"I need to get stronger, I need to surpass the handicap of signs, destroy Koraaz and move Turunda to safety. Decontaminate our lands of mages and foreigners - and *elves*. *Anyone* who would do it and its people harm..."

But Salus was fully aware that the thought was preposterous. He was *already* strong. His arsenal of spells was unvaried, he ruefully acknowledged, but he had power, *immense* power, and the instruction of the elves. He could push magic, manipulate it directly which, as far as Erran had led him to believe, was supposed to be impossible. That feat alone was testament to his power, and it was one he already had a handle on - was there not some way he could use that against Koraaz? If he could avoid wasting time learning new things and just hone what he already had...but how could he turn that into a weapon?

He sank into his chair, unaware of Teagan's continued protests, and stared deeper into his own musings.

He could use the chasms to his advantage and direct the magic through those lines and strike him with deadly intent. But he would have to be at one of those chasms at the time, and it would have to be one he'd linked up - or another formed at random that he was waiting at the other end of.

Or he could try to manipulate the magic beyond inciting and directing it - try, perhaps, to weave some of it into a spell of his own and send that along the chasm chain - or just plant a spell and wait for him to wander within range. But just where he was going was a mystery, which would make predicting it near-impossible and downright dangerous to anyone else who might get caught in his place... But just how would something like that even be achieved?

He hadn't seen Liogan since she'd dragged him out to Halen nearly a month ago, and there was no knowing at all when the wretched harridan would return. He'd have to work it out on his own.

A nerve-shattering crash ripped him out of his deliberations and his eyes bolted up into the aged face of fury.

Malson slammed the door behind him without breaking his blistering stare. "I thought you were watching the cities!" He yelled with no regard at all to Teagan's presence. "Why didn't you see this?! It's *your* advanced intel that's supposed to *stop* things exactly like this!"

"My lord," he replied tightly, "it happened outside the--"

"And your *vast* resources can't climb *over* walls?! Step *through* the gates?!"

It took more power than Salus had to control his outrage. He only managed by channelling the majority of it into his feet as he rose dangerously from behind his desk, but the insolence that met him, smouldering in the man's eyes, threatened to break that flimsy restraint. He found neither strength nor will to even attempt a soothing smile. "The perpetrator wasn't within the walls. He never was; there was nothing for us to see. There were no stirrings of an impending attack, let alone anything this elaborate."

"We both know you're watching the mages," he hissed accusingly. "You must have heard *something* - unless it slipped by you."

"My lord, *nothing* slips by me if it is there to be seen. This was kept quiet."

"Plans of this magnitude could *never* be kept quiet. Do not take me for a fool, Salus. You've slipped up, *again*. The Crown will call for *both* of our heads at this rate."

The two held each other's gaze for a solid minute, until Salus felt a faint and derailing twitch of his eye. "Was there anything else?" His pleasure at the curl of Malson's lip didn't reveal itself.

But then the old man straightened and adopted a strange look of almost genuine regret - almost, if not for the slightest, most negligible smirk that hovered just beneath his grimace. "Your funding is being cut." His certain pleasure at Salus's paling didn't reveal itself, either. "The Crown has decided to concentrate finances on the military and sustaining the refugees. And you're to send more agents out towards the forces holed up in Glensmoor. Doana has poisoned their water supply with blackbane, most likely in an attempt to provoke them. It was caught quickly, but General Moore won't risk acting on it. Not until he knows exactly what they're planning."

Silently, Salus raged.

"Search for how they did it - how they got into the camp, how they crossed the moors without being seen, and how they managed to leave only the single smallest yet clearest clue behind them after taking all that care." His eyes burned again, and the accusation was clear. But Salus held his stare without emotion. Malson waited, but Salus offered nothing.

A knock at the door snatched the focus of the room's near-tangible strain, and at a bark from the keliceran, the woman stepped inside. She inclined her head to the liaison then fixed her gaze stolidly past the others, approached her superior and dropped a roll of parchment upon the walnut desk.

Malson barely spared her a glance. He fired Salus a final look of warning, then turned away in a flurry of rich, blue robes and left the office with the words 'get it done' falling as heavily as lead behind him.

The moment the door slammed shut, Salus's brittle restraint snapped. Teagan and Taliel waited, still and silent, their eyes fixed rigidly, almost desperately to the furthest wall to avoid glimpsing his abrupt, ghastly pallor, raven-black eyes and monstrous, fanged expression while he raged and thrashed in his torment.

With a single, deliberate sweep, the neatly stacked papers were cast clear of the desk. Candles followed, extinguished by the force of their displacement, and spilled their wax over the dark rug while quills and inkwells added yet more black stains to the aged collection. Paperweights landed with a dull thud and rolled out noisily onto the wooden floor.

He kicked the desk; he threw his chair; the teapot set safely upon the sideboard at the edge of the room shattered, it seemed, even before his malicious contact. And he yelled. He cursed. He vowed that, in the end, *he* would come out on top, and that *all* Turunda's enemies would crumble under his hand, be they man, elf or king. He vowed it to Teagan, to Taliel, to himself, to the stars that twinkled indifferently outside the window. He would see it done. Whatever it took.

Exhaustion forced him at last to stop. He leaned over his desk, bracing himself against the dizziness while his body continued shaking in fury, and he stared through the wood grain for an explanation.

His spells *couldn't* be failing him. They *couldn't* be. *He* hadn't seen anything preceding Koraaz's strike, but he couldn't be in that room watching those mirrors forever. It could only have been one of the handful he'd left in charge of it - because the accursed old coot had gotten one thing right, at least: someone *must* have heard something.

Unless the elves were using their magic to keep Koraaz's movements hidden, in which case his arcane eyes could *never* have caught him. And they never would.

His fingernails, as sharp and tapered as claws, raked deep into the polished wood. He forced himself to breathe. It was only a theory. If the elves were concealing him so dearly, why had he ever been spotted at all? It could be tactical, but too often he'd been spotted and followed with no ill consequences, which suggested that the elves were either doing a *poor* job of hiding him, or weren't hiding him at all.

His fingers relaxed a little.

But whatever Malson *had* gotten right, he was remarkably incorrect in his assumption that it had been an act of the Order. Koraaz - he was now *certain* - was not working with the Order. He'd seen enough from Liogan to know that *he* was disdainful to her. Fully-human mages - or as close to human as one possessing magic could be - would be too far beneath her to even be looked at. He suspected most elves would feel the same. Which would explain why Koraaz was never seen around another Order mage. He was working within a whole other league.

But allegiances aside, it seemed that Koraaz and the Order alike were about to be joined by a new internal threat. Like an old man whose stubborn convictions were finally revealed as little more than a mask for his own fear and elderly confusion, General Moore was proving himself more fool than wisened tactician. At this rate, if Doana *did* finally make the first strike, he wouldn't move until they were already razing the palace.

And Malson seemed almost *pleased* that he hadn't taken Salus's poisoned bait! Did he *want* this to drag out? Or was he just naive enough to believe that all was well while no blood was being shed?

He exhaled tightly. Moore would need yet another push - something far more direct.

As his heart returned to a near-normal rhythm, he pushed himself away from the desk and lifted the ink-spattered roll of parchment from beneath the disarray of folders and reports. He didn't cast either subordinate a look, and so he didn't notice the fright within Taliel's wide eyes, nor the edge of uncertainty that had creased Teagan's face into an expression of concern.

He read for but a moment before his rampage resumed.

"*Fools!*" He bellowed finally, screwing up the ripped parchment and hurling it violently to the ground. "The magic *couldn't* just 'deplete', not just like that!"

"How can you be sure?" Teagan asked, lifting the missive from beside his foot and glancing over the contents.

"Because I have *felt it*, Teagan," he hissed. "I have *touched* it. No. It isn't so simple. It was Koraaz, it *had* to be. He appeared in Ferna out of nowhere, he could just as easily have been at White Barrows, too. Why not?! He's been teleporting around since Dolunokh!"

"And another strike by non-humans." Teagan cocked an eyebrow at the parchment while Salus swore disdainfully. "Harpies and ditchlings, together. Again."

"And that *surprises* you? *Nothing* we do stops them! They hide in trees and holes in the ground, well out of sight! How can we *ever* be sure an area has been cleared without burning the trees and flooding every hollow?! They're like rats! They're everywhere, hiding *just out of sight!* And they've killed *another* of my men!"

"Perhaps we're underestimating them?"

"Evidently," he replied dryly. "They've been getting bolder since they started working together. It's proving successful for them, and they recognise that. For those that lack intelligence, there is strength in numbers..." His eyes searched the air, and the hard edge to his face, human once again, softened as thought descended. Both Teagan and Taliel sent him a brief glance, each successfully concealing their own private concern. His expression brightened for a fleeting moment, the darkened once more. "Burn and flood the forests."

"Sal--Sir," Taliel stammered in shock, "forgive me, but that would--"

"Not at the same time," he growled tediously. "Flood some, burn others - whichever will have the smallest impact on the nearest settlements. We have to keep them apart!" His searing gaze dropped to his bare and splintered desk, then to the mess that surrounded it. He uttered not a sound of irritation as he gathered the papers from the floor and dropped them back onto the table, sorting through them quickly, filtering out the folders bound with white string and those bound in brown. The phidipan and portian waited in silence while he compared and discarded, made notes and muttered curses beneath his breath. Then, finally, he handed a selection to Teagan and fixed him with his still-searing eyes. He seemed not to carry the same fret as his colleague. "See it done."

The portian inclined his head and left.

Taliel eased only slightly when the door closed behind him, and Salus sank, defeated, into his straightened chair, covering his face with his hands. When he finally dropped them, he found her gathering up the rest of his things. "Leave it," he said more coarsely than he'd meant to, and she rose swiftly, placing the map, inkwells, quills and candles she'd already collected carefully back upon the desk. But when he looked up, expecting an empty expression, he found her looking right back at him, her beautiful face twisted in worry.

His heart jumped and softened in an instant, the memory of the first such look she'd given him only a few months ago rushing back to strangle him into shame. His eyes slipped away. "Don't fret about me."

"You're stretched too thin," she said softly.

"I'm fine."

"Have you looked in the mirror? And I don't mean your enchanted ones - you have new lines on your face, you have shadows under your eyes, your jaw is rough, not to mention you're not thinking clearly--"

"I'm *fine*." He smiled in an attempt to offset his waspish tone. "Really."

"No, you're not." She reached out and brushed her fingertips gently over his stubbled cheek. He flinched at first, but didn't pull away, and let her lean in and kiss him. He discovered only then that he'd been yearning for her touch all day. The moment her lips met his, he felt the shadow that had been hanging over him since morning vanish like a fog.

Every knot in his muscles released. His fingers slipped into her hair and he breathed in her scent - the faintest trace of golden juniper, he finally placed, but not of perfume - and lost himself in her.

Until a detached, dutiful voice spoke up in the recesses of his wandering mind.

In a heartbeat his fingers pulled free and he pushed her back, and he rose to stand over his desk, dragging the map out from among the things she'd gathered to stare over it with sudden purpose.

He heard her breathe the softest sigh of frustration, but he didn't let himself look up.

"Why won't you let me help?" She asked softly. He heard the helplessness in the back of her voice, like a shadow beneath her words, but he didn't let that move him, either.

"It's distracting."

"If your mind can wander so easily, perhaps it's trying to tell you something."

"Like what?"

"That you're exhausted. You can't concentrate, you haven't properly rested in a month - you need to take time out. If you keep ignoring what your body is telling you, you'll make yourself ill."

"Old wives' tales."

"Steeped in truth nonetheless."

"I'll sleep when Turunda's safe."

"I didn't say 'sleep', I said 'rest'." She stared at him, willing him to meet her eyes, but he didn't even lift his head. Disappointment bloomed in her chest like a thistle. She moved around to the other side of the desk, and though he didn't show it, he was acutely aware of her every step. His mood dampened further at the crispening of her tone. "You've not sent me out in twelve days. You've given away my previous station in the palace. What are the others doing that you think I can't?"

"It's not like that." Again his voice was involuntarily sharp. "It's too dangerous."

"I will be fine."

"Non-humans are killing operatives, Taliel, Doana are spreading distractions, the Order is attacking, and now Koraaz is..." He didn't have the words. He growled and let it drop. Her slender hands slipped into view as she leaned intently upon the desk.

"I can handle it."

"No."

"Salus, I'm trained to--"

"I said *no!*" His gaze tore free from the map at last and he fixed her with a powerful, scalding look that warned her sorely against challenge. But she didn't flinch back from him, and her brown, copper-ringed eyes were equally as forceful.

"I understand what you're trying to do, but, *Keliceran*, it is my *job*. I have been trained. I am capable. My record doesn't have a scratch. And not all of your subordinates have been so reliable as of late. Your attention is being pulled in too many directions and yet you're not using the Arana's full potential. Count *me* among those pinpointing the non-humans' homes and burrows and you can rest *assured* of results." She held his stare for a long moment and watched him weigh the odds. She'd been a phidipan for near a decade - she was capable, and he knew it. He had no reason to keep her trapped within the walls of Arana House.

No *rational* reason.

She watched him until his gaze dropped again. "I need you here."

"No, you don't. You have Teagan. I am not an *advisor*. I am not a *doll*. I am a *phidipan*, Salus! For the love of the goddess will you let me *help?* You're doubting others, you're under pressure, and the world is trying to race ahead and out of our control! This isn't the time for being *protective*, Salus, it's a time for doing what you must! And who can you trust if not me?!"

His mouth opened to respond ahead of his aggravation, but no sound made it out, and her steady, challenging stare flustered him all the more until his shoulders sagged and he shook his head with a rough sigh of defeat. "You're right." He said it quietly. "Fine. But, *please, be careful*."

"I am never anything but." Then she moved back around at his reluctant gesture and pored over the map beside him, observing various locations while he outlined the regions most likely in need of cleansing.

Lanterns and torches flickered ominously about the city. The tension in the room seemed to escape through the windows to deepen every shadow, and that blackness seeped back inside like a pestilent cloud.

A great sigh heaved in the dark. "We have no idea what he's up to."

"And no communication?"

"None. Not since the first."

Another exhalation, feminine but no less troubled. "Mage hunters will have a field day with this. He needs to be stopped. He needs to be brought in."

"And he should be so easy to find?"

"He may be, if we go about it the right way. We could always try *asking*..."

"He wouldn't do it, Delas. He thinks we turned our backs on him, and there's also the very simple fact that he hasn't come to us for help with the matter, even though he must have realised that it is far beyond his capabilities."

"What if Owan asked him?"

"He would see through it."

"So we're going to abduct him?" Her voice was thick with scepticism.

"I know you're fond of him, Delas, you practically raised him when he came here. But he is not a child anymore."

"And so that justifies it?" She sighed again. "You really think this is wise?"

"Not at all. But I suspect we will have some time to work it out. We can't do much until we know where he is."

"The sparrow seemed to find his companion well enough. A simple beacon attached to--"

"And when the sparrow flies too near an arcanised zone and the hills crack for miles around?"

"Blast. Has Owan discovered a way we can deal with those yet?"

"Not yet. He's working himself ragged with it. Just yesterday I had to *order* him to take a few days off."

"And I expect he bowed and agreed, then scurried off and stitched himself right back into his work."

"As it happens, he did. His wife is watching over him now."

Delas chuckled. "Poor girl. She's about to have a baby and now she has to chase around after her *husband* to make sure he does what he's told. It's good practise, I suppose." She sent Arator a steady look. "I will send word to preservers. They will search for Rathen outside the cities. He won't show his face again so soon."

"No, he won't." The old grand magister met the elder's gaze. "As soon as possible, Delas."

"As soon as possible."

Chapter 45

The tamer woods of the Eswolds were no less virile than the Wildlands to the south. Thick boughs dominated the stifled air at head-height, the light was smothered, the dense, green ceilings were filled with the heavy scent of damp wood, fungi and moist earth, and the shadows by the calls of predatory beasts that didn't quite conform to any known profiles. But though the inescapable sense of a watchful presence reached even this far north, it was neither as potent nor as ominous as that which had previously dogged them, and the forest itself impeded in no way out of the ordinary. Three days of difficult trekking passed uneventfully but for crossing paths with a kvistdjur, who dismissed them after a quick assessment, and a run-in with an indignant wood-grouse which Rathen was very insistent about keeping their distance from, to the ends of moving their camp ten minutes from its territory.

But that afternoon, the light had finally brightened, the trees had slimmed, and the air had become cleaner and easier to breathe. An hour later, they emerged at last into the summer sun, its warm glow bathing their faces from across the pastures.

Garon cursed immediately. The sun should have been behind them.

"How did we get turned around?!" He demanded furiously of no one in particular, but as the others looked around in equal confusion, Eyila sent him an impish grin. He met her flatly. "If you say 'winds', I'm leaving you here."

But while Aria declared that she hadn't been woken in the night by any such force, Rathen was pondering his own theories. There was a strange idea coalescing that perhaps another natural force was at work - one with tempestuous eyes of painite - but he couldn't gauge why. Unless, of course, the great Root Mother had finally come to realise that the matter was well beyond his capabilities and simply sought the quickest end. That wouldn't come as any great surprise. But he wasn't about to complain. For once, things seemed to be going his way.

The others stepped out of the trees and into the open landscape. He moved to follow with Aria in hand when a peculiar melancholy set over him. Compelled by something unfathomable, he hesitated at the threshold, lingering in the last reach of the trees as he looked out across the empty fields. The sorrow grew only deeper.

Unbidden, his eyes pulled longingly over his shoulder. At the sight of the leaves, trees, bark and moss, his anguish waned, replaced by that same, singular welcome that had met him when they'd camped in the High Dells. A mournful sigh slipped from his lips.

Aria noticed. With a wonderful, reassuring smile and gentle squeeze of his hand, she encouraged him out behind her. He followed reluctantly, until he heard his name spoken from back along the trees.

All six snapped around to find a lithe figure hurrying towards them on silent feet. Rathen's strange mood evaporated at the sight of her. "Elle? What are you doing here?"

"Warning you."

His smile slackened as she reached him, but he embraced her fiercely never the less. She matched it, and they remained in each other's arms for a long moment while the rest looked on uncomfortably.

"Warning us of what?" Garon interrupted, earning himself a mix of reproach and disapproval from the others, but he ignored them when Taliel's soft, thoughtful eyes hardened gravely and swept over them all as they parted.

"Salus has made a deduction. One I *presume* he's wrong about, but there is no evidence to convince him or anyone else otherwise." Her gaze returned to Rathen, who looked back at her nervously. "He thinks you're working with the elves. If you aren't one yourself."

His harsh face broke into a sudden grin of confusion, and he laughed at the absurdity. She proceeded to explain the connections her superior had made between his sudden appearances and disappearances, his power, his absence from the Order, his acquisition and use of the Zi'veyn, and how he'd tied it all so neatly into the incident at Ferna.

"The thorns and guardians receded yesterday," she informed them as he stared at the ground and sifted the matter.

"Two days of watch," Anthis mused. "In keeping with holy observations - it took two days and two nights without food or water for Thu'ulak to repent his slaughter of a neighbour's prize pig. The spells were meant as discouragement, though, so--"

"Thank you, Anthis." Garon looked firmly back to the phidipan. "What does he plan to do about this?"

"As of yet, I don't know."

"Well what *else* has he been doing? In the last three to four weeks - what's happened? Where has he struck? And when?"

"Easy, Garon," Rathen bristled at his aggression, and turned back to her himself to poise the question more calmly. "What has he done since we last met?"

And she told them. Eyila was appalled by the report of his attempts to provoke both Doana and General Moore into battle, Anthis was personally uneased by both sides' focus upon his resident city of Kora, Rathen was worried by both his array of surveillance spells and his successful extension of a chasm all the way across the northern border from the Pavise Mountains to Dustwatch, and Taliel was, herself, more than a little surprised that the union between harpy and ditchling was their own doing.

But every one of them took on a deathly pallor when the attack on Bowden was raised.

"He was *there?*"

"Yes," she replied tersely. "Searching for Doana's lockbox at the very same time *you* were there, pushing your luck. It's fortunate that you didn't cross paths! Vastal knows what could have happened. Though, it is ironic that if he hadn't been there himself, he would have seen you in one of his mirrors..."

"Mirrors?"

"He's feeding the surveillance spells into them - the idea was that he could look in, but those he was looking at couldn't look back." She shrugged while they exchanged looks of abstract amusement. "As it is, one of my...like-minded colleagues was monitoring them at the time. You got away with it by nothing more than sheer dumb luck."

"It seems to be a recurring theme," Anthis noted.

"And as for what he's doing now, his attention is focused on Doana, but you are a close second for priority. He's no doubt trying to find a way to stop you, and more enthusiastically than before."

"Isn't there something *you* can do?" All eyes turned to Garon at his flagrant accusation. "You're working with Elias Malson and other 'colleagues', as you call them, but what are *you* all doing about it? What have you done to slow him down? Impede his magic? You're in the best position out of *all* of us to make a difference and what have you got to--"

"*Enough*, Garon." The inquisitor's black, challenging glare flicked sharply onto Rathen, and he met it with his own caustic scowl. His voice dropped dangerously. "Don't you forget for a *moment* that Elle is risking her life by telling us this. *Every* time she comes to us she puts her life on the line, and she knows better than any of us what her punishment would be. Don't you dare question her loyalty."

"The very fact that she's here telling us all of this *at all begs* the question of her loyalty."

Rathen's lip twitched into a snarl, and he squared towards him with an expression that turned even darker against possibility. But he said nothing beyond that powerful stare, and Garon presented no challenge beyond holding it for a moment, then turning away of his own accord and surveying their surroundings instead.

Rathen straightened in silent victory, but he quickly joined the others beneath their thick cloud of fret.

"There must be something we can do," Petra said at last, stirring the heavy silence. "If he's taking on tasks himself rather than leaving them to others, and if we're going to carry on running around, removing the magic he's trying to use *and* he thinks Rathen is working with elves..." she let it hang. Everyone looked back at her; they knew what she was moving towards, but they each hoped they were wrong. She sighed and finished if just to shake off their anxious eyes. "It's inevitable that we're going to come to blows with him. Directly."

"Then we use his weaknesses to our advantage," Anthis said with a thick frown, arms still folded tightly in thought. "He's relying on his magic - these watchful spells, mirrors, handling matters himself. And, no doubt, he's overestimating himself because of it. Who wouldn't, after gaining magic out of the blue like that? And *elven* magic, no less. But he's only been in tuition for a matter of months, and with Rathen *and* the Zi'veyn...I think we could have some kind of fighting chance. We just need to find out what those weaknesses are..." He looked up hopefully towards Taliel, but the phidipan could only shake her head.

"I would tell you if I knew. But you're right: his knowledge is thin, and he does have too much confidence in it."

"That isn't enough..." Rathen picked at his lip as he spiralled deeper into thought, staring through the grass and well beyond while his face twisted slowly in repugnance, an inward battle raging between mutually unfavourable choices. When he finally looked up, kneading his unhappy decision into more delicate words, he found Garon and Elle each watching him.

"You want to provoke him," the inquisitor said in a quiet voice that belied his disbelief.

"We have the Zi'veyn," he explained quickly, "and he *knows* that, so he won't come after us alone. But if we plan ahead, find out where he'll be, we can *stay* ahead."

"He'll bring *mages*," he reminded him pointedly, still shaking his head, incredulous to what he was hearing. "And - Anthis said it - he has *elven* magic, Rathen."

"Could we not use the Zi'veyn against him?" Eyila suggested, but Rathen had begun shaking his head, too.

"If we forget that he's only *part*-elf, then, at best, it will weaken him. But it'll occupy my magic to use it whether it works or not, and if he brings mages with him - *human* magic, which the Zi'veyn *can't* affect - then there will be no one to stop *them*. You've not been trained as I have, *or* as Salus's mages have, and while you are, frankly, incredible at what you *have* been taught, in this situation there's only so much you can do." He glanced towards her apologetically, but she didn't seem at all offended, and nodded instead at the compliment.

"Could you not bind them, then?" Petra asked.

"If he brings two mages, the second could counter-spell the first's bonds before I can get to him."

"Unless you taught Eyila how to do it."

"Yes," he said slowly, "I could - but that would still leave Salus unoccupied."

"Only for a moment."

"And that could be all it takes."

"And while he is over-confident in his own abilities," Taliel added, "he's shrewd. He knows you're powerful, Rathen. He wouldn't bring just one mage."

Garon turned away slowly in bewilderment, still shaking his head to himself and muttering something beneath his breath. He looked out over the fields, awash in golden light, but of course he didn't see them. Finally he spoke up. "This is...mad... Madness. That's what this is."

"It's also inevitable."

He sighed heavily and hung his head. The others watched him in patient silence until he rolled his head back and looked hopelessly towards the sky. "It is. I know it is... And...far better that we're prepared for it when it does come crashing down..." He sighed again and turned back to them, but though his grey eyes pinned each of them with severe consideration, he didn't speak again for a while. His eyes locked onto Rathen. "Can we be sure the Zi'veyn won't work on humans?"

"Yes." He shrugged the bag off of his back and withdrew the palm-sized relic. Garon and Anthis each looked quickly to Taliel, but she only peered at it with a touch of wonder and her hands remained behind her back.

When Rathen turned with it directly towards Eyila, the young woman stumbled back a step, her eyes wide in alarm. He held it loosely and closed his eyes, leaving her to look frantically across the others, hoping someone would step in and stop him. But it had already begun to float between his palms.

"Uh, Rathen--"

"She'll be fine." His tone was unaffected; he seemed to have no trouble at all in operating the relic while there was no magic around to addle him, and his ease silently impressed a great many of them. "Eyila: cast something."

Though frightened, she found some kind of reassurance in his poise. So she collected herself and raised her hands to her chest, aware all the while of the beat of her heart and the heat of the blood in her veins. Her fingers twisted into brief, swift signs. Rathen flew backwards and struck the trunk of a tree.

A gasp of surprise burst from the group, and a few may then have chuckled. Aria, trying to hide her own amusement, rushed to his side to make sure he was okay with Eyila close behind her, apologising all the while.

"She did tell us she could defend herself, as I recall," Petra reminded him with a grin as he rose stiffly back to his feet, and Anthis hurried to snatch the Zi'veyn from the ground.

"Yes, I remember... Well, my point is proven: it won't work on human magic."

Garon nodded gravely while Rathen winced and rubbed his tailbone. "Shall we assume, then, that it won't work on him at all?"

"We might be better off."

"In that case, we won't be able to do much with just the six of us. We can attack and use the element of surprise, but to test weaknesses we'll have to linger, which means we won't be able to flee in the confusion. We will need allies. Allies Salus wouldn't expect..."

Rathen frowned at him carefully. "...You mean Elle's--"

"No. Others." He looked pointedly at Taliel. "And we'll leave it at that."

Rathen glared, but he didn't attempt to argue. Whoever these 'others' were, he would reveal it when it mattered. And...perhaps it wouldn't hurt to keep one or two things from her...

"When can we do it?" Eyila asked.

"Not for some time," Garon replied, and even Rathen was forced to agree.

"We're not remotely ready. It will take planning. And we're getting ahead of ourselves either way - the Order is still our best bet."

"All right," Garon snapped, whirling on him like a viper, "you're pushing for it. How *exactly* do you propose we get into Kulokhar without getting ourselves arrested? Or *killed?*"

"You want to go to the *Order?!*" Taliel stared at him in such horror that he shrank back a step. "Rathen, have you lost your mind?!"

"No, I haven't--look, just calm down - they can *help* us."

"Help? Rathen, they're *hunting* for you, they want to bring you in!"

Garon barked a humourless laugh. "My question stands."

"Why are they looking for him?" Anthis asked more calmly, but it was Rathen who gave the bitter answer.

"Because of Ferna. Of course. I've put the Order in an even worse light. The rebellion is bigger than me, but the threat *I* pose can be eradicated by just imprisoning me." He closed his eyes tightly and pressed the heels of his hands against his forehead as if to push together a solution to his once-perfect plan.

Anthis, however, merely blinked. "Well...doesn't that mean we have our in, then? Can't we just *let* them find us?"

"No, we'll be taken as prisoners. Ferna or not, whatever it is that has forced the Order to acknowledge I'm out here and try to bring me back can't be good for us. It's best that *we* go to *them* and pick carefully who we reveal ourselves to. Maybe we can...sneak in somehow..."

"'Sneak in somehow' - plan of the century," Garon retorted dryly. "Look, you may have some idea where these transformations come from, but the Order is still none the wiser. They *will* prosecute you without question."

"That may be true," Rathen growled impatiently, "but Owan has said that no one in the Order believed it was as simple as--" His face suddenly lit up. "Owan! We can send word to Owan!"

"The lone, aggressive mage we found lurking around Stonton?"

"Aggr--what? No, he--"

"And what if *Owan* doesn't trust you anymore? What if the incident in Ferna has altered even *his* stalwart opinion of you? What if he agrees that you need to be brought in?"

"No." He shook his head almost petulantly. "No, we can trust him."

"You've said that before and there's been little to confirm it."

"And nothing at all to deny it. We can trust him."

"My sister," Petra offered slowly.

"But she's in the military, isn't she?" Anthis asked. "They're mobilised..."

"That doesn't mean she's outside the city...but, no. She *could* be against me. Owan, I know, but your sister joined the order *after* my banishment and no doubt shares the popular opinion that I am a monster, some black mark on the Order's past. She could vouch for *you*, but she'd take no small amount of convincing for me, and if she's not receptive, that's the end of it. But Owan knows me personally, and he knows what we've been doing. Don't make faces, Garon, he's a scholar, he's intuitive. And if he *has* been persuaded against me, it will still be a far easier matter to bring him around. He's our only option..."

"We can use Midsummer to our advantage," Anthis suggested. "Everywhere's alive with it - it would help us slip by unnoticed. We could be there in a week, maybe less."

"And Owan has some means of using the White Hammer's sparrows. If we go to the nearest White Hammer outpost, we can use a sparrow to get word to him and he can find some means of shielding us from the Arana's eyes in the city."

"*If* we do this," Garon sighed with sufferance, "we need a solid plan. There's an outpost in Eselon; we could be there in three hours."

"A solid plan in three hours?" Petra looked doubtful.

"Not necessarily - if we let Owan know that we're heading his way and that we need his help getting into the city without being seen, *he* can work something out and send the details back to us."

"It would all be in his hands. You're putting an awful lot of faith in him."

Rathen sighed irritably. "Yes, well, friendships are like that."

"But I thought you weren't that close anymore."

"Who *am* I close with anymore? Bonds aside, this is the only reliable option we have." He gave the inquisitor a long and steady look. "We *have* to do this. People are in danger, Garon."

"You realise that our antics at Ferna will have undone all our sneaking around?" Petra reminded them carefully. "Those posters are doubtlessly still up, and it seems that people *are* looking for us."

"But surely the incident at Ferna would discourage anyone else from confronting him? Assuming anyone even believes he was there - stone thorns and moving statues are unbelievable already. Throw him into the mix and it's nothing short of ridiculous. Surely..."

"One can only hope." Garon loosed a flat sigh and shook his head to himself one more time. "I'll go into Eselon alone either way. And all of you...you just be careful." He fired Taliel a warning glance, but this time Rathen could only find it comical. He sorely doubted that Garon was capable of seeing through any such threat towards her.

She certainly knew the same, but she returned it with a nod of assurance anyway, and the look in her own eyes was one of familiar promise. Rathen knew that an assurance given with that look was one she had no intention of breaking - by her efforts or anyone else's.

But those eyes then turned onto him, and they softened with a more personal concern. "Can we have a moment?"

"Don't you always?"

While the others turned to their own business, the pair stepped back into the trees, leaving Aria in Petra's vigilant care. Rathen felt himself relax as leaves closed around him once again, until Elle considered him with a despairing confusion.

"Why ever would you want to go to the *Order*, Rathen?" Her voice was soft as she wrapped her slender, sun-kissed arms comfortingly about herself. "After...after everything that's happened?"

"Because if Salus is going to keep stressing these chasms and he's that over-confident, someone is going to get hurt. The Order needs to be informed of his strength and plans so they can raise defences and save lives from his foolishness."

"It will be dangerous. You *know* this."

"It's necessary."

"The Arana has spies in there."

"The Arana has spies everywhere."

"And you will bring Aria into their reach?"

His eyes hardened into steel. This time, she shrank back. "She will be *safe* with me. I am *not* leaving her behind again. Anyway: why are *you* out here? You only slip out when you have orders. What are you doing?"

"I am hunting."

"Let me guess: for harpies and ditchlings?" He sighed as she nodded. "Here?"

"No - Korovor."

"You *can't* let Salus kill them, Elle. He surely doesn't see them as a real threat, just a nuisance - but I can't shake the feeling that they and their alliance will be *crucial* for us before too much longer, if just because he underestimates them. We *need* to use that - *both* of us do. We helped them settle their dispute, even if it's just for the moment, and for that, they've already given us their aid."

"Scrambling into the keliceran's office? A daring group, I have to admit..."

He blinked. "*You* were in there?"

"I was. And I told no one. They left a muddy mess, though, so I had to send someone in to clean up. Daring, but none too mindful. If I'd not been in there at that moment, Salus would have identified the prints and...well, I shudder to think of the 'preventative' measures he'd have taken." She cocked an eyebrow at his confusion. "Why did I leave them alone? Who are you talking to, my love? I knew you had dealings with them - though I have to admit, I didn't realise you'd entered into such levels of *diplomacy*."

"That's using the term a little wildly, there." His gaze hardened imploringly again. "We *need* them, Elle."

"Yes, I know you do. But there are many holes and eyries studding our forests - not all of which are occupied. Perhaps they saw me and fled."

"Reporting abandoned warrens? That won't cast a good colour on your record."

"I'm sure it will be fine."

"Elle, you can't afford to slip up. You could...if he finds out that you're *sabotaging* him--"

"Then I'll think of something else. Let me worry about it, my love. I know the danger he poses far better than you. And he won't suspect me of sabotage."

"How can you be so sure?"

She smiled at him softly, with the most earnest promise. "Because I know what I'm doing."

He searched her eyes for a long moment, seeking any clue to the source of her confidence or for some hint she was laying down to soothe him without saying too much. If anything was there, he couldn't find it.

A cool breeze rustled through the branches above them, carrying the scent of meadows. Finally, defeat weighted his shoulders. He sighed heavily, shaking his head, and his eyes paced over the tree roots and thin, shaded grass. They bore a whisper of heartache when they lifted back to her. "You can't keep coming to us. You're going to get caught. We're being tracked, you know this - why risk it?"

Her smile didn't change as she brushed his hair back at his temples. "You seem to forget who I am. What I've been doing for twenty five years." She took his hand as his pale face twisted in exasperation, but rather than challenge her skill, he squeezed her fingers and pulled her close. She returned the embrace fervently. But as she rested her cheek against his collarbone and allowed herself to get lost in his familiar hold, decade-old memories shattered the unobtainable moment. She held him tighter as fear crept up her spine. "Are you all right?"

He didn't need to ask what she'd meant. His own memories merely days old and whose confusion was still much too fresh strangled his own peace away. But he didn't answer. She squeezed him softly, as though she'd heard his silent thoughts.

When she stepped back, dragging with her the last of their contact's bliss, she offered him a smile both sympathetic and heart-wrenching. "You have things to think about."

"No, Elle--"

"I'll find you tonight. You'll know when I'm there." She leaned up and kissed the dejected bow of his lips, closing her eyes against his disappointment. He was late to return it, and pulled her back when she began to leave. They remained with each other, troubled, daunted and shaken, neither speaking a word of it. When he finally let her go, she stepped away backwards, and they watched one another until she disappeared.

He found leaving the pacifying trees twice as hard the second time.

They'd discussed the matter at length by the time the old and unremarkable town of Eselon appeared over the hills, but they had agreed upon nothing. Rathen was the most qualified to comment on what was and was not magically possible, and what was and was not within the skills of the mages on hand during wartime, but he had also not set foot in the city for eleven years and had no idea of the advances the Order had made, never mind changes to the city itself. Garon, on the other hand, advised on the best routes into the city, none of which worked with Rathen's information, and stood rigidly against alternative suggestions.

Among all of this was talk of who best to avoid - Rathen wanted to speak to the grand magister, while Garon wanted to avoid the head of the Order at all costs. Then just how much to tell them - Rathen was prepared to answer their every question and defuse their hostility, while Garon felt it was only necessary to get in, tell a single reliable individual what *Salus* was doing, and leave.

And so, by the time they'd found a suitable hiding place beside a small if much too recent rockslide, they'd reached no decisions at all. But Garon left anyway, presumably to write more than 'help' and hopefully not naively confident of his own colleagues' trust. Rathen wished someone could go with him and make sure he didn't do anything stupid.

They waited under tension, but the inquisitor was quick to return, message sent and curt words questioning the inherent intelligence of the officer on duty still ringing in the poor man's ears.

"'Under orders of the First Commander'?" Anthis had asked with some scepticism.

"It's not unheard of to incriminate one's self if it means successfully completing orders," Garon had explained, setting them off away from the ominously loose rocks without a moment to lose. "There's no better way to earn a criminal's trust, and it makes for tidier arrests."

"And what if he *does* check up on it?"

Garon grunted in amusement at a thought he failed to share. "He won't."

They didn't stop until the thick of night, recent experiences still riding on their heels, and were rewarded for their patience with an abandoned shack along a hunting track, long-overgrown in the hills. It was cooler within the wooden walls, and they ate their usual rations without a fire beneath the sounds of chirping insects and the occasional creak of wall panels.

Rathen was quick to finish and vanish outside to stare intently through the trees, leaving Aria in Anthis's company, who was only too pleased to watch her - if even a little relieved. The pair sat together with Eyila in a shaft of blinding moonlight to continue reading their book.

Noting and ignoring Rathen's silent departure minutes later, and satisfied by the implications of Taliel's frivolous arrival, Garon watched the three through the broken doorway with a mind of absent thought. As odd as it was to watch a child teach an adult how to read, the young woman appeared to be making progress, and she beamed with no small amount of amazement at her every success. Anthis smiled even broader, and his gaze when it lifted from the page she wrote upon lingered with the most blatant affection.

Garon couldn't understand it, himself - Eyila was much too quiet. She had a firm hand occasionally, but she spent too much time watching, weighing and observing, never giving input. He'd seen little of her personality. She was impossible to read, and her expressions set him on edge sometimes - another culture, perhaps, but being unable to predict her reactions nor read them when they occurred made plans and encounters potentially hazardous. He couldn't bear to think of what would happen when she stepped into Kulokhar. She couldn't be left outside, and they could be subject to the Order's hospitality for a very long while. Imprisoned by it, some might say. The thought made him anxious.

Ten minutes later, Eyila exclaimed victoriously while Aria clapped and Anthis gave her another of his foolish grins. She'd made it ten pages. Of course the script was large and each bore around eleven lines, never mind the illustrations that often occupied half to a full page, but progress was progress and it rounded her education of their own tongue - a tongue she already spoke so smoothly. He wondered absently how many others she could speak - the tribes learned from trade, even the isolated ones, and more countries than Turunda traded in their wares. And it wasn't as surprising as it should have been that the village healer was among those most fluent. Out in the desert, she was traders' only hope of aid if they fell foul of some beast, plant, dust storm or sun beam, and no matter how hostile they might be to 'cityfolk', if they wanted trade to stay open, they needed traders alive.

But Garon couldn't help wondering, as Anthis stared at her again for a fraction too long before tearing his eyes a touch desperately back to the parchment, what had caused the awkward young man to finally shed his discomfort around her. Or, shed enough of it in Aria's company to be able to function rather than turn crimson and babble.

He grunted bitterly to himself. Rathen must have yelled at him, too.

Suddenly, the idea that Anthis could be braver than him rankled like name-calling among toddlers, and his mind stopped free of all other thoughts. Even recognising that juvenility, he continued to let it chafe.

Then he turned away from the house and headed purposefully further up the hill.

Petra wasn't hard to find. Some ways up, overlooking house and slope, she sat quietly against a rock. Her sword, daggers and bolas were piled on the ground beside her, her locket in her hands, but this time she stared off into space, lost in her thoughts while her thumb slowly polished the moon-bathed silver. It wasn't difficult to guess what was on her mind.

Garon slowed his approach and skirted around a short ways so as not to put her off. He came to a quiet stop beside her, and after a silent debate, hushed the domineering voice in his head and sat down on the rock. She didn't look up, and he didn't say anything. When she finally spoke, her tone was so soft that he wondered if she'd confused him with another.

"I'd never killed anyone before I joined you."

That surprised him a little as he thought back to bandits and their near-miss with the phidipan at Nestor. "You've never had any trouble with it..."

She scoffed in distinct disagreement, but didn't elaborate. "The world's better off without them. But the...the bounty hunter was the first who didn't deserve it."

"But you didn't kill him."

"I was going to."

"He had bleak intentions."

"He was doing his job."

He decided not to comment on the fact that his 'job' was entirely voluntary and that no employer was going to hound him over it. As a 'professional' duelist, he supposed she had some unique understanding of the man that escaped him completely.

"I should have killed him," she continued sullenly. "It would have been kinder. I knew what was going to happen...but I thought I could keep Rath...Rathen's attention. I should have known better..."

"And if you had kept his attention, Rathen would have turned on *you*."

She said nothing. Even through the darkness he could see doubt flickering in her eyes as she stared away down the hill, her fingers fiddling unceasingly with the locket. She seemed to become aware of it and clasped them around it instead. "What will my sister think when she sees me?"

"Why should she think anything?"

She didn't seem able to find an answer.

He shook his head at her foolishness, but his tone didn't harden. "You think you've changed. You haven't. You're as stubborn, determined and impossible as ever. She won't see any difference."

"My, you do know how to flatter a girl."

"All right. You're as graceful, beautiful and surprising as ever. Either way, she still won't see any difference." He missed the frown that flickered across her brow, but she didn't raise her head. "You killed in defence. Every single time. Your sister - Celise? She's a soldier. She will be able to appreciate that."

Her lips twisted, not unattractively, and she breathed a heavy sigh. "I guess... She never fully supported my choices, but I suppose she'd be glad to know I can defend people, too. Not just knock seven bells out of them..."

"Yes, well, we can't all choose what we're good at." His lips bowed ever so slightly, but her own remained downturned. His smile quickly fled. "Don't carry shame, Petra. Whether because you killed someone, or because you didn't. You needed his help. How did you expect to throw that bolas if Rathen was running after *you?*"

"I'd have managed." Her tone turned suddenly flat. She was finished with the subject, and seemed to have detected some hint of a phantom insult in his words.

He eased his sigh into a long, silent breath and looked back down towards the old shack. The two sat in silence for a long minute until a red scent, spicy and floral, drifted towards him on an uplifted breeze. He looked back towards her and finally noticed the depth of her hair through the night. "Your hair is red again." He regretted the stupid statement the moment he said it. "I thought you said it stood out too much."

"The copper beneath stands out no less. And the posters aren't in colour. A face is a face. Besides, the Arana is too advanced to go by hair colour alone." She raised her head then, and looked at him askance, hazel eyes suddenly swirling with all too familiar mistrust. "Why are you here? I'm too tired for an argument."

"Good," he replied lightly. "So am I. I'd rather talk."

She cocked a cynical eyebrow. "Talk? What about? Why I'm sitting up here by myself? Why I'm not patrolling? Or, perhaps it's about my father again." She fastened the chain back around her neck and tucked the oval away. "Like, 'why am I not at the Crucible where he would want me to be?' Or, 'why am I not out there looking for his killer even though it's clear there's *nothing* I can do here?' Because I'd love the answer to that, too. Or is it something stupid, like my favourite jump-rope game, or my favourite kind of cake? Why my hair is red? Why I put my life on the line to protect people who are ultimately strangers? Why I worry about *you* when you're so set on doing everything yourself? Why I don't just leave you alone, return to my world, to what I'm good at, and rid myself of your sheer, relentless...*contemptible* pigheadedness?!"

He watched the tempest gather in her eyes, and he wanted to answer, to calm her sudden ire, reassure her that he wasn't out to hurt or belittle her, but out of nowhere a hammer-strike of shock rattled his thoughts to an utterly useless end. In the helpless grip of those screaming green-brown eyes - their volatility suddenly so clear, presenting a keening truth so often shut away, so often manifesting as hatred whenever he was around - he found in them a terrible familiarity.

Instantly, he was thrown back to that misty, elven island, to the moment when those very same eyes had gripped him the first time, as equally unable to suppress the turmoil raging behind them then as now, but through whose chaos he had discerned but one single fact...

He'd thought that hatred was aimed at him. Only now did he realise that it wasn't. Not entirely. He had shut that moment on the island away, dismissed it as nonsense on *both* their parts. But Rathen had been correct - and he had known it himself all along. He'd just chosen to...

'To protect myself.'

He could answer her every question. Now he understood. She'd found something else. And it speared him with shame.

"...Yes." The word slipped out before he realised his lips had moved, and his eyes, he knew, were stupidly wide, and yet he couldn't seem to reduce them.

She didn't seem to notice. "Yes?!" She stared back at him, exasperated. And hateful. "What does 'yes' mean?!"

But still he could only stare, searching her blazing eyes, vexed and wounded and confused. She was distressed. *He* was distressed. He knew it would be best for both their sakes to turn around and leave even before the voice in his head rose to a commanding bellow against the childish and unruly voice that egged him on. Somehow, among the chaos, he managed to find his hands and push himself up. But his feet didn't follow. He leaned over instead, his heart thumping in his skull, and kissed her without a thought.

A cold heat flared swiftly across his cheek, and he heard her voice hiss. "*What* do you think you're doing?!"

He blinked and stared back at her, stunned and stammering, but before he could catch up with the escaping seconds, his heart, dropping in his chest in repugnant humiliation, leapt back into his throat.

Her cheeks had darkened. Her body stilled. Her eyes emptied of every rage and sorrow, glittering instead with a nervous, aching hope that shortened her breath despite the guarded turn of her head. She searched his eyes. He searched hers. They both found confusion; they both found comprehension.

His chest tremored as her eyes dropped to his lips, his own breath quickened, and slowly, assertively, she began to lean in. He didn't let himself shy back.

He caught her warmth, her scent, rosehip and spices, and he breathed it as insatiably as he had that first time. A heartbeat later he felt her breath brush his skin. He braced himself, but still her lips met his long before he was ready. Again her walls crumbled. But this time, his came with them.

In that moment she was, to him, perfectly simple: fragile but convicted, troubled but driven, honourable and moral to a fault. And there was again that thriving flame of passion that drove her every word and reason, concealed beneath that thin, fragile glass guard, carefully contained, easily released, and burning brighter and hotter than anyone could know.

How had he ever let himself ignore this?

'Because it had been for the best.'

His chest sank as a sudden, extinguishing wave of despair crashed over him.

She would not be safe.

His work was dangerous, his orders long and varied. He could be gone for weeks, he could be gone for months; if his quarries discovered her, now or then, whomever they may be, she would be at risk. It couldn't work. There was only one way it could end.

She felt his spirit drop, and she withdrew with a disappointment so fierce it seemed to physically strike him. He opened his eyes as she did, discovering the pained twist to her exquisitely sharp features, and found his head already shaking and his hands grasping her imploringly by the shoulders. But she only looked back at him in helpless confusion, one that ignited both desperation in his eyes and self-loathing in his gut.

She shrugged herself out of his hold. Her voice was whispered torment. "I don't understand. You...Garon, I just...you keep sending me all these mixed signals--"

"No." His hands returned, and he locked her eyes with a mixture of regret and promise so powerful that it could have stood tangibly between them. His jaw hardened, and he shut down the voice in his head, once and for all. "Not anymore." He leaned in and kissed her again, firmer, hungrier, and she moved in to meet it despite herself. His hands ran down her toned back, hers around his waist; the warmth of the other's breath prickled the skin to chills. Both of their minds rolled to a stop, the movements of the other silencing all thought and concern for what could have become eternity.

They remained on the hill beneath the moon for some time, the night quiet but for the hoot of owls, breathy whispers and the occasional rattle of steel as discarded blades were knocked with foot or elbow.

Chapter 46

It was dark; the first grey traces of morning were just beginning to glow in the north-eastern sky. Before long the birds would start to sing, chasing out the insects' layered chorus and heralding the forage of animals within the tangle of trees and undergrowth. But, inside the shack's broken walls, it was still as black as pitch, what holes in the wood offering little entry to the bleak, washed out light. The squatters would sleep longer with no daylight to rouse them. But that was just as well if they couldn't see, as they'd certainly stumble over one another if they were to try to leave - unless, of course, one sat still in the darkness for long enough. A practised eye would adjust, and in time would be able to make out the bodies and blankets and belongings littering the dusty floor. Like the beaten and tired old notebook that lay on the ground just inside the doorway, pulled back into the confines of shadow and out of the path of any beast or deluge that might ruin it. Or the equally weathered satchel that stood on the other side of the sleeping body. The body that lay still and silent beneath the blanket, back turned trustingly to the door, a part of the shadow itself.

A fragment of the darkness broke off towards it.

Anthis opened his eyes, awakened by a rough kick to his shin. He grumbled inwardly, his throat too dry to manage itself, and he peered slowly through the darkness for who or what had been so rude when it was still quite clearly night time. It took a while to adjust to the smothering darkness, and he thought for a sluggish moment that his eyes were still closed until he spotted vague movement in the shrouded doorway.

It still took a gruelling length of time to process it, at which point he concluded that it was a beast, then moved to wake the others. If it was a wildling, it may not attack - but there was no knowing if Hlífrún had spoken to this one or not.

The beast had already vanished by the time he reached out to whomever lay behind him, and only then did it sink in that the beast had been awfully top-heavy. And had had four lifeless, dangling limbs.

It was only as his hand finally found and shook a leg that he spotted the scuffed and empty blanket beside him. The blanket - this, he processed much more quickly - was Eyila's.

The situation crashed down around him like a deafening clap of thunder.

He scrambled to his feet, sleep forgotten, and dug around for his knife while a voice distorted by the grip of slumber answered the rude awakening. He didn't respond, but his haste was enough. As he fled out of the door, only just missing the book on the ground, Rathen roused himself, made sense of the matter as rapidly as he could, and immediately raised the alarm, shaking awake every limb he could find.

Anthis bounded through the woods. He ran blind in the heat of panic, loping over the hills, tearing past trees, snapping fallen twigs and dry roots beneath his feet. He had no idea how many minutes had passed since he'd watched her be carried away, nor if he was even running in the right direction, but his mind wouldn't focus long enough to muddle anything out of it until his foot finally caught on some rock or root and he hit the ground hard enough to hear a crack in his wrist. In the time it took him to scramble back up, he'd lost his bearings completely, and logic was finally given opportunity to beat its way in.

'Stop,' he told himself as he panted for breath, 'and think.' There were no tracks to be seen in the darkness, and he could hear nothing over the insects. But these people wouldn't leave tracks, and they wouldn't make a sound. But he didn't need them to. He was a hunter, himself - and he rarely used tracks *or* sound to find his targets.

He closed his eyes and breathed, concentrating as best he could, wrangling his desperation back under control as he had so many times before.

It took only three racing heartbeats to find them.

There should have been few to no noteworthy souls out in these woods, and those that were, he could account for. There were four behind him - that added up - and two more up ahead, moving quickly away from him. One had a familiar feel, a radiance he recognised immediately, but the other was much darker, a shadow in comparison, and desolate. He recognised this one, too, if distantly; he'd passed many like it throughout his life. And increasingly often, as of late

His blood ran cold. There was no doubt. It was the Arana, after all.

He needn't have coaxed his feet to move.

Anger rapidly thawed his veins and he set off with honed determination, Rathen and Garon falling in behind him, pounding their way along the kidnapper's trail without a word between them. The sky had begun to lighten - or perhaps there were more frequent breaks in the leaves - when another chill clawed up Anthis's spine.

He stopped abruptly, the others almost tripping behind him, and his eyes grew wide with fear.

There was another presence, a lone individual even darker and more desolate than the first, to the point that he wondered if that soul was a soul at all. It seemed almost empty, and yet so very exquisite at the same time; someone who neither loved nor hated what they did with their lives, but carried it through with the utmost dedication. Someone who lived for it, but did not thrive - *couldn't* thrive. He'd felt something like this a few times in the past, too, and he liked it even less now. Perhaps because, this time, he understood what it was.

And the pair were making straight for it.

His jaw clenched tightly. "There's a portian out there..."

Garon snarled a vile string of oaths. "Did Taliel lead them here?!"

"*Of course not!*" The blanching mage hissed in return, then turned to Anthis, forcing control back into his eyes. "How do you know it's a portian?"

"Because I can feel it," he replied impatiently. "We have no hope of winning against it, do we? *Then we need hurry up!*"

Garon nodded agreement, at which Anthis immediately darted ahead, and sent Rathen a single, instructing glance before rushing on after him, his hands ready at hilt and scabbard.

Rathen stayed where he was and scrutinised the darkness with purpose, beating his thoughts into submission and his efforts onto what he could do. His ears pricked at the two pairs of footsteps approaching quickly from behind, one smaller and slower than the other.

"What is it?" Petra whispered from beside him, but the soft waver in her voice suggested that she already had some ideas.

Aria gripped his leg tightly, panting from the exertion, and he laid a comforting hand on her shoulder. As twisted as it was, he was glad she was there. Even if Petra hadn't guessed the extent of the trouble, she couldn't have left her behind. She wouldn't have had a chance even had it been the Arana's lowest ranks skulking through those hills.

Petra similarly paled when Rathen corrected her assumptions.

"I'm going to locate him so we can keep him at a distance - distract him, delay him, anything I can from here. Anthis and Garon have gone on ahead to intercept the other." His hands were already freed, and while Petra and Aria stared sharply through the woods, his fingers began to twist in a rapid chain of shapes.

He hissed in surprise as he faltered. The pain that immediately seared in his arm was quick to dampen his effort. It was only in that moment that he realised he'd not suffered more than an offhand warmth from the cuff since Rowan's Repentance almost a month ago.

He growled dangerously and heaved it to the back of his mind. As racking as it was, he couldn't afford to think about it. He increased his efforts even as the burning swelled again, and pushed forwards with urgency.

It caught like an oiled rag. His shoulder, neck and skull were set aflame, his eyes saw white, and agony rampaged through his body along every nerve from his spine. He arched, convulsed, hit the ground as hard as had he thrown himself down. And it didn't stop with his casting.

"Rathen?!" Petra whispered sharply, but he didn't reply beyond involuntary grunts between spasms. She tried again, and Aria beside her, eyes as big as saucers, but he curled only tighter into a ball. Intense torment deepened every line in his face. His eyes and jaw were clamped shut.

A curse slipped from the duelist's lips. She dropped her sword and knelt beside him to shake him out of his fit instead, but the moment her fingers touched him, she hissed and withdrew, stung by a spark of light. She frowned in confusion, shook her head and tried again, but was rewarded with another bite from a sudden tendril of lightning.

"Do something, Petra," Aria begged in a heart-wrenching panic, "*please!*"

But there was nothing she could. A shield enveloped him, cast from some kind of magic, though she hadn't seen him weave it - assuming it was his doing at all. Perhaps the portian had done this to him - Rathen was the greatest threat in their company, and now he had been removed.

She caught Aria before she could try to shake him, and fired her eyes back into the trees while the child thrashed and wailed in her arms, both of their hearts breaking.

They were moving fast. Too fast. Eyila and her captor would reach the portian in minutes, or the portian would break away and come to them. Urgency set a fire beneath Anthis's feet, and he stalked even further ahead of the inquisitor. He could feel they were close - but they must have known they would pursue. They had a plan, he was sure of it. And he was likely charging right into it.

Shouts from ahead shattered the encroaching dawn. Thoughtlessly, Anthis broke into a run. He barrelled through the trees, grunts and growls and snapping twigs leading his way, until he came upon two figures grappling in the dirt. A shaft of moonlight illuminated Eyila's hair and glinted from the blade in the hand of the man pinning her down. They were both bloodied, but it was impossible to tell who it belonged to in that single moment he granted himself to gather his bearings.

Garon didn't stop beside him to assess, but Anthis was still faster.

He closed the space in three bounds and in a single, powerful leap, threw himself into the phidipan and ripped him clear off of her. Garon was there in an instant, pulling Eyila away to safety, but the young woman fought him in a vehement attempt to move back in, her visage a mask of ferocity. Garon restrained her easily enough, but her relentless strength and venom surprised him.

Securing his grip, his attention fell immediately back to the others. Anthis wrestled with the kidnapper in equal fury; they grunted, kicked and punched, drawing injury on the other with every third strike while the moonlight bounced indifferently off of blades and smears of fresh blood.

He saw the look in Anthis's eyes.

Garon turned Eyila away from the skirmish, but she spun back immediately. He turned her again and she replied with a new unreadable look, but one that could only have been frustration. "I need to help him," she declared in a tone just petulant enough to muddy courage into foolishness.

"He doesn't need any help. Do not turn back around." He fixed her with a firm, dark look, which she challenged with eyes of icy fire. But she obeyed.

Her body turned rigid under tension even as she shaped a flame at Garon's command, and despite the sounds of struggle just paces away from them, he began calmly checking her over for injuries. She soon began to shake, which was to be expected, but the swaying and crumpling were not. He caught her as her knees gave out beneath her and sat her down on the dirt, looking into her drowsy face which only a moment ago had been so alive and enraged. This was more than shock.

"You've been drugged," he surmised, straining against the thin dawn light to examine her eyes, and she nodded sluggishly.

"Er...raani..."

Eraani. A numbing solution of alcohol and poisonous plant extracts from the mountains. She'd recognised it even in her disorientation. That had probably saved her life. Rather than the temporary paralysis that would come with the heat of panic, she would only suffer from lethargy and heavy limbs. It was fortunate that it didn't react to adrenaline.

And then, in a moment, it was done. A decisive plunge of a knife, a string of murmurs, an alarmed gurgle that faded into a final breath, and then a single sigh of relief.

Eyila held her dizzy breath. She didn't dare to look around. Her only spark of hope came from Garon's lack of concern.

It took a long while for footsteps to sound behind them, but Anthis said nothing when he returned, as composed as he could be, and Garon still didn't look up from searching the blood on her legs. Only then did she begin to notice her own state.

There were streaks all over her, some thin and dark, others wide and vague, and her dirty, forest-mottled clothes were torn. But her injuries were minimal - a few cuts and scratches, a few marks that would bruise green, others purple, and for the most part, the blood was not her own. Garon noted with approval the bloodied rock on the ground as he rose, then turned his attention to Anthis.

Her drowsy eyes landed on him at last, and her heart dropped instantly. He was as bloody as she was and yet had suffered worse, but while Garon searched out the young man's wounds through his equally torn clothes, and one notable cut down the inside length of his forearm, she frowned sadly at the strange quality in his eyes. Elation, perhaps, mixed with shame. Then she felt the hum of magic that surrounded him.

Much too late, she understood what had happened, and why he couldn't bring himself to meet her eyes. So she took care of it herself.

He blinked in astonishment when she pushed herself up and slipped her shaking arms around him, and thanked him in a breath from the very depths of her heart. Slowly, his arms wrapped around her in return, and he held her as she teetered.

"We're not done yet," Garon reminded them ominously, stepping back from the historian, satisfied that none of his wounds were too serious for his arcane payment to fix, "there's another. We have to be away from here *now*--"

It was as slight as a whisper, and yet it oppressed all thought and function; a rustle of movement, a twig snapping as if by courtesy to inform them of their impending annihilation. All three of them froze. And in one immediate, offensive moment, the situation unravelled.

The air shook with a blast of power, deflected from the darkness as quickly as Anthis had loosed it to ricochet back through the trees, towards and past them, trailing heat and static to end with a crack and a grunt. They followed it, and found a form caught within a tree trunk, crashed with force into the hold of the bark. At that fleeting glimpse, he appeared, to their horror, as a common traveller.

A dark shape surged past them, faster than the wind. A rasp, a choke; the dazed traveller's hands rose sluggishly to his throat where the figure had suddenly snatched him, and his body lifted from the indented bark, raised as if he weighed nothing. Then, an unholy snap. His head rolled to one side, what little resistance he'd offered gone.

His body dropped heavily to the ground.

"Well done, Mister Karth," spoke a familiar voice, but there was none of its characteristic warmth. There was only steel.

Garon's hand stilled in its reach for his sword, and Anthis paled as the figure turned around, realising much too late who he had fired at. She bore no humour. Her eyes were frightfully dark.

"Come," she commanded, but before any could turn or take a step, the forest shifted, the darkness deepened, and the air chilled. And a desperate, heart-rending sob reverberated all around them.

"Thank Vastal," they heard Petra breathe beneath it.

Without a word, Kienza summoned a warm ball of light and dove to her knees beside a form huddled in the dirt. The others moved around beneath a silent cloud of dread. Rathen lay as still as death.

Kienza reached towards him despite Petra's sharp warning, and began probing meticulously every six inches along his body. Small sparks of light fired around her fingertips with each contact, but nothing roused him. They looked on in horror as Aria spun helplessly into Petra's arms, burying her face in her chest and bawling uncontrollably. "Eyila," Kienza said firmly as she busied herself, "what happened?"

"S-someone grabbed me," she managed, shaking even more as she watched the cold sparks while Anthis sat her gently on the ground, suddenly too dazed and frightened to think to offer any help. "Hit me at the back of the head, I-I think...and a cloth, eraani...and carried me out..." She swallowed hard, unable to pull her eyes away from the body beneath with sorceress's passing hands even when Garon moved around to check the back of her head again. "B-but it wasn't me, he wanted Anthis."

"You were bait?" Garon growled, his anger incensed by his own worry.

"N-no, he thought I was him. He s-said so - something about a b-book next to m-me." She swallowed hard, trying and failing to fight back her tears. She said nothing else. No one did. The silence lasted for an age.

Finally, Kienza withdrew her hands and sat back with a deep, troubled sigh. But she didn't turn her eyes away from the still body. The tension in the darkness mounted. "It's his magic," she said at last. She sounded as though she was going to elaborate, but seemed unable to decide. It became gradually clear that she wouldn't.

"Is it the loose magic?" Petra asked, stroking the girl's curls, doing her best to soothe her. "Is it...getting to him?"

"No." No one liked the hopeless certainty with which she'd said it. "It's something within him. Which means there's nothing I can do." The sorceress's emerald eyes closed achingly at the worsening of the child's cries. She gestured to Petra, who passed her gently into her arms. Kienza held her close and rocked her with a hush, then kissed her softly on her forehead. Her sobs began to subdue, then diminish, then she seemed to fall asleep. She carried her a few paces to the side of the large, soily den and lay her down on a thick, soft blanket that appeared on the ground.

"Could the Order not help him?" Garon asked as she stroked the girl's hair away from her face and covered her from the chill, but she shook her head all too readily. She said nothing else as she returned to her lover's side, where she leaned over and placed a long, gentle kiss on his forehead.

A swift exhalation startled them as she smoothly pulled away, and Rathen sat up in a fever, eyes wide and haunted with a terrible shadow, flicking unseeing through the darkness until, finally, they settled on Kienza. She smiled back softly while the others cursed and laughed in their relief, but the joy didn't touch him.

"Where is he?" He demanded, searching through the black again, eyes grim with purpose beside the lingering darkness as he pushed himself to his feet. Kienza placed a firm hand on his shoulder before he could manage.

"Dealt with," she assured him. Then she turned a look to the others, friendly, but one that brooked no argument nor offered explanation. "I must speak with him. You don't need to leave."

"Where are we?" Garon asked quickly, guessing what she as about to do.

"Inside a sett. It's abandoned, don't worry."

"A sett? Ditchlings?"

"No." She turned her back, a campfire sprung into existence, and a wall of silence dropped between them.

Rathen frowned at the eerily quiet flames and the looks of unease on his companions' faces. His own relaxed a great deal, however, when he saw Eyila beside the fire, instructing Petra in her search through the healer's collection of herbs and plants, Garon and Anthis standing over them while Aria slept with unnatural serenity close by. He recognised the touch of Kienza's magic on her sweet, round face.

Partially subdued, his gaze returned to find her staring back at him with an indecipherable expression. It stirred a new terror in his gut. He swallowed hard. "What happened to me?" He wasn't entirely sure he wanted to know.

"In suppressing your transformations," she replied almost clinically, "your magic gets squashed down. Even if you don't succeed in stopping it, the magic is still restricted. But in consciously letting that transformation out and trying to control it, there was nothing to constrict it. It was freed and it was welcomed, as a whole, for the first time in your life." She watched his eyes drift down to his hands. There was nothing to see, but he stared all the same. In time, his gaze rose and penetrated well beyond the thickest depths of the darkness.

"I'd not felt anything more than a warmth in my arm since we were in Banmar Dells," he whispered pensively, "when my...magic..."

She nodded. "I know. And you barely used it after that."

"Only when I had to."

"And it has burned on every occasion since?"

"Yes... I felt something different when I used the Zi'veyn on Eyila, it was just starting when her spell interrupted it and threw the Zi'veyn from my hands. Or, rather, me from the Zi'veyn..."

"And that was the first time you'd cast anything since Ferna?" Her eyes didn't move from the metal band concealed beneath his sleeve.

"Yes."

"And this was the second..."

"What's happened?" His voice was quiet. Vulnerable. Despairing. "What have I done?"

Her eyes lifted to his. They glittered in the light of her orb, his distress laid bare. She smiled sadly. "You accepted it."

"And that means...what? That I'm going to be overpowered like this every time I use my magic?"

"Yes," she replied simply, "you will. So you will have to use it carefully. Shrewdly."

"...I...I don't know that I can push through it..."

"No, you fool, of *course* you can't. You're not *listening*. You cannot hide from these pains. You cannot turn a blind eye to them just because they only affect you and no one else. You cannot brush them off as if they are nothing. They are *serious*, Rathen, but they *aren't* immediately debilitating, and if you're going to the *Order*, you're going to need to have your wits about you and be ready to do whatever you have to, and that means you need to face your situation."

"Why?" His brow dropped guardedly. "What do you know?"

"In this case, as much as you do. And you, my love, know as much as *I*. So don't try to attack this head-on and don't shy away from it. I will do my best to find a solution. But, in the mean time," her tone softened, and she placed her hand upon his and squeezed it gently, "if anything should happen, I'll be there."

He observed her carefully. "Will you?" He said at last, and she nodded without breaking her gaze.

"I give you my word."

"But you also told me I could control this."

"I did. And you can. But there was...an element I hadn't accounted for, until recently."

His eyes flashed in fright. "Which is?"

She smiled softly, then leaned in and kissed him. Quite suddenly he found his mind empty. He couldn't recall the thought, if he even noticed it was gone. "Now, my love," she said warmly, "are you all right?"

"I...I think so..."

"And...Ferna? The harpies weren't too rough?"

He nodded to himself in understanding. "You sent them. Yes, I'm fine. I'm...fine."

Her head tilted thoughtfully. "But you're ashamed."

A sudden loathing spiked through his eyes and curled his lips from his teeth. A loathing that had been hovering just beneath the surface. He looked briefly towards the others, but they still spoke and moved without even the thinnest sound. They couldn't hear him, either. But as his eyes caught on Petra, crushing two plants together in a small, stone bowl which Eyila took and drank from, all he could see was his own insurmountable disgrace. "I let it happen, Kienza," he growled quietly, turning his head away to stare at the wall of excavated soil beside him instead, embedded with bones, roots and insects that seemed to shy away from the presence of the light. "I could have stopped it but I let it happen. I fought to control it - I thought I *could* control it, but...I killed the bounty hunter. First I just wanted to scare him off so we could flee somewhere, but once the...once *it* set in, killing him was the only acceptable solution...and after that, the screams...the...people being crushed by the...the things...I wanted to help them. I don't know what I was going to do, what I *thought* I could do...they were *stone*, they would have probably killed me first...but..." he shook his head in growing discomprehension. "What if I'd gotten out there and lost control? I-I could have...I..."

She threaded her arms around him and held him close against her. He was shaking and slow to react, and she could feel the rigid knot in his jaw. Tears pricked her eyes and she wished, not for the first time, that she could take it all away from him. Helplessness railed against her in that moment, but she shut it away with cold and efficient determination. She had learned long, long ago that such thoughts and feelings served no purpose at all.

"But you did control it," she whispered, her lips against his ear. "The bounty hunter was the reason you let it out, and he remained your focus. And then you sought to protect. Tell me: have you thought anything else while under such influence?"

"...No. Not that I can remember..."

"And I doubt you ever have."

He stroked her hair as she squeezed him, his thoughts twisting and contorting. He shook his head at their mercy. "How could something like this ever *only* be a *deterrent?*"

"You are only half-elf, my sweet. You don't have the inherent control. But you will get there." She gave him one final squeeze before releasing him. His eyes remained shadowed, but the lines in his face she loved so dearly weren't as deep. "I have to speak to Anthis."

He nodded, still lost in his lingering torment. With a kiss, she rose and stepped away, leaving him sitting upon the blanket he had yet to notice had appeared, knees pulled into his chest, absently watching the insects. She sighed to herself and turned towards the suddenly audible fire. "I apologise," she said to the others as she crouched beside the sleeping child, checking on her needlessly as a devoted mother would, "but I need to speak with Anthis."

"Kienza?" She looked inquiringly towards Eyila while the others began moving away. There was some restlessness in the girl's eyes. "I'm quite all right now - is there anything I can do for Rathen?"

Her plump lips pursed as she considered her, then bowed into a flawless smile, her doubt hidden away perfectly. "Bring him water," she replied, seating herself gracefully beside the young man. "And slap him if he mopes for much longer." Eyila blinked in surprise, but Kienza offered no hint as to whether or not she was joking. When she departed uncertainly to fetch a waterskin, the sorceress turned towards the historian and another wall of privacy set about them.

"Well done," she told him, pulling his eyes from the tribal girl onto her. "Those were quick reactions. And powerful magic. How long does it usually last?"

"Oh...uh...a few days..." He shifted quite uncomfortably.

"Mm. To save yourself, no doubt. In case something goes wrong after the hunt. ...Eyila seems awfully understanding about it." She smiled briefly as he brightened at the mention of her name, but sobered in a heartbeat. "Tell me."

He needed no elaboration, and Kienza nodded without reaction throughout his report of Rathen's increasing urgency and mutterings beneath the pressure of the magic. Until she pressed for anything 'less important'. Then her eyebrows rose. "'Boastful'?"

"He could have caught Garon with magic when he slipped," he explained carefully, wary of offence or being overheard, "but he made the rope coil around him like a snake. It was showier. And he referred to his magic as a power that the Root Mother, the vakehn, and no other man possessed. And that the world would crumble if it wasn't for his help."

She nodded slowly, her captivating face made somehow more beautiful by its slightest crease of concern. He began to wonder if he wasn't being unduly fastidious, until she looked back from the fire with even more severity. "And his magic usage? Aside from zoomorphic ropes?"

His eyes flicked back towards the mage, beside whom Eyila now sat, probing him with some spell or other. He fought down his instinctive jealousy. "He, uh...may have used it against me." He turned a hurt look back at the sorceress for her sudden laugh.

She pursed her lips to catch it. "I'm sorry - he *'may'* have?"

"Well I...can't really remember. There was a, uh...misunderstanding. It happened a bit fast..."

"Well we'll just gloss over that one, then," she grinned. "Anything else?"

"Yes. In the Wildlands, he retaliated immediately. Without thought. He didn't hurt anyone, but he dispelled the Root Mother's attempts to capture us." He shrank back at the sudden incredulous widening of her eyes.

"He *dispelled* it?"

"Oh...well...yes, there's a difference, isn't there? Of course there is. I don't know. He stopped it with magic, and quickly. Roots rose and wrapped around us, then they loosened and retracted. It happened a couple of times..."

"...And?"

"...It was a little *too* quick. I didn't see anything, but I've...been wondering if there was anything *to* see...if you understand."

The disturbed look on her face suggested that she did. Her eyes travelled towards the dark-haired mage, and she thought back to the shield he had apparently cast about himself. Petra had presumed it had been the portian. But Kienza had destroyed that man, and there hadn't been a trace of magic about him.

It was all coming together too neatly.

There was someone she had to speak with.

"Did he have any pain through this?" She asked, drawing herself out of the dark thoughts.

"Not that I'm aware of. A bit of discomfort, maybe, but it never slowed him down."

"Mhm. And what about when he was retaliating 'too quickly', specifically?"

"He...well I don't know, there was a lot going on..."

"Think, Anthis."

He swallowed hard as her emerald stare speared him. "He had no hesitation. Before or after." Again she lapsed into thought. "Kienza," her eyes flicked back to him, "what is this about?"

"Elves," she replied simply.

"I had gathered that much, to be honest," he said. "It's almost as if he's *becoming* one."

She chuckled briefly. "Fortunately not."

"Is there anything we can do to help?" She shook her head. "...Are we in any danger?" She shook her head again, but it was slower to come than the first.

"Please keep watching him." She rose to her feet, ignoring his disquiet. "I may have a solution soon - but in the mean time it must not get worse."

"And if it does?"

She reached out, took his hand and pressed something small and round into his palm. "Then I will come. But only if you believe it is escalating. Use your judgement, Mister Karth, and trust it. Always trust it."

The wall of silence dropped and quiet conversations from the rest of the room spilled over him, whispers as loud as a tavern. Kienza turned towards the others, and all looked back at her unspoken call for attention, finding at last the natural congeniality she had been missing. "You are safe. The shack is half a day behind you and I've cast a protection about this sett. Leave only when you're able and ready." Her gaze touched Rathen, Eyila and Anthis, but a humourless grunt drew her attention towards Garon. She raised her sleek eyebrows and smiled patiently. "Yes, Inquisitor?"

Quite foolishly, he barely flinched. "We're grateful for your timely arrival, of course, but you must know that *this* isn't as helpful as you think. Every few days we seem to be picked up and put down somewhere else - it's *exactly* why Salus thinks we're working with elves." He bristled as her fair voice burst into a peal of laughter.

"Is *that* what he thinks?! Well, then you have him at a disadvantage, don't you? He's confused and looking over his shoulder for your pointy-eared 'allies'."

"Perhaps - but it *also* has him hunting us even more aggressively! This whole *abduction* happened because of it!"

"Would you rather I put you back?"

He didn't reply.

"That's what I thought. Come now, Inquisitor Brack, I understand your concern, but as long as you keep ahead of him and step carefully past what webs he may weave, you will be fine. He has other things to think about than the six of you, does he not? His position is a demanding one. He cannot pour his every resource into hunting all of you. Now," the slightest waft of breeze ruffled her skirts, ridding them of bugs and soil as she strode through the enormous burrow. She paused beside Aria to kiss her brow, then bestowed another upon Rathen, but his forlorn expression stalled her. She smiled sadly back down at him, took him by the chin, whispered something in his ear and rose again while he nodded sullenly. "I have things to see to. I will be back when I am needed. The exit is that way," she pointed past Petra, "it's not far to the surface." Then, with one final, decisive sweep across them all - and a vague but far too knowing glance from Petra to Garon - she wished them all luck and vanished.

"I doubt we'll get any more sleep this morning," Garon sighed with frustration even as he looked towards the slumbering child. "We'll eat and set out in an hour."

As he and Petra began dividing the rations, Rathen dragged his blanket closer to the fire and sat beside his daughter with a heavy heart. Staring into her peaceful face, he lost himself in his own seething worries.

Eyila had been taken. That was unacceptable. But what if it had been Aria? Salus was resorting to kidnapping in a bid to remove them as a threat, and his subordinates had gotten far too close to success. Had they wished, they could have killed Eyila and any number of them while they'd slept - and as Rathen was supposedly the only one capable of standing against him, Aria would remain in constant, direct danger for as long as they were involved. And...*this* was what would happen to him if he tried.

His jaw clenched, his knuckles turned white, his eyes sparked like a hammer against steel. He had to get rid of the Zi'veyn. He had to get out of all of this, for her sake. The Order could handle it. They may not be able to use the Zi'veyn itself, but they could surely construct this spell of his; he had no inconsequential number of notes he could give them to get them started, and they could probably dismantle the Zi'veyn while they were at it and learn all they needed to from that. As well as keep it out of Salus's hands...

Yes. The sooner they got to the Order, the better. For everyone. They would be able to find a solution far quicker than he alone, and then the whole matter would be at an end. No more chasms, no more afflicted mages, no more reactive magic. The matter would be done, and Aria would be safe. The Order could do it. The Order would *have* to do it.

It was only then that a distant thought began to prod at him: Kienza hadn't asked him *why* they were going to the Order...

A sudden strike across his cheek startled him out of his melancholy, and he blinked several times into a scrutinising bronze face.

Chapter 47

The smoke rolled in. Channels and currents of chilled breeze dragged it up and over the frozen mountain. It hung several feet too high to choke, but the sweet scent of burned resin, noxious itself in its concentration, stooped just low enough to reach him. Salus tolerated it, a sleeve pressed over his mouth and nose.

Crouching beside one of many jagged outcrops, its farthest face encased in snow, he stared up into the black cloud. And watched. Waited. Scoured the sky from the tops of the firs in the pass to his left, to the edge of the towering peak to his right. The smoke had filled the sky.

Finally, they appeared, dense specks forming in the roiling shadows. They had become familiar. He watched them grow, watched them near, constantly noting their shape. Would they lengthen? Or remain four fine points?

He blinked. Lengthen.

He remained where he was and watched as this newest volley of hewn-stone bolts broke through the cloud and embedded themselves in the snow with a dull and heavy thud, six safe paces to his right. That was their fourth far-miss. They'd lost him. Which meant one thing.

He focused his hearing. Bolts were quiet, but not silent. Silence was intentional. He stared harder, straining against the smoke, the aroma finally seeping through his sleeve and into his throat. It tasted foul but he brushed it from his mind, forgotten in an instant beneath the dictation of his training.

Then he heard it: a deliberate stillness, as though all living things held their breath. His sight intensified, picking out the slightest shadow in the smoke. He had three seconds.

He breathed, he tracked, he raised his hands.

Like a dart from a ballista, the shape burst through the cloud and shot low overhead, buffeting him with a single powerful beat of its wings. With an ear-piercing cry that shook the frigid air, the mighty falcon banked at speed, turned, and stooped straight towards him.

In an instant, its feathers were aflame.

But he was already too late. Its speed had surprised him, and that briefest hesitation had given it all the time it had needed. With its guiding cry, its handlers had located him - but they were low on weapons. He'd heard them say as much, in that obscure tongue of theirs. This would be their last volley. But it would be precise.

Before the blazing falcon had hit the snow, he dashed off to the right and climbed higher up the furthest side of the slope, twenty paces from where he'd been reported. The mountain wind tribe's warriors would aim unerringly for where their pet had indicated, and, reasonably, no ordinary man could have escaped the spot through such deep snow so quickly. Unfortunately for them, he was no ordinary man.

Sure enough, the stone bolts rained down with eerie precision, embedding themselves in the flattened snow right behind the rock.

He didn't make a sound. If he feigned death throes, they would investigate. As it was, they were out of ammunition and unsure if they'd hit him at all. If they had any sense, they would re-arm themselves before taking a look. And with their last bird dead, the smouldering remains of the first two similarly melting the snow where they'd fallen, they had no more scouts. Not even savages would be so foolish as to move ahead, blind.

Salus straightened in satisfaction as he listened to uncertain mutters and then slow, retreating footfalls, then slunk off in the opposite direction himself, moving deeper into the Pavise Mountains of the west.

He pulled his thick cloak tighter about himself. As much as he favoured the colder climes, he couldn't understand how or why anyone would choose to live up in the mountains. He could only conclude that they were unaware of the world around the next peak. But those were conundrums for another time - along with the issues stacking on his desk. For all his mirrors, his phidipans, his orders, his assets, everything seemed to be coming up fruitless.

So for this moment, out here in the cold, desolate, blissfully simple mountains, he focused on what he could rely upon: his own two hands, and their safeguarding of Turunda.

His woes numbed as he concentrated on climbing the sharp and jagged ridges, sliding carefully along the icy slopes and bracing against the biting frost that not even silver takin wool could ward away forever, and by the time the thinning air finally forced him to a stop, his mind had fallen silent. It was then that the dusking world around him at last drifted over his awareness, as gingerly as a child's tug on his sleeve.

He took a long, deep breath even as the sight tried to take it away from him.

Surrounded by snow and grey stone, the familiar verdant expanse of his country burst with the vibrancy of a sea of emeralds, even fogged by the low-hanging cloud as it was, and it was no less precious. Unbroken. Unbreakable. Not a torrent of floods nor an army of fire devils from the plains could strip the land of its sylvan riches.

His heart stirred. Peace settled in behind a ragged breath; it was impossible not to be moved. No one of Turundan blood - touched by the forest, as it was said - could resist the debilitating sensations of such a sight of their home: from one side a gentle and maternal embrace, comfort, an assurance of welcome and belonging against all worries and strife, and from the other a direct and steely punch to any doubt or disconnection of one's place and importance, a firm hand of order and purpose that reigned above small and fleeting personal ambition. A touch both corrective and soft, like the hand of Vastal Herself brushing grace and indomitable certainty.

The sight, the perception, each were a privilege. And perhaps, if others were to experience it as he did, they might see sense and abandon their efforts to incite such chaos and menace and unite their strengths against Turunda's *true* enemies.

Assuming any of them were as devoted to the Emerald Kingdom as he was. Personal ambition was a powerful lure. It had broken people and countries for centuries. It had broken the elves.

The thought sobered him, and in the shadow of such a humbling sight he felt more strongly than ever that what he was doing was right and good. This was his land, his home and his charge. He would not let harm befall it nor the people it sheltered while he drew breath - not beyond what was necessary to safeguard it for as long as possible. Whatever it took, he would give; whomever against, he would face. Or he wasn't fit to be buried beneath its soil.

Resolute beneath the cold, he turned his eyes away. But they were pulled helplessly towards the darkness he felt looming to his left, growing in his peripherals and becoming harder and harder to face. But face it, he did. Because this abhorrence could be twisted to Turunda's benefit.

An abyssal black scar cut through the Pavise range, snaking down from the north from beyond even the Northrage River, cracking mountains that had stood since the beginning of time.

It set a contrast so heartbreaking that, for a moment, he was almost sick. But discipline forced him to steel. As terrible as it was, and as much fault as was his, it would do good. And once that good was done, there would *be* no rend to mar the landscape. It would be as if Turunda had never been shackled here at all.

He didn't allow himself to linger. With a final glance east across his beloved home, he turned towards the chasm and covered the final, craggy stretch, and when snow-covered arches and crumbled walls rose on the pass above him, the familiar touch of magic softened the horror like flowers over a mass grave.

Even before he stood among them, the blissful peace that preceded his every such endeavour reached out towards him like a silk ribbon, setting a calmness over his mind and easing away the pummelling ache of his muscles. The terrible landscape, too, began to soften with every step, and though the mountains could never compare with the sight of the eternal forests, theirs was not a natural beauty. But even in knowing that, he was, for a time, captivated.

Bathed in the soft, silver light of the waking moon, the frozen shelf was littered with leaves that shouldn't have been, strewn around like autumn and glinting as though solid gold, the snow itself of powdered pearl, encrusting ancient statues of time-lost watchers. A delectable mix of tobacco and spiced fruits glanced through the air and tickled his nose on a breeze, transporting him back to a moment lost in memory so distant he was unsure it was even his own, while a whimsical, tinkling melody persisted beneath the ghostly howl of the higher winds, casting the surreal nook ever closer to a fairy tale.

He couldn't help but marvel. It was truly a wonder that something so destructive could be so beautiful. He still had no idea why each sundered place was so diversely affected, and on some suppressed level it fascinated him - but he was there to work, not gawp or study.

As easily as the enchantment had set in, it was shaken off, and his mindset turned towards his task.

Slipping beneath a crooked arch, he took up position at the edge of the chasm, filled here with yet more of the golden leaves, and closed his eyes. With a breath, his muscles relaxed despite the precarious drop just inches from his toes, and his magic danced attentively in his veins. He sent it out with a thought, ignoring the strange and familiar sensation that came with opening himself up to the world, and settled in on the pulse of the reservoir. He found it quickly; the effort became easier with every attempt. With another trained breath, he gathered his strength, reined in his adrenaline, twisted his fingers and dropped his intent into the chasm.

A near-immediate tremor started violently beneath his feet. He ignored it completely. He heard the edges of the chasm crumble, felt the gap before him widen, but his concentration was unharried.

The intangible force moved, and his spell formed a gulley, leading the incensed magic choicelessly along a route of his choosing, its rebellion helpless against its practised walls. He watched in his mind's eye as the dreadful rift surged south at his bidding, striking out towards Víla's Rest to deepen the Red Canyon.

The familiar throb began in his head, but he rose above it, as necessity had taught him to do, and the sweat passed like a phantom over his skin. And then, quite suddenly, the magic seemed to join him. As if convinced by his commanding power, it ceased its struggle and began rolling along the gulley with zeal, spreading further into the world on his efforts and its own momentum.

Progress hastened until the chasm was well beyond his reach, but even when his eyes opened and his quickened breath escaped him in a ragged puff, he knew it would continue as instructed even without his guiding hand.

It took only a moment to regain himself. This time, dizziness hadn't touched him. His strength was improving. But any sense of victory was obliterated before it could form by a single utterance of praise.

He turned, darkening despite the overwhelming peace of the place, and stared into the face made almost truly silver in the moonlight.

Liogan smiled back with nauseating sweetness. "Oh, what is it?" she cooed. "Too old for a pat on the back? Mm...well, perhaps you are. Perhaps you'd prefer..." But her nose scrunched up instead. Apparently even a perverse joke was too sickening for her if it involved one not entirely elven. But it still piqued his irritation. "Regardless, I am surprised you've managed this much." Her tone hardened with condescension. "You're getting distracted again, Salus."

"It can't be helped," he replied venomously.

"Oh, but it *can*. You know your priorities, *Keliceran*, and yet, somehow, not only are you letting yourself get distracted *at all*, but by the wrong thing! You went after that lockbox based on a hunch and then you *held back* when mages attacked the town."

The irrational fire that had sparked at her arrival all but raged in his eyes. "How do you know about that?"

"Ohh, my dear, how do I *not* know about that? Do you think I just pop in when I feel like it and ignore you otherwise? Do you think *any* of us do? Oh, no, we *watch* you, my dear, and we watch you *closely*."

"And yet, it happened over a week ago."

"Oh!" Her hands rose to her mouth, concealing a feigned look of surprise. "Silly me! I forgot! Suddenly you're older and wiser now - you've corrected it all, and you would *never* let such a thing happen again, would you? Such a *distraction* happen again?" Her hands dropped to her hips, and she regarded him with a bitter, mocking smile. "No. Of course you would. You're a child, Salus, chasing whims like butterflies, dividing your attention so far that you couldn't possibly linger on one thing long enough to get bored of it." She continued over his bluster. "You need to set your priorities straight, once and for all, or there is no hope for you. We will turn to another. You are not the only one of elven blood among your people - I believe you already know of one other..."

His blood boiled and his tongue fell suddenly paralysed behind his teeth. He seethed so violently that he could have thrown her into the chasm, and he was made angrier by knowing in his gut that, on some level, she was right. But he also knew, behind his rage, behind his insult, that Doana was just as genuine a threat; he wasn't working to this elf's whims, he was working to his own ends, towards Turunda's safety, and he was *not* going to play so deep into her hands that the moment he saved it, it fell.

But...he had let mages attack. He'd turned away from that fact to spare himself the shame that now stared him full in the face with her blunt and intentional words. Because he *could* have stopped them. But he'd chosen not to. He'd chosen to let people get hurt instead.

But...only a few. A handful. For the greater good. And none had actually died.

His eyes returned to her from their haze. She was studying the leaves with some interest from over her shoulder.

"There's a general riling within your magic, you know," she told him as casually as if she were pointing out the weather. "It's making you angry. And it's born of doubt. I can feel that much." Her cold eyes flicked towards him. "Doubt of your subordinates. Doubt of your king. Doubt of your wench's love - an *older* wench, I note - and doubt, even, of yourself..." She straightened and began to wander about the curious little nook, unconcerned in her sleeveless gown by the chill that bit even deeper to the bone now that night had truly descended. "The only thing you seem certain of *at all* is that your beautiful country deserves saving - but, how much of it? Certainly not *all* its people, not the king, nothing that isn't human...and...oh, well, dare I even ask the question?"

His eyes bore into her. "Ask it."

She turned and smiled sweetly again. "*Can* you even save it?"

His rage sparked anew and, this time, he lunged for her. But she only chuckled, teleporting back just out of his reach, and knocked a bolt of fire aside with the back of her hand as though it was a fly. Then, an instant later, she was before him, filling his blood-hazed vision, and his wrists were clasped in a single, sharp-nailed hold. "Never," she smiled as he tried in vain to free himself from the impossibly powerful grasp, "raise your hand against me again. Or you will discover just how far beneath me you really are."

She released him and turned casually away as his hands dropped like lead. He stared at her in castrated fury as she peered at the pearlescent snow over one of the statues. "I'm afraid I have some bad news for you. These papers of yours - in the lockbox you valued above the welfare of your people - ooh," she sucked air through her teeth. "You're not going to like them."

"Why?" His heart raced in a sudden frenzy. What was it? Were the plans a threat? Absolute? Unstoppable and already in motion? *'Or,'* his eyes narrowed *'is she just toying with me?'*

But "you'll have to wait and see," was all she said. "Oh, and, also, that ratty little girl got away from you." Her expression didn't change at his confusion. "Oh yes, two days ago - hadn't you discovered that yet? They didn't catch the one you wanted, they botched it and grabbed the desert rat instead. Your people were killed. Both of them. One was stabbed to death with some kind of...taint...ugh, oh, it was--" she gagged animatedly.

He stopped listening. He fell as still as stone even while the voice bellowed in the depths of his mind.

Koraaz.

There had been nothing for five days, not since they'd vanished from Ferna, and he'd had too much else to deal with to try to chase them down. But he'd sent a phidipan and portian after them, and...*both* of them had been killed?! ...How was that even possible?

Success rates had improved drastically since he'd rid himself of the phaeacians, but now it seemed the phidipans were heading in the same direction. The portian himself was a new elevation - a bad call, evidently. He should have known better. He should have pulled a mage out of cover to go after them, and sent a more experienced portian. Koraaz was important enough. But he had them all stationed in other locations - the Order and the palace, among others...

So, the fault was his.

But they should both have been capable. Neither, so far as he had heard, were killed with magic beyond that which Karth was capable of - and if the first had been foolish enough to be killed by his 'taint', then the second would have been easily overpowered with a Sulyaxist's magic.

So what had Koraaz done during all of this?

He tuned back in at the mention of Kalokh. "Where?"

"In the northern pass," she repeated witheringly. "Their numbers are few - but *you* know better than most that it takes but one persistent woodcutter to fell the oldest, tallest oak."

"The northern pass..."

Liogan rolled her pastel rose eyes at his distraction and summoned a méridienne, flared out her skirts and lay languidly across it, staring up at the stars.

The northern pass. The Crown had just ordered them away from that border - ordered them *explicitly* - and now Kalokh were moving in? They had probably already been waiting for a window, and their withdrawal had provided it...but Skilan had stomped them into the dirt just *months* ago. They were in no state for war right now, especially against a country whose military was this close to pristine - but that military was also distracted by Doana.

And yet one would think they would wait for fighting to actually break out if their numbers were that small. Why risk drawing any attention at all? There was more to it. They knew something...

...Or did the *Crown* know something? It had been *their* order to withdraw - from that area, specifically. Salus had felt at the time that the Crown was almost *trying* to blind themselves so he'd kept a few individuals out there just in case, but with his numbers thinned, he could only do so much. And now Kalokh were marching towards them through that very pass, and far too soon. As if they'd known his people were going to be ordered away. Had prepared for it. Had *trusted* it.

And the Crown had ordered them away. Did they *want* Kalokh to strike? It would force the military away from locking in Doana to deal with an actively hostile force - Doana would secure their foothold. They would have all the time they needed to turn Kora upside down.

None of those umber-skinned wretches had been seen in the city, but they knew they would stand out. They doubtlessly had less conspicuous people working for them. People of his own colour, his own nation...

The thought struck him as absurd, and yet it seemed to fall so perfectly into place.

Perhaps King Thunan himself had people working for them. Malson seemed almost pleased that Moore hadn't reacted to Doana's movements or his own efforts, as if he wanted this stand-off prolonged - as if he didn't want *either* side to attack at all. But why would he or the king want Kora to find evidence that would compromise the throne?

Unless he had no intention of giving it up, and was preparing instead to negotiate. But...for what? And what was he willing to give up to succeed?

History told him it was most likely that he sought to marry the eastern queen, to maintain his seat and take Doana and its military for his own by marriage, strengthening his forces, gaining new farmland and eradicating a threat in one bejewelled and celebrated move.

But there was one problem. The queen was a child - malleable and callow - but her advisors were not. They would not allow it. *No* respectable governor would. They would be giving up their cultural identity, and no leader - no *honourable* leader - could do such a thing.

And so Thunan, naive in his victory over a child, would inevitably be manipulated once the negotiations of word or marriage were complete, perhaps even killed...

And then they would all bow to the child queen of Doana.

Liogan had said he wouldn't like what he found in the lockbox.

But...*why* would the king think to concoct this?! To oppose Skilan? It was as certain as the moon in the sky that they would bring war down upon them again, and they were still too powerful for even Salus to do anything final about - but that alliance alone would provoke them into war, if not King Jalund to try the same thing. And then where would they be?

King Thunan had always thought himself clever. Malson did, too. It was a failing that seemed to come from a close proximity to the courts. And his advisors were all yes-men, sold on that very illusion. Salus was glad that he was so rarely summoned. His intelligence was still intact.

But if this *was* the king's plan, what could he possibly do about it? And so late?

He quickly stamped that hasty thought out. He needed proof first, above all else. And with eyes in the palace, it would be no long job. There may have already been signs. Why else would he have come to this conclusion so neatly if not because the information had already been laid out in the tiniest of pieces, cut and sanded for assembly?

A sudden shift in the wind drew him out of his thoughts, and he loosened the cloak from about his throat, sweating in his anger and humiliation.

Liogan, he discovered, had gone. But he had no questions. There was only betrayal.

But, up here in the mountains, there was nothing he could do. The nearest

462

translocator was a day behind him and he would never make it back without rest, no matter his determination. That was why he'd brought a pack with him. But he knew he would get no sleep even in this affected and empyrean peace with his blood surging so.

His eyes drifted slowly back down the mountain.

Two birds, one stone.

There were tribes that needed wiping out.

Chapter 48

Three days did little to smooth his temper. Despite returning victorious from the mountains, Salus had immediately shut himself away in his office with troubles he had no desire to discuss, yet could clearly be heard both muttering and raging over long into the night. He let few in, took reports curtly, barely ate - he'd only visited his private chambers once during Taliel's absence, and that was solely because he'd gotten sick to the point of madness of the sight of his office walls.

In the end it took nothing less than another mountain to free his chest of the constraints of duty and breathe again freely, and the chill to invigorate and chase away his mental fatigue enough to grasp a clear thought. But even as he planned and pondered in the seclusion of those frozen heights, a new concern was gnawing.

Salus regarded the ancient barrows carefully. Koraaz had meddled here. He could feel the disturbance if just because nothing at all appeared out of place. And yet, even while nothing looked, sounded or smelled unusual, there remained a distinct and striking abnormality to the air. A silence. Another deliberate silence - deliberate, but not conscious.

He wandered slowly about the menhirs, pausing beside the altar whenever he crossed it, and considered the magic warily before he dared upon a conclusion. But the moment the thought shaped gingerly in his mind, his certainty hardened. The magic was still there. He was sure of it. As sure as had it been bound, gagged and hidden behind one of the standing stones. There was nothing wrong with it but inactivity.

A malicious smile tugged at his perpetually grim-set lips as he felt at least one of his woes evaporate. Koraaz had failed. Despite reports, the magic was still here. Whatever the accursed rogue had thought he'd done, he'd only made it safer for him.

He straightened beneath his cloak and breathed deep the frozen air. What a fine gift for Midsummer's Day.

With a smug bounce in his step, he passed on through the ruins and continued his climb until he reached at last the gaping chasm. But when he extended himself down into its blackness, his confidence slipped. The magic, when provoked, was sluggish to respond, and when it finally did it seemed confused, twirling aimlessly like fallen leaves in a gasp of breeze.

He frowned, though he knew who to blame and an inkling of what to do. If the magic was going to be lazy, he would need to be firmer. It could be that Koraaz had found a way to 'dampen' it, to get in his way and slow him down. But surely that could be overcome. If a child stuck its fingers in its ears, one had only to shout louder or slap its hands away.

Salus redoubled his efforts, bullying it into motion, goading it to wake up, to liven, to rejuvenate, to recover its previous vigour until, finally, its stupor buckled. With a momentary flush of victory, he felt the magic shift and contort beneath his pressure, mustering slowly, moving at last in line with his efforts. He quickly adjusted his spell, paving its way southwards with a sigh of relief. For a moment, he'd thought--

Something was wrong.

Like a fallen tree damming a river, the flow suddenly clogged. It swelled and spilled out over the trail behind it, escaping his lane of control for no reason his frantic search could find. Like wasps, it swarmed recklessly out over the precarious ledge, inciting yet more clusters of magic as it expanded, reaching back as far as the barrows until a storm of ephemeral frost suddenly raged around him.

His blood turned cold.

Koraaz had trapped it after all.

Teeth clamped tight, Salus steeled and fought back for control. But the magic was vigorous now. Wild. Clots of power ruptured at random all around him, faster and more violently the harder he fought, and with each burst, the air about it changed. Something took shape from within the magic - or revealed itself from its hiding place - potent, raving, and unstable. He noticed only at the very last moment that another was forming beside him.

Instinct tore his eyes open and threw him back towards the safety of the trees, but in doing so, the last vestige of his control collapsed. He was spared not even a moment to reel in panic before something struck him on the back of the head.

Salus whirled furiously, a sign already shaping in his fingers, but he did not find the wretch he'd expected.

A dog-faced creature leapt with a scream from the tree's shadows, paws open and grasping for his face. It took only a confused backhand to knock it out of the air. Another large nut immediately struck him from his left, clipping his eyebrow, but as he turned and snarled towards this second beast, a third leapt at him from behind.

One by one, five of the lanky creatures descended upon him from their place in the firs, attacking from all sides with whooping and barking, spinning him around as he tried to hit one away while throwing another off. But they were relentless. Urgency boiled in his blood. The magic was rushing away from him.

He gave up trying to deflect them. With a short string of gestures, the creatures screamed and their thick, furry coats erupted into flame. Their holds failed immediately and they dropped writhing to the snow. He wasted no time watching their futile rolling.

Salus took off, thudding through the snow in the wake of the snaking, splintering chasm as it pushed off towards Doana, vaulting over tremoring rock and miraculously keeping his feet even as his mind surged ahead, groping haphazardly after it. A minute took a lifetime, but finally he drew level, and exceeded. His feet slowed while his hastily revived spell tightened and hemmed it in, and he steered it with all his might, pulling it back together, beating it into submission until it was at last heading southwards again.

His breath shook with relief and exhaustion, his feet finally stilled, and he swallowed his heart back down into his chest. Control was his again. The magic was still riled, and the exploding pockets were still discernible though mellowed and diluted among the rest, but it obeyed. He kept a tight hold despite his flagging strength until the flow's impetus was enough to carry it to the next rend, then, finally, with another ragged breath, he withdrew.

A moment too soon.

The chasm had extended for miles, and just at the edge of his reach, something else had gone wrong. Like spooked horses the magic suddenly jumped and scattered again, and this time he knew there was no hope of saving it. It splintered once more, and veered westwards.

He stared after it in terror. Sweat beaded, dread roiled in his gut and panic spiked through his limbs, trying ardently to paralyse his thoughts against his fevered search for a solution. But the truth spiralled relentlessly in his head: there was nothing he could do. It was too far, too fast, and his disordered mind was already weighted by fatigue.

He cursed himself desperately. *'No!* No! *I don't believe that. I* can't *believe that.'* There had to be something he could do. *He'd* set this in motion, and it was his loss of control, his *failing*, that had let it loose to obliterate Turunda. But if he was powerful enough to start it, he was powerful enough to reclaim it. He just had to reach it. He had to get ahead of it.

And so he ran without a thought of futility, shrouded in his determination, blood surging in his ears as the snow melted beneath his feet. He ran, he reached, and he willed.

The mountains shifted, the land levelled, and his feet pounded over frost, following the tremors, following the scar, racing beside it as it carved out its destruction. Until something terrible compelled him to look backwards.

Shock held him for a single step. His eyes fell not upon mountains, but upon Toakh. The old, eastern border town. And it had been ripped in two.

And Tamley lay directly ahead.

He was almost out of time.

Fire burned in Salus's eyes as they returned to the front, and his fatigue had long since evaporated. He slammed himself to a stop, gathered his focus, and fired his magic straight into the rampage.

It caught violently. His strength jolted under its powerful momentum - too powerful to break, but not to be diverted. He rooted himself, physically and mentally, gritted his teeth against the strain, and swept his spell around, dragging the magic with it like a leash. But it took more than he had to return it to the mountains. He thought rapidly, puffing under the exertion. He knew he couldn't join it to the next rift he'd planned to - something deep and primeval told him not to even try - but if he could bow this one far enough, he could connect it to the second later and keep damage to a minimum.

Judgement was critical.

He held his breath and released the spell.

The world blurred. The ground struck his knees. His mind swirled and muscles numbed, but, distantly, he felt the tremor swing. The magic hurtled south. And the trailing cloud that had hung just beneath sight and sense burst and gasped out across the land.

Green meadows and pastures were bleached grey under the creeping sheets, and the lazy breeze drifting over them chilled. Cattle stamped uneasily on the crunching silver frost, rabbits scurried deeper into freezing warrens, and rushkins dove to undisturbed depths. Lake surfaces cracked, streams flowed beneath glass, and Bowden's water carriers swore and read omens, while rain froze mid-fall, pummelling Rul's wooden roofs and Bridgend's rickety stables.

Kvistdjur abandoned their tendings and rose in twists of leaves to sing their mournful lullaby as the woods emptied of birdsong, and a skogsrå staggered back in shock, her heart breaking and stitching back together in fury as a thin sheet of ice glazed each and every leaf. Ditchlings shivered in Ziili, harpies fluffed up in Korovor, and vittra roaming outside cities muttered anxiously over the chaos that ensued within.

Beggars huddled, elderly stumbled, children ran and whooped in fear and wonder. A scholarly mage looked out from a tower over a glistening city, thoughts already bent towards a logical cause while another, far older, leaned towards the consequences. Soldiers east of Kora sheltered from hail and remapped against frozen water sources while their umber-skinned counterparts listened to alarmed mages just north in Greentop.

And a sylvan sorceress soothed an agitated goat, watching with a beautiful knot of worry in her brow as moss and lichen shrank and shrivelled under the touch of the unnatural freeze, and a grievous song rose from the depths of the scowles behind her.

Salus lay beside the gaping black scar, staring listlessly up into the madly swirling clouds. He didn't feel the cold through his clothes, sweating and steaming in his exhaustion. He wasn't sure yet if he'd actually noticed it, if he'd seen what he thought he had or if he'd imagined it even as he'd watched the frost spread. He'd been in the Olusan Mountains just minutes ago, and now lay half way between Toakh and Tamley. But even as his dulled and muffled thoughts tried to make some sense of it, the only thing he could concentrate on was that the dog-faced creatures had lost him his pack in their skirmish, and that he needed a blanket.

'I have noticed the cold, then,' he thought disjointedly, but the fact that it shouldn't have been was still slow to arrive.

He was so tired. Everything ached, ached as though he'd climbed mountains. And he was hungry. And drained.

But he was victorious.

His eyes closed and a smile eased across his weary face. Victorious. And now, he wished for home. For warmth, for food, for rest. Not to have his name spoken with such alarm, nor be shaken so roughly by the shoulder for not answering quickly enough.

"Leave me be, Teagan," he managed, moving only to bat his hand away. "Or get me a blanket. I want to sleep." He soon felt a sheet laid over him, which he pulled about himself gratefully as the smell of drying ink wafted towards him. It was a strange thing to smell in the meadows, and he was surprised that Teagan had found him so soon, and that he'd brought both a blanket and a teacup with him, for the clink was unmistakable. But it had been a strange afternoon. A little too strange.

He mustered the strength in his curiosity to open his eyes, and found not the bright and blinding sky he'd expected and failed to prepare for, but a dark and vaulted ceiling that triggered a lurid conflict of dread and relief in his heart.

And yet, he couldn't help but smile sardonically to himself. He had wished himself home. He just hadn't expected that 'home' would be his desk rather than his bed.

"Where is Liogan?" Teagan asked in tight and unsettled tone, but Salus sat up slowly in his chair, shaking his head before he could find his tongue.

"It wasn't her."

"It wasn't her?"

"No. Somehow..." he smiled as the obscure and fatigued understanding finished falling into place, and he eased back into his blanket. "It was me. Desperation, I think. Like the blue fire."

"What happened?"

He missed the continued tightness of the portian's tone and told him of Koraaz's sabotage and all that had ensued since. He was too tired and distracted to notice the shadow of concern that had already been in Teagan's eyes, growing as he spoke, nor that they seemed to linger through the window.

They drifted back onto him when Salus mentioned far too casually the jump he'd made from mountain to meadow, and Teagan found a weary and satisfied smile upon his face. *'He teleported. Twice.'* The thought sent chills clawing up his spine and a steel rod through his shoulders. He kept it all from his face.

"What's happened while I've been gone?"

"You're tired," the portian reminded him, stepping forwards to tidy the papers he'd left across his desk, arranging them according to his progress. "You should rest, first." He stopped when a hand slipped in and pressed the remainder to the surface. He looked back to Salus. His eyes were pink, but serious. Teagan stepped back in obedience. "As you wish. Kalokh has attacked."

Salus blinked. "They've...*attacked?* But we sent people after them to deal with it. How could they have *attacked?*"

"They were few enough to lose their tails. And a few were dealt with--"

"*Too* few if those remaining can still 'attack'! Where are they? What have they done?" His good and placid mood was as good as dead.

"They bypassed Rega entirely, it seems," Teagan reported dutifully, "but they struck Eddon and Whiteheath simultaneously after burning Kruuz and what remained of Redgrove. They're hitting hard. They want our attention."

"Tell me Moore didn't stoop."

"I'm afraid I can't. And Doana were quick to take advantage of it. They looted the afflicted areas and when Moore sent two regiments to deal with Kalokh, Doana took the opportunity to obliterate them from the rear. Over four hundred dead, and Kalokh slipped away. They've vanished into Korovor."

"Korovor?" He paled. *'Taliel...'* "Where was the Order when all of this was happening?!"

"None were stationed at Greentop, and in many cases, they're not trusted to act. A few commanders are holding them back."

He rose in anger, biting off a snarl. He understood that so very well, but they *could* have turned the tide, if... He grunted. *'If they could be trusted.'* He turned hopelessly to the window, but hesitated in shock at the sight of the frost that clung to every roof, wall, tree and road like a thin film of silver. *'It's reached...this far...? What does this mean?'* He pondered it for only a moment before recoiling from the dizzying consequences. "What happened to the trackers? In the Pass? What happened to them?"

"A number were killed by tribes. The earth and water on either side launched fresh raids on one another and the phidipans were caught in the crossfire."

Salus whipped back towards him. "*All* of them?!"

"Many, but not all."

"Then why didn't the *rest* do anything about this?!"

"About the tribes or Kalokh?"

"*Either!*" He squeezed his fists against the shake of his hands and ripped the blanket from his burning shoulders. "We're too vulnerable - who else is going to storm in to take advantage of that? Skilan?! They're already occupying our eyes for what *may or may not* be their own impending march. We're being chipped away at from all sides! Doana, Kalokh, the tribes, *non-humans* - even Ivaea and Kasire have impeded us! How long until *Antide or Dweron* land on our shores?! Because it looks like every *other* war is turning our way!"

"Each of which you started."

"*I am aware of that!*"

Teagan fell silent. The room shook beneath his bellow, and for a long while all that could be heard was the keliceran's seething breath and the occasional shouts of dismay from the neighbouring nobles and their servants outside. Finally, his breath calmed. "War has worn them all down. Their numbers are thin, just as we planned. All of them. Doana are the only ones we need to contend with." He turned back to Teagan, who saw the whites of his eyes grow brighter as the darkness he'd been spared receded. "Kalokh will be dealt with. We need eyes back on Doana. Now that they've finally attacked, Moore will have no choice but to move on them. What else do you have?"

Teagan didn't ask how he'd known. "The papers have been decoded."

His grim face seemed to transform at his flash of hope. "And?" He was already hurrying back to the desk and began rifling through the piles spread over it, until Teagan stepped forwards and raised a single sheet. Salus fell perfectly still as his eyes landed upon it. They pulled back to him a long moment later. "I don't understand."

"It was all gibberish. This was the only thing it contained."

"Well, maybe the code was wrong after all. Maybe we need a different one..."

"No, sir, you misunderstand. It all translated. Into a children's story about a spider. We're picking it apart in case there's more to it, but this is all we've found that is...relevant."

His eyes dropped slowly back to the only four words on the page.

All hail Queen Yejide.

Chapter 49

The humming sensation was mild, but the foreboding Rathen felt creeping over him with it was enough to stall and whip him around on the spot. Eyila was beside him in an instant, and together they stared sharply back through the trees in fixated silence. The others noticed. Uneasily, they followed their gaze.

They saw it just before Aria could whisper the question. A low cloud of white dust rolled at speed over the grass towards them, stretching endlessly in both directions of the thin forest, leaving trees and bushes as steel in its wake. And it was immediately clear that it couldn't be outrun.

They braced themselves, some managed to draw weapons, and heartbeats later a terrible cold froze them in place. They puffed and gasped, fighting for breath as their chests tightened in shock, until Garon's own ragged voice assured them that they would breathe just fine once they relaxed.

Petra was the first to manage some kind of composure. "W-what *was* th-that?" She demanded as she hugged her shivering body and rubbed vigorously the sides of her chest, watching with dismay as the frosty cloud continued along through the trees, unhindered.

"Magic," Rathen replied gruffly. He was hurrying Aria's feet back into her shoes and removing her oversized cloak from her pack, bundling her up in it before fishing out his own. The others followed his lead as quickly as their comprehension would let them.

"What m-magic would d-do this?!"

"Clumsy magic."

"Salus." Garon growled. He drew his hood closer about his neck and searched furiously between the trees, fingers tightening about his sword.

"W-what reason c-could he have to do *this?*"

"I don't th-think it was intention-nal," Rathen said distractedly, pulling his own grey cloak tighter about himself and looking back through the frost, adjusting as quickly as he could to the cold. "It feels...familiar..." His dark eyebrows drew together. *'It feels like White Barrows. But how?'*

He glanced towards Eyila. She didn't seem encumbered by it. And, he realised, neither was he.

Dissatisfied, he turned and started back along their heading, drawing Aria close and brushing past the others' disquieted looks. Eyila shortly followed, then the rest fell in tow, soothed if only a little by the two casters' resolution.

The clouds soon appeared through a break in the trees, and they were thicker and greyer than they'd been half an hour before. It had been threatening rain all afternoon, and now it looked distinctly worse.

Within another hour, it was snowing, and by nightfall the thin, white blanket that had settled reflected any and every surrounding light, exposing the landscape but rendering their fire equally less conspicuous. While it burned happily a ways behind him, their blankets set close by to warm, Rathen looked out from the treeline across the half-frozen river to the vast city on the hilltop. The three twisting towers loomed even from their great distance, their ebon facades appearing as polished steel in the snow, while the gold and silver spirals and braces glittered like the trim of the royal pennants.

He took a deep breath to subdue the racing of his heart. They would be inside those walls the next morning, if Owan's disturbingly simple plan worked out. But it wasn't the threat of capture or the Order's own intentions with him that weighed on his mind.

He heard footsteps approach behind him and locked his frets away.

"Will you have to cast anything tomorrow?"

Rathen shook his head. "Not if Owan comes through."

"Do you think it will work?"

Rathen breathed a laugh and cast Anthis a look torn between cynicism and faith. But he didn't answer. Uneasily, they looked back towards the towers and the flickering Midsummer lights.

Anthis shook his head in dismay. "Ironic, isn't it?"

"That's one word for it."

"Aria doesn't seem too disappointed, though."

"No," he smiled, "she doesn't. Her most memorable Midsummer yet, I should think."

The young man nodded in agreement. Rathen looked towards him when he failed to continue, and Anthis felt his gaze. He turned him a soft but doubtful look, which Rathen met directly, straightening in defence. He asked the question anyway. "Are you sure you want to bring her with us?"

Unsurprisingly, Rathen turned and stalked off back into the trees. "I'm sure I'm not letting her out of my sight."

He returned to the camp with a scowl on his face, but his darkness slipped when he found Aria kicking the snow by the fire, her face lowered and a great big pout on her lips. She seemed even smaller in her much too large cloak, and his first instinct was to scoop her up and squeeze her. Which he did.

She giggled, struggling to keep her pout in place. "I can't find Petra," she complained, fighting back her smile. "I wanted to practise with her."

"She's probably patrolling," he said, sitting himself on the driest rock in range of the fire, and lifting her onto his lap. "We're very close to Kulokhar."

She sighed dramatically. "I know." Her big blue-grey eyes lifted hopefully. "Can I see it?"

"You'll see it tomorrow, little one. I don't want you wandering off now, anyway. It's dangerous. Stay close to me." He spotted a fallen stick nearby and leaned over to fetch it. When he presented it to her, however, she regarded it with disgust, shook her head, and scurried off a few trees away. She came back within moments, a shorter, thicker branch in her hands which she turned over thoughtfully as she walked, paused to take her knife from her pack, and settled back down beside her father, running the blade across it without a word.

He smiled and sat back against the boulder, pulling his cloak tighter about himself. He watched her for a while, and beneath her broken humming and the constant shunk-shunk-shunk of quick, confident strokes, he soon drifted off into thought. But when he found himself entrenched in the matter of the coming day, he forced his mental march around and wandered instead onto other matters, both trivial and grievous. Until those, too, morphed into issues he didn't have the strength to face.

By the time he returned to himself, roused by one of Eyila's grunts of frustration from across the camp, Aria had fallen asleep. Huddled in her cloak beside him, wood shavings all over her lap - as well as his own - and her knife forgotten on the ground.

He smiled softly and kissed the top of her curly hair, then found what remained of the branch poking out from her cloak's folds. She'd fashioned it into a crude horse's head - the beginnings of a hobby horse, he was sure, though one much too small for herself. But not, he mused, for a doll. He had no doubt that it would look perfect when she was finished. Her skill was freakish. He adored that. But even as he smiled, the corners of his lips pulled downwards in guilt. He leaned over her and reached carefully into her bag. He found it buried at the bottom. He was sure that wasn't an accident.

A sigh eased free as he turned it over in the firelight. The woman carved of the dark elm of home, cocooned in a lacing flower bud, its sepal leaves etched with mind-numbingly intricate symbols. Yes, her skill was freakish. And her dedication to her task was something else to be admired.

But they'd found the Zi'veyn. Her dedication had been for nothing.

That thought clamped around his heart like a vice.

As shame crept over him, he traced his fingers over the twisting lines of the bud, from base to tip and back again, and his tormented rumination stampeded away.

And then, quite suddenly, he had it. A flicker of a notion, an idea so small and so obvious it didn't even announce itself. A thought that had been there all along, standing in plain sight like a single bird within a flock, a tree within a forest, a pebble within a stream, revealing itself with an incidental clearing of its throat and changing his view of everything around him.

"What are you doing with that?"

His wide eyes snapped onto the girl. She was looking back at him with poorly concealed injury, her tone guarded. But he was still catching up with his spiralling calculations. Even so, he spoke loud enough for the others to hear. "I think I might have something."

Anthis and Eyila looked up from their paper, relief on the latter's face for the distraction, and Garon and Petra stepped in together from the trees. Rathen found himself suddenly pinned under their critical stares. He rose to his feet and addressed them carefully. "I'd already worked a few things out, but since Anthis's last discovery, I've been onto a little more. It's not enough, but it's *something*..."

Garon fixed him levelly. "How far from 'enough'?"

"...Potentially," he shifted as he said it, "it could affect a single, specified spell."

"That's not enough."

"Didn't I just say that?"

"What *have* you got?" Anthis asked before Garon could fire another unhelpful statement.

"I can't modify the Zi'veyn. I can't risk damaging it. But I *can* use the Zi'veyn's spell as a base for my own. I've figured that out to the point that I should be able to target and suspend a small amount, and I've also been working over the notes Vorik made--"

"Vuthal. Kruik Vuthal."

Rathen blinked. "*Vuthal* made regarding dissolving the magic. I'm making progress there, too, I just need to expand them to affect magic as a whole rather than one spell at a time." He laughed to himself, then, a brief, sardonic chuckle. *'It's the difference between pebbles and mountains.'* He kept his doubt to himself. It wouldn't be his problem for much longer. "But combining them without degrading their individual strengths and purposes is a problem. I've been considering various methods of layering and merging, but in every case, one or the other looks likely to collapse. I've not tried casting them, but if it doesn't add up on paper, I can't risk applying it in practice."

"So you have half-finished spells and no way of combining them."

He let Garon's flat response slip by and, to their surprise, smiled instead. "No." He raised the wooden carving and tapped its base, the only point where the vined flower bud and the woman inside touched. "Connection. The spells don't *need* to be interwoven or cast one over the other. They just need to be *connected*. And while they both do different things, they have the same target, which means they only need to be connected at the *start*."

"Wouldn't it be easier to just take the Zi'veyn's targeting command and replace the suspension half with the command to 'dissolve'?"

"Yes. Would it not also be easier to kill suspected criminals on the spot rather than drag them away to the bailiff? Garon, if I start removing screws and nails when I don't know exactly what I'm doing, things are going to fall apart and nothing good will come of that. We've already seen for ourselves what half-formed elven magic is capable of. I'm trying to put together a spell beyond even the grand magister's capabilities using elven notes and the Zi'veyn as a framework. What I have is *already* a crude reproduction, but I have no intention of cutting things out, not until an elf tells me otherwise while I'm drunk off of my face."

"How much help do you think the Order could give you?" Petra asked hopefully. "Do you think you could have it finished before we leave?"

He stared through her for a moment before answering. "I think they could help the matter a great deal."

"But if you're using the Zi'veyn as a base spell, does that not mean that it'll be too big to cast?"

"For one person? Certainly."

Garon growled at the mage's lack of concern. "You want to recruit the Order to cast it, don't you? And what will happen when one of them takes the finished spell and--"

"Yes, yes, *or*," he held up the carving and smiled again. "Bit by bit."

They each blinked in sudden realisation. It seemed that he wasn't the only one to have overlooked that obvious detail.

A sudden squeal startled them, and Aria began bouncing up and down on the crunching snow, relief and excitement radiating from her like heat from the fire. But while the others grinned as she hopped madly around him, Rathen felt the awful shame and vice-like grip return. He didn't have the heart to tell her that he planned to hand it all over to the Order, especially not now that her carving would be put to use. Progress or not, they could complete it far more quickly than he, and they were in a much better position to cast it. No matter what Kienza had said, he doubted he could even light a torch without doubling over.

It was better for everyone that they took it off his hands. And since he'd already done most of the work for them, and planned it out as a human spell, they had no reason to refuse it aside from the deliberate bruising of a few scholars' egos. In fact, whoever could assemble it first would no doubt take all the credit and have a garish portrait hung in a tower corridor for their monumental achievement.

They were welcome to it. He wanted no further part in it, for himself or for Aria.

She jumped up at him, threw her arms about his waist and squeezed. He smiled and knelt, wrapping her up in his arms, and forced himself to smile. Tomorrow, this would all be over. And she - and the others - would be safe.

Few slept that night. Morning was painfully slow to come, and they broke camp before dawn. The snow had frozen through the night and remained strikingly reflective, and they made their way nervously by frost-light towards the capital city's walls, ducking behind rocks and beneath the riverbank to evade the sight of patrols along and below the battlement. But cover was sparse, and with every quiet, stooping, slippery dash they made, they were more and more likely to be spotted. Only once they reached the shadow of the walls did any semblance of safety return, but so too did their risk equally double.

No one dared speak a word as they pressed themselves into the shadows, willing themselves to disappear into the stone. It was here, within sight of the East Road and Gate, that Owan had instructed them to wait, but whether he would appear, or a score of Rathen's hunters, weighed even upon his trustful mind.

Despite the hour, the night was not still; the faint smell of smoke and freshly hewn wood drifted over the top of the wall, and repetitive strikes of hammer against copper and steel could be heard a short distance beyond. They listened to it, tuned into it, and worried silently that they wouldn't hear the toll of the bell tower over it, and that the sign they awaited would drift by unnoticed. But among their fret, they stopped hearing the rhythmic clamour, and after an age, three great chimes finally rang through the chill air, very loud and very clear.

They roused themselves to attention and began watching the sky, worrying now that they would miss the sign over the final flits of nightlarks. But before that concern could burrow too deep, another and far more real problem moved into sight along the road, sending panic jolting through their hearts.

A platoon of thirty of Turunda's soldiers marched in formation towards the East Gate, clad in glinting silver armour behind their lieutenant's silent lead, an emerald pennant flowing proudly upon his spear.

The group fell perfectly still until Garon made the call to slip further back. But Rathen stilled them. He watched the approaching men closely, and spotted a single bird dancing in the air close above them, a nightlark itself, but with a tail too long for a female and too short for a male. It was a thoroughly uninteresting example of its species. But despite the certainty that set in place, he reached out towards it gingerly. Only then did he relax and nod. "That's our sign."

He moved out towards a rock to arc through cover towards them, leaving the others at the wall behind him in a panic. Eyila was the first to follow, then Aria, and the rest were left with no choice.

The soldiers didn't react as he neared, and Rathen slipped in among them like a ghost. Or perhaps, the others thought, it was the other way around. The soldiers appeared perfectly corporeal from even as close as a foot away, but when a hand, elbow or shoulder touched them, they passed straight through.

Eerily, the group melded in and moved with them towards the gate, continuing on through when the guards stood aside and opened the way with a salute.

And then, all of a sudden, they were inside the great city of Kulokhar.

Rathen stifled his sudden wash of terror and focused on following the false soldiers, until he spotted a street branching off to one side, dark and empty - almost of snow, entirely of people. He gestured, and they dove into it at the first opportunity, leaving the platoon to continue its phantom march.

Now, they were alone.

Pulling their cloaks about themselves, they moved on quickly.

The artisanal district. It was evident even before they'd set foot in the city, and it wasn't empty. But the trade district and its main gate had never been an option; the stately district would have been quiet but guarded, while the poor district was thin on guards yet always alive, and the royal district had neither gate nor forest to enter through. But while this area wasn't asleep, everyone around them would be focused. It also made the ideal place for soldiers to enter the city without causing disturbance or being hindered by the populace. The streets here were wide and the buildings generously spaced apart; while it wasn't as compact as the rest of the open districts, they were dotted with crates and carts instead - providing the perfect cover for six who may wish not to be seen.

The smells that had drifted over the walls outside had become more concentrated, and were joined by that of leather, dirt and heat, while the noise itself was almost deafening to walk through in the twilight: clanging, hissing, repetitive puffs of bellows and grinding of saws, orders barked to apprentices, and more they couldn't identify. Such early work seemed ridiculous, especially in such low light, but the open lanterns gave off more than enough for practised craftsmen to see by while paying the courtesy of deepening the shadows, and few lived this close to the workshops. There were only craftsmen and intermittent guards around, and while the former were focused on their work, the guards were weary under their shift and appeared both distracted and eased by the arrival of the phantom soldiers. There wasn't likely to be any trouble while they were close by.

They moved deeper into the district, and where the snow had been burned away from the heat of the forges, beggars and homeless sat under the feet of tolerant smiths. One or two even appeared to have been put to work, and their haggard expressions looked more relieved than those of their sleeping counterparts, huddled but warm despite the noise. But not one of them were paying the group any attention. Each of them, in their own ways, were busy.

Anthis noticed Eyila staring at each person they passed, careful to keep the light from catching the subtle burnish of her skin by pulling her hood lower. Her bemusement finally slipped out in the faintest whisper. "These people don't seem unhappy..."

"Because," Anthis whispered just as carefully, "they're not." *'Though any other district would be a different matter.'* Thank goodness it had been this one.

A low growl rumbled in Garon's throat as he noticed a set of posters fixed to a dusty, smoky board, but he said nothing. Assuming Taric had done his job, they would be gone in a week.

Rathen, meanwhile, felt a loathsomely wistful pang of sorrow as he walked like a felon through the city that had once been his home, watching the snow gleam in the broader streets empty of forges, beautiful despite the clouds of smoke and dust. He imagined how the rest of it must have looked, from the towers that had once been a sanctuary. But a familiar and cruelly practical voice reminded him that this city had turned its back on him, and that his adoration was biased. Had he grown up anywhere else, Kulokhar would have been no more appealing than Mokhan or Carenna.

He pulled Aria closer and shut his longing away. She was his life now.

A figure wrapped in a travel cloak stepped suddenly out from the shadows, sending their hearts into their throats. Rathen recognised him quicker than the rest, but not before he'd pulled Aria behind him and considered a means to incapacitate him. He sighed shakily in relief. "Owan."

"Sorry," he smiled briefly. "You got in all right. Good. Come with me."

Rathen moved without hesitation; the others were less convinced.

Owan looked around at him as he fell into step beside. It took him a moment to speak. "There's something different about you." His eyes narrowed as Rathen failed to meet his stare. "What's happened?"

"I'll explain it all later. You don't need me to cast anything, do you?"

The man's brow knotted tighter. "No..."

"I thought there was a prohibition against magic," Garon said suspiciously.

"The grand magister declared this an exception."

The inquisitor glared unhappily. The mage had brought the matter to the grand magister's attention after all. He should have been more explicit in his message. He glanced towards Petra as she brushed her shoulder silently against his, and found a brief, reassuring look. He managed a flicker of a smile in return, but it did nothing to quiet his concerns.

They moved through empty streets, dark alleys and dusty lanes, encountering few souls as they went. A beggar or two sleeping in wagons, choosing soft hay and cloth-filled sacks over the warmth of forge fires, and a cat that followed them for a few turns until a mouse caught its flighty attention. From others, however, Owan could not conceal them, but he could at least cast a distraction. When they weren't waiting patiently for a patrol to round a distant corner, a simple spell could open a path around a watchful guard.

They waited until the illusory thief-child ran off around a corner, laughing mischievously while the guard dutifully chased it down with only minimal swearing.

Anthis watched curiously. "What happens when he catches it?"

"He won't catch it," Owan assured him. "Children have a way of vanishing through small spaces. He knows that. He won't think anything else."

"What about the soldiers?"

"They'll march back out through the North Gate."

The smells and noise thinned out as they moved deeper into the city, the buildings drew in, and the darkness grew heavier. They tightened together, looking over their shoulders, jumping at every sound. Owan frowned at them, but the equally anxious look on Rathen's face explained enough that he decided not to ask - not out here, anyway.

Mercifully, the streets soon began to widen again, and ahead loomed the three immense towers that bore the city's namesake: Kulokhar, Ebon Star Rise. Though they'd been visible from the approach beyond the walls, now so close, neither Eyila nor Aria could help but gawp, and Anthis and Petra noticed features they never had before. Notably that the famed Twisting Towers were only vaguely coiled, an optical illusion cast by the gold and silver four-point spiral that twisted around them in the opposite direction, making the architecture as a whole appear much more dramatic.

The black faces were dotted with tall, arched windows and finer gold flourishes, but above all were the invisible details revealed only in a shift of the light: washes and whirls that seemed to ripple over the onyx surface with every step they took forwards, backwards, left or right.

Eyila frowned with a touch of disappointment when she saw the holes and notches along the otherwise pristine spirals, cut very precisely as though it was quite intentional vandalism, until Anthis explained the musical intent behind the design, coaxing rainfall into beautiful melodies. Half of the group looked hopefully towards the sky, but if anything were to fall from those clouds, it was certain to be snow. The chill was relentless.

"These towers are bound to be watched."

"The Order took care of that some time ago," Owan assured Garon with ease, just as he had his every other thinly-veiled suspicion.

"And what of the Arana's spies?"

"They're known to the grand magister. They've been redirected."

The area took a sudden shift, and they knew they'd passed into a new district. Gone were the tightly-packed homes and store-houses, dusty streets and fulfilling sense of purpose; instead the cobbled stones became abruptly smooth, clean and uniform, laid to elven standards, the roads themselves had widened, and the buildings, though smaller, were no less opulent than the towers themselves.

Domed roofs, gilded facades, arched windows and ornate, oversized doors; meticulously tended gardens and trees, a pond so vast it verged on a small mere, a miniature rock bridge over a stream that trickled across a turquoise glass bed which, had it been day, would have been exquisite in colour as it wound its way among the classrooms, training grounds, dormitories and kitchens. Or so it would have been had every leaf, lily pad, and drop of water not been frozen solid.

Again, Rathen pushed aside that mournful ache and continued along the main road, leading straight to the towers.

"What's in there?" Aria asked, staring straight up at them with giant eyes. "Books?"

"Yes," Owan chuckled, "books. Libraries, archives, offices, meeting chambers, elders' dormitories--"

"Are we going in there?"

Rathen squeezed her hand in affectionate warning, but as she turned him an apologetic smile for her volume, a shadow broke away from one of the frozen gardens and moved out in front of them. Panic befell them all again, but the figure quickly dropped into step beside Owan, who hadn't broken his stride. After a few quiet words, the figure looked suddenly around to Rathen, who shrank back from the force of the awe in the man's eyes.

He returned briefly to Owan for another exchange, then moved off and disappeared around a corner.

The rest of them watched him leave uneasily.

They were so very close to the towers - closer than any but Rathen had ever been - and well within the range of any entrapping spells that may be lying in wait. If Owan *was* going to betray Rathen's trust, it could come at any moment.

Rathen was quite aware of this, and moved back up beside Owan, watching his old friend closely as he assured him he was only clearing the way.

When the towers stood just ahead atop a twenty-step dais, he stopped, turned, and looked them all over. None could tell what he was thinking. Rathen cursed himself for the failing of this friendship, until he realised that there was no longer *any* single person in the Order he could read completely.

His fingers loosened, and his heart began to race. He hadn't a clue what he could do. The memory of his last debilitating attempt to use magic shackled his imagination, but he had to be ready to do *something*, even if it was just throwing a punch.

Each of them tightened when Owan's eyes fell and lingered upon Eyila, as though he'd only then noticed her. But shrouded in a cloak as she was, and surrounded by magic all the time as *he* was, why would he notice her at all?

He considered her for a moment, then looked quickly back to Rathen. But Rathen had guessed what he was about to say. "Yes, and she's my responsibility. She's coming with me. They *all* are."

Owan looked across them all again before nodding his understanding, and it seemed to them that a brief glimmer of faith shone in his eyes at his old friend's resolve.

He turned and gestured for them to follow him around to the back of the dais, assuring Garon once again that the matter of spies had been taken care of.

"I'm sure all this mystery is very exciting, but I'm beginning to tire of vague answers."

"I apologise, but I'm sure you can appreciate that I'm not permitted to explain, Inquisitor."

"Actually, since you're the one who has been sent to meet us, no, I can't."

They were escorted through a small and unassuming door that almost vanished into the ebon facade. But, as they stepped over the hidden threshold, there was nothing within of the exterior grandeur. It was not a meeting hall, modest or otherwise. It was a small kitchen, dark, lit only by a few candles set upon a table, and occupied by a shadow. Garon's hand finally moved towards his sword. Petra's swiftly followed.

The door closed behind them. The figure moved into the light from the far side of the room. Blades were drawn. Aria was shuffled back into Anthis's care. And Rathen was hit by a sudden punch of nostalgia. But the panic that came with it was not that which the others shared, and this man, he was forced to remind himself, no longer had cause to invoke it. He was no longer his superior.

Rathen forced himself to straighten. The task was needlessly difficult. But the old man smiled not unkindly for it. "Sahrot Koraaz."

"Grand Magister." Rathen bowed his head on instinct, then looked around to the others and saw, with horror, the points of their blades angled towards him. He pulled Aria back to his side and demanded them to sheath. When he turned back, he found the old man looking down at the young girl with unconcealed surprise, while Aria peered back at him first in fear, then with growing curiosity. Finally, her eyes flicked back to her father, and the grand magister composed.

"I'm glad you're here, Rathen," he said in his kind voice, a voice that had thinned and weathered over eleven years, yet still had the power to render him contrite without reason. "There is a matter I'd like to discuss with you."

Rathen sobered. This time, it seemed he had reason. He straightened again and nodded. "And I, you."

"I don't doubt it. But my matter can wait." The grand magister smiled apologetically. "You didn't come here to answer a summons. Your own business is far more immediate." He looked across the others, lingering first upon Eyila with Owan's same curiosity, then upon Aria in another flicker of shock. He composed himself quickly once again and swept them a warm and hospitable smile before formally taking introductions. "It is a rare honour to have one of the tribes among us," he said softly to Eyila, who looked back at him with obvious surprise from beneath the concealment of her hood.

"It is?"

"Certainly," he smiled. "Especially a caster. I am a man of arcane academia, but anthropology is a special interest of mine. I would enjoy a talk with you, if you would grant it - at a later time, of course."

She dropped her hood and nodded somewhat falteringly in her surprise.

"Wonderful," he smiled again. "Now, if you would all please follow me. There's tea waiting upstairs, and a fire burning - it's preposterous that we should need it, but such are the present...complications."

Rathen led the way behind the grand magister while Owan took up the rear, leaving the cramped and modest kitchen for the magnificent hall beyond, its deep burgundy and walnut-panelled walls lit by elaborate sconces. Vast portraits set within ornate golden frames hung at regular intervals and followed them up the great staircase, where exquisitely carved busts of mages notable only to those acquainted greeted them at every half-landing.

They rose floor after floor, increasingly unsettled by their growing distance from the exit, and their legs quietly ached by the time they stepped off of the wide and winding staircase and down a dimly lit corridor. More busts stood along these walls, but they were outnumbered by the books that lay open upon periodic stands and lecterns and the occasional display of curious trinkets, most of which broke through Anthis's alarm to draw his insatiably academic eye.

His misgivings returned, however, when they were drawn to a stop beside a pair of doors. Even Rathen hesitated.

The room they were ushered into was vast and circular, with a large mahogany table set upon a raised platform, ringed by high-backed chairs. Another collection of portraits, books and busts stood silently along the walls, with the addition of bright green plants and ivory vases between and atop the cabinets.

But the most striking feature was the room's single window, so vast that it occupied a full quarter of the encircling walls and gave a near panoramic view of the city outside, interrupted only briefly by one of the exterior golden spirals, cutting across over the top corner. Facing north-west, all was perfectly positioned to catch as much light throughout the day as it could. Despite their crippling reliance on magic, the elves had maintained their penchant for daylight.

For now, though, the sky was brightening from indigo; the sun was rising, dawn approaching, and the dying twilight cast itself all throughout the room. The candelabra were lit, and the large fireplace flickered quietly in the corner. There was no arcane magic in their flames.

Two imposing figures moved around to the front of the table; a silver-haired woman, sublime in robes that complemented the contrast of her delicate form and powerful bearing, and a younger man in military dress, with broad shoulders, dark hair and a harsh, humourless expression. They looked over the arrivals with distinctly different intent.

The woman was the first to step forwards, but she did so with a smile even warmer than the grand magister's had been, and embraced Rathen in a gesture which shocked the group. He hesitated only a moment before returning it. "Young Rathen," she murmured affectionately as she released him, and smiled at the childish reddening of his cheeks as he inclined his head.

She looked then across the others, and introductions were given. Aria took her liking immediately. She crouched down to speak to her while giving her a surreptitiously close and appraising look, then her eyes flicked briefly up towards Rathen. But she didn't voice her conclusion. She smiled back at Aria instead. "The most beautiful young lady that has ever graced my sight," she declared softly, and now Aria's plump cheeks burned bright red, and she couldn't help the smile that pulled at her heart-shaped lips.

"And this is Sahrakh Roane Forlin," Arator continued. The man only took a few steps forwards as courtesy and acknowledgement, but did not offer his hand. Rathen made no move to, either. Instead he returned the soldier's viperous gaze and decided upon him instantly. Owan cringed, but kept it to himself. As did Delas and Arator.

The grand magister nodded towards Owan, who promptly turned to close the door, and escorted the group to their seats. Roane watched as Rathen pulled out a chair for Aria, who scrambled into it and looked about the room from the chin-high table in awe. Rathen caught his look, and the brief glance he sent back blistered with challenge. The sahrakh saw, and took it. "With everything that's at stake, you would bring a *child* to your summoning?"

"I'm not here on anyone's command," he replied bluntly as he took his own seat, his dark eyes unmoving from the soldier. "I don't answer to the Order."

"No, though you have no problem dragging our name through the dirt."

"Why ever would I bother when there are so many others doing such a fine job of it themselves? Tell me, Sahrakh," his tone was dangerously light, "what *have* you been doing about it?"

"As much as I can while balancing war, training, defence - against Doana, mage hunters *and* impaired mages - and trying to offset the chaos *you've* been sowing--"

"Oh, children, *please*." The pair silenced immediately beneath Delas's dramatic sigh. She turned apathetically towards the teapot set steaming upon the table, twisting her fingers to draw it nearer before Arator cleared his throat. She tutted to herself and rose to drag it closer by hand, pouring a cup for each. "It's much too early for this. Now, have you all eaten? You all look so very weary." Her concerned gaze lingered on Aria the longest. "We have some cakes--"

"Yes, please!"

She chuckled and turned to fetch them.

"Rathen."

At the burdened tone of the softly spoken voice, all eyes fell upon the grand magister. He'd fixed the mage with a sudden shadow of solemnity in his eyes.

"What are you doing?"

Rathen straightened and matched the severity. "Handling the magic."

"How?"

He reached into his bag in answer, but Garon objected with a single word. His eyes flicked instinctively towards Roane. He withdrew his empty hand. He knew Arator, Owan and Delas - but not him.

But while Garon had won that much, Rathen proceeded to explain the entire situation despite his every subsequent attempt at protest: what the magic was, where it had come from, and how they were handling it. And, through it all, the grand magister showed no mistrust or scepticism, only a level of passive attention that Rathen found nostalgic if also familiarly infuriating. But he knew all the while that every word was being absorbed, chewed and weighed - and, at least initially, a surprising number of points didn't appear to be news at all.

Until the depth of Salus's role in the matter was raised.

The expressions of all three, and Owan to the side of the room, darkened dubiously. Finally, Delas spoke. "Why have you come here, Rathen?"

He and his companions frowned in confusion, even Aria as she nibbled at a sugar bun. "What do you mean, 'why have you come here'? Didn't you hear anything I said?"

"Of course," she replied calmly. "But what can we do about it? We cannot move freely to do the things you're expecting of us. The Arana are here too - they are easily circumvented and our cloaking spells are far too complex for them to comprehend, but only a handful of us are capable of casting them, and for the rest of us it means that there is one more thing to think about with *every* move we make.

"Before all else, we need to deal with the rebellion and re-stabilise our own situation. They strike every few days; if it continues and escalates, our power will be scattered and then what will become of us all? Turunda's mages are among the best treated in Arasiin, but that could be about to change."

"Yes but it's that very instability, that ease of falling from grace, that forms the basis of their rebellion!"

"It is. And the rebellion itself is chipping away at that instability, making it even more hazardous. Already we will not regain the trust lost through any of these actions, be they intentional or not--"

"Which you are making worse--"

"Roane, *hush*." They blinked at the head of the preservation department in surprise, while Arator merely shook his head tediously between them. "Damage control is *critical*," she continued, "both for us and for future mages. Only then can we consolidate our power and form an organised front. As it stands, we don't know who among us we can trust - or who among us might use the opportunity to cast these defences to strike a crippling blow instead."

"Then what exactly do you plan to do about it? Persecuting already oppressed mages will only make the Order one of their enemies, and you won't be able to rely on any other authority's support against them. The Order, *and* the rebellion, will be left completely exposed!"

Delas splayed her hands. "Such is the Order's dilemma."

"But it *must* be overcome!"

"And it will be. But it will take time. We will never win the *absolute* trust of the Crown *or* the populace, we are under no illusions about that. Those without magic will always feel inferior, and without possessing magic one could never understand it. And when something isn't understood, especially something of such power and potential, it will always be feared. It is easy for someone possessing that power, who truly understands it, to tell people they have nothing to fear from it, but to doubt, mistrust - and to deceive - is human. No one can ever know another's thoughts or intentions, and so they could never trust the one trying to soothe them. But that doesn't mean we shouldn't try. To give in to that line of thought will lead to acting out and giving it base. Therefore, *every* mage needs to be the picture of honour and trust, regardless of whether or not the populace will believe it."

"But, as you said, to deceive is human. They will *never* believe it. You won't gain that trust, if anything even *near* it."

"No," Eyila's musical voice cut in, catching even the sneering soldier's full attention in his surprise, "but neither will anyone else. Mistrust is just a symptom of ignorance. You cannot teach people how to read minds, but you *can* teach them how to read spells. Magic *can* be understood, and once it's understood - its limitations and its capabilities - then it won't seem so mysterious. It will become little different to a skiving knife, it simply takes training or affinity to use it. And as far as it being a weapon - it is quite possible to kill without tools *or* magic."

"Would that we could all live under the same simple and gratifying trust as the tribes," Arator sighed to himself mournfully.

"Educating the masses will not satisfy the rebels," Delas replied carefully, still minutely in awe of the remarkable voice. "They're tired of being worse than disrespected by the people they are trying to protect, and even if we *did* impart such tutelage, results would be too slow and too few. Which brings us right back to damage control. And we are still scoping out the instigators."

"And in the mean time, the rest of Turunda will fall around the city's walls."

Her eyes turned back to Rathen with regret. "There is nothing we can do. We cannot leave to cast these spells. Turunda needs protecting against the keliceran's campaign, but with the impending war spreading us out, rebels abandoning their posts and a sickness of some kind afflicting and killing mages at random, we haven't the forces or the trust to handle it. Not yet. I am sorry, my dear."

Everyone but Roane braced themselves for Rathen's outburst - a cry of outrage, an accusation of dereliction of duty, a threat of one kind or another that no one was quite sure he wouldn't follow through. But none came. He remained under complete outward composure but for a knot in his jaw and a dangerous glint in his eyes. His tongue and temper remained in check. No one was quite sure who was more surprised. Even Arator appeared relieved.

Rathen's eyes flicked then onto him. "Why did you want to bring me in?"

"Because you are a menace. Not just to our name, but to the whole country."

He flashed immediately towards Roane, and whatever anger or frustration had been suppressed leaked out now in his direction. "And what do you plan to do now that I'm here, *Sahrakh?* Lock me up? Execute me? And then what will you do once my 'menace' has been put to an end? Step up and handle the magic yourself? Face Salus? Or stick your head in the sand, ignore every person and creature who have been made to suffer by either, put Aria in an orphanage and move on as if I had never existed to muddy the vaunted Order's precious name?"

Rathen saw his eyes flash. "At the very least, she'd be better off out of your 'care'."

He exploded to his feet, and Roane quickly followed.

"Stop."

They both restrained themselves with clear effort at the grand magister's gentle warning, while a number of those around Rathen scowled towards the soldier in shock or disdain. But neither's burning stare moved from the other.

"Know your place, Koraaz."

"Oh, *believe* me, I know my place."

"We won't be detaining you."

Both snapped towards the grand magister in surprise.

"What?"

"What?!"

Arator continued to regard Rathen in deep speculation, and while Owan displayed the same amazement as the rest, Delas seemed to be considering something in the ex-sahrot herself. "I don't believe it's necessary."

"Sir, with all due respect--"

But Arator waved the soldier away. "I'd like to speak with you privately, if you don't mind, Rathen."

"No, of course..."

Delas, her musings still clear in her eyes, rose elegantly and brushed down her robes with a single, delicate sweep before addressing the others, who rose in turn to be escorted out quite reluctantly by herself and Owan. Roane followed after another brief, heated glare, and Aria lingered doubtfully, looking between her father and her companions, a spiced fruit tart in her sticky hands.

But Rathen smiled warmly, a transformation that surprised the mages, and promised her with a hug that he would be along in a moment. "There's something I'd like to discuss with the grand magister, too."

She looked past him carefully towards the gentle old man, then slowly back to her father. Then her eyes travelled towards Roane, and she glared at him most deliberately. Delas stifled a chuckle.

Her big blue-grey eyes settled back upon the grand magister, and she nodded with acceptance. "All right. He seems nice. But don't be long."

"Of course." He kissed her on the forehead, which somehow tasted of sugar, and watched her hurry to take Petra's hand and leave with one final glance back through the door.

The air almost groaned with released tension once the latch fell into place, and Rathen felt his shoulders ease. Until the revered old man spoke.

"Something feels different about you."

Chapter 50

Rathen turned witheringly towards the old man, and his heart sank under the acute and deliberate conjecture in his eyes. He rubbed the sides of his head, chasing away the returning tension, and moved wearily towards the window. "You wouldn't believe me if I told you."

"Phantom magic, broken mages, Doana's invasion, the world ripping itself apart..." Arator returned casually to his seat and watched him with his distinctive patience. "Try me."

Rathen's eyes dragged away from the city, tinged gold by the early morning sun, and considered his former superior. He knew well how this would go, but equally that the dogged old man wasn't going to let him get away with not answering. So, easing cautiously into the chair beside him, he decided to give him what the old man thought he wanted. "My mother was an elf."

The words, spoken perhaps a little too lightly, struck even himself as utterly absurd, and he suddenly felt keenly close to the seven year old boy who had just been inducted into the Order. Even his palms began to sweat - a fact that grated and forced him to sit taller in his seat, as if to remind himself that he was an adult now.

Arator, however, simply stared back at him blankly. As expected, and not unreasonably, he didn't believe a word.

"We ran across an island of them," he continued despite himself, "and they...helped me."

Now Arator's wrinkled brow flickered at the flat disdain with which he'd said it, and bewilderment slowly seeped in. Rathen proceeded to explain the whole matter to the best of his ability, though his own recollection was foggy at best, but this time, while the old mage listened, he seemed torn between an outright refusal to believe and a complete lack of surprise. "Elves?" He said once he'd finished.

"Elves."

"And you found them while you were...searching for this relic? The Zi'veyn?"
"Yes."

"And they 'helped' you to control your magic and your...ability, with that cuff, but you don't know how? And that's how you're able to operate the Zi'veyn?"

"Elven blood, yes."

He nodded slowly, his furrow set firmly in place. "Can I see this 'Zi'veyn'?"

Without even cursory hesitation, Rathen rose, seized his bag, and withdrew the onyx-gold pyramid, laden with thorns and sharp corners, that fit snugly in the palm of the hand. He brought it back around and placed it upon the polished wood right in front of him.

Arator's cynical expression immediately dropped, and the years seemed to catch up with him. Clearly, he felt the power of the unsuspecting little thing.

He reached charily towards it, eyes unblinking, and lifted it reverently, turning it slowly in the candlelight. "*This* can silence magic?"

"*Only* silence. It can't remove it. The chains I've used it against out there are broken, but the magic remains in concentration and there's still no telling what it could do if it's left alone. Or what someone could do *with* it." He nodded at the doubtful look. "I know, but this very thing is proof that it's *not* impossible to directly affect magic. *I have* directly affected it. I've pushed it, I've manipulated it; someone else could do a lot more if they put their mind to it. I've been working on a spell that can finish the job before they get the chance, but it's slow-going."

"...I see... And the Zi'veyn can be used against casters?"

"Only elves. It won't work on humans."

"You know for sure?"

"Yes, and I've proven it. On Eyila. It didn't work."

"You're sure you were using it correctly?"

Rathen smiled hollowly. "I've studied it inside and out. There is only one way to use it."

Arator turned it over a few more times, touching the lines, admiring the arcane craftsmanship and, quite certainly, attempting to analyse the spell inside. Rathen's brow rose in surprise when the old man shuddered and visibly recoiled from it, and he put it down in sudden onset of exhaustion.

There was something frightening in those implications. Frightening, and empowering.

"Forgive me for saying so," Arator puffed, "but I'm shocked that you worked it out at all. Not because it's you, but because...it's..." He abandoned his hunt for words and looked towards him with a speculation so powerful, he was almost physically struck by it. "*No one* here could have done this."

"No one here is half-elf." He regretted that immediately.

Arator's expression didn't change. "You're realising your power."

'And there it is.'

"So many of us sensed something within you, Rathen; since the day you came here, you've been different."

"Yes," he turned away tightly and stared back out of the window. "Because I can turn into a monster."

"No, that is clearly only a small part of it, and a part which you *can* learn to control. Ferna - could you have stopped that from happening?"

Rathen chewed the inside of his cheek while a war raged in his mind. Did he admit to his former mentor that he could have, and fuel this obsession? Or lie and risk satisfying the imperious sahrakh's misconception instead?

Resentfully, he discovered that he cared a great deal about the grand magister's opinion, and under that compelling stare, he had no room to fight the exhausted sentiment. "I had my reasons..."

He looked around at the following silence and watched Arator watching him. He was again a picture of profound contemplation.

"Many mages view you as a disgrace. A villain, even."

"I know."

"Myself and a great many of your peers disagree. I know you, Rathen. You may think you've changed in eleven years, but you haven't. I can still read you like a book. When Owan came to me with your message, I had my suspicions, and the moment I laid eyes on you again, they were confirmed. You are weighted by your task, you're frightened, and you seek help, and not just by means of the defence you spoke of.

"But, regrettably, what Lady Delas told you is true: we must deal with the rebellion before all else - regain our strength in numbers and trust, and then we will be able to act. But when that time comes, we cannot take this task off of your hands. And I wouldn't allow it if we could. It fell to you for a reason, and it seems increasingly obvious that you are the only one with the potential to achieve it."

"Potential," Rathen snarled, gripping his folded arms tighter, "*potential!*" He whirled around on him, any trace of his lingering veneration and inferiority snuffed out like a candle. "For *years*, all I heard growing up here was 'potential'. I am *sick* of it."

"Are you sick of it simply because you know that it's true but wish that it wasn't?"

That, he refused to admit. "There is too much weight on my shoulders," he growled, snapping away again, "you're right. But it has *always* been there - your expectations *put* it there! And it's...*unbearable*. I don't want the weight any more. People are getting *hurt* because of it."

"Is that why they're getting hurt? Or is it because they sense something worthwhile in you and choose to follow you for it, wherever it might lead them?"

Rathen's eyes darkened in exasperation. "I cannot let anything else happen to them. I cannot let anything happen to *Aria.*"

"I'm afraid, Rathen, that that weight was put there by yourself," Arator replied with such simplicity that Rathen felt his head might explode. "Perhaps we did encourage it, but after awakening magic at the age of seven, you expected great things of yourself, too. Which you have achieved - you just can't see them through the seven year old's heroic and grandiose dreams. The dreams born of stories your father once told you - stories that didn't come to pass as you imagined them to, and that you grew to blame him for. The stories that some part of you still clings on to."

His back became rigid. "Things have changed."

"Have they?"

"Yes." He eyed him darkly. "Many things. Above all else, I have a daughter now. She is eight. *She* has grandiose dreams - of peace and of happiness - and I want to see them come true. Getting the both of us killed won't help towards that."

"Even so, you *are* the only one capable of wielding the Zi'veyn, crafting this spell and all else you've sought to do. All these heroic dreams could yet be realised."

Rathen barked an irritated laugh and snapped away in dismissal, whirling towards the window, the table, the wall. But there was nowhere in that room that Arator's voice or thoughtful gaze couldn't reach him, and the idea of leaving his distinguished presence didn't dare occur to him. He was trapped.

He settled for the window. The sight of the waking city at least created the illusion of distance.

Arator said nothing for a while. He rose after a few moments and stood beside the window himself, but he allowed Rathen his privacy. He became aware of it only once his seething thoughts began to exhaust themselves, and then the deference that had been drummed into him since he was a boy marched in to vanquish his contempt.

"Tell me," Arator spoke at last, his voice quiet and sombre, "does Salus happen to be acquainted with any of these elves?"

"...Yes."

He grunted softly and nodded his head, eyes tracking absently across the scape of the royal district. "I see. Now the story makes sense. The mages of the Arana aren't bound by our rules, and there are many things they can do that we cannot - or *would* not. But applying elven theories to their own meagre arsenal of spells, well, that was too much. They don't have the capacity for that, magically or academically. You should have known that wouldn't add up."

"I did," he sighed, "but I was desperate. I didn't want to...frighten you off."

"I quite understand. I dare say Roane would have flown into a fit at the slightest suggestion of the truth."

"I doubt it would take much."

"He isn't a bad man, Rathen. He's just...he's a tactician. He intentionally pushes buttons--"

"To get the best read on someone. I know. I can see what he's doing. But it's not a game I want to play with him."

"No. Most people don't." Arator sighed and leaned his hands against the windowsill. He sent Rathen another thoughtful look, but one softened by some small hint of apology. "I know you're tired of hearing it, Rathen, but whether you like it or not, a great power resides in you. And with...well, the experiences and encounters you've had, surely you've accepted the fact of that power by now; it's no longer an inkling on your elders' part but a truth you've been shown for yourself. And if your...if your abilities are a part of that, then there is hope - *great* hope - for control and for help. And, above all else, we finally have an explanation."

The small sigh that escaped the old man surprised Rathen. It was as though an ancient personal strife had finally been eased. Had the matter troubled him that much? *'More for the name of the Order, no doubt.'*

And yet something in his heart told him that it was more than that...

The knot in Rathen's shoulders released itself as he looked more easily across the city. The old man wasn't wrong: Tekhest had presented him with an explanation for everything. He didn't like the explanation, nor its source, and everyone seemed to be overlooking the fact that an explanation didn't mean a solution, but...it was *something*. And he *was* gaining control.

Or, he *thought* he had been...

Rathen looked up at Arator's sudden chuckle as he forced the events of that night away from him, and found the old man shaking his head. "Elven blood... Well well. I have to admit, I'm not wholly surprised. And that in itself *does* surprise me. And that this whole matter should wind up in *your* lap... It seems our assumptions were prophetic. Oh, scowl all you like, but I find the whole matter quite satisfying."

"Oh *good*," Rathen drawled, "I'm glad for you."

Arator laughed again, more heartily this time, and he turned from the window to clasp him on the shoulder. "You've not changed at all. You may have behaved in my presence all those years ago, but there was always a fire - oh, you kept it in check, but it was there, and I'm sure it was that which ensured you always did what had to be done." He considered him for a brief moment, then nodded with another shameful smile. "You would have made a fine sahrakh."

Rathen scoffed.

"You were in line for it. Perhaps, if things had gone differently, you could even have made Sivaan, in time."

"And perhaps, if I cross my fingers tightly enough, I'll wake up back in my own bed and we won't be having this conversation."

"Anything is possible." But then the humour faded from his steel-blue eyes, and the intent of his stare made Rathen shift. "You can do this. You're in the perfect position. You're not tied to our rules, you have broad field experience with the magic, with the Zi'veyn, and you know the spell inside it well enough to dare to make one of your own variation. Have you gotten far?"

"Yes," he said eagerly, spotting an opportunity. "Very far. I've written everything down - ideas that worked and those that didn't, processes, reasoning--"

"It sounds like a dissertation."

"Well I supposed I took something away from my studies, then. The point is, it's all there, on paper; it would be no trouble for someone wiser to take over and finish it, and *much* quicker than I could."

"One would think. But what about the small, subtle connections you've made that you didn't think to write down? The connections that experience and experimentation with the Zi'veyn itself produced? The ones that seemed so obvious, you didn't even notice them?" Arator smiled sadly at his loss for words, even while his dark eyes revealed his desperate, raking thought. "There is a reason studies are rarely reassigned, and why so few succeed when they try to continue an idol's work, no matter how much research they put into it. It's because they lack the inherent understanding for the matter, whatever it might be. And it will often times have nothing at all to do with intelligence, but personality. If anyone in the Order - even myself - were to take your notes and try to complete your spell, it would take years, whether you were on hand to help or not. It would be far too late. You are the only one who can do this."

Rathen sank helplessly into his chair and stared down at the woodgrain in defeat. "But I'm not an academic."

"Which makes it all the more surprising that you took on the task in the first place." He cocked his head as he sat back down beside him. "Or is it? You were drawn to the military not because you weren't good at academic work, but because you weren't *interested* in it. You have an innate understanding of magic - you always have. It is, dare I say, in your blood, and in every sense of the term. And that no doubt has shaped the construction of your spell without you even knowing it. You may have been raised as a human mage, but your perspective is most likely more in tune with your magic than I am with my own, and that means that you have made yet more connections, and greater leaps, than any one of us could reasonably comprehend."

"What you're saying is that no one else can make *this* spell. But what if you were to just use the foundation - disregard all my connections and progress and just use the *concept*--"

Arator raised a silencing hand. "The matter remains unchanged. You have been able to grasp the foundation, but it's the foundation itself that our magic is not capable of. We cannot construct the spell. Even a foundation as simple as the *theory* of making a spell to suspend magic isn't within our comprehension. Ask us to create a spell to *remove* it, and you would have more luck getting ditchlings to fly."

Rathen felt his last desperate flicker of hope burn out like a candle thrown down a well. It must have been clear on his face, as the old man patted the tabletop for his attention, but he didn't lift his gaze.

"You *can* do this, Rathen. You have grasped that foundation, you have used the Zi'veyn, you have formulated a spell from it, even if it remains unfinished. That is...simply astonishing - and there is no reason you cannot complete it."

"I never said I couldn't complete it," he replied distantly.

"No...I suppose you didn't, did you?" Arator studied him for a long moment, until Rathen finally tore his eyes from the woodgrain and the old man smiled. He straightened in his chair and pulled across the teapot. "Now," his tone lightened in a manner that struck Rathen as wholly inappropriate in his torment, though he accepted the fresh cup of tea, "if it doesn't put you out, I should like to talk with you."

"What about?"

"Oh, nothing in particular," he smiled kindly, "though, I admit, young Aria has piqued my curiosity above all else. You left here heirless and return now with an adoring and healthy daughter in tow. I just...wonder what fortune banishment seems to have granted you."

Rathen couldn't help smiling at the irony. "Looking for a change of lifestyle, Grand Magister?"

"Allayment of guilt, if I'm honest."

"It wasn't your doing."

"I should have fought them."

"It's done. And the Crown's plan failed, anyway - I'm still breathing."

"Yes, you are." Arator grinned, an expression Rathen had rarely seen in his twenty seven years in the Order, and raised his teacup enthusiastically. "To your ongoing health. Now: how in Vastal's name *did* you survive?"

The sitting room was vast. It was large enough to sit twenty people quite comfortably with still room for privacy, and its broad windows had long since eliminated the need for candles, the mid-morning light smiling through the lace drapery while prying eyes were shut out.

The walls remained the subdued and tasteful burgundy and walnut that had lined the staircase and corridors, but was accented now by the soft and rolling lines of cabriole sofas, wingback chairs and chiselled circular tables, and the neutral tones of landscape paintings and encased leather books. The air, too, was mellowed by the scent of summer flowers arranged in vases beside the windows, and the fireplace that crackled quite excitedly against the chill of the frosted world outside. The combination of florals and warmth could have fooled anyone into thinking that nothing at all was out of place.

Jugs of water sat upon the low table central to a three-quarter ring of seats, as well as a steaming teapot, frequently refreshed, raisin-studded bread, and scones with butter, cream or jam, which Aria had initially set to devouring but now ignored entirely. Worry had gotten the better of her and she'd spent the last hour staring intently towards the door from a large chair she'd dragged around and angled directly towards it.

But she was not the only one.

She turned her eyes briefly towards the inquisitor, who kept a similar if more subtle watch over the door. "What did he want to speak to the mage-ister about?" She asked, not for the first time, to which Garon equally replied no differently. She didn't believe him, though. There was something in his eyes, an idea or suspicion. He just didn't want to tell her.

She sighed quietly and returned to her vigil.

Then, the door opened, and her little heart burst into her throat. But the man that stepped inside was not her father. She sighed again and slumped deeper into her seat.

Petra turned away from her pacing as the mage approached her. He was an older man, certainly no older than Rathen, and had been the one to startle them outside and clear the way of lingering mages ahead of their arrival. His sharp nose and the scar across his otherwise dimpled chin marked him out quite distinctly.

Garon stood and drew himself up as he neared.

"I'm afraid I was correct," the mage said to her, his strong voice softened by privacy, "Celise Dalton has been deployed."

She was already hugging herself, but her expression fell even deeper in fret. "Where? Is she all right? She's not...behaving unusually?"

His face softened sadly. "No, she's just fine. Everyone is watching each other closely." His green eyes narrowed at her thoughtfully. "She's your sister, isn't she? I thought there was a likeness. She's in the west, moving to head off Kalokh."

Petra frowned at that, and Garon stepped forwards. "Explain."

"They moved in from the mountains two days ago," he told them. "They hit a few towns and villages simultaneously, and the military was quick to divert and confront them, but Doana took a cheap shot from behind. Reserves have been deployed to combat Kalokh while others reinforce the watch over Doana - Celise is among the mages accompanying the reserves."

Petra found little relief in that fact, and the both of them frowned in growing concern.

"We saw very few soldiers in the city," Garon noted.

"Most have been called away. Only Kulokhar and a handful of the larger internal cities still have any such guard at all, but we don't know how much longer that will last." He looked across them both patiently. "Is there anything else I can do for you?"

Petra smiled and shook her head distractedly. The mage bowed, then turned and left. Aria tracked him suspiciously before returning her watch to the door, until Eyila left Anthis to distract her with a game.

Petra sighed and sank heavily into her seat a ways from the others. Her eyes were distant as her fingers traced the locket through her blouse, and Garon didn't miss their fret and sadness as he moved surreptitiously to stare out of the window behind her.

"You heard what he said," he reminded her quietly without turning. "She's fine."

"For how long?" She replied similarly.

"You're disappointed she isn't here."

"Of course I am. At least then I'd *know* if something was wrong - we've seen the signs, we could get her help."

"I doubt very much that *they* haven't learned the signs by now. He said they were watching each other closely. If she falls ill to it, it will be spotted."

"And what can they do about it?"

"What can *we?*"

She didn't reply. He cast a careful glance around and found her sitting forwards now, her face in her hands, and he realised he'd handled the matter poorly.

Garon abandoned the window and moved to sit down beside her, though not as close as either of them would have liked. He said nothing, though, and neither did she, but the gesture seemed to be enough. She cast him a subtle, grateful smile.

Forcing himself to soften was taking some getting used to.

Time progressed sluggishly, agitating their impatience. Their only real relief came from the opportunity to finally sit down for longer than twenty minutes, and for being out of the elements for the first time in longer than any of them could remember. And the room itself was spacious, warm and comfortable, a fact they were grateful for following the sudden and unnatural turn of the weather - but it was difficult to forget the fact that they were in the middle of the capital city, within range of the Arana's command hidden somewhere in plain sight, and surrounded by any number of proficient spell casters who, up until a few hours ago, wanted to catch and detain Rathen indefinitely. No one was in any state to enjoy the apparent comforts.

Though his stomach rumbled, Anthis turned away from the selection of breads, cheeses and warm meats recently brought in to them, and heaved an anxious sigh.

"Worried about him now?"

He jumped in surprise, then looked sheepishly back towards Petra and her wry smile. "We've had our misunderstandings, I admit, but I don't *dislike* him..." His eyes travelled back towards the door. Aria's had been fixed to it despite Eyila's attempts to distract her, and now they all seemed to participate in her watch. He looked back around towards Garon. "What if they've detained him after all?"

"Then we'll break him out."

Anthis frowned incredulously. "*How?*"

"With magic."

His eyes shot towards Eyila at her own steady reply, and watched the determination harden her ice-blue eyes. Garon's were identical. Had the two concocted a plan somewhere in the dismal silence?

He had little opportunity to ponder. The shift of the latch snatched back their attention and prompted the same futile hope it always did. This time, however, it was not for nothing.

They all rose to their feet in relief when Rathen stepped inside, escorted as he was by the same mage who appeared to have been assigned to tending them. Aria leapt up immediately and charged at him like a bull, earning a smile that broke the troubled lock of his face.

"Where have you been?" Garon demanded as Rathen knelt and scooped the child up, gesturing for the mage behind him to wait.

"Where you left me," he replied evasively. "There were some things the grand magister and I needed to discuss."

"So you said - care to elaborate?"

"Not particularly." He kissed Aria on the top of her head, then rose and turned towards the escort. "Thank you. Could you tell Owan that I need to speak with him as soon as possible - in the fifth floor archives."

"You're leaving again?"

He smiled softly down at Aria and gently mussed her curls. "Not yet, Owan will be busy." He looked briefly back to the mage. "Have him send word when he's ready." Rathen was about to turn away when a hint of familiarity tugged on his memory, and he frowned speculatively at the mage. "I know you..."

The scar-chinned man stood suddenly straight and saluted with his fist to his heart. There bloomed a surprised and honoured gleam in his green eyes. "Seyir Caiden Vi'rah, Alokh Battalion."

The gesture didn't seem to discomfort Rathen as he stood and scrutinised the man, but Aria stared up from beside him in open shock at the bold and strictly executed show of respect towards her father.

"You were my soviin in our part against Qenra's campaign in the year Seven Hundred and Three."

"What's a soviin?" Aria asked in a hushed voice, quickly whirling towards Garon.

"A captain," he replied quietly. "He led a company."

"A company? How many people is that?"

"In the Order's case, about twenty mages."

Her eyes bloomed. "*Twenty people?!*"

"It's not that many, and Qenra were already finished by that point," Rathen assured her deprecatingly. "We were just accompanying a few soldiers to ensure they didn't get near Turunda."

"A battalion - and under his command we saved almost four hundred lives because he and he alone noticed a concealment spell. If not for that, Qenra's advance company would have cut down half of us in a surprise attack."

"Why didn't the rest of you detect it?" Garon asked suspiciously.

"It was an extremely advanced spell - what are you doing here, Caiden?" Rathen asked in an attempt to escape the focus, but the mage's boldness swiftly collapsed.

"Administration," he replied ruefully, "for the war. The same as Sahrakh Forlin, really."

Rathen's eyes hardened inquisitively. "Roane? What do you make of him?"

"He is a fine and proficient leader."

The absolute conviction of Caiden's statement deflated some of Rathen's doubt, but the next question that presented itself - one born of his own loyalty - trapped itself behind his teeth. Arator had told him everything he needed, and he knew in turn that Rosh wouldn't have allowed the man's promotion if he wasn't suited to the task of succeeding him. But he remained stubbornly unsatisfied.

The sergeant must have seen it in his eyes, for he answered the unspoken question anyway. "There is no doubt over Sahrakh Forlin's capability. We will follow him willingly."

Reluctantly, Rathen straightened and gave a single nod of acceptance. "Very well." Again he began to turn away, but the soldier stunned him with a wholly unexpected question. He turned back slowly and shook his head with such remorse that he surprised himself. "No. The Order doesn't need me, and I don't need its rules. And there are...things I need to do that those rules would hold back."

Caiden studied him for a moment, then his eyes dropped to Aria who stood at his side, still looking up and between the two with awe. He looked back to Rathen and nodded. "I understand." He saluted again, then, upon Rathen's withering consent, turned and left the room.

Rathen sighed in relief as the door clicked shut, but shortly discovered the rest of them looking at him rather oddly, as though they were suddenly rearranging their opinion of him.

He cleared his throat uncomfortably and slipped past them towards the food on the table.

Chapter 51

The air was heavy with the musty smell of old parchment and ink, a smell that had the strange ability both to comfort and unsettle in its invoking of whispered memories: the unreasonable fear of chastisement for the slightest mistake, the catastrophic punishments for tardiness, the fifteen minutes of detention that spanned a lifetime, while interwoven was the safe certainty and routine of every day life, of lessons, of classrooms, of mentors and peers, of knowing what each day would bring.

Now, though, it spelled out hope, and with that hope came a distinct panic under the roaring possibility of rejection.

Rathen watched Owan leaf carefully through his notebook, through Anthis's translations, through their joint workings and individual musings, but for every passing moment the scholar's face betrayed none of his thought. Despite the grand magister's refutation, Rathen still had hope, and its increasingly fragile existence hinged upon their location and its inciting aroma. Surrounded by knowledge and the achievements of his predecessors, Owan might be more inclined to entertain the idea of taking the task for himself. He might even fathom an idea and be able to carry it through on the spot if the references he needed were on hand. He chose to overlook the fact that his old friend had never been selfishly impulsive.

The concentrated frown deepened, and Rathen felt his impatience rise a step higher. Finally, Owan set the papers down with a sigh, sat back in his seat, and regarded his old friend with a curious look. "It could work," he said carefully.

"It could?"

"I...I think so...to be honest, it's a little over my head..."

"Well that's probably just because it's unfinished. It looks a bit of a mess right now, but it will all come together when the few final areas are worked out - just little things, like how to make the connection at the base: where to link the two spells, for how long, and where to split them apart, because I don't believe they need to be intertwined completely. Then expanding the spell to touch all the magic at a location rather than just one spell chain - but that's more a matter of usage than construction, and confining the power to do what it has to rather than break out of control and falter. It's not a question of personal strength," he added quickly, watching the dubious frown grow deeper on his old friend's face, "casting the spell bit by bit will satisfy that, but more the reinforcement of the edges of the spells. It really is just little things..."

Owan blinked slowly. "Yes, just little things." He shook his head. "'Bit by bit'?"

"...Why not?"

"*Why not?!*" He bit his incredulity back behind a rasping whisper, and his eyes suddenly blazed with a mixture of insult and desperate calculation. "Because it's...it's..."

"It's how the elves did it."

"Yes, Rathen: *elves*."

He felt his heart suddenly flutter in panic at the abrupt crumbling of his manipulative plan. The very roots of his confidence shook at the scholar's alarm, but even while the steady voice of reason was quick to remind him that there were a few key details his old friend was unaware of, he found himself somewhat disinclined to share them after the grand magister's conclusion.

Rathen forced himself into composure. If he was to convince Owan to take the task off his hands, he couldn't let it seem as futile as he was right to think. "It can be done."

"The idea is preposterous."

"There is no other choice." He held him in a morose stare, and Owan's stubborn conviction began to deflate.

"No," he sighed finally, slumping back into his seat, "I suppose there isn't... All right..." He sat forwards and looked over the papers again, a studious air of deliberation falling over him even as his doubt remained as thick as a storm cloud above. "Right. Well...first, if the two spells are going to be connected, there's no need for *both* of them to start with a nominative chain; if the foundational spell begins with the nominative chain then the obliteration spell can be linked in subsequently rather than doubling up. It would be less effort but just as effective, and there's less room for something to go wrong. But, once they're linked, they'll begin acting simultaneously and there's going to be a break down if both spells are trying to act on the same thing at once - one can't suspend the subject if the other is obliterating it. So they'll need to be just short of synchronised. If the spell to suspend *has* to be involved--"

"It does."

He glanced up, and Rathen saw the dubious look creeping back in. "Then that one will have to come first, if only barely. There will need to be a timing or deferral chain added to the obliteration spell the moment they split apart, which should only be once the full parameters of the subject are described. That should allow the suspension the room to satisfy and give the obliteration the opportunity to act in peace, while at the same time keeping each spell separate enough that their respective purposes don't get confused."

Rathen nodded slowly, trying to work out just when Owan had lost him.

"As for reinforcement..." A glint of enthusiasm suddenly caught in his eye. He jumped up and hurried down one of the many cramped aisles of neatly stacked and towering bookcases.

Rathen smiled to himself as he disappeared, and abandoned his desperate attempt to recollect his words. His plan was working after all.

"There are a few tricks," his voice floated back towards him, "and for so...*ambitious* a spell, it might pay to try them all..." He reappeared with a particularly average-looking tome open in his hands and an absorbed pinch to his face. "You can make the spell stronger by being more precise - don't gloss over things, make it as detailed and tedious as you can, leave no room for error... You can also double-link the connections - but in such a complicated spell that might not be a wise idea, you might accidentally duplicate a command. Forget I said it... Weaving a reinforcement spell through their spines can strengthen the bonds, and if it's through the spine of the spell it won't muddy the chains themselves, it'll be like a shadow - unobtrusive but always present..." He fell quiet for a long moment and flicked back and forth through a few pages. "You could also try laying a more literal reinforcement spell into the object you plan to cast it into."

Rathen frowned. "That would work?"

"It should at least prevent degradation or loss of power if the spell *does* fall apart."

"...Like the Zi'veyn..."

"Yes." He closed the book.

After a silent moment of thought, Rathen discovered that his eyes had drifted onto him in another hesitant consideration, but one marked by a personal dilemma rather than anything serious. He knew what was coming. Arator had given him the same look.

"Can I see it?"

He restrained his optimism and removed it from the bag. Owan reacted in much the same way as the grand magister had, though he took longer to probe the spell, and recoiled much sooner. He looked back at him in harrowed awe. "I can't believe you got this to work."

"That's a popular sentiment."

"How do you turn it on?"

"Uh...well you don't, really..."

He turned it over once more before his eyes slammed up onto him. "Rathen, this is a *channelled* spell. You have to *fuel* it."

"Yes..."

"It's an *elven* spell."

"What gave it away?"

Confusion further darkened Owan's eyes. "I...don't..." He fell back onto Anthis's notes in a frenzy, muttering incoherently to himself. He spoke up only barely. "You couldn't possibly fuel it with our kind of magic, not an elven spell...but how could you possibly bypass it? It's a rule of...of nature!"

"It was troublesome, I won't lie. Owan," he slipped around beside him while he continued his frantic debate and fixed him seriously. "I don't have the disposition to take this spell where it needs to go. Anthis Karth found and translated the elven notes, and I applied an arcane perspective to pull it all together, but that's all, and the remaining connections are beyond my capacity to make. I'm not like you, Owan, I took a different path. I have no interest in this kind of thing, nor the training or experience to see it through."

Rathen saw his thoughts finally slowing down, and a moment later he was staring back at him with equal severity. "I can see your angle, Rathen, but I can't take this off your hands."

Carefully, he steeled his frustration. "Why not?"

"Because the very *utilisation* of the spell is over my head! Notes or not, I can't work out how you managed to put this together in the first place!"

"Necessity had a large part. Look, you've only been reading over these notes for a few *minutes*--"

"We've been here for two hours."

"And how long is two hours in the grand scheme of things? You *wouldn't* grasp it in an instant, and yet you still managed to come up with some solutions--"

"I came up with *suggestions*--"

"And look at all the studies and references you have around you! Pair that with everything I've given you and you could have it down in a *week*."

"And destabilise the country in a fortnight."

His hopeful persuasion evaporated. The misery lines in his face deepened. "You wanted a solution to this catastrophe."

"Yes. And I dare say I've found one."

"And if you took it off my hands, it would all be done much sooner - but if it's left with *me*, there's no telling how far Salus is going to get nor how many pieces Turunda is going to be in by the time I finish it! Why are you looking at me like that?"

Owan's narrowed eyes harboured a shade of suspicion so powerful that, for a moment, Rathen's heart stopped. It took great trouble to force aside his instinctive defence and meet his stare levelly. Again, he knew exactly what was coming.

"There's been a change in you. Magically. Don't think I haven't noticed that you've still not explained it - and now I'm increasingly certain that it has to do with your operation of the Zi'veyn... Something has awakened in you."

He tried to suppress it, but Rathen couldn't keep his gaze from flicking just past him, nor the intolerant lick of fire from flaring within it.

Owan caught it and watched his jaw harden as a sudden charge coursed through the air. A charge made cautionary by nostalgia's warning.

With the slightest sigh, the studious mage's shoulders rounded in defeat, and he finally sat back down at the small, paper-strewn table, watching him with consideration. "Have you spoken to the grand magister about this?"

"Yes," he replied crisply. "I've told him everything."

"Everything? Or everything he needs to know?"

"Everything."

"And he's not changed his mind about detaining you?"

"No." Rathen returned at last to his seat, and the charge began to dissipate. "I have his support."

"Then I suppose I don't need the details. No matter how much it's going to scratch at me. But - and brace yourself, Rathen, because this is going to hurt - *you are* the solution to this catastrophe."

"No, no, I'm not. The *spell*--"

"The spell is impossible. And in your case, that should go doubly. And yet, somehow, I have this really quite...*frightening* confidence that it *isn't* impossible as long as you're involved. You've...*you* have grasped ideas that are beyond anyone in this place. *Destroying* magic? *'Killing'* it, your notes say - it isn't a living thing! But...but somehow...your reasoning..." His eyes grew harrowed as his crisis of conviction set in deeper. "Even the *notion* of casting a spell 'bit by bit' is absurd! But the elves...they *did* do it, and...Vastal save me, somehow I think you could, too. Rathen, I *can't* take this off of your hands."

"*But I don't want it.*"

"Yes, you do."

Rathen faltered. "What?"

"This spell could save everyone. It could stop Salus in his tracks."

"Yes, and that would remain the case *whoever* finished it."

"'Finished it' is the key phrase here."

"Yes, and anyone could."

"No, they couldn't." He sat forwards, his eyes blisteringly astute. It made Rathen itch. "Why is it so important that you get rid of this? It doesn't seem dangerous, just...impossible..."

"No, the spell isn't dangerous. But *I cannot cast* it. And even if I could--"

"Why not?"

"...I don't have the power."

"'Bit by bit'. But that's not how you said it." Owan's disconcerting speculation grew sharper, and Rathen suddenly felt as though he was training an arrow on him. "You didn't want to cast anything when we were coming in. Why? What's wrong?"

"Nothing - I'm just tired from all the travelling - and I simply mean that if *I* cast it, *I* stay in Salus's line of sight. I can't do that. I have a daughter and...it's too much responsibility. If it fails, it's on me, and there will be no one out there to pick it all up if I'm the only one who knows anything about it. That can't happen. I have to put her first. Anyone else can take my place - *you* could finish it, you could even be the one to *cast* it."

"Except I never wanted to be a hero. That was always your part to play."

The reminder stung no less from Owan. "I'm no hero."

He smiled sympathetically. "You're a soldier, Rathen; you're a hero in practice and in heart. You were *banished*, and yet here you are, out in the world, facing off against the most formidable threat in recent history, with a spell impossible even to *conceive* now near completion by your own hand. And for that reason alone, it could just work."

The room fell quiet. Candles flickered and lapped against the air, footsteps passed through the corridor outside, and the low, constant drone of city life hummed beyond the windows.

The chair creaked while Rathen leaned back in exhaustion and closed his eyes in defeat. Owan spared his old friend his gaze and traced back over the words of the open pages instead.

"I didn't want any of this," Rathen said, finally.

Owan looked up from the confusion on the page and gave him a sympathetic smile, though he stared now at the ceiling. "Yes, you did. You could have turned away, abandoned the matter, continued in banishment. But you didn't. Instead you stepped out here, with Aria in tow, to try to save all of us, even those who wrongly spurned you. You may wish you were a cynic, Rathen, but you're not. You're a romantic. A romantic with the perfect soldier's heart: devoted, responsible, enduring. Don't kid yourself. And don't insult me by trying to convince me otherwise." His voice remained soft, apologetic for the truth being what it was, but not for delivering it. When Rathen didn't look back at him, he leaned over, lifted a file box from the floor beside his seat and set it quite deliberately upon the table. "My apple for your pear?"

Rathen finally sat up, pulled by a reluctant curiosity. "What have you got?"

"While you've been out there playing with relics and running away from ghosts, I've been working on the matter of magic and elements to the ends of stopping these chasms - the ones Salus *isn't* responsible for." He pushed the box towards him. "It might be a little more wordy than you're used to, but it could be useful."

"You've not really met Anthis yet, have you? What do you want from me?"

"You need to ask? You've been out there splashing around in it for *months*. People here are more than just a little hungry for information..."

A smile of disbelief suddenly tore across Rathen's face. "And *you* want to get ahead."

"Academia is a competitive world," he replied loftily, "but I'm hungry, too."

Rathen said nothing. He sat back in his seat and stared at him, one eyebrow slightly cocked, arms folded across his chest, and continued to grin like a viper.

Owan groaned painfully. "You're a wretched man."

"I know."

The curtains were drawn; candles flickered on the table in antiquated candelabra and the fireplace continued its quiet seething against the cold. Another steaming teapot sat upon the central table, and empty bowls and crumbs of bread were all that remained of a nauseously eaten supper. The endless wait had finally exhausted them.

Petra sat dozing on a sofa with Eyila curled up in a blanket beside her, Garon stared almost wild-eyed towards the door or out through the slightest gap in the drapes, and Anthis watched Aria toddle sleepily back towards him, her bag in one hand, dragging along the floor behind her, and her doll clutched absently in the other. He sighed sadly, both for her sake and his own. "Perhaps you should get some sleep," he said softly once again, trying to stifle a yawn, but she shook her head quite firmly.

"Can't."

"Aria, it'll be fine - he'll be back before you know it."

"In a few minutes, maybe?"

"Yes, maybe."

"Then there's no point in sleeping." She dumped her small bag on the table just in front of him, rummaged through, withdrew her wooden carving, shoved it into his hands, took a few sheets of paper then climbed back up into the seat beside him, pinning him under an earnest look with her tired, red eyes. "I need your help."

Anthis frowned as his gaze dropped to the crumpled parchment. He was used to all kinds of scriptures, all kinds of diction, sociolects and short-hand, but now, he hesitated. He could feel her hopeful eyes on him. Rather than risk insulting her by guessing at what she'd scribbled, he tried a different tact. "You've given it a name."

She smiled and nodded, not noticing his evasiveness. "'Sentinel of Ruins' - what is that in elven?"

"In elven?" He thought for a moment. "'Asulzahn'."

Her heart-shaped lips pursed and twisted strangely. Anthis returned it in question.

"I hoped it would be longer."

He nodded his head slowly. "I see..." His smile stifled, he rose to meet her own solemnity instead. "Well...this is going to be able to remove magic that shouldn't be present, and restore ruins to their previous...ruin...yes? So...how about..." This time, he let his knowing smile through. "How about 'Sahfeikrahsulniir'."

She blinked at him.

He gestured for a pencil and began writing much too fast for her to keep up with. "Sah of 'sahkein', the soldier, active defender; feik of 'fein', existence and continuity; sul of 'suln', time everlasting - *not* 'qísul', which is age, hour, era and so on; and niir of 'puniil', proper, intended or natural state. 'Champion of Balance, Reclaimer'."

Her eyes had transformed into bright discs of wonder as she watched the words form on the page, but they dulled suddenly with suspicion, and she fired it up towards him. "Where's 'reclaimer'?"

"The elves didn't have a word for that. It's 'puniil' in the given context."

She nodded slowly and sat back into the sofa, considering the wood in his hands. He held it up to aid her contemplation. "Sah-feek-rah-sull-nair."

"Sah-fayk-rah-sool-neer."

Her red eyes narrowed and lips pursed tightly. Then, finally, she smiled. "I like it." She beamed up at him. "And now we have to shorten it."

"Shorten it?"

"Like the Zi'veyn."

"I see... Uh...Sah'niir?"

"*Perfect.*"

He chuckled and wrapped an affectionate arm about her as they looked out towards the remarkable thing. "You did a wonderful job on this, you know."

"I guess."

He looked askance towards her, but he found that, for once, she wasn't pouting.

Garon hurried suddenly through the room, startling the pair and rousing the sleeping women. Then came the sound of footsteps.

Sleep was forgotten in a heart beat as all eyes fell impatiently upon the door, but when Rathen entered, only Aria closed the distance. Even as he knelt and hugged her close, there was something terrible in his eyes that made the others hesitate, and the concerns that lay just beneath their skin rose and bloomed into certainties.

But while panic gripped them, Eyila softened in empathy. She was the first to speak. "Rathen, are you all right?"

"Yes." His distant eyes lifted too quickly from the floor, and Aria's voice came muffled from his shoulder.

"You're lying."

"It's not important." He squeezed her again and pushed resolution into his bearing. He didn't seem convinced by it himself. "Nothing that can be changed now, anyway."

He avoided everyone's gaze as he stood, Eyila's in particular, and so he didn't see the sadness in her eyes nor her approach before she embraced him. Surprise eased the lines in his face, but he didn't reject the gesture, and Aria was quick to add her own comfort again.

The others looked at one another uneasily, but no one voiced their questions. Not even when the pair stepped away in silence and let him walk past sullenly to pour a glass of water at the table. His unspoken need for space was respected by all but Garon.

"You've been in the archives all this time?"

"Yes." Rathen's voice was terse. "With Owan."

"Why?"

"Because I thought maybe he could help with the spell. He's a scholar. Why else?"

Garon moved around beside him and speared him with a flinty look. Rathen's own dark eyes remained fixed to the furthest wall. "This might be your old territory, but things have changed, and right now, in this place, *you* are the only guarantee of safety for the rest of us. Don't get complacent."

"I'm not getting complacent. I'm trying to get help."

"Through private conversations? You're being secretive."

"I've been out of touch with everyone here for over a decade. There are a few things and people I wanted to check up on while I had the chance."

"Meetings?"

Rathen's lips tightened. His stare didn't move. "No. We're at war. Anyone I'd like to have spoken to isn't here - some never will be again. And I hadn't intended to try, anyway. We have other things to deal with."

"Who were you asking after?"

"Did I probe after your discussion with Taric?"

"You heard everything we said and I didn't try to hide it."

"You're paranoid, Garon." Now his gaze moved, and its sudden softness surprised the officer. He turned and walked away, glass unfinished, and nodded to Caiden as he poked his head around the door. "Get your things," he told the others, "we can't stay in here all night. There are rooms--"

"What?" Garon flashed back around in front of him and faced off against the flicker of annoyance on Rathen's face. "We need to leave the *city*."

"Not before twilight."

"Garon," Petra spoke up before he could object, "Rathen's right. It'll be quieter if we leave in the morning, and you don't really want to traipse through the snow all night, do you? You must be at least as tired as the rest of us..."

"Get some sleep, Garon," Rathen agreed, moving towards the door ahead of them. "Make the most of a bed while you can. There's no need to patrol tonight."

"Complacent."

Rathen's jaw hardened, but he didn't look back around. He took Aria's hand even as she continued stuffing her things back into her bag and strode out of the door behind the sergeant's lead.

They rose two more floors before reaching another identical hallway, and stopped outside a door about mid-way along where their guide began to apologise.

"It's far more than we're used to," Rathen assured him. "Aria, you stay with me; Petra and Eyila can take the next room, and Garon and Anthis the other." He noted Anthis's shoulders sag in dread and offered an apologetic smile.

"Owan will be here to escort you out at the third hour. I'll ensure the way is clear."

"Thank you, Caiden."

"It's an honour to be in your service, Sahrot." He saluted, and Rathen's own shoulders slumped, but he made no attempt to correct him, deciding it easier to formally dismiss him instead. That seemed to please the soldier, who pained him with another ceremonial salute before stiffly walking away.

Rathen made a point of avoiding even brushing the others with his gaze. He turned curtly and all but dragged Aria into the twin room behind him.

Chapter 52

For almost fifteen minutes Aria had done nothing but stare at her father from her bed, her feet kicking about beneath the luxuriously soft, thick covers, making the most of the vast space even despite the intense seriousness of her gaze. Rathen had ignored it for as long as he could. "Stop looking at me like that."

"Yessir."

He sighed witheringly and squeezed his eyes shut tight. "Vastal save me."

"You never used to say things like that."

"Say things like what?"

"Anything about gods." Her feet continued wriggling. "Not by name."

"Well...company has a habit of rubbing off on you." He peered closer at his book in an attempt to escape the analysis. "*You* never used to carry a sword."

"It's not a real sword."

"In all honesty, Aria, with what Petra's been teaching you, I'm pretty sure you could do some damage with it all the same."

"Not to you, though."

"I can only hope." He felt her stare continue. Finally, he closed his book, left the bed upon which he sat and moved across to her side. She rolled over to face him and grinned. Her eyes were puffy and her cheeks were red. She was tired. She must have stayed awake all day and night until he'd come back. He smiled sadly and brushed a curl from her face. "I'm sorry for being away for so long."

"It's all right. I understand. You were trying to get help."

"Yes, I was."

"Did Owan not want to take over the spell, either?"

A hot flush of panic squeezed his heart up and into his throat; outwardly, he merely blinked. "What do you mean?"

"Well you wanted to give it all to someone else to finish so you could cast it and use it quicker, didn't you?"

"Oh...yes, of course that's it... I didn't realise I'd told you..."

"You didn't. But it's okay. And you'll finish it on your own - you've come so far already, I know you can do it. I'm so proud of you."

His eyebrows rose as her big eyes glittered with adoration, and he felt that much too familiar shame flood into his chest. He realised then that he was profoundly sick of it and the self-loathing it dragged along with it. '*This,*' he vowed, wholly and silently, '*will be the last time.*' And with every possible avenue of aid now exhausted, it shouldn't be a difficult matter to keep.

He reached out and placed his hand gently upon the side of her face, the only part of her not bundled beneath the blankets, and fixed her steadily. "I promise: I will never keep a secret from you again."

"What about everyone else?"

"That is a promise I refuse to make."

She giggled, nestling her cheek into his hand, "that's okay - we can have secrets from them as long as we don't have any from each other."

He laughed and kissed her forehead. She yawned immediately. "Get some sleep, little one. You've been up for much too long. We're moving again in a few hours."

"Yessir." She closed her eyes as he kissed her again, but they quickly flickered back open. "You won't go anywhere, will you?"

"No, sweetheart. Not this time. Now sleep. I love you."

"I love you too, Daddy."

He tucked her in and returned to sit upon his own bed. She was asleep in minutes. He envied her that, but his mind was much too awake to follow. And so he noticed quickly the sound of uncertain footsteps shuffling around outside the door.

He listened closely as they faded, and again as they returned, lingering in the hallway between the three rooms. Carefully, he rose and hurried towards the door, his own feet as quiet as he could make them to avoid waking Aria or startling the intruder. When he opened the door, however, he found only Eyila moving towards Garon and Anthis's room. Fear of intrusion passed. Now came the fear that it had already happened. "What is it?" He whispered urgently. "What's happened?"

"Nothing," she blinked, startled and wide-eyed, gesturing back towards the door on the opposite side of the hall. "Garon wanted to speak with Petra, so I'm giving them some privacy."

She turned away from the handle, however, and stepped towards him slowly, her young, peculiarly beautiful face suddenly twisted in sympathy. When she spoke, her musical voice lilted with care. "Are *you* all right?"

His shoulders rounded beneath that painfully familiar look. "I'm fine. It was a while ago now."

"It doesn't matter. You only just found out. It may as well have just happened."

"I put that life and its friendships behind me when I left."

"That doesn't matter, either." She nodded through the door behind him. "Talk to Aria. Talk to Petra. Talk to me. Don't bottle it up."

"This all sounds familiar..."

"Then it shouldn't need saying again, should it?"

Rathen considered her soft little smile with no small degree of wonder. She cried, she mourned, but she lived with the fate of her people. She was, ultimately, very strong for someone so young. But while he appreciated her words - or, rather, his own - truthfully, he was more surprised by the news than anything. He was a soldier, and, among other things, a soldier was trained in a few certain truths: life happens, death happens, war happens, and people are lost. But if those people - friends and strangers alike - live and fight for what is good and right, then not one of them is any more or less worth remembering than the rest. He would pay his respects by finishing the job he'd started and protecting the land his oldest friends had died for.

His back straightened more easily with that thought in his mind. "Thank you," he said, for she had forced that buzzing sentiment into a coherent state. "Oh - I can call Caiden back and see if there's somewhere he can take you so you can meditate tonight--"

"No, no it's fine, thank you," she smiled honestly, "I don't want to be any trouble - perhaps I'll just read with Anthis instead. Or, try to..."

"How is that coming along?"

"Slowly," she sighed. "It was wonderful at first, but now it's...becoming more difficult... *Why* would someone follow a trail of cakes left in the woods?"

"Aria's asked me the same question. Hunger will do that." He smiled at her helpless look. "Good luck. And don't stay up too late."

"I don't plan to." She turned and knocked at Anthis's door. "Toa'uuya, Rathen."

"Toa'uuya, Eyila. Sweet dreams."

The night hadn't moved when they descended into the tower's deserted foyer early the next morning. Candles and sconces continued to flicker, the chill continued to seep, and the sky outside through the cracks between the curtains remained as black as ink. None but Aria felt restored - if anything, the alien luxury of soft beds had made their night that much more agitated. Owan, Caiden and the three elders, however, each appeared perfectly refreshed.

"Thank you for putting us up," Rathen said politely all the same.

"It's our pleasure," Arator replied, and then a formality fell over him, one Rathen felt it was much too early for, but he awaited the old man's words patiently. "You all took a great risk in coming here. Greater, I think, than any of us realised. But with all that you've given us, the Order can organise itself. We now know exactly what we're dealing with and where our attention will be best focused for the good of Turunda, and we will do all that we can towards it under present circumstances.

"But, while it seems that magic is only a small part of the problem, I regret that we cannot touch Salus. One authority moving openly against another beneath the same crown, be they corrupt or not - it cannot be done. Not by us in the poor light we now stand in, nor even by the White Hammer, so few in number. Not without the king's order. But," he straightened and looked with encouragement over the weary group's disappointment, "you came here seeking defences against the magic, and that, you will have. They will have to be done by the book, but with the information we have 'stumbled upon' suggesting the reason for the arcane turmoil, we can do it."

"Will the Crown buy the claim that it all fell into your lap?" Rathen asked while the others frowned. "The Order weren't officially looking into it."

The grand magister paused, then, and looked at him for a moment. "You're looking rather old, Rathen. Dry and leathery. And there's a great deal written all over your face."

Their confusion deepened, edged even by a little insult on his behalf, but Rathen merely shook his head. "As you're no longer my superior, I have no reservations in telling you that your sense of humour leaves *much* to be desired."

Delas chuckled quietly while a brief flicker of injury passed over Arator's face. "One mention of a dusty old tome and Lord Riken will switch off," she explained for the others' benefit. "It will be a trifle. What these defences will be capable of is another matter, but, at the very least, they will be able to detect the encroachment of more magic and the expansion of the chasms. With any luck, we'll be able to avoid or prevent another incident like the one at Toakh."

"It's just as well it had already been evacuated," Rathen replied remorsefully. "The only people who would have been hurt are looters, and they knew better than to venture in." He bowed only briefly, but that in itself was far beyond his usual gesture. "Thank you for reconsidering; defences are all that we hoped for. But Toakh's destruction was the result of Salus's interference - any chasm he sets his eye on is probably already beyond your help."

"But not," she smiled, "beyond yours."

"Only once the spell is finished. While the magic remains, it seems he'll be able to continue doing it. He stretched that chasm from White Barrows *after* I'd silenced the magic there..."

"Then I wish you haste as well as luck. We will do our best to protect settlements. We can hold a few mages back to protect Kulokhar and look for anything suspicious, and divert a few elsewhere to reinforce mages in settlements near magnetic sites since they're at greatest risk."

"He has surveillance spells."

"They've...been dealt with..." Arator's old face furrowed in consternation, a look that discomforted even the two elders. "We had detected them, but we'd thought that they were the workings of rebels...but how they'd managed it, we couldn't work out, and they wouldn't admit knowledge of them... If we could cast spells like that--"

"Then you should keep such things to yourself."

"We didn't want them to know we'd discovered them so we didn't counter-spell them. We've only interfered with those within these walls. What they relay is not the truth."

"That's just as well. Perhaps it's better to let Salus think he has the upper hand rather than put him in his place and have him come back at you with something worse."

"You have a high opinion of his skills," Delas remarked, but Rathen merely shrugged. Evidently the grand magister hadn't yet shared with his fellow department heads *all* that he'd been given.

"Far better to prevent than fight against."

"I can hardly believe you're the same man."

"People won't like the Order's increased presence," Garon reminded them.

Delas drew herself up contentiously. "The Order is *not* guilty."

"Not as a whole, perhaps, but even setting the rebellion aside, mages are still being driven mad and appear to be attacking on their own. They're drawn towards the magnetism rather than the source now that it's been cut off - is there not a greater risk of these...incidents if there are more mages in populated areas?"

"It has affected so few, and of those few only two were ever positioned near any such places. If anything, especially with the information Owan has delivered us, the more mages around, the lower the risk becomes."

"This is beside the point," Roane spoke up for the first time, his voice rough though not indelicate. "Now we know what is happening, we have to act, regardless of the risk. Mages can intervene if another seems to be losing control, but these defences are a priority for the sake of the people *and* the Order's honour. We will do all that we can." He looked directly at Rathen, his eyes hard and guarded; professionally offended, personally threatened, and touched by a shadow of grudging respect. "As, I trust, will you."

Rathen looked only briefly at the bag he extended towards him. Neither's stern expression moved as he took it. "All that we can."

"There are horses waiting outside," said Delas with a curious glance between the two. "Where will you go now?"

"West. We'll try to reach one of Salus's targets before he can, and with any luck we'll punch a big hole in his plans."

"I see...well, luck, haste and the will of the Goddess, then." She stepped forwards and embraced him again, which he returned immediately. "Take care of yourself, my dear," she said quietly, and he nodded his promise. She then crouched to embrace Aria. She delighted in it and accepted eagerly the small bundle of cloth the older woman handed her with a few whispered words. Delas then straightened and bowed to the rest while Arator shook their hands. Once again, Roane kept to himself.

"Rathen," he looked around towards Owan as he stepped forwards from the side, "a word, if I may?"

He nodded respectfully to the elders and followed him towards the wall, leaving the rest to offer their own thanks.

Outside of earshot, the scholar's sharp eyes became tentative, yet decided. "You say you're gaining control over your transformations." He ignored Rathen's brief, uncomfortable shift. "Could you, in time, have it fully under control?"

"In time," he sighed quietly, "perhaps. I hope so."

"And when that day comes...would you consider returning to the Order?"

"What?"

"You were always a valuable asset to the Order's military wing - your skills, your leadership - even I know that. And now we have an explanation, we could petition the Crown to reverse your sentence."

"No, Owan. They would need proof, and there's nothing to guarantee I wouldn't lose control in the future. Look at what's happening to other mages - if that happened to me...it doesn't bear thinking about. Even if this whole matter was brought to a decisive close by my own hand, the Crown would never accept it. *No one* would. Not after what I've done."

"If the grand magister vouched for you--"

"With all that the rebellion and this magic have done, the grand magister's word probably doesn't carry the weight it used to."

"It's true they would take some convincing, but he would do it with facts and they'd be left with no reason not to trust you."

"Paranoia would give them one. Listen to me, Owan: put the thought out of your mind. It isn't going to happen. Mages are out of favour; they'd rather see our ranks thinned, not bolstered, *especially* by someone like me. No amount of grovelling will change that."

His eyes became frosty. "Despite the general consensus, Rathen, the Order is *not* guilty. We will not walk with our tails between our legs, we will not shy away from our duties or our rights, *not* in the shadow of false claims. That would only give us further to climb. We will not grovel for anything."

"Wise words, but walking tall will seem like hubris."

"But it will be *innocence*. The Crown will see that in time."

"You give them too much credit."

A lopsided smile touched Owan's lips. "I have to believe some reason remains. Otherwise I might just escalate the rebellion myself." Then the gravity in his eyes changed; they became less worldly, less expansive, and suddenly his concern became personal. Rathen frowned and turned directly towards him. "I have a daughter of my own along the way. If you get this spell wrong--"

"A phrase I've been just *dying* to hear," Rathen smiled helplessly. "You don't need to tell me, Owan. I know. I know well. I also know what will happen if it isn't done at all. So it looks like we're all going to have to hold our breath and pray to the gods that I *don't* get it wrong."

"Gods?"

He smiled smoothly. "A slip of the tongue." He extended his hand and grasped Owan's firmly with a broad smile. "Congratulations. Truly. Prepare to have your heart stolen."

"I'm sure I can handle it," he said with a foolish grin, to which Rathen merely laughed. "I'll keep studying where I can. If I learn anything useful, I'll pass it along."

"Thank you. I'll need it. Now let's get out of here before the sun comes up."

No one spoke as they wove their way through the quiet, frosted streets. While they stalked among or within the wake of illusions, the city guards continued their listless watch and craftsmen their noisy trade by lantern light. Not one lifted their eyes towards them.

The city was no different for their exit than it was for their arrival, but the familiar tension they shared was spiked now by the anticipation of passing through those towering gates - a task made easier this time by their direction. No one was likely to make trouble *leaving* the city, and the authenticity of the coffin wagoner accompanying them negated the need for questions. Craitic burials often took place at dusk or dawn.

Their silence remained well beyond the reach of the city's walls, with many backward glances cast to ensure that no figures were following them. They saw nothing even in the expansive snowlight, but still their urgency persisted.

"Are we sure we weren't seen?" Anthis asked at last, his voice careful as the louring sky began to wake.

"I don't believe so," Rathen replied, forcibly loosening his gloved hands from their tight grip on the reins, "but there's no knowing just what Salus's spells are capable of. He may have seen through whatever deception the elders cast against them." *'Assuming they managed to pull the wool over his spies' eyes in the first place.'* He shifted uncomfortably in the saddle. His bones ached against his sleepless night. "It might be best to assume we *were* seen and act accordingly."

"Wouldn't we have been attacked?" Aria asked sceptically, but her father's lips tightened.

"The Arana isn't so direct," Garon informed her. "And if they think Rathen has gone rogue or is working with the elves, they'll be intrigued by his visit to the Order. So, either they'll wait and find out his purpose, or...we'll be attacked on the road." He looked back through the trees in the direction of the city, though it was long out of sight. "We should hurry. We need to put as much distance between us and him as we can."

"Should we not just strike him now?" Eyila asked as she clumsily urged her horse on after the rest of them, struggling to feel its ribs through her thick boots. "He won't be expecting it..."

"No, he wouldn't, but neither are we. We have no plan - we don't even know where exactly the Arana is. And regardless, he would have immediate reinforcements. We wouldn't stand a chance." Garon's eyes now shifted onto Rathen at the lead, and narrowed in private suspicion.

"It feels wrong running away."

"We have no choice, Anthis. We don't stand a chance against them. And, for the record, we're not running away--"

"We're running away," Anthis confirmed.

"We're not running away. It's a tactical retreat." He cast a brief but dark look back towards the historian. "Eyila is fine, but she *won't* be if we go charging in with revenge on our minds. *None* of us will."

Rathen's eyes burned through the trees ahead. His voice growled low with convicted promise. "We will be back for him." He looked around at Garon as he reined his horse in alongside him. He saw the darkness now meant for him and knew well what was coming.

"West?"

"Well he's obliterated the east," Rathen replied matter-of-factly, assumption confirmed. "There's littlewhere else to go."

"Where did you have in mind?" Anthis asked, hurrying up beside.

"Whitemouth."

"Whitemouth? But there's nothing at--...the one beneath..." His eyes fell anxiously wide. "But there's never been any suggestion of *anything* beneath the--"

"Beneath the sea, yes, you've said, but Salus has an *elf's* help so I'd imagine his information on the existence of elven ruins is pretty reliable."

"Meanwhile, we have *none*." He stared at him levelly. "I *can't* find it, Rathen."

"I'm afraid you'll have to; none of the rest of us would stand a chance. And we have to get there before he does."

"And just what is it that makes you think he hasn't already?"

"We'd have heard something, and Taliel would've put in an appearance if his plans were that close to completion."

"Then he could already be on his *way*."

Rathen shook his head and steered his horse across a ford to avoid the upturned wagon further along the river. It had seemed the perfect spot for an ambush when they'd passed it two nights before, and he didn't like to stretch their luck needlessly when it would be crucial later on. "I doubt it. Now that Kalokh has attacked, his attention will be divided, and his accident at Toakh will have shaken him. Either he's exhausted, or something went wrong. Despite the evidence, he *doesn't* want to put lives at risk. He won't strike again until he's recovered or has figured it out."

"How can you be sure it *was* an accident?" Petra asked.

"Rathen is right," Garon agreed, "the town was deserted, but it was the closest outpost to the Doanan border and a valuable location for that fact alone. Salus wouldn't have wanted it broken, and the fear it has doubtlessly spread through the populace wouldn't have been of any benefit to him. People are angry enough with the mages, but anything more than the present animosity will be a hindrance."

"Fine," Anthis grumbled, pulling one of the coats the Order had given them tighter about himself, "so he's not heading there *yet,* but even assuming I *did* know where to find it, it would take us nearly three weeks to get there on horseback! Never mind all this...*this!*" He gestured animatedly at the snow all around them.

"He's right," Petra admitted uneasily. "He could sort himself out in that time."

"Can we not delay him?" Eyila asked. "If we hit him hard enough we might be able to slow him if he's licking his wounds."

"You *did* want to test his weaknesses..."

"The Zi'veyn didn't work against me, but could it work against him?"

"The Zi'veyn?" Rathen hesitated, chewing his cheek. "I don't know - *maybe*. But we've been over this, it's a huge chance to take, and even if it *did* work it would only stop him for as long as I was using it."

"But it could be enough to give him a reason to hesitate. Confront him, use that, and we'll frighten him."

"And he'll respond by attacking hard and fast when he recovers." Garon shook his head with confidence. "We won't stall him for long with that. He's a devoted man, and when people like him get an idea wedged in their head, it burns everything else away and they get very dangerous very fast."

The group fell tensely silent as they trotted through the snow.

Finally, Eyila's musical voice rose. "We need to do *something*..."

"...She's right."

"And just what *exactly* would that be?"

"We provoke him," Rathen replied with worrying ease, despite the fret he felt creeping along his spine. "We've already talked about it - we're going to be thrown in against him at some point and we *need* to know what he's capable of."

"Look around you. *This* is what he's capable of."

"This was a mistake. He can't replicate this - it's what he can do *consciously* that we need to know about, because those are the abilities he'll build his plans around." He watched Garon from the corner of his eye. It was clear by the fretting of his scowl that he was still far from convinced by the idea - none of them were, really, because now it felt like far more than just brainstorming. But just as he was about to inform Garon that he knew he was right, the inquisitor's expression softened in helplessness and he sat a little lower in the saddle.

"This is madness...but...you're right..." Even so, he turned the mage a cynical look. "But what exactly do you have in mind? What if you cast something and you keel over again? Without you we'll all be--"

Rathen raised a finger. "He would expect magical attacks - so what if we *avoided* them? He would build his plan around the certainty that I'd use magic and his defences will be tailored to it. If we go against his expectations, he'll be unarmed and we can strike hard and fast."

His brow flattened. "Yes. Very good. And what about when this highly intelligent man, trained to think and act seamlessly on his feet, abandons his defeated plan and decides to attack using magic himself? *We* won't have any defences, and we can *guarantee* he'll use it. We'll be entirely at his mercy."

"I'll teach Eyila a few things - she already has binding down and we know she's capable of knocking people off of their feet. A mage can't cast if he's worrying about hitting his head when he lands. And anyway..." His tone suddenly darkened ruefully. "It's me he wants, so it's me he'll be watching. He won't be paying attention to any of you."

"And what will *you* be doing in the meantime?"

"Luring him wherever we need him to be. Dragging him into traps."

"Or...you could...transform..."

All eyes turned onto Anthis in shock, but, slowly, reluctant reasoning stirred among them, and their gazes soon fell weightily back upon the ex-sahrot. Rathen however had fallen still, and his was the most reluctant look of all. Evidently, the thought had already occurred to him.

Aria looked up at him worriedly from the front of his saddle as he straightened and raised his chin. His expression was chillingly resolute. "If needs must."

"It's the only way it could possibly work," Anthis said carefully. "And it'll be a powerful ace up our sleeve..."

"But can he not transform, too?"

"Not fully," Rathen replied unhappily.

"What if that's changed, though?"

He released a deep sigh and smiled unconvincingly down at his daughter. "We'll find out, I suppose."

"How would we go about it? It won't be difficult to draw his attention, but how do we make sure we get him and not just Joe Lackey?" Petra looked between Rathen and Garon uneasily. "And how do we make sure we're ready when the time comes?"

They were all quiet for a while, wrestling at first with the weight of the matter, then with the futility, while their horses picked their own routes through the rocks and snow.

"We set the whole thing up," Rathen concluded long before the others could direct their thoughts onto anything useful. "A place of our choosing, somewhere we can control, somewhere with cover, and somewhere empty of people."

"We can use a tail to relay the location back to him," Petra added. "It won't be hard to find one. Showing our faces in a town could be enough. We wouldn't need to do anything suspicious, we just need to make sure we're seen..."

But Garon was already shaking his head. "Salus is the leader of an organisation of *spies*. They're trained to look for *hidden* information; they don't trust anything they find too easily. Suddenly walking around in the open in a town square will be too suspicious, he may well think we're up to something and send in his subordinates instead."

Petra sighed hopelessly. "So what are we supposed to do, then? Keep sneaking around and hope they spot us through the trees? That could take a very long time - I mean, they're surprisingly inept; it doesn't seem to take much to lose them..."

"We give him reason to think we're distracted enough to make that mistake ourselves, then we can plant bait without making it *look* like bait, to be picked up by sagacious people who are trained to be sceptical and to know a ruse when they see one."

"You want to deceive the deceivers... It will need to be convincing..."

"Tensions are getting high. We're falling behind and Salus is looking more and more likely to succeed."

Rathen turned a boldly bitter look towards the inquisitor. "That's not as helpful as you think it is."

"What I mean is that *we* will be under pressure, and tensions between *us* will rise. It's only natural - as is the practise of venting them on each other. If we make it seem as though a rift is forming between us, Salus will think we're growing careless and vulnerable. He's more likely to come for us directly, and come for us *himself* if the odds are in his favour. Taliel said that he's aware of your power. He wouldn't face you if he didn't think he could win. But that means that he *will* bring reinforcements."

"If we knew how many to expect, we'd have a better shot at success..."

"We'll need Taliel's help, then."

"And a tail, as Petra said. Someone to observe and report a change in behaviour."

"But," Anthis frowned worriedly, "it would be a *sudden* change - won't that be suspicious?"

Garon looked around at him lightly. "Bickering, arguments, hostilities, the occasional punch..."

His cheeks turned pink, and a few sheepish looks passed among the others. "No, not so sudden, I suppose..."

"Which means this won't be a huge leap."

"So we need a tail to observe fake arguments? And they won't act on us because Salus will want to know what's going on - or he'll want the rift to widen further?" Petra nodded slowly. "Clever - but how do we let him know we're ready for him without making it obvious?"

"By making the 'mistake' and showing our faces, just for a moment, and dropping a single, very subtle hint to where we're going. We'll have to be careful if we have a tail - if it gets out too soon, he'll have too much time to plan against us. Otherwise, there are surveillance spells up in most towns and cities now, so our arrival won't be missed...but it will need to be somewhere low-profile or it might look *too* careless..."

"All right, hang on," Rathen said quickly, shaking his head in confusion while Aria merely blinked, her little mind racing furiously to keep up. "We find ourselves a tail, we act up, give them something to report back about straining tensions, we get Salus's interest, then we 'slip up' and mention our travelling plans out loud in a town square or some such? It seems a bit..."

Petra turned towards Garon. "You must know someone. Your contacts have to be nosy to pick up information, and I'd bet that one or two are chatterboxes."

"My contacts aren't chatterboxes."

"They might be, for the right price."

His frown evaporated. "*We* pay them..."

"But just where would we do this?" Anthis looked towards Rathen. "You must have had somewhere in mind?"

"Nowhere in particular - but we...*want* him to attack us," it almost physically hurt to say it, "so there are lots of places that *won't* work. It will need to be empty of people, and open, but not so open that *we* don't have cover, and he might not come out if there's none for him, either. And if it's in the wild, he could potentially get the jump on us, and so could we on him... The only advantage we can have in this is that we'll know he'll be there..."

"A ruin." Aria looked up with a pensive knot between her eyebrows. "Somewhere open like a village but empty of people, and where we can still jump on him from the trees."

They each looked at one another, then towards Anthis, who blinked at the little girl in surprise. "I suppose I'll get to work on finding us a spot, then."

"It's perfect. It will look like we're going there to repair it - he'll think we're distracted and that his luck is in..." Garon nodded, thoughts racing through his eyes. "We'll need a solid plan first, and the sooner the better. Then we can find ourselves a tail - and once we do," the gaze he cast back across them all was steel, "we don't speak of this again. In the mean time, if we're heading for a ruin, we may be able to call upon some of our allies."

Rathen frowned. "You said that before - who exactly do you have in mind?"

Aria gasped, and beamed at them all in knowing. Garon smiled with satisfaction. She turned her father a devious look.

Chapter 53

A fool. He'd been taken for a fool. He'd been taken for a fool from the very beginning. He should have seen it. *Why hadn't he seen it?!* They *knew* the Arana would get to their intel at some point, they'd recognised their skill, they knew it was inevitable, but rather than try to *hide* it, they *let* him find it, and laced it with one single, subtle thread that enticed him into a wild goose chase!

It was *exactly* what he would have done. And it had yielded precisely the results he would have sought in their position: now, Salus was second-guessing everything.

There was only one certainty that had come from obsessively turning everything upside down and inside out: Kora couldn't have been a distraction. The thread towards the wretched lockbox was planted deliberately to lure him away from it. He knew better than most that a lie is always more credible when delivered among truths.

No, they were putting too much into Kora, too much subtlety. It was far too calculated. The presence of the city's archives was not known to the public; Doana had gone through a lot of trouble to discover that what they needed in order to secure ownership of the throne was kept in that city. And all the while, their army had held Turunda's eye and kept its forces contained, weakening their fighting power.

The impasse had unsettled the country, drawing soldiers away from smaller outposts and reserves in anticipation of a great strike, for the longer Doana bided their time, the more devastating it was sure to be. Which meant more and more eyes were fixed on the two armies, leaving smaller forces - *individuals* - free to move unnoticed.

And move they did. But not onto Kora alone. Some had begun spreading out, heading into insignificant areas for no good reason at all. One had been followed into the Sotwolds and watched while they set traps for jackalopes, another into Hoarwood and observed while they practised bird songs, and another into Green Hills where they climbed up into a tree and simply sat, staring at the frost on the leaves for an hour before moving on to another. There was no mistaking the intent behind the activity: Doana were mocking him.

His fingers tightened, hands in his hair, and his grotesque scowl set deeper. He couldn't afford to capture any of them for intel or to make an example of, no matter how much he itched, and neither could he afford to dismiss them as a distraction. He *needed* to keep an eye on them. But despite the open movements of individuals, Doana as a whole was another matter. Because the moment Moore had *finally* decided to make a move on them, they'd already vanished.

Salus hadn't seen it. No one had. And he knew why: the spells he'd planted overlooking Doana's camps had been deceived. There was an image playing in front of them. Somehow, they'd been detected and overridden, and now the curs could be anywhere - they'd sneaked their armies in once, after all. Perhaps now they were moving closer to Kora - perhaps they'd almost found what they sought. Or they were getting desperate and pulling their forces in to take the city by force and scour it from the floorboards to the rafters. And all because he had presumed his spells were enough. Because he had underestimated Doana's mages. Because he had been a fool.

He released his grip from his hair and dropped his fist heavily, clipping the edge of the table beside him. The teacup rattled in its saucer, drawing him at last back to the office and the sofa upon which he'd dejectedly cast himself, and squinted against the suddenly blinding light. The cold sun's reflection from the fresh snowfall bounced in through the windows, ricocheting through the room from one shining surface to the next. It was broken with an adjustment to the milk jug.

With a lengthy sigh, he looked purposefully towards Teagan, sitting across the room at the desk, his face a mask of concentration, surrounded by small, neat stacks of reports. "Moore needs to know about Kora."

The portian looked up from the parchments without a trace of surprise.

"Doana can't hide for long; we have people looking, and so does he. The moment they're rediscovered, he needs to engage them - with radical tactics if need be. Stun them and stall them, then redirect them - push them away from Kora, straight north, and fence them in against the mountains. Push the armies away so that only the individuals are left, and *we* will deal with them directly. No more sneaking about - we'll obtain White Hammer uniforms if we must, and apprehend them in public."

"It will cause a disruption."

"War is disruptive."

Teagan bowed his head in accedence. "But what of Moore's efforts against--"

"Kalokh is already being dealt with." He sat up, rubbing the kink out of his neck. "They delivered a swift blow, but their numbers were too small - that was the only reason they were able to hurt us at all - and now they're being crushed for it. Their motive remains a mystery, but we'll acquire a prisoner or two to find out and prevent it from happening again. Kalokh is no longer an issue. We have the means to strike Doana - we just need to *find* them..." His scowl hadn't diminished, and it drilled now into the floor in pensive thought. When two second knuckles rapped furiously against the door moments later, his suffering fell even deeper. With the quickest twist of his fingers, the lock clicked into place.

"Salus!" The imperious voice yelled indignantly outside. "Salus, I need a word!"

"I can think of two," he mumbled to himself, then lay back in his seat and threw an arm over his face while Malson continued to rage. Salus grunted when he finally gave up minutes later, abandoning the assault on the door and storming away in a huff. "He's quick to point the finger. The military's scouts didn't notice anything, either." He rose and moved towards the window, watching for the liaison's departure. "It's rather suspicious, really. We still have nothing on the old fool?"

"No. The tail lost him in the city."

"Mm. Which means he moved deliberately. He knows we're following him. And that means he *is* hiding something... What of the palace?"

"Nothing untoward on the council or the king."

"Which means we need to dig deeper. *Something* is going on. They keep rejecting my requests for meetings, they're consistently dissatisfied, they expect us to deliver results immediately even when they order us in the opposite direction - it's reaching the point that I wonder if they *want* us to fail. They're keeping the Arana at arm's length but they still expect us to do their bidding. We're not dogs..." A growl rumbled in his throat as he watched the pompous old man stride down the long garden path and climb into his carriage. He whipped with disdain from the window. "And the mages are moving with purpose now..."

"There's no unusual activity in the Order, either."

"That means nothing. We missed Doana's movements..." If Doana had tampered with the spells, the Order could have done the same...and what could he do about it if they had? The whole situation was getting away from him. He needed to regain control.

Salus laughed derisively while Teagan read aloud a new report. Here was a matter he'd never thought could have *become* a problem. "Torching and flooding may not be enough. It looks like it's time to pull out all the stops."

"What does that mean?"

Salus smiled grimly and looked towards the portian. He didn't notice the faint shadow of unease in his favoured's eyes. "Most of them live in the woods. I can steer the chasms through and demolish homes. They'll be flushed out, their traps destroyed, and we can kill them directly. Non-humans will be eradicated in one fell swoop."

"And what if you lose control again?"

A perilous darkness flickered through Salus's eyes, and his cruel smile twisted into another terrible grimace. "I won't."

"You may. What will be lost then?"

"Nothing." His tone was dangerous. "I will not lose control of it. Not again."

"How can you be sure? You didn't intend to the first time. The mistake could happen again just as easily. There's no telling the repercussions from the freez--"

"*Enough, Teagan.*"

The portian fell silent. But the strange compulsion that fluttered in his chest wouldn't be ignored. Despite his efforts to prevent it, Teagan heard himself speak. "What will you do once you've cracked all the borders? You've been pushing the chasms, but how will you ever break the *underbelly?* Arasiin does not float, we've learned this - what chaos could you reap if--"

"*I will not lose control!*"

The compulsion was snuffed out like a candle. Flooded and drowned by the instinctive terror that arrived long before he could process the sight of the gaunt and skeletal cheeks, white skin and jet-black eyes. He swallowed hard and felt himself begin to sweat as those coals glowered through to his soul, and averted his eyes at last to the wall as those long, sharp teeth bared in a monstrous snarl.

"Where," Salus's voice, tainted by some awful rasp, came through those teeth, "is your faith?" He turned fully towards him. "Nothing else to say? You've been increasingly doubtful over these past weeks, Teagan. Why is that?"

"No--"

"Oh, yes, you have. It's concerning."

"I'm merely--"

"Trying to provide an alternative point of view?" He stepped towards him. His tone remained frightfully soft, and the dreadful visage didn't waver. "Don't you think I've considered it all? That I weigh everything before making a decision? I don't act lightly. I have *never* acted lightly. You know this better than anyone - frankly, it disappoints me that I should have to spell this out to you, of all people. And this isn't the first time either, is it?"

Teagan remained as still as stone.

Salus grunted and stepped past him. He looked down at the desk, as calm as an impending storm, and studied the reports laid open. He didn't notice Teagan flinch when he finally spoke. "The phidipans are failing. Handle it."

"They're failing because they have too many orders--"

"Then *prioritise* them. Re-issue, re-assign, filter out the unreliable and stick them somewhere they *will* be useful. You were handling this, Teagan. Don't let this fall apart. Or the Arana will fall with it."

Salus turned away from the desk, and Teagan listened acutely as his footsteps moved much too quickly through the room. There came the small click of the door latch, the soft, brief whine of the hinge, and then the decisive slam that set cupboard doors rattling.

His breath shuddered in relief and his heartbeat slowly returned to normal.

It was some time before he dared to approach the desk.

The bustle of the trade district hadn't suffered despite the gnawing cold. Not even by the flurry of fresh snowfall that dampened the creeping evening, still much too light for the winter skin. Bundled in wool hastily retrieved from lofts and cellars, people moved through the streets with as much or as little purpose as usual, some seeking to complete their errands as quickly as possible to return home to a warm hearth, others instead ambling towards the warmth of tavern fire or tankard.

But despite the flow of ale, the bartering of goods and the roll of day-to-day routine, panic had gripped the people.

Beneath that biting wind, there were stifled whispers of the coming of the sulyax, the arrival of the end of times. Craitic prophecy held that the end of the world would come just as it had for the elves, preceded by the same inescapable snow and ice. Under that evening snowfall, Zikhon's name was on everyone's lips.

Many buried their heads in the sand, stocking up on supplies wherever they could in the hope of hiding from it, but there were some who were doubtful over the intended victims. The Temple itself had declared that only the unfaithful would suffer, and many believed that it would not be man that fell, but mage. Sceptics, on the other hand, were adamant that the snow was the Order's doing entirely, an alternative brand of terrorism with nothing divine about it.

The only agreement: it was not natural.

Elias Malson pulled his cloak tighter about himself and his hood lower over his face. He wasn't sure whom to believe, but unlike the other nobles, who scoffed at the peasantry and allowed themselves to become charmed by the glittering powder, his mind was nailed to the dangers that *would* follow, whatever the source. Crops and livestock were not prepared for this disaster, and there were no stores of food, no surplus to see them through. All there had been, the brimming war had occupied, and a number of desperate measures had been taken to prevent Doana from using any of Turunda's bounty themselves.

He passed by a general store as the tall and lanky owner hung a sign on the door outside. *'No wood til Tuesday'*. It was Friday. Loggers and merchants were surely making fine business, but, as with meat, grain and vegetables, the demand was too high to keep up with and there were no premeditated stores of wood, either. That was built up when demand was low over spring and summer to meet the winter market. Now, there would be far too little to go around.

The war had already promised an onerous winter, but now, with summer frozen, the hardships were set to cut deeper and sooner with every dazzling snowfall. People would die. Children, sick, elderly, vagabonds; they would freeze, or they would starve. And there was nothing at all that could be done for it.

The old man sank deeper into his grim, pensive thoughts, but still he noticed as he walked the shadow that had been trailing him for so long.

He watched it for a while from the corner of his eye. It was a distance away, but always present, and if he lost sight of her, she always reappeared a short while later, moving down a parallel street, sometimes even waiting ahead of him and appearing to peruse wares. But whenever he saw her, she was always at the same distance. She never lost sight of him.

He turned away and ignored it, as he always did, and focused instead on his surroundings. Just ahead stood a bakery, watched sharply by pockets of desperate shoppers, while a cart unloaded sacks of grain and partially blocked a narrow path between the adjacent buildings. Another group of people were approaching in a hurry from his left to join the impatient customers, and the wet clop of hooves over slushed ice announced the arrival of another cart, heavily laden, moving along the road from the right.

He slowed down, picking his steps carefully as though navigating a patch of ice. He was aware of his shadow's distance, and that she hadn't slowed. Of course not. It would have been too obvious that she was following him. If he stopped she would probably keep walking on ahead and duck out of sight to wait for him to pass, then slip back out a suitable ways behind him.

He sped up after a few moments and made towards the narrow, cart-blocked path, apologising as he bumped into one of the wagoners busy pulling the final few sacks from the cart. He heard the soft, wet thuds of two sacks hitting the ground behind him, but he didn't stop to look back as the man groaned and scrambled to collect them before they could soak. Then came the desperate scrape of hooves over iced cobbles, a neigh of alarm, an abrupt *'woah!'* and the splintering of wood. As cries of anger rose, the way had closed behind him.

He allowed himself only the briefest smug glance before vanishing around a corner.

His pace increased as he stepped out into the wider street behind another group of people, and walked in their tracks for a while before breaking off down another lane. After a few further twists and turns he returned to the broad, busy streets, and the familiar old tavern, its windows well-lit and laughter spilling from two open panes, soon loomed ahead.

As always, Lord Malson slipped into The Cockatrice unnoticed.

Weaving his way through the patrons warming by the fire, he ascended to the second floor, making towards a particular table among those overlooking the tavern below. It was occupied by a lone, miserable man staring dismally into the depths of his mug. He didn't look up as Malson neared, nor as he stopped, pulled aside the curtain just behind the man's seat and slipped into the room beyond.

"Marie may not be joining us," he announced as way of greeting, throwing back his hood and stopping beside the candelabra on the table, warming his hands rather futilely over its candles. The six gathered men and women didn't stir.

"It's a stroke of luck that she should be the one charged with following you," the dark-haired fellow beside the window remarked, staring relentlessly through the smudged, veined glass to the street below. "Though she'll be under scrutiny for failing the order a second time."

"With everyone wrapped up in hats and cloaks, and tracks crossing in the snow, it will be more reasonable."

But the man shook his head, his eyes still fixed to the people outside. "Salus is not in a reasonable mood. How did you lose her?"

They nodded in approval as he explained.

"You're getting better," David told him, "but you caused a scene. She saw the direction you'd taken, she could have caught up. And as Bheid said, Salus is not in a reasonable mood."

"Well I've not mastered the ability to turn invisible *just* yet." He withdrew his hands and rubbed them together, attempting to spread the candles' feeble warmth before eagerly taking the cup of steaming tea the chestnut-haired woman had poured for him. After a sigh of relief, he sat down and looked across them all dubiously. They mirrored his tone immediately. "The Crown is becoming more and more private. There are more meetings taking place without liaisons. It feels like something is going on, and they're cutting the other authorities out of it."

"Such as?"

"I don't know. But I don't like it. The king won't see me."

"You think he's scheming something?" The chestnut woman asked.

"Or he's afraid. The Order's attacks are becoming more frequent. He may be getting paranoid - and not unreasonably so if Salus has people in the palace. And Salus won't see me, either, so I can't gauge for myself his present state nor what he might be up to. He's becoming reclusive."

"And reckless," Taliel added grimly. "This snow is his doing." She looked across their startled faces with some surprise of her own. "You didn't really think it was the *Order*, did you?"

Malson shook his head, his cup held between both hands while its steam licked his face. "He needs to be stopped. We need to escalate our efforts. We've been pulling strings for too long, we need to take *action* once and for all." He looked back towards Taliel. "You say Rathen was going to the Order?"

"Word is they've been and gone, my lord, and with the suddenly purposeful movements of mages, it seems he has said or done something to spur them into action."

"Or has he further incited the rebellion?"

Her eyes hardened. "You wanted us to involve ourselves with him," she said with only the faintest trace of insult. "You must trust him. More likely, he has successfully encouraged them to increase defences and prevent more disasters by either Salus's hand or the magic itself."

His youthful eyes watched her closely. "There's more."

Her austerity slipped. "Yes. He spoke of provoking Salus in order to get a read on him. I don't know what he has in mind, but his companions didn't seem averse to the idea. When or how, though, I don't know. Knowing him, however, he would want as much control over the matter as possible. It's likely that he would set a trap so it would take place on his terms."

"Mm. If he sets a trap then he'll have to plant bait, and if he wants a read on Salus, he may just be the bait himself. Which Salus will take - but not directly or easily. Which means that he would have time to plan. Probably not much time, but some - which in turn means that there's an opportunity to learn of it and pass it on. And there's no doubt that Rathen will want *your* advice on the matter before it happens."

"We should do what we can to put everything in their favour, then," David declared. "If Salus knows he'll be going up against Rathen Koraaz, he will take precautions. He won't go alone, but there are a few key individuals he's likely to choose. Those he trusts. We can distract them, ensure they're unavailable when he discovers the bait so he can't call them back as easily."

"And perhaps ensure that one of *us* goes with him instead. He'll take mages - what about Vari? Or Kaz?"

The chestnut woman shook her head. "Vari is out on a prolonged assignment and I'm not strong enough. He might be open to taking Oliver, though. He's a cell guard, after all. He's always close by and is more accustomed to combat than Vari and I put together."

"You may be right, there," Malson mused. "But sending one of us along with him is a wise move. Internal sabotage and a reduced chance of fatalities. Otherwise, we find out what Salus will plan to do - perhaps try to steer those plans ourselves - and give Rathen Koraaz as much information as we can." His eyes fell upon Taliel. She stared back levelly without protest. He nodded and returned to the others. "But as brave as Rathen and his group are, it won't be enough. *We*, however, can go further. He has agents in the palace, I will find a way to hamper them, but we need to reduce his numbers elsewhere, too."

"We can knock his confidence if we strike the right people," Taliel suggested. "He's paranoid and still questioning the capabilities of his subordinates. His attempts to reinforce our results with promotion and further conditioning don't seem to have had the results he was hoping for. He rushed into it, and not all the conditioning has taken. But if we break his confidence in just a handful of his preferred agents, we can knock him further off balance."

"Portians, you mean?" Kaz asked, but Taliel shook her head.

"They would have the greatest impact, but they would also be more difficult. Phidipans will give us faster results and dig deeper into the doubts he already has."

"And you know who these trusted phidipans are?"

She looked back at Malson and smiled strangely. "I do."

"Good. Then make it happen. If we whittle away at his confidence, he'll hesitate."

"Or he'll strike harder and faster," one of the others remarked dubiously, but Malson shook his head with a calculating look, and slowly his eyes drifted back onto Taliel.

"No. He'll hesitate. Because we can make him doubt himself as well as his subordinates. We can discourage and delay action, we can encourage responses. We're already burrowing into him." He watched Taliel's expression. It was hard and unreadable, but while there was no enthusiasm, there remained no protest either. She didn't break his stare. "We can break him from the inside, and then we, *and* Rathen, will have a fighting chance."

Her chin rose decisively, and he nodded his approval.

"How exactly are we supposed to knock his confidence in his favourite operatives?" Kaz was asking, but when the curtain was pulled back and Renan, the grim drunk outside, slipped into their meeting, their hearts jumped into their throats.

"What is it?" Malson hissed, rising from his seat in a frenzy at the sight of alarm in the man's eyes.

"There's a mage here - I'm sure it's a mage - and he doesn't look right." He didn't wait for response or reaction. He slipped immediately back out through the curtain and returned to his spot outside, perfectly positioned to survey the entire tavern and the comings and goings of anyone that should pass through.

"Kaz," Malson began, but she was already moving towards the curtain. No one missed the foreboding look the candles caught in her eyes. She sensed something, and it unsettled her greatly.

They stared after her under tense silence. A moment later the incessant noise outside rose into shouts, but the panic that incited them into motion passed as raucous laughter quickly followed. But their guard didn't drop, and when Kaz returned, her eyes were wide and harrowed, clouded by terror, as though a personal fear was being realised and demonstrated right in front of her. They stared at her warily, reading the situation in a flat second. Taliel and Bheid hurried past her to see for themselves.

A scream shattered the air like broken glass. Startled shouts followed, chairs screeched across the floor as people leapt from their seats, and feet pounded frantically over wood in all directions.

"An attack?" Malson asked in utter disbelief as Taliel and Bheid burst back in, but Kaz's quiet voice cut through the chaos like a knife.

"It's not an attack. Get out. Now."

No one waited for clarification. They fled the room in an instant, splitting off in different directions and finding their own way out, avoiding the conspicuous crowds that barrelled towards the doors and clambered out through windows, a handful of mage hunters among them. Flashes of light flickered through the previously jovial tavern, bright, blinding lights that shunned the lanterns and sconces, while cracks, pops, cackles and sobs created a dreadful symphony of ruin the walls wouldn't soon forget.

Making for the privy door that lead into an alley, Taliel threw one final glance behind her. She saw the figure of flaming chestnut hair approaching the mad-eyed mage with a scar on his chin. She didn't try to stop her.

The tavern was in flames before she reached the end of the alley.

Chapter 54

Convinced that she'd missed something, Petra strained to listen through the darkness. The snow had muffled the air into a deathly silence; no nightlarks sang, no owls hooted. There was nothing but the occasional dampened thump of snow sliding from overloaded branches. Her measured footsteps stopped periodically in case the rhythmic crunch of snow was masking something, but there was nothing at all to be found.

She breathed uneasily and forced her hands away from her sword. Despite it all, she knew in her gut that there was nothing in these wooded slopes, and that the ominous feeling hounding her all evening was nothing more than general tension. It had been hanging over the whole group since they'd broached the idea of provoking the Arana four days ago - and that no one faced up to it seemed to make it even thicker.

She rolled her neck and dropped her shoulders, fighting the knots between them, and looked up to the sky through the frozen leaves for distance. There were no clouds overhead that night; the sky was as black as jet, studded with billions of silver pin-points. The snow's own brilliance shied back beneath it, but its chill remained rigid, made colder by the depth of the darkness, and the stillness felt unbreakable, as though even time hadn't been spared the frost's bite.

No one had seen even a trace of wildlife since the previous afternoon, and nothing - not even an Aranan agent - could trek across the ground or climb through the trees without announcing themselves. But, even though they couldn't be taken by surprise, and she was certain that these woods were empty, patrol remained a habit best left unbroken.

Petra drew herself back in and focused, setting aside the nagging feeling for vigilance.

Until another half hour passed and marked the fifth time she crossed Garon's route and found him absently rolling his shoulder. Finally, she stopped, and extended her blade from a practised grip. "Draw your sword."

He blinked at her in confusion. "I beg your pardon?"

She pointed it towards the shoulder he was still absently rolling even then, and fixed him with intention while he straightened somewhat defensively. "Exercise it."

"We'll wear ourselves out."

He sighed as she stepped out in front of him, blocking his path of escape. "We've been through this before. I'm not letting you get out of it this time. Draw. Your. Sword." She stared at him rigidly, then smiled with satisfaction as he complied at last, though with no small degree of objection.

He was barely ready when she struck him from the right, but he managed to deflect it all the same. He glared at her, but she merely grinned, withdrew, and struck quickly once more from the left, which again he blocked. When she withdrew a second time, however, he moved into a swift lunge led by two quick stabs, the first caught in a hurry by the flat of her blade, the second knocked aside. She darted immediately to the right and used his own momentum to get around behind him, but he slammed to an abrupt stop and spun about, lashing with his blade to catch her again. She was still grinning. He was not, but she saw his enthusiasm in his strikes. She knew he would walk away if he wasn't enjoying himself, and for that, she beamed all the more.

Their game came to a sudden halt at the sound of frantic footsteps, and they both spun with their blades at the ready, humour lost for gravity. Rathen slowed and looked from one to the other, his dark eyes wide with alarm. The pair sighed with relief. "It's fine," Petra assured him.

"I heard swords..." his brow dropped in bewilderment.

"We were just sharpening our skills," Garon explained, drawing himself back into his official demeanour. "Everything is fine. If there's a problem, rest assured we will call for you."

"Okay..." He looked again from one to the other, then slowly turned away, heading back towards the camp. Moments later, the clanging rose again.

The camp was nestled in a hollow beneath three towering boulders. The small fire burned brightly at its centre, though its light was hidden from the few passers by who might be out in this weather, and its heat bounced back from the stones that rose and met above to encase them. It was cramped, but it was warm, and that counted for the most.

Aria lay asleep in a tent beside the crackling flames, bundled in one of the Order's thick blankets, a little smile on her round and rosy face. Eyila and Anthis sat at the doorway of another, book and paper laid out beside them.

Eyila didn't look up as Rathen passed to stand beyond the boulders and stare out into the night. Her eyes were tied to the papers, looking between the two with great determination, considering the black, inky shapes on the page. Most she'd come to recognise - names, places, conjunctions, the marks that denoted questions and exclamations - and though there were a few words that had multiple spellings for the same sounds, she'd decided she would work out their distinction over time. Instead, her biggest challenge came from the subject matter. She was often sure she'd made a mistake when in fact she hadn't all, because the choices the characters made were so outrageous. Lost children who followed trails of cakes rather than searched for their own tracks to find their way back home, an old woman who loved children but lived alone in the woods, and who ultimately wished to *eat* said children rather than the cakes she slaved over or the game that roamed outside. And why weren't the parents looking for them? Had they so easily decided them lost beyond a hope? Could a parent truly be that incompetent? The idea had set an ache in her heart for the past two days. No, it made absolutely no sense. But these were the final pages. Confusion aside, if she could finish these two pages, she would have read a book.

Despite her concentration, she gradually became aware of Anthis's eyes upon her. There was nothing strange in that, nor in the flush of her own cheeks at the discovery, but while his eyes would flick away seamlessly the moment she looked up, she made no effort to try to hide her embarrassment. Their pale complexions had the strangest tendency to lay bare their feelings, but hers merely glowed. It made him stare a little harder, but she rather enjoyed it. No one had ever paid her much interest before. From the age of eleven she'd been a novitiate to the priestesses, then at sixteen an apprentice to the village healer. Her time had been scheduled, her future determined, and if she were deemed worthy of marriage, her partner would be chosen accordingly.

...And yet here she sat in unnatural snow, beneath the interested eyes of a near-stranger, a foreign book in her hands, far from a home forever lost to her. And a family forever lost to her.

The black shapes began to blur, and a lump formed in her throat.

"Are you all right?"

She looked up quickly and smiled at the furrow of concern that ruffled Anthis's handsome brow. "Fine." Her voice managed to escape the constriction. "Thank you."

"Are you sure? We can stop if you--"

"No." She smiled again to placate his confusion, and forced softness into her suddenly hardened voice. "I'd like to finish this tonight."

He nodded slowly as she returned to the book without waiting for argument, his concern flickering deeper, and listened as she read aloud and transcribed the words of each sentence as she went. She stumbled a few times, caught again by the characters' absurd decisions, but she made her way stubbornly towards the end.

His eyes tracked the words beside her voice, and upon the completion of the last, Anthis was already beaming with pride. It took him a moment too long to notice that her own smile was hollow. "Eyila..."

"Yes? I'm fine." But again she failed to convince him. Regret eased some soft honesty into her eyes. "I'm sorry, I'm just tired, that's all."

"Oh...well, it is late...and it's not an easy thing to do. Well done - truly."

She softened for a moment at the warmth of his smile and the affection he suddenly tried to hide from his eyes, but it didn't last. She doubted if she could even pull her lips into a smile with her hands.

But she didn't want to smile.

She rose abruptly to her feet, and he scrambled to follow, his face set in what now seemed to be perpetual confusion limned with a hovering injury. She didn't notice it, however; she'd turned her face away towards the gap in the hollow and the frozen world beyond it. "Thank you, Anthis. I'm going to meditate before I sleep. My mind is busy. I'd like to quieten it."

Her voice had an edge of stone. Anthis said nothing as she walked away.

Rathen didn't notice her walk by. He didn't notice the countless minutes pass, nor the end of the distant, ringing swordplay, nor even the snow as it began to fall and melt upon his face. He was lost in yet another labyrinth of torment, caught in an endless, desperate struggle, racking his brain for a solution to the problem he'd been unable to shed and had tumbled far beyond his control. But he couldn't get past that first towering obstacle. Initially he'd ignored it and thought on ahead, but it seemed to grow while he wasn't watching it, until it loomed like a thick, black cloud that smothered all hope of the sun ever returning.

How, *how* was he ever going to do this?

His cold, stinging hands clenched into fists. Even as his thoughts cascaded, he was acutely aware of the magic humming in his veins. It surged like a mountain river, powerful, unstoppable yet contained within its frozen banks - but should he try to touch it, it would snatch him from the edge, toss him around and squeeze the life out of him in moments.

He hadn't dared to try for almost two weeks. There was no point. Nothing had changed. He couldn't use it. And yet, somehow, Kienza expected him to do just that even after rescuing him from the hands of his own magic *again*, and had offered her usual lack of helpfulness in the form of 'use it carefully' and 'face your situation', neither of which could reasonably fall into the category of 'advice'.

The Order had sensed nothing amiss in him; they couldn't see past his blood - which had undoubtedly been a mistake to divulge - and in knowing that, they would have considered him beyond their help before sparing even a moment to try. And so he hadn't asked. There would have been no point.

Which ultimately meant that the matter - *every* matter - rested squarely and entirely upon his own slumping shoulders.

They rounded further beneath the amassing weight. What he wouldn't give to be back beside his fire in his rock-shell home, listening to Oat bleat indignantly outside while Aria tried to plait her wool. When life had been quiet, simple and free of responsibility. And safe.

'You could have turned away, abandoned the matter, continued in banishment. But you didn't. You're a hero in practice and in heart.'

Rathen stiffened. It wasn't heroism, it was *necessity*. Nothing more. Because, according to everyone else too frightened to take the matter on themselves, he was the only one who could do it. He didn't seek fame for it, he never had. He didn't care what people thought of him or of his skills, he just wanted to live in peace.

...So why did Owan's words bother him so much?

Rathen loosened his fingers, suddenly aware of nails digging into his palms, and straightened belligerently in the face of it. They were that certain that he could save them all? *'Let's see how well-placed that confidence really is.'*

Tentatively, an idea formed, and he bent down to scoop a handful of snow. It wasn't as powdery as it looked, almost snapping apart from the rest of the sheet, and was squeezed easily into a rough ball that held the impression of his fingers. With a deep, steadying breath, rooting his consciousness to the banks of that raging river, he raised his empty hand and reached into the magic.

Right away, he felt the cold of the snow spread further over his palm. He watched as its surface began to smoothen and shine, and steam rose silently from beneath. But the searing pain he'd been waiting for ignited suddenly beneath his flesh, and surged up from his bicep and into his shoulder.

He withdrew in panic and dropped the snow as though it was on fire. Water ran across his temples, melted flakes or sweat, he couldn't tell, and his breath released in one ragged shudder.

His hands dropped helplessly to his sides. He couldn't do this.

"Still?"

Rathen spun in shock to find Anthis standing a few paces behind him. The splinter of worry piercing his green eyes only made his defeat sting deeper.

He sighed and looked away. "I'll manage."

"I hope so."

"You didn't need to say that."

"I know, but I also couldn't not." Anthis moved up beside him, holding the blanket bundled in his arms closer to himself, and followed his thoughtful stare out along the steep-sided ravine. The pair stood in silence for a full minute before the gathering suspense forced Rathen to look around at him, and the indecisive draw to his lips made it clear that the young man had something he wished to say, and that Rathen probably wouldn't like it. The timid smile confirmed it, and he looked away to make his guesses. They turned out to be wrong.

"Aria..."

Rathen felt his heart sink.

"She can't be around for this. She came with us to the Order, and we managed to get away with it, but this...we're *luring--*"

"I know."

Anthis quietened obediently at his fully expected glacial tone, but he had not expected him to soften so quickly. He regarded the mage regretfully as he slumped in torment.

"I know. You're right." A smile flickered at his surprise. "Garon's already given me this speech three times over."

"Yes, of course he has... What did you say to him?"

"I told him she wasn't going anywhere." Anthis baulked at that. "But," Rathen continued, much to his relief, "in truth, I never had any intention of bringing her into that kind of danger. I've been reckless with her as it is, but this...this is too much." Anthis had only seen the lines around his eyes so deep once before: when he'd sent his adopted daughter away at Ronar Cove. But the sorrow this time was far more pronounced, haunted no doubt by her ordeal in his absence.

But Salus's hands would be more perilous than a chance attack by bandits, and though it visibly hurt him, it was clear that he was well aware of it.

Anthis clapped him firmly on the shoulder and did his best to smile. "She'll be all right this time."

Rathen said nothing. He barely managed to nod. Anthis decided it best to drop the matter. He'd got what he'd needed for his own peace of mind. No one wanted Aria to get hurt. So he forced a lightness into his tone as he turned towards his original intent, but he found even that to be a struggle. "Did you see which way Eyila went?"

"Eyila? Why?" He looked down at the blanket the young man was carrying, holding it so close to himself that it seemed he was trying to give it warmth rather than take it, but his first assumptions were shattered when he recalled by chance how quickly her feet had trampled through the frost.

His sharp eyes flicked keenly down the slope and through the depths of the trees. They'd ridden through there earlier, along the riverside. The wind had been channelled into a consistent and biting stream.

Dreadful realisation warmed him against the cold, and he set off at a run with Anthis immediately behind him. "How long?" He called back to him, and cursed as Anthis replied with almost an hour. She'd departed just short of a flee, and he'd been too confused to notice she hadn't taken a blanket with her.

They split up at the river; Anthis headed north, Rathen south. There had been nowhere that stood out along the route they'd taken that evening, so she may have followed the river along until she'd found somewhere suitable. Rathen cursed over and over to himself as he hunted, staring up into every bough of every tree, around every boulder, even, fearfully, into the water itself as it ran black against the ice beneath overhangs.

When he finally heard Anthis's voice echo through the still air, he ran so fast he almost fell into the water himself.

It didn't take him long to find the historian waving frantically from an overhanging rock, and he dashed with him down and behind it, where relief fused with fright to create a powerful rage. "*Oh, you stupid girl!*"

The bronze body was impossible to mistake, even as it lay as still as stone in the dark among the rocks. Her eyes were closed, her hair dishevelled, one arm sprawled and her hand limp in the flowing black water. Anthis snatched it out immediately and felt for a pulse. "Unconscious. She can't have been here for long..."

Rathen was already tilting her head back and lifting her chin, then turned his cheek to her mouth and looked down the line of her chest. A fraction of alarm faded from his eyes. "She's breathing."

His attention turned immediately to her injuries. Countless cuts covered her left side, and though little blood marked the snow, a thick stream of it glistened across the side of her face and matted her white hair. He looked up at the rock. She must have been sat upon it before falling off to the left, landing face-first into the ragged, crumbled rocks. The cold had gotten to her, and to make matters worse, she was barely clothed. But it was still impossible to tell if her skin had paled beyond the diminishing of its strange, metallic sheen.

He muttered chastisement again, then began looking close into her eyes and for discharge from her ears. "Why did she leave?"

"I don't know," Anthis replied, desperate to help but unwilling to risk getting in the way, and opted for rubbing her frozen hand instead. "We were reading, she started to seem a little down towards the end, then we finished and--"

"The book. What was it?"

"Old Gruel." He watched as Rathen's eyes closed beneath a sudden and tightly knotted frown. Understanding dawned within just a moment of racking his thoughts before he was drowned in shame. "The children thought they'd lost their family for good..."

"Until they escaped Old Gruel and were reunited in the end." He finished examining her wounds. "Get the blanket ready." Carefully, he lifted her sodden body from the rocks and Anthis was quick to wrap her, then he kicked away as many rocks as he could and lowered her onto her side. Anthis began to object when Rathen took her icy hand and contorted the fingers of his other. He turned him a stern, resigned look. "It's this, or she loses them."

Anthis watched his expression twist in pain, his fingers unravelling in shock before stubbornly repeating the sequence. After five attempts, he released her and threw snow into his reddened face. Anthis took her hand to tuck it into the blankets. It was warm.

Exhausted, Rathen looked slowly about at the surroundings. There was nothing remotely resembling shelter. They'd made camp at the only possible spot, a ways back up the slope. "There's nothing for it," the mage panted, staggering to his feet, "we have to carry her to the fire. Keep her as still as you can."

They made it only half way up the slope before two figures came thundering down towards them, swords drawn and alarm in their eyes. "What's happened?!"

"Adolescence."

"She went to meditate, then passed out from the cold," Anthis replied instead, and flinched under the expected heat of Petra's sudden outrage.

"*Meditate?* Anthis, she was with *you* - why would you let her go off in this?!"

"Leave it be, Petra, it's not his fault," Rathen sighed, "she wouldn't have been stopped by anyone."

"She would have been stopped by *him*."

"*Leave it,* I said. It's not helping."

"She's not tried to meditate since the frost set in." Garon looked dubiously across to the historian as they hurried carefully on up the slope. His head already hung in shame. "What brought this on?"

"Old Gruel." His voice was small and bitter with self-reproach. "She finished the book. I think the ending hit her too close to...home..." He looked up at the judgemental silence. Rathen's disappointment hadn't changed, though whether at him or at her, he couldn't tell, and the others stared down at Eyila's still body with grave understanding. Anthis's guilt tripled when Petra eventually spoke.

"So, did she try to *kill* herself?"

It grew even further when no one rushed to deny it.

"There are easier ways to go about it," Garon said at last, but Anthis shook his head with desperately seized conviction.

"No. No, she meditates to feel closer to her people. Maybe she just needed it more than usual tonight, and underestimated the cold. She's not used to this."

But again, no one rejected the possibility. Beyond Petra's muttered declaration of '*I knew something was going to happen,*' they continued back to the camp in silence.

The following morning began with a clamour. No one had slept well, Anthis least of all, but what few hours they had stolen were rudely broken by a raised and blistering voice. Peering out from their tents, they found Eyila sat at the middle of the camp beside the breakfast she'd made them as thanks or apology, while Rathen paced and yelled heatedly in front of her. And whatever gentle sympathy she'd expected from her ordeal, she was not granted, as not one of them moved to calm the mage. Though they winced at his brutal truths, they were all in silent agreement.

The fireside seemed to have been enough to bring her back around, and her injuries were negligible. She'd been lucky. And Rathen made damned certain that she knew it.

And so, that morning, she rode along in the middle of the group in silence, tightly wrapped and harbouring a familiar, Aria-esque contrition that plunged her into a well of shame and self-pity. Whenever she dragged her eyes up from her reins, Anthis was looking back at her, but the disappointment in his eyes clawed at her gut and each of them quickly turned away from the other.

Rathen rode at the lead beneath a roiling and onerous cloud, edged by the enduring traces of last night's panic that just wouldn't unlatch. Increasing copses of trees marked an end to the blanketed pastures, and the village of Ramstead stood close by to the south. In such poor humour, he met the discovery of spells with only a grunt of surprise. The Order was quick.

He led them along a branching route that curved away from the village, and before long the copses turned to thickets and a woodland loomed ahead. The road narrowed, snow piled lower, and small, wooden cones stood in clusters between the trees. Aria stared at them curiously for some time before finally turning to her father.

"Apiaries."

She blinked at him.

"Bee houses. Honey farms." He looked at the icicles that hung from the lowest edges. *'Though I doubt any survived...'*

They rode on until a small house appeared among the trees, the home most likely of said honey farmer, but were given no time to branch off around it before an old man shuffled out of the door, wrapped in full winter wools of rich red hues. Rather than raise suspicion by avoiding him, they continued forwards guardedly.

He gave them only a glance as he fumbled to unlock the cellar door, and they nodded innocuously in return. Then froze in their saddles at the sound of his rough-hewn voice.

"Some friendly advice," their wide eyes flicked quickly towards him, "turn y' horses about. The woods aren't fit for travel."

"Much obliged," Garon called back to him as their route drew them nearer, recovering the quickest, if he'd needed to at all, and settling himself easily into a far more common air. His face seemed to change and soften with it. "Much obliged indeed - but we can handle the snow."

"Snow and ice can be prepared for, and y' do look prepared - but what lurks in there, y' can't."

"Oh? What's the problem?"

With the strength of a man who had taken well to a life of labour, he heaved the cellar doors open, breaking their seal of ice, then turned and approached them while dusting off his hands. He was, they saw, wearing two thick hats. Aria stifled a laugh. "Time was people'd *heed* locals' knowledge, not question it. But, times change. Monsters, 'tis. The wilds come t' life. All to do with that magic, I have no doubt."

"Magic - yes, who knows what the Order is up to?"

But the old man was shaking his head. "No, I don't suspect 'twas the Order. It's something else. These beasts, they were always there, but they kept t' themselves. Now they've grown in number, and they're aggressive, wandering out of the deeper woods and closer t' the village. They've all but shut down the mines, driven the miners out and killed the rest. I tell people t' keep away, but they won't listen. Something's upset them, and they've reacted, I think."

"'Reacted' how?"

He gestured around at the snow. "Strange weather, this. What's stranger still is that this forest doesn't seem too troubled by it. In fact, it's thriving and growing, spreading like a buxom young--" his eyes flicked quickly towards Aria and Petra, and he tugged at one of his woollen hats. "My apologies, young ladies. It's fertile, and those monsters are responsible. Wild magic, I'm sure, and they're taking it back for themselves. The roads are blocked - there's no way through, so wherever y' planned t' go, you'll have t' go around."

"We'll take our chances," Rathen stated bluntly, then encouraged his horse forwards. The old man simply shook his head and trudged back towards his cellar.

"Of course y' will. Well, no one's going t' send in a search party, so I wish y' the best of luck in there. Vastal knows I warned you. I'll sleep easily enough for that."

Once he'd vanished beneath his cottage, Aria looked around at her father with distinct disapproval. "That was rude."

He sighed beneath her admonishment, but said nothing until Garon rode up beside him and swiftly cut off his protest. "No. We go through. It's cover. Especially if the forest is 'fertile'. It could stave off some of the cold."

"And we'll be killed by wildlings in the process."

"I don't think we will."

Garon grunted cynically. "You're putting too much trust in Hlífrún."

Again he fell silent and they rode onwards into the woods.

The old man's words were quickly proven true. Though still white and bitterly cold, the snow within the confines of the trees was thinner, and crystalline casings of frost were nowhere to be seen. It was as though the heat of life itself was opposing it. There were flickers among the black trunks, too; Petra was the first to distinguish the eyes. But whatever these hidden wildlings were, they showed no signs of aggression. They remained within the shadows of the trees and watched them pass in sedate silence.

Beneath the reach of wild magic, travel was hard; sprawling roots formed walls that blocked the main roads almost deliberately, while wildlife trails were tight and overgrown, negotiable by beast but a hazard for any on their backs. For hours they were tripped, lashed, turned about and hunted, and the experience as a whole was far too familiar. By evening their horses were waning, and an accident was long overdue.

Riding through a dusk-darkened holloway, the quiet was shattered by a squeal of panic and a human yelp. Each of them snapped around in a startled instant, but the hoof had already broken deep through the tangled brush, and with a thick, hopeless crack, both Petra and her mount dropped heavily from the edge of the road, vanishing through the overgrowth. Along the cramped trail, no one could manoeuvre quickly enough to do a thing to stop it.

Garon dismounted immediately and raced clumsily for the ragged hole, throwing himself down it without a thought. Rathen shouted a futile protest as he rushed to stare down after them. The drop was sheer, eighteen feet or more, and carpeted by thick brambles. They'd been travelling obliviously across the edge of an escarpment. That set no small alarm through his blood.

Below, the horse was hauling itself to its feet with a wild look in its eyes, but Petra had already grasped the reins to keep it from bolting before she'd found her own, the both of them littered with fine scratches. Garon was untouched as he helped her up with some urgency.

"Everyone all right?" Rathen called down while the others gathered frantically beside him.

"Fine," Petra grumbled, steadying and dusting herself down while Garon took a respectful step back and looked over the surroundings.

"It doesn't look like we can get back up from here," he said after a moment.

"We'll come down to you."

"No - you stay there. We'll find another way around."

"No," Rathen replied just as peremptorily. "We should stick together." He looked along the holloway, then down into the overgrown vale below, and soon spotted a slope at just the right gradient to descend, albeit ungracefully. Ignoring Garon's continued objections, he led the others along.

"He's right, you know," Petra told him as he made his quiet remarks. She returned his flat look with a soft smile, then led her horse out of the thorns and towards the unseemly slope the others were gathering at the top of, speaking lightly to soothe it. At her next sharp yelp and halting tug on the reins, however, it startled again. She hushed it quickly, in part to calm herself.

The corpse must only have been a few days old; there was little sign of decomposition, but the blood that stained the shirt collar and chest had long since dried up, and there was far less than there should have been around the shafts of the dozen arrows that pinned the torso to the tree. Its jaw was agape, lightless eyes stared at the ground, head and shoulders weighted by snow, and not a weapon for defence in sight.

"His throat was cut first," Garon said from beside her, his tone soft but clinical. He looked around the dense woods and grunted. "The silver mines are nearby."

"Bandits looking for easy pickings, then," she replied disdainfully, turning and pulling her distressed horse away. "Somehow I doubt wildlings would use arrows."

It wasn't long before another body was found, hanging by the neck in the growing darkness, and another slumped at the foot of a tree. With each corpse discovered, the group's guard rose higher, and though their eyes darted anxiously through the compacted, twilight landscape, they found no route of escape from the vale. They dismounted and led their horses, choosing not to risk being carried into a low branch or another ditch by a panicked mount should they be ambushed, and swords were quietly drawn. But despite their efforts, despite the eerily muffled silence, despite the tell-tale crunch of snow underfoot, when the ambush inevitably came, they were still caught by surprise.

Garon and Petra's blades flashed and sang against the formidable weapons of the nine attackers. The previously controlled short temper that had plagued Anthis since the morning drove him dagger-first into their backs while they were occupied, and Eyila threw aside those who threatened to overwhelm them. Horses roared and reared in alarm, adding to the confusion, and Aria was bundled back into Rathen's keeping while he resorted to watching helplessly, warring internally with himself while his fingers itched to move.

The skirmish wasn't over quickly. The tight space seemed to work in the bandits' favour and they played off of one another like a choreographed dance. When one seemed defeated, another jumped in before the killing blow could occur, wearing the trapped defender down. Eyila managed to finish two of them off with blasts of energy that propelled them backwards into solid tree trunks, but the rest were too fast and too close to her companions to strike without clipping them at the same time. And so she was soon as helpless as Rathen.

When three suddenly broke away, Petra immediately gave chase.

"*Leave them!*" Garon roared after her, but she didn't even glance back.

"They'll only come after us later, maybe even with reinforcements!"

Garon growled as she disappeared, and quickly blocked a powerful strike from a wildly grinning man. "Anthis, go after her!"

The historian delivered his opponent a final brutal slash across the face before obeying. Eyila seized the opportunity to dive back in to the remaining skirmish, and Rathen restrained Aria who seemed to have roused from fear into foolishness now that the numbers had thinned, and declared with wooden sword in hand that she had to help. There were tears in her eyes, and Rathen was suddenly struck with the imagined memory of his own father's death at her feet.

Petra had already forced them to a stop when Anthis caught up with her; one marauder lay still on the ground, entangled in bolas beside a fallen tree, his head at an awkward angle from his body, while another was rising quickly to his feet after having tripped over his fallen comrade. But the third, a woman, had turned and pinned her beneath an assault of strikes far too quick and precise from her short sword.

Anthis rushed forwards to prevent the rising man from outnumbering her, but he didn't bare his back, and whirled on him instead with daggers of his own. Anthis didn't retreat. He grinned like a beast and allowed the bloodlust that promised a satisfying offering to Vokaad to take over. Theirs was not a quick fight, and with each jump his opponent made for distance, Anthis threw a look back towards Petra.

She and her adversary had appeared frightfully well-matched at first, but after a minute or so, Petra's face had become twisted by concentration and her movements were growing slower. Her clothes and skin were nicked, small red stains soaked into her blouse, and she was shifting further onto the defensive; she blocked and parried, but her ripostes were fewer, and she began falling for feints. She was rewarded for one with a solid kick to her gut, and dropped to the ground and through another patch of overgrowth only a few feet deep.

Despite having downed and weakened her, the bandit did not turn her attention onto Anthis. She stepped back and gave Petra the room to rise, swinging her sword about insolently. When Petra managed to pull herself back out, the woman dove right back upon her, twisting her blade to strike with the hilt instead. She struck a combination to her side, hip and ribs so quickly she almost crumpled on the spot.

Anthis's anger erupted in a bellow, and with a single, calculated thrust, he shut down his own struggling opponent. But as he turned to kick aside Petra's would-be killer, he saw something suddenly glint in the duelist's hazel eyes. In an instant, all fatigue evaporated.

Faster than he thought possible, her sword swung around, her grip tightened, she pushed off of her back foot and her steel flashed clean into the woman's shoulder. The short sword dropped from a limp hand. Before it could hit the ground, Petra snatched her own blade free and drove it swiftly and precisely through her chest.

Silence hung for a long moment until a startled gasp confirmed Petra's victory. Curtly, she withdrew her sword, and the bandit dropped to her knees, collapsing as the life finally left her.

Anthis looked quickly back up at her and watched a mild and honest weariness descend. He turned and knelt beside his own rousing victim. "A trick?" He asked as he retrieved the ornate knife from beneath his shirt.

"She was too quick for me," she replied with a steadying breath, and turned away herself to look back up the path while the bandit behind her began to whimper. The others' fight also seemed to be coming to an end. "It's worked for me before." She steeled at the elated sigh.

"Clever," he replied in a weakened voice, "but you could have been killed."

"I knew what I was doing."

When the others rushed around the corner a moment later, Garon was far less understanding.

Chapter 55

What chill the forest's wild magic had restrained seemed to strike in full force at the first brush of moonlight. The group had ridden as hard as the terrain would allow them to, and were finally just about satisfied that the bandits' camp, the mine and any lingering marauders were far enough behind them to stop safely for the night. Finding a suitable spot, however, was proving another challenge.

But, while sleep tugged at the others as the horses trudged just as wearily through the snow, Aria, shivering beneath her blankets, continued to scribble ardently into a notebook. Finally, she looked up and broke the silence with chattering teeth. "H-how do you spell 's-sahrot'?"

"S-A-H-R-O-T."

"'T'?"

"It's silent." Rathen frowned down at her as she huddled back over the pages. "What are you doing?"

"I'm writing a diary."

"A diary? Why?"

"Bec-cause if no one else is going t-to write about our adv-venture, *I* will."

"Whatever for?"

"Bec-cause I think it's v-very important." She looked up and around in the saddle, then, and fixed her father with a thoughtful pout. "You were h-happy in the Order, w-weren't y-you?"

He looked back in surprise as he pulled her small, shaking form closer against himself. "Happy?"

"Some k-kind of happy, yes. Those p-people showed you a *l-lot* of respect."

He grunted and looked forwards again. His expression darkened while the others turned careful glances his way. "Yes. Strange."

"Why d-did-d they?"

"You heard what Caiden said. That's all."

"No, your father earned it well beyond chasing off Qenra."

The look he fired Garon was acidic enough to melt his skin, but it didn't seem to discourage him.

"He co-ordinated on battlefields, led critical attacks, and both located and countered extremely violent spells. But the most notable--"

"Enough, Garon."

"No, Rathen," he replied shortly, "given everything ahead of us, I think she needs to hear it. In fact, I'm rather surprised she doesn't know already." The ease with which he broke the mage's iron stare left Rathen slightly stunned, and he looked instead towards Aria, attempting to soften the severity in his own eyes. "Fourteen years ago, we were in the middle of another war with Skilan. They were trying to cross our borders, but we'd blocked off every route south of the

Pavise Mountains. They continued to try to break through, and we continued to hold them off, but losses eventually forced their general to turn his eye to the north, to enter through Kalokh instead. The widest pass in the northern mountains was too narrow for a full army, so he sent men in smaller groups to try to sneak by and trickle into Turunda instead, but with orders to avoid the most obvious pass. We kept eyes on it all the same, but spread ourselves over the others while the main body continued fighting them off at the south. But the Arana's eyes were deceived."

"Salus was d-d-deceived, you mean?"

"No, Salus wasn't in power yet; it was his predecessor. A single Skee mage managed to sneak along that widest pass the others had been ordered away from, toppled the largest watch post and its ranks, and Skilan quickly and quietly overran it to control the whole pass, keeping just a few bodies to maintain it and avoid drawing attention - no platoons, no banners, no carousing. It was to appear as business as usual. They would have had no problem moving troops through that funnel and out into the country, they'd have become much harder to track or stop. But they made one mistake: they thought they'd left no one alive and that their small victory had gone unnoticed, but one Aranan watcher remained to report the matter.

"It would take time to move so many through, so we had the opportunity to stop them - but, to keep the element of surprise, the matter was kept a secret and the military remained engaged at the south. Only a small number were sent to remedy it. That included your father, as Sahrot.

"The Arana had sent triple the number of agents this time to ensure the information they gathered was correct, and under their intel, his orders along with those of the military captains beside him were to retake the site, with a secondary goal of discovering what they were planning and compensating for the blindness.

"They remained hidden for as long as they could while the mages probed for and countered spells, and the soldiers prepared to pour in through a known weakness maintained for just this kind of occasion. The Skee mage hadn't used it, so it was a safe assumption that they were unaware of it."

"And they weren't?"

"No, they were. They were then to attack, capture what few maintained it and preserve the location. But, though the agents' intel was correct, there was one single detail which had been very carefully hidden: one of the few Skee mages present was Ake Sjorend - a hero of his people and renowned across borders for being quick, clever and extremely powerful. He far outranked your father. The pass was vital to Skilan's success, so they'd sent him to reinforce it. A prudent move we should have expected. While Rathen's mages removed the wards Skilan's had set in place, Sjorend had laid one more right beneath them. It was missed, and the soldiers ran right into it. They were frozen in place, their critical first charge was compromised, and the enemy had been alerted to their presence and moved in to defend.

"It was Rathen who detected that hidden ward, though a moment too late; the other spells had just been countered and the soldiers had moved immediately. Only a handful were caught, but they blocked the way for the others. Rathen was the only mage strong enough to counter the spell, so it was left down to him while the others felt out for Sjorend and the soldiers formed up to attack. The only advantage they had at this point was that, though the triggered spell had told the enemy where they were, the Skees still didn't know about the weakness in the lower wall, nor how to get there quickly, so they were able to spill in and salvage some of the surprise. Mages on both sides attacked and defended while trying to give their soldiers the advantage, and the soldiers themselves clashed and fought to force Skilan into a position of surrender.

"Sjorend soon saw his own advantage start to slip and began breaking the place apart. Skilan only needed to blind Turunda to the pass, so destroying the watch post would serve that purpose, as well as keeping any intel from leaking out. Rathen remained the only one remotely capable of standing against him, and so he fought to counter-spell, keep the place together, prevent others from being crushed in the collapse and stop Sjorend from escaping."

Aria's eyes glowed up in awe at her father, who stared forwards with retiring indifference, deaf to the story as he watched the route unfold through the snow-laden trees ahead of them.

"And he managed it," Petra picked up before Garon could continue. "He kept the place up, saved the lives of soldiers and mages, and distracted Sjorend with a feign attack to take him out at his own cost. As I understand it, he cast a fire spell, but adjusted it just before release so that it exploded just in front of himself rather than at Sjorend. He leapt through it and captured him while he was preoccupied with trying to cast a redundant counter-spell."

"He leapt through the fire?" Aria asked in a wonder usually reserved for characters in her books, and turned her awe back upon him. "Didn't it hurt?"

"He was burned," Garon replied, nodding, "but the exposure was brief. He bound him and those that tried to free him, rallied his own forces, and with one final push, they retook the northern pass with only three losses on his side."

"Three too many," Rathen said bitterly.

"Sahrot Koraaz..." Anthis shook his head while Eyila stared at him from beneath a growing cloud of intimidation. "I didn't realise...that was you..."

"It doesn't mean anything. Not any more."

"It doesn't mean anything? Daddy, you ended the *war!*"

"I didn't."

"No, but he confounded the opposition enough that they ended up losing very quickly afterwards."

Rathen grunted irritably. They rode on in a silence torn between astonishment and oppression that made his skin crawl. Fortunately, the aching dirge of a kvistdjur soon snatched away their attention, and their focus remained fixed to their surroundings until they finally happened upon a patch of sheltered ground just level enough and bare enough to sleep upon.

"We're near a ruin," Anthis declared as they pegged their tents to the frozen ground and Eyila silently started a fire. "Quite a significant one, actu--"

"We're not going near it," Rathen replied absolutely, sorting some food and ignoring the young man's frustrated bluster. "I can't do anything about the magic, so it's best just to leave it."

"But it's a site known for creationism--" He stopped short at the mage's warning look and almost visibly paled. "Okay, sorry, you're right."

Rathen turned away and collected the pickings of meagre vegetables and bread, suppressing his disappointment at the young man's intimidation. It was far from unusual, but streaked now by something wholly irrelevant that propelled him back into his hounded days at the Order. *'You were happy in the Order'* - had Aria actually come with them, or had he taken along some other curly-headed, round-faced little girl by mistake? She could be perceptive at times, but at others, she could be downright ridiculous.

Anthis hurried over to Petra as she adjusted her sword and turned to head out on a sorely-needed patrol. She looked at him curiously while he watched Rathen with slightly unsettled eyes as he began to prepare a stew, and shook her head to herself. "He hasn't changed from yesterday, you know."

"No, well, he was formidable then, too." He dragged himself away and turned almost accusingly towards her. "How did you know about Rathen's past?"

"I eventually placed his name and asked Garon about it. And my sister is a soldier, remember."

"Oh, of course... I'm sorry you didn't get to see her."

"Yeah..." She smiled meekly, her hand rising absently to the chain about her neck. "I suppose I should have expected--" Her eyes flashed suddenly wide, sending a jolt of panic through Anthis's bones. "Where's...?"

"What? What is it?"

"My locket - it's gone!"

"Gone?" He frowned, glancing over her neck for himself. "How could it be gone?"

"I don't know, I didn't--" Realisation dulled the wildness of her eyes and stilled her frantic hands. "Earlier - the fight. It could have broken off..." She spun around and the two stared back along their darkened path. Her shoulders slumped beneath the force of her exhalation. "It's gone, then..."

"No, no, we can find it--"

"Anthis, it's dark, and it would take hours even if that thicket was right around the corner!"

But he'd already turned away, and within minutes the whole camp was up and searching the area, inside bags, her horse's mane and tack, and retracing their steps along the path. No one complained that it was a waste of time, not even Garon, which Rathen found curious, and before long, Anthis spotted something glinting in the snow beneath the small and rickety bridge they'd crossed just half an hour before.

Skidding down into the creek, he lifted the small silver chain from the snow, complete with the circular Craitic talisman and unadorned oval. Aside from the unlikeliness of it belonging to anyone else, he'd seen her fiddle with it often enough to recognise it. It had probably come loose during the fight after all, but hadn't slipped off until they'd dismounted to reduce the strain on the bridge.

He turned and hurried immediately back towards camp, slowing to catch his breath only when he heard Petra approaching. He opened his palm as an after-thought to check for damage, and realised then that the locked was slightly ajar. His heart shuddered at the thought of returning water-stained pictures, and flicked it open to check - though he was unsure what he could do if they were.

Fortunately, he needn't discover a solution.

He moved on slowly, lingering for a moment on the image of her sister. The resemblance was uncanny - and she looked far too kind to be a soldier. But Petra, too, when she laughed or smiled, was free of a fighter's edge.

It was only as he moved to close it that his eyes fell onto the picture of the man and woman on the other half of the locket.

Petra raced around the corner with Rathen and Garon close behind, and he looked up at her in sheerest surprise. "Durhan the Bastion..."

She nodded, all but snatching it from his open hand and searching for any damage herself. "Yes," she replied, her beaming relief quite abruptly dulled by just a touch of intense anguish, and caught her own breath with a single, practised puff. "My father."

"Your father was Durhan the Bastion?"

"Who's Durhan the Bastion?" Rathen asked with a frown, and Garon and Anthis each looked back at him in surprise. "I remind you that I was banished for eleven years..."

"He was a gladiator," Petra replied quietly, staring down at the portrait. "In the Crucible. He trained me. We were very close..." She raised her chin, and her eyes were hard. Frightfully so. Rathen saw the sorrow around them, and the hunger for vengeance - the vengeance she'd sought for years, the vengeance she'd confessed to him after she'd discovered his own dark secret. The confession that had been eating her enough that it had grown, in her eyes, to the size of his own, and haunted her just the same.

"Until he was murdered." Rathen watched the edge of her jaw harden, and he struggled to put the facts together. "But...he was a gladiator? Was he not killed in the Crucib--"

"No, he was *murdered*." The violence lacing her voice clogged his words in his throat. "He was attacked in the *street* - mugged, assaulted, purposeless *whatever* it was meant to be. He had nothing to steal, no winnings on him, *nothing*, but dead all the same by a common *thug* or some deranged gambler who'd taken a risk, betted against him and couldn't handle the loss. My father...my father was a *champion*. And he was cut down in the *street*, stabbed in the back and then *butchered*...just...*covered* in cuts..."

Rathen stepped forwards and embraced her as her voice caught into ragged sobs. Garon stood stoically in silence, his face twisted in a muted scowl. Clearly, he already knew the story.

She sniffed and thanked him, but didn't let the gesture linger. She stood taller after that, stubborn and proud, her hand tight around the hilt of her sword and words spoken hatefully through her teeth. "The bastard had expected to defeat him in one blow, so he must've fought in a panic when he turned around. He won - but my father would have given *far* more than he'd got before he was left to bleed out. And the fact that no other bodies were found means that the bastard survived by luck alone. But *I will* find him."

"But what if he's already dead?" Rathen asked softly, though he knew before the words left his mouth that his attempt at reason wouldn't land at all. "What if he didn't die on the street but died at home instead? Or has already been caught--"

"I would have been told about it," she hissed. "I would *know*. He's still out there, somewhere, and I *will* put my father's spirit to rest *myself*."

The locket snapped shut between her fingers. The sharp, keening sound reverberated through the cold.

She turned around and walked away, tall, powerful, rigid against the anguish of her freshly opened wound. Rathen sighed sadly, wishing dearly that he'd never asked the question to begin with, then turned to follow her back through the snow at a respectful distance.

Half an hour later, while eating their thin but welcome stew in the smouldering shadow of an aggrieved silence, a rumble shook the camp. It was slight but certain, deep, colossal, and lasted for four frantic heartbeats. They looked across one another with wide eyes before Aria broke the silence.

"What was that?"

"I don't know," Rathen replied, already rising to his feet. They waited for a few minutes, but it didn't come again.

"Do you think it's Salus?" She asked, looking cautiously back in the direction she thought it had come from. "Pushing chasms?"

"It..." He frowned as he reached himself carefully out beyond the camp. "No. I don't think so... It is magic, but it's not... Stay here." He stepped away from the sheltered fire without another word. Garon was quick to hurry after him.

"I have a thought," he replied before Garon could ask his question, but didn't elaborate, and before long they found themselves standing at the edge of a forested chasm, a scar that stretched off far into the darkness yet stood narrower than others they'd seen - or perhaps that was an illusion cast by the hundreds of foot-thick roots that reached across the gaping void.

Staring at it, Garon quickly put the mage's guess together. "Hlífrún."

"How else would these woods be so 'fertile'?" He started as Garon suddenly drew his sword, and saw then what had provoked him. Some way along its length, the furthest they could see through the trees, was an abnormal mass of rocks and pebbles, speckled here and there with dark patches of moss and lichen, free from a shroud of snow.

And moving.

"Stendjur," Rathen surmised very quietly. "A young one."

"Does it answer to her, do you think?"

"Maybe, but I'm not willing to wander over and find out."

Slowly and ponderously, it drew up its bulk and moved to the edge of the chasm, where it appeared to stoop and examine the lacing roots. The ground shook with its heavy steps, but it was shallow, a surface rumble that lacked the strength of the first. After a long and apparently pensive moment, it moved away and settled itself back on the ground a short ways from the edge, and appeared quite suddenly as nothing more than a pile of highly natural and highly inanimate rock.

Rathen's eyes narrowed in thought. Was the stendjur guarding the rend? Or observing it? With the presence of wildlings and their cryptic magic, it wasn't beyond the realms of possibility that the rumble had been the earth itself, dragging itself back together.

Preferring not to overstay their welcome, the pair quietly slipped away, and

Garon promptly renewed his patrol with an eye for suspiciously compact mounds of stone. Rathen jumped some moments later when Anthis appeared out of the shadows.

"Vastal's *Blood*, don't sneak around like that," he whispered hoarsely, forcing his heart back down his throat. But he frowned when Anthis remained silent. Gradually, he noticed through the darkness the profound stillness of the young man; his expression was drawn and harrowed in the vague moonlight, his eyes wide and traumatised, his feet level as though he had no intention of taking another step, and his hands, trembling, hugged tightly about himself. It was as if he'd seen a ghost.

Rathen's pounding heart skipped a beat. "What is it?" He swallowed hard. "What's happened?" He stared past him towards the hidden camp, and as a blinding panic fuelled a surge of violent images, he moved to storm on past him.

"I think I know who killed Petra's father."

Surprise stunned his feet to a halt. He spun around, staring back at him in confusion. "What?" But Anthis said nothing. Slowly, painfully, the wide, tormented eyes began to form the answer.

Rathen felt his blood run cold. The truth struck him like the bone-shaking ring of a colossal bell. Again, just as it had happened in the desert, the young man offered no denial to his unspoken conclusion. "Oh, Anthis..." The two stood and stared at one another like statues of an ancient tragedy. "What have you done?"

Chapter 56

Garon looked up at the distant approach of faint but familiar footsteps and immediately forced a softness into his bearing. It was a trial every time that threw him well out of his comfort zone, but he was gradually finding his way through. When Petra finally strode out of the trees, however, her face was tainted with that same distress it had been since the return of her locket. Compassion found him a little easier as he stepped calmly out into her path. "Are you all right?"

"Fine," she smiled, looking up suddenly as if startled from her thoughts. But her smile was hollow, and her gait didn't break.

"Petra," he caught her gently by the elbow. The jerk with which she pulled herself free was much too sharp. He didn't address it. "You didn't have to tell anyone anything, you know."

"It's no secret."

"That's not what I mean."

"I know. Look, it's nothing. Really. I'm just fine."

Her smile hadn't moved. Garon considered her for a brief but intense moment.

Her face was a mask; she was trying too hard to feign cheer, and she was failing. Her injury was too deep and still too fresh even after half a dozen years, and instead of concealing it, her efforts were fusing into her anger and becoming something terrible. Her smile and cold, dead eyes were chilling. "Petra--"

"Leave me alone, Garon."

"No. If I leave you alone, I run the risk of making you think I don't care."

"But you do. So it's all right."

He didn't like the way she said it. It was almost spiteful. "Have I done something?"

"What ever could you have done?" She was impossible to read. On a phantom cue, she turned and walked away. "We're being watched, Garon. There's a patrol to see to. I'll see you later."

Confused and powerless, he watched her leave, and after violently racking his brain managed to turn up but one thought: he hadn't comforted her. That was all it could be. He'd let Rathen embrace her rather than reach out himself. But public displays weren't his way - she knew that. There was order to maintain. She understood why he distanced himself...didn't she?

He breathed a long, weary, helpless sigh. There was little he could do if she didn't. But beyond the others' prying eyes, he could at least try to comfort her now. Better late than never had to ring true at some point.

...But what if she *didn't* want it?

Anthis didn't breathe any easier with distance between himself and the camp. He had hoped, foolishly, to flee from his guilt, but it had followed him like a hungry dog. Like a shadow. Like his own skin. He had imagined their stares, their hatred, he *knew* he had, but even out here he could feel their eyes on him, hear their whispers. Supper had been agony, and he couldn't bring himself to look at Petra nor bear to remain within reach of that oppressive sorrow, knowing that it had been caused entirely by his own hands.

He stumbled over another root as he ran blindly through the trees. He felt sick to the depths of his stomach, as though his guts had decayed to pulp.

He'd explained *everything* to Rathen, and he had listened without vocal judgement. He'd thought, perhaps, that he was beginning to understand, but he didn't say a word once he'd finished.

He wasn't sure what he'd hoped to gain from the admission, but his guilt had remained unmollified - as so it should. But the matter wasn't so black and white, either, and he knew that Rathen had at least seen that much, otherwise, surely, he would have said *something*...

Anthis squeezed the strap of his satchel to still the incessant shaking of his hands. He felt himself begin to sweat again at just the thought of that dark and disappointed stare, a stare that had made him feel now as strongly as it had then that he was under the scrutiny of a high bailiff, as though Rathen had the power and the right to judge and to punish. And absurd as that was, he'd found himself desperately seeking his ruling, whatever it might be.

But he'd received nothing but the horror of hearing himself say aloud that he had murdered their friend's father, and of seeing Rathen's own disgust sink in with terrible permanence.

His stomach convulsed. He braced himself against a tree and wretched over the snow.

She had to be told. And he had to be the one to do it. He knew Rathen well enough to know that he wouldn't intervene, but also that he wouldn't stand by for long. The guilt of knowing and holding the secret would weigh on him, too, and he couldn't risk losing what few opportunities he had to soften the blow. If she heard it from someone else, she wouldn't get the whole story.

The whole story. How could he possibly break that to her? And what would she do when he did?

He staggered and wretched again.

He knew what she would do. Even if he caught her in the most rational mood, even if he explained it with perfect composure and reason, he knew what she would do. The only question would be whether she'd use a sword or her own bare hands.

No. He had to escape. Just for the moment. Just for the night. He had to get away.

The tangled woods flashed by as his feet pounded wildly across the undergrowth, his frozen fingers clutching desperately around his satchel. Guided by some vague notion of his only chance at distraction, he ran and stumbled until he fell at last into the disconcerting air of magic, the same quiet, uncomfortable taint that had loured upon him at every other ruin. The sudden shift into preternatural danger was all that soothed his frenzy.

Half-cautiously, bushes and saplings were brushed aside, and he ducked beneath the clawing limbs of ancients. He stepped slowly, feeling for any more roots or worse hidden beneath the snow, and listened closely for any changed beast that called this place home. He found nothing. The ruin was as overgrown as the rest of the woods, layered with the same thin mantle of snow, just as cold, empty and silent. But its atmosphere was far removed from the vibrancy of the surrounding nature, and imposed itself upon him grimly. Beneath that weight, nothing around him sat right. In his distraction, he only vaguely noticed the fragments of a moon spread across the underside of the laden trees, their faces and etchings identical to that which hung in the sky, a perfect likeness, just as silver, just as bright, as though it had been deliberately plucked and shattered.

He gasped suddenly and his jittery heart vaulted into his throat as the ground gave way beneath his foot. He jumped back as the snow sank along a crack, dropping slowly with the litter beneath it.

A chasm. It shouldn't have surprised him. And neither should his concern have been for the ruin itself, but once he discovered that this highly-treasured and studied site of Doru, the God of Mind, was unrecognisable even beyond the snow and magic, it stole away his entire focus.

The slanted stone walls had shifted with the cracking of the earth, some crumbling into a worse state of disrepair while others had fallen completely, their timeworn carvings swallowed by the ground and baring new faces covered in moss, lichen, soil and fine roots. A few walls were nowhere to be seen at all. The needless destruction ripped apart his shaken nerves.

In a fit of desperation, he fell upon the wreckage, gathering the shattered fragments despite the bite of the snow, pushing upright the tilted stones without an inch of success, lifting with all his might the tragically toppled walls. He tried to sketch out what he could still see, and what he couldn't he dragged from memory, all the while turning himself obstinately away from the hopeless truth of the matter.

The ancient inscriptions, the centre of the most heated academic debates, the only such record of creation known in the southern world, was lost.

But he refused to give up. The cold stung, the force exerted on the sharp and shattered rock cut his hands, the chill and torment tightened his breath. But his own insurmountable guilt wouldn't let him abandon it. Every cut, frost burn and dropped stone added to his self-punishment.

His guilt had forced out of his mind the fact that its every face had been copied out by hundreds of historians over hundreds of decades, the figures of gods and of various peoples, transcribed and interpreted throughout the third era, then transcribed and interpreted again. There were abundant ideas with abundant support, so many that even the Temple was disinclined to choose but one as gospel, the vague series of images of all the gods' faces looking down upon smaller, near-identical figures, then upon men that looked like animals, and then, finally, upon the elves.

Some believed that, before Vastal and Zikhon's hatred, the pair had left half of Their power behind so that They could step down and live upon the fragile world, where Vastal soon began to create in Her boredom, and Zikhon began to destroy out of jealousy. Over time, She created increasingly stronger creatures as custodians over all else She'd made, culminating in the elves, before departing to regain Her full power and hold back Zikhon's tirade Herself.

Others said that Vastal created a copy of Herself, which changed itself into a beast to be different from Her, then divided itself for company and began to walk on two legs, first appearing as an animal and eventually becoming the elves. But it had divided its power too far and only Vastal could protect its many bodies from Zikhon's disgust.

Some that Vastal had created the elves, and that Zikhon had created a terrible plague that changed a great many of them into feral beasts, but enough had survived to live on and flourish in spite of Him.

But perhaps they were all wrong. Perhaps the first elves, the beast-men and subsequent elves were all different creations; the first elves were more akin to gods, made too close to Their own image, rich in magic if to a lesser degree, but they were too familiar, they didn't grow or learn or change, and they became dull to watch. And so the beast-like 'wild men' were created to be the far opposite of Themselves, but they were too slow and primitive and were eventually abandoned in disgust. The elves that came next were the perfect balance between primitive and omnipotent, and held the gods' interest until the eventual gift of magic ended in offence and obliteration.

As well as being too complex for the masses, Anthis's theory was hailed as one of the more ridiculous; that Vastal could be capable of disgust was in itself disgusting, and the idea that the first elves - dubbed hatefully by his mocking peers as 'lesser gods' - possessed such powerful magic and transcendency was declared as blasphemy. But after his recent discovery that the various faces of Vastal and Zikhon were in fact separate gods, and that none of these gods were exclusively good or evil, it became increasingly plausible that they could have suffered the same kind of arrogance the elves eventually did. All-mighty creators that made something too familiar, then too different, before settling at last on the middle-ground.

And while everyone else shrugged the beast-men off as having either died or changed into elves, his was the only theory that had worked the origin of men into the equation. If the beast-men had indeed been abandoned out of disgust and left alone and ignored while gods focused on the prettier elves, then it was probable that the elves would have placed themselves above the beast-men, too. Just as they had above humans. In the passage of so much time, was it not possible that these wild men might walk a little straighter and learn to talk, like children did? And elven oppression would have introduced them to culture and civilisation, which they would have slowly adopted for themselves beneath that oppression. And 'lesser gods', though he loathed the term, also lent itself to Vokaad's existence and reinforced his desperate hope that the Sulyax Dizan was not killing for nothing.

But here his validation lay in dust.

Finally, despair dropped him to his knees while broken sobs cut through his shivers, and he slumped against a fallen wall, exhaustion and cold racking his body. He looked down at his hands. They were mottled red and white, and shaking violently. He'd left his blanket behind in his rush to escape. But he wondered if that would really matter all that much.

He cursed sluggishly as water seeped through to his skin, and he discovered that the snow had frozen to his shirt. He pulled himself free, but the compacted snow came with him, as well as a clump of frozen soil, roots and moss. It was by chance that he was still capable of noticing that the stone beneath it was bare.

He frowned and sat up, breaking the snow off of his shoulder, then pulled at another patch from the broadest surface. Another sheet of humus broke away. And there were etchings beneath. Unfamiliar etchings. Etchings that had been embedded in a soil mound, a mound into which many thought the stone had been intentionally embedded like so many others. Not a mound that had built up against it over such time only the gods could account for.

Suddenly, the cold was forgotten, and he desperately began pulling, ripping and digging the snow away, resorting even to using the edge of his notebook to scrape off the more stubborn patches.

Quick, light footsteps padded swiftly across the ground. He turned at the very last minute and instinct ejected a blast of energy from his palm, hitting the speeding shape directly and throwing it backwards.

Panic tore his eyes wide, and a curse tumbled from his numb lips. It was a sword after all.

With frightening speed, Petra was back on her feet. A fury of red, she fell upon him again, led by the tip of her sword, sharp, glinting and driven by a hand free of any restraint. Not a sound crossed her lips as she descended. But her eyes screamed for blood.

"Rathen told you..." He scrambled away, throwing another clumsy spell out behind him, and kicked up as much snow in his wake as he could. But she easily side-stepped the strike, which crashed and splintered a tree, and stormed on through the billowing snow. He found his feet at last and dashed witlessly back towards the chasm. She caught him before he made three steps.

"*It's not what you think!*" He cried, hitting the snow with a thump. "I'm so sorry! Please! Please, believe me!" He flipped over to find her standing silently above him, her sword raised, as dark and obdurate as a revenant. With a pathetic gasp, he threw himself immediately to the side. The tip came down right beside his ear. He heard the force of its impact reverberate through the steel. His blood turned to ice.

Desperation threw another blast into her left leg, and he rolled away to the right as she crumpled beneath her weight. She growled a curse and set after him again, but swore as she stumbled and pain shot through her inner thigh. The murder in her eyes darkened.

"Oh, Vastal save me..." He wheezed, turned and sprinted once again for the chasm, reluctant to fire a fourth ungainly strike and risk stoking her bloodlust. The rend was within sight.

The rattle of chains clinking through the chill air sent a sudden heat of alarm through his limbs, and panic threw him swiftly to the side. But he was too quick. Only after his adjustment did the repetitive whooshing and rattling end, and he processed it too late to evade again. The chain wrapped itself heavily about his legs.

He hit the ground hard and skidded a few feet further across the snow, stopped only by the reversed impetus of his own confused direction of magic towards the edge of the hidden chasm.

But the next strike didn't come.

He shoved himself quickly to his feet while the foulest oaths tore free behind him, and discovered her suddenly restrained. One arm barred across her chest, another about her waist, she thrashed, howled and kicked, but Garon remained as firm as a statue, his arms locked and immovable. Her sword was on the ground. His own was still in its sheath.

"*I heard you telling him!*" She was screaming even as she slipped her arm down and behind herself for one of the daggers at her back. "I heard the lies!" Garon pulled her tighter against himself. She may have had the blade, but she couldn't free it from its sheath, nor her hand from its entrapment.

"They weren't lies!" Anthis explained quickly, desperately, wrestling his legs free to run if Garon's hold failed. "Your father was a *killer!* He *murdered* people, Petra!"

"*No!!*"

"*Yes!*" He stepped towards her imploringly, foolishly, then jumped back as she began kicking savagely at the air in front of her, using Garon's sturdy frame to her advantage. "He was an unknown bounty - I had a hunch, so I followed him, I watched him, I waited - I wanted to make *absolutely sure!* And I s...I *saw* him do it! There was no mistake, Petra, I'm sorry!"

"*LIES!*"

"*They're not!*" He pressed, eyes fixed to her entrapped hand. "He didn't enjoy the fight, Petra, he enjoyed choking the life--"

"Anthis."

His pleading eyes flicked quickly towards Garon. He was giving him the chance. He couldn't waste it. "He wasn't the man you thought he was."

"*He was a good man!*"

"*To you!*"

"*An honourable man!*"

"*Beneath an audience!*"

"Anthis." Garon's voice was steady. "Leave. Now."

He stared at Petra helplessly. She hadn't stopped thrashing, and her eyes were bestial. There was nothing he could say that she would hear. And the moment she escaped the inquisitor's grip, she would kill him.

While excruciating shame twisted knots in his gut, he turned, and he fled.

"*How much did you get for him? Huh?!*"

"He didn't turn him in," Garon said calmly. "He had no physical proof." Trapping the crossguard with his hip, he pulled her dagger hand free, but she whirled on him before he could grasp her shoulders. Screaming and crying in rage, she hit him relentlessly, her fists tightly balled, but he braced against every strike and lifted his chin away to protect his face. She fought him zealously as he tried to steady her, and forced her instead to the ground.

She spat in his face while he pinned her legs and held down her wrists. "*You bastard.*" Her voice was venom. "You *knew* Anthis had done it. You *lied to me* when you said you didn't know back on that damned island! You knew! *You knew!*"

"I *didn't* know, not then--"

"Oh-hoh - so you *worked it out*, did you? *When? How?!*"

"I read the reports of Durhan's murder, I recognised the wound down the length of the arm. But as for Anthis, it wasn't until he gave you back your locket. I saw the look on his face when he saw the picture. But his claims weren't unfounded - the murders stopped after your father's death."

But she had stopped listening. Though she speared him with a caustic glare, her thoughts moved clearly through her eyes. She was recalling the horrendous sight of her father's slashed body, and seeing, perhaps for the first time, the long, insignificant cut down the inside of his forearm. Her eyes softened in disbelief. "It was in front of me all along..." The poison returned. "And in front of you, *O Wise Inquisitor.*"

"All right. Say I *had* known sooner. What would it have done if I'd told you?"

"Why? Because we *'need'* his skills?"

"It has nothing to do with that. You would *kill* him for vengeance."

"*I still will!*"

"*Petra!* You must know that I - *none* of us - can let that stand! For his safety *and* yours! You can't let hate and vengeance consume your existence! You can't let yourself be defined by it! Life is so much *more* than that - *you* are so much more than that!" He said nothing while she laughed, and let her kick herself free. He stormed back onto her once she found her feet, gripping her tightly by the shoulders. "Laugh all you like, but you've been screaming these kinds of sentiments at me for long enough. I'm doing my *best* to create some kind of existence alongside my work, and I'm doing that for *you*. Because, as *irritating* as you are, I knew that you were right. Just as you know now that *I'm* right. You can spit on me, you can kick me, you can drive your blade right on through me, but that won't change the facts. Vengeance doesn't quiet the heart, Petra. It consumes the soul."

She snatched herself free. Again, he let her. Her eyes were filled with nothing but hate.

He sighed to himself when she turned and ran off, but she'd headed in the opposite direction to the camp. He let her go, counted to ten, and walked on after her, following her tracks. People got hurt in the cold. He wasn't about to let it happen under his watch.

Chapter 57

Salus grunted as the August sun bounced in through the window from the snow-blanketed city and blinded him out of his thoughts. His foul expression darkened. With a restless sigh, he ceased his agitated pacing. "A rescue is too big a risk. Doana will have planned for it. But leaving him there is absolutely *not* an option."

"Grant is a portian. He will not speak."

"Teagan," he snapped with the same pestilent irritation that had fringed his mood all morning, "Doana *knows* about us. They know how to kill us, how to deceive us and how to *capture* us. They will also know we won't be broken so easily, and if they employ the same kind of tactics we do in response to that, willingness will have nothing to do with it! Doana *cannot* be underestimated again!"

"And neither can your subordinates." Teagan didn't flinch beneath the bristling look. "What are you proposing?"

"We need to remove him."

He stared for a moment in disbelief. "You mean *dispose* of him."

"It's the *only* way we can keep Doana in the dark and avoid losing any more of our own."

"And what of the others? He isn't the only informed agent out there - the others haven't been captured, but what will you do if that changes?"

"They've not been captured because they've not made the mistake to *learn* from," he growled. "But that one mistake could be as good as handing over our war plans and the key to our back door. Grant has made that mistake. He will have to be their lesson."

"Sir, after all he's done--"

"And all he's *learned*--"

"This is his first mistake!"

"And it will be his *last!* We can't risk them extracting his information!"

"So you wish to kill him?"

He speared Teagan with a venomous look. But as his next words formed on his lips - the reminder that *he* was Keliceran, and they were *his* decisions to make - another voice spoke up in his mind. A familiar voice, considered, archival; a voice that rang with detachment and truth. It repeated an ancient thought. A bygone conclusion. A conclusion he had reached himself in the bitterest moment of his life. *'...done too well...perfect record...inevitable...threat to the safety of the country...'*

'You give the order of death to the guilty and innocent alike.' The voice had changed. He realised with horror that it was his own. *'And even to your own kind when they've outlived their usefulness, or if they may possibly become a threat.*

And yet you believe that I am the one who is dead inside.'

He swallowed hard.

Suddenly, for a terrible moment, he understood what Elina had done. He saw the necessity of his predecessor's actions because, this time, he was the one making that very same decision.

'But with one difference,' he was quick to amend, *'Grant has already been captured. I had not.'*

He could feel the wideness of his eyes and looked up quickly to find Teagan staring past him towards the wall. But he was a perceptive man. He'd seen it. Salus wondered what he was thinking, as Teagan had once been the one tasked with such a duty, and had refused to do it.

He swallowed again, forcing his horror aside, and straightened in defiance to the past. His was the right decision. "We do what must be done."

"Of course, Keliceran." Teagan's voice had steeled. Perhaps he had reached the same conclusion.

They both snapped around at the sudden knock on the door, then Taliel burst inside and thrust a tiny scroll into Salus's hand. "Word from Stoke Rass," she explained quickly. "They're heading to Sagestone."

His anger collapsed to fervour. Salus pulled open the parchment urgently, a glint of mania in his eye. "How can Dana be sure?"

"She overheard it," she replied, even as he read the shorthand. "The inquisitor asked the bartender if there was any talk of trouble around Sagestone - specifically magic. The bartender was wary, asked why he wanted to know. Made out that he was following a lead on the rebellion, heading off an impending attack. The bartender believed him and talked."

"Overheard? That was clumsy..."

"Or was it intentional?"

Taliel glanced nervously towards Teagan while Salus descended back into harsh-eyed thought. "No," he said a moment later, "they'd have made more noise if it was intentional. As it is, it's *too* subtle. An accident brought about by distraction. From Rae's reports, they're preoccupied with fighting amongst themselves. Whatever they're up to, it's putting a strain on them."

"That doesn't mean they're heading to Sagestone."

"They wouldn't have asked after dangers if they weren't, Teagan."

"What if this is just another case of mistaken identity? Why would they slip up now?"

The look Salus gave him was deadly, but brief. When he turned back to Taliel, the volatility in his eyes had shifted towards excitement. "We know where they're going to be, and they're distracted. This is an opportunity. Get me a report on Sagestone, as detailed as possible - then I can get out there and stop them in their tracks."

"Go up against Koraaz yourself?"

"Perhaps we should consider this further before--"

"*Quiet!*" The pair obeyed in a heartbeat. "I remind you that they've thwarted *everyone* else I've sent after them - even *killed* a *portian*. But for once, *we* are a step ahead, and I'm not going to lose this chance by leaving it in someone else's hands! Whatever he and the elves are up to, *it must be stopped immediately!*"

"Forgive me, sir," Taliel appeased hurriedly, "but at the least, you mustn't go alone."

"I don't intend to. Koraaz is strong, and if he's working with the elves, there's no telling what tricks he's learned... No, I won't be going alone." His eyes flicked deliberately onto her, and for a moment, dread crashed like a wave over her face. He smiled apologetically, affection softening his eyes a frightening degree. "Don't worry, I would never put you in his path. But you've been asking to help, and now I think you can. And it's important." He moved towards the desk. "I want you to go to Gennith's Point and plant this." He withdrew a small and strikingly ordinary pebble from a drawer and placed it in her hands. She frowned down at it in open confusion. "Erran created it for use against the Order. It will react to the presence of others' magic, but not to mine. Place it like you did the surveillance spells and then look around. I want to know if anyone else has been sniffing around - Koraaz or otherwise."

"A trap?"

"Gennith's Point is *crucial*, Taliel. I can't risk it being compromised. It may not react to Koraaz, but if the Order or his pet tribal goes near it, it will trigger."

She turned it over in her hands, peering closely at its weather-smoothed surface. "What will it do?" She looked up when Salus didn't reply, and found his lips tight. Whatever it was, he didn't wish to explain. Her eyes sobered. "Very well. Consider it done." But he caught her arm as she turned to leave.

"Not yet. Wait two days, until Sagestone. Then we'll know for sure he's nowhere near and you can plant it safely. I won't risk him teleporting on top of you."

"Yes, Keliceran." She turned and began to leave, but again Salus caught her and spun her back around. He kissed her firmly. Her heart jumped, her cheeks burned and her blood raged for the endless seconds it lasted.

"Thank you," he said when he released her.

She forced the colour to leave her cheeks and inclined her head respectfully. "I'm only doing my job." Forcing herself into composure, she turned again and was allowed at last to leave. The door clicked shut quietly behind her.

"What do you plan to do?"

Salus's mood darkened again as he returned to Teagan. "I will kill him."

"You will need mages."

"Yes...mages..."

Teagan looked around from the window at the musing note in his superior's voice, but his eyes were following his thoughts. Neither noticed the concerned crease in his own brow.

"Mages I can trust. Mages who are loyal..." He began again to pace. "We're in the middle of unusual events...perhaps it's time to change the mould and *ensure* their loyalty. The Order's rebellion is on a tightrope, and when it finally snaps, whether I like it or not, I'll need mages to handle it. And it *will* snap. And *soon*..."

"Your mages are already loyal," he said carefully. "None of them are of the same mind as the Order."

"That's not where the danger lies," he snapped. "There are so few of them...and they're all phidipans..."

Panic flashed behind Teagan's eyes, and he couldn't stop himself from taking an urgent step forwards. "No, Salus, mages are too *powerful* to be given that kind of conditioning - think of the destruction they could wreak! And what if it doesn't take properly? Portians aren't trained to reason, they're trained to *obey* - they don't think of 'right' or 'wrong', only their orders exist. Completing them is all that matters! If a--"

"And yet," he replied absently, still absorbed in his own frantic thought, "that is not so for you. Which is why I keep you around. You're able to balance that necessity with reason..." His lips turned down further in decision. "It's the only way."

"But--"

"I want all available mages in here now." A sudden thought dragged his eyes towards the window, then spurred him purposefully for the door. "In three hours. Call them in, as many as you can. See it done."

The door closed with Teagan's objections wedged firmly beneath the lump of panic in his throat.

For a while Salus mulled his decision over in the carriage, but the details were shortly settled, repercussions established, and his mind soon tumbled onto the looming matter of the rapidly impending meeting.

He'd had no choice but to reel in his temper; Taliel's arrival had been a temporary buoy, but now the bitter mood that had plagued him all day dragged him even lower. Though he'd been vying for this audience for what felt like months, this had not been his making, and that fact had dogged him for the past two days, not least for the short notice. Meetings with the Crown were always scheduled at least a full month in advance, and authority heads were rarely invited. The fact that he'd been summoned in place of Malson meant that the matter was serious.

Though, he could make a guess easily enough: their 'dissatisfaction' had reached new heights.

But while his irritation warred with a begrudging nervousness, his heart was steadfast in its certainty. He was dealing with matters so much bigger than those they threw around across their vast and excessively polished tables, and acting against things they hadn't foreseen despite all of their celebrated wisdom. But while he knew, when it really came down to it, that their opinion meant nothing at all, he couldn't overlook the fact that they possessed a crucial power that he did not. There were more than a handful of situations in which political strength outmatched magical - not to mention that they held the purse strings.

But, summoned or not, he ultimately knew how this would go, and so his mind turned towards ensuring he got the best of the situation. It was, after all, a fine opportunity to observe the palace and the council for himself.

He'd thought hard on the evidence over those past two weeks, and had concluded that the Crown's attempts to send the Arana on nonsense tasks away from critical areas were intended to keep him from discovering the king's plot, to usurp Doana's throne from its child-queen by marriage. There was no other explanation for the backwards orders, unless he was prepared to admit that the Crown was *entirely* inept, which he found himself unwilling to do. That surprised him, but no one could happily stomach the thought of a country in the hands of a *single* moron, let alone a whole flock of them.

He would see what he could find. He was duty-bound to do so.

Resolve drew him up taller in his seat, then he irritably tugged the hem of his gold-trimmed doublet back down. Salus wasn't unaccustomed to costumes, but the palace always demanded the worst. Apparently nobles were offended by practicality.

The royal district passed indifferently outside, growing more ornate and self-involved with every turning along the swept roads. The people paraded importantly in their regalia, though not one had anywhere worthwhile to go, moving in close groups thick with gossip they made no attempt to keep among themselves.

Like the stately district, secrets here were not kept under silence, but beneath garish claims and displays of wealth. Their nature, too, was just as frivolous - but nothing that couldn't be useful. Nobles heard their share of rumours, a good many of which were born of truth, and blackmail was so common across the richest districts that his own subordinates used the tactics openly and effectively without drawing suspicion. And such dissipated people would do and tell a great deal to keep an affair, debt or disgraceful child from ruining their social status. It was a ridiculous and valuable practice.

The buildings were just as ostentatious, needlessly grand and overdone, and seemed to get bigger the closer they were to the palace. But the palace itself overshadowed them all from its position atop the hill, standing in a strange combination of elven elements - twists, braids and elegant curves - and simple, angular human, all of which had been painstakingly carved by hand from the stone, without a spell in sight. That was something Salus felt he could be proud of, despite the people within it.

The road took its final turn, and the carriage began its ambling climb up the long avenue. Buildings gave way to gardens, walls to hedges and trees, city guards to imperial, and the number of carriages thinned. Dramatic iron gates opened in time with the horses' pace, and they followed the empty road towards a second pair which opened into a vast, green courtyard. At the foot of the excessive stone stairs that preceded every palace, the carriage drew to a slow, dignified stop.

Salus looked out at it wearily. Beneath the enormous doors made to accommodate egos, a primly dressed valet stood waiting upon the third step. He recognised the unaged man from his last visit, and suspected again that he'd been born with a crick in his neck. Either that or there was a rather short puppet string fixed to the end of his nose.

The carriage door swung open at the hand of the coachman, and he stepped out onto the swept, slushy road with all the pomp that was expected of him. The cold soaked far too quickly through his flimsy doeskin boots, but he showed no trace of it. There were a number of court-goers milling around outside, and each to a one cast him an uninterested look even while their eyes tried hungrily to work out his trade and cast their judgements.

He didn't entertain them with even a glance, and felt the deflation, insult and rising enmity spreading quickly around him with every step. Behind his lofty and disinterested grimace, he was quite enjoying himself.

The valet bowed deeply as he ascended towards him, and Salus returned it with the expected nod once he stood one step above. Salus knew that the bow was meant in mockery - every bow that was not to a member of the royal family was subtly limned in satire - but Salus suspected that he was just as aware of the derision in his own. There was a mutual disrespect between them, but malicious on neither side. Salus could see right through the poor fellow and pitied his weary, prostrated existence, regardless of his substantial wages.

The middle aged man straightened and his nose returned to the air. "If my lord would follow me..." He turned without waiting for a response and began back up the steps, free of haste despite his lack of a coat, as either might appear unseemly, and Salus duly followed, continuing to ignore the stares.

A wall of heat hit him the moment he stepped through the doors. A colossal fireplace burned at the head of the foyer, consuming wood like it was oil, and cast a welcome glow across the uncountable gold surfaces. The flowers that filled every vase had been swapped for deep winter colours of summer blooms, as though to avoid offending any royal sensibilities, and he was sure for a moment that he smelled cinnamon.

Salus decided to spare himself the headache of thinking about it and followed the valet up the winding, sprawling staircase.

All too soon he was drawn to a stop outside one of the many meeting chambers, its twin doors framed by two imperial guards, neither of whom paid him any outward attention. The valet knocked upon the engraved mahogany with a practised weight, and at the muffled call of admittance, opened the door with a deep and ceremonious bow which was, to a careful eye, another perfectly hidden mockery aimed at anyone who might feel important enough to deserve it.

Salus steeled himself and stepped inside, and immediately fell under the glacial stares of twelve pairs of imperial eyes, already peering down their noses at him before the latch fell back into place. Instinctively, he drew himself up to meet them, and tightened his hold over his rapidly spiking fury.

"Keliceran," the gilded man at the head of the table began as Salus bowed sardonically and took his place in the furthest seat. The man's voice was a sneer, no attempt made to hide his dislike or distrust, and the others present peered at him in much the same cavalier manner. Here sat the royal council, the Crown in absence of the king's presence, and they each bore their authority far too easily. The head councillor looked shortly back to his parchments to further the deliberate affront. "Thank you for coming."

"It is my honour."

Not one of them replied, too busy perhaps trying to locate the sarcasm in his perfectly tempered tone. He looked across them neutrally and, one by one, they turned warily towards the council's head, who still seemed absorbed in the papers. "We're all busy men, so I'll step to the point: the Arana is slipping." He glanced up, then, no doubt to see how the statement had landed, but Salus offered him nothing. His dark eyes narrowed and he straightened in his seat, turning his full attention onto the commander of The Crown's Fang in another attempt to intimidate. "Too little information is coming in, and what does is often too late. You've provided us nothing at all with which to take the upper hand - the stalemate went on for far too long, and when Moore finally moved, Doana were gone, and *none* of your people had seen it."

"Moore's reluctance to move was not our doing," Salus replied coolly. "We provided what we could, and he chose not to act on it."

"But it *was* your doing that allowed Doana to slip in in the first place."

"We are not the only ones who are supposed to be watching the borders."

"Kalokh also slipped in."

"After you ordered us away." He stifled his victory at the wave of darkened, foolish looks that passed along the table, and didn't miss the lack of any attempt to deny it. "I admit," he continued with perfectly feigned deference, "I've been unable to work that one out, but it is my duty to obey the commands of the Crown, and I trust that the reason will become evident in time."

"You might think to hold your tongue, Keliceran," the council head rebuked, straightening the gold-hemmed sleeves of his perfectly pressed robes. "You are adept at pointing the finger, and had you been employed among the court scribes, it might well be your job to devise excuses. But you are not. It is, rather, to provide the information that His Majesty's enemies would prefer to keep hidden so that we might turn it against them - or prevent them from turning it upon *us*. But instead you make covert strikes that get two out of three of your men killed, deliver nothing of use, and allow them to overrun us while we're weakened by internal affairs!"

"The Order is a hazard--"

"It is not your business to discuss the Order. The Arana is the subject upon the table at this moment--"

"Perhaps you have your priorities muddled, my lord, but the Order has made it clear that they will tear this country apart and they're undoubtedly going to use the distraction of the war to do it."

"Is this information, Keliceran, or guesswork?"

Salus bit back his snarl.

The councillor straightened with the slightest smile of victory. He was terrible at hiding it. "I thought as much."

"What is the White Hammer's role in all this?"

"The White Hammer does not concern you, their interest with the populace lies within the borders, the Arana's lies beyond."

"And yet the Arana is still expected to provide information on enemy forces *within* while we're being *sent* beyond. And Moore's scouts, they can't do it?"

"The military does not concern you--"

"When the safety of the country is involved, *everything* concerns me."

The councillor flashed him a look of poisonous consideration. "And yet," he spoke calmly, "the fact remains that the country has been invaded twice in four months."

And there it was. The bitter, stinging truth. No matter what conflicting orders he might remind them of, no matter what victories he had secured, no matter what the other authorities might be doing against it - no matter even their enemies' own covert skills - the country *had* been invaded, *twice*, and the Arana, who *should* have been the first to see it, hadn't been able to stop it.

He straightened in defence, but said nothing, raging internally at the councillor's most recent flicker of success.

"There is talk of dissolving the Arana."

And then, suddenly, he was standing beside himself, as though the words had knocked his consciousness clean from his body. He observed that endless moment with a strange detachment that was capable of noticing only the remarkable irony.

"But, many are against it as a permanent measure. Most say it is a necessary evil. Personally, I believe the Arana is due for restructuring. But it is not my decision alone to make. So, we have agreed to give you another chance." His eyes glittered with a subtle dare. Regaining himself, Salus did not stoop to it. "The Grey River has run dry. There is concern that some may try to use its route as passage. Ivaea, or the tribes. The Arana is to survey the area and report any and all movements."

Twelve pairs of eyes turned patiently upon him. His expression was mild as he stared back, thoughtful, as though already weighing the most suitable candidates. Privately, though, he was sceptical.

The region they proposed was empty, and for good reason: it was treacherous, not least for the chasm he'd steered through it himself, cutting off that very river, and more trouble than it was worth for even a desperate felon to reach. *No one* would use that sheer-sided river bed for travel, even had it been whole.

But, more than that, he had eyes among Ivaea. Recent evidence may have proven that lack of obvious motive meant nothing at all, but Ivaea were embroiled entirely in their own affairs, with no resources to pour into a surprise assault. They were in no position to attack them. The tribes, too, had been almost eradicated within Turunda, and they had no reason to come further inland.

The suggestion had been pulled from the soles of their boots. And it was, he felt, not the first.

Any recent orders he'd obeyed had happened by chance, missions he'd assigned on his own initiative and only received official orders for up to four weeks later. But though he knew watching the ravine was a waste of resources, this time, he *would* obey - and if this *was* an attempt to probe the Arana's skills, then he would use it to probe the Crown's intentions in return. Because this didn't add up.

Once again, it seemed as though the Crown was trying to divert their attention, if not outright remove them from the picture. The council seemed to be doing their best to keep him in the dark on the other authorities, too, even though it was far from unreasonable that he should ask after the military given the present state of affairs. It was as though they *wanted* to keep the two apart. And he still had no explanation as to why Moore had taken such a ridiculously long time to move - and why, when he finally had, Doana had already vanished without the Arana's knowledge. Suddenly, it all seemed too convenient.

Despite himself, he was curious. So he would obey this command - but he would do so cautiously. And he wouldn't waste one of his best on jumping through the Crown's hoops.

The councillors continued to watch him. None of his thoughts had shown through, so he smiled obligingly. "Whatever the Crown wishes. But it is a secluded place - it will take some time to get to, and it will be troublesome in this weather."

"You will manage."

"What about our funding?"

"Earn it."

Salus's expression didn't waver.

The head councillor returned curtly to his parchments, sparing not even a glance as he proceeded to dismiss him.

With perfect composure, Salus stood, bowed briefly, turned, and left, stepping silently out through the door which had opened in perfect time, as though the valet had been waiting outside with his ear up against it. Wrapped in a veil of crystalline thought, he allowed him to lead him back to his carriage.

His suspicions were gaining ground. He would handle Malson more meticulously now, and would soon find his answers. The Crown had been vague, using disdain as an excuse to withhold all the details - a foolish choice to make when dealing with a man trained in uncovering the truth, but such was the Crown, and such was he. It was not so straight-forward. But they had at least been right about one thing: the Arana *was* due for restructuring - but that was a matter that only *he* was qualified to oversee it. And oversee it he would. It would happen on his terms. And it would begin in just over an hour.

That hour couldn't come soon enough. With all need for decorum and finesse lost, he stormed through the Arana's halls, stopping only to change his ridiculous attire, and stood now in the oppressive safety and mastery of his office in front of seven stalwart faces, expressions and eyes tempered to steel, nailed to the furthest wall. And so few. Before him half of the Arana's mages - and one had recently been lost to a sudden attack in their very own city.

His mages were valuable; he couldn't afford to lose any others, but more crucially, he couldn't afford to lose their loyalty. Without loyalty, their power was a risk, and how could he possibly rely on them to strike true in the face of Koraaz, a half-elf demon, if they were not loyal and dedicated?

His eyes panned over them, evaluating them intensively, one by one. None looked back nor showed discomfort, not even when he finally addressed them, his voice clear but weighted and retaining even now a degree of bite from his ordeal with the council.

"No mage has ever been allowed to ascend beyond the ranks of phidipan. For decades, you have been prevented by blood from reaching your potential, because past kelicerans have never trusted you. Yet they readily used your magic as a tool and ignored your every other skill, like using a knife to butter bread rather than to cut, stab or sever. Over time, the blade will dull until all it *can* do is butter bread." An edge crept into his eyes, and his tone heated with resolution. "Today, that changes. Today, I give you the chance to excel. Today, each of you is being given the opportunity to become the first portian mages. Whether you embrace that opportunity or not is entirely in your hands."

Nothing disrupted the stillness of the room. There was no excitement, nor uncertainty.

Teagan watched impassively from the side as Salus stepped towards Erran. A 'breaker' - an expert in torment and the ripping of secrets. He was his most trusted magic-wielder. He'd been teaching him how to utilise his own long before Liogan had imposed herself, and there was no one he would rather gift with the honour of being the first.

The black haired mage didn't move when he stopped in front of him, and yet somehow stood both taller and straighter, and there came only now the slightest trace of anticipation. "Erran - will you accept it?"

"Without question, Keliceran." He spoke calmly. Absolutely. There was no doubt that his training would take perfectly.

Salus stepped then towards the shorter man beside him, much rounder, and common in every way. He was often overlooked and taken for a fool, and he used that to his advantage. He overheard much and was quick to find his mark, he cast flawless distractions and always took his targets by the sheerest surprise. He was also much faster than he looked. Here was a mage who could deceive other casters. "Roland - will you accept it?"

"In the flash of an eye, Keliceran." He, too, was explicit in his decision.

The next was a tall, slender man, certainly by comparison, and a guard among the cells; a mage versed in offensive magic and was perfectly capable of both taking and containing prisoners, as he had proven time and time again. But now there was the slightest whisper of discomfort around him that made Salus suspicious. "Oliver - will you accept it?"

"Yes, Keliceran."

His eyes narrowed the faintest degree. There was a vague hint of doubt in this phidipan's tone, too. Trained as he was in unspoken language, every quiet detail came together as loud and clear as a town crier's bell. He looked across the others. "Three of you so far have agreed to take on the training. I admit, I am surprised. It's no small decision to make, and yet you've each made it so intently."

"We live to obey."

Speaking was his mistake.

A knife appeared in Salus's hand, and with the sharpest, swiftest movement, without a breath of sound, it cut across the man's throat. Another knife cut into his abdomen. With a soft gurgle, Oliver dropped heavily to the ground.

No one moved. They had each sensed it coming. His haste to reassure his superior had revealed his doubt in him, and each knew to the depths of their bones that Salus wouldn't tolerate it. Not even Teagan appeared surprised.

The knives vanished as quickly as they had appeared, and the wildness rose higher from the depths of Salus's eyes. Silently, he moved along to the next mage, a woman, who he viewed with challenge. Her face was as much a mask as everyone else's. "Vari - will you accept it?"

"Unquestionably, Keliceran."

He stared at her for a moment, but she didn't flinch. There was no tremor, no sweat, no quickening of the pulse in her throat nor charge in her eyes. And she had spoken with perfect conviction. Satisfied, he moved on to the next mage in line. If she or anyone else had had any doubts about agreeing, they were silenced. It was regretful, but it was necessary. Far better to lose the service of one man than the loyalty of two. And he would need that loyalty in the days to come...

Chapter 58

The landscape of the past four days had been almost a pleasure to travel through; the ground had been flat, if thick with fresh snow, and the beech trees as they entered Greentop swayed and rustled mutely in the gentle summer breeze, standing wide of one another like a cathedral's columns with few wandering roots to snag the horses' hooves. The sky, thinly overcast, had cleared the previous afternoon, and now shone a vast and brilliant blue. They were sure they'd even felt some brush of warmth to the air, though that could have been the power of wishful thinking.

Instead, it was the atmosphere that had made the days torturous, an inescapable sense of waiting for something dreadful to happen. That sense was at its worst that afternoon.

They'd stopped for lunch rather than eating on the move, a habit they'd revived for the benefit of their tail, but all six of them were silent and keeping to themselves. Garon sat at the edge of the group, tending his sword as he ate, while Petra sat a little further out by herself, looking over her arsenal. Eyila appeared to be meditating though she remained among the others, and Anthis fretted, staring deep into his books while his lips moved with his worries, his own food untouched. Aria watched them all nervously, sniffling and rubbing her eyes, while her father paced behind her. The apprehension was suffocating.

"Rathen." Garon didn't look up from the edge of his blade. "You're putting me off."

"Stars forbid I should put you off." But he forced his feet to a stop all the same and sat back down beside his daughter, where once again he read and re-read the small roll of paper that had been delivered by sparrow the previous day, signed simply with 'E'.

The tense stillness hung heavily for what felt like an hour, though it could only have been minutes, before it was suddenly shattered by the rough, scathing cackle of a crow. Three bated breaths later came the chip of a sparrow, and then two more, another crow.

Every heart leapt.

All was in place.

"Come on," Garon said cursorily, "we best move on." He slipped his sword back into its sheath and rose to his feet. It seemed painfully slow to the others, and slower still as they joined him, and no one uttered a sound as they tidied their belongings away, mounted their horses and rode on through the trees.

Petra took the lead, and Garon let her, while Anthis placed himself deliberately at the back. All cast her a wary look. A new darkness had seeped into her eyes, furious more often than not, but occasionally broken, as though some part of her, some small, deep mote of consciousness, was fighting against her rage to forgive him - a part of her that knew, though she had forever turned away from the thought, that something of what Anthis had said could have been true.

Now, however, they were murderous.

Feeling their chill, Rathen pulled his eyes away from the back of her head.

"I've spoken to her," Garon said quietly from beside him. "She won't let Anthis distract her."

"She wants Salus crushed as much as the rest of us. And, all things considered, she's handled this well."

"You mean she's only tried to kill him the once so far?"

"See? She's handled it well." What little humour had wheezed into Rathen's voice dropped like a stone, and a remorseful sigh eased out. "So much for having to force the arguments, eh? I was almost looking forward to it."

"There's still time."

The belligerent air that had plagued them for four days was heightened now by a new tension, and no one was able to escape it by hiding among their own thoughts. Rathen least of all while Aria clung to him possessively as they rode. Her eyes were still red, and his own lips dragged downwards. He wrapped his arm around her and pulled her close, coaxing a ragged, anguished hiccup that only further cracked his heart.

A drystack wall rose along one side of the hidden road at waist-height, and the ground beyond it began to slope upwards. The ruin was nearby, so close they must have stood just on the brink of the magic, and they'd have to leave the road to reach it. But beside a collapse in the wall, Garon called a halt. He turned towards the back of the company and fixed Anthis with a steady look. "Anthis." His tone was just as serious. "There was some confusion last night. Are you *sure* this is the best ruin to use?"

"It's a bit late to change it if it isn't," Rathen murmured.

Anthis ignored him. "Yes. Sagestone - there's little left of the original structure, but it's rich with magic. The elves used to honour Zikhon here before burying--"

"What?"

Anthis blinked. "'What' what?"

"Anthis, you said Sagestone was used to honour *Doru*."

"...No, I *explicitly* said 'Sagestone is where the elves used to honour *Zikhon* before burying them in a blessed shroud.'"

"No, you said *Doru*. That's the only reason we were coming here at all!"

Anthis's eyes darkened. "You're mistaken, Inquisitor. 'Doru' never passed my lips once."

"I heard you say 'Doru'."

His eyes flicked onto Rathen. "Don't you start."

"Vastal's Blood, Anthis!" Garon shook his head with a long-suffering growl. "We can't afford to waste time like this. We need a shrine to *Doru* - figure it out. Now."

The darkness deepened. "It won't be quick."

"So be it." Garon dismounted while muttering something under his breath, and the others followed with much the same irritation while Anthis found himself a seat on the wall and began poring over the pages of his books. Every one of them tensed at the sound of snow crunching just behind them, but Rathen had already sensed her presence, and only looked up when he felt the gentle touch of familiar magic. He breathed in relief, and the others relaxed minutely.

Aria immediately began to cry.

"Hush, little one," Rathen said softly as he seized her in a fierce embrace. "Do you remember what we talked about?" He felt her nod and wipe her eyes. "You'll be safe with Kienza."

"I won't let you out of my sight," the sorceress promised her pointedly.

Aria nodded again, but continued to sob as her father lifted her down from the saddle and stood her in the snow, and Kienza quickly pulled her close, smoothing the thick woollen hat that encompassed almost her entire head right down past her eyebrows. "It's going to g-go the same as l-last time," she hiccuped, clinging now to her dark, forest green skirts.

"It won't. I *promise* you that."

"What i-if you're wrong?! W-what if *you* get h-hurt?!"

She was about to answer, when Petra stepped forwards. They each looked at her warily, Aria especially so. Her movements were curt and to the point; whatever swagger of confidence or feminine sway they had never consciously noticed had been lost, and there was a lingering brusqueness to her voice. For the most part, she had been civil for the past few days, if silent and distant when interaction wasn't needed. Anthis, however, she kept unerringly in her sights whenever she wasn't out on watch. But now there was a new kind of significance in her heartsick hazel eyes.

Without a word, she knelt down in front of Aria and removed the wooden sword from its shirt-sleeve sheath at her waist. Then, she withdrew one of the lesser-used blades fastened at the small of her back, complete with its scabbard. She extended it towards her, flat across her palms, but gripped her eyes in a purposeful stare before she could take it. Aria met it with slow recognition. "What is this for?"

"Defence," she replied firmly, despite the break of her voice.

"What is it *not* for?"

"Its physical function."

"Which is?"

"To cause harm."

"Why is it at your hip?"

"So my hands are free to try other things first."

"And when it is in your hand?"

"I protect what's dearest to me."

"Good girl." Petra leaned forwards, lifted her hat and kissed her on the forehead. "So now you know: Kienza *will* be safe." She lowered the sheathed blade gently into her hands, gave her the first smile anyone had seen of her in days, then straightened and looked out through the trees. Her expression was quick to darken. "I'll check the area. We could be here for a while."

"Good idea. I'll go too."

As Garon and Petra set off in opposite directions with their hands upon their hilts, Kienza turned towards Rathen, still maternally stroking the child's head as she pulled the blade free of its scabbard. "Your tail won't notice this, but I can't cast much else or I risk being detected. I'm sorry."

"It's all right," he replied, watching his daughter peer at the razor-sharp edge without too much concern. "Far better you get her out of here safely."

"She'll come to associate me with losing you if you keep waiting until the last minute to tell her." Her voice was suddenly frosty. "I warn you: I will not have it." Then, as he formed some helpless apology, her demeanour softened once again and her gaze drifted across Anthis and Eyila, both of whom sat lost in their own heavy thoughts. Her rich, emerald eyes slipped gently back onto him. "Will you be all right?"

"I think so. I might even be able to manage a few things myself."

"Well, if not, you're the most attractive piece of bait I think I've ever seen."

He smiled briefly, then found Kienza's soft, plump lips upon his own, and Aria clinging tightly to his leg. Sadly, and with an unwelcome plunge of anxiety in his chest, he returned their affections with a touch of the desperation he'd been stamping down through his every waking moment.

All too soon, Anthis exclaimed and called Garon back, and Kienza slunk away with Aria quiet at her side. Rathen forced himself not to watch them leave.

They gathered around as he spoke at length, pointing things out between the map and his books, intentionally using jargon that not one of them could accurately follow. But no one called him out, no one cut him short, no one demanded he got to the point. Every false and cumbersome word he said was another moment of delay. They listened intently, and no one paid even an ounce of attention when Eyila got up and began chasing something around and vanishing after it into the downhill trees. But Garon and Petra's hands never left their hilts.

"So," Rathen said chafingly once Eyila had returned, her abrupt hunt finally finished, "to numb a painful story, you led us here, and now you're saying we need to be miles *east* from here?"

"Y-yes, I'm sorry, it was--"

"You're sorry? You're *sorry?!*" His anger caught quickly.

"Leave it, Rathen," Garon warned as he glanced worriedly around them, "it's done now."

"No. No, he's made too many mistakes, Garon! Or have you forgotten the merry chase he led us on to find this damned relic in the first place?! What were you thinking bringing him at all? There *had* to be others more qualified than him - he's a *kid!*"

"How dare you--"

"Quiet, Anthis," Garon snapped, dampening the young historian's ire, then turned to bring his own down upon him. "Don't you *dare* question my decisions."

Rathen laughed. A sick, derisive laugh. "Question your decisions? *Question your decisions?!* I haven't even *begun* to question your decisions! I wouldn't even know where to start! I'm still scratching my head over things you did *months* ago! Above all else, why you came to me in the first place - and why I even *agreed* to it! I've *had it* with this accursed errand you tricked me into, I'm sick of being out here and suffering for it! I'm sick of sleepless nights spent worrying about tomorrow! I'm sick of looking over my shoulder all the time, of jumping at the slightest movement! I'm sick of sleeping on the dirt, eating stale bread and dried meat, drinking nothing but water, of the wind, the rain, the heat - the *snow!* And you let me bring my *daughter* into this!"

"It's too late to turn back now."

"Yes," he hissed, further vexed by the inquisitor's apathy. "It is. And I'm sick of hearing that, too."

Genuine alarm shuddered through the group when he turned and stormed away. "Where are you going?"

"A safe distance from you. Or I fear I might just kill you."

They watched him leave. Backs were rigid, muscles tight, ears strained through the forest. Hands tightened around hilts.

The bait was loose.

Heartbeats later, two bodies leapt silently over the wall.

Garon and Petra spun immediately, meeting them blade-first while Eyila was thrust back behind Anthis, already armed with his dagger. Petra's sword was a blur of motion long before the mage could release her spells, and the other, armed with a frightfully thin-bladed knife, was trapped beneath Garon's barrage of strikes. Eyila's fingers twisted quickly into the trained signs, and the blonde mage was near-instantly rendered helpless, her hands pinned to her back by unseen bonds, her fingers as good as broken. She resorted to fighting with her feet instead, aiming high a series of steady, powerful, lateral kicks, but Petra easily read and evaded them.

No others raced to join them. The third and fourth had been successfully taken out at the ruins.

Rathen's heart was in his throat. He could hear the frenzied footsteps hammering ever closer behind him, but even as he felt the hum of stirring magic and the reactive shake of the ground beneath his feet, he kept his eyes forward and wrangled his panic and the primal stirring in his gut under control. He could take him, if he focused. And if he kept ahead.

His eyes searched quickly over every tree he pounded past, but so few bore the tell-tale notch that the worry he'd missed one was very real.

The hum ceased, and another lash of fire reached out for him. But the spell was clumsy. He avoided it easily, and heard another growl of frustration for his brief victory. But the footsteps didn't slow, and the air shortly hummed again. Salus was attacking clumsily, but relentlessly, and Rathen had no chance at all to respond to the assault.

Finally, he spotted it: a rough but deliberate crosshatch in the bark. He veered towards it, careful not to trample too close to the trunk, and passed it without incident. Two seconds later a curse and a deep, muffled puff rose behind him, and the footsteps faltered at last. Salus had hit the trigger.

A powerful rush of snow blinded him, thrown up by a concealed and inflated waterskin.

Rathen changed direction immediately and raised his fingers. There was no time for doubt, and his mind was clear beneath the power of adrenaline despite the surge of his deafening heartbeat. He cast as he ran, a brief spell, but effective, and another muffled thump and foul oath shortly rose.

Squeezing his fists tight against the heat in his veins, this time he dared a glance. The heavily-laden branch had dumped its load right on top of him - but he was already back on the move, and his face was that of thunder, with sharp, focused eyes that were void of anything but hate, laced with a mad if calculated menace. Rathen knew he wouldn't be caught out like that again.

He veered again, leading him swiftly towards another trap. But this one missed. By chance, he was sure - he *hoped* - Salus had passed the trigger. He felt a lump of desperation rising higher in his throat, but he beat it down long before it could strangle him. His fists tightened again, and he sought out another.

He missed the next hum of magic. The brightening of the snow was his sole warning. Leaping swiftly to the side was all that saved him from the latest bolt of flame, and that escape was far too narrow. In his moment of alarm, he missed the marking on the next trunk, and this time it was luck alone that he missed the trigger himself. He cursed himself to focus while a pile of stones tumbled into Salus's path, and glanced back to gauge the distance. It had grown, but Salus was still on his feet, light and steady, chasing him down like a wild cat.

"Hurry up, hurry up," he murmured tightly to himself, fighting back the creeping edge of fatigue, but his voice caught in his throat as a projectile whizzed close by his head, too small and shiny to be an arrow, though it embedded itself deep in the bark of a tree straight ahead of him. His heart launched quickly back into his throat.

But then came a new sound over the padding of feet, grunted oaths and steady panting breath. A rough, mad and familiar cackle, followed by the scream of yet more projectiles flying from the opposite direction. He caught motion high in the trees to his right, but kept his focus on the trunks and the placement of his own feet. He didn't need to spare them notice.

There were grunts and thuds as the stones found their marks, but the disturbance of magic this time set a new panic in his chest. He couldn't afford to shout a warning. But the attack was skewed, distracted, and the ditchling scrambled several boughs up and out of the way of the flames. There came another flash of movement to his left and another volley of stones, but this one was not so lucky. With a short bark of surprise, it toppled and fell, hitting the snow with a limp thud where it smoked black against the still, pallid landscape. It didn't move again.

A piercing surge of guilt tightened Rathen's jaw. His fingers moved before he could think, weaving themselves into another spell.

The footsteps stopped short with another abrupt thud. The snow had grasped Salus's feet and frozen him in place, his momentum threw him to the ground, and his fingers too were encased within the air's hardened chill.

Rathen saw this only vaguely as he staggered against a tree, fighting back the spinning behind his eyes. But it took an age to dull.

He couldn't afford to wait. He steeled himself against the fire in his veins, already deadened by adrenaline, and pushed off from the tree. Within moments, Salus was giving chase, the ice encasing his fingers shattered against another trunk, his feet wrenched free by force and magic.

And so the game began anew.

Until the trill of a chaffinch changed the cards.

The others were close behind him.

Another wave of adrenaline fired through his blood, and he deviated again, dragging Salus through another pressure trap. His fury had blinded him to the tell-tale marks. A curse and a foul-smelling odour quickly pervaded the air, a burst of fluid from another hidden waterskin rather than a puff of snow, and Rathen changed direction again, the last of many acute adjustments to lead them back towards the road.

A sudden weight struck him from behind, knocking his breath free, and the snow rushed up towards him.

He braced and twisted as he landed, throwing himself onto his back to grapple madly with his attacker. How Salus had moved so fast, he didn't have time to work out. Or perhaps he'd slowed down himself. He was exhausted, his veins burned, yet his skin and bones were succumbing to the cold, and the clinging, sour smell of what odorous concoction Eyila had planted choked him. But he could see the same kind of delirium in Salus's dead eyes, too. However much elven blood he had, he hadn't learned to pace himself. Fatigue was getting the better of him.

Rathen tried to force the man off of him, who in turn kept him pinned down, but the fight descended into a tired and frantic race to catch the other's fingers as they tried to cast between physical strikes. Every movement was agonisingly slow, and Rathen was sure every time that he wouldn't get there before he finished his signs.

The spinning inside his skull began again and desperation intensified, and so he wasn't sure just what his fingers had done to blast Salus off of him, nor why it had succeeded. But the villain continued to rise long after he should have fallen, with giant talons grasped about his shoulders. Only then did the ring of the harpy's squall register to his senses.

But the victory lasted just seconds. A glinting sliver appeared almost immediately in Salus's hand, from thin air or his sleeve, and even as his terrible, black eyes remained pinned upon him, he drove the blade up into the scaled leg. With a shriek of pain, the harpy released him.

Rathen's heart sank in the pit of his chest.

Then lurched when he was hauled suddenly to his feet, and as Salus made a near-perfect landing several paces away, a second pair of arms moved in to restrain him.

Black gloves. Garon.

The scent of spice and flowers receded as Rathen was released, and Petra quickly jumped back for distance, loosing her bolas from her cinch. Anthis was suddenly there, too, guarding Eyila who was moving up to cast the binding as quickly as her frozen fingers could manage. Relief set in like a tidal wave.

As unbounded time began to slow, his eyes returned to Salus. The stare he was burning into him would have made his skin itch if he wasn't already numb. His eyes were black, his face gaunt and deathly pale, and his teeth as he roared and cursed and swore their downfall were as sharp as a wolf's fangs. Rathen had seen it before, and there was a streak of personal familiarity to it which turned his chilled blood to ice. And though he thrashed like a man possessed, Garon's hold didn't slip. His inflamed savagery was only wearing himself down further.

"Garon--"

"I know." He didn't need reminding. They were all aware. Even once Eyila's spell was complete, he would still be capable of casting without signs, especially in a state like this. That it hadn't happened yet meant nothing at all. And he may still have had a plan.

But Salus was exhausted, beaten and desperate, though his eyes and muscles screamed against it; shivering, bloodied, raw with the cold, and just beginning to realise that he was alone. And yet each of them knew if they let him go now, he was liable to kill them, and none of them were capable of holding him off as things stood. But if they tried to stretch their luck any further, he may well succeed.

Whether they had what they needed or not didn't matter; their plan had run its course. All that remained was to get out of it alive so they could put whatever they'd gathered to use.

They had to make him run. It was the only way they would get out of it. And if he thought Rathen was working with elves, then he had no idea just exactly what Rathen was capable of. He wouldn't risk sticking around if it looked like he was going to kill him on the spot.

While Eyila's fingers continued to twist, Rathen drew himself up and stepped slowly towards him. He put away as much of his fatigue as he could and assumed an air of power, his eyes menacing, lips grim, and raised his fingers where Salus could clearly see them. Then his, too, began to twist, slowly and deliberately. Salus watched with wide eyes, and for a moment his struggle faltered.

The tension was deafening. Their hearts hammered in their ears. All eyes flicked between Rathen's fingers and Salus's black, murderous eyes, waiting for him to free himself when Garon's grip slackened at just the right moment, prepared to fight if they had to. Their focus was such that when a call rose to the right, neither of bird nor beast, only Petra caught it. She turned quickly and spotted the black-haired figure running towards them through the trees.

His fingers were contorting rapidly. And his eyes were fixed on Anthis.

Rathen spun around the moment he noticed the stirring of magic, but he was already too late. Eyila stumbled as the historian staggered into her, her concentration broken and spell lost to surprise.

Rathen's own masquerade collapsed in panic. But he had no time to bend to it. Magic rose again in an instant, but this time he was ready, and perfectly deflected this second incorporeal projectile, sending it into a tree instead. It entered the bark tidily, like a surgical incision, until a moment later the sides of the trunk exploded outwards. He chanced no time to stare in horror, and Anthis was already back on his feet, no worse for wear, if as white as a sheet. The first attack had been a distraction to break their spells; the second had not. Whatever came next would be worse.

A grunt snatched his attention back towards Salus just as he wrenched himself free with a blunt and powerful kick into Garon's leg. It shouldn't have worked, but the inquisitor's iron grip had already faltered. Only Rathen stood his ground while the rest staggered back in alarm.

Salus's face, weary and pink with the cold, creased into a wolfish grin, and while his eyes were blue again, their malice made them far from human. His fingers rose quickly and Rathen's hastened to follow, but they didn't shape; he whistled sharply instead, then turned and fled through the trees. The black-haired mage dashed away in the opposite direction.

Time slowed. After a moment of bated breath, bones shaken by the hammering of his heart, Rathen loosed a long, deep sigh and felt his adrenaline begin at last to ease. It was done.

He turned back to the others. "Anthis, are you all right?"

But his voice stalled in his throat at the spread of ashen faces.

Anthis stood in horror, staring back towards the trees where the mage had fled, while Garon was fixated upon the ground where Eyila knelt. His heart clawed up into his throat as he followed his gaze.

The snow, once brilliant white, was stained red where Petra lay. Her body was contracted, and her trembling hands hovered about the smallest rip in the weave of her crimson blouse, no larger than the smallest coin. The wound beneath it couldn't have been any bigger.

But the blouse, Rathen realised, had been white.

A metallic taste seeped onto his tongue at the sound of her short, ragged breaths. A dreadful kind of gravity rolled out through the trees, smothering the world into silence.

Eyila was already kneeling over her, her young face gripped by professionalism, her heart bricked up. Her hands began busily tracing the wound. Rathen felt the stir of her magic as she delved deeper. And for the first time, he saw her bronze skin pale.

But whatever she'd found didn't discourage her. He felt her magic engage again and watched her fingers twist, and he hurried down beside her to help. She was quick to put him to work, and he followed her instructions meticulously.

Small, slight whimpers slipped out between Petra's gasps, shattering the forbidding silence. Despite her pain, she turned her head, and set her misty eyes upon Anthis. He stood motionless, right where he had been when she had slammed into him. He was staring back at her without a trace of colour in his face. "You..." she winced and gritted her teeth, "stupid...fool..."

"Hush," Eyila commanded, "keep still."

She nodded and tightly closed her eyes, but jolted suddenly a moment later with a cry and a hiss as agony racked her body. The blood trickling from her abdomen swelled and darkened. Rathen held her as still as he could on Eyila's order, but her own hands were shaking. Her teeth were gritted, a tear rolled from her hair-shadowed eyes, and he heard her muttering something beneath her breath in her own musical tongue. He caught a few desperate words. His grip recovered on her immediate chide.

Finally, Petra eased a pained and ragged breath as the torment passed. Her eyes were hazy when they opened, and they scanned across their faces for a long while before registering that Garon was not among them.

Her head turned slowly to the other side, where she found him standing further back, deathly still, his grey eyes a fraction wider than usual beneath the perpetual furrow in his brow. She grunted, trying to find her voice. Her breath had thinned, and each had become a labour. "Ga...Garon..." She saw his chest heave with a brief shudder, and her lips curved into a reassuring smile, beautiful, exhausted, and filled with heart. "I..."

A deep, gentle sigh eased through them. Her head wilted slowly against the snow.

Eyila's fingers continued to work, twisting faster and faster, her voice rising in desperation against the crushing, leaden silence.

Rathen didn't try to stop her. He was paralysed. He barely stirred when Garon turned and sprinted away.

The inquisitor's feet pounded silently through the forest. The tracks were clear. He ran with no care of traps, but expertly avoided them; he ran with no care of roots, but every footfall was certain; he ran with no care of fatigue, but didn't tire. He didn't feel the thump of his heart, he didn't feel the burn in his legs, he didn't feel the whip of branches or the chill of the snow. He didn't feel anything.

He closed in on the sound of feet ahead. They were urgent, but not alarmed. And Garon's own were barely a whisper. For, this time, he was the hunter.

The black-haired mage was visible through the trees, standing out like a beacon against the pure white of the snow. Once in Garon's sight, he never escaped it.

He drew his blade silently, missing even the rasp over the scabbard's locket, and set his soundless feet to speed.

The mage turned too late.

His blade ran straight through.

The forest seemed trapped in a daze. Rathen stood, though he couldn't recall rising, and stared down at Petra's small, still form. Eyila sat just as still beside her, though tears rolled freely down her wooden face, and Anthis hadn't yet moved from the spot at which the tragedy had happened. The shock and confusion in his face hadn't faded.

No one moved, as though they found some sense in reasoning that if they stayed still for long enough, time might just reverse. But it hadn't yet happened, and the stricken silence reached in all directions and lay so thick that not even Aria's desperate wailing in Kienza's arms could touch it.

The sorceress wore a mask as thick as the rest of them, but Rathen had seen the regret in her eyes. He hadn't asked. For all her powers, not even she could bring back the dead.

His mind had stopped. No solution nor remedy presented itself, and he stared down mindlessly, watching the colour slowly leave her face. Her hazel gaze bore dull and vacant through the trees. Her eyes hadn't closed. They'd been locked on Garon when she'd died, and no one had dared to break that line of sight. But as a gentle snowfall drifted through the trees and soft white flakes settled within them, a furious compulsion drove him forward to close them himself.

The snow crunched behind them as Garon returned, but no one said a word. His face appeared no different to usual - grim, purposeful - but his eyes were flat and empty. There was blood on his clothes. He came to a stop nearby and stood stone-still, staring at her again.

Rathen turned away. The words came out as though spoken through someone else's lips, and he resented hearing them himself. "She should be buried." No one responded. He had no energy to push for it, but the slow relent of his shock was building a lump in his throat and he looked around at the surrounding forest for anything that might make the situation more bearable before it could choke him. Only then did he spot the two harpies perched in a tree a respectful distance away, their heads bowed gravely and one's foot held curled in injury. He doubted their sentimentality, but they understood the atmosphere. That angered him. They *should* have felt the loss, and keenly.

He turned at the sound of smaller footsteps, and three ditchlings approached carrying their own fatality, the girl Salus had incinerated to a husk. The smell of burned wood rather than flesh muddied that of Petra's blood. Unlike the harpies, these three looked upon Petra with tears in their huge eyes. This angered him, too. They didn't even know her - how could they dare claim such grief?

While one of them broke away to hug Aria, another turned those big eyes up to Rathen. He noticed, by chance, that a closed walnut shell was strung about each of their necks. "We know a good place," he said with surprising compassion. "'S quiet and pretty, and none too far. Ain't nowhere her dreams'll be disturbed. By us nor no one else."

"I can see to the excavation," Kienza added softly.

Rathen tightly nodded his thanks, then lurched out of Garon's way.

Without a word, the inquisitor spread a sheet out over the ground beside her, a blanket he must have fetched from the horses, and lifted Petra's body from the crimson snow. He lay her upon it with profound tenderness. Everyone watched as he stroked her red hair back from her face and closed her pale lips, his thumb lingering for only a moment before reaching gently behind her neck. He removed her locket and placed it in her left palm, clasping her fingers about it, and lay it over her heart. In her right, he placed her sword hilt, covering her wound while its blade pointed down her body with nobility.

Without a sound, Eyila rose and stood over them. Anthis managed to move forwards, and Kienza led Aria closer.

Delicately, Garon wrapped the blanket about her, secured it with his own belt, and lifted her up into his arms stained red with her blood. His dead eyes fell onto the ditchlings. "Lead us."

Kienza fell in beside Rathen, her voice the softest whisper. But whatever she began to say, she didn't finish. His jaw was clenched hard enough to crack his teeth, and his voice was ice as he spoke through them. "We lured Salus out here because the ruins were too dangerous... The charade...was meant to..."

"You couldn't have known what would happen."

"This was my fault."

"No, my love, it wasn't."

He didn't argue. He didn't appear to have heard her, if he'd noticed she was beside him at all. Kienza didn't attempt again to soothe him, and his eyes didn't leave the blanket Garon carried ahead of them.

The ditchling hadn't lied.

At the head of a small, declined glen hidden among the thickening beeches stood a single, dignified ancient. An iron tree, four feet across and rising even above the heights of its neighbours. Its thick boughs, softened and rounded by snow, all pointed skyward, and plentiful red, six-point leaves coated in a silver lace of frost hung like silk from tapered branches. A tree that had earned its place in the oldest stories as a symbol of hardiness and resolve. It was a fitting spot.

A deep hollow formed in the snow at its foot, where Garon lay Petra's wrapped body with as much care as had she been sleeping. But his step back wavered, and his shoulders heaved with a single broken shudder before he fell chillingly still. The others gathered in an equal daze.

Slowly, Aria stepped forwards. Petra's dagger lay in her shaking hands, and her knuckles were bone-white as she clutched it. But as she bent down to lay it upon the blanket, Kienza quickly stopped her. "I think she may have wanted you to have that."

Tears exhausted, Aria's dry, bloodshot eyes turned emptily up at her, then drifted slowly back to the sheathed blade. Her fingers tightened possessively around it again. But she lingered reluctantly.

Suddenly, she set the knife on the ground and took out her wooden sword, but she hesitated as she looked over the aged notches and dents along its blunt edge, and shame fell over her. She looked around at her father, but he didn't seem to notice. Kienza, however, gave her the small, encouraging smile she needed.

Her heart-shaped lips tightened in grim purpose, and she lay the wooden sword carefully upon the blanket instead. Retrieving Petra's precious blade, she stepped back with a dry sniff.

"Would you like me to send word to her sister?" Kienza asked delicately, but Rathen replied with a curt shake of his head and a poison to his voice that forbade any further words. It was their fault she had died, and their duty to inform the bereaved and face the blame they were due.

He reached his hand out towards Aria, who came to his side at once and clung graspingly to his leg. Her tears began again at her father's touch, but no one noticed. Shock and grief shrouded them each in a numb cloud.

Chapter 59

He couldn't grasp how, nor indeed why his magic had waited until the situation was done before asserting itself, but the sprawling and ragged beech and chestnut trees Salus tore through were suddenly not those of Greentop. He had no capacity to think on it, and he wasn't even sure he was grateful. But it was done, and at least it wasn't his accursed office. He needed to move, to storm out his rage, and Blackbrush was more than fit for purpose. None moving through those bleak, chilling woods would dare to get in his way, and doing so now, he was certain, would be fatal. It was almost a shame that none of those vile, opportunistic, non-human wretches dwelt within these woods.

A tree limb broken in a recent storm hung down in his way. He ripped it off and cast it aside without breaking his gait.

Once again, *once again*, he had let himself be taken for a fool! Professionalism dictated he prepare for the possibility of a trap, but when it was clear they weren't heading into the ruin after all, he'd panicked and reacted too quickly. He'd fallen for the bait. And he had run. He had *run*. He shouldn't have had to, he could have taken Koraaz out right then and there! But he hadn't, because he'd *exhausted himself* like some over-eager *novice!* That fact angered him just as much as the lost opportunity.

Koraaz had gotten away, and what damage they *had* done was negligible. Erran had only managed to take out the brainless duelist who'd gotten herself wrapped up in their games with too little sense to realise they were trouble. He resented that she'd been the one to fall, ultimately one of the most innocent among them; she had no part in their plan - but she had stood right beside them to oppose him all the same. And as regrettable as her death was, it served a purpose. The rest of them would be shaken. They would re-evaluate their position, and it would, at the very least, slow them down.

He lashed out against another unoffending branch, and ignored the streaks of blood the bark left across his palms.

He never thought he'd have to fight to convince his own people to *let* him protect them.

But it wasn't just rogue civilians, was it? No, no it wasn't just rogue civilians *at all*. Even the *Crown* was muddying the water, twisting things, allowing their own country to fall into war, allowing people to *die*, all so they could steal the throne of *another! Why?!* Doana had *nothing* that Turunda needed! Turunda's army rivalled theirs, they had no exceptional farmland, no valuable minerals, no wealth or strategic value - just wet, mountainous forests and oversized cats! And yet the Crown felt *compelled* to pursue it all while keeping the whole matter a secret, which could only mean that there was so much more going on than it seemed. But none of his people had found anything on it. *Nothing*. They were keeping their cards much too close, and he had no way of knowing how close they were to reaching their goal. It could already be too late.

Malson had suspected something long ago, but he'd never alluded to anything specific - and then, out of the blue, he'd clammed up and all mention of the matter vanished. And no one had been able to find anything on him, either - nothing but the fact that, from time to time, he donned a large, surreptitious cloak and ventured off into the trade district, which was also the only time he ever happened to lose his tail. Which meant that Malson *knew* he was being followed, and only took action to shake them off when he needed to. When it was most *crucial* that they be right behind him. That said nothing good about the tails, but it did at least confirm that he *was* up to something and being very careful about it. Perhaps even deliberately waiting for distractions to pull his surveillance spells away. Did that mean he knew about them? Or was it just chance that, in this time of nation-wide upheaval, there was always something worse happening, every single time?

He kicked at a frozen patch of woodruff. The stems made a satisfying snap.

All of them were working against him. *Every single one of them.* And now the Crown was ordering him to 'earn' their funding, shipping his people out to ridiculous places to keep them occupied and diverted, and then, *no doubt*, they would use that as an excuse to claim dereliction of duty and dissolve the Arana completely! It was *sabotage*, and Turunda - his sworn charge - was going to pay the price for it--

...Unless he stopped it. Unless he stepped in. Desperate times, desperate measures, and if his people could find no secrets within that house of mirrors, they were buried too deeply. It had happened before, centuries ago, under King Arish, and it had plunged Turunda into a costly and bloody civil war. He'd deliberately dug the records out of the archives a fortnight ago and compared the symptoms. Too much matched. But this time, the Arana stood in its way - and he was not about to let it happen again.

...But what if it was already too late?

The trees thinned out and the picturesque gardens of Arana House opened before him. He was in no mood to seek out the concealed tunnels. He cut across the grass and stormed in through the terrace doors instead. Servants, employed for appearance's sake, looked up in startlement, then recovered themselves and averted their eyes as they'd learned to do from others around them, and he proceeded unmolested up the stairs, a haze of fury and self-rebuke serrating his thoughts. It had been the perfect opportunity. Trap or not, the *perfect* opportunity. And it was *his* fault it had slipped through his fingers.

"*Where have you been?!*"

His eyes snapped up from the landing. Malson. At the top of the east wing's flight, glowering down upon him. Imperial. Undeserved superiority. Entitlement. Nothing more. Here at the bidding of his gilded masters while who knew what worked away in the background. A puppet who had learned to pull but a few of his own strings.

Loathe. A threat. A man who dared the audacity of thinking he could hide his secrets within these walls. If he wasn't working with the Crown, he was working against them. Against him. Against Turunda.

A traitor.

There was no chance for alarm to flicker through the nobleman's eyes.

Salus closed the distance in an instant. His slender knife flashed. His left hand clasped firmly over the old man's mouth, and the blade plunged up through his chin with soundless precision. Youthful eyes screamed with desperate confusion. All trace of dominance evaporated in a single, sputtering heartbeat.

Slowly, warm lifeblood trickled and dampened his hand, and a deep-seated weight lifted like a feather from his mind. A smile spread across Salus's lips, malicious and ecstatic.

He withdrew his hold from his mouth. Blood lined Malson's lips; bubbles formed and burst as he tried to shape a question, but all that rasped out was a sickening, doomed gurgle. Salus ripped the knife free and stepped back as the Crown's liaison dropped to the floor with a heavy, satisfying thump.

His heart soared. *Freedom.*

But its flight clouded just as quickly as his eyes lifted to Teagan, standing several paces down the hall, staring at the dignitary lying lifeless between them. His expression was as empty as always, but an instinctive defence took a hammer to Salus's triumph and set a fresh strain of irritation crawling across his skin.

Beneath the dense silence of the foyer, he stepped over the body and the blood-sodden rug without sparing it another glance, and strode on, tall and powerful. The amateur's plots were stymied, and his secrets *would* be broken.

He didn't pause as they levelled, and drew his voice in cold. "We'll have our proof soon enough."

By sundown the following day, they did.

No one had ever seen a rage like it. A quiet rage, chillingly still, while a fire blazed in Salus's eyes and hitched his lip, betraying the cataclysmic fury corroding his thoughts inside his skull.

He'd stood behind the gate in silence while the breakers worked over Malson's coachman and two footmen, but not one had yielded a thing. Fortunately the Arana were capable of looking further than the end of their nose, but what they'd ultimately uncovered in a locked and hidden drawer in the desk of Malson's home study had shocked and insulted him deeper than he cared to reveal: notes written in code - a *crude* code that had been cracked within half an hour by comparing the recurring patterns even without a key - and vague, but not vague enough. As though he thought it would be enough to addle them.

And yet, even so, they'd doubted what the amateur had tried to hide, until a flicker of panic in the phidipan's eyes had confirmed the truth, and his attempt to flee from arrest sealed it.

A part of Salus was pleased, if frustrated, by the fact that David hadn't talked. He'd managed to withstand even Nolan's exquisite efforts as lead breaker, and that was no small thing, especially for a fresh promotion, and he'd died with his lips sealed. He was almost proud. And his silence was no bother, because three other names had been uncovered alongside his. While Oliver, the mage who had rejected promotion, was in no state to either plot nor answer questions, the two remaining traitors, phaeacians discarded to far-flung posts, were recalled, and between them were far more obliging.

Malson had indeed been working under ulterior motives, striving for a higher seat among the royal council, and had recruited the four of them to help him with promises of a better country. In their loyalty to Turunda, they'd believed him.

Which had been a lie. But while Annette had died before she'd hinted at the *real* truth, young Jora had not. At the edge of death he gave only a single, vague answer, but in his final moments seemed to find perverse enjoyment in the choler it set within the keliceran.

Salus had killed him himself.

He stood now, looking at the body tied to the old, torment-stained rack, head hanging forwards, bruised and bloodied face hidden by scraggly hair. But he could still see a trace of that defiant smile.

His own lips dipped further into their grimace, and he tossed the knife to the ground beside the steel contraption. He'd spoken to unnerve him, that was the sole reason he'd told him anything at all. And that meant that there were more involved than just those mentioned in the notes, otherwise who would there be to reap the benefits of that discourage and doubt? And he had no way of knowing who.

But all had been phidipan or lower, and if he couldn't weed out the traitors, he could harden the loyalty of the rest...

But there was one other glaring matter that needed seeing to first.

Nolan and the guard were quick to move aside as he stormed from the cell without a word, and the sound of fast, thundering footsteps boomed across the rounded stone walls in his wake. Ascending into the house, no one dared let themselves fall into his sight.

Teagan rose from behind the desk as he surged into the office, and watched in dismay as he began immediately rifling through the files in one of the grand bookcases. "Another?"

"No," Salus replied quietly, his voice low and coarse, "not just 'another', not 'another' at all." He moved further along the shelves, at first stuffing the folders back in place, then laying them impatiently along the top of others before discarding order completely, muttering furiously beneath his breath.

Concern coaxed Teagan slowly around the desk. "What is it?"

"Koraaz. He has help."

"From who?"

"One of us."

Teagan's eye widened in a shock that not even portian training could suppress. "What?"

"*He has help. From one of us.*" He threw a handful of folders to the already work-loaded sofa beside the bookcase. "We pulled a tag number from Jora before he died, but it could have been false. Something to light a fire, to incite mistrust amongst us all."

"Then he's lying?"

"No," he snarled, moving immediately to the next shelf up, "no he's not lying. A phidipan *is* helping him. It's the only way to explain how he's managed to stay ahead of us, and how he always loses tails so efficiently... This is my fault. I've surrounded myself with masters of deceit without assuring maximum *loyalty*..."

"But why would--"

"*Because Malson got to them all, Teagan! He* did this! I don't know what he's promised them, but they're on *his* side, and whatever he was plotting, Koraaz was a part of it! *And Koraaz is still out there!*"

"Why would Malson turn against the Crown?"

"*Did* he turn against the Crown?! The king *himself* is up to no good, I'm certain of that!" Suddenly the wild look in his eyes sharpened and focused, and they flicked ominously onto him. "Has a report come in from Kyrie yet?"

"Yes. Both were found dead near the Grey River. Geographical hazards, as predicted, nothing else..."

His eyes narrowed. "And?"

"And a report came in from Hower. Erran's body has been found. He was barely recognisable."

An ugly string of curses accompanied the files he ripped violently out from the shelves. "How many of Malson's actions were sanctioned by the king?!"

"The king? Why would they be? He was suspicious of the Crown, himself."

"Or was he just trying to *bond* with me? Lend himself some credence by taking *my* side occasionally? He wasn't a mindless official, but, curse it all, I've not been able to work out why he would even *toy* with the idea of defecting! He *must* have had orders, it's the *only* explanation..."

"Then Koraaz is working with the Crown, too?"

His blue eyes darkened. Once again, wildness gave way to quick and focused thought. "No. He has other motives. He's as much a pawn as Malson was, but that doesn't make him any less of a threat. Both sides are still undermining Turunda's safety. And its honour.

"The king wants the Arana suspended - or perhaps me removed from command - and he's starting by reducing our numbers. Why else order us to remote, dangerous and tactless places? And if he believed that Malson had picked a few things up from the Arana in his decades of service, he probably thought that Malson would be capable of circumventing *my* position and getting to the others, realigning them to himself, to the Crown and to the king. And Malson had believed it... But how far his success goes is in our hands. We can cripple it *right here*. Before Turunda can fall."

'*Before everything I've given my whole* being *for can turn to dust...*'

Teagan observed his frenzied search carefully. "What do you propose?"

"We secure their loyalty."

"...I...see... But phidipans make up fifty six percent of the Arana. At best, thirty percent of them will take to the conditioning. It doesn't seem--"

"Then we get rid of the rest of them. They've proven time and again that they can't be trusted! And this is the final straw! I want them gone - away from Koraaz and away from here, with nothing to learn and nothing to report, to *anyone*. And those who already know too much...we lock away."

"We will not have the room to imprison them all. And we risk thinning our numbers to the point of vulnerability."

"...Which is exactly what the Crown wants..." Again Salus pondered. He abandoned the bookshelves and his scouring of folders' numbers and began to pace. The glint forming in his eye was unsettling. "No, they won't all take to the training, but success rates will drastically improve and loyalty will no longer be a question. It's worth the risk."

"You wish to train all of them?"

"...Most of them. Those we can trust. The rest, we lock away. Or frame and leave the city guards to deal with. Or..." His stride paused, but the thought was left unspoken. Another was quick to stampede in and spur him towards the window. "And the *military* implants - there's no knowing who among those are involved..."

"We can't remove them, we'll be blind--"

"We'll handle it. Give them one final message, *disinformation*; make them believe there are changes happening, then abandon them." Salus leaned against the windowsill. He stared out over the city, wearied by the unrelenting snow but going about its business without complaint, and his eyes drew towards the north. The palace was out of sight, but clear as day in his mind's eye. "But even with phidipans handled, the king remains a threat," he mumbled pensively. "We need answers...and I'm not leaving it to anyone else. I'll handle it myself. And plant one of our best portians onto the council to find out just how deep the conspiracy goes. The Crown is no stranger to plots or lies."

"...And what of this phidipan?"

His eyes slid from the city to the bookcase. "...I can make it work for us..." He strode back towards it and returned the operative profiles he'd strewn across the floor. "It needs thought. I have the number. I'll find who it is, and a way to turn it to our advantage. But for now, we leave it alone. We have other things to take care of." He took then to his desk, pushed aside the papers Teagan had been tending to in his stead, and began scrawling over fresh sheets, drafting recall missives and plans to enforce the transition with minimal disruption to the Arana's work.

Teagan watched him from beneath a storm cloud of apprehension, and stood by as the matter moved ahead, unable to find his voice to speak a word of protest or reason even as his heart screamed against the morality of an army of mindless assassins.

That awareness only added to the fright he knew he shouldn't have been capable of feeling.

Chapter 60

The deep howl of wind hummed through Turunda's forests like a monastic chant. Trees bowed in deference, stiff old limbs creaked with the strain, and what frosted leaves that had yet to snap off seemed to tinkle in ceaseless exuberance.

Clouds hung low above their frozen crowns, racing along on the frigid currents. No matter how far one travelled, no edge showed itself nor revealed a hint of the azure sky beyond. The world had been plunged into darkness; dim mornings crawled into dark afternoons, merging seamlessly into night until the next dawn arrived without announcement. Hours blended, the days became inseparable. The single assurance to the continued passage of time was the coming and going of snowfall.

The flurries loosed from the black veil were the most sinister yet.

Grass, soil, roots and roads were lost beneath a deepening white cloak. The landscape became tidy with a beautiful treachery. Straying was invited, leaping encouraged, and ankles were broken for the pleasure, while small villages, isolated homes and the downcast were thrown to the cold where hunger and hypothermia reined.

Cattle was sparse. Many fields were empty. What crops that could be harvested early had already been collected, while the rest had been left to freeze. Hunters wrapped themselves thickly and tracked the larger beasts, but the snow was quick to fill in their steps. Their findings were thin, and what they did manage to catch was leaner than the market demanded. Fishermen, too, were having less luck, but those willing to brave the ice lakes for the warmer core of the water brought in a better catch, and much of it was smoked and dried for harder days with enough held back to feed their own families.

The wilds appeared hopeless. Despite the unnatural regrowth of pockets of riven woodland, landscapes knitting themselves back together over equally unnatural scars, they appeared still, quiet and empty. Occasionally a bird might sing and shatter the void, or snow might slip from an overburdened branch, but the disembodied sounds only heightened the eeriness. All appeared not dead, but vanished, as though life had never graced it, as though the trees had no memory of squirrels' dreys nor the soil of rabbits' warrens, and neither could they imagine them. There was no sense of expectation, no preparation for anything. The forests had lost their purpose, and the life of the trees themselves seemed to have taken full precedence.

*

A fine snow, soft and gentle, drifted like fog between the silent yet virile trees and cast a pale, melancholy haze that greyed their black trunks. All colour seemed to have been frozen out of the world until the stark, orange coat of a fox broke the monotony, stalking effortlessly through the snow and revealing by its own presence the existence of lesser creatures.

But no one noticed it.

The world and all its struggles continued to pass by without consequence.

Four days vanished in their stupor. There was nothing to recollect; they rode along, blind and deaf, lost in a maelstrom of thoughts they tried desperately to escape whenever they noticed their entrapment, only to be dragged right back in. Strength to fight it on that fifth morning was thin.

An involuntary squeak drew Rathen's arm about Aria, but his dark, aimless eyes didn't retreat from their thousand mile stare.

Anthis watched him quietly. It wasn't difficult to guess at what was going on behind them. The doubts he'd had about his own abilities, the struggles he'd endured just by using his magic, the increasing peril, Aria's safety - he'd probably been toying with the idea of abandoning the matter already. But now that...now that that peril had come to a head, because he was the soldier among them, the experienced leader, he took it too personally. As though it was all a result of his own failing. He was probably only continuing to ride with them because he was still in shock.

His eyes brushed over Eyila as he looked around behind him. She had drifted into a familiar silence, but where before her grief for her people had stunned her into a perpetual trance, now she wore a sharper edge and a grim-set line to her lips. There were streaks of tears upon her face, but her expression showed not a trace of sorrow.

He shrank away, though her gaze, too, was lost, and looked towards Garon instead. He rode at the rear, as absent in his saddle as though he wasn't even there, and his eyes were beyond empty. Where the others had said little, his silence was the most profound, speaking only when it was necessary and with as few words as possible. The loss had affected him most of all, and no one had seen him sleep for days. His thoughts, Anthis couldn't guess at. Or he simply didn't wish to try.

Answering his rising discomfort, he returned his attention to their heading, drew the map from his saddle and noted the altered landmarks. For his own part, his shock had quickly given way to perplexity, but where Garon and Rathen alike had retreated from the role of leadership, he had seen little choice but to step up in their place. They *couldn't* let Salus get ahead of them, otherwise Petra's death would have been for nothing at all.

They hadn't discussed what they'd learned from the encounter; any observations made were still swilling around at the back of their thoughts, but if nothing else, they now knew for certain that both Salus *and* his people were more than happy to kill to complete their task. And, Anthis deduced, if they were all to just give up and call it quits, let him win and suffer the consequences, Salus probably wouldn't believe it.

But even as he picked their course and reasoned their destination with no small degree of doubt and second-guessing, the nausea that had set in a week ago with the recovery of the locket had begun to boil. He knew, though he couldn't bare to look at it, that he would be hounded by her father's murder for the rest of his life. He had no chance at all of making suitable recompense to the one person he knew it had hurt. He only killed those who deserved judgement, wherever he could help it, and had comforted himself in the knowledge that the world was better off without them. But, for the first time, he'd seen the damage one such judgement had caused. And that, he would never be able to hide from.

His blood froze in fright when a voice spoke up, melodic, if glacial, shattering the mournful stillness. The first needless words any had spoken in four torturously numb days.

And he wished she hadn't, for the question only stoked his guilt.

"He didn't," Anthis replied quietly while the others remained in the grasp of their thoughts. "She wasn't his target. He wanted to kill--"

"He wanted to kill Anthis."

Rathen didn't look around despite the intensity of the confusion in Eyila's eyes, while Anthis dropped his gaze remorsefully back to the map. The mage's voice was strangely hollow, rough with neglected use, and distant and disconnected, as though he was unaware of the movement of his own lips. "Salus was about to call the retreat. It was his only option. So they had to do the most damage in the smallest amount of time. A single, crippling blow..."

Her hard eyes sharpened. "Then why didn't he go for *you?*"

He chuckled bitterly. It was a low, rattling laugh filled with nothing but loathe and contempt, not all of which was for their enemy. "Because," his knuckles turned white around the reins, "I'm off-limits. Salus evidently wants me for himself. Next to me, Anthis was the biggest threat."

"But Garon was restraining--"

"He could have gotten himself out of that easily enough. And Petra was too far away to be a problem. But you were casting the binding. Their escape would have been harder if you'd managed."

"Then *I* was the--"

"But Salus thinks Anthis is our source of information," he continued, unaware she was speaking at all. "Without him, he thinks our plans will fall apart. We wouldn't be a threat to him. So if only one person could die, it should be him. And our attack would fail in the distraction. As it did."

Eyila abruptly spurred her horse forwards and drew in beside him, piercing him with her pale blue eyes, as frigid as the snow. Rathen didn't flinch. His own were still fixed miles away. It only envenomed her stare. "Why didn't you change?"

The plod of the horses' hooves sharpened as the covered ground turned momentarily from soil to stone. A sheet of rock, or an ancient flooring swallowed by time. Anthis found he had no interest at all in discovering which. Instead, he worked out the response Rathen refused to offer.

The need for a cool head had forbidden transformation during the chase, and by the time he'd understood what had happened, grief had already paralysed him. He guessed that was also how he'd worked out how and why it had happened at all. He'd had more than enough time to think on it.

But though Anthis had thought the matter over just as extensively, why she had dove in front of him to take the strike herself continued to elude him.

Eyila's impatient, accusing stare seared into him like frostfire. "Where did he *come from,* Rathen? You should have sensed him. *Why didn't you sense him?!*"

"*I don't know!*"

Aria squeaked in fright, but Eyila didn't flinch as he snapped around at last, turning his own ferociously grievous eyes upon her.

"He got out of the trap, somehow! Is that supposed to be *my* fault?!"

Anthis quickly drove his horse forwards and between them, and both of their black stares transferred condemningly onto him. He didn't let himself waver. The fault he held against himself was greater than all of theirs combined. "The snow has covered our tracks, but there's no doubt we're still being followed. We wouldn't be forgotten just like that. And *we* can't abandon our senses. If we let ourselves get caught because of this, Petra will have died for nothing. Giving up *isn't* an option. We *owe* it to her - it's not just Turunda we're doing this for anymore."

He held his breath and steeled himself as their glares smouldered for a long, awful moment, and sighed with relief when they finally snapped away and drew their horses out to their own distance. He may not have been a natural leader, but he had, at least, defused this incident.

They rode on in silence as he consulted his map again.

Even as dusk fell, no one had spoken since.

Anthis called a stop for camp, their horses weary, riders drawn, and, as had become routine, they ate without conversation. But none were interested in food; most plates were picked at and left alone, and Anthis's was little different. But he made certain that Aria finished hers.

As usual, Eyila fled almost immediately. He'd followed her a couple of times, and she always sat within a tree or upon a rock or overhang in search of meditation, and always with a blanket by her side. But she never seemed to find peace. She fidgeted, muttered, cursed and cried; while she'd found her people on the Wind, it offered no solace for her newest grief and did nothing to quell the deep and personal anger that had come with it. The loss of her village had sent her into shock, but there had been nothing she could have done for them. Petra, however, had died in front of her. No doubt she'd been over the event a hundred times trying to pick out what she could have changed, what she could have done differently, how she could have saved her. But if anything had presented itself...well, it probably only made her feel worse.

He shook his had sadly and slunk away, leaving her to her present spot in the boughs of an enormous elm.

Rathen and Garon were still sitting against the trees and sprawling roots nearest their modest fire, lost in their thoughts. Anthis left them alone and returned to his own distant spot to pore over the ditchlings' charcoal map, until small footsteps and the drop of a shadow drew his attention back to the camp.

"Are you okay?"

"I'm getting by." It took effort to smile up at Aria as he set the map aside. Her eyes were still red. "How are you?"

She needn't have answered. His heavy heart dropped even further as he watched her little lips, which tried and failed to find a smile, tremble and clamp together, tears spring into her eyes and her hands wring anxiously around her doll.

He moved to embrace her, until his own shame stopped him short. But she had already leapt upon the opportunity and surged into his arms, grasping him tightly and shaking as she cried into his chest. His defeated spirit settled itself deeper as his arms wrapped about her.

The sound of her sobs stirred Rathen from his distant stare, but he didn't come to her side. He seemed to drift back into thought as he watched them. Anthis wasn't sure if he'd imagined the accusation in his eyes. The mage was expressionless, but what else could he be thinking while he was looking at him? It had been his life that Petra had died for, and...*why?*

His shame rose and his hold turned rigid. Aria wriggled out of it and looked at him sadly. Her big, glistening eyes broke his heart all over again.

"I put Petra in my diary," she said timidly. "People need to know about her. But...I don't think I wrote it very well..."

"I am certain you did her justice. She would be honoured."

She nodded, but doubtfully. Even the bounce of her curls seemed unconvinced. Then her voice became strangely guarded. "The elves were clever, weren't they? They made all these things with magic in them. Things even Daddy can't do."

His smile was meant to be reassuring, but he wasn't sure he'd even managed to turn his lips in the right direction. "He'll manage the spell."

"I know. I didn't...mean..." Her eyes dropped briefly to her thickly gloved hands, then back to him. There was a dreadful hope in them, and one he knew with a horrible lurch in his gut that he was about to crush.

He sighed with soft resentment and pulled her in again. "I'm sorry, Aria, no. Not even the elves could do such a thing."

She nodded, but didn't cry again. She was terribly bright. She'd already known it was a desperate hope. But she stayed in his arms for a while longer, and Anthis held her close for his own undeserved comfort.

When they parted again, she sat herself on the edge of the log beside him and peered down at the map, dragging herself into an imperfect composure yet one still unsuited to a child. "Where are we going?"

"Whitemouth. But we're taking a detour to shake off anyone that might be following us. We'll head north a little more," he trailed his fingertip across the map, "then cut west into The Ghost Patch before following the river down to the coast."

"Is it working?"

He sighed unfavourably. "I hope so."

In time, everyone retired to their tents, but sleep eluded them all. A soft shuffling in the snow half an hour later told him that Garon had given up on the pretence and stepped outside to freeze out his thoughts instead, but the rest fought their nocturnal battles in silence.

Another quarter hour passed before Anthis followed Garon's lead to escape the internal assault.

The inquisitor stood like a spectre at the edge of the camp, still, dark and silent. But his usually straight and proud shoulders were rounded, and the slight cock of his head revealed the depth of his absorption. He didn't turn, deaf to the world, and Anthis stepped quietly to keep it that way.

Once out of the reach of the tents and any danger of intrusion, he steered his thoughts stiffly forwards and slumped almost immediately into a trudging walk, plagued by another kind of helplessness.

A ruin, at the bottom of the sea.

It was there, according to Salus's elf, but none among the historical society nor even amateurs had ever suggested the possibility. And even if he knew that it *was* there, *getting* to it was a whole other matter. He'd discovered ruins in the past, of course, including one or two of note, but the worst of them had been in swamps or snow. Not miles off of the coast, drowned and flooded for hundreds upon hundreds of years.

...But...what it could hold if it existed...it had the potential to harbour secrets, brand new insight into the lives of pre- or short post-magic elves. It could be the opportunity to make a discovery that would *really* rattle his peers' cages. They disliked him as it was, but for petty reasons; his youthful passion for the elves had propelled him into the profession, and his constant presence in isolated or overgrown ruins rather than libraries and discussion groups had given him more opportunity for discovery than they'd given themselves.

That impotent jealousy was precisely why they launched savage attacks onto almost every claim he made, and while he'd proven most of his cases, his suggestion towards the origin of elf, human and the rest had been perhaps just too much to swallow. And with so little proof, he'd offered it to them on a golden platter. He doubted if even the upturned rocks beyond Ramstead could change it. Nor even if the gods themselves slapped them in the face.

The gods...who just so happened to be a part of the greatest and perhaps most insulting discovery he or anyone else could ever make. A discovery he had no choice but to keep to himself, or risk both his career and perhaps even his life.

A discovery that made him feel sick in the darkest depths of his consciousness.

He turned away from the shake in his bones. None of that mattered. Not any more. In fact, the moment he'd spent entertaining it filled him with a keening shame.

As a tenebrous shadow of blame and grief thickened, he turned away from that, too, and pinned his focus back onto the task at hand. Discovering new ruins and their secrets was of no consequence if their task failed. They had a job to do, and he had to keep everyone focused on it. Himself included. Otherwise...all this...it *couldn't* be for nothing.

He would find it, and they had the means to reach it. Rathen seemed to be getting a handle on whatever was aggravating his magic, and 'punching a hole in Salus's plans' had opened back up into a theoretical possibility. How Rathen planned to do it, he hadn't a clue, but Anthis's job was to get them there. That was all that mattered.

He walked on resolutely and forced a straight line into his shoulders, until a flicker of movement stole away his attention. He fell stone-still and stared through the trees to his right.

It was impossible for anything to hide in the snow even in the dark, and yet there was nothing at all to be seen. Or his eyes were flicking around too fast to spot it. He reined himself in with a careful breath and steadied his racing nerves.

He saw it in an instant.

A kvistdjur, but taller and more slender than those of the Wildlands, as though formed of the roots and twigs of another kind of tree. Her woven wolf-skull head bore branchlike horns that pointed upwards rather than reached out, and she watched him from around an equally narrow trunk, her firefly eyes blazing and unreadable. They gave no hint at all to the strike waiting behind him.

After a white, blinding flash erupted behind his eyes, all went black.

The next thing he knew was a thick pressure wrapped around his head and the dreadful sensation of hanging upside down. It took some time before he had the thought to open his eyes, and when he did so he found the world sideways and steadily throbbing. Slowly, he realised it was his own pulse.

It took longer still to push himself up on muscles that were painfully slow and heavy to respond, and decided, after a moment to gather his thoughts, that it was still night.

But all concern for the passage of time left him when his eyes focused at last on the backs of two semi-armoured figures standing a few paces away.

His heart leapt into his throat.

Quietly, he spun around to discover Rathen, Garon, Eyila and Aria grouped around beside him. Rathen and Garon were each awake, sitting in silence, though the latter bore little outward awareness, while the mage watched the two figures with a measuring gaze. Aria sat huddled beside him, burying herself in the crook of his arm, while Eyila lay curled up with her back to them, wrapped tightly in a blanket. He couldn't tell if she was awake.

Rathen's eyes brushed him momentarily, but there was no message nor signal within them. Anthis realised then that he wasn't as alert as he seemed.

He turned back to the men and stared at their clothing. His first conclusion was discarded almost immediately. If they were Aranan hunters, they wouldn't still be sitting out there. They probably wouldn't even be alive. Though he entertained his second thought a while longer, it didn't add up, either. He doubted that tribals would wear such expertly crafted leather. The cut, fit and thickness were too strong and precise to have not been made with professional tools. It was true that he had little experience with the tribes, but this didn't seem of their make. And again, if the tribes had caught them, he doubted that they would still be sitting out there.

But his deduction that the garments were made for both stealth and combat brought him slowly onto another thought. His eyes began scanning furiously. The bearing, the arming, the patience - but none of the green and ivory of Turundan colours.

Only then did he notice that there were no bars or fencing to contain them, only an earthen wall at their back and trees all around. There was nothing but these two men to stop them from leaving.

He looked to the others again. Garon had been disarmed, but he doubted he was in any state to use a weapon, and Rathen's hands lay limp in his lap as though his nerves had been cut. It was clear that he'd been magically bound. He suspected the same was true of Eyila.

His own moved to the hem of his shirt, but his hope sank even before his fingers brushed his abdomen rather than the hilt of his dagger. The ceremonial blade was in his bag. The other...he'd left behind in his distraction. He'd never had it to begin with.

He looked about quickly and spotted a cluster of steel nearby, a collection of blades set upon a blanketed rock maybe two or three times his distance from the guards. It was close enough to chance.

Slowly, he rose to his feet and tiptoed across the snow, eyes fixed to the weapons and ears tuned sharply to the guards. Carefully, one step at a time. Finally he reached out towards them, holding his breath against the impending scrape of shifting steel. But it didn't come.

A hot flare of spidering light spread through the air where his hand struck an unseen barrier, and he recoiled with a hiss of surprise. His eyes shot back towards the guards, his heart in his throat, but they spared him only the briefest glance over their shoulders before continuing to ignore him. Their faces were dark umber.

His plan thwarted, he slunk cautiously back to the others, and Rathen's calm, dead eyes drifted back onto the guards. The faintest glint of life soon touched them, however, and he sat a little straighter. Anthis turned and watched two more dark-skinned, leather and steel-clad men approach, one of whom Rathen fixed a little more closely, while the other, with a more ornate single pauldron and plate vambraces, drew Anthis's eye.

This one nodded to the two guards as he approached, and the pair promptly stood aside. The other who trailed behind him then stepped forwards, and with a twist of his dark fingers, a line of gentle light sank from twice head height and down to the floor like a long, drifting feather. Then he, too, moved aside, and the decorated man strode through the de-spelled space.

Dark eyes bore down on the five of them, but whatever degree of intimidation was intended, Anthis suspected that it fell short. Rathen stared back with eyes now tainted by hatred and disgust, Aria watched them warily, Eyila, who must have been awake all along, stared back with a deadly challenge, and Garon seemed entirely untouched by it, barely rousing from an open-eyed doze. Anthis found himself also fairly unimpressed.

The soldier barked something in Doanan, at which the guards turned and moved in around him to begin pulling them all to their feet and corralling them towards the invisible doorway. They kept close to one another and followed them out, and though the plated soldier took the lead, Rathen's eyes again drifted towards the mage who had taken up position behind them.

Anthis followed his gaze and realised that the man looked long broken. Void of all passion and will. It was clear from his dull eyes, the forced rigidity and false pride in his movements, as though it was the armour that enforced the posture and that the man within it was little but a doll being propped into shape.

Anthis thought he saw some small semblance of pity in Rathen's eyes as he turned away. It was well known that Doana did not look fondly upon mages, and was said that they were as good as slaves. Denied free will, thrown into the army, taught only battle magic under the tightest security, and had been beaten into believing themselves too low to attempt to do anything about it despite their unique armoury. Suddenly, Anthis doubted that they were the only prisoners here.

They were steered through the camp like cattle, following long, straight paths pounded into the frozen grass by frequent patrols and hemmed by an embankment on one side and the face of an escarpment on the other. A natural trench, thickly wooded and well-concealed, and occupied by surely no more than fifty men. But the numbers meant nothing, for those few soldiers they passed, all clad in leather, showed not a trace of weariness or defeat. On the contrary: they appeared as though their goal was within sight despite the absence of classic warfare.

Anthis turned his eyes to their surroundings, and moved closer to Rathen. "I thought Garon said Doana didn't have a camp in Greentop anymore."

"Clearly, he was wrong."

"And I saw a kvistdjur right before someone knocked me on the head."

"They tend to live in forests."

"I mean it didn't do anything."

"Why would it? it's not their problem."

He wasn't in the mood for conversation, so Anthis left the matter alone and took to absorbing as many details of their surroundings as he could. His eyes weren't trained for tactical observations, though; instead they began to seek out unusual prints on rocks and deliberate shapes sculpted into the ground. He caught himself a number of times and redirected his focus. He was very glad that Rathen had roused, if only a little.

They were drawn to an abrupt stop outside a long, narrow opening in the cliff face, where the mage and two guards promptly encircled them while their leader stepped on into the darkness. Their eyes adjusted as they stared in after him. There were boxes and crates stacked along the walls, blankets, medicines - supplies to last a good number of men for a few months - as well as a few larger tents erected beneath the rock ceiling, and a broad table strewn with maps, surrounded by a number of other semi-armoured figures.

The soldier approached them, and they all turned as one to look back towards the captives. A few words were spoken, and the soldier came back. They were then roughly escorted inside.

One man broke away from the group. He wore leather, like the rest, and a few choice pieces of steel, but his were even grander and more numerous than the last, as though they served as badges of rank themselves despite the choice of subtlety; while others wore engraved vambraces, his were paired with rerebraces, and while they had one elaborate pauldron girding their shoulder, he had two, each of which extended lower over the shoulder and were inlayed with traces of red steel, as were the half-breastplate, cuisses and greaves. There was no doubt at all that this man was the commander of the entire camp, even without taking into account his elite bearing and the speed at which the others stepped respectfully out of his way.

He turned his head towards the soldier and spoke low and studiously in his native tongue while his eyes drifted over them.

Aggravation rumbled behind Rathen's teeth. "Of course we're not spies."

Anthis winced as the commander broke off and fixed the group directly. He turned from his subordinates, the importance of his conference forgotten, and approached them with slow, ominous footsteps. But his menace, like the first soldier's, only grazed them.

He stopped and drew himself up against Rathen's impudent gaze. "What are you doing out here?" His voice was rich, thickly accented, but it draped across his words rather than strangled them.

"I'm not sure it's your place to ask that question."

A shadow of a smile flickered across his lips, one either amused or contentious. "Perhaps." He looked across the five of them for a moment, evaluating each in turn. Finally, his eyes returned to Rathen. "You were sent here."

"What?"

"Well you're not here by chance. There is a notable...grimness in all of your eyes much too close to the surface, and it's not one of hatred but purpose."

A toxic smirk pulled at Rathen's lips. "You think so, do you?"

"It's one of the more likely reasons," the commander replied indifferently. "So why are you here?"

"We were passing through *our* territory--"

"Oh, no, not *your* territory." He pointed a straight finger towards Eyila. "This one is Ivaean."

"Yes. Well done. Her tribe was killed, so she came with us. It's no business of yours."

Anthis watched something awful flash through the commander's eyes. "Her tribe was killed, you say? The whole tribe?"

"By another."

"Mm. I see..." Rathen didn't deign to turn his head as the middle-aged man began to slowly circle them, but his awareness was pinned onto him. "And you saw it happen, did you?"

"No."

"No. Did *she?*"

Rathen's eyes narrowed in suspicion. "No..."

"No. But the evidence suggested--"

"It can mean nothing else!"

He paused at the abruptly savage tone as his dark, slate-grey eyes slipped onto Eyila, who stared back at him in reckless outrage. But he straightened as he resumed, and inclined his head courteously. "I apologise, of course, young lady. There have been many conflicts all across Arasiin. Many losses. These are...very troubling times. And yet," he turned ever so slightly towards them, "Turunda has been largely untouched by it all..."

"We've been fortunate," Rathen replied icily. "Up until the point that you, Skilan and Kalokh all attacked."

"Ah, yes - three armies. Very unfortunate, that. And yet, somehow, you've managed to fend us all off. Hold us at bay. It's remarkable, really, even if one of those armies *was* decimated before it started. Kalokh were hardly prepared for another fight, and yet..." He sighed a touch dramatically. "Yes, troubled, troubled times."

He circled onwards, and the apathetic contemplation suddenly dropped from his tone. "Of course, when one really thinks about it, it becomes notably less alarming. Well, there's not a war-bug going around, at least - that's how you use the phrase, isn't it? A 'bug going around'?"

"What do you want with us?"

"So you won't deny it, then. There's nothing in the water at all, no maddening illness that drives kings into a blood rage. We thought that unlikely. No, it turns out there's quite a *simple* explanation for it - an explanation that was confirmed when we found three Turundan spies within our own military, feeding information back to your king, and others in the palace attempting to strain existing animosity with Voent and send us both into *war!*" His voice rose as accusation burned brighter in his eyes. The guards suddenly closed in around them, and in a single rapid movement, drew their daggers and pressed them firmly to their throats. "And *why?!*"

"What are you talking about?" Anthis tried not to yelp.

"The Arana..."

"Yes," the slate eyes bore into Rathen, "the 'Arana'. What does your king intend to gain from all this subterfuge and sabotage?"

"Why would we know?"

He stormed towards them, clearing the distance in three powerful strides. "You aren't as innocent as you seem. This child? The Arana uses children. It doesn't mean *anything* towards your innocence. Now tell me: what does your king stand to gain?"

"We are *not* with the Arana."

"Of course you're not - you were captured far too easily. But you're up to something yourselves, and you're meddling with *magic* to do it. Now tell me of your king's *plans!*"

"We have nothing to *do* with the king!"

He moved quickly. The guard pressed the blade harder against Rathen's throat as the commander wrenched Aria out from his tightened grasp, filling the cave with a panicked wail as she reached desperately back to her father.

Anthis had seen what was coming. He looked sharply towards Rathen and found the rage already manifesting in the darkening of his eyes and the paling of his skin, and he heard the shortening and cutting of his breath as it infused with a wrath and agony he made no attempt to suppress.

In his own apprehension as he thought furiously for a solution, the movement behind him only just caught his eye. With the briefest twist of his fingers, the Doanan mage subdued Rathen as though he'd physically struck him. All ire melted as his blackening eyes suddenly clouded, and he slumped briefly against the soldier threatening him, addled and disconnected even as he struggled to regain his bearings.

Aria sobbed in fear, for herself or for her father, and Anthis suddenly found his own lips moving.

"The chasms," the words came out in a panic, and the grey eyes shifted weightily onto him. "You've seen them, great big rips in the land - there's one cutting this forest in half, and I'm sure they're spreading into your country from the mountains, yes?"

"You--"

"*No!* No, we have *nothing* to do with them, we're trying to *stop* them *and* the magic that's causing them! Look, we have an elven relic, a spell vessel, and we've been using it to break up the spell chains and stop the magic from spreading and reacting and cracking the land any further."

The commander regarded him with unvarnished suspicion. "Or are you drawing the magic up in preparation to unleash it against the rest of us?"

"*No*," he urged quickly, "no it doesn't work that way, but I don't know why-- look, the Arana, yes? They're *not* working with the king, they're working *against* him. Salus, their leader, he's deluded, he thinks everyone is working against him, he's paranoid, and he's got this mad idea that we're working with *elves! Elves!* So he's--"

"Where did this magic come from?"

Anthis blinked. "Well it's elven, and it leaked out of...a place they built in Dolunokh. But, Salus is--"

"Why is it cracking the land?"

"...Because..." Desperately, he forced his mind to slow into cohesion. "Because...magic is unique - like an element - there's nothing else like it, just like there's nothing else like rock, or water, or fire, or air, the things that make up the world - but it's...*not* an element, I don't know why. But the magic is a mass of spell fragments and some of them are just complete enough to keep working, and they're using the other elements in place of a subject--I don't know the details, but it's *imperative* that you let us *go!*"

The commander shook his head and folded his plated arms. "Forgive me if I don't seem convinced, but there seems to be an awful lot you 'don't know'..."

"It's not my field!"

"Oh? And what is?"

"History!"

"History... Yes, you don't seem like much of a leader."

"I'm not."

"Who among you is?"

He looked towards Rathen, who had yet to reclaim himself, and Garon, who still appeared passively indifferent to their situation. Anthis felt his hope deteriorate even further. "One of those two."

"And why are they not speaking up while you dig their graves for them? Did I use that phrase correctly? 'Digging your own grave'?"

"What? Yes, I suppose so, and...well, you've...Rathen is..."

"Mm. And the other?"

"I don't know," he lied. Suddenly, he found himself disinclined to explain.

The commander's cold eyes fixed him directly. "Why *are* you here?"

"We were passing through - heading to the coast--"

"You were heading north."

"We were trying to lose a tail--"

"Why were you being followed?"

"*Vokaad give me strength*," he growled desperately, trying his hardest to control his hysterical urgency, and failing. "I've told you, haven't I?! *The Arana is after us!* Salus thinks we're working with *elves* and he's more than prepared to *kill us because of it!* Whatever you want to know, *we can't tell you!* All we're doing is trying to stop him from breaking the land away - I don't know *what* he's thinking, but he just wants us--"

"Breaking the land away?"

Anthis howled in frustration, and the guard moved in closer. His eyes flashed viciously up to him even as the blade drew a bead of blood from his neck. "If you come any closer to me, I swear I will kill you."

"You are unarmed."

"I don't need a blade."

But the soldier then stepped back, retreating at a single nod from his commander. When Anthis returned his attention, he found him looking back with a suddenly more critical eye. He finally noticed the twist in his brow that had been deepening slowly throughout the exchange, and read another kind of suspicion there - a curiosity rather than any kind of belief.

His eyes drifted then across the others, and that curiosity began to clear.

He nodded to the soldiers. Each looked back doubtfully even as they obeyed, lowering their blades and taking a step away. "Get them blankets," he said without switching tongues, "it's a cold night." Then he looked back towards Anthis and gestured deeper into the cave. There was a table with several vintner's crates and ale casks nearby. "We will speak more, historian."

Chapter 61

The cave was bitterly cold. Icicles hung from the ceiling, water frozen mid-run from channels in the rock above, and what little breeze passed outside hooked in through the low, wide opening to throw wicked shadows from tormented flames. The torches and candles were the sole illumination to break the stiff blackness, itself made deeper by the glowing snow outside. Blankets warded off the worst of it, small sheets of wool the colour of granite, but thick, soft and comfortable - a fact that surprised, until one considered that a well-rested soldier was an alert soldier, many of whom were already fast asleep in preparation to demonstrate the fact. Only about five were seen to be up and patrolling in the snow.

But the only trace of their activity that touched Rathen's attention was the brief, routine movement at the edge of his vision among the languid flutter of red and ochre flags, washed out by the night. But he ignored them. His eyes didn't once trail outside. He was watching the commander.

The man sat at a table across the cave, a pocket of light in the darkness, with a severe look upon his face, listening intently with only the slightest degree of cynicism as Anthis spoke animatedly. Rathen couldn't hear the words, and with Anthis's back to him, he couldn't make a guess from his lips, either. But he found himself curiously without a care for it.

His eyes drifted absently towards the command table nearby. A number of candles were set upon it. If just one of them toppled, the maps and missives would catch quickly. Plans would become cinders in moments. But it would do little to stop any attacks, so there was no point hoping for it to happen. Orders would have already been read and committed to memory, and this was only one of several enemy camps. If this detachment fell or failed to act, others would fill in. And it was possible that there were more such encampments than officials believed. This one had certainly not been marked on any map, public notice or private correspondence.

But, ultimately, soldiers' movements could be anticipated.

His eyes moved briefly towards the umber mage who lay asleep on a cot nearby, his back turned to the world. He appeared no less broken in rest. And yet, to be so close at hand to his commander, the power he wielded must have exceeded that of the average Turundan mage. Not Rathen's own, of course, but that of the average soldier. And yet he did nothing about his poor treatment. None of them did. They had not rebelled, and it seemed unlikely that they ever would.

As such, their power and obedience made them far more difficult to predict, which in turn made Doana a greater threat.

He became suddenly aware of the rattling of his heart against his ribs, and bitterly realised that it wasn't that he didn't care, but that he was so completely focused upon ignoring that care and turning in on himself that he'd succeeded. In fact, the mage worried him. Their situation worried him. And Anthis acting as their representative particularly worried him.

Movement drew his eyes sharply back towards the pair. Anthis was approaching him. The sorrow in his young eyes appeared both closer to the surface and dulled, which made the streak of solemnity that pierced them even graver. He'd drank probably three or four pints of ale and yet still seemed to be holding himself together.

He stopped just short, at the edge of the nearest flame's light, and steadied that serious look onto him. "Rathen. Come." He hadn't slurred, but his few words seemed tactical.

Rathen said nothing in return. But after a moment of stubborn hesitation, he slipped Aria from his side to sleep alone upon the provided cot, and followed him guardedly back towards the table. His mouth, he realised, was bowed firmly in a grimace. He couldn't recall the last time it hadn't been.

The commander rose at his approach and began pouring ale into a third, slightly dented mug. He offered it towards him with a stare a little too gentle for a military man. "My condolences."

Rathen barely paused for thought. He took the tankard and drank. It was shockingly bitter, with the slightest aroma of burnt orange, but he found the heat quite welcoming. The accompanying handshake was spurned.

Untroubled, the commander seated himself, and Anthis followed. Rathen sat a moment later. "Mister Karth has told me everything."

"Has he really?" Rathen grunted, setting the mug down, a third drained already, and fixed the soldier at last with cold indifference.

"And while I find it unlikely," he continued easily, deliberately meeting the look, "I'm also inclined to believe it. At least insofar as your having nothing to do with your king or the Arana."

"But not towards the Arana's rogue."

"A king could not lose control over one of his assets like this."

"Would that the world were so simple."

"Oh it's far from simple. I also cannot personally wrap my mind around the idea that a single country could invoke war among eight - Skilan and Kalokh, Ivaea and Kasire, Dweron and Antide, and the attempts upon us and Voent, of course. And yet that, we have confirmed, *is* true."

Rathen continued to watch him carefully from beneath a veil of disdain. The commander stared back at him steadily. Anthis drew back into his mug.

"The Arana is trained in deception and passing unnoticed," Rathen spoke at last. "But you found them in your military. How?"

"Ah - that was a stroke of genius on the part of our Ma'as - lieutenant general - Lord Monatt'. He was shrewd enough to view with suspicion the wars the other nations dove into so zealously. When a few of our own councillors began pushing for war with Voent, he tiptoed aside and began to dig. He discovered the young women who had been whispering into their ears, and the individuals responsible for inflaming our general. None of them were who they seemed to be, but rather than making allegations without solid proof, he acted carefully and dug deeper to find what he needed to convince the council against it, utterly. In time, a few individuals were apprehended and questioned, and they were...*persuaded* to reveal the others."

"They spoke that easily?"

The man studied with intent the dents in his own tankard. "They were not given a choice. We have our methods, as I'm sure your Arana does; we pressed the right buttons, read them well enough to find the right leverage - the ma'as was a genius when it came down to that. We sent false reports in the spies' place to conceal our own actions while observing your own, which subsequently confirmed our suspicions that Turunda, curiously untouched, was orchestrating it *all*. Whittling down your enemies without taking off your gloves." His slate-grey eyes hardened as he looked at the pair, accusation clear at the surface despite his previous acquiescence to their innocence. "And so your claims that the king is not involved, we cannot believe. King Thunan is not a slow-witted king. No authority under his command could break away and continue to function as you suggest."

"Except that's exactly what the Arana has done," Rathen replied sedately. "The king may have ordered spies, but I can't believe that he would have invoked all of this war across the entire continent. Salus, on the other hand, I can."

"You know him well, then?"

"Well enough. And we have our own eyes and ears on the inside. We know what he is capable of. Sorely."

"Do you really? There is dissent? Or are you being fooled, yourselves?"

"Dissent."

"You sound certain."

"I am. As you should be."

"Mm." He leaned forwards then, his eyes slighting in open suspicion. Rathen didn't flinch. "But, now, if you're not tied to the Arana, and you're not working for the king...how did you come to be affiliated with these 'eyes and ears'?"

"Because they are working for the good of Turunda, as we are. Forces pulled us together. Don't get distracted."

"The epitome of vagueness."

"You'll live."

"Rathen."

He didn't spare Anthis a look. He raised his mug back to his lips and turned his eyes deliberately off into the darkness.

"He's telling the truth," Anthis assured the soldier a moment later.

"But there is, of course, no proof you can give me."

"Short of the king's word. And would you believe it?"

"Horses can lie."

"...Pardon?"

His dark eyebrows rose in a strangely keen, tentative hope. "'Straight from the horse's mouth'?"

Anthis blinked in bewilderment, but Rathen was still staring away into the cave, apparently no longer listening. "Uh, maybe, I suppose... But do you have any proof that the Arana is really to blame for *all* of these wars?"

"You doubt, and yet you act against them yourself?"

"I only point out that your proof is just as immaterial as ours. But...no, I suppose I don't doubt. He is just that driven..."

"It would seem so. And, unfortunately, we do have proof. On most counts.

Kalokh were eager to aid us against you despite their losses when we informed them of your role in their downfall. And so I'm afraid that your word, and that of your king, would never be enough. Only time will prove your king's innocence, and we are not prepared to give time the chance."

"What are you doing here?"

His eyes flicked onto Rathen, who had grown only more acrid in his distance. "Putting an end to the sabotage."

"By skulking in the woods? Attacking retreating forces before running off yourself?"

The commander responded with only a tight-lipped smile. Rathen's grimace dropped suddenly in understanding. He sat forwards, abandoning his previous irritability entirely, and his voice contracted into a tight hiss. "You're going to kill the king."

"What?" Even against the yellow candlelight, the colour had visibly drained from Anthis's face.

"You plan to march on Kulokhar."

"Oh, *goodness*, no. That would be too obvious."

"But the king *is* your target."

"Naturally."

"*But the king isn't involved.*"

"Your word."

Rathen beat his tankard against the table in frustration, interrupting the nocturnal peace. "We *will* find proof."

"I can't imagine what you have in mind. But you haven't the time."

"Why not?"

"Because I'm afraid we will be in position to resolve the situation in a matter of days."

"Then call it off!"

He chuckled with a bemused smile. "Call it off? Do I look like a general to you? I am a *captain* with only half of a company. I can't issue those orders."

"And when you kill an innocent king--"

"No king is innocent."

"He is innocent in these circumstances. What will happen then? Turunda will *crush* you."

"I'm afraid I'm not at liberty to discuss our plans."

"No. Only confirm assumptions." He leaned forwards darkly. The candles sent fiendish shadows across his face. Anthis watched uneasily from the edge of his cup. "Then confirm this: you're a distraction. All of your encampments, your indirect attacks and withdrawals - you're here to occupy our military. You suspected spies, you found them, you caught them, and you 'persuaded' them. You deciphered their line of contact and intercepted it. And successfully convinced the Arana that nothing was amiss. And you have your own version of the Arana, to some degree, and it is they who will kill the king. They're in the palace right now, aren't they? Under orders to strike as soon as the opportunity arises, at whatever personal cost."

"You're a perceptive man."

"No, just a cynic exposed to too much deception and sacrifice."

"And what would you have me do? Inform my superiors that our intel is incorrect according to a ragtag group of *enemy* vigilantes? That the Arana has gone rogue and is *not* acting upon their king's orders? While their king somehow *doesn't notice* the insubordination taking place all around him and so does nothing at all to stop it?"

"Yes."

"Oh, look at that, I'm convinced!"

"Sarcasm is unbecoming of an officer."

"Isn't it just?" The captain put down his tankard and sat back once more in his chair, considering his two Turundan captives carefully. His air of confidence hadn't once shaken, set in place as firmly as stone. Rathen's own severity was equally fixed, and Anthis, too, had settled into a similar state. Finally, his dark lips pursed, and he spoke carefully. "You are trying to stop this 'Salus', yes? And he is the one you say is responsible for the carnage?"

"In a nutshell."

"Nutshell. I like that." He pondered again for another long moment, and neither said a word to intrude upon his deliberations. Unfortunately, others weren't so careful.

A man in unplated leather appeared beside him in the candle light and whispered at length into his ear. The captain's gaze didn't move from the pair until he'd finished, at which point a distasteful curl warped his lip. When he rose to his feet, Rathen and Anthis followed in protest. "It is late. You will rest here as my guests. You were abducted on my order, after all."

"We *can't* stay here."

"You *have* to call off the men in the palace!"

His eyebrow cocked disapprovingly. "Full of demands, aren't you? You could just as easily be my prisoners."

"As if we aren't already."

"I suppose that's true. But you still have your shoes."

"Our shoes?"

"Bare feet in unhappy circumstances does strange things to a man." He turned and marched away, gesturing towards another plated soldier to follow him. "Good night, gentlemen."

A deeply frustrated sigh vented from Anthis's lips, his eyes boring after him in irritation, while Rathen's stare was as hard as granite beside him. It was a long moment before the mage finally turned and moved rigidly back to the others at the side of the cave. Garon was the only one awake, sitting upon his cot and carelessly half-wrapped in his blanket, but his eyes were glass and his mind was far away. A state that had become his norm.

"We could try to leave," Anthis began quietly, falling in beside him, but Rathen cut him off with a sharp shake of his head.

"Not until he's called off his men. It shouldn't take long. If they're already in place and it's too late, he and all the rest will know soon enough."

"So for now, we just sit here and wait?"

"We have no choice." He reached the cot and immediately scooped the slumbering Aria up into his arms, the most open affection Anthis had seen him display in a week. For the vaguest moment, he managed to smile himself. And then his own conscience elbowed its way back in.

The night stood still. Though they were safe from the elements and lay upon a surface softer than rock or snow for the first time since Kulokhar, rest was impossible. The internal torment that paralysed them whenever they sought sleep continued to follow them like a spectre. Anthis doubted he'd caught more than a few minutes, and he suspected that Rathen, like Garon, hadn't even tried. But between the fitful and senseless images his own conscience subjected him to, the haze began to lift as summer light brushed over the snow.

When he opened his eyes, sleep having finally found him only half an hour before, the soldiers were already moving around. And Rathen and Garon were each red-eyed and wide awake.

They were offered food, rations little different to the dried and salted meat, stale bread, cheese and fruit they'd been sustaining themselves with along their journey, which seemed to Anthis to have started a lifetime ago, though he suspected that was simply what stress and loss would do. It had been early March when they'd first set out, he recalled, and Midsummer had only recently passed. Somehow, it couldn't have been any more than five and a half months.

While he relished in the distraction of the mundane thought, the captain approached and promptly apologised. "An army marches on his stomach," he explained, gesturing to the modest fare.

Anthis smiled wearily. "It's fine, thank you. But if you'd allowed us to leave, we wouldn't have had to intrude at all."

"Ah, but then I wouldn't be able to tell you that I am inclined to believe you."

"You told us that already," Rathen reminded him tersely. Another sleepless night had done little to reinstate his manners. "What's changed?"

"Oh you're hard to please." The captain dragged over a stool and sat among them while they ate. Each looked at him warily, but only Rathen wore any hostility. "You have suffered a loss. That much, I can see, is not a lie. And at the hands of Salus who, we can also agree, is enemy to us both, whether your king is involved or not. You seek to stop him. And you believe that that will also end the unrest?"

"It will prevent further stirrings. But the results of monarchs' actions are their own to handle."

"Of course, that goes without saying. But if I were to - and I make no promises - but if I were to try to get word to my commanding officer--"

"By the sounds of it, it will be too late by the time you manage to convince him."

The captain's grey eyes slowed. "I'm already considering the idea of overstepping martial boundaries, but do you expect me to leap *fully* into the realms of insubordination?"

"I expect you to complete what you came here to do, but with a single amendment: *don't* kill the king. Stay your hand."

"Until...when? You're proven right? Or we are?"

Something flashed through Rathen's eyes then, something that, for the first time either he or Anthis had witnessed, sent a touch of hesitance through the soldier's cocksure demeanour. "I can get word to the king far quicker than your superior can to your assassins. I can even get word to the Arana. In a matter of *hours*, all of your plans will crumble, and not one of you will live long enough to be choked by the dust."

"A matter of hours?" The speed at which he'd regained his composure betrayed the depth of his uncertainty.

"The Arana will leap on the intel, and it won't be difficult to draw them right to it. Right to *you*."

"...You leave a man no choice."

"Then you'll do it?" Anthis asked charily, at which the captain sat forwards, a grave obligation lining his brow.

"As I said: I'm inclined to believe you. And if the Arana's leader truly *has* gone rogue and has started all of this on his own initiative, then removing King Thunan will not stop it. We will have only incensed you all and be left with nothing to show for it."

The commander paused for a long moment. Rathen and Anthis watched him patiently, concealing their hope where they could. Finally, he straightened. "I will send word to the assassins to stay their hand once they reach the king *until* the order is given. Assuming that it is not already too late. But I will not be able to delay them for long - my superior, and his above him, will wonder what the hold-up is. We only have so many supplies, and the assassins will take the opportunity as soon as it arises. They know they will not get out from it alive, and we know we will be the only suspects, so they have little intention of being too tactful."

"Which means we would both know if it had already happened."

"Unless it's *about* to happen. But if I can manage that, we will move our attention and efforts onto Salus instead and eliminate him in the king's place."

"...*You* will?"

"Of course. I said I was inclined to *believe* you, I never said anything about *trust*. I have to cover my backside."

"But you said you believed that we weren't involved!"

"And yet you have eyes and ears on the inside and are remarkably perceptive yourselves. You may not be involved in the execution of the misdeeds, but you are not unsuspicious."

"And in the mean time--"

"You will be detained."

Rathen darkened. He spoke through clenched teeth as fire danced in his eyes. "If you do that, you may as well go ahead and kill the king. The country will collapse either way, and you will have painted a glowing target on your foreheads."

"Come now, you can't *honestly* suggest that we let you go--"

"It's that, or Salus destroys your god-forsaken country as well as ours. You won't be able to get to him - you might have gotten a few over on him already, but your luck *is* going to run out, and quickly. You will not get near him."

His eyes narrowed. "You seem rather sure of that."

"Oh I am. And I can be *certain* even *without* numbering in his ranks."

"Mm..." Once again the captain descended into silent contemplation, his gaze fixed to each of their faces in turn. His thoughts, however, were impossible to decipher. He was secretive and tactical, considered and receptive. He was clearly suited to his post. He would probably be in line for a promotion if all this worked out. Or, Anthis thought, more likely court-martialled. And yet he was prepared to break orders anyway. Here was not a villain, but a man trying to do the best for his home and people - and those even beyond his charge. Perhaps that was where Salus's problem stemmed from: Turunda was his world, not his country. But Doana, to this man, was a part of something bigger, and while that 'something bigger' had its dangers and differences, and while informing Kalokh of Turunda's deception was probably little more than a tactic to strengthen their own position rather than any kind of camaraderie, he did not immediately view anyone unlike himself as an enemy. And if he did, he was open to being corrected.

"Very well."

Anthis blinked in surprise despite himself.

"If you're telling the truth - and you're as capable as that vengeful, malevolent glint in your eye would have me believe - you could solve our problem *for* us and save us a great deal of Doanan blood. Assuming you are truly so brave, or so foolish, as to move against a group like the Arana yourselves. And that you are, indeed, to be trusted. In which case, I release you and wish you luck. Know, however, that should you fail or be lying, we will kill your king, kill Salus, and kill you, for whatever part you play in it, deliberate or not."

Anthis suddenly found himself a little less sure of his conclusion.

Rathen, however, was unrattled. "If you truly believed we couldn't be trusted, you wouldn't be entertaining us."

"Unless I was knitting out a read on you."

"Knitting out?"

"Ah - pulling a thread until it's long enough to take shape."

"Or be forced into one."

"Perspective."

"Then it's just as well we're telling the truth." To their surprise, Rathen's shoulders relaxed fractionally and he sat a little more easily on the edge of the cot. "Your superiors will find out you've interfered."

"Of course they will. Which is why I will begin drawing up a report immediately afterwards in the hopes of softening the punishment."

"If you know you'll be punished, why help us?"

"Mister Koraaz, are you always so disagreeable? For the moment, we have a shared interest, and I am confident enough in your...*attitude*...that you are genuine, and could quite possibly see the matter done. There are fewer of you, you know the lay of the land and the Arana itself better than we, and that opens the avenue for an alternative strike. But we will not be sitting idle. And if that mutuality turns out to be false, then your punishment will be far more severe than my own. I am not known to be as hard-headed as my colleagues, but I am also not known to make an uninformed judgement. And as time is of the essence, this is the most informed I can be. But I may only be able to manage days - two weeks, at most - before your throne sits bare."

"Will that be long enough?" Anthis asked worriedly.

"It will have to be." Rathen extended his hand. "Thank you, Captain...?"

"Kemba. And I am not doing this for *you*, understand. My country stands to gain from it."

"And mine stands to lose a little less. The gratitude remains."

"Fair enough. Oh," he added, rising to his feet, "if I may, perhaps you might consider introducing more restrictions over your magic-wielders. If all this has come from magic, then a lock-down on freedom would go a long way to quietening tirades and delusions of grandeur."

"Thank you for your advice. May I also suggest that you watch your fingers? Those who are treated as dogs are likely to bite."

Captain Kemba regarded him for a moment, and the slightest smile crept across his face. "Very eloquently put. Mister Koraaz, Mister Karth." He nodded to the rest, and left.

They were allowed to leave once they'd eaten, and were escorted back to their campsite by the messenger who had interrupted the night before. Rather worryingly, it was quite close by.

"Now what?" Anthis asked as they packed up their tents and supplies, which had either been investigated by a fox or torn through by a small, silent hurricane.

"There is no 'now what' - we do what we've been doing all along. Because you're right."

"I am? About what?"

The single, heartfelt look Rathen gave him set a familiar if unintentional edge of guilt through his bones. "We owe it to her."

Anthis's heart hardened. Resolutely, he nodded, and finished strapping their things to the horses. Tying the reins of the riderless dun to the back of his saddle, they set off out through the August morning light. "He let us go too easily," Anthis said after a while.

"No he didn't. We're being followed, you can put your life on that." But Rathen then cast him a thin, weak smile. "But what's another tail?"

Chapter 62

Few corridors of the palace were ever empty. On every floor of every wing, servants and caretakers hurried about, carrying out their tasks with the utmost urgency as though their lives depended on it. Every member of staff seemed to be eternally busy. And for the footmen in particular, that industriousness was genuine. Their tasks - the petty things the valets were able to shuffle off onto them - would bring the palace to a stand-still if they weren't seen to. After all, who would open doors or serve the prepared food if they didn't? Such was below the valets, and the cooks and pages were under strict rules and forbidden from many areas of the grounds.

Footmen were the valets' whipping boys, in truth, but as menial and thankless as the work was, they also had the greatest freedom. Free from the short leash of the master a valet was so often tied to, they were sent all over the palace day to day to tend to whatever routine emergencies might arise. They did, after all, still outrank the majority of servants in the king's employ, and aside from the Palace Steward, were the highest subservient ranks to wander the halls unaccompanied.

Striding in his livery of fern-green and ivory, one such footman moved through the large, opulent halls with his nose held suitably high, given way by every servant who passed him. Guards, formidably trained and exquisitely dressed, stood as still and shiny as empty suits of armour beside doors and within recesses, ignoring him at the immediate sight of his uniform. Cinnamon wafted through the halls, punctuated by coriander and cloves, though the kitchens were at the furthest end of the wing, and the Yuletide decor was equally in keeping with the aberrant frost that penetrated the summer air inescapably.

He paused for a moment to straighten up a vase beside the staircase; burgundy tulips, baby's breath and twigs of red summer berries all bunched into two diverging groups with a few stems of stragglers standing out on their own. Tutting and shaking his head at the disarray, he jostled and fluffed them into a presentable state for the benefit of the next nobleman to come along, before proceeding with satisfaction up the stairs.

Servants continued to melt out of his way without even a glance as he moved through the gallery and into another labyrinth of corridors, through which he wove confidently by way of identical doors and matching portraits. Like so many of the servants, he was so intimate with the palace layout that he could have navigated with his eyes closed.

Before too long he was winding through the private apartments and making for the small breakfasting room, when a young woman approaching from the opposite end steered directly for him. Her head was bowed, but with a glance at her kirtle, her position among the general staff was clear. Individual identity didn't matter.

She extended a silver tray, its load hidden beneath a draped silken cloth, and thrust it into his hands. "For the Good King Thunan," she said with an uncertain half-curtsey, so intimidated by the footman as she was. But that was not unusual. Any who served the king and royal family directly were awed and feared by those denied such a presence.

With the slightest nod of his head, he took it, and deduced immediately by the shape and weight of the tray where it was to be taken. The king, it seemed, had broken his usual morning routine. He adjusted his path, continuing along the corridor, but turned past the breakfasting room and on instead towards the royal bath chambers.

Two guards stood like stone sentinels outside of the door. Immediately, he dropped into a walking bow and approached low, as was expected when the king was on the other side. One must always enter subservient.

The guards didn't move. They would only have done so to bar his way. They had observed his livery and the tray in his hands through their visors, and hadn't seen need to impede him. The footman opened the door and stepped inside, still stooping, the miasma of peppermint, rose and mallow so dense as to hang as steam by itself.

King Thunan lay in the tub of cedar wood, and only raised his lightly greying head from the velvet cushioning for a moment. A young groom was washing him, who paid the footman even less attention as the king settled himself back down and closed his eyes again.

The footman shut the door behind him and removed the silken cloth. "Fresh undergarments, Your Majesty. Steamed and pressed."

"In the corner on the stool, thank you, Lynel," he said perfunctorily.

"As Your Majesty wishes."

"And have Elandé treat Danai's burgundy gown. She's finally made up her mind."

"Right away, Your Majesty."

"Oh - and have the guests housed in the north wing's third floor, garden side - I want to keep Countess Creo's eyes away from the riding grounds...Anten? Why have you stopped scrubbing?" The king opened one eye when the groom failed to move or respond, and found him sitting quite still, staring with glazed, daydreaming eyes across the room, one hand remaining about the king's wrist and the other absently holding the steaming cloth to his arm.

"Anton," the king said again, shaking his wrist to reclaim his attention, but the hand did not move with him. The grasp was as constant and unbreakable as stone.

Alarm set in rapidly. He sat up and began attempting to tug himself free in confusion, reprimanding and threatening him as he splashed in a panic. But his voice slurred into a weakened gurgle before he could complete the first curse, and his body slipped limp back into the water.

A vaguely metallic aroma rose with the steam and laced into the herb-choked air; the trickle of crimson joined beads of sweat, clouding and seeping through the water.

Old eyes wide and bulging, his voice lost and strength slipping away, the king watched helplessly, deliriously, as Lynel moved into view, a fine, bloodied knife in his hands and void of any sentiment. But his face was not what it should have been.

The footman walked, calm and collected, to stop beside the boy. He was still frozen, but a silent, desperate scream invaded his motionless eyes. But Lynel didn't respond to it. He drew the knife across his throat and waited for just a moment, for his blood to run freely and stain his spotless livery. Then the spell was released. With a gurgling sigh, he slumped forwards and draped over the edge of the wooden tub, out of the line of the king's empty stare.

Calmly, he removed a kerchief from his sleeve, red with an ochre hem, and tied it about the late king's wrist. Then he rose, moved backwards towards the door and bowed to the sodden corpse. "Of course, Your Majesty." His volume was just right, tone firm and unshaken.

He left the room, stooping just as he'd entered, and closed the door behind him. He resumed unhurried along the extravagant corridor. The guards did not react, and he did not let the victory touch his lips.

He made discreetly for the staircase. The palace would be in lock-down within half an hour.

The footman walked without the slightest urgency through the foyer, an elegant box in his arms that could only contain a noble's personal effects being toted out to a waiting carriage. There wasn't a trace of regret, fear or doubt in his proud bearing.

The image within the golden frame hazed in Teagan's eyes.

He stood frozen before the wall of mirrors, countless trivial scenes playing out in blissful ignorance of the Arana's watchmen and spells, and their movement too was lost to his sight.

His thoughts were spinning. His pulse raced and thundered through his veins; sweat beaded and dampened his shirt.

It had happened. Soon, every authority would turn upside down, morale would plummet, Doana would make their move...and Vastal knows who else...

And it would be his fault. He'd seen what was happening. He'd seen where it was going, and he had done nothing. He had *let* this happen. King Thunan was dead by Salus's hand, regicide of the most extreme order, executed by the reach of his own royal arm.

His hands were shaking. He could feel them trembling. He dug his fingers into his folded arms and squeezed them closer into his chest. His heart was rattling his bones, and his eyes, he could feel, were unnaturally wide.

He recognised the emotions - feelings and sensations, he realised with growing horror, that had been present for weeks, guiding his forgotten dreams and compelling him to speak out against his superior, but that he had turned a desperate blind eye to in the hope that they would disappear, or that it was a fluke, or that he was simply unwell and that all would fall back into place in a few days' time. But it had happened too often, and for much too long, and only now had it seen fit to click into place.

But he could hazard a guess at when it had started: right when Salus had begun poking into magic.

And now he was pierced with dread. Panic. A desperate compulsion boiling up inside him to escape the situation, to reverse time or flee and wrap himself in ignorance. But most of all, he'd been speared by doubt - the most crippling self-indulgence of all.

It shouldn't have been possible. It was supposed to have been trained out of him; he was supposed to be untouched by emotions, focused entirely on the matter at hand. These states should have been beyond him.

Just as anger, frustration and love should have been beyond Salus.

But the fact that he was still capable of considering his state rather than succumbing to it entirely as Salus had revealed something else - a point that gave him some hope. His training was slipping, but it hadn't broken; cracked, not crumbled - which meant that it could be fixed.

It wouldn't be quick. Salus would notice his absence, and perhaps even find out what he was doing. He had pointed out his lack of faith, but had done nothing about it - perhaps he'd gotten away with it. But it wouldn't last. And he couldn't let him find out for certain. Perhaps that was another creeping indulgence: pride. Or was it shame? It didn't matter; they were two ends of the same stick in a bundle he was already forbidden to touch.

Forbidden... Taliel. She'd been gone for six days. She'd be back soon, if not that very day, and Salus wasn't likely to send her out again in a hurry. She would keep him occupied. With her around, he wouldn't notice if Teagan was missing for a few days... He wouldn't notice a lot of anything.

His composure stormed back in place and crushed his confusions with a steel fist. His back straightened, his eyes hardened, and he turned with resolve from the mirrors, leaving the room and the portian mage who had been assigned to oversee it.

He would regain his control, and with it Salus's trust. And then he would be able to step in and advise the keliceran the moment it was needed. And the keliceran would listen to him again. A rational hand was all Salus needed, an unbiased, uncompromised point of view delivered in the least offensive manner. It would take a portian, nothing more, nothing less. Only then could Salus be steered back onto the right and honourable path.

And he had to be. And it was Teagan's job to do it.

The sky was dark and overcast. Soured with salt, the air was doubly coloured with the aroma of fish and the squawking of swooping gulls, never to be discouraged from their scavengery by even an anomalous winter.

Salus pulled the sleeves of his livery down even further against the chill. He hadn't stopped to change; the need to regain control from all that was slipping away from him forbade any waste of time. But he had, at least, turned the jacket inside out.

There was no time, either, for deliberation. With the greatest caution, his fingers formed a spell - the same caution and the same spell that he had in Whitemouth just days ago, cast with the same perilous attention. Then, with a deep, saline breath atop Bear Bone Cove's highest point, he lowered his hands and stepped out into the thin, sea air.

His heart thudded in apprehension at that first step, but his doe-skin boots immediately found a peculiarly soft surface, neither truly solid nor incorporeal, and he walked on with the vaguest relief, descending a flight of delicate, crystal-clear stairs. He gave himself no opportunity to contemplate the fact that he was indeed walking over nothing at all.

The sprawling sea grew nearer, and he soon saw that what waves and ripples should have disturbed its great grey surface had been overpowered instead by a violent vibration, as though thousands of tiny needles were being pushed up repeatedly through the underside. He'd witnessed the same phenomenon at Whitemouth, and could guess just as easily at the cause.

The water indented as he reached it, an imprint of nothing that grew deeper and deeper as he continued his descent, until the sea moved around him as though he were surrounded by a sphere of twisting winds that pushed the water safely aside. Then, ultimately, the sea closed over his sphere, and the convulsing surface was left without a trace of his passing.

With every nervous step the expanse grew colder, and while the shell diverted the worst of it, the predating hum that rumbled from the depths beneath him became only stronger. The seabed was moving, and violently, a reaction shared with that of dry land upon almost every other such occasion. But he steeled himself with effort against it, and against the knowledge that his own protective spell was antagonising it, and fixed his thoughts upon his task. There were none here to be injured, and he had no intention of letting the magic escape him again. He'd been obscenely fortunate that Toakh had already been evacuated.

An orb sparked into light against the enclosing darkness - a notably slimmer challenge than the first time he'd tried to juggle two spells - and cast a cold, deathly glow through the water. There was nothing to see but an abyss in all directions. If anything, it compressed the darkness.

Foreboding began to claw at the back of his mind, so thick and tangible that he turned twice to catch whatever was behind him. But there was nothing but the blooming fret of his spells' integrity. A fret that had sat upon his shoulders the last time, too.

And just like the last time, he beat it forcefully from his mind. There was no time to waste on panicking. He had a task to carry out, the most important task he or anyone else would ever be charged with, and one that stood, absolutely, for the good of all.

Doggedly, he followed the pull of the magic, and the seabed eventually loomed into sight. His feet shortly hit the swirling sand and he walked at last over a surface, shaking but existent. But he had not arrived, yet.

It was most disconcerting to feel none of the weight of the sea nor its current, but even with his glowing light, it was so dark that it was easy to imagine himself instead in a large, unlit and spacious room. His focus had become quickly rigid, as had his back, shoulders and jaw. He would not be beaten. Not by anyone or anything. Not so close to victory.

He began to move faster, running unimpeded, sand and seaweed swirling aside with the water, until the light at last began to bounce back from straight-sided stone. But it was not deliberate architecture; it was too vast and uneven to be an imbued ruin. It was the seabed, cracked and elevated, sheared in two, a pure black void gaping open into the barren vacuum between them.

Lights then began twinkling out of the darkness just ahead of him, drifting like marine snowflakes; fish scales, catching and reflecting the orb, and a single, colossal, ghostly eel surely the length of the palace road slipped languidly through the chasm, its undulating, ethereal form rising and vanishing beneath the lowest cliff top.

And the pressure of magic; the thrum of power excited in his own veins.

He had arrived.

Cautiously, he stopped at the cliff and peered tentatively over the edge. The eel had disappeared, and if anything else lurked beneath, it was invisible to his eyes and obscured by the void-black shadow his orb enhanced. Falling here, he knew, was impossible, but the bottomless gulf still sparked some echo of atavistic dread. But he had to remain close. The closer he was to the magic and the chasm, the more control he had over it. Surely, logically, that was the case.

But...if he was wrong, and his sphere shattered...

As his eyes turned unwillingly towards the distant surface, the voice of doubt - the voice of *reason* - seized him with so tight a grasp he felt that the seabed had suddenly closed around him. Whitemouth had been too close. He couldn't take that chance again.

Twisting his fingers, his heart racing and shuddering, his shell of swirling winds rose from the sands and carried him urgently towards the surface. Every second was an age; black turned much too slowly to indigo, then azure-tinted grey, and by the time he broke through to weightless air and the sweet, distant ceiling of snow-laden clouds, he felt weariness edging in.

Relief. And there was no time for it.

He collected himself swiftly and focused into his magic, reaching with it straight down, back into the blackness, and began to coax the wild magic before that weariness could coalesce into something worse. Because there was no time to succumb to it. Not now. No time to waste.

The magic responded eagerly, jumping and skitting like a young colt, leaping and bounding, ready to take advantage of the briefest weakness in his assault. But he wasn't going to let it get away from him again. Through magically-paved gulleys and channels, he steered the magic, controlling it through every crack and splinter, subduing its energy into obedience, pushing directly westwards from this easternmost border.

It was only minutes, though it felt like hours, and by the time the chasm had been tamed and collected, a muffling blanket of dizziness rolled through his skull.

He released the spell willingly before his vision could cross and double, and began to shiver. He was exhausted. And soaked. He looked down at himself, bobbing up and down in the water, and realised with some disconnection that the sphere had broken after all. But he found he had little strength to be surprised, relieved or alarmed, and turned his eyes instead towards the horizons. Shore was visible, but only just. He could never swim that far.

Fortunately, he didn't have to.

Almost immediately, the water beneath him turned to blissfully solid ground, a fact he appreciated after another passing of vertigo, but the chill was unremedied, and the snow and frosted stone were blinding. But at least it wasn't water. Here, it was possible to start and sit beside a fire.

There was no time for that, of course, nor for his briefest moment of gratitude to his past-self for pouring effort into grasping self-teleportation. He was alive, and staring into the face of the final step. That was all that mattered.

With a deep breath, he steeled himself against the cold and looked around, warming himself up by stamping his feet and rubbing his hands.

Gennith's Point. A ruin; a single, large menhir accompanied by little more than time-worn fragments of others, arranged randomly and pummelled by age and element into stumps. However they had once looked, whatever their significance, every surface had been beaten smooth by the salty coastal winds, and yet more had been lost to the sea. But the site's distinction had been renewed by clods of earth hanging suspended in the air, bare soil black against the snow, and rocks shaped like well-pruned topiary trees that seemed to have no relevance to the ancient stones at all. And the strange darkness that pervaded the scene.

He frowned as he looked up at the sky. No, not darkness, just...dim. Like evening. Like sunset. And yet the sun was still high, if obscured by the clouds.

Salus quickly turned away from it. He was wasting time. It bore no relevance. And the magic here was raging. His heart was raging. He was already exhausted, and his attention was slipping. Completing this would truly test his magic and his strength in a way he'd never anticipated. But complete it, he must.

His eyes pulled eastwards. He could feel the magic approaching, travelling at impossible speed, its progress hastened by a small modification to his gulleys, covering half the length of the southern coast in what amounted to eleven minutes. And it was almost upon him.

Again, he reached his magic out towards it, paving another gulley to steer it on its final stretch. Another chasm, filled with petulant magic, lay beneath the sea before him. He could feel it if he couldn't see it, and had only to join them up. Then...then...

The magic almost spilled. His guidance had slowed down.

'Focus.'

He was ahead once again. The distance was closing. Closing. The ends were almost within reach.

The ground shook violently beneath him. The cliff began to crumble, rock, soil, snow, then the outermost of the remaining stones slipped and plummeted into the roiling sea. Floating rocks fell, others rose, and a few began to spin and whirl, dancing around the ruin and colliding with one another with a terrible crunch. Chance alone saved Salus's life, for he dropped to his knees in immersion just as one passed over him. But his focus didn't break. The two ends joined.

The ground ruptured. Earth and stone spewed into the air to land with a crash and shatter upon one another, firing even greater tremors through the ground. With an expended gasp, Salus's mind latched desperately onto the shaking of his bones, out of sync with the rest. Against the chaos surrounding him, how, he managed to wonder, was he still upright?

He wasn't for long.

He hit the ground as heavily as a horse, and a great warmth washed over him on impact in spite of the surrounding snow. He'd pushed himself too far. He knew he would, but it had been necessary, and he was certain that it was not a wasted effort. And he would survive the repercussions. He had to.

His bones ached. His head spun, his breath caught, but a smile crept over his lips, and a single thought reverberated through his being in the passing of the strain: it was finally coming together.

He was almost there. And he was ahead. *Truly* ahead! Nothing could get in his way now - nothing and no one. Malson, the king - they were redundant concerns, and the country was better off for it. People died - *kings* died - but the country had survived it each time before, regardless of the circumstances.

And as for Koraaz, that mongrel was far behind him. The distance was insurmountable.

Footsteps passed nearby, and he realised that his eyes were closed. Even when he opened them, it took him a few moments to realise that he stared not at the clouds but at the dark, vaulted ceiling of his office, and that the warmth he felt was not - at least in entirety - due to any sudden sickness or hypothermia, but to the fire that burned happily in the fireplace. A fire that burned for no one, for no one else was there.

Hurriedly, he pushed himself up onto his elbows and looked around. Indeed, the office was empty. Teagan was nowhere to be found. He struggled to his feet and immediately staggered sideways, crashing into the bookcase.

He cursed and steadied himself against the frame to look around instead. Teagan had certainly been in, as the desk, he could see from there, was meticulously tidy. Tidy, at least, but for a single report folder placed just so in the middle. He frowned at it. There was something significant about the placement, centred upon the leather blotter, but at a gentle angle, just off from perpendicular, favouring the left. Teagan wouldn't have left it like that...

His bearings were further from his reach than he'd thought. As yet more footsteps passed outside the door, understanding tumbled clumsily over him, and his juddering heart burst up into his throat. His smile returned in strength.

Taliel was back.

A ridiculous, guileless energy snatched him from out of nowhere, excitement, enthusiasm, subduing at least for the moment the spent shake of his bones. He had to see her.

He raced mindlessly for the door, and though he tripped twice, he decided to collect himself along the way rather than waste any more time. He had to see her right away. He would find her, he would hold her, he would kiss her, and he would tell her the good news. She would be so proud, so impressed! She would love him all the more! And she would know without a trace of doubt that he could protect her to the ends of the earth, just as he could protect Turunda.

He would find her, and he would tell her right away.

And...he would tell others. The distance was vast, that was undeniable, but it wouldn't hurt to widen it a little more. And he had just the thing.

Chapter 63

Every evening the August sun blazed the snow into gold. It was the single event to break the black and white monotony of the landscape and, for a blissful moment, enabled one to set aside their worries in favour of hope, even if that hope felt wrong, foolish or absurd.

But that phenomenon had passed an hour ago, and now the light was fading. Night was creeping in; the chill became sharper, the silence denser, but they kept moving, the horses only drawn to a stop once darkness had truly set in. Within the safety of an abandoned and overgrown barn at the edge of The Ghost Patch, Anthis handed out bowls of stew. It was thin, but warm, and was eaten in silence. Aria fell asleep almost immediately, cocooned in a blanket on the rotten-wood floor beside her father, exhausted by her ongoing grief. But while Eyila and Garon remained in their silent stupors, Rathen sat more consciously at the young girl's side. When Anthis collected their bowls, he discovered the mage fiddling with his daughter's wooden carving.

The need to break the torturous silence was overwhelming, and he cursed himself for his clumsy outburst. But, somehow, the whisper that moved like a roar through the chill went largely unnoticed. "How's it going?" He tried again, this time barely above the crackle of the fire.

"I don't want to tempt fate."

"That sounds promising."

"And that sounds like tempting fate."

Anthis turned to resume his desperately collected chores, until Rathen's next quiet words stalled him. His eyebrows rose in surprise. "Why 'thank you'?"

"For taking the lead. You're the only one of us that hasn't fallen into...self-indulgence, I suppose."

A sneer, thin but rueful, broke his confusion. "I wouldn't say that. I've just been trying to keep my mind off of it..."

"It's not been working."

"No, of course it hasn't." Even so, he busied himself with rearranging the stack of bowls in his hands, but succeeded only in spattering a few remnants of stew over his already dirty shirt. A tight puff of air escaped his nostrils and he abandoned the childish pretence, looking helplessly towards the mage instead. "Why did she do it?"

"Because," Rathen replied patiently, nodding his head towards a spot on the floor beside him, "she was a good person."

"But what I did--"

"Was beyond unforgivable." Anthis hesitated in taking the seat, but Rathen's stare didn't change. The hard edge that had been present in his eyes for so long had eroded away. "But," he continued softly, "not deliberately personal. Some part of her knew that."

His head dropped helplessly into his hands.

"Or," Rathen continued once again, "perhaps it was just that she knew we needed you. Or maybe it was just reflex. I can't speak for her, so you'll have to take from it what you will, but knowing her as we did, the answer should be obvious. She was a protector, despite the rest. Devoted, but not to just one single thing. Don't destroy yourself if she gave her life to save you. And my thanks still stands."

The pair sat in silence for some time. Anthis didn't lift his head from his hands and stared instead into his thoughts. He couldn't fathom how Rathen could be right in the slightest. What he did *was* unforgivable, and he didn't hesitate to remind himself of that.

When he finally raised his head from the suffocating heat of his breath, he found that Rathen had sunk back into his ponderings over the Sah'niir. Again, desperation charged his tongue. "Can I help?"

"I doubt it. It's a matter of magic, not elves. It's my problem."

"Oh..." he turned slightly at the arrival of another concern. "How's your...uh..."

"*'Use it shrewdly'*, she said." He ran a thumb thoughtfully over the smooth wood. His eyes didn't once peel away from it. "I took that as 'only when it's necessary', but I think she meant the duration, not the frequency. If it's cast in quick bursts, nothing prolonged or channelled, I seem to be able to do it. But searching for that lackey in the woods, using the Zi'veyn..." he shook his head.

"...What exactly has been happening?"

"Honestly, I don't know. Tekhest, the elves, they did...something. I have more control over the transformations, but...everything else...seems..." He sighed, and his shoulders twitched in a feeble shrug. "It's come at a cost."

"But a cost that might have been worth it?"

Finally his eyes lifted from the figure of carven elm, but they had turned frigid as they stared into the flames, touched by doubt, by grief, and by purpose. He didn't speak for some time. In the end, he didn't speak at all.

Anthis quickly regretted the question. Perhaps it had been a subconscious decision that had restrained his transformation that hateful afternoon, not shock. But...would he really have made that decision, even unaware, while Petra...?

No. He couldn't believe that as a possibility. It wasn't in him. It just wasn't.

But he didn't say so. He followed his stare instead. "Can you overc--"

"I can. I *am*. I've already managed to--"

A soft crying interrupted the dampened stillness that surrounded their conversation, and in a single broken heartbeat, the ice melted from Rathen's eyes and the stone crumbled from his voice. He reached over and held the weeping child close against him, rocking her softly, hushing her, whispering promises that everything would be all right, whatever little comfort that offered. But she soon calmed, by his words or his hold, and fell slowly back to sleep.

Anthis watched them wistfully. No one had recovered. Over the two days since their abduction, any outward trace of Rathen's self-pity had vanished as suddenly as summer rain. He'd resumed the mantle of leader while Garon followed, lost in a daze behind them, and Anthis had been only too pleased to hand it over, even if it meant he fell deeply back into his own.

But it was still there. It was, he suspected, either his soldier's heart that had kicked him back into form, or the same heart that had him continue to whisper and rock comfort even while his daughter slept. He might wish to seem the careless, brooding, grudge-bearing outcast, he might threaten to abandon the matter and leave Turunda to its fate by man or magic, but it was all a front, a front that collapsed whenever things became serious - when someone needed to act. A soldier's heart, spurred into action by an imperishable compassion.

The fact that he'd wallowed in grief and 'self-indulgence' with the rest of them showed just how deep that care went. Too deep, perhaps, but maybe that was also a good thing. And that he should spare a few comforting words even for him, when it had been his fault that Petra had died... No one else would be so considerate. He knew he wouldn't.

Anthis rose and silently slipped away, making instead for the distraction of his satchel across the barn, until a quick movement of the statuesque figure outside the wall's splintered hole startled him. Both he and Rathen looked Garon's way. His head had turned. The campfire caught just enough - there was something new in his eyes.

Rathen rose, slipping Aria gently to his own folded blanket, and regarded the inquisitor nervously. "What is it?"

His gaze flicked onto him quickly from the eastern darkness. "We leave. Now."

Neither missed the wildness in his eyes.

They moved immediately, rousing Aria and Eyila each and collapsing the camp without a moment to spare. They gathered belongings, throwing them carelessly into bags, fired by the grim watchman's sudden animation. Something dangerous was close. Or some*one*.

Rathen's heart raced as he fumbled to strap a bag to his horse's saddle. Was it Salus? If it was, this time, he wouldn't fail. He wouldn't let him win. He wouldn't let another fall at his order.

His teeth grit against the adrenaline, and he steadied his nerves as he turned to snatch up Aria's bag. When he staggered backwards in sudden fright, the others fell equally still around him, and the horses reared in a panic.

At the centre of the barn, cast half in spectral shadows from the campfire at his feet, stood a man with dead eyes. He didn't wait for them to find their tongues. "I have a message," he said plainly in way of introduction. His voice didn't shake. There was no trace of any concern for his own safety, nor of any threat. Yet the way he stood, so still, so composed, warned that his tone was clue to nothing, and that he was capable of attacking so quickly that none would see him move until they were already struck down.

Yet Rathen's instinct to attack pre-emptively was frozen, dulled by the drowning of his heart. He stared at the passive man, his unremarkable face unknown to him or forgotten, and sought in it some suggestion that his conclusion was in error. But he found nothing. He did his best not to let his dread show through. "He's done it, hasn't he?"

"The borders have been cut."

Somehow, his heart sank further. A foolish hope against all rationality. And he could feel the truth in the words, the pride. It was not a bluff. He knew the others sensed the same.

"The king is dead."

These words didn't land as quickly. Shock had further slowed his mind. But he knew just as certainly as the last declaration that it was true, and also by Salus's doing. How he'd managed it didn't matter, but he tried to voice the question anyway. His tongue didn't move.

"Lord Elias Malson, is dead. Your alliance has been severed."

Now, Rathen's heart stopped. He was sure his eyes were wide, gripped by a terror that threatened to burst something inside him. But they were just as dead as the messenger's.

"And we know," his list continued, cold gaze passing briefly over those gathered behind the grim, black-haired mage, each reeling beneath the messenger's mental assault, "that one of you is not what you seem."

Alarm slipped seamlessly to confusion. Frowns drew over each face despite themselves. The previous declarations hadn't been unreasonable in the state of things, but this...this was nothing more than a sudden and desperate attempt to rattle them, to the point that the message as a whole was cast quickly into doubt.

And yet, no one was prepared to say it. If that brought any satisfaction to the near-lifeless messenger, it wasn't shown.

"What does he mean?" Anthis finally managed while the others stared at the man in silent vigilance. "One of us...isn't...what does he mean?" The man's eyes had returned emptily to Rathen. All others followed, and each realised at once that he was not talking to them, but exclusively to him. Anthis felt his heart leap in terror. "Rathen - Rathen, what does he mean?"

"What he said. That one of us..."

There was nothing in the man's face. "Is one of us."

Rathen continued to stare at him. He read what little he found, chewed over the delivery, and deciphered at least one thing as a certainty. *'He's not talking about Elle... They don't know she's involved or he'd have said so, said so by name...'* He kept the flare of hope from his eyes. "What are you saying?"

"You know what I'm saying. You know something isn't right. You've known for a while. Otherwise you wouldn't have understood so quickly. You wouldn't have believed it. Trying to predict and out-think deceivers would lead inevitably to the conclusion that you aren't out of reach of it yourselves. But you've only briefly entertained the idea. Most of you have. But you've not voiced it, and you've not been able to work it out. You haven't tried hard enough, to spare yourselves. But you suspect each other, all the same." His razor-sharp eyes flicked then towards Garon. "Is it the one about whom you know so little?" Then onto Anthis, who flinched at the gaze. "Or of whom you know too much?" And then onto Eyila. "Or, perhaps, it's the most unassuming and mysterious of you all."

"This is absurd," Anthis announced fervently. "Of *course* we're not Aranan! None of us--you're just trying to turn Rathen against us, trying to split us up because you can't take that we've been ahead of you for--"

"Quiet, Anthis."

"Rathen, he's--"

"Be quiet."

"No! No, come on!" He looked across them imploringly, fighting against the suspicion that lay so openly in their eyes and fell inevitably then onto him. "No! *None* of us! It's all just lies to drag us apart! To keep us out of his way! You can't *possibly* believe him! Rathen!"

"*Quiet*, I said." The ferocity hidden within the collection of his tone silenced him at last.

Rathen stared at the messenger. A dark, pensive shadow had clouded his eyes, and he stood motionless as his mind moved faster than a loosed arrow.

The messenger's dead eyes followed his progress. They hadn't left him once. After a while, he broke the agonising silence. "You have it, don't you?"

Slowly, compulsion turned his head. His dark eyes were sharp. Any words on his companions' tongues were lost immediately. But it was not a speculative look. It was not suspicion or mistrust. It was realisation. Reluctant, but undefiable realisation.

The horror in his eyes chilled their blood, and the ferocity in his tone crumbled, a whisper steeped in disbelief. "It's you, isn't it?" The words stuck in his mouth. And Garon said nothing.

The others followed slowly, bewildered, sceptical, brows furrowed in the sheerest dismay. Still, he did not waver. The inquisitor held Rathen's stare, grey eyes as dead as steel.

The silence that dropped was filled with screaming questions their tongues couldn't shape. The moment lasted an eternity.

Rathen turned towards him. And Garon ran. He was out of sight in moments.

When Rathen spun back around for answers, the messenger, too, had vanished. Only he, Aria, Anthis and Eyila were left.

Anthis blinked towards the barn door. The fire crackled quietly behind him. "...Why did he run?"

"Because," Rathen snarled poisonously, eyes searing through the wood, fists balled tight at his sides, "he is guilty."

Anthis turned him a baffled frown and searched across the rest for comprehension. "What? No, no, look: that bastard was just trying to turn us against each other. No, we made a play of it, the wedge between us, remember? Salus is just trying to *widen* it--"

His voice caught as Eyila whirled, a brief but shredding breeze snapping around her and denting the wooden beams, tears of fury in her ice-blue eyes and a voice as tight as a bowstring. "Then *why* did he *run?*"

"No, no, you're--Garon's on *our* side!"

"If he was, he'd have told us who he was by now, especially after everything we've been through."

"Rathen, there's nothing to tell! He's been working *against* Sal--"

"You're sure? Are you?"

"He's been hiding from him just like the rest of us. Why--"

"Because he was staying in character! Keeping us from getting suspicious! Anthis, *he ran* rather than even *try* to fight the accusation! He's *guilty! Nothing* less! Salus is probably calling him in right now!"

Anthis adamantly shook his head. "Rathen, you're confus--"

"No." He spoke firmly, turning square towards him and pinning him beneath ferocious eyes. Anthis shrank beneath his intensity. "No, Anthis, I'm *not*. He was right - I *have* wondered. A *few* times. How we always managed to keep ahead, how things were never quite as bad as they should have been - but I didn't want to look at it too closely, I didn't want to find issues because I wanted to stop the magic, and I wanted to stop Salus. But the fact is that he knew *everything* he needed to know about me - he told me that right at the start. And he *found* me. As skilled as the White Hammer are, the ability to track me down out there was a tall order even for them! He wasn't surprised about your 'condition' either, was he? He probably knew all about that before we even tracked you down. We were always near enough to a settlement when your 'needs' arose. He knew *all* of this before we even set out, he didn't figure it out along the way! He's known *exactly* who we all are all along! He probably worked out who Petra was as soon as she ran into us, too!"

"B-but Petra--he kept trying to--"

"Get rid of her - because she wasn't a part of his plans! She was dangerous, she would draw attention to us, maybe even ruin whatever he had planned! He was *always* in control! The point is, *he knew everything!* And--and Salus," his eyes widened and flicked past the desperate young man, "he was there at Khry's Glory--he was there *right when we were!* If you hadn't stayed behind and gotten us both trapped, we would have carried the Zi'veyn *right into his hands!*"

"It was chance," he blustered, "we managed to keep away from him at every *other* point--"

"When we didn't have what he *wanted*. When we hadn't found the Zi'veyn's location. When we hadn't opened the door to it. He was there *in person* only when he *needed* to be."

"But the messenger said he was working with *Malson!*"

"No, he didn't! He said that one of us isn't what we seem, and then Garon ran. If *he* was working with Malson, Elle would *never* have come to us; it would have put her *and* their association at risk! But she *did*, and she gave *me* her messages! She never *once* shared them with him! Because I am the only one who would believe her! And trust her!"

"But if he was feeding Salus information on us," he said with sudden confidence, "why hasn't he told him about *her?*"

Rathen's face paled. "She needs to be warned."

"Rathen, you're slipping."

"No, Anthis, *you* are! You're blind to what's staring you in the face! He *ran! Explain why an innocent man runs!*"

The young man's jaw tightened, and his eyes narrowed, coloured with frustration, anger, and steadily growing remorse. His voice was small when he finally spoke. "I can't. But it doesn't make sense...he's made so many mistak--the ditchlings, we stumbled--"

Rathen nodded zealously. "Right into them. And what *perfect* allies they've made. Telepathic allies, who can relay messages over vast distances *very* quickly."

"You're saying the *ditchlings* are working for Salus?!"

"No. That, I don't believe. But whatever his plans were, he knew we'd need more eyes and ears and thought they'd be more efficient and reliable than humans."

"Rathen, the ditchlings weren't going to ally with us, they wanted us *gone*, remember? They wanted nothing to do with us! We only cleared the air by *saving* one of them! And *that* only happened because Aria dropped her knife. That was the only reason we crossed the attack!"

"Dropped the knife she hadn't been using from the very bottom of her bag?"

Anthis shook his head again, squeezing his eyes shut tight against his own madness. "You think *he* dropped it? On purpose? What else are you going to pin on him? Getting lost in the Wildlands? Finding the elves? Every damned time you've lost control of yourself? Every time *I* have?!" He flinched as Rathen closed the distance between them in a flash.

"*He ran, Anthis!* Whether he's guilty of all that or not, *he ran!* If he was working with Elle, if he was working with Malson, he would have stayed and explained himself! Instead, he said nothing, turned and ran, and left the messenger untouched to slip away in the distraction!"

"*All right!*" He bellowed back. "Okay! Say you're right - what reason could Salus possibly have for telling us about him and blowing his cover after all this time?"

"Anthis, *think*. It's to shake us. Sow doubt. Mistrust. Widen the wedge - if it wasn't there before, it damned sure is now."

"And now? If Garon *was* sending him messages, Salus has lost his eyes among us."

"He doesn't *need* them anymore! He's succeeded! He's cracked the borders! And now he can't be *stopped!*"

Anthis fell silent. They stared at one another, Rathen at the reluctant curl of his lip, Anthis at the fervour in his eyes. The silence was filled only by the crackle of the fire and the heave of enraged breath.

And then Eyila's hard eyes crashed onto them, her fury and insult immovable, but accompanied now by some kind of condescension. Aria's eyes had shifted the same way, but she remained quietly trying to calm the horses. "You don't believe that, do you?"

"Why else would he--"

"No," she interrupted him smoothly, "I mean that he can't be stopped."

Her direct gaze squeezed the wildness out of him and pressed him into consideration. Rathen sighed as his shoulders rounded in defeat. "He's cracked the land," he replied calmly. "It's all linked up. The magic has been pushed and joined; it's probably coursing all around the country like a whirlwind. What can we do against that with the Zi'veyn?"

"Nothing," she shrugged. "We use the Sah'niir."

His gaze dropped and shifted. Her own didn't soften. "It's not ready yet."

"It's not? Or *you're* not? You can use it to break up the magic."

"No - Salus probably already knows about it. To play his hand now, he must have an ace up his sleeve! And it's already too late! He's--"

"He's cracked the borders, that's *all*." She stepped around, fur boots silent over the wooden flooring, and forced herself into his sight. Her eyes had truly turned to ice. "Rathen, we have a *job* to do. After everything, we *cannot* give it up. Whatever or whoever Garon is, whether that's really his name, whether he's working with Salus, Malson or even someone else - none of it changes the fact that Turunda won't move *anywhere* just because of a crack down its *sides!*"

"*That's* what all this is about?"

The three spun around as quick as lightning at the harshly cut voice, sorely prepared this time with loose fingers and blades. But the dark figure standing tall in the doorway wore a familiar face. Though that didn't make him welcome.

"He really is quite mad."

"Eizariin?!" Anthis broke away from the others and rushed towards him with a relieved grin, tucking his knife away in haste to eagerly shake the old elf's hand. The fire caught the shine of black-blue hair, half loosely gathered, the rest flowing free, and the lively curiosity in his pastel eyes that seemed to be a part of his natural expression. His robes, however, remained as grand as those he wore upon his first interruption on the mist-shrouded island four months ago.

Charily, Rathen and Eyila lowered their hands as the two historians greeted one another enthusiastically. "Can he do it?" Rathen interrupted, extending the elf's own absent discourtesy. "Is it really possible that he could move Turunda away from the rest of Arasiin?"

"If he's responsible for the destruction of your borders, then I wouldn't want to float too many raaohz on the idea that he can't." He approached, nodding and smiling in recognition of the others, though he peered curiously at Aria who stared wide-eyed from around the horses. "It's no mean feat."

"Which means we *must* stop him," Eyila concluded needlessly and quite for Rathen's benefit.

"That it does."

"Are you here to help us?"

"Certainly, Anthis," he smiled, but a fraction of his good humour slipped away as he looked back towards Rathen. "But first, I'd rather like to know just how *all this* has been able to happen. You destroyed Khryu'vahz, so I *assumed* you found the Zi'veyn. But now it's snowing in August."

"I can't say I appreciate your tone," Rathen replied loftily.

"This was Salus's doing," Anthis explained in his place. "The Zi'veyn didn't go as far as we thought it would, it only *silences* the magic, it doesn't remove it."

"...Ah."

"...What do you mean, 'ah'?"

"Well I'm not exactly an expert on the thing," he replied with an evasive smile, "but even *I* thought it would be the perfect solution..."

"That's still an underwhelming reaction."

"You said you could help us?" Anthis asked, preventing any more of Rathen's dry remarks, and the old elf's geniality hesitantly returned.

"I can - but I warn you, I also can't interfere. If the others detect me, I'll be punished. And I rather prefer my hands this way up. I'm only here to put right my peers' own meddling." He began gesturing towards Rathen, waving his hand towards his right arm, but the mage stepped backwards instead. Eizariin tutted and rolled his eyes. His harsh elven voice became abruptly more pertinent. "Do behave, young man."

Suddenly Rathen's coat began to remove itself from his arm, and his sleeve rolled itself up as Eizariin stepped forwards to examine the silver cuff clamped about his bicep. "The magic is extremely dangerous right now," he informed them as he began probing the cuff, and Rathen watched with open concern while the elf's peculiar magic began to weave its way through the metal, "and my people still refuse to accept responsibility. And, as I said, I cannot interfere. Not here, anyway. But your 'Salus' fellow has thrown Turunda and outlying regions into elemental and magical chaos. His magic is strong to manage such a thing, and completing the linkage has been like tying a knot in red-hot steel. You will not be able to undo it."

"Then what *can* we do?" Eyila asked pointedly, and frowned at Eizariin's simple, handsome smile.

"Melt the steel."

"Is that possible?"

"Most things are, when magic is involved." He looked up from the cuff when Rathen started towards something behind him, and turned to find Aria moving tentatively into view. She froze when all eyes snapped onto her. Eizariin smiled again, then glanced around at the rest. "There are fewer of you. The red-haired girl--"

"Petra," Rathen replied dutifully. "Her name is Petra. And she...died."

His old, angled eyes softened and his mouth drooped into an expression much too powerful for one who had barely spoken a word to her. An expression that spoke instead of an experience that weighed heavily upon him, and had perhaps for an age. "I am so dreadfully sorry. My deepest condolences. ...May...I ask--"

"Salus killed her." Rathen pushed successfully past the lump in his throat. "As for the other..."

Eizariin glanced about at the sudden frost in the air. "I have the sense that the less said about him, the better?" He nodded then turned back to the cuff. The heartache remained in his eyes for some time.

Anthis soon noticed a dark mark upon the elf's neck. A scar, steel-grey against silver skin. The elf's black-blue hair quickly shifted to cover it. "She's already punished you, hasn't she?" Anthis asked in quiet horror. "For helping us to escape."

Eizariin pretended not to notice the shamed slump of Rathen's shoulders. "I don't regret helping you."

"Can they not be healed away?"

"Not scars like these, no." The elf's bleak tone was enough to end the matter.

"How did you find us?" Anthis asked instead, a few long moments later.

"A, ah...mutual friend."

"A mutual friend? Who?"

"It's not my place to say."

Rathen sighed with far too belated understanding. "Kienza."

Eizariin popped his lips and refrained from meeting his eyes. "For the record, I did not say it."

"How in the world do *you* know *Kienza?!*" Anthis burst.

"Gods..."

"What?!"

Eizariin shook his head and increased the flow of magic over the cuff. His silver face had become lined with disgust. "What has she done to you?"

Rathen's eyes widened in alarm. "What is it? What's Kienza done?"

"What? No, not Kienza - Tekhest. Whatever she told you when she interfered with this, she lied."

"H-how do you know she lied if you don't know what she said?"

"Because," he replied severely, "if she'd told you the truth, you'd never have left that room."

"Explain, and quickly."

Without warning, he reached out and grasped the metal band. Concentration fell over his face. Even so, he spoke. "Mages - you humans - you have only a small amount of elven blood in your veins, a trace of it. It's weak - but you've inherited just enough of the right bits for it to work, and how well it works depends on resilience as well as the amount of magic."

"I know all this--"

"In elves, the balance is perfect. In humans, it varies drastically. These do'osos are given to elven children for their safety - they're designed to limit the potency of the magic in the blood, rendering much of it inert so that they can learn to control a smaller amount of it. The do'osos is tweaked as they age so that less of it is restrained and they can adjust to increased strength, and so on, increasing incrementally until it's fully unleashed. It was a practice that came into use in the Kerenik Dynasty, the middle of the Third Age of the Second Era. You wouldn't give a three-year-old free rein over a sword or crossbow, would you?"

"And what does that have to do with me?"

His eyes closed in his focus, but still he continued his patient explanation. "You were given this cuff because your magic is much stronger than a typical human mage's - by your mother, no doubt, but it was never adjusted or removed. Perhaps she was concerned you wouldn't be able to handle it--"

"Or because she died when I was three and never had the chance to make that decision."

"...I apologise again. But when Tekhest interfered, your magic was released and clarified - clearer elven magic, clear enough to control your transformations, but not enough to rival us in strength. But she released too much and chained back any hope of your resilience keeping up with it. Or so she thought. It has managed, against the odds, because you're close enough to us physiologically to be capable of adapting. But not in full - not yet. Your power and resilience is stronger than an elven child's, of course, but the rate at which the magic has been released...the harmony the do'osos provided is gone. Because of this, you're also not as strong as you probably feel. The sudden increase in power must be quite a feeling, and I envy you the experience, but that means you're more likely to incite the loss of control yourself by trying to do more than you're capable of." Briefly, his eyes opened and turned him a deliberate look. "And with such pure power, not so muddied by human blood, if your magic gets out of control...it could be catastrophic."

Rathen looked across the others and found similar expressions of alarm on their faces, as well as Aria, who had taken refuge between the two while she watched the elf with a wary fascination. "Lose control?" Anthis repeated, though everyone wished he hadn't. "Like...the other mages?"

Eizariin pursed his lips with a deep, pensive breath. "It wouldn't be *quite* the same thing. It may not kill him – not directly. Drive him mad, perhaps, or plague him with convulsive fits, seizures and the like. If he were to bite his tongue and pass out... In such a moment, he could clear a third of the forests for fifty years along with anyone and anything in them."

"That's ridiculous!" Rathen almost yelped, his voice tainted by the hue of alarm at the much too familiar suggestion. "If anything, it's crippled me! I wanted to give all this over to the Order - I can't finish it!"

"Oh that's nonsense, and you know it is," he declared with sudden impatience, as though scolding a blustering child. "That's fear talking. Fear of failure. Of proving you're not as powerful as you feel - or, perhaps, of proving yourself right. You wouldn't wish to be like us, would you? I know *I* certainly don't."

"You said you were going to help?" Anthis reminded him, intercepting any potential altercations, and the elf nodded decisively.

"Yes. By removing the do'osos."

Each face blanched as yet another blanket of apprehension descended over them like fresh, muffling snowfall. "Seriously? After what you just said? Are you *mad?*"

"I might just be," he smiled, which did nothing to soothe Rathen's thundering heart, "but thinking about it will only make it worse, so..." he glanced over his shoulder to the others, "stand back." There came the slightest click, and the cuff fell inertly into the elf's open hand.

In a single heartbeat, Rathen braced himself with instinct while his surroundings melted away, as though he'd been thrown into another existence. The surge of heat formed immediately in his bicep and passed through his arm, shooting down to his fingers and up into his shoulder, moving as quickly as it always did, and he gritted his teeth in preparation for the agony that would follow, helpless to the impending torment of his own physiology.

But the pain didn't come.

Instead the heat quickly began to wane; rather than burn and sear, it warmed and emboldened, and in its wake came power, strength, invulnerability, flowing freely like a river. His blood practically buzzed with it, surging and coursing through his veins like wild animals tamed by the strength of some primal compulsion. It felt unusual, peculiar - but...good. Enjoyable. *Incredible*. He almost laughed. What power! The Order's elders had been right after all. This had been inside him all along!

The power continued to mount; with every moment he felt he could achieve more and more - enough, even, to protect Turunda from a magic-wielding madman. He would avenge Petra, he would free Taliel from her shackles, he would protect Aria to the edge of the world and over. He wouldn't be stopped, especially not by someone whose only skills were limited magic and lying. Even if he was a professional in the latter.

The buzzing in his veins grew stronger and his head began to spin, adding to the confusion in his blood. It continued to swell with the power, and he continued to enjoy it, until a thumping began to creep into his skull.

He began to stumble. The power grew, the thumping increased, and it steadily overwhelmed him.

It was as though there were a thousand horses suddenly stampeding in his chest. The magic was becoming too much, moving too quickly, and the thought that he would never find control over it until it utterly consumed him accelerated his state. So much so that the fact that he was keeping up with it so easily escaped him entirely.

He became suddenly aware of the terrible sounds and sensations of his body changing, and true panic set in. But it was different this time; disconnected, distant, numb, and where in the past he had been almost incapacitated by the pain, now he was acutely aware of every shift and growth. And the fact that it didn't hurt equally escaped him. Instead, he felt it, understood it, and predicted it. His mind began to slow down as it focused on the details, and his own riled magic seemed to slow in the distraction. His grasp finally closed.

The moment he seized it, those details blurred and distorted, and he lost them in seconds. His efforts crumbled.

Frustrations roared through him, and his eyes, squeezed shut in his torment, ripped open.

Chapter 64

The barn Rathen had forgotten he stood within was bright - much brighter than it had been before he'd closed his eyes. So bright, in fact, that it really should have hurt. And yet it didn't. Instead, everything was impossibly sharp, crystalline in its clarity. He saw every crack and splinter in the old, wooden floor, surprised he hadn't noticed them before; he saw every grain in the planks, every straight and crooked nail holding them together, while the floor itself seemed further away than usual, as though his perception of distance had become more acute. He even grew certain that he could predict the shift of his shadow cast by the campfire behind him. All after-effects of his dizziness, most likely; delayed responses; a moment to marvel at mundane details before their reality sank in.

He ignored the peculiarities and looked up towards the elf for an explanation as to just why his power had fizzled out, but his voice caught in his throat when he found Anthis, Eyila and Aria seized by wide-eyed horror, while Eizariin stood beside them, notably untroubled.

'We've been tricked.'

The realisation hit him like a kick to the head, but just how, and why, eluded his rapidly churning mind. It took him a long moment to notice that the horrified stares were directed towards him, and as his eyes flicked past them at a sudden, sharp, equine squeal, he found the horses gathered tightly in the corner where they were hitched, rearing and pawing at the air with their hooves, tusks bared forwards, eyes wide and rolling.

He swallowed hard. A dreadful thought coalesced. And though his heart warned against it, he looked down.

The cracks and splinters in the floor. He'd not noticed them before; they hadn't *been* there before. The planks had been raked and shredded. It wasn't age or rot; they had been torn up by claws. And there were splinters nearby, shards of wood scattered across the ground. His eyes tracked them unwillingly. The support beam standing closest to him had been almost obliterated. It probably wouldn't hold for much longer.

His throat closed. And while his heavy arms refused to obey, even as his heart now screamed against it, he looked down at his hands.

His fingers were too long; slender and tapered, almost fleshless, like bony talons, and white - white as the dead. His eyes widened as distress and revulsion rapidly swelled.

Heart in his throat, his monstrous hands rose to his face, passing his still-fleshy, black-veined palms tentatively over unfamiliar features. His breath caught short. His cheekbones had never been so sharp.

"Rathen?"

He looked up towards Anthis, who flinched back from his gaze. His movements seemed slow.

"...Are...you...?"

'Myself?' A deep, reluctant breath filled his lungs and, slowly, he nodded. Then his attention crashed grievously upon Eizariin. "*What did you--*" But it was not his voice. He bit his lip to cut back the foul and guttural sound, but cut his own flesh instead. His teeth were as sharp as needles.

His black eyes grew even wider, until the elf stepped forwards and filled his enhanced vision. Menace returned as he stared down at him, talons cutting into his palms as he squeezed his fists in rage, but the elf merely smiled back soothingly.

"You can revert," he told him in a calm voice made sickening by his rough and brutal accent. "You have full control, so go ahead. Don't wait to be asked."

Hope sparked through him so quickly that he spared no time for his suspicions, and dove back into his magic on the blind faith that instinct would show him how. The thumping was swift to return to his skull. "Breathe," he heard the elf say as he fumbled desperately to find the spell to retract his bones and return his colour, "ease back into your body." As if it could be so easy.

But it was. As some abstract part of his mind considered the suggestion, a strange relaxation laced through his blood, diluting his adrenaline and widening his veins, and as quickly as that, he felt his body begin once again to shift.

The pain that finally forced his eyes open was decidedly more than uncomfortable, and while his fingers were red with blood and a trail trickled slowly down his forearms from his elbows, his skin had coloured fair once again.

Eyila hurried towards him immediately.

He smiled shamefully as Aria followed her, surging out from behind Anthis to throw her little arms around his leg. She cried while she smiled, blood smearing her coat, but she wouldn't release him. He squeezed her tightly while Eyila busied herself with his wounds.

"Congratulations, Rathen Koraaz," the elf declared ceremoniously. "Your magic is freed."

"What happened?" Anthis asked, stepping forwards a little more warily.

"He reversed it," he explained as he his eyes fell upon the tribal girl with open curiosity. "When I unleashed his magic, it surged, then settled, like water breaking out from a dam, and that triggered the transformation."

"Did you know it would happen?"

"Absolutely. But it won't happen again now that it's out - not unless he wants it to."

"Why is he still injured?"

"Well," Eizariin stepped aside to peer even further around Eyila's shoulder at her fingers, "he is only *half*-elf. The Vahzik'i'kaan ukhsuun was never going to be perfect."

"...The...what?"

He sent Anthis a slow look. "Becoming the image of Zikhon."

"...I see... So now, he's..."

"His magic is unrestricted, but his resilience will take some time to catch up."

"So he's at risk?"

"Only if he's foolish enough to try to exercise the limits of his power in the next few days. It will take some time to catch up, as I said, but there's no knowing just how long. He is a...unique case."

"How did you find out about the cuff?" Rathen asked, his voice and eyes having also returned to normal, and were remarkably strong for his ordeal. "Tekhest couldn't have told you, not with your differences."

He sighed and folded his arms ruefully. "Indeed she didn't. Kienza told me. She had ideas, said it seemed to her that the cuff had weakened rather than been turned down, but she couldn't work out why. It turns out that she simply didn't expect my people, at present, of sabotage. And she came to me, I answer before being asked, because it was out of her ability to fix."

"Out of *Kienza's* ability? How could that be?"

"Because the very nature of the do'osos prevents tampering – apparently – for everyone's safety, including the individual's. The spell is highly refined. When she realised what it was, she came to me. But I suppose I wasn't easy to find, even for her. There are spells in place on the island to detect and misdirect non-elven magic from the outside. Young lady," he walked now to Rathen's other side and openly stared at the healing, "how ever did you work out how to do that?"

She spared only a brief moment from her concentration. "Work *with* magic, don't force it. Then it will work with *you*."

"...My, that's wise."

"I thought elves could heal," Anthis mused.

"Yes, *we* can - but you're human."

"A fair point. And you never did explain how you know one another - you and Kienza."

"Well," he chuckled evasively, "we're both very old. I myself am in my third teens."

"Third teens?"

"Two hundred and seventeen," he said proudly. "You're as old as you feel."

"...And Kienza?"

He frowned disapprovingly. "A gentleman shouldn't ask."

"Enough," Rathen grunted impatiently. "How did you do this? Tekhest needed the aid of several--"

"No, she didn't," he sighed, "it was a show to frighten you and set herself above you, and probably above everyone who 'helped'. That's all. Anyway--"

"I thought your people worshipped Zikhon - that you were 'enlightened'--"

"'Enlightened' has many definitions. The one you're thinking of is the only one that doesn't exist. Everyone suffers some kind of greed, some kind of vice, and hers is power."

"And yours?"

He smiled. "Knowledge. *Now:* this 'Sah'niir'..."

Aria suddenly clambered away from his side and reached for the wooden carving still standing where her father had put it before the night fell into shambles. She handed it wordlessly to the old elf who proceeded to study it for some time, and watched him with big eyes, glimmering with a hunger for approval. Rathen pulled her gently back towards him and kissed her remorsefully on the head, but didn't discourage her hope.

His black-blue eyebrows eventually rose, and he nodded in concedence, turning it over in his hands. "I'm impressed."

"Thank you."

His eyes drifted down onto the big-eyed child who seemed ready to burst, somehow with both pride and modesty, and frowned in bewilderment. "Pardon? No, no, I--oh...*oh*." He looked again at the carving, seeing for the first time the wood rather than the spell, and his eyes brightened in marvel. "Oh my...you, young lady...you would surely have been worth your father's weight in gold to my people in the old days..."

"And she's worth four times my weight right now."

He smiled joyfully. "That, I'm sure, she is! You have a highly enviable talent, my dear. Treasure it."

Her cheeks burned pink, and she sat happily back beside her father, her arms slipping around him like a steel vice once again.

"As for the spell..."

"Will it work?"

"It's already in there?!"

"Yes, it may work," Eizariin replied, neither of them paying Anthis any attention as he stared somewhat agog at the wood, but his tone was hesitant, and the crease in his brow didn't buoy Rathen's hope. "But it's complex. It's a job to get my head around it, if I'm honest... But, these are no longer the spells my people would cast. I can't honestly offer a verdict until I see it applied, and I suspect the very act of doing so would render the need of said verdict redundant. But I am in awe of how *you* managed it, though, what with your rudimentary tutelage and impure descendancy."

Rathen's brow flattened. "Thank you."

"...Well?"

He blinked. "...'Well' what?"

"The spell--*oh*." He snapped his fingers. "A moment. Anthis, come closer, please. And bring the horses - you'll want them, I suspect."

The dizziness that followed was as unpleasant as always, but Rathen recovered quicker than usual. Aria, meanwhile, groaned in a moment of misery, Anthis staggered off-balance, and Eyila dropped to her knees, but while the former rather delicately shook it off, Eyila's eyes had glazed. Rathen rushed down to help her, but he quickly recognised the state. The surrounding magic, softly brushing against his senses like downy feathers, confirmed it.

And yet it barely touched him.

He rose slowly from the pebbles and looked out across the flat horizon, from the blaze of the lighthouse set out upon the still-standing tip of a collapsed headland in the east, to the edge of the foreboding Pavise mountains in the west. The white-capped sea roiled between them, studded beneath the surface with small, golden-sunset fish, and the rotten mast of an ancient wreck which broke the surface two miles out.

Whitemouth.

Silently, Anthis stepped up beside him. "Are we--"

"Looks like it."

"I can't see any--"

"It's under the water." Rathen's teeth gritted even tighter. "The bastard didn't lie. Salus really has done it." He sensed Eizariin join them. Dutifully, he took the

Sah'niir from his outstretched hand and turned it about cynically. "If not now," he muttered, "when?"

Without leaving himself another moment to doubt, he raised his free hand, twisted his fingers into a brief spell, then took hold of the piece with both. The two watched closely from either side, apprehensive and curious, while Aria stared hopefully from beside Eyila.

A shaking began immediately underfoot, but it stopped shortly after it started, and Eizariin smiled to himself in satisfaction. The water surface continued to tremor, but the surrounding pebbles fell still. Anthis sent him a cautious look, but his attention was quickly dragged outwards.

The three listened, watched and waited, but the results were few and hard to discern. There may have been some unnoticed sound, though he heard nothing at that moment, and perhaps a smell or sensation already overpowered by the salt, but Anthis couldn't detect it. If Eizariin had noticed anything in his attention, he didn't share it. There appeared to be no change at all until the fish quite abruptly vanished, but whether they had ceased to exist, returned to darker camouflage or simply retreated to the depths was unclear. The sea didn't calm its unnatural boiling, and nothing else seemed to change.

His wondering ceased only upon Aria's warning cry.

Anthis was already turning when she hit the ground with a startled gasp, but Eizariin was faster. With a mildly confused glance around towards the charging tribal, he froze her immediately in place, even as Anthis rushed to her side.

"*No!*" He yelled, earning himself a bemused look of his own. "Release her, I'll hold her back! She'll be fine!"

"Do as he says," Rathen said gravely from beneath his concentration.

Eizariin glanced curiously at the two for a moment, but when he landed upon Anthis, his confusion passed instantly. His attention returned to the Sah'niir, and Eyila began to move. Anthis caught her as her vicious surge faltered.

"Aria, give Eizariin the Zi'veyn. Use it on her."

"What?! No, Rathen, he's--"

"Aria, do it."

Despite Anthis's protest, Aria obeyed her father in a heartbeat, fishing the Zi'veyn out of her pocket, stuffed inside when the first strange man had appeared in their barn, and thrust it into the elf's unwilling hands. He stared at it, eyes filled with foreboding, even while Aria pushed him physically towards the struggling tribal. "Help her," she ordered. "It will still her magic and calm her down. Hurry!"

Looking from the child's urgent expression to the tribal's blind madness, reluctantly, he did as he was told. A moment later Eyila sank limp into Anthis's arms, and he pushed the ebon artefact back into Aria's hands with such haste it was as though it was diseased before his attention was pulled directly back towards the growing power of the Sah'niir.

Rathen's face was lined deeply in concentration. His skin shone with sweat in the nocturnal light, his shoulders almost trembled, and the crease in his brow inched closer to pain than to focus. He was beginning to exhaust. He felt as though he was a pot boiling dry on the stove.

"Don't try to use your full power," Eizariin said from beside him, but no matter how softly he spoke, there was a note of alarm in his voice that did little to help Rathen's struggle.

Not that it made any difference. A ragged breath later, his knees collapsed and hit the pebbles, and the Sah'niir tumbled from his hands. "I couldn't...if I tried..." He struggled to catch his breath, and rose from his hands with Aria's help to sit back on his heels. The others gathered around him. Eyila, as always, began to tend to his spent energy, and Eizariin watched again with interest. "It's broken."

"Broken? What is? The spell?"

"Well, frayed. But it comes down to the same thing." He accepted Aria's embrace, but didn't return it, shaking his head in self-reproach. "It didn't work."

Eizariin frowned. "...But it did."

His head rose sharply and he looked more carefully around the dark beach.

The water surface had fallen still. Even the tremors that had formed when he'd first cast the spell had ceased. And Eyila was fine - and looking back at him as she worked in astonishment. She felt it. So did he. There was no magic here.

All the creases vanished from his face, and his dark eyes widened in sheer wonder. "...It...worked..."

"Congratulations, Rathen Koraaz," Eizariin beamed, "you've just made history."

"That's not a first," he replied grimly, finally returning his daughter's vigorous hug, "but I'd rather take credit for this."

"Now you just need to fix it."

"Oh, is that all? It *broke*, Eizariin. It will break again."

"Unless you find the problem. The Zi'veyn didn't require a sign to use, did it?"

"No," Rathen admitted, suddenly a touch sheepish, "that was a safety precaution I added. In case Salus got a hold of it. A sort of...password. Why are you smiling? Is that the problem?"

"Oh, no," he grinned, "not as far as I can see. And I'm smiling because I'm just so...humbled. Your seals are such a handicap! Your Order's manner of thinking means there are things you just can't do. You think in seals and signs, and if you don't know the signs, you can't cast the spell. It would take too long to train that out of you, both as an adult with decades of such tuition, and with the impending matter...and yet...you've done *this!*"

"...So it's a compliment?"

"Absolutely."

Rathen nodded slowly, but he was too tired to try to pick out any hidden insults, and in truth, he didn't really want to notice them. He reached out and collected the Sah'niir, undented or scratched, and rose to his feet with the two girls' help. He held the wooden carving out towards the elf. "I don't suppose you have any suggestions?"

"Mmm...a faulty connection, perhaps. Your power leaked out, or over-charged it. Or the reinforcing spells were poorly cast. Or a bit of all three. It's over my head, really; history is my field."

"But you're an elf..."

"And? You're a human. Can you educate me on the finer points of smithing?"

"Fair enough."

"Well," Eizariin began to straighten his silver-embroidered robes, though they seemed decidedly uncreased, as though they had just that moment been pressed, and passed the inert do'osos back into Rathen's hand, "it would be best if I left about now. This was a powerful demonstration and I really shouldn't be discovered near it."

"Wait!"

Eizariin blinked at the young historian. "No need to shout, I'm still standing right here..."

"Well, I...you don't use signs, so--"

"The elves will know where we are?" Eyila asked for him.

"Precisely where you are, yes. You had better leave, too."

"They *are* after us, then?"

"I said they would be, my dear."

"But we've not seen them," Anthis said hopefully, despite the elf's suddenly bleak look. "Not a trace."

"But they've seen *you*."

"Eizariin." Rathen stepped forwards, and on a strange, unspoken command, the others immediately fell silent. There was something in his tone that demanded precedence, some subtle detail in his voice and his bearing that had, for that brief moment, changed him entirely. Everyone felt it. Not even Aria, beaming and clinging onto his leg, took anything away from it. Only Eizariin found the courage to meet him directly. "*Why* are they after us?"

"Because you are raising the dust of the past. Some fear you will reveal our existence, and others believe we should come back to the world."

"And you?"

He smiled sadly. "It is not our world anymore. On that, Tekhest and I agree. But while I have no issues with being revealed - we are powerful enough to defend ourselves, should it come to that - others would just as well that we were hidden. For good. Keep the past in the past and focus on our future, remaining separate, avoiding a convergence of cultures and the repeat of our mistakes. But some of them are not above the idea of killing to keep it that way. And one or two...well, then we step into the realms of supremacy so many of us think we've left behind."

"What happened?"

"Magic, Mister Karth. What else? Power corrupts. Always. In one way or another. It can change the way you think, it can change what you believe. It can change a whole civilisation for the better, or the worse. We had it right, for a while. And then we didn't. 'Convenience' is a dirty word, my friends. We have since learned that. But the young are inclined to forget the old lessons - no offence, of course."

"None taken - but how many of those lessons are they actually *taught?* You might not want to reveal your ancestors' shame, but how will your people ever be able to grow past those mistakes if--"

"I know, Mister Karth. Believe me." He forced a smile into his staid eyes, but it didn't stick for a moment. "I must leave. Congratulations, Mister Koraaz, on your monumental achievement. Truly. I am honoured to be a part of it. I am just sorry it was necessary at all."

"As am I." He extended his hand, and the elf clasped it gladly. "Thank you for your help, Eizariin. Truly. I..." His harsh features softened with only a touch of contrition, and he smiled with honour in his eyes. "I am in your debt."

The old elf bowed his head, black-blue hair shimmering in the window of moonlight. Then, he vanished.

Rathen's eyes sank down to the Sah'niir. The others gathered and stared at it with their own curiosity. Aria, however, peered up through the gaps in the wood and into her father's face. She smiled proudly. So very proudly. "You did it, Daddy."

"Yes, sweetheart," he replied softly, smiling back down at her as heady disbelief began to set in. "...I suppose I did."

Epilogue

The night air was thick. It barely shifted in the lazy breeze, and hung heavy with the scent of smoke. Snow drifted through it as listlessly as soot, while the dusty glow of amassing candlelight far below chased out the darkness, bouncing across the snow-covered rooftops as though the buildings themselves held vigil. A sombre bell tolled gravely from the Temple to the west.

The whole city was shrouded in mourning. The country would follow, once word spread. Dirty smudges of light could already be seen flickering along the slush-trampled roads as outlying villages came to pay their respects to the fallen king.

Salus looked down across them from the heights of the palace's twisted dome roof, lost in thought, hypnotised in his weariness by the thousands of tiny, entrancing flames. The people were restless; they were frightened, they were uncertain, but they were outraged most of all, and all of that anger was pointing towards the red and ochre flags of the king's assassins. It was upon the military to deliver that fury, the condemnation of the country, and not least that of the young Crown Prince Ellory.

Named for his grandfather, His Royal Highness would be pushed hastily onto the throne, for the country would need a ruler during wartime, even if only a figurehead - and at the age of thirteen, he could lead no one but his nurse maid. But he would do. If just for the sake of his father's memory, the people and the military would rally behind him, and he would solidify his position without anyone batting an eyelid.

But there were benefits to his youth: he was malleable. Provided the Crown didn't sink their claws in too deep before he could, the boy could shape up into a very fine king indeed, with the right encouragement. And the Crown itself, the royal council, they would be in shock and turmoil. They were in the perfect position to be manipulated, too. It was the prime opportunity for change.

The Arana was prepared to leap at Salus's command. The boy-king would be snared. Portians could be trusted. And while they leapt, Salus would deal with the bigger issue himself. For no one else but he possibly could.

Something stirred in the air behind him. He didn't turn. The caustic chuckle that followed its disturbance didn't elicit the usual degree of disgust, but he stood instinctively taller all the same.

"Look at you," Liogan said softly, her rough, brutal accent injecting a natural venom into her words. "On top of the world. Well, I suppose you're allowed *some* posturing today." She drew up alongside him and peered over the edge of the cupola to the sea of candles below. "Congratulations, Salus. In spite of all your distractions, you've succeeded in cracking the borders. And upheaved your dear, beloved Turunda - albeit in not quite the manner I had in mind."

His eyes turned stonily upon her.

"Oh now, now, now," she cooed, "I conceded you your congratulations. Don't be ungrateful." She stepped back from the edge and began a leisurely pace around him, dusting the snow from her finely tailored shoulders. His eyes turned back out over the city. "You're almost done. Just one more simple little step, and your cherished Turunda will be free. Just crack the underside. Break it away, and carry her off to safety at last."

"How?"

She blinked. "...What do you mean, 'how'? Shift the force. A forward momentum with a lateral expression rather than a vertical one. I seriously need to tell you to break *through* it, not *across?*"

"So there's magic within the earth?"

"Why ever would there be magic within it?"

His eyes snapped sharply back upon her at the sound of the elf's light but sudden gasp. The smile that now wrapped around her plump and bitter lips stoked his irritation. What patience he'd had at her arrival was rapidly searing away.

"*Oh.* Oh, I see... I apologise. I thought you were stronger than that - you know: *mentally.* I didn't realise you would become trapped in such a *secure* way of thinking so easily. Well, don't fret your tangled little head about it." He jerked back as she patted his snow-sodden hair. "I'll find someone else to finish your dreams."

Her skirt flared as she turned away, and his hand flashed out to snatch her by the arm. His iron stare was piercing. "*Tell me.*"

She met that stare directly, and all humour rapidly vanished from her pastel eyes. "You must come to know the country you love so dearly. Know it *intimately.* Know it from top to bottom. Inside and out. Seep into its very bones, and breathe there. If it means as much to you as you claim it does, it should be an easy matter."

His fingers tightened through her damask and doe-skin coat. "Enough. A straight answer. Now."

"But that would be too easy."

His eyes narrowed. His lip curled. He could see she was playing with him. She was *always* playing with him. Even now, while the task she'd set him on was so close to fruition, she played games. And while he'd never turned upon her the force he had over Denek - perhaps because he knew it wouldn't touch her, or perhaps through some redundant sense of chivalry - he was quickly tiring of his own restraint. '*Just one more simple little step...*'

And this wasn't the only game she and her kind were playing...

He closed the distance between them, his voice dropping like a stone, and spoke at last the question that had hounded him for so long. "What are your plans for Koraaz?"

But her lips only curved into a gleefully malicious smile.

"Why have you pitted him against me? Answer me!"

"There are tests in life," she replied with that same, unwavering smirk, "that must be overcome. Only then can one's true strength, of mind and of magic, be realised."

"So it's survival of the fittest?"

"No."

An exasperated hiss leapt from his lips, and his fingers tightened again. *"Enough riddles!"*

"But, my dear Salus, wherever would the fun be in that?"

Her foul smile seared itself into his sight. She vanished behind it despite his hold on her arm.

An instant later, he was standing alone on the sloping tower roof, clutching the falling snow and staring into the darkness, the people's grief glowing at his back while the endless toll of the bell hammered against the thumping in his skull. As the night's chill crept in beneath his rage, he could feel the elf's venom crawling through his blood. And noticed despite himself, lost in the smothering scent of burning wicks and oils, the indomitable trace of cinnamon in the air.

The story of The Devoted continues in *Veysuul*.

Out 2020

Thank you. Truly. You have no idea what it means to me that you have read this far. Seriously. Not a clue.

I *really* hope you liked it.

If you did enjoy it, please consider taking a moment to leave a review – even just a few words - on Amazon, GoodReads, Google, Instagram, *whatever*. Even just a quick tweet. All authors rely hugely on the support and feedback of our readers, and this goes doubly for self-published authors.
We won't know what we're getting wrong if we're not told.

www.KimWedlock.com
@KimWedlock

48360692R00356

Printed in Poland
by Amazon Fulfillment
Poland Sp. z o.o., Wrocław